VALERIOS

ROAD TO MASTERY

6

aethonbooks.com

ROAD TO MASTERY 6

Aethon Books
www.aethonbooks.com

Print and eBook design and formatting by Kevin G. Summers. Artwork provided by Kaion Luong.

Published by Aethon Books LLC.

ALSO IN SERIES

Road to Mastery

Road to Mastery 2

Road to Mastery 3

Road to Mastery 4

Road to Mastery 5

Road to Mastery 6

CHAPTER ONE

THE BEGINNING OF THE END

A GROUP WAS GATHERED IN SPACE. A DOZEN WHITE-DRESSED PEOPLE, EACH more brooding than the last. Wreckage surrounded them. Parts of what used to be an Elder-level starship. The distant stars felt cold, and the universe was suddenly much less inviting.

"This is useless," a man said. "The Hand will find and kill us. We're just delaying the inevitable."

"You need to believe, Borg," a woman replied. "The Old Gods will arrive. The Arch Priestess depends on us. We cannot give up."

The man named Borg raised his head. "I don't *want* to give up! I believe in the Old Gods like all of us, and I hate the cruel Immortals with every fiber of my being, but this is just hopeless. We are sheep to the slaughter. We just barely managed to teleport away this time—the Hand will find us again, and they'll kill more of us. We'll die few by few until we're all gone, and for what? A hope that will never bear fruit? A doomed war? Even if the cause is noble, dying in vain is not."

"But the Arch Priestess—"

"I don't give a shit about the Arch Priestess. She's lying to us, Katie! Can't you see this war is a lost cause? She has us holding the front lines, but the Hand of God is so much stronger. They've got double the people. Stick it in your goddamn head, we cannot win! We have already lost!"

"The Old Gods will arrive," an older man said. "The tide will turn. We must stay strong."

"How can I stay strong, Father? How much longer do we have to wait? I feel scared and alone, and I fear we will all die in the darkness between the stars like we never existed. I... I cannot do this anymore." All his energy left him then. "I want to go home."

The older man frowned as a heavy silence spread between the gathered cultivators. It was hard to fight a losing war. Hard to watch your friends die beside you, one after another, as you persisted for an ideal that might or might not come to be.

The current state of the Second Crusade was worse than advertised. The Black Hole Church was pushed back on every front. They'd split their forces and hidden them in a Systemless galaxy, merely delaying their inevitable defeat. The Hand of God was searching, finding them piece by piece, killing them slowly. While the Church hid, their disadvantage only grew, and the mental pressure on their people was growing heavier.

Everyone felt like prisoners on the execution block, waiting for the blade to fall. They knew that any of these days could be their turn. Yes, the Old Gods were en route, or so the Arch Priestess said... but would they arrive in time? Or was everyone going to die first?

The army of the Black Hole Church had started the war by being ambushed, losing their headquarters—the Cathedral—and forced to flee all across System space as many of their hiding spots were discovered. They'd suffered serious losses before they could even fight back, and it had only gone downhill from there. They'd managed to delay their defeat by hiding and fighting a semblance of guerilla warfare, but morale was crumbling everywhere.

The cultivators of the Church were losing faith. They desperately needed a victory, to strike back, *something*. They needed hope.

Except, with the state of war as it was, how could the Church achieve anything?

The dozen white-robed cultivators still stood silently in the darkness of space, surrounded by the wreckage of their starship. Many were injured. Their moods couldn't be worse. Suddenly, a younger woman lifted her head. Her voice trembled with excitement.

"What!" she exclaimed. "That's... Are you sure?"

The others threw her questioning glances. Their heads drooped lower. "What is it this time?" asked the older man, the leader of this group. "Which of our comrades fell?"

"It's not that. Not that at all!" the woman exclaimed. "I... I don't know if I believe this, but I actually received good news. Great news!"

Their eyes shone. "What happened?"

"Do you remember Jack Rust? Who was about to break into the B-Grade?"

The cultivators nodded. Jack's breakthrough hadn't been broadcasted, for fear of revealing his position, but the Church had secretly spread the news.

"Well, his breakthrough just finished. And he, he..." She hesitated, as if struggling to believe her own words.

"So it went well," the man who'd had a meltdown before, Borg, spoke before she could. "I don't think that really matters to us. How much did he get? Seven thousand miles? Eight?"

"Not even close!" the younger woman exclaimed, her face growing red with excitement. "I am receiving this news from multiple sources. Elders Boatman and Heavenstar have both confirmed this. It cannot be wrong!"

"Out with it, then!" the older man exclaimed.

"His inner world reached ten thousand miles across!"

The news fell like a nuke on a summer day. Choking attempts to speak fell silent. The older man's face scrunched up. "Is that a joke? This is not the time, Matilda."

"It's true! I swear it on my mother's grave! Everyone is saying the same, all my communications are lighting up! Jack Rust rewrote history! Nine thousand wasn't the limit—it's ten!"

The older man snorted. "That's absurd."

"And yet it's true! Not just that, either—even his spiritual companion, the brorilla named Brock, reached 8800 miles! They're an unprecedented duo! Even the Arch Priestess herself congratulates them, and she sent a faction-wide message confirming this. It is absolutely true!"

"Hmph!" the older man harrumphed. "Ludicrous. If you're lying about this, Matilda, we will have a problem. Let me speak to them."

He reached out to touch her shoulder, and she let him tap into the soul connections they used to communicate. Every squad of the Church had someone with this ability—that was how they could communicate efficiently even outside System space.

A moment later, the older man pulled back his hand, his aged eyes growing wide.

"Well?" the others asked, desperately needing but not daring to believe.

"It's true," he said slowly. The trembling excitement of Matilda had invaded his voice now. "I saw the Arch Priestess's Dao signature. Elders Boatman and Heavenstar, too. This is not a joke. I have no idea how it happened, but Jack Rust really broke through the nine-thousand-mile limit."

The cultivators exchanged bewildered looks. Their dead hope began to shimmer. They wouldn't have believed this in regular times, but they were now neck-deep in war. They believed for dear life. It was the first good news they'd received in a long time—someone achieved an impossible feat, and they were part of the same army!

It is incredible how much strength a desperate person can derive from a single piece of good news.

All of them felt like someone had taken a torch, reached into their chests, and lit up something in there. The darkness and despair dissipated.

Their hearts turned warm. They clenched their fists, shedding tears they didn't even know they'd been holding back. Somehow, the pride they felt grew until it was overwhelming. The Church had achieved something. They hadn't fought so long in vain. If miracles could still happen, not all was lost. Who knew how powerful Jack could become? This war wasn't over yet. They had hope!

"There's another message," the communicator girl, Matilda, said. She gasped. "It's another faction-wide message by the Arch Priestess. She says this is proof that fate hasn't abandoned us. We are still here. We are still fighting. With such a heaven-defying genius amongst us, how could we possibly be destroyed? How could we lose? The enemy is fighting for power, but we are fighting for survival. We are fighting for what is right, for our friends and families and the weak people of the universe who need us. We may be fewer, but our hearts burn brighter. This is our war—and we *will* win!"

She'd gotten swept by her own words, and the surrounding cultivators, already vulnerable, raised their arms and roared into the void. The surrounding space lit up. The stars were no longer cold, the emptiness no longer scary.

They'd always believed in the Church, that's why they were fighting in the first place. All it took to reignite their flames was a single spark.

Yes, things remained terrible for them. They knew they would probably die. They were scared. But dying meaninglessly and sacrificing yourself for a worthy, attainable cause were two wildly different things. These cultivators would fight. They would endure the darkness.

Their battle was not in vain, but for freedom. A surety of the universe they gladly carried on their shoulders. They were heroes.

"Fuck the Immortals!" the older man shouted, and the others echoed, their voices rising through the cosmos.

Reality was often negotiable. In war, each army's commanders claimed they were winning. Each side painted themselves as heroes. The crowds back home were always filled with hope and heroism, while those at the frontlines always felt they were in hell. They were the ones who came face-to-face with the reality of war. Killing others, fearing for your life, and watching your friends collapse had a way of tying one to the present, shrouding the mind in darkness through which they could only trudge, an endless march through the night, seeking a sun that might never rise.

The Church could endure for a long time. Their scattered and hidden forces ensured that. The problem was that every month of survival required a blood price, the death of the least capable or the most unlucky. To those who participated in this massacre lottery, the wait was unbearable. Their morale was bottomed out, and many held thoughts of deserting. At the current state of war, the Church's greatest problem was maintaining their army's morale until the Old Gods arrived. They needed something to recharge their people's faith.

Jack's ten-thousand-mile, unprecedented breakthrough came like a gift from the gods.

Once the Church leadership recovered from the shock, they spread the word far and wide. This was proof that fate hadn't abandoned them, and was exactly what they needed.

The news spread like wildfire. Everyone in the Church army knew about Jack's breakthrough within the hour. In the span of a single day, even the most clueless, non-combatant drunkard in the remotest pub of an Elder-level starship had heard the story at least three times. Through various communication channels, it spread even to System space, infiltrating all seventy-three galaxies. Before long, almost everyone in the universe knew about Jack's breakthrough.

Such a legendary event had many consequences. To the positive, the morale of the Church army was uplifted, at least temporarily. The dark despair gave way to burning, warm heroism. People set their jaws, determined to give their lives fighting if necessary. They'd hated the Immortals and their System with a passion—this was their chance to truly strike back. Brave roars and laughter filled the Church starships. The celebration of dying men. Of heroes.

On the other side, the Immortals posted a sky-high bounty on Jack and Brock's heads, and they even sent an Archon to personally hunt them down. It was just how things worked.

The greatest impression, however, was made on the people in and around the Death Boat. They'd witnessed everything with their own eyes. Seen Jack's inner world blow outward again and again, each time surpassing what they thought possible. They'd witnessed him charge into a tribulation which could even annihilate A-Grades, and even watched Brock and Elder Boatman stand alongside Jack to face the tribulation together.

All these sights would forever remain carved in the hearts of everyone watching. They'd branded themselves indefinitely. Jack had become a god in their eyes—a universe-class hero. They desired to see how far he could go. His breakthrough had easily surpassed every Archon's ever. Could he be the first person to take the final step beyond the A-Grade? Could they have witnessed the birth of an eternal legend?

Pubs and gathering places everywhere buzzed with discussion about Jack and Brock. It'd become the Death Boat's favorite conversation subject.

As for Jack and Brock themselves, they'd gone into seclusion after their breakthrough to stabilize their cultivation. It was only three days later that they finally opened their eyes.

Their final—and greatest—adventure was just beginning.

CHAPTER TWO
GUM WORMS

Stars hung in the distant space. They were above, below, and to the sides of the Death Boat, framing the world. Each was a different color. Blue stars burned the hottest, while red were the largest. Outside a planet's atmosphere, the different colors could all reach the observer's eye unfiltered, further amplifying the beauty of the universe.

Jack currently couldn't see that. It was just him and Brock in a dark room. All he heard was breathing, following a steady rhythm. In and out. In and out. His own spirit was in his inner world, calmly observing it, harmonizing himself with the changes that had occurred in himself.

After breaking into the B-Grade, Jack had been reborn. A whole world now existed in place of his soul. A ten thousand mile wide sphere, supported by his Daos. Tiny particles floated about—barely enough to be called matter. It was empty otherwise.

Well, almost empty. A large, purple, fist-shaped meteor dominated its midst. The empty Life Drop was plastered on its middle finger like an encrusted gem, and Copy Jack lazily floated about, exploring this newfound space. Jack had tried talking to him, but

Copy Jack maintained his non-committal stance like he cared about nothing in the world.

Jack recalled how the Dao Soul's eyes had sharpened during the breakthrough. There was something hidden under the surface. Something wrong with Copy Jack. He just had to figure out what.

He opened his eyes in the real world, releasing a long sigh. He'd finally familiarized himself with his inner world. He wasn't particularly stronger than he had been right after his breakthrough, but he now understood it more intimately. His cultivation was stabilized.

Jack gave a sideways glance, finding that Brock was still meditating. *No problem,* he thought. *Take your time, bro.*

Meanwhile, he opened his status screen.

ERROR: PLEASE REPORT TO THE NEAREST AUTHORITIES IMMEDIATELY OR FACE EXTERMINATION.

Name: Jack Rust
Species: Human, Earth-387
Faction: Bare Fist Brotherhood (B)
Grade: B
Class: Paragon of Cultivation (Legendary)
Level: 400

Strength: 8480 (+)
Dexterity: 8480 (+)
Constitution: 8480 (+)
Mental: 1200
Will: 1200
Free sub-points: 2

Dao Skills: Meteor Punch IV, Iron Fist Style III, Brutalizing Aura III, Neutron Star Body III, Supernova III, Space Mastery III, Fist of Mortality III, Death Mastery III, Titan Taunt III, Immortal Commune I

Inner World Size: 10,000 miles
Matter Condensation: -
Titles: Planetary Frontrunner (10), Planetary Torch-bearer (1), Ninth Ring Conqueror, Planetary Overlord (1), Grade Defier, Planet Destroyer, Challenger

The error warning at the very top remained. Having been there since he first absorbed the Life Drop, which was considered a taboo item to the Immortals. He'd just learned to ignore it.

Besides that, a lot of things changed. His Dao Roots and Dao Fruits had disappeared, replaced by the new entries of Inner World Size and Matter Condensation. The meaning of the first was obvious. He had some suspicions about the second, but he'd ask around to make sure.

Besides those, he'd acquired a new Class and a new title: Challenger.

Challenger: Most people conform. You fight and struggle to carve your own path. You will either defy the heavens... or fall and be forgotten. Efficacy of all stats +10%.

He liked the sound of that. It was ominous, sure, but it was his path. Plus, that 10% increase was just broken at this point.

Unlike previous Classes, the legendary-tier Paragon of Cultivation had only given him a single skill: Immortal Commune. It allowed him to directly contact the Immortals for guidance. This was probably something hardwired into the System, assuming every cultivator sided with the Immortals. It could have been a tremendous boon to others, but to Jack, who was their enemy, it was pretty useless.

No, not useless, he corrected himself. I can't use it for guidance, but I'm sure it will come in handy.

His stat points had shot through the roof. His Physical was at almost eight and a half thousand, or almost twenty thousand after all the efficacy increases from his titles. Considering the average pre-System human had an average Physical of *five*, that was a lot. Especially if he used it in conjunction with his Dao.

After familiarizing himself with his new level of power, Jack was finally ready to cultivate again. In fact, he looked forward to it, but he chose to wait a moment. He'd already been meditating for three days. Who knew what had occurred in the meantime.

Jack closed his status screen and left the room. He paced down a well-lit corridor. His previous cape had burned to nothing during the tribulation, and he hadn't gotten a new one. His only remaining piece of clothing were his enchanted brown shorts which reached down to his thighs. His bare feet rubbed against the metal floor. His muscular upper body dominated the corridor.

It still felt weird to walk around a futuristic starship half-naked, but he had more important things to worry about. Plus, those shorts could magically enhance his durability, so they weren't going anywhere. He couldn't wear anything else either, as the shorts' Life Dao amplification field couldn't penetrate fabric. He was, unfortunately, in a perpetual state of commando.

The corridor led him past a glass window overlooking the top floor of the Death Boat. He saw endless people going about their lives, living, breathing, working. It was an entire world down there. An almost nostalgic sight.

He walked past the one-way glass unseen, then turned down a bend, reaching a meeting room. He'd already received a mental message to come here.

The door swung open. A twenty by thirty foot meeting room appeared, with a long table in the middle and little else in the way of decoration. A wall-sized window overlooked the Bone Belt, the current hiding place of the Death Boat—an astronomically long strip of astral dust and flying boulders ranging from tiny to moon-sized. The light of a million distant suns augmented the brilliant image.

Despite Jack's expectations, only a single person awaited in the room. It was Starhair—a peak B-Grade cultivator with fluorescent hair like galaxy branches. Jack didn't know how strong this man was, but given he was part of Sovereign Heavenly Spoon's elite squad, he had to pack a punch.

The two of them had already met on the way to this galaxy. Starhair seemed to dislike Jack, for whatever reason, but they'd always kept things cordial.

As Jack entered, Starhair turned around. A condescending look was plastered to his face. "Here comes the champion. Should I kneel in worship?"

"Don't be a dick, Starhair. Keep your mouth shut."

Starhair froze. Jack grinned.

When the peak B-Grade had been feisty before, Jack had always kept his composure. He didn't give ground, but he also didn't desire to make new, unknown enemies. That was all different now. Jack had achieved a ten thousand mile inner world. He didn't give a flying fuck about Starhair's opinion.

The other man was surprised. "What did you just say to me?"

"I told you to shut up. Clearly, you've got something against me, but I'm in no mood for your silly games. Spit it out or be quiet."

Starhair puffed up like an angry rooster. "You are seriously overstepping your boundaries, Jack Rust."

"Fuck off, man. The only boundary I overstepped recently was with your mo—"

A door at the other side of the room slid open before Jack could finish his words. Sovereign Heavenly Spoon walked in, his face covered by a lazy smile, followed by the Sage, Min Ling, and Bottomless.

"Good morning, guys," the sovereign said. "Had breakfast yet? I brought food." He swiped a hand over his space ring, filling the table with snacks. Jack spotted everything from croissants to bacon sandwiches, along with a menagerie of alien stuff he'd never seen before. Among those a bowl of fat, writhing, green worms. There was also tea and coffee.

Jack raised his gaze from the table, meeting the Sage's intrigued eyes. Min Ling waved at him. Bottomless remained under his hood. Despite traveling together for a week, Jack still hadn't caught a glimpse of the person's features. He didn't even know if they were male or female.

Starhair remained with his mouth open, ready to spit bile at Jack, but he finally harrumphed and turned back to the window. Jack shrugged. He grabbed a paper plate from a pile and scanned the snacks.

"What's that?" he asked, pointing at the bowl of worms.

"Protein!" the sovereign exclaimed jovially. He manifested a silver spoon in his hand, then used it to sweep two worms onto his plate. "I guess you come from an area where you don't have something similar, but don't worry. These are called gum worms, a very popular dish across the universe. They may appear disgusting, but you have to remember that the world is a large place, and disgust is only a product of your mind. Keep an open mind. Try some."

Jack observed the worms. Each was the size of his pinky, slick in shape and not at all oily. They were plump, too. If not for their faces and little legs, he'd have assumed they were fruit.

He reached out, then gulped. "Maybe later," he said, and picked up a sausage instead. "How did you even store these, anyway? I thought you couldn't put living creatures in space rings."

The sovereign gave him a stare. "Come on, Jack. They're worms. Food. Don't be that guy."

"They don't have souls," Min Ling explained from the side. "I'm not sure why, but it makes them very convenient to transfer. They're certainly alive, though."

Jack shrugged. "Whatever. So, how have you guys been? It feels like ages."

"It's only been three days," the Sage replied. "Three eventful, important days. The kind that counts like a hundred dull ones."

"Who cares about us?" Min Ling said, her voice filled with excitement. "How have *you* been? You broke all records! You are immortalized as a legend! Tell me, how did that feel?"

"Scary," Jack replied. "I really thought I was going to die. But, you know, I'm used to that."

"Oh, don't dodge the question. Spit it out. How did you manage to reach ten thousand miles?"

With the exception of Starhair, who was still looking away, and Bottomless, whose expression was hidden by his hood, the others all sported expectant smiles. Their squad should have taken off the day before, but they'd stayed precisely to ask Jack about his experience. They hadn't had the opportunity after his breakthrough as he'd been exhausted and injured, and he'd rushed off to meditate.

Jack rubbed the back of his head. He considered lying, but most of these people had helped him greatly in the past. As for Starhair... Well, screw that guy. "I developed a tenth fruit mid-breakthrough. I thought my nine were perfect, but as I was about to break them up into an inner world, I suddenly realized they weren't. I took a risk to form a tenth one. Luckily, it worked out."

"Just like that?" Min Ling asked. "It can't be that simple. Everyone would have ten fruits."

"It wasn't easy. The first nine fruits felt natural, but this one showed resistance. It was like the laws of cultivation refused to accommodate me. I had to push real hard. I almost failed."

"And that's coming from someone who would have reached close to nine thousand miles even without the tenth fruit," the Sage said. "I suspect this tenth fruit really does go against the laws of cultivation. Perfection of the nine is the prerequisite of pursuing the ten. Even then, Jack achieved perfection of the ten fruits, reaching exactly ten thousand miles."

"That's what I think as well," Jack agreed.

"Do you believe there can be more fruits?" Sovereign Heavenly Spoon asked as he tossed a grape into his mouth. "Beyond the tenth, I mean."

Jack frowned. "I don't know. My Dao system feels pretty perfect right now. Maybe I could have tried to develop an eleventh fruit if I knew beforehand, but I think it's a good thing I didn't. The tribulation would have slaughtered me, Elder Boatman or not."

"That's the point of cultivation," the Sage said. "We pave the way for future generations. Now that we know it's possible, the apex talents of the universe will try to reach ten fruits. Some will succeed. Maybe they'll make more breakthroughs later. And the cultivation world marches forward, every generation one step higher."

Jack nodded. "Exactly. Even my idea about a tenth fruit didn't come completely out of nowhere. The inheritance of Archon Green Dragon contained a hint. I think he suspected it was possible, but long after he'd reached the B-Grade."

"I feel for him," the sovereign said with a sigh. "If I wasn't already at the B-Grade, I would try to go for a tenth fruit myself. Maybe more. Seventeen is a nice number."

Jack smiled. In his experience, manifesting a tenth fruit was as difficult as reaching well over eight thousand miles, but he chose not to say anything. No sense discouraging his friends.

"What are we gathered for, anyway?" he asked. "Elder Boatman had told me to come when I was ready, but he didn't mention a reason."

"I don't think he knew either," the Sage replied. "Many things happened after your breakthrough. This is the time to find a way forward."

As if hearing his name, Elder Boatman suddenly appeared in the middle of the room. He didn't teleport in. It was like part of reality perished, defaulting to him instead of death. "Greetings, everyone," he said. "Let's get started. Are those gum worms?"

CHAPTER THREE
CLONE

Elder Boatman grabbed a gum worm between two fingers, slurping it in. Jack cringed. The worm disappeared down the vampire's throat, dead the moment he touched it.

"You have achieved great merit, Jack," Elder Boatman said. "News of your breakthrough have spread far and wide. The failing morale of our army has temporarily recovered. You've given our cultivators a source of inspiration, and our enemies one of fear. You've also made me proud. Good job."

"Thanks, Master," Jack replied, trying to keep his mind away from how the Elder was still eating worms.

"Of course, everything has consequences," the vampire continued. "The Immortals are aware of your existence, and they'll do anything they can to exterminate you. Don't be surprised when they send A-Grades to personally hunt you down."

Jack stood straight. "I can handle it."

"I know. But we can't. My starship houses tens of millions of people, and I'd rather not invite the enemy's full attention to my doorstep. Besides, if they really do find us, I may not be able to protect you. You will leave the Death Boat in a few hours and head towards the New Cathedral, our current headquarters. The Arch Priestess herself wants to see you. She may even accept you as a disciple, so I suggest making a good impression. Maybe consider wearing a shirt."

"What?" Jack said. "Hold on, I'll be leaving? But I just arrived."

"I'm sad too, my disciple," Elder Boatman replied. "However, even if I hadn't received direct orders, it would be irresponsible of me to keep you here. Protecting you is my duty as your master, but I have to accept I may not be able to. It's a shame."

"You saved my life," Jack replied. "And Brock's. We are extremely grateful."

"It was nothing," he replied, waving a pale hand. "Now, as I said, you'll be transferring to the New Cathedral for training. Brock will join you, and I will also separate a small part of my soul to follow you and keep instructing you on the Dao of Death."

"Part of your soul?"

"It's called a clone. I believe you're familiar with the concept. One soul simultaneously inhabiting multiple bodies. It's the basis of all our communication systems, but that's besides the point."

Jack opened his mouth and closed it again. This was a little too much information. And had Elder Boatman mentioned he might be apprenticed to the Arch Priestess? The head of the Black Hole Church, who was most probably an Archon?

He shook his head to clear it.

"And I guess," he said, motioning toward the Spoon Squad who were idling nearby, "they'll be the ones taking me there."

"Sovereign Heavenly Spoon and his squad are needed at the front lines. They've already wasted precious time here," Elder Boatman said, striking the sovereign with a glare. The other man didn't even pause eating. "You will be escorted by a different vessel. We won't reveal the details until the final moment for security reasons. However, Envoy Starhair has also been recalled to the New Cathedral, so he will be joining you."

Oh, fuck me.

Jack and Starhair locked eyes. The Envoy smiled grimly.

Wait. I'm also an Envoy now. Nice.

"I don't know what's going on between you two, nor do I care," the Elder said. "We are fighting a losing war. We cannot afford infighting. I expect you to act as responsible individuals and put your differences aside."

Jack raised his head. "Yes, Master."

"Yes, Elder," Starhair replied at the same time. He sounded earnest. Jack didn't believe him in the slightest.

"Good," Elder Boatman replied. "Meet me at the throne room in three hours." He reached for his plate, grasping no gum worms. He'd run out. "Oh," he said. Ten of them teleported from the bowl to his paper plate, then he abruptly disappeared. The bowl was now empty.

Sovereign Heavenly Spoon hissed. "I wanted those!" he said, then sighed in displeasure. He grabbed a large cup of tea and swirled it with the silver spoon which also doubled as his planet-eating weapon.

Jack swept his gaze over his fellow Envoys. Min Ling was the first to meet him. "We still have a date, cowboy," she said. "You promised to spar with me when you reached the B-Grade. I'm right here."

He grinned at her. "Do you really think you stand a chance?"

"Only one way to find out."

Jack laughed. "Good! I look forward to testing out my powers, too."

"We can do it now."

"Sure. Just give me a moment." He turned his gaze to another person. "Hey, Sage. Think I could talk to you alone for a minute?"

The homeless-looking man, just like every other time, showed no surprise. The extent and nature of his powers remained a mystery to Jack.

Jack and the Sage stood alone in a different room. There was another large window here, but no table, only a set of chairs at the back. The two men stood next to the window, gazing out.

"Do you remember what you told me once upon a time?" Jack asked.

"I've told you many things."

"That your soul resonated with Enas. That you could use that connection to share in the god's Dao and reach the B-Grade with basically no bottleneck. That the whole reason Earth was Integrated was because the Church wanted to find you."

The Sage nodded. "That is correct."

"But is it the whole truth?"

A pause. "Why do you ask?"

"I was stranded in a strange place for a year—a place called the Black Hole World," Jack said. "It was occupied by the descendants of an old Archon, trapped there since the First Crusade a billion years ago. They had a stone tablet about that event. It portrayed the Old Gods and the Immortals, as well as their armies."

Jack faced the Sage, then continued, "There was a person there, in the army following the Old Gods. A person who looked just like you."

The Sage smiled. "It was a stone tablet. How accurate could they make the face of a small figure?"

"Don't dodge the question, Sage. It was carved in great detail. That person had your likeness. What's going on?"

The Sage remained silent, and almost looked pained; almost. He sighed. "You shouldn't have seen that," he said. Jack instinctively raised his guard, but there was no attack coming, only words. "This isn't really a secret. It's just something we'd rather not share to the common cultivator."

"Am I a common cultivator?"

"You were, last time we talked about this."

Jack frowned. "Keep talking."

"The truth is, I am not just a human whose soul vibrates with that of Enas. When he was trapped in the black hole, he was not content to remain there for eternity. Enas embodies the Dao of Life, whose core tenant is survival. Soon after his imprisonment, Enas split his soul in two, then shattered one half into innumerable tiny pieces. Those pieces were nothing but soul-infused collections of Life Dao particles.

"Over time, they slowly seeped out of the black hole, making their way through the universe in search of suitable bodies. Of course, that was an extremely unlikely process, which was why Enas had created so many. There needed to be someone with a compatible soul, which was already extremely rare, and then there also needed to be a soul piece very close-by when that person was born. The fusion could only be carried out shortly after birth.

"A billion years later, those coincidences finally occurred. One of those innumerable tiny soul pieces happened to land on Earth, where it fused into a compatible baby. And thus, I was born. A human with a tiny, tiny part of a god inside me. However, even that part of a god's soul is stronger than a mortal's, so the fusion wasn't perfect. I spent thirty-three years on Earth being insane as the two sides warred inside me. I had flashes and visions of things no mortal could witness. It was only when the Integration happened that an agent of the Church arrived at our planet, helped the divine part of my soul overwhelm the other, and made me into who I am today."

Jack gave him a suspicious glance. "So you're, like, a clone of Enas?"

"In the wider sense of the word. I possess my own personality and almost none of the god's powers. What I do have is random visions, as well as an extreme affinity towards the Dao of Life. Specifically, divination."

"Extreme affinity? Really? Nobody has mentioned your B-Grade breakthrough as anything outstanding."

"Dao affinity doesn't always translate into a deeper cultivation. In any case, it's a good thing my breakthrough was low-key. It helped me avoid attention. My cultivation and combat strength—

which has always been shit—are secondary. The real purpose of my existence is to remain alive, so the Church can use me as the key to summon the true soul of Enas outside the black hole."

"What!"

The Sage smiled, showing yellow teeth. "I am to be sacrificed. Thanks to me, the remainder of Enas's soul and body will escape their eternal prison, reclaiming his rightful position as god king of the universe."

"Wait. So the Second Crusade is happening to stop that?"

"No. The Immortals suspect some things, but they know nothing. The Second Crusade coinciding with my appearance is a humongous, terrible coincidence."

"...How is that possible?"

"The Heavenly Dao works in mysterious ways, my friend," the Sage replied with a sad smile. He put a hand on Jack's shoulder. "The person in the tablet was another clone of Enas. Before his imprisonment, he was experimenting with infusing his soul into cultivators and controlling them. His fellow gods betrayed him before those experiments bore fruit."

Jack wasn't really listening now. Various puzzle pieces clicked into place in his mind. "Is that why you wanted the Life Drop in Trial Planet? Because it was kind of your blood to begin with?"

"That's right. I would be able to resonate with it and use it much more effectively than anyone else, including you... but, as I said, my combat strength is secondary. It was average back then, and it's even worse now. A fragmented soul like me could never reach the A-Grade. I was supposed to take the Life Drop to the Church and help it find a suitable candidate, but I deemed you good enough."

"Hmm," Jack said. He frowned, saying nothing for a moment, then changed the subject. "Still, man... You only exist to be sacrificed? That's so incredibly sad."

The Sage shrugged. "It's not as bad as it sounds. I will reunite with my whole like a tributary flowing into the river. The person I am now will die, but my soul will live on."

"...Oh."

"Is that all you wanted to ask me?"

Jack looked at the Sage. This homeless-looking, yellow-toothed, rag-wearing man had always been an enigma. The more he learned, the more questions he had—some of which he felt were better left unasked.

Thing is, something wasn't right about the Sage's story. There was still something missing. He just couldn't place a finger on what.

"Yeah, that's all," he finally said.

"Good. Then, let me give you a piece of advice before you go fight that little girl," the Sage said, leaning closer. "Do you know why the Heavenly Dao sent that tribulation for you? During your latest breakthrough?"

Jack was immediately transfixed. "Because it's an asshole?"

"Because you took a single step outside the lines. That by itself isn't much, but defiance is a plague. It spreads from person to person, and one step turns into ten, which turn into a stampede. What starts slow can become exponentially fast, and before the universe knows it, it might lose control of you cultivators. So, remember this, Jack. That was neither your first nor last tribulation. The universe will keep trying to take you down. If you do survive, however, then your defiance will become a superpower. You and Brock can spread that shit and change the world. Even the Gods are afraid. Don't sleep on it."

Jack stared into the Sage's eyes, finding them glowing with a fierce, excited light. The next moment, it was gone. The Sage stood back to his full height, which wasn't much. "Well, that was my advice, anyway."

"Do you want to elaborate? That was cryptic as fuck."

"You will understand when the time comes. Now go have fun out there. I believe your date is waiting."

CHAPTER FOUR

SPARRING MIN LING

Jack floated in space. The Death Boat floated to the side, a looming behemoth, while the Bone Belt surrounded them in all directions, partially hiding the stars beyond. On a careful glance, Jack noticed this wasn't the same part of the Bone Belt they'd been at before. The Death Boat had moved since his breakthrough. That made sense—he'd raised quite a ruckus.

"Ready when you are," his opponent called out. She raised her spear, pointing it straight at his nose. Red lightning danced on its tip. She grinned. The crowd cheered.

Min Ling was a pale-skinned, dark-haired woman Jack had first met while training at the Cathedral. They'd been C-Grades then, with her at the very top of the rankings. Despite that, she wasn't an asshole—a stark difference from many other cultivators.

The two of them had adventured together in the Green Dragon Realm and spent three years meditating in a cave. They were good friends.

Now, they had both reached the early B-Grade. Their once-uneven cultivations had caught up, and any clash between them would depend entirely on talent. That was what Min Ling wanted.

She didn't think she could win, but she was a warrior. Facing the unprecedented genius of Jack Rust, she wanted to see how she stacked up. Her anticipation was through the roof. She'd never been more excited.

So was the crowd. They also didn't doubt the conclusion of this spar, but who would miss the opportunity to see two great talents go head-to-head?

Who would miss Jack Rust's first battle since entering the B-Grade?

Jack smiled. "Prepare yourself, Min Ling. Here I come."

"No need to warn me! And, just so you know, I will be going all-out. If I accidentally kill you, it's your fault."

He laughed. "You can try your—"

The spear point was between his eyes. Power blasted out of Jack, slowing her down just enough to let him duck, dodging the strike. It zipped over his head, unleashing a straight thrust which penetrated the entire Bone Belt for a thousand miles. Rock and dust went flying. Space frothed like water currents.

Jack narrowed his eyes. *That was fast!*

His already clenched fist shot out, faster than Min Ling's spear. A cage of sparks appeared to block it. Intense lightning snaked into his body through his arm, trying to paralyze him or slow him down, but he easily shook it off. His fist kept going, smashing into Min Ling and sending her flying. She'd barely managed to block with the body of her spear.

"Again!" she shouted. Her body blurred. Three Min Lings spread across space, each moving in a different trajectory. They flew in a complex pattern. Even Jack's accelerated perception couldn't differentiate them.

This wasn't just an application of Space Dao, but more of her extreme speed. Even Jack had to admit that, on this subject, he was outmatched.

But speed was just one facet of battle.

He also blurred. Two Jacks appeared, smashing into the three

Min Lings. Spears met fists. By this point, Jack's knuckles were hard enough to clash directly against the tip of her spear. They were by far the most tempered part of his body.

Blows rained from either side. The two Jacks and three Min Lings maneuvered around each other. It was a spectacular sight.

"Look, she's winning!" an audience member cried breathlessly.

"No, you idiot. Can't you see he's pushing her back?" another replied.

Though there were two Jacks and three Min Lings, in truth, it didn't matter at all. Jack didn't practice this technique. He was purposely matching her strong attribute with his weak one, but even that wasn't enough to overpower him. As the two sides struggled, Min Ling was pushed farther and farther back. She was faster than Jack, but not enough to secure an advantage. Meanwhile, he was stronger, more durable, with deeper insights into the Dao, and with significantly more energy at his disposal thanks to his larger inner world.

Jack burst with power. The feeling was almost ecstatic. He no longer needed to use the ambient Dao as he did in the D and C-Grades. It flooded out of him, an exorbitant amount of energy perfectly attuned with his Dao. It filled every spot of his body with firecrackers. This power was so explosive, so potent, he moved at the speed of thought. His punches cracked out. Starry purple aura flowed outside his limbs, splashing back every time he attacked. To the spectators, he looked like a god.

Min Ling was a boat in a storm, struggling just to stay afloat. She fell into a defensive position. "Hah!" she shouted, her joy evident as she pulled back to disengage. Her form-fitting leather armor was torn in places—her hair was disheveled, and she was panting, but her eyes remained spirited.

"You're good, Jack! I've never lost to someone at the same cultivation level, and I don't plan to start now!"

"Then come!" Jack replied. He, too, was excited. This battle was the best opportunity to familiarize himself with his new powers.

Energy flooded his inner world, an amount incomparable to anything he'd ever wielded before. It was a ten thousand mile wide sphere which answered only to him. He could quite literally blast a planet with pure energy and destroy it.

Red sparks emerged from Min Ling's body. Purple flames burned. She was clad in lightning and fire, her two main Daos, and Jack could feel her power rising. Space was quivering by her mere presence. "This is my strongest form," she declared. "I know you possess a similar technique. Bring it out, and let's fight to our heart's content!"

Jack smiled. "Make me."

She snorted. Space rippled, and she disappeared. Her speed was vastly superior to before, as was her strength.

Jack leaned forward. A spear appeared over his head, having stabbed at him from his blind spot, then curved down to smack him. He punched its body, sending it off course. Min Ling stayed on him. She pressed her advantage. Hundreds of stabs and strikes assaulted him. She was like a dancer, twirling and turning, maintaining her spear's momentum as it pelted him with an increasing number of attacks. The lightning gave her explosiveness, the fire tenacity. She had him cornered and wasn't going to let go.

Jack twisted and turned. He ducked under a swing, leaned sideways to avoid a stab, then slapped another off course. As she danced, so did he. Min Ling teleported behind and below him, already mid-thrust. He teleported himself upside down, punching the tip of her spear. Sparks erupted. Fist and spear both recoiled, but Min Ling twisted around herself, borrowing the momentum of Jack's attack to maintain her momentum.

She was good. Very good. Jack's eyes flashed with appreciation. Her technique was immaculate, her body strong, and her Daos deep. Against any other opponent, she would have seemed unbeatable, as if she had no weakness. It was a shame that the one she fought was Jack, who was also a well-rounded fighter, but better. His every attribute except speed was a tier above hers.

Min Ling pelted Jack with attacks. This form she was using could pressure Jack, but she was also spending tremendous amounts of energy to maintain it. If he just defended, he could probably endure until she grew exhausted.

But where was the fun in that?

Jack homed in. Spacetime warped around him, enhancing his movements while obstructing hers. He was like a fish in water—like a leaf in the wind, untouchable. No matter how many spear strikes surrounded him, they couldn't even scratch him. His eyes were focused. Every movement of her spear was clearly reflected there, as Jack gathered his energy and waited for his chance.

He leaned back, then to the side, flew up and teleported behind her. She matched the movement, still stabbing. He dodged every attack by a narrow margin, saving enough time to dodge the next one. His eyes remained glued on hers, sensing her frustration, her growing sense of impatience.

A single spear strike went wide. Jack's eyes flashed. *Now!*

Lightning erupted from his body with a boom. Thunder Body activated. His speed and power shot up. To her credit, Min Ling reacted instantly. She abandoned her strike and brought her spear back to defend.

Jack reached out, grabbed the spear body, and yanked it out of the way to expose her face. His strength was vastly superior. Min Ling had no way of stopping him. In the same movement, his other hand was clenched into a fist, shooting forward. He met her panicked eyes. She saw death.

Jack's fist froze an inch before her face. She just remained there, unable to react in time. She was still blown back. He might have stopped his punch, but the momentum remained. Min Ling flew backward like a broken kite, her body warped by the extreme speed, crossing a thousand miles in the blink of an eye. Only then did she manage to stop herself, yet the force of the strike kept going. The entire asteroid belt behind her exploded. A wide cone of emptiness cut right through it, sending rocks and dust and everything else flying away. A clear, starry sky was revealed at the far back.

Min Ling stood frozen. She turned her head around to look, gasping at the sheer amount of destruction Jack had wrought. And that was just the escaping energy. If he hadn't stopped his strike, all that energy would have gone into her face. Her head would have disintegrated.

She turned back to the front and chuckled helplessly, not even registering her disheveled hair or the blood that flowed from her nose. "I lost," she declared. Her voice reached the crowd. Voices rose in cheers, while many others spoke encouraging words.

"You fought great!" they said. "That was awesome!"

"Keep rocking, Min Ling!"

"We love you!"

Jack also received words of congratulations, but he only chuckled in amusement. Back during the Integration Tournament, the cheering audience had been made up of F-Grades, while the D-Grade mentors stood arrogantly at the back. Now, the least of his audience was D-Grades, with even B-Grades thrown in the mix. They were reacting the exact same way the F-Grades once did.

It had nothing to do with individual power. Once a person joined a crowd, they were all the same—and that wasn't a bad thing at all. It was a reminder that appearances were made-up. They were all humans at heart—or, well, whatever species each of them belonged to.

Or, maybe, personality had nothing to do with one's level. Every level had assholes and good people. Take Starhair, for example—the man had reached a level of power most would wet themselves just thinking about, yet all he could do was sit away from the crowd and grumble like a loser.

Jack turned and gave the man a thumbs-up. Starhair snorted.

"Good fight," Min Ling said, appearing in front of Jack. "I lost fair and square. It was my honor." She extended a hand.

Jack shook it. "The honor was all mine. You fought well. It wasn't as easy as it seemed."

The crowd erupted in cheers. Unlike most of Jack's battles, there weren't any bad feelings involved here. It was just a wholesome show.

She stuck out a tongue. "Liar. You didn't use a single skill."

"Thunder Body is a skill."

"Yeah, but you only used it for show."

He winked. "Really though. It seemed I was just dodging everything back there, but it was pushing me to the limit. You are by far the strongest opponent I have ever faced at the same level."

"I'm not as great as you make me out to be," she said. "Spoon once lowered his cultivation level to the early B-Grade and sparred with me. He completely kicked my ass."

"Really?" Jack felt a sudden interest.

"Yeah. But, he already told me he won't do that for you. He wants to fight you at full power once you reach his level."

"Who says I haven't?"

She laughed. "Trust me, Jack. He's a whole different beast. When he reached eight thousand miles during his breakthrough, it was because he had an accident mid-way. The Elders thought he could have gone higher. Much higher."

Jack turned his head to the side. Sovereign Heavenly Spoon sat there, calmly sipping on his tea. They crossed eyes. "*I'm ready whenever, big guy,*" Jack messaged him. Spoon smiled and ignored him. Jack smiled.

Sovereign Heavenly Spoon had been the Head Envoy of the Black Hole Church since he was at the middle B-Grade. That meant he was the strongest B-Grade around. Now that he'd reached the late B-Grade and was approaching the peak level... Just how strong could he be?

Jack felt a rare hint of excitement rising inside him. He really looked forward to fighting that man. Of course, if Spoon didn't feel like it, he couldn't force it.

"*Next time,*" the sovereign's reply reached Jack's mind, and he nodded, satisfied.

"*Next time.*"

"Jack," a new voice came. It was Elder Boatman's, though it sounded oddly weakened. "*Come to the throne room. It's almost time for you to go.*"

Jack looked around. Besides his master, he didn't have anything tying him down to the Death Boat. Dorman, who'd arrived here alongside Jack, had already left to join the front lines. Even the Spoon Squad would depart soon. He turned his gaze to the Sage, who was sitting there as if untouched by anything.

A clone of Enas... Jack thought. He shook his head. Whatever was going on there was beyond his current paygrade. Once the time came for him to be involved, hopefully things would become clear.

He looked back at Min Ling. "I gotta go. I'll see you around?"

She smiled. "You bet."

The two exchanged a hug, then he teleported away.

CHAPTER FIVE

CULTIVATING IN THE B-GRADE

JACK TELEPORTED INSIDE THE BONE THRONE ROOM. WHITE MARBLE WAS ALL around. Black columns supported a high ceiling, while a massive, bone-adorned throne stood at the far back, atop a small flight of stairs. The middle of the room held a table with twelve seats, and at the first of those seats sat Elder Boatman.

He also sat at the second seat. There were two Elder Boatmans.

"Master?" Jack said.

"Jack, let me introduce you to my clone," the first Elder Boatman said. Both of them stood up.

"I remain one individual," the second Elder Boatman said. "I just split a small part of my soul to create the low-power clone you see before you. As long as they are in the same dimension, my two bodies can communicate instantly regardless of distance. My clone will accompany you to the New Cathedral."

"Oh," Jack replied. Scanning the two Boatmans, he noted that the second was only at the early A-Grade level of power, while the first remained at the late A-Grade but had lost some intensity. "You know, this would have been very useful while I was alone in System space."

"Creating clones is not easy, Jack. You weren't worth it at the time. Plus, I didn't know all this was going to happen."

The second Boatman wore the same clothes and held the same weapon as the original body. On closer scrutiny, Jack found that his scythe radiated far less power. Like a replica.

"I understand," he said. "Thank you, Master. I hope this wasn't too hard on you."

"Nothing you need to worry about," the first Boatman replied. "We can leave as soon as your—Uh. They're here."

A door opened, letting in Brock and Starhair. The two were ignoring each other. Starhair had never shown animosity toward Brock, but he had against Jack, so Brock naturally followed suit. "Hey, bro," the brorilla said with a huge smile. "Hello, Master Grandpa Dead. Hello, uh, twin bro of Master Grandpa Dead."

"Hey, Brock," Jack replied. "That's a clone. He's still your Master Grandpa Dead, just in two bodies instead of one."

Elder Boatman groaned. "If you could stop encouraging this farce, Jack, that would be great. Welcome, Brock, Starhair. I trust you've been informed."

"Yes, Elder," Starhair replied reverently. "With your clone by our side, we are certain to have an uneventful journey. Thank you for your protection."

"What an ass-kisser," Jack whispered to Brock, loud enough for Starhair to hear.

"Ass-kisser Bro indeed."

"Uneventful journeys are the worst kind," Elder Boatman replied, ignoring Starhair's flattery. "Since you're all gathered, there is no need to keep waiting. You can leave immediately."

"Yes, Elder," Starhair said as the space around them died, replaced with a different scenery. They were in a starship floating alone in the Bone Belt. The Death Boat was barely visible in the distance through a window. Jack whistled, impressed once again at the efficiency with which Elder Boatman manipulated space.

This starship was the sleek, metallic kind designed for security.

The windows were small and enhanced, while the walls were extra thick. The entire thing was shaped as a needle. Spreading his perception outside, Jack also discovered that the exterior of the starship felt fuzzy, as if his perception slid right off.

"Anti-detection," the clone of Elder Boatman said, not explaining further. The starship was empty when they arrived. It was just the four of them.

"Oh wow," Jack said. "Our crew is one-fourth asshole."

Starhair turned his head around so hard it could have cracked, while Boatman frowned. "You will be civilized, Jack. Don't make me repeat myself. We cannot afford infighting."

Jack sighed. "Yes, Master."

Brock went around and knocked on the walls. They replied with muffled thuds—not the hollow kind. "Good ship," he said. "What's it called?"

"The *Iron Maiden*," Elder Boatman replied.

"The hell? That's an ominous name if I've ever heard one, Master!" Jack protested.

"There is a reason for it, Jack. There is always a reason. Now, I will handle the guidance of this thing. I don't specialize in the Dao of Space, so while I am not slow, I am not as fast as Bottomless, either. Moreover, we'll be operating in stealth mode. It will take us a few days to reach the New Cathedral. We'll probably encounter space monsters on the way, as this galaxy is chock-full of them, but they shouldn't be a problem. You are free to stay in your rooms or walk around during the journey, but *no infighting*. Am I clear?"

"Yes, Elder!" Starhair replied, standing at attention. Jack and Brock agreed a moment later.

"Good. Jack and Brock, I will approach you later to discuss your cultivation in the B-Grade. You are all dismissed."

Despite Elder Boatman's assurances, Jack believed the *Iron Maiden* was not aptly named at all. There was no way it could be. The real iron maiden was a medieval device which killed the person inside it, and this starship was supposed to do the exact opposite. Sure, Jack could sense an odd Dao current flowing through the walls, but what function it could have and how it correlated to an iron maiden was beyond him.

The starship didn't care for his concerns. It flowed smoothly through space like a propelled needle through the ocean. With Elder Boatman at the helm, space constantly warped around them, shooting them forward at tremendous speed. Stars twinkled all around. Despite the Elder's warning about space monsters and the war raging everywhere, this galaxy seemed oddly empty.

Jack's mind was calm. He had his eyes closed, breathing to a steady rhythm. His chest rose and fell.

He was cultivating.

An endless expanse comprised his inner world. It was so large he almost couldn't see its limits, though he knew it was exactly ten thousand miles across, shaped as a perfect sphere. A fist-shaped meteor floated in the very middle, while Jack sat cross-legged on it, meditating.

His real body was still in the outside world, and always would be, but he could manifest his willpower as a second body inside his inner world. Here, he was a god. Everything bowed to his desires. He wasn't cultivating either of his bodies, but the world itself.

The inner world had once been filled with energy, and Jack had expended it all during his breakthrough. Now, the remaining energy was pitifully sparse. That didn't mean it was little in quantity, but that the area over which it spread was simply humongous.

In fact, the energy density was so low that it couldn't even condense into matter. It was just lonely, fist-shaped particles floating around.

Jack focused. He took another deep breath, using his powers to draw in the ambient Dao particles of the real world, filtering them so they were compatible with his Dao. He then poured those particles into his inner world. They immediately dissipated into their surroundings and disappeared. Jack persisted. His real body became a funnel similar to a black hole, relentlessly drawing in the energy of the universe and absorbing it into his inner world. The surrounding space stirred. Vacuum strips trailed behind the quickly-moving starship. Had it been sitting still, Jack would have already sucked dry the surrounding few miles of space.

The volume of energy entering his inner world felt great. Yet, the moment it actually arrived, it wasn't even a drop in the bucket. The inner world boasted a volume of over four trillion cubic miles. That was just absurd. It was double the volume of the Earth, and his gathering of energy felt like using a teaspoon to fill the ocean.

Jack sighed, running out of patience. *This is pointless*, he realized.

In the B-Grade, the System quantified one's progress using two metrics: Inner World Size and Matter Condensation. The first was self-explanatory, indicating the diameter of one's inner world. The second metric, as Jack found out after asking Elder Boatman, was a fancy name for energy density.

The B-Grade worked as follows:

A cultivator started with a certain world size and abysmal energy density. To progress from one tier to the next, e.g. from the early to the middle B-Grade, they had to absorb energy into their inner world to increase its density. Once it reached a certain point—which was at 100% Matter Condensation, or double the starting density—the inner world would be dense enough for the energy to condense into matter. That's where the fancy name came from.

After matter appeared, the inner world's stability would increase. The cultivator then utilized that extra stability to expand the world again, increasing its diameter by one-fourth, and therefore, due to math, doubling its volume. That had the effect of reducing their energy density, pulling it back to 0%. The cultivator had stepped into the next minor tier, and the process began anew.

In short, he had to cultivate until Matter Condensation went from 0 to 100%, then break through and double the volume of his inner world, then do it all over again. After completing the third cycle, he would have reached the peak B-Grade, and he could then proceed to break into the A-Grade.

It was simple in theory. Easy in practice. The problem was that it was damn time-consuming.

Even the smallest inner world with a thousand-mile diameter had volume counted in the billions of cubic miles. Jack's volume was a thousand times that. He was extremely powerful for his level, but the drawback was that breaking through each minor realm would be far more difficult for him than for other cultivators. Even with his deep foundation and Dao insights, which allowed for faster accumulation of energy, cultivating was simply proving to be pointless.

Inner World size: 10,000 miles
Matter Condensation: 0%

He had spent an entire day cultivating, and all he'd managed was to activate the Matter Condensation metric, turning it from a single dash to 0%. He wasn't even close to 1%. Wasn't even close to a thousandth of a percent. The volume he had to fill up with energy was so endless, he could spend his entire hundred thousand years of lifespan cultivating and only reach the middle B-Grade.

He grumbled and sat up. Regular B-Grades often spent tens of thousands of years in cultivation between each minor realm, but he had neither the time nor the patience for that. He was at war. If he wanted to have any sort of impact, he'd have to break through within a few years at the most.

Cultivating like this is a waste of time, he decided. I will progress by killing others to level up or using treasures. My time is best spent on the Dao.

That was the real path of cultivation. The Dao. And Jack, having just broken through and surpassed a heavenly tribulation, had a bunch of things to meditate on. He also had a Dao Vision to cash in. First, though, he wanted to get some fresh air.

He exited his room, finding himself back at the bridge of the starship. Elder Boatman sat cross-legged at the very front, facing a window flashing with the light of teleportation, while Brock stood before another window to the side. He seemed relaxed and casual. He'd even found some peanuts somewhere and was chomping them down.

"Hey, Brock," Jack said, approaching his little brother. "You're also bummed out, huh?"

"It's pointless," Brock said. "The world is too big. Waste of my time."

"Yeah."

"Peanuts?"

"Yes, please. Where did you even find these?"

"Master Grandpa Dead gave me."

Jack threw an amused glance at Elder Boatman. Another door slid open, revealing Starhair, who was shaking his head at something. The moment he saw Jack, his face soured. He chose a different window and approached it without a word.

Jack rolled his eyes and walked over.

CHAPTER SIX
DAO TALK

"Hey, man," Jack said, stepping to the side of Starhair. "Can I ask you something?"

The other cultivator didn't turn his head. His voice came aloof, almost dismissing, "What is it this time?"

"Why are you being a dick to me? I don't remember doing anything to offend you."

Starhair gave Jack a long stare. Jack scoffed.

"Not that I particularly care," he added. "I've had my fair share of assholes. It's just that we're stuck here for a few days, I'm annoyed that my cultivation is slow, and I figured that maybe asking you would ruin your mood."

Starhair snorted. "Of course it's slow. The B-Grade is adjusted for difficulty against a cultivator's potential. With your stupidly large inner world, it won't surprise me if you remain at the early B-Grade forever. It would suit you just right."

"We both know that won't happen. I'll find a way." Jack smiled. "Is that it, then? You're jealous?"

"Please."

"Then what is it?"

"You killed a family friend of mine. A C-Grade from my galaxy. You know who I'm talking about."

Jack scoffed again. "I haven't the slightest idea. I've killed lots of people."

Starhair turned quickly, his galaxy-like hair whipping around, eyes shimmering with anger. "Don Cranxiao, you imbecile. An heir of the Iron Fist Empire. He was from the Hammerhead Galaxy, same as me, as you very well know."

Jack blinked in surprise. The name was familiar, from a long time ago. When he first arrived at the Cathedral, Don Cranxiao had been an obnoxious, low-level bully. He was sheltered by his high-rank cousin, Baron Longform, and often beat up or stole the Dao Stones of the bottom-rankers. He'd eventually made the mistake of messing with Jack, who executed him in a public duel. It was what kick-started his whole enmity with the much more dangerous Baron Longform.

In Jack's mind, Don Cranxiao was nothing but a throw-away minor villain, one of the dozens he'd faced throughout the years.

"First of all," Jack said, "I don't give a shit about which galaxy you come from, let alone Cranxiao. It's my first time hearing about a Hammerhead galaxy. What stupid name is that, anyway? Second... Really? You were friends with that clown? He was nothing but a little bully. I know you're an ass, but even you can do better."

"Don't insult the dead. Cranxiao was a family friend. I had the implicit responsibility to protect him," Starhair said, puffing out his chest. "Because you killed him, I received a chastisement by my galaxy's A-Grade Overlord."

Jack couldn't help it. He laughed.

"What are you laughing about?" Starhair said, frowning deeply.

"I just can't," Jack replied, still laughing. It wasn't out of mockery. This justification was so jarringly soft, so ridiculous, that he'd been ambushed with laughter. "Let me tell you something, Starhair," he said, wiping a tear off his eye. "You and I are not the same kind of people. I'm a warrior, and you are just a spoiled, powerful brat. Do you know what happened between me and my last real enemy? He tried to enslave my planet. I killed his son, his best disciple, humiliated him publicly, cracked his Dao, and got him exiled from his family and home faction. In retaliation, he yet again invaded my home planet, abducted my son and killed him before my very eyes, then orchestrated a massive hunt for me.

"I had to go through hell and back to recover from my son's death and gain the power to face that man and his backers. Our conflict was the focal point of a constellation-wide war with casualties numbering in the tens of billions. In the end, not only did I defeat him and kill everyone who supported him, not only did I destroy a B-Grade faction with a million years of history, I also forced his millions of descendants to change their last name so he would be dishonored for eternity."

Jack had stopped laughing. He wasn't angry, just amused. Meanwhile, Starhair had gone pale.

"So you can understand, Starhair," Jack continued calmly, "that when you use your peanut-sized brain to insult me only because you received a scolding from your galaxy's big daddy, you do not intimidate me. I'm not even offended. You are so refreshingly mild that all you achieve is to amuse me. If you want my advice, give it up, turn your life around, and stop being such a little bitch."

Starhair took a moment to compose himself. He seemed both mortified and angry. "I don't need your advice," was all he managed to say.

"Ha! Just stay out from under my damn feet," he said, walking away. "Clown."

He approached Brock again, ignoring Starhair's burning glare on his back. Brock, who'd listened to the conversation, shook his head. "What a silly little bro."

"I heard that!" Starhair called out, only to be ignored by both.

"I guess that's one worry off my head," Jack said, shrugging. "What are you going to do now? Meditate on your Dao?"

"Yes. Time is precious. We must work hard."

"Agreed." Jack sighed. "After everything that happened, not having a time limit over our heads feels pretty nice, but we shouldn't laze about."

Brock gave him a good look. "Are you okay, bro?"

"Yes. It's all in the past now, but thank you for worrying."

"It's my job." Brock nodded. "Okay. I'm going to meditate."

"See you, bro."

Brock made to walk away. In the same moment, space warped between them. Elder Boatman appeared—the clone who was driving their ship. "Disciples," he said in his gravely voice. "I have some time. Let's talk about your paths."

"Oh, hi, Master," Jack said.

"Hello, Master Grandpa Dead. Thanks for the peanuts. They were very tasty."

"No problem. Brock, you go first. Tell me about your inner world."

The brorilla grinned. "Okay! I have the bro world. It is gold and big. All my bros live there."

"As phantoms, I assume?" the Elder asked.

"Yes. All real bros have phantoms in the central temple. There are also brorilla bros flying around."

"That's so much more than mine," Jack said. "I just have a meteor and empty space."

"Different Daos manifest differently, but it doesn't mean much," Elder Boatman explained. "Does your inner world feel stable, Brock?"

"Yes."

"Good. That's an important point. It means you can just focus on gathering energy. Not by yourself, obviously—the New Cathedral contains many resources which I suspect they'll let you use."

Jack and Brock's faces lit up. "Thank you, Master!" Jack said.

"Don't thank me. The Arch Priestess controls these things." Boatman waved a hand. "What Daos do you focus on, Brock?"

"Brohood."

"Just that?"

"Yes. The rest of the Daos are just helpful bros."

"That's good. I would normally be worried, but since you've reached this stage without a problem, brotherhood must be one of the rare Daos which can be cultivated by themselves."

"Of course. Brotherhood is everything."

"For the early B-Grade realm," Boatman advised, "you should try to exercise your Dao as much as possible. Make bros. Do things with them. Help them and have them help you. I don't know if the New Cathedral has any Dao Visions suitable for you, but your path is very simple regardless. Just stay pure and true."

"Of course. Thanks, Master Grandpa Dead."

"And stop calling me that."

"Okay, Master Bro."

Boatman closed his eyes and released a long, tired sigh. "Never mind. Call me whatever you want. Now, Jack—your path is significantly more complicated than your brother's. I understand you cultivate Life and Death alongside Time and Space. Is that right?"

"Right," Jack replied. "The Fist is the core of my Dao, and it represents Life. The rest are built around it. Life and Death are my primary duality, and Spacetime is secondary."

Boatman nodded. "You understand it is a difficult path. Even most Archons only pursue one or two Daos to the apex. You want to go for four, and you have very little time to do so because of the looming war. Tell me the truth—is there any way I can talk you out of this?"

Jack grinned. "No."

"I assumed as much. Then, here's what you need to do. Pursue Life and Death concurrently. Use all the time and resources you can on those two Daos, making sure you reach as far as possible and that they remain balanced. Spacetime will hopefully follow by itself. It's okay if it lags behind a bit—you'll have time to make up for it in the A-Grade."

"Yes, Master."

"As for your cultivation, there is no point wasting your time, as you've no doubt realized yourself. The process would take tens of thousands of years for each minor realm. Just look for treasures and other opportunities to advance quickly. I want your Dao to remain as your focus, at least for now."

"Okay."

"Good. You're listening—that already surpasses my expectations. Tell me about your Class."

"It's something called Paragon of Cultivation," Jack explained. "A Legendary Class."

"Legendary?" Boatman raised a brow. "What do you mean?"

"That's its tier. It's not King, but Legendary. I think that's better."

"Are you sure? I've never heard of anything like that."

"The System said it's because I pushed a new boundary in cultivation, opening the path for future generations."

"Hmm. Well, yes. That makes sense. It's just that I've never heard about it." Boatman scratched his pale head. He seemed intrigued. "Then again, you did reach ten thousand miles during your breakthrough. I suppose it's possible. You wouldn't lie, either. Based on your description, such a Class should have been awarded to other cultivators in the past, but I'm not surprised it never reached my ears. People tend to keep their Classes a secret. It can serve as a clue about their strengths and weaknesses."

Jack shrugged. "I don't know if it's a big deal or not, but the Class did come with certain benefits. It gives me more stats per level. It also grants me a top-level Dao Vision at every minor realm, and it came with a skill which lets me contact an Immortal directly to receive guidance."

"Contact an Immortal?" Boatman's eyes widened. "That's important. Immortals possess virtually infinite knowledge and resources, and they almost never accept disciples. Having one of them as your mentor would be a huge deal—and, depending on your allegiance, maybe not something you'd want to share. That would explain why there is no mention of this Class in the

Church's records. It's an easy path to treason—nobody would reveal this."

"Uh." Jack scratched his head. "I'm not planning on actually contacting the Immortals. I'm not a traitor."

"I know you aren't. It's a good thing you let me know—a direct channel of communication to the Immortals could be a strategic advantage, if you don't mind sharing this with the Arch Priestess as well. But it probably won't work unless you're inside System space."

"Then it's useless."

"We'll see. There are some things we can do. Those Dao Visions you mentioned should also need the System to work. They obviously aren't stored in the little System core inside you—you will need to be in System space to receive them."

"What!"

"Don't worry. I told you—there are things we can do, but we'll need to reach the New Cathedral first. Just focus on your Daos for now. Stabilize your foundation. Get ready to leap forward once you receive those Dao Visions. Each will only be about a single Dao, anyway, so most of the heavy lifting will be done by yourself." He sighed. "See how easy this would be if you focused on just one or two Daos?"

"Perhaps, but I think I can handle four."

"What else I can do except believe in you?" Boatman shrugged. "That's all I had to say for now. If there is nothing else—"

The starship shook. The teleportation was cut short. Jack looked out the window and saw the inside of pulsating suckers surrounded by bright pink flesh. Something had grabbed their ship and ripped it directly out of the deep spacetime layers. Something big.

CHAPTER SEVEN
FIGHTING A-GRADE

THE *IRON MAIDEN* GROANED. METAL BENT. JACK AND BROCK TOOK A STEP to steady themselves while Elder Boatman gazed outside the window. Finally, he relaxed. "What are you sitting around for?" he asked Jack. "Go out there and kill that thing."

"Excuse me?"

"You heard me. You should hurry, too, or it will damage our ship."

More sounds of creaking metal. Something gave way. A piece of the hull was torn apart. Jack cursed out loud, then teleported outside the starship, staring at it and the space monster from a distance.

It was a monstrosity. A large, bright pink mass of flesh with eight thrashing limbs, one of which was wrapped around their starship. The monster was significantly larger than the ship, over three hundred feet from end to end, and it used its tentacle to bring the ship closer to its single eye, inspecting it carefully. Jack saw the Elder waving.

"Fuck me," he muttered. This was an octopus. He had traveled to a different galaxy to fight an octopus.

Despite its small body compared to other space monsters, the octopus contained a vast amount of energy. It felt more like a natural disaster than a creature. Every inch of its form was saturated, hinting at extreme physical power. The fact that the starship hadn't instantly imploded in its grasp meant there were Dao protections at play.

Unlike lower-rank space monsters, which relied solely on their physical superiority to crush their opponents, this octopus comprehended the Dao as well. It'd reached into a deep layer of space to pull them out of their teleportation, something Jack hadn't even known was possible. Spacetime fluctuated around it like the surface of the sea in a storm, creating an area of danger several thousand miles wide. If a C-Grade cultivator was placed in this range, they would be immediately torn apart. Thankfully, Jack also cultivated the Dao of Space, so he could resist with little effort.

At least, this space monster wasn't of the intelligent variety. Jack wasn't sure how that worked, but he knew that starting from the D-Grade, more and more space monsters were intelligent. He guessed some species were more bestial than others.

This was outside System space, so he couldn't just inspect the creature. He could, however, use his experience to estimate its strength from the Dao fluctuations it emitted. The result made his heart clench. This octopus creature possessed strength squarely at the early A-Grade.

"What the fuck?" he muttered. Elder Boatman had mentioned this galaxy being overrun with powerful space monsters, but randomly bumping into an A-Grade was just too much. Too coincidental. There couldn't be more than a couple of them across the entire galaxy. Had the Elder driven them here on purpose so Jack could fight the giant octopus?

The monster opened its beaked mouth and screamed at the starship. Spacetime rumbled. Jack reinforced the spacetime around him in a bubble so he wouldn't be affected. The starship shook but held—it was absolutely fine. Elder Boatman was on the case.

Two flashes arrived beside Jack. One was Brock, calmly floating in space surrounded by a golden sphere. He didn't comprehend spacetime, but he could use raw power to protect himself. Starhair did comprehend spacetime. His hair formed into six thick strands, each glowing like a river of stars. They swirled above his head like an entire galaxy, and they released a discreet aura which kept the octopus's area attacks at bay.

"This is an A-Grade space monster specializing in spacetime," Starhair said, offering no new information. "I know you're stupid, but follow my instructions. We need to work together."

Jack and Brock exchanged a glance. Brock brought his hands together, pulling the Goldenwood Staff out of his space ring and twirling it once. A golden aura spread over Jack, enhancing him.

Jack released his Dao. Power surged from his inner world, filling him to the brim. Every cell in his body activated. A purple aura erupted, almost corporeal, dying the world. It was quickly joined by lightning sparks as he activated Thunder Body. He flashed forward, his aura trailing behind him, and every movement released new strands of purple.

"I didn't order you to attack!" Starhair exclaimed.

The octopus had noticed them from the start, but it ignored them. In its eyes, they weren't worth bothering. Only Elder Boatman's early A-Grade clone, still inside the starship, was its real opponent. Even when Jack charged at the octopus, it just swiped a tentacle at him without even looking.

But Jack wasn't your average early B-Grade.

He grinned. The octopus used the Dao of Spacetime, but so did he. He charged up a massive punch. The fabric of reality was wrestled from the octopus's control. Every aspect of the universe and every Dao particle was sucked into Jack's punch, compressed to the extreme. The world around him turned to void.

The tentacle swiped, and Jack forcefully bent spacetime and teleported out of the way. He appeared over the octopus's head, fist already coming down. "Supernova!"

It felt like a mortal punching a wooden wall. Jack's hand barely held. A massive explosion followed, showering the world in white and purple light. The void disintegrated for ten thousand miles. The octopus screamed, sent careening downward as it let go of the starship, which spun away. A powerful shockwave still spread, disturbing the surrounding space. The light persisted for a few moments, and the heat was enough to disintegrate metal.

When the explosion receded, Jack gazed at his bloodied hand which had already regenerated. He chuckled. "Tough motherfucker."

The octopus screeched. It had been thrown a long distance away, but it just teleported back. It no longer ignored him. A crater was formed on its head, with milky, almost transparent blood flowing out. The octopus glared at Jack, and space coagulated around him. The pressure intensified. He could no longer move.

It swept two tentacles at him from different directions. They moved at almost the speed of light. Jack turned toward one, clenched his fist, and shot it out. The second tentacle came for his back. Brock appeared at the last moment, holding out a palm. A thousand golden brorillas overlapped with him, copying the motion. The tentacle slapped against his palm, which shone golden. Brock was forced a few feet backward, and his arm creaked ominously, but he held.

Jack punched his own tentacle away.

"Now, Ass-Kisser Bro!" Brock shouted.

"What did you call me!" A scream came from above, where Starhair appeared and fell onto the octopus. His six strands of starry hair spun like a saw, each elongating to resemble a blade. They hacked into the octopus's head where Jack had hit it. The monster screamed in pain.

"That's not my fucking name!" Starhair shouted as he retreated next to Jack and Brock. "I'm the leader here! You follow my commands! Listen well: Jack and I will—"

"Too late, ass-kisser," Jack interrupted him. "Here it comes."

The monster was utterly enraged now. A pulse emanated from its body, locking down spacetime. Even Jack couldn't teleport. At the same time, all eight of its tentacles elongated, growing from a hundred feet to several miles long. Only its head remained at its former size, making it resemble a weird kind of jellyfish. It opened its beak mouth to screech—and then all eight tentacles shot forward at once, moving at the speed of light, eviscerating the distance.

"Brock!" Jack shouted.

The brorilla shone golden. He brought his hands together, facing the storm of tentacles. "Good bros are everywhere!" he shouted. A hundred illusory, golden brorillas shot out of his body, spreading in all directions. Their bodies warped. From golden brorillas, they transformed into Brock, Jack, and Starhair, hiding the real ones in a sea of illusions. Even their Dao signatures were almost identical to the originals.

The octopus didn't care. Its tentacles slapped forward, tearing through the illusions. A dozen cultivators disappeared every instant. Brock's defenses would last less than a second—but that was enough.

The real Jack swam between the tentacles, flying at extreme speed. He didn't just have to avoid their tips; the entire length of the tentacles danced wildly, striking from every direction without warning, tearing apart the void. The closer Jack approached the main body, the tighter they were packed. He shot under a tentacle, dodged the random swipe of another, then pressed against it with his feet and launched off. The locked spacetime shivered as he passed. A river of starry purple was left behind him. Sparks rose from his body, further increasing his power as he sailed closer to the main body of the octopus.

The illusions were mostly gone by now, and Jack was too eye-catching. He was also too close. The octopus screeched and coiled one of its tentacles, attempting to swipe him out of the air. Jack ignored it. "Starhair!" he shouted.

The other man was attempting a similar plan, but he was being much more discreet about it. He still hadn't been noticed. Unfortunately for him, he also happened to be right between Jack and the swinging tentacle. His eyes widened. "Goddammit!" he screamed. "I'm not your shield, Jack Rust!"

He could have tried to dodge. To his credit, he went with Jack's plan and used all six of his hair strands to block the tentacle. There was a wet, slapping sound. Jack rushed through. Starhair remained tangled with that one tentacle, his hair wrapped around it and seething in rage. Brock also rushed through, following Jack and shouting, "Good job, Ass-Kisser Bro!"

"That's not my fucking name!"

The octopus hadn't expected its attack to be blocked and it had no more time to react. Jack was upon it, almost face-to-face with its main body. The single eye of the octopus widened as it saw his fist approach. It abruptly rotated its body, and Jack was now facing not its soft eye, but the beak it had for a mouth, surrounded by the roots of all eight tentacles.

He rushed into it regardless and pulled back a fist. The beak opened to bite down on him, revealing a gaping darkness.

Jack reached the mouth. At the last moment, he abandoned his punch. A new pulse of power erupted from his body. He straightened himself. As the beak clamped down, ready to tear him apart, he stepped on its bottom half and grabbed the top one with his hands. For a single, terrible moment, he thought he'd miscalculated. The beak pushed itself closed with terrible force, and Jack's body was bending under the pressure. His arms and legs were shaking. He pulled more and more power out of his inner world, flooding his body, using everything he had to keep the beak open.

Space monsters specialized in physicality, but so did Jack, and he had an effective twenty thousand Strength. It was about damn time he put it to use!

A moment later, the closing beak slowed. Its momentum faltered, and the pressure reduced. Jack was left in the monster's beak, holding it open with all his strength. He felt like Atlas holding up the sky. His entire body was on the verge of breaking, but he possessed enough strength, just as he suspected.

He was stuck. Any moment now, the monster would wrap a tentacle around him and squish him to death. However, he'd temporarily kept the beak open. That was enough.

"Staff Bro, I choose you!" a shout came from behind him. A golden arrow flew by his head—the Goldenwood Staff, overcharged with the Dao of Brohood. It flew right into the octopus's open mouth. Golden light illuminated the darkness, revealing a vast emptiness. As it turned out, the octopus's head was hollow. But not for long.

The golden aura around the staff erupted. A hundred brorillas appeared, wielding various weapons, and they started attacking the octopus from within. Transparent blood flew everywhere.

This space monster possessed extreme durability, but so what? Its insides were naturally softer than its outsides, not to mention the brorillas could attack it freely. Even if the damage they inflicted with each strike was minimal, it rapidly added up. The octopus screamed and thrashed, growing more panicked by the second. It even released Jack, who managed to slip out of its mouth, his limbs trembling from the effort.

He and Brock remained nearby. Whilst being torn apart from the inside, it couldn't focus on them. Its attacks were wild and predictable. Both of them could easily dodge, pelting the space monster with their own attacks to expedite its fall. Starhair also assisted—his strands of starry hair possessed great offensive power.

The octopus weakened with every passing moment. Soon, it completely lost all power to resist, and then it was over.

A massive body lay across this ravaged part of space. Spacetime was returning to order as a sea of milky, transparent blood slowly spread out. "Good fight," Brock said, grinning. "Nice teamwork, Ass-Kisser Bro."

"How many times do I need to tell you? Stop calling me that!"

"Man, fighting in the B-Grade is so fun," Jack said, clenching and unclenching his fist. He had so much power at his disposal. He could sense himself growing stronger. There was an addictive element to this progression—an almost euphoric sense of improvement.

"That was stupid, by the way," Starhair said. "Going into its beak like that? It's a space monster. They're supposed to be strong. You're lucky to be alive."

Jack winked at him. "I knew what I was doing. The monster was very fast and extremely durable, but when it struck me at the start, I could tell that its strength was lacking. As for me, I specialize in Physical. I was pretty sure I could overpower its beak. Even if I couldn't, I'm also durable—I wouldn't die."

Starhair snorted, looking away. A flash came between them all. Elder Boatman appeared, calm and collected. "Good work, everyone. I'm glad I didn't have to help."

"Did you bring us to this monster on purpose?" Jack asked.

"Of course. It is known to inhabit this territory of space, so we took a little detour. It was a good opportunity for you to practice fighting together."

"Why would we need that?" Jack asked, eyeing Starhair.

"Because we're all part of the same faction. We're an army at war. All battles are group battles, and the faster you get used to that, the better." He swiped a pale hand. The body of the octopus and its sea of blood disappeared, leaving only Brock's staff hovering in the middle. There was also a little pink ball. Like a miniature version of the octopus, except fist-sized, perfectly smooth, and without tentacles. Elder Boatman opened his hand, and the ball flew to him.

"What's that?" Jack asked.

Boatman gave him a look. "Have you never killed a space monster outside System space?"

"It's not as common as you make it sound."

The Elder smirked. "This is the monster's core," he said, raising the ball so Jack and Brock could take a better look. "The condensed energy source of a space monster. Very useful for cultivation. If you kill a space monster in System space, the System automatically disperses this core and grants you its energy as levels. That process, and space monster cores, are what the entire leveling aspect of the System is based on. You will have to do it manually, but it's the same thing."

"Oh," Jack exclaimed.

"Since Brock delivered most of the damage, this core belongs to him," Boatman said, tossing it over to the brorilla. "It should have enough energy to give you a dozen levels. Use it wisely."

"Thanks, Master Grandpa Dead. I will share with my bros."

Boatman nodded. "However, I am not pleased with how you two acted. As the one with the highest cultivation, Starhair is automatically in charge. You should have followed his orders."

"He would have given dumbass orders," Jack said. "He's not familiar with us and our fighting styles, plus he's less intelligent than the octopus."

"You may have your differences, but Starhair is an elite peak B-Grade with thousands of years of experience. You, on the other hand, have been cultivators for less than a decade. It would do you good to practice some humility."

Jack and Brock deflated. They made fun of Starhair, but they had to admit Boatman had a point. "Yes, Master," Jack said. Next time, he would wait for the stupid orders to actually arrive before disobeying them, so nobody could complain.

Starhair puffed up. "Serves you right, younglings." He ignored their glares.

"Now, let's get going," Boatman said. "We're only halfway there, and we don't want to leave the Arch Priestess waiting."

CHAPTER EIGHT
IT AWAKENS

It's important to have a way forward. A guiding line, pulling you toward where you need to be. Jack meditated on that as the starship shuttled closer and closer to the New Cathedral.

What is my path now? he wondered. I've saved Earth, destroyed the Animal Kingdom, and avenged my son... Now, where is my fist aimed?

At the Immortals. That much was easy. In the previous years, Jack had matured greatly and understood many things. The reason he and Earth suffered so much was due to the Immortals. The Animal Kingdom was just a symptom—the System was the real cause. It sank the galaxies into permanent war, encouraging everyone to kill each other. It rewarded levels for blood. Of course it would create tyrants. In such an environment, any system of government not based on raw power was bound to collapse.

The Immortals and their System had made the universe suffer for a billion years now, all to create as many warriors as possible. Trillions of lives had fallen for their cause. It didn't have to be this way. Cultivation was meant to be a slow, peaceful process. There would always be enemies and killing, even war, but the world order should try to prevent that, not actively encourage it.

Jack had attained his own freedom. He'd liberated his people. Now, he fought to save the world.

He was certainly against the Immortals. As for whether the Old Gods were a good alternative... That remained to be seen.

His rumination was interrupted by a constant whisper at the back of his mind. He sighed. Just a little bit ago, he'd made a mistake.

He'd opened his space ring to find The Stone, a blabbering pebble he'd once picked up from the corpse of Eva Solvig. He hadn't given it much thought at the time, but The Stone was lonely. The moment he took it out, guilt-ridden into keeping it company for a while, it had launched into a ceaseless barrage of questions.

"Oh, hi!" it had said in its high-pitched voice. "Long time no see. How are you doing? All good? Where are we? Nice room, by the way. I love the window. Is that the Spiral Stair galaxy? You have a little bit of spit on you, by the way. Did you face a Spitting Salamander? Those critters are vicious!"

The Stone had just rattled off the name of this galaxy, which it should have no way of knowing. It couldn't overhear from inside the space ring.

"How do you know this is the Spiral Stair galaxy?" Jack asked, wiping his hair.

"Good question. I wish I knew. So, anyway, how have you been? Tell Daddy everything."

Jack had opened and closed his mouth to no effect. He'd persisted for a bit, but The Stone really seemed to not remember much. It just instinctively recognized this galaxy, and the mystery surrounding it deepened with the moment. According to Eva's notes, she'd found it on an asteroid in the Milky Way. What connection did it have to the Spiral Stair galaxy? And how did it get from here to there?

Unfortunately, he got no new information out of it. After humoring The Stone for a half hour of ultra-high-speed chatting, he got an idea. He placed it in his inner world, where it could hang out with Copy Jack, who had nothing better to do anyway. Meanwhile, Jack could ponder on his Dao guilt-free.

That idea backfired immediately, since Jack maintained a constant awareness of his inner world. The Stone's speech barrage reached his mind like a persistent, distant whisper, frequently breaking him out of his thoughts. It didn't matter that Copy Jack only replied with grunts and, "Is that so?" The Stone just kept going. If there was a competitive talking league, it would have swept the trophies.

Jack took a break from meditation, massaging his temples. This can't go on, he decided. I don't care how lonely it is, it's going back in the space ring.

He entered his inner world, finding The Stone flying around the head of Copy Jack. Even he seemed annoyed.

"Oh, hi, real Jack," The Stone said the moment he appeared. "We were just discussing whether you should put on both socks before both shoes or one at a time. *I* support that the most organized people..."

It just kept going and going. Jack hardened his heart, and he was about to pull it away when a mighty roar blasted throughout his entire inner world. "KID!" it screamed. "For the love of Enas, make it stop!"

Jack looked up. His gaze brightened with surprise. "Turtle! You're awake!"

"My name is Venerable Saint Thousand Shell, and you will make that chattering thing shut up or I will break it to pieces!"

Jack raised a brow. "But you can't exit the Life Drop."

"Oh yeah?"

A green ray of light emerged from the inactive Life Drop. Venerable Saint Thousand Shell appeared in Jack's inner world. It was even larger than he remembered—almost a mile from head to tail. Yet, compared to the size of his inner world, it was nothing. It had a wide shell of interlocking plates, the head of a snapping turtle, and wise, beady little eyes. If not for its power and intelligence, it could have been a magnified snapping turtle.

As Jack inspected it, he realized he'd now grown to the point where he could estimate its strength. It wasn't at the B-Grade, as he assumed, but at the early A-Grade.

"Don't tell me what I can and can't do, kid!" It snorted, satisfied at Jack's surprised expression. "I am the senior here. If I tell you to shut it up, you will..." It trailed off, looking around, eyes going from annoyance to wonder. "What the hell did you do, kid?" it asked in a whisper. "How large is this place?"

"Ten thousand miles," Jack replied with a grin.

"Hi!" The Stone exclaimed. "Nice to meet you. I am The Stone! From what I understand, you are The Turtle?"

"Who—Fuck you. I am Venerable Saint Thousand Shell."

"That is no way to speak. Politeness is the cornerstone of civilization. Let me recite you a sermon I seem to recall hearing somewhere. It all began when—"

"Just... Just stay quiet," the turtle said, deflating. "Jack. Kid. What the hell is going on here? How long was I asleep?"

"Almost five years," Jack replied.

"Nonsense. You're telling me you went from a middle C-Grade to this in just five years?"

"Yeah."

The turtle choked. "You damn monster," it said, but Jack could hear the pride in its voice. "I'm glad I exhausted myself to save you."

"So am I." Jack smiled. "Did you sleep well?"

"It was okay. Just a little power nap. I can't believe I was awoken by a prattling stone, of all things."

"Do you know what it is?"

"Annoying."

"But besides that?"

"No clue, kid. Do I look like an encyclopedia to you?" It snorted at its own joke. "Anyway. I'm glad I woke up. There are many things to talk about, and—Kid! What did you do to the Divine Blood? It's empty!"

"Oh, yeah. That happened. I used all of its energy in my B-Grade breakthrough."

The turtle looked like it would have an aneurysm. "You used it all up? A billion years of accumulation, and you *used it all up*? You just reached the B-Grade! This is absurd!"

"If it makes you feel better, it was very helpful."

"Helpful? Ohh, kid, I'll fuck you up!"

The turtle rushed Jack, who just willed it back into the Life Drop. It may be an almighty entity, but it was now inside his inner world. Here, he was a god. It couldn't do anything to him.

Not that it really intended to harm him, anyway. It was just playing around.

"Okay, I give up!" the turtle's voice echoed. "Bring me out again, we need to talk!"

"In a moment," Jack said, suppressing his laughter. "Attacking me wasn't very senior-like of you. Therefore, you should embrace your responsibilities and grace the younger generation with your knowledge. Here's a perfect candidate."

With a tug of will, he transported The Stone into the Life Drop.

"No!" the turtle cried out in horror. "I'll be good, I promise! Just take this thing out of here!"

Jack could already hear The Stone's endless chatting. "Have fun!" he said, then sealed the Life Drop. He laughed. The turtle liked to act tough, but it had a good heart. It wouldn't actually harm The Stone. If anything, maybe a few hours of chatting would sap away The Stone's energy so Jack could have a proper chat with it.

He also had a few things to talk about with the turtle, but they could wait. Anything for a moment of quiet.

———

The stone was inexhaustible. Even when Jack unsealed the Life Drop several hours later, he found it still chatting away. The turtle had used its own energy to seal The Stone in a bubble, effectively muting it. The Stone didn't seem to notice.

"I'll be good, I promise," the turtle said as Jack pulled it out of the Life Drop. "Just, for the love of Enas, make it stop."

Jack laughed. "Sorry about that. The Stone is lonely. It needed some company."

"I'm also lonely, but I would rather bury myself in an active star than stand its chattering for a single moment longer."

"Oh? I didn't know that."

"How much clearer could I make it?"

"Not that. That you're lonely. I didn't know."

The turtle fell silent, then promptly changed the subject, "In any case, now that I'm awake, there are a few things to get in order. First, what the hell did you do to become so powerful so quickly?"

Jack briefly explained everything that happened since the turtle fell asleep at the Green Dragon Realm.

"I'm sorry about your son," it replied when Jack was done. For the first time, Jack thought he heard genuine care in its voice. It then sighed. "Maybe it's good that this happened when it happened. Your road had been too smooth. You needed a setback. It builds character."

Jack shook his head. "Master Boatman said the same thing, but let's not talk about that. I have some things to ask you. You've been alive for a long, long time. Have you been in the Life Drop since after the First Crusade, when Enas was imprisoned?"

The turtle settled down. It rested its huge body on the fist-shaped meteor in the center of Jack's world, then sighed deeply. "Some things are blurry..." Its voice had lowered to a whisper. "I was in intermittent stasis until you awakened the Life Drop. I understood it's been a billion years, but... Mortal bodies are not meant to last that long. Not even mine. Even asleep, part of my mind has deteriorated."

"That's alright." Jack placed a hand on its shell. "As much as you remember. Don't push yourself."

"Don't worry about me. Anyway. I wasn't going to give you this information before, but since you've now reached a decent level, it's best if you know." It took a deep breath. "My name is Venerable Saint Thousand Shell. A space monster. I am—was—the spiritual companion of the man you call Archon Black Hole. His real name was Claude."

Jack had suspected this much. Archon Black Hole wielded great power during the First Crusade and had founded the Black Hole Church. He was also the creator of the Black Hole World, where Jack had spent a year of his life. After all that, Jack expected him to be somehow related to the Life Drop, though he didn't expect the turtle to be that man's spiritual companion. It was to him what Brock was to Jack.

"Claude," he said, tasting the name. He chuckled. "That's so normal."

"What did you expect? It's not like people knew he'd grow up to be an Archon when he was born. Most high-status people have normal names, which is why they prefer to use their titles. It makes them sound cooler. I think that's stupid."

Jack raised a brow. "Is that so, Venerable Saint Thousand Shell?"

"That's my real name, kid!" the turtle shouted. It proudly raised its head. "It was given to me by Claude."

"Right. So, you guys were bros?"

"Bros?"

"Friends. Sorry, boomer."

It gave him a funny look. "We were close, yes. Of course we were. I had left my homeland and was escaping through the cosmos when I ran into Claude at the fringes of a Systemless galaxy. We fought, and he subdued me. However, surprised at my intelligence, he didn't kill me. We talked, bonded, and decided to travel together since we were both alone in the universe."

Jack almost thought this was touching before he realized what the turtle just revealed. "Wait. I know the Archon was an outlaw, or kind of, but what about you? You mentioned you were escaping from your homeland?"

"That's not important. You'll never get anywhere close to it, anyway. Just know that space monsters are divided into the sapient and beastly types, and the sapient ones have their own world in another galaxy. Back to the point. I met Claude while he still pretended to be allied with the Immortals. I helped him sow the seeds of an uprising, culminating into the organization now known as the Black Hole Church—a group of individuals fed up with the tyrannical and warmongering Immortals. We worshiped Enas, who, if freed from his prison, might possess the power to unite the Old Gods and once again assault the Immortals. That was the only way to bring them down—they were too powerful otherwise."

"So you intended to launch a reverse Crusade?"

"Essentially, yes. But rescuing Enas was a long and difficult road. Bluntly put, we had no idea how to do it. All solutions we could come up with required a set of near-impossible coincidences, and the time horizon of our plans was discouragingly long. Finally, some of us couldn't take it anymore. We broke away from the Immortals and officially formed the Black Hole Church, trying to save as many people as possible. Since we knew the plan would be inherited by our descendants, we set up various contingencies. Claude had secretly installed the Life Drop in one of the Trial Planets, placing me as its guardian spirit. His life was running out, anyway, so he was tying up loose ends. He was also working on the Black Hole World you discovered. I'm glad he succeeded, though it saddens me to hear his descendants have been trapped there ever since."

"They'll be free soon," Jack replied. "As for that set of coincidences you mentioned... I believe they've finally occurred. The Church is close to rescuing Enas, though I don't know the specifics."

"WHAT!"

The shout was so loud and so sudden Jack was flung back. The resting turtle broke away from its reminiscence and jumped to its feet, regarding him with almost dog-like excitement. "Start with that next time, kid! That's amazing! It's the best news ever!"

"I sure hope so," Jack replied, holding his ear.

"It is! I won't ask if you won't say, but ohhh, kid, how my old bones are tingling for a fight. I'm so glad I slept for a billion years. I get to carry out Claude's last wish! This is great!"

"Yeah, I'm happy for you," Jack said. The turtle was even wagging its tail. "So, uh, is there anything you want to tell me? Some instructions on how to use the Life Drop? And with less shouting, please."

"Hmph. If I want to shout, kid, then I will shout. And, oh, *now* you care about the Life Drop? After you wrung it dry of its billion years of accumulation?"

"What else was I supposed to do? You were asleep."

"Hmph. I seem to recall, kid, that you owed me some life energy from before I fell asleep. You'd borrowed some to create your silly little life stones or whatever and we'd agreed you'd return it."

"I would, but again, you were asleep."

"Well, I'm here now. Hand it over. And with proper dues—it's been four years since your deadline to pay me back, so let's just say you owe me double."

Jack didn't know whether to laugh or to cry. "I don't have any life treasures at hand," he said. "How about I help you fulfill Claude's last wish and destroy the Immortals? Would that be payment enough?"

The turtle considered it. "I'll allow it."

"Deal."

"There are a few advanced ways to utilize the Divine Blood," the turtle began, instantly launching into an explanation, "but they're useless when it's empty. You should try to refill it. It can be very useful, even to B and A-Grades."

"I'll give it a shot."

"Good." The turtle stood to its full height. "It was nice catching up. Now go meditate on your Daos, or play ball, or whatever it is you youngsters do. I will relax. And no matter what you do, kid, don't ever put that stone in my territory again. I *will* break it."

Jack sighed. "Alright."

He'd actually been planning to leave The Stone with the turtle, given that they were both immortal, lonely existences. But he couldn't force it. He'd just need to find a better candidate. Copy Jack wasn't suitable either, as he was in Jack's inner world, and the endless chattering there reached his ears as an annoying whisper.

Hmm. If I create a separate place in my inner world, however...

It was an interesting idea, though not for right now. Jack summoned The Stone from inside the Life Drop, cutting it off in the middle of a sentence. "Oh," it said, looking around despite its lack of eyes. All it had was a mouth. "Hi, Jack. What's up? Did you know that embroidery was considered a rebellious act in ancient times?"

"That's very interesting. Listen. I will need to put you back in my space ring for a few days, but then I promise I'll find you some company, okay? It's just that I'm working on something right now and I need some silence."

"I can be silent."

"Can you?"

The Stone shook from side to side. "Okay, I can't. But promise you'll take me out again, okay? Don't just throw away the space ring. I don't want to be alone again. Please?"

His heart was touched. "I promise," he said. The Stone nodded, uncharacteristically quiet. Jack took it out of his inner world and into his space ring.

I'm carrying so many different dimensions right now.

"It's not bad," said the turtle. "That talking stone. I don't know what it is, but I can sense its pain and kindness. You really should find it some company. Just not me."

"I will," Jack replied. Copy Jack just watched from the side, silently, like a ghost.

Jack returned to the real world and meditated, slowly advancing his Dao. The hours turned into days until, without incident, they arrived at the New Cathedral.

CHAPTER NINE

ARCH PRIESTESS

The New Cathedral was built on a sprawling expanse. A prairie stretched for endless miles. Blades of grass danced, occasionally trampled by the hooves of farm animals. Civilization had slowly started to appear on this beast-inhabited planet, brought about by the Church.

This planet had no name. It was just one of the many inhabitable planets that dotted this and every galaxy. It'd been chosen because of its location deep inside a cluster of stars, and also because, while it possessed life, no intelligent life forms had developed yet.

This world was covered in moist jungles and populated by creatures suspiciously similar to Earth's dinosaurs. A brontosaurus head peeked out of a jungle in the distance, calmly chewing on wide leaves. A pterodactyl flew overhead. Deeper in the thick trees, a beast roared.

Asking around, Jack discovered that giant lizards were a common life form in the universe. Unfortunately, them developing sapience was rare. Something to do with their cold blood. Jack would have liked to explore the subject, but he had more pressing problems.

The New Cathedral was a vast temple surrounded by a city

complex. Construction had only begun two years ago, but it was carried out by high-level cultivators, so everything progressed at a rapid pace. Rows of residences already lined the city outside the temple—a mix of fairy-tale and high-tech standards. Construction sites littered the surroundings. There was water, sewage, and electricity, all dependent on a large nearby lake. People crawled around this place, seeming like ants from up-high, while farmers had already begun transforming the surrounding prairie into rich farmland.

The temple itself was made of wood, glowing with life in the sun. Its shape was similar to a set of four joined spheres, with one in the middle and the other three surrounding it.

The center sphere was the largest. Its domed roof reached several hundred feet in size, while the other three were only half as tall. Balconies were visible at the top of the domes, and the open entrance of each building revealed an austere, powerful interior. Windows were everywhere.

The temple had smooth walls decorated with statues and paintings of heroes—maybe past Archons—fighting all sorts of enemies. In one prominent piece, two humanoids and what looked like a centaur faced down five robots. Numbers were painted on each robot head—from five to nine. Jack could tell they were Immortals, though the meaning of the numbers was lost on him.

"This is pretty good work for two years," he commented. Their starship descended toward a landing base sandwiched between a park and a medieval pub.

"It's nothing," Elder Boatman replied. "The city is just an afterthought. All the real effort goes into the war."

Brock pointed in the distance. "Look, bro. Big lizards. Girl Bro would be happy here."

Jack smiled. Nauja's tribe originally lived in the Barbarian Ring of Trial Planet, a place also inhabited by dinosaurs. This planet would have given her nostalgia. Unfortunately, she was an incalculable distance away, so she would probably never see this.

"The New Cathedral is a military base, not a sightseeing attraction," Starhair said with a snort.

Jack laughed. "Keep it in your starry pants. There is always time to sightsee."

"Hmph."

"Hmph to you as well."

"The Arch Priestess wants to see you, Jack and Brock," Elder Boatman said. "I will take you to the main temple now. Do you know the way, Starhair?"

"Certainly, Elder," Starhair replied. "Thank you for the trip." He vanished.

"You know, he's actually not that bad," Jack said, pointing his thumb at Starhair's previous location. "Just needs to loosen up a little."

Brock shook his head. "Ass-Kisser bro still needs an ass-kicking. Otherwise, he will backfire."

"Well, if you say so."

Their starship changed course. From the landing spot they were aiming at, they were now headed toward the temple. Elder Boatman steered them to the entrance—a thirty foot tall archway depicting a kind, scholarly man at the top. The man was opening his arms as if to hug whoever entered.

"That's Enas," Elder Boatman explained. "It is said that life originated from one of his experiments, so he's often portrayed as a scholar."

Jack simply nodded as they disembarked the starship and entered the temple proper.

The interior of the temple was as expected. Rows of wooden benches led to an altar featuring another image of Enas. Cultivators of various levels lined the benches, praying, though they didn't seem too devoted. Some chatted with one another, while a pair of children ran down the aisle. A white-robed priest silently read a book in the back.

"We're going to the upper floor," Elder Boatman said. He led them to a spiral staircase upward. Just like everything else in this temple, it was made of wood. Flowers sprouted from various places, like the entire temple was a living, still-growing tree. Jack could even sense his Dao of Life invigorated inside this place.

"Oh wow," The Stone said from his inner world, where he'd placed it again after it grew bored in his space ring. "If I had a credit for every time I've been inside a living tree building, I would have two credits. Which isn't a lot, but it's weird that it happened twice."

"You've been to a similar place before?" Jack asked back.

"Not similar. I think I was stuck inside a tree hollow once. Nobody came to save me, and I obviously couldn't dislodge myself, being a stone and all. I waited until the tree grew older and its hollow wider, and then I just slipped out."

"You know it's annoying when you remember random stuff but not the important ones, right?"

"Sorry, my friend. It's not on purpose. Maybe if I speak enough, the right memories will surface! Okay, let's see. My favorite food is—"

It couldn't even eat food. Jack tuned out The Stone as they ascended the staircase. He counted three landings, and they kept going up. The higher they reached, the less noise suffused their surroundings, though nobody questioned them being here. Eventually, they reached the top of the stairs, greeted by a door made of twisting tree branches.

"It can't be that simple," Jack said. "The Arch Priestess is an Overlord of the universe. Surely she has her own dimension instead of sitting behind a wooden door."

He couldn't quite tell, but he thought Elder Boatman smiled. The old vampire knocked on the door. A moment later, a voice answered, "Enter."

The door swung open, revealing a place Jack could only describe as sacred.

Flowers grew from the wooden walls. A hole in the ceiling let in a column of light, with dust particles lazily floating about. The world turned quiet the moment Jack entered—he was surrounded by reverence, piety, the sound of a gentle stream. An earthly scent permeated the room, punctuated by the dirt which made up the floor. There were even ants walking back and forth. The few columns were made of wood and had vines growing around them. Everything was natural and at peace.

On the dirt floor, a lone path stretched from the entrance to the back of this dome-shaped room, leading to a throne of roots and flowers. A woman sat there—the only other person in the room. Her presence was ethereal. She was like a goddess of nature, a part of the natural world. White robes covered her entire body, revealing only a pair of smiling golden eyes and tanned, bare feet. Her toenails were unpainted.

The moment Jack laid eyes on this woman, he knew she was the Arch Priestess, the leader of the Black Hole Church. And he knew that with absolute certainty, not because of the context of his arrival here or because of her commanding position in the room, but because of the sheer amount of power which left her body. It was indescribable. The strongest person Jack had seen so far was Elder Boatman, but even his power paled before hers, a firefly to the moon. She was so powerful that Jack had the momentary illusion that she was the entire world, and he had been pushed outside of it.

Despite her great strength, her aura bore no pressure at all. It was like staring at the sky—beautiful, vast, but not suppressive.

Jack was lost for words. The Stone in his inner world, for whatever reason, wasn't. "Oh wow. If you and that woman pool your clothes together, you might be able to make two properly dressed people."

Jack was snapped out of the illusion and had to fight not to laugh. He wore only a pair of shorts; she, robes covering her entire body, and who knows what else underneath.

The Arch Priestess regarded them kindly, yet without speaking. Elder Boatman fell to a knee. "Boatman greets the Arch Priestess," he said. "May your life be ever blooming."

Jack and Brock followed, also bowing. "Greetings, Arch Priestess," they said as one. Even Brock spoke with more respect than usual.

She still regarded them silently. Right as Jack was beginning to wonder, her entire being brightened. He couldn't see her face, but he knew she'd just given a radiant smile. "Hello, Boatman, Jack, Brock." Her voice was exactly as expected. Ethereal, beautiful, yet heavy with authority. Hearing it made Jack feel warm inside, but he would hesitate to interrupt her.

"I have heard many things," she continued. "It's a pleasure to finally meet you."

"The pleasure is all ours, Arch Priestess," Jack replied.

"I'm sure it is. Don't worry about offending me. In private, you may address me freely and speak your mind."

Jack looked up. He didn't straighten his back yet because neither had Elder Boatman. "Your temple is beautiful," he blurted out. He wasn't sure why he said that. To lighten the mood?

Her smile—which he still couldn't see—grew wider. The feeling was like every flower in existence blooming at once. "The Immortals live in temples of metal," she replied softly. "They worship themselves and hold no respect for life. I hope we can be better. All life is sacred, even the simplest trees and flowers. When we live in harmony, our hearts are at peace—with our hearts at peace, we can truly live."

Jack's Dao of the Fist resonated with her words. A casual phrase had awoken his Dao of Life. The sign of an Archon.

"Well-spoken, Beautiful Bro," Brock said, nodding in agreement. Jack's heart seized. Elder Boatman tensed up.

"Oh!" The Stone said. "Your bro has a crush on the leader lady! Maybe you'll all become a big family and have half-monkey, half-priest children."

The Arch Priestess, however, only laughed—a light, cheerful sound.

"Thank you, Brock," she replied. "Your ancestry resonates with my temple. If we have the time later, I look forward to discussing your view of life and nature. It is rare for a beast-born cultivator to reach such high achievements."

"Sure thing," Brock replied.

"Time is precious these days," the Arch Priestess said, standing from her throne. She was taller than Jack expected—slightly more than himself. Her white robes cascaded, elegantly covering her whole body. "You may take your leave, Boatman. I will instruct your disciples and ensure they take full advantage of the resources the New Cathedral has to offer. When I'm done, I will return them to you, so you can guide them more consistently."

"Yes, Arch Priestess," Elder Boatman replied. He bowed again, then walked out of the room, closing the door behind him. Jack suddenly felt vulnerable. The Arch Priestess smiled at them.

"Let's talk business."

CHAPTER TEN

BEING WITH ONE'S FAMILY

At a wave of the Arch Priestess' hand, roots grew out of the dirt floor, forming into chairs before Jack and Brock. She sat back down, and they followed suit.

"Your breakthroughs were sensational," she said, her voice taking on a more hands-on quality. "Especially Jack's. It came at the perfect time. The war situation is unfortunate right now, and our army was in dire need of good news. We spread the word, giving our cultivators something to believe in, and morale temporarily recovered. Unfortunately, it will not last forever. Sooner or later, new things will happen, and your breakthroughs will become old news. We must ensure there is more to come."

"What exactly does that mean, Arch Priestess?" Jack asked.

"It means that I intend to make you one of the faces of our army. It's a gamble, of course, but one I am willing to believe in. For that to work, we need to keep your progress rolling." She looked deep into his eyes. "If you agree to shoulder our army's morale, I can give you access to a vast amount of resources you otherwise wouldn't be able to touch."

Jack considered it. This sounded too good to be true. "Is it that simple?" he asked. "I just cultivate, and you use my progress to maintain army morale?"

"Sort of," she replied. "We have morale experts. They will curate your exploits and publicize them at regular intervals, making you into a celebrity. There is no downside to you besides the fame, which you may or may not welcome, and the fact that being in the spotlight makes it easy to create enemies."

He just stared for a moment. "You want to turn us into influencers? Seriously?"

"If by that you mean influential people, then yes. It's a proven technique. You won't need to do anything; just focus on your cultivation, and we will handle the rest."

Jack didn't know whether to laugh or cry. *What the hell.* In the end, he chose to laugh. "Whatever. Fame is fine, and I like having enemies. However, I have to ask... Is that all? As arrogant as this sounds, I thought our breakthroughs and potentials were enough for the Church to invest resources into us. I didn't think we'd need to make a show out of it."

"You are not entirely wrong," she admitted. "Your potential is outstanding, a hope to be cultivated. If you enjoyed your privacy so much that you attempted to refuse my request, we would still invest in you, just not as heavily. There is an entire war happening. Our resources are distributed to thousands of Envoys and dozens of Elders. Meanwhile, you are just an early B-Grade. No matter how talented, your ascent is a very uncertain thing. You are a high-risk, high-return gamble."

"I understand," Jack said. "So, if I agree to become a public figure, that coupled with my potential will be enough for you to invest a disproportional amount of resources into me. That will, in turn, create enemies in the people who will lack those resources."

She smiled. "Correct. Just to be clear, this offer is extended to both of you. Brock's breakthrough wasn't as breathtaking as yours, but it remains extraordinary. Plus, I can sense he has some sort of magnetizing aura, and we can use that."

Jack and Brock gazed at each other. There wasn't much to think about. "We accept," Jack said.

They were already used to being public figures and having a plethora of enemies. As for enjoying an almost unfair amount of resources, well... They'd earned it. If someone wanted more resources than they were given, they could only blame themselves for being weak.

"Excellent," the Arch Priestess said, clapping her hands.

"Can we get an overview of these resources you mentioned?" Jack asked.

"The most important ones are space monster cores. They will allow you to increase your cultivation much faster than normal. I cannot give you unlimited access to our vault, but I will make sure you're allocated a very generous amount."

Jack nodded. Increasing his cultivation was his main problem right now. If the Arch Priestess could help, that would be great.

"Besides that," she continued, "I can provide you with treasures tailored to your Dao. Is there anything in particular you would like?"

Brock shrugged. "I'm fine," he said, while Jack replied, "I would like a treasure with a lot of life energy." He needed it to both temper his body and partially refill the Life Drop. The turtle had made it clear there were uses he hadn't discovered yet, but they needed life energy to activate.

The Arch Priestess nodded. "It is done."

"Good. Can I also request something related to Death?"

She hesitated. "There is a treasure that would suit you well, but it is borrowed by another cultivator right now. I won't have it back for thirty days. I can give it to you then if you'd like."

"Sounds good. Also, I have a question. Has Master Boatman informed you of my new Class?"

She gave another smile. "He has."

"Good. It offers me Dao Visions, but Master Boatman said I need to be in System space to receive them. He said you may be able to help."

"That's easy," she replied. "We'll just make you a clone."

"A clone? Like the one Elder Boatman sent to accompany us here?"

"Better. That's just a temporary energy clone. Real clones are difficult to manufacture, but thankfully, you're still only at the B-Grade. We can handle it."

Jack was intrigued. If he understood this correctly, then maybe, just maybe... He didn't dare to hope just yet.

"I suppose we'll shoot this clone into System space and have it communicate the Dao Visions?" he asked.

"Correct, though there will be no need for communication. You and your clone will share one soul. You will be one person in two bodies."

Jack's heart was pumping. "Does my clone have to stay in System space?"

"Of course not. Ideally, we want it somewhere outside System space where it cannot be located by our enemies. You will only pop into System space to receive Dao Visions or carry out other tasks."

"Then, can my clone reside... on Earth?"

His breath caught in his throat. Being away from home had plagued him for so long. When hope suddenly appeared, he didn't dare to believe.

The Arch Priestess read his emotions. She smiled. "Sure."

Jack felt a weight he didn't know he carried be lifted. Two bodies. One would stay here, cultivate, and fight, while the other would be on Earth, accompanying his family. It was a dream come true. His life had just become ten times better.

"Thank you. I will remember this favor," he said, unable to keep the emotion out of his voice.

"Don't worry," the Arch Priestess replied. "It's not a favor. Your clone will need to be near System space anyway. If you want to conveniently place it on your home planet, that really doesn't change much."

"Wait," Jack said, suddenly worried. "That won't place my planet in danger, will it?"

"Not if you're careful. Locating a single planet in a mostly un-Integrated galaxy is too difficult, even for the Immortals. You being there doesn't change anything. The only way to locate it would be if you were detected in System space and then followed outside, but even then, you can just take a detour and wait on another planet for a few hours. Even if they catch you, you will only lose a clone; they won't find your Earth."

"Perfect. I... Thank you, Arch Priestess. My family will be overjoyed."

"I'm sure they will," she replied. "Since you're so excited about it, we can make creating your clone our first order of business. I won't oversee this personally, but I'll send you an expert."

"Alright!"

"Thank you," Brock said as well. "You help my bro, you help me. You good person, Beautiful Bro. I owe you one."

"My pleasure," she replied. "It was interesting meeting you, Jack and Brock. You may go now. I have already assigned you a helper and instructed them on what to do. If I find the time, I will drop by your residence and personally guide you through the Dao."

"We look forward to that. See you, Beautiful Bro," Brock said, then rose to leave. Jack followed him outside, also bidding his goodbyes. He had more things to discuss with her, like the Black Hole World, or the fact he housed one of the Church's founding members in his inner world. However, he was too shaken. Too happy. Those things could wait until next time.

They left the room and closed the door. Only then did Jack turn to Brock.

"Do you really have a crush on her?" he whispered.

"I didn't mean it like that. Her soul is beautiful. Her aura. She knows."

"Okay," Jack replied with a small smile. He'd suspected as much, but he couldn't help hoping. How funny would it be if Brock got the

Arch Priestess, of all people? "By the way, you could have asked for a clone as well."

"It's fine," Brock said. "They sound expensive. I don't need one. I've left the pack; they live without me."

Jack nodded.

They climbed down the spiral stairs, traveling all the way to ground floor. On the way, Jack realized they had no idea where they were supposed to go now. He hoped there would be someone waiting for them downstairs.

And there was. He just didn't expect who it would be.

Starhair stood at the entrance of the temple, looking terrible. His face was scrunched up. His arms were crossed. His star-like hair was stuck to his scalp, occasionally spasming in rage. Everyone gave him a wide berth.

"Sup, Ass-Kisser Bro," Brock said. He made to clasp the other man's hand. Starhair, very reluctantly, returned the motion.

"What are you doing here?" Jack asked.

"I was ordered to be your helper," Starhair replied through gritted teeth. His expression was so sour he could have been eating a dozen lemons while waiting.

"Wait. *You're* our helper?"

Starhair was not amused. "I'm as surprised as you are. That's not why I came to the New Cathedral. I was supposed to train. I will follow my orders, but I still despise you."

Jack looked at Brock, then shrugged. "Fair enough. Lead us to our residence, helper."

Starhair gave him a glare so scalding that Jack thought his eyebrows would implode. Still, the man trudged away, and Jack and Brock followed him through the city.

On the way to the New Cathedral, Boatman had employed some magic to hide them from the crowd. That was no longer active. People pointed at them. A few cultivators—all below the B-Grade—approached for a greeting. Jack could tell he and Brock were somehow already celebrities. The only question was, how did everyone know their faces?

"There was a city-wide projection," Starhair explained when asked. He was even more annoyed—if possible—because everyone ignored him to greet Jack and Brock. "They played scenes of your duel in Hell, your battle over the skies of Earth, and your recent extermination of those leonines. They also showed your breakthrough and tribulation—it wasn't broadcasted live, but someone recorded it and brought it over."

"Oh," Jack replied. That projection had happened before they arrived. The Arch Priestess must have been pretty certain they would accept to be the face of their forces... Then again, maybe they never had a choice. She was only asking nicely the first time. If they protested, she could just order them to do it.

After all the grand visuals and space-rupturing battles Jack had experienced lately, this simple city was an almost relaxing sight. The fact it was mostly inhabited by D-Grades was a different story.

Eventually, they made their way out. Starhair led them to a mansion in the suburbs, complete with its own walls and garden. It had three floors, each covering almost a thousand square feet.

"That's a big-ass house," The Stone said.

Jack, being more polite, simply said, "Woah. It this all for us?"

"Mostly," Starhair replied in ultra-salty territory. "There is also some room for me. But don't worry, it's not like I enjoyed living in my own mansion, which I possessed until a few moments ago. I *much* prefer being the servant of you two idiots."

"That's not right," Brock said. "You're Ass-Kisser Bro. You should flatter us. Then, maybe, you'll get a tip."

He waltzed forth into the house, followed by Jack. Starhair remained outside, steaming from the ears. Jack thought he would explode.

CHAPTER ELEVEN

CELEBRITY IN TRAINING

"Let's come up with a catchphrase!"

Jack groaned. Brock groaned. Even The Stone in Jack's inner world groaned.

As it turned out, being famous was hard work. Starhair had been assigned as Jack and Brock's personal assistant, but there was a different person working on their public image. Her name was Sophie, and she was so insufferably full of energy that Jack considered giving her The Stone.

Sophie was an E-Grade djinn: toddler-sized, blue-skinned, wearing silken robes which sometimes revealed what little she had to hide, and wore a pink turban on her head, under which cascaded brown hair. She wasn't bad; in fact, Jack quite liked her company. It was just that she was so damn excited to get her work done.

She'd arrived at their mansion shortly after they had, and brought with her a storm. There were a dozen members of staff ranging from photographers and videographers carrying projection stones, to make-up artists and accompanying beautiful models. Before Jack knew it, he was taking pictures and videos with the models—only one of which was a human—in various poses and attires. Sophie was running around, scheduling Brock's photo session, maximizing their time together.

It was so disorientingly before-the-System, that Jack briefly wondered if he was still a PhD student on Earth, dreaming everything up about robots and cultivators and planet-shattering fists. Then again, this wasn't the life of PhD students, either.

"Is this really necessary?" he asked as Sophie sat them down at *their* fluffy couch, eating *their* gum worms spread over the counter. Jack still didn't like those.

"Not necessary, but a very good idea!" she replied, taking a bite off the worm in her palm. Due to her small size, she couldn't slurp them up in one go. She chomped happily. "A catchphrase makes you easier to relate to. It's free real estate in the minds of your fans!"

"...Like what?" Brock asked.

"Something simple, yet powerful. Memorable. How about... *I'll punch you up!* No, too meh. *Prepare to be destroyed?* We can also try something corny, like: *Only my punch is eternal!*"

Jack and Brock glanced at each other. "No offense, but those are all terrible," Jack said.

"That's okay. It will definitely sound terrible to you, but your fans have a different perspective. Anyway, we'll figure something out. Brock is easier. I remember something you said in one of the projections... *Bro army, assemble!*"

Brock gave her an apprehensive glance. "Why do I need a catchphrase? Bro is the celebrity."

"Both of you are. You're a duo. We need to prop you both up and make the fans debate who is cooler between you. That way, they will never consider following other celebrities."

"What other celebrities?" Jack asked.

"The Arch Priestess, for example. Or Sovereign Heavenly Spoon." A dreamy look briefly entered her eyes, then disappeared. "Your competition is hard, but you are harder! Oh, maybe that should be your catchphrase, Jack. *I'm hard.*"

"...You're just messing with me, aren't you?"

She laughed. “Anyway, try to come up with something. I’ll also prepare a few alternatives by tomorrow—we need to get this done as soon as possible to implement it in our campaign.”

“I know I will regret this,” Jack said, “but what campaign are we doing, exactly?”

“All sorts of things. There are newsletters, projections, audio broadcasts, paid storytellers and bards… We are even preparing a series of plushies and t-shirts. The audience is receptive to you, so we scale quickly.”

“You’re making plushies? And t-shirts?”

“Oh yeah! The pre-orders for the Brock plushie are through the roof. The Jack one… Well, in any case, we have a lot of things to work on. The galaxy wasn’t built in a day, so if we want to scale up, we need to rush, rush, rush!”

Jack groaned again, pressing his eyes shut. “Can we just shush, shush, shush for a moment? My head is about to explode.”

“That’s fine. Just remember to—Oh, hi, Starhair. Is the clonemancer here already?”

“Yes,” Starhair said, stepping through the door. He was followed by an elderly, green-skinned cultivator whose head split into two like the humps of a camel. Jack vaguely recognized this species as bactrian, and the only reason he could tell this person’s age was the tell-tale white beard hanging from his chin. He was also a peak B-Grade.

“Hello,” said the bactrian. “My name is Envoy Yoshi. Pleased to make your acquaintance.”

“The pleasure’s all ours. I’m Jack, and this is Brock.”

“Oh, I’m well aware,” the bactrian said. He reached into his bag and removed what seemed suspiciously similar to human body parts. “Don’t mind me. Do your business, and I’ll just be over here setting up.”

“Are those…” Jack trailed, but the bactrian shook his big, green head.

“Artificial, obviously. Clone parts made of highly-compressed life energy. These materials alone cost an astronomical amount, so let me congratulate you in advance about your new clone."

Jack's heart beat faster. "And we can start now?"

"Just a second, let me finish here."

"*My fist is inevitable!*" Sophie cried out. "What do you think about that, Jack?"

"It's not bad, but let's think about it a little more."

"Alright."

"How about You deserve a good fisting?" Brock tried.

Jack gave him a glance. "Et tu, Brute?"

"I don't know what that means."

"I like that," Sophie said. Jack swiveled at her.

"You can't be serious."

"Oh, don't worry. I think it can work. The obvious innuendo is a little crass, but maybe it fits with your persona. We want to make you powerful, brutal, but also approachable. A dash of humor would go a long way."

"There's nothing funny about that catchphrase."

"There will be when it's said—repeat after me—at scale."

"Absolutely not," Jack said, shaking his head. "I agreed to be a celebrity, not a fool. Let's find something less idiotic."

"Hey, I'm just trying to do my job!" Sophie replied, seeming a little hurt.

"I know, it's just... Ugh. I'll come up with something, okay?"

"All done," the bactrian said. He'd drawn a red pentagram on the floor and placed the mock body parts at each of the five ends. Jack stared at it.

"Yeah... That's not creepy at all."

"Clonemancy is creepy business. Hop in. The sooner we start, the sooner we'll finish."

Jack took a good look at the bactrian, the pentagram, and the clone parts. When he found nothing suspicious, he slowly stepped into the pentagram. Envoy Yoshi did his thing. The red paint went up in smoke. A reddish aura appeared, clinging to Jack's skin like moisture, and he even felt it seeping through his body to scan his organs. It wasn't painful, just profoundly uncomfortable. Like receiving a gastroscopy and a colonoscopy at the same time.

The smoke and red aura finally receded, coagulating with the now-floating clone parts to form a naked copy of Jack. He could see his organs and cardiovascular system appear out of thin air, coupled with endless neurons, then slowly be covered with skin. He fought the urge to look away. The clone parts docked in like the limbs of a transformer.

"Now, Jack!" the bactrian said.

Jack gritted his teeth. He reached into his inner world and dislodged a tiny piece, barely a hundred feet across. It wouldn't affect his strength. The pain was terrible, but he endured. He slowly pushed the piece away, into the new body, which felt extremely compatible. The piece of inner world anchored itself near the clone's heart, disappearing, and just like that, Jack now possessed two bodies.

The clone blinked as it awakened. Both bodies tumbled to the floor as Jack struggled to deal with the doubling of his senses. "Ugh," he cried out.

"The process is done," the bactrian said softly. "Adjusting to your new condition can take up to an hour. When you're done, you will have successfully created a permanent clone. Congratulations."

"Congratulations!" Sophie echoed. "If this wasn't a secret, we could publicize it as yet another of your achievements!"

"How do you feel, bro?" Brock asked.

Jack slowly raised his body. He sat on all fours, retched once, then shakily got to his feet. The clone and real body stared at each other. They then looked around. Their wobbling bodies steadying. "I think I got the trick," Jack said—from his real body.

"Less than a minute," the bactrian muttered, shaking his big head. "Impressive."

"Can I have some clothes?" the clone asked. The bactrian waved his hand, summoning a few sets of garments from his space ring.

"Take your pick," he said, and the clone body quickly chose a set of elegant purple robes. He put them on, then stared at the real Jack. Jack stared back. This clone was identical to the real thing, with the exception of his aura, which was less steady and significantly weaker. This clone's cultivation was only around the late C-Grade, compared to Jack's early B-Grade, and it could never increase. His body was also much weaker than the real Jack's. Their Dao understandings, however, were the same. Despite the clone's weaknesses, he could stand his ground against most late B-Grades. More than enough to protect Earth.

"I am you," said the clone.

"And you are me," the real body replied. They smiled at each other. "Funky."

The two Jacks exchanged a fist-bump. "This is actually pretty cool," said the real body. He placed both hands on the clone's shoulders. "I am entrusting you with a very important task, Jack. Go home and take care of our family. Be there for them. And do that other thing we talked about, too."

"I will, Jack. Don't worry about anything."

"You know we can tell you're just talking to yourself, right?" Starhair asked. "You have one soul. There is literally nothing to discuss."

The clone nudged his head toward Starhair. "He's a difficult one, huh?"

"Yeah. I think his parents dropped him when he was a baby," the original replied.

Sophie giggled. "Can you repeat this snick with Brock so I can record it? We can make Starhair into the humorous sidekick."

"I am neither," Starhair replied grumpily.

"Not yet," Sophie corrected him.

"If you're ready, please come with me," Envoy Yoshi said to the clone. "There is already a ship waiting for you."

"Sure thing," the clone said. "By the way, is it possible for the ship to make a small detour on the way to my planet?"

"That is something you will need to discuss with the captain," Envoy Yoshi replied.

"Then lead the way," the clone said. He exchanged a fist-bump with the real Jack and Brock, waved goodbye to Sophie, then followed the bactrian out of the room.

"Hey, Jack!" Jack shouted. "Want a stone?"

"No thanks!" the clone shouted back.

Jack sighed. Of course, he controlled both bodies. This was just an inside joke with himself. Part of the reason he was so exhausted dealing with Sophie was because The Stone remained in his inner world, and it kept spouting one-liners non-stop. It was like having two Sophies, one of which replied to the other and sometimes demanded Jack transfer its jokes.

The Stone had come up with at least a dozen catchphrases since Sophie mentioned it, the most imaginative of which was *It's Fisting Time!* Which wasn't bad, if Jack was being honest, but he'd be damned if he encouraged The Stone.

In fact, this whole catchphrase thing was a hit in his inner world.

"Make it something good, kid!" the turtle demanded, having exited the Life Drop to participate. "I have a catchphrase for you. Venerable Saint Thousand Shell is the Best!"

Even Copy Jack had entered the fray. *"Fists and stones will certainly break your bones,"* he offered, which wasn't very good, but Jack liked seeing him engaged.

Jack's inner world residents then got into a fight, because the turtle insisted on being in the catchphrase, The Stone was speaking incessantly, and Copy Jack fanned the flames.

"Guys, guys, guys," Jack said. "If you all backseat me like this, I cannot focus. Just be quiet for a moment."

They grumbled but complied. Jack sighed. *How did my inner world turn into a bar...* he asked himself.

"Okay, guys, my time with you today is up!" Sophie exclaimed, looking at her wrist which had no clock. "I'll be back tomorrow at the same time. You come up with possible catchphrases in the meantime, and remember: Rush, rush, rush!"

"And then we'll crash, crash, crash," Jack replied humorlessly. "See you around, Sophie."

"See you, TV Bro," Brock said. The djinn left the mansion, dragging together her hosts of models, photographers, and videographers who'd been busy filming something in another room. Jack and Brock were finally left alone. They released a long, long sigh. Jack wanted nothing more than to sleep.

Instead, he went to his room, grabbed the space monster cores he'd been delivered earlier, and started cultivating.

CHAPTER TWELVE
ABSORBING CORES

JACK TOOK A DEEP BREATH AND OPENED HIS STATUS SCREEN.

Name: Jack Rust
Species: Human, Earth-387
Faction: Bare Fist Brotherhood (B)
Grade: B
Class: Paragon of Cultivation (Legendary)
Level: 403

Strength: 8630 (+)
Dexterity: 8630 (+)
Constitution: 8630 (+)
Mental: 1200
Will: 1200
Free sub-points: 2

Dao Skills: Meteor Punch IV, Iron Fist Style III, Brutalizing Aura III, Neutron Star Body III, Supernova III, Space

Mastery III, Fist of Mortality III, Death Mastery III, Titan Taunt III, Immortal Commune I
Inner World size: 10,000 miles
Matter Condensation: 6%
Titles: Planetary Frontrunner (10), Planetary Torch-bearer (1), Ninth Ring Conqueror, Planetary Overlord (1), Grade Defier, Planet Destroyer, Challenger

After their fight against the space octopus, Brock had gotten its core, which he shared with both Jack and Starhair. However, Starhair said he was already at the very peak of the B-Grade, so it was just Brock and Jack. They absorbed the core together. Both rose by three levels. The squid's Dao was more compatible with Jack's, so his absorption rate was higher, but his inner world was also wider, so his rate of growth was slower.

Despairingly slow, in fact.

Half the core of an early A-Grade space monster had given him six percent Matter Condensation, or three levels. Given that the B-Grade comprised of 150 levels, from 400 all the way to 550, it was bound to be extremely slow-going. Unless, of course, he found a den of A-Grade space monsters to hunt.

On the bright side, his stat gain per level was insane. He currently received fifty points every level thanks to his Legendary Class. Over the course of the entire B-Grade, that would translate to seven thousand five hundred points, which would almost double his already towering Physical. Given the bits of body tempering he planned to sneak in, it really would double. He would become a monster.

From what he'd heard, most B-Grades received twenty or thirty points per level depending on whether they possessed Common or Elite classes. The super talented ones with King classes, like Min Ling and Sovereign Heavenly Spoon, received forty. His advantage over everyone else would be exponential. And that wasn't even taking into account the extreme amount of energy he possessed due to his wide inner world.

By now, Jack really was on the path to greatness—and he planned to take the next step today.

He sat cross-legged on the floor. An office room surrounded him—his very own office—but he preferred the floor. The mahogany chair just felt wrong.

A large sack lay between Jack's feet. The sheer energy radiating from it blinded his senses—if not for the energy-proof material used on the sack, he couldn't just keep it there. This sack contained the greatest resources he'd been given so far.

Reaching into it, he removed the first item. It was a glowing orb the size of his head, green like mold. Life energy flowed off of it in waves, saturating the room. His Dao resonated, and his inner world yearned to absorb it.

This was a space monster core. According to the small description attached to it, it'd come from a peak B-Grade monster called a Mold Worm—a species which took a planet as its shell, carved mountain-sized troughs through it, and eventually consumed it like a regular worm consumed an apple.

Jack placed the orb against his chest. Tendrils of energy leaked out, drawn towards his heart, where his inner world resided. Energy flowed into him. The tendrils widened like water drawn to the waterfall, transferring energy at a faster and faster rate.

Before long, a green vortex hovered before Jack's chest, rotating so violently it threatened the room's integrity. Endless energy flowed into his inner world, dispersing without a sign. No matter how vast the energy, his inner world was even vaster. This was just a drop in the sea.

Six hours later, Jack was done absorbing it—two times faster than he'd taken on the octopus core. He opened his eyes from meditation, finding the energy inside him marginally increased.

Level: 404
Matter Condensation: 8%

He groaned. Two percent. That was all he'd gained from a peak B-Grade core, and only because that core was highly compatible with his Dao.

This will take forever, he groaned inwardly.

"Not forever!" The Stone unhelpfully exclaimed. "Just a really, really long time! But don't worry—I'll be right here keeping you company!"

He groaned again. "*Thanks, Stone.*"

"*No problem.*"

Thankfully, he also had some A-Grade cores in the sack. They would give him more meaningful increases. If not for the full support of the Church, he had no idea how or when he'd reach even the middle B-Grade.

For now, he would just get a little bit stronger every day.

The days flowed. Before Jack knew it, he'd lived in the New Cathedral for two weeks, and he'd developed a routine. Sophie came by almost every day to discuss a new marketing approach or take silly pictures and interviews. She, Starhair, and Brock had somehow caught on to the *It's Fisting Time!* suggestion for a catchphrase. He rejected it. Yet, it somehow got out, and his fans liked it enough that it'd become his unofficial catchphrase.

Whatever Sophie was doing, it was working. He received more looks every time he left the house. People eyed him in the streets, pointing and speaking in hushed tones. He saw interviews of himself playing on big screens, and he cringed every single time. They'd somehow edited his words to give him a brutal, bloodthirsty, warrior-like feel. It wasn't that he disliked it, nor did he mind the attention. It was just weird. He couldn't fathom how this enhanced the army's morale.

"Jack! Jack!" Two E-Grade human girls rushed up to him in the street. "Can we have an autograph?"

He shrugged. "Sure. Where do you want it?"

They raised their shirts all the way. Jack bolted out of there.

Another time, he was walking by a clothing store and almost jumped when he saw his face, magnified, stuck against the glass. It was on a t-shirt which also featured the words "It's fisting time!" in a large font size. Taking a step back, he saw more shirts—himself drawn as a bare-chested superhero, Brock posing with sunglasses and surrounded by female models, a coffee mug with a purple meteor fist... There was even a hoodie portraying him spanking a blushing Artus Emberheart.

"Are people buying those?" he wondered aloud, just as a set of youths left the shop wearing their brand new t-shirts. They froze when they caught sight of him. One of them panicked and muttered, "It's fisting time?"

Jack sighed and walked away.

It wasn't all stupid. Jack caught projections of himself which were actually pretty strong. He slaughtered leonines, standing against entire swathes of enemies with nothing but his bare chest. "This is for freedom," he heard himself say. "I might die, but I will never kneel!"

He didn't remember saying that, but it wasn't impossible. He gradually began to see just why the Church had done all this. If the cultivators were suffering on the front lines, struggling to persist and believe in their cause despite the difficulties, then seeing someone do the exact same thing would be encouraging.

It just made Jack sad that he wasn't at the front lines alongside them.

Nevertheless, he understood his place. Right now, the important thing was to grow stronger quickly. That was how he could best help the army. If he succumbed to the pressure and went to fight with them now, he would be throwing their lives away.

His form in the big screen blurred, revealing Brock clad in golden power. "Bros of the world, lend me your power!" he shouted, raising his hands. Inspiring music played. Jack spied multiple people staring at the screen and raising their hands as they laughed. He sighed again.

"I hate war."

Inhabiting two bodies was a disorienting experience. Jack's way of handling it, which was the same as most people's, was to isolate the thoughts and perception of each body from the other. It was like closing one of your eyes. Harmless and easy to get used to, while maintaining all the advantages of having a clone. The two bodies could reinstate their communication whenever they wanted and for as long as they wanted.

Souls, it seemed, were something that stood above the constraints of space. Through Jack's experimentation, he'd come to realize that any communication between the main body and the clone occurred instantly regardless of the distance separating them.

It was a great boon, and also solved one of his long-standing questions, since the System regularly used faster-than-light communications. It must have relied on a similar principle. Maybe a bunch of tiny soul pieces of... something... scattered across the universe?

While Jack's main body remained at the New Cathedral, cultivating as fast as humanly possible, the clone was shuttling through space. This Jack was also meditating. His eyes flashed open, and he looked out the window.

"Hey, Captain," he said. The small, gray-skin alien piloting their starship turned around.

"Yes?"

It was just the two of them here. To travel as fast and discreetly as possible, they'd used a starship barely large enough for two people. Jack didn't even have his own room, sharing the ship's single communal space with the captain, an alien called Druk-Druk. Despite her odd name, she was actually quite competent—as well as a middle B-Grade.

"Is that the Heaven's Egg galaxy?" Jack asked.

The alien glanced outside the window. "Why?" she asked.

"I've left something there. Do you mind if we make a quick stop to pick it up?"

She raised a brow—or rather, the bony ridge over her eye, as this species had no hair whatsoever. "We cannot enter System space here. Too dangerous."

"We don't need System space. This galaxy is not fully Integrated. As long as we can get somewhere close to the edge, it will be fine."

She hesitated, but relented. "Sure. What are you looking for?"

"Oh, just a little separate dimension." He laughed at her surprise.

Years ago, Jack had entered a hidden realm called the Green Dragon Realm. That was where he received the inheritance of Archon Green Dragon, an ancient dragon specializing in spacetime. He'd also spent three years meditating in the center of the Green Dragon Realm alongside Brock and Min Ling—that was the single longest meditation session he'd ever had.

Green Dragon's inheritance included the realm's Realm Heart, the core of that place. Once he reached the B-Grade, Jack could use it to absorb the entire realm into his inner world, strengthening himself and protecting it at the same time. That absorption was something he really looked forward to.

Unfortunately, he'd only reached the B-Grade in the Spiral Stair galaxy very recently, and he hadn't had the opportunity to come pick up the Green Dragon Realm yet. Now was a good chance—he knew they'd pass by, so he'd kept an eye on the window.

Their starship angled to the side. Galaxies surrounded them like islands in the sea, and they dove toward one. With Druk-Druk specializing in spacetime, they were extremely fast. The galaxy grew in their sights.

Jack actually suspected he could take the starship even faster, but he didn't want to offend his captain.

Before long, their entire field of view was occupied by multicolored stars, arranged as a vast, egg-shaped galaxy. There were no spirals on this one.

The stars look so small, Jack thought, once again admiring the beauty of the universe. Galaxies comprised of billions of stars. Each was humongous, orbited by several planets, each a different world. Most weren't inhabitable, but so what? There were hundreds of billions of worlds nestled in each galaxy, seeming so small from afar.

And there were a trillion galaxies in the universe. With the cultivation world occupying exactly seventy-three.

Jack would have snickered if he wasn't so humbled.

The Heaven Egg galaxy wasn't fully Integrated. Just like the Milky Way, it was one of the newest additions to System space. Still, around eighty percent of it was occupied by the System, leaving only the fringes on one side. It was precisely there that Jack and Druk-Druk headed.

Once upon a time, he'd entered the Green Dragon Realm through an entrance portal situated in System space. That portal had since closed, but its location remained the realm's anchoring point to the universe.

Jack, however, didn't need to go through there. He possessed the Realm Heart. If he came anywhere close, meaning anywhere in the entire galaxy, he could just use the heart to create a new connection, accessing the realm directly.

Of course, the heart remained in the inner world of the main body, not the clone, but the two were connected. Using the aura of the heart to open a portal was possible.

"Here should be fine," Jack said.

Druk-Druk brought the starship to a stop. She looked around questioningly. "Right here?"

"Right here."

A multicolored portal ripped open ahead of them. It was egg-shaped and pulsing with dimensional energy. Just behind it, Jack could see a thin tunnel twisting through an expanse of colors—the dimensional sea.

"Can you wait here?" Jack asked. "I'll need a few hours."

Druk-Druk just stared. He gave her a thumbs-up, flew into the portal, and disappeared.

CHAPTER THIRTEEN
VISITING THE GREEN DRAGON REALM

JACK'S CLONE FLEW THROUGH THE WORMHOLE, SURROUNDED BY DANCING colors on all sides. They weren't really colors—that was just the best way his human brain could translate the chaos of the dimensional sea. In truth, it was a place where spacetime lost all meaning, a place existing on a higher dimension than Jack could comprehend.

He imagined that, if a higher-dimensional creature existed, and if it was watching him right now, it might see him as a drawing jumping from one piece of paper to another. It was a mind-twister. He wondered if he'd ever have the power to actually enter the dimensional sea instead of cheating his way through.

Maybe not. Even the Old Gods of Space and Time couldn't perform such a feat. Still, Jack could hope. As he'd recently realized, the cultivation world occupied a tiny fraction of a fraction of the universe. They were basically infants at the start of their journey. Who knew how far they could reach given a few billion years.

One step each generation... he thought, watching the end of the tunnel approach. He popped through. A familiar sky welcomed him, containing the occasional flying beast. He watched a bird seemingly made of vines cross the air. As soon as it caught sight of him, it swooped in, releasing a low squawk. Jack laughed and petted its head.

As the master of this realm, the native creatures weren't aggressive towards him. They felt the same kind of respect and excitement one would feel toward their father. The fluctuations of the Realm Heart rippled out of him, cultivating a sense of camaraderie in their hearts.

He could sense their souls aligned to his.

The flying vine creature buried its head in Jack's chest, rubbing against him like a puppy. Ironically, the creature's head alone was larger than Jack, but it wasn't bothered. Neither was he. The hard vines, which would have torn a mortal apart, couldn't even scratch his skin.

Looking at the creature confirmed one of Jack's suspicions, and he was very glad for it. He couldn't use the System to inspect it.

The last time he was here, this entire realm had counted as System space. The System had seeped in through the previous portal and claimed it. Now, after losing contact with the wider System for so long, whatever constituted System space had faded, returning this realm to the virgin state it had always existed in.

It also meant nobody could spy on Jack.

"Wanna go on an adventure, buddy?" he asked, rubbing the nose of the vine-dragon thing. It squealed with joy. He flashed, reappearing on its back. "Let's go!"

The vine dragon flapped its wings. Though made of vines, they were coated with sticky dense leaves, giving them the aerodynamics necessary to fly through the sky. Not that this monster needed it—as a late D-Grade creature, it could fly even without wings. The wings were mostly useful before maturity.

Jack and the vine dragon flew high, crossing the realm where Jack took it all in. Any flying creatures he met squawked at his appearance, filled with joy and respect. Dense jungle spread below his feet, occupying almost the entirety of the Green Dragon Realm. Jack could see hundreds of creatures as they flew by, consisting of an endless variety of life forms, some of which he hadn't encountered during his last visit.

There was a hill-sized bush walking around, like a large turtle with dense shrubbery instead of a shell. He caught sight of dragons living above the clouds, their scales glowing green as they absorbed the light of the artificial sun for sustenance. Using his sharp eyesight, Jack even saw a little creature darting from branch to branch—a mouse-sized, wingless dragon.

The diversity of this realm was staggering. It made Jack proud—and also increased the respect he harbored toward Archon Green Dragon, the progenitor of this place.

Like the last time he was here, the dense Life aura surrounded him, attempting to cut down his power to a fraction of its usual level. Unlike the last time, he was very familiar with the Dao of Life. The aura couldn't affect him.

As master of the realm, Jack had an understanding of where everything was. He could instinctively sense the direction of the massive temple at the center of the realm. He was moving closer to it, though the temple wasn't his goal. His real destination was the little village he knew existed near it—where the remnants of the expedition forces were staying.

When Jack had first arrived in this place, over four years ago, he was accompanied by elite cultivators from both the Hand of God and the Black Hole Church. When he later left the realm, he hadn't taken them along, as he wasn't confident in handling the strongest of them.

Now that he was beyond their strength, he intended to resolve this issue before attaching this realm to his inner world.

The vine dragon carried him across mountains and endless jungle. It was slow, by Jack's current measure, but flying on its back was fun. He was pretty close, anyway. Only three hours later, the mountain-sized temple rose in the distance. It looked exactly as it had the last time he was here. To the side, he could even see the volcano in which he'd fought Baron Longform. He'd then escaped through the lava tunnels under it, swimming all the way to the temple and nearly dying in the process.

The cultivator village was somewhere between the temple and the volcano. Jack used his Dao of Spacetime to cloak himself and the vine dragon as they approached, ensuring they escaped detection. Thanks to his current understanding, and these people being at most early B-Grades, it was child's play.

Soon, a small village appeared below him. He was impressed at what he saw. Elegant buildings spread in a circle, with a wide range of trees cut down around it to offer visibility of any incoming enemies. The houses were small and simple, with a unique sense of aesthetics. Vines crawled up the walls, which were made of polished wood. Chimneys released tufts of smoke.

Jack also saw the people. Most had abandoned their previous cultivator guises and now wore green, silken clothing formed of this realm's native plants. It made them resemble elegant forest people. There was no visible distinction of who came from which faction. Such things became meaningless when they thought they were trapped forever.

They seemed happy, too.

Groups of cultivators were gathered in gardens, laughing and playing games. Little animals ran around, domesticated as household versions of the realm's fauna, while larger animals waited in pens or in a nearby field, taken care of by loving cultivators. Jack even spied a few cultivator couples, which he was certain were not a thing four years ago. There was a single little boy running around, constantly tailed by his mother.

This little village didn't need walls, but Jack did see a plaque erected at the entrance, facing the jungle. It proudly declared them as the *Green Cultivator Town*.

Life really had moved on. These cultivators probably had a hard time adjusting, but they'd created a new life for themselves, one that seemed much more fulfilling than being disciples and Envoys of two warring factions.

Jack felt a momentary doubt in his heart. These people seemed so happy. Was this how it was meant to be? Was this the future the Immortals were stealing from the inhabitants of the world?

He shook his head. It didn't matter. Unlike others, he did not go to war because that was all he knew. He did it because he had to. To ensure that his friends, family, and the world would be free to select a more peaceful life than his.

Jack gazed at the town again, more inquisitively this time. His perception spread out. Thanks to being so much more powerful than everybody at Green Cultivator Town, they couldn't detect him. The difference in power was especially prominent since they were suppressed by the dense life energy, while he was not.

He looked inside the buildings. Within the central one, which was larger than the others, Monk Uruselam was discussing with a few other cultivators—something about domesticating an animal called Leaf Sweeper. Jack had no idea what it was. All he cared about was that Monk Uruselam had become the leader of this small community, which wasn't a terrible idea. The monk wasn't nearly as kind as he seemed, but since there were no conflicts of interest here, he was a competent leader.

Jack looked for certain others , too. Shi Mo, the middle-aged warrior who'd become friends with Jack in the past, had a little house where he cultivated. A pet draconic twig was curled around him, breathing in and out in peaceful sleep. The warrior himself had foregone his sword for a wooden hoe—a touching image.

The only other people Jack had interacted with were Borkuren Madiba, a frog-like humanoid Church Envoy who'd helped him a few times on the Cathedral, and Sassa, a talented C-Grade of the Hand of God, whose last name he'd never gotten. That young girl had been a massive bitch during the banquet battles before entering the hidden realm, to the point where Jack had gloriously kicked her ass.

To his great amusement, he discovered that Borkuren and Sassa were now a couple. In fact, they were the sole couple whom had children. Sassa was the mother of the boy running around earlier, it was just that she'd changed so much Jack hadn't recognized her.

The once aloof, arrogant young girl had transformed into a caring mother. Her entire aura was different. Jack had no idea how that came to be, but he guessed that getting trapped here, presumably for life, had deeply impacted her and completely turned her life around. That was a good thing. Jack had planned on killing her to eliminate future trouble, as he did to all his enemies, but the less blood he had to spill, the better.

He watched Borkuren step out of a house, kiss her with his frog-like mouth, then wrap her in a big hug. She giggled as she hugged him back.

Yep. Loving couple alright.

Jack planned to appear before the town and explain what was going on, but not yet. The final person he looked for was his old enemy—Spacewind. He was the leader of the Church side of the expedition, as well as a massive dick who'd bullied Jack on various occasions and even tried to kill him.

Jack found him in the only house outside the town. While everyone else lived together in harmony, Spacewind was alone in a stone building, stubbornly cultivating. It was unclear whether he isolated himself or others did it for him, but Jack thought it was fitting. A sad ending for a sad man.

"Thanks for the ride, bro," Jack told the vine dragon. He patted its back. "Go live a happy life."

The creature squawked once more, then flew away. Jack was left hovering in the sky. He slowly lowered himself to the ground and flew into Spacewind's house through the window. His cloaking remained active. The other man, who prided himself in his understanding of space, didn't have the slightest idea there was someone standing right in front of him. He was meditating. Jack could kill him as easily as blinking.

He dropped his cloaking. Instantly, Spacewind jumped back, terrified to the ends of his wits. His hair was disheveled, his clothes raggedy, and his eyes bloodshot. Those hadn't come from Jack scaring him—they were his natural state now.

"What?" he cried out. "It's... It's you! Jack Rust! That's... What? I will kill you!"

True to his station, Spacewind recovered quickly. He straightened his palm and slashed it out like a knife. Jack raised a hand and caught it. Spacewind's strike was frozen midair. He paled.

"What?" he muttered.

Jack gave a sad smile. This clone body wasn't nearly as strong as the original, and his cultivation was only at a level similar to the late C-Grade, but his Dao understandings remained. Dealing with an early B-Grade like Spacewind was easy. He'd just wrapped space around his palm to easily catch Spacewind's hand.

The man seemed like he was about to have a stroke.

CHAPTER FOURTEEN

ENDING SPACEWIND

"You have no idea what's going on, and that's okay," Jack said, firmly holding onto Spacewind's attacking hand. "I'm Jack Rust. You once mocked me, bullied me, and tried to kill me. I'm here to repay the favor."

"How?" Spacewind cried out. "How can you be alive? How can you be so strong!"

The poor man didn't even realize he was seeing a clone. In his mind, Jack going from the middle to the late C-Grade in the span of four years was already a great pace.

Jack didn't plan to correct his misunderstanding.

"You've made a sad life for yourself, Spacewind. As much as you deserve it, it pains me to see you so isolated... but it no longer matters, does it?" He shook his head. "You hate me. Therefore, you must die."

He punched out faster than Spacewind could react. A hole was blasted in the other man's chest. Spacewind fell to his knees. Even as life abandoned him, the look of incomprehension never left his wide eyes.

He had once sworn to destroy Jack Rust. He remembered his own words clearly:

Jack Rust, you took my woman, took my treasures, and took my reputation. If I don't cripple you and feed you to the dogs, I am no man!

Since then, revenge had been his driving force. He'd cultivated intensely, never resigning himself to remaining trapped in this place. He'd clearly fantasized escaping and dealing Jack Rust a hard blow. Picturing himself laughing over the corpse of his enemy.

Yet, things had changed so abruptly. Spacewind was dying. His enemy had appeared out of nowhere, ruthlessly exterminating him. He hadn't had the slightest chance to fight back. Despair and unwillingness warred inside his heart.

This is... unfair... were his final thoughts before all life left him. His eyes remained glued on Jack, burning with hatred until their light faded.

Jack waited until Spacewind really was dead. He shook his head and sighed. Did he enjoy this? No. As much as Spacewind had been his enemy before, executing someone was never a happy affair, just a necessity.

He would never let an enemy get away again. Artus Emberheart had taught him this lesson.

Then, Jack teleported, appearing right in the middle of the city. He was no longer hiding his presence. Every single cultivator jumped and rushed to surround him, while Sassa took the boy in her arms and prepared to teleport away.

Monk Uruselam stood at the very front of the gathering, with Shi Mo next to him. His wooden hoe had once again been replaced with a sword. Jack was surprised at their reaction speed.

"Jack Rust?" Uruselam asked, as if recalling the name from the depths of his memory. Unlike Spacewind, he didn't react immediately. He scouted Jack with his Dao perception, sensing the depths of his aura. That gave him pause.

"Hello, everyone," Jack said. "It's been a while. I hope you've been well."

"What is going on?" Shi Mo asked, narrowing his eyes. "Are you really Jack? You feel different. And where's Brock?"

"I will explain everything," Jack replied, and that's exactly what he did. For the next hour, he recounted how he'd gained control of the entire realm and sealed them in—without going into details. He informed them about the outside world and the ongoing Crusade.

They were stunned, of course, asking him all sorts of questions. They struggled to believe him. It was only as the hour passed that they came to terms with the world-altering reality Jack presented them—and only because he demonstrated his prowess, enough to easily overpower everyone here combined.

"So, you are responsible for trapping us here?" Uruselam asked.

"I am, and I'm sorry about it," Jack replied. "I couldn't risk releasing you without the strength to control things. Now that I do... I have come to give you a choice."

Before Jack actually saw this place, one of his potential plans had been to exterminate all the Hand of God cultivators and release the others. However, he hadn't been satisfied with it, because it felt too brutal. Now, he was glad to see that things had changed. These people had lost their edge—in a good way. He no longer believed any of them deserved killing.

"I will soon attach this entire realm to my inner world," Jack said. "To those of you who will still be here, you will likely experience no change. You won't be able to harm me either, as the connection between this place and my inner world will be... special. After I do that, releasing you from this realm will be much more difficult, and I may not be able to achieve it for the near future. Therefore, you need to make a decision now."

They watched with rapt attention.

"Those of you belonging to the Hand of God, I am sorry to say, but I will not release you. I cannot risk you joining the war and killing any of our cultivators. I will not kill you unless you wish for it, but you can remain here and live out the rest of your lives in peace. When the war is over, then I might let you out.

"Those of you belonging to the Church... You can make your choice. If you want to leave, I will take you just outside System space and help you reach the Church forces. I cannot escort you, however. Your survival will be up to you. If you prefer to stay here and live in peace, then you may do so, until the day comes that I offer to release you again. What do you choose?"

Jack looked everyone in the eye. He expected the Hand of God people to be angry. Instead, they seemed almost... relieved? It was the Church cultivators who showed signs of internal struggle.

"I will stay," Borkuren said. He reached out to hug Sassa and his little son, who was gazing at Jack with wide eyes. "I never had a family, but now I do. I will not abandon them."

Jack nodded with approval.

"I will stay as well," Shi Mo said. "I'm approaching the limits of my life, and after sitting around for four years, my blade has lost its edge. I am no longer a warrior. Just an old man." He chuckled. "Are you disappointed, Jack?"

Jack smiled. "I'm happy for you, old friend. I liked you as an honorable warrior, and I like you equally now. There is nothing wrong with change."

Shi Mo laughed, not saying anything else. Besides him and Borkuren, however, all other members of the Church chose to exit; that included two Envoys. They all had families and friends on the outside. As happy as they were in this place, hiding here and letting their people fight alone would be wrong. Nobody reached this level by being a coward.

Jack watched as these people set their jaws, saw how torn some of them were. He wondered if, perhaps, he should never have said anything. Then, these people wouldn't have to go to war, and they could continue living here in happiness.

But that wasn't the right way. Everyone deserved to make their own choices.

Jack gave them some time. There were heartful goodbyes. These people had all bonded with each other, regardless of their faction of origin, and having to completely uproot these new lives in the span of a few hours must have been difficult.

Unfortunately, Jack couldn't give them too long. He was also on a mission. Six hours later, after everyone had a huge party, he returned to bid his own goodbyes.

"I'll visit sometimes," he said, clasping the hands of both Borkuren and Shi Mo. They pulled him into a hug, laughing.

"We'll be looking forward to it, old friend," Shi Mo said, still drunk from the party before. They'd managed to make liquor strong enough to affect them.

"Hey, Jack," Borkuren said with a drunk smile, "do you know what we named our son? Jack. After you. Because we thought you died too early."

Jack swiveled, his eyes widening. He looked over at Sassa, who waited by the side. She gave him a coy look. "I did think it was a silly name," she replied. "But when Borkuren likes an idea, you just can't get it out of his mind."

The frog man laughed. So did she. She did not resemble the arrogant young girl of four years ago at all. If Jack didn't know it was impossible, he would have thought she'd been replaced by a shapeshifting monster.

"Thank you," he said. A child was named after him. That hit home hard. He'd even lost his breath.

The couple laughed again. Their son, too young to speak, waved at Jack and laughed with his little baby face.

Jack was suddenly emotional. He shook his head to clear it. "See you guys," he told everyone who remained as he took to the sky. "Enjoy this place. It's all yours!"

With that, he wrapped the people who were leaving in a spacetime bubble and took them along, teleporting rapidly. It only took him a couple minutes to reach the location of the portal. The cultivators he was dragging along had tears in their eyes. They looked down, memorizing this happy jungle they'd never see again.

"Heads down," Jack said, flying into the portal. A few minutes later, it snapped close, and the realm was isolated once more.

They were now floating in space, between the stars. The cultivators he'd brought along were teary-eyed. Druk-Druk was not amused. "Where am I supposed to put all these people?" she asked. "Our starship is tiny."

"I'll keep them in a space bubble," Jack promised. "Once we reach Earth, I'll give you a larger starship for the way back. Consider it a gift."

The space bubble would also ensure these people didn't figure out the location of Earth, but Jack didn't mention that. Instead, after chatting with the cultivators a bit and introducing them to Druk-Druk, he formed another space bubble, shrank it to the size of a desk, and took it into the starship with him. It was larger on the inside, so the cultivators wouldn't be crowded.

Maintaining this for the rest of the trip would be taxing, but as long as they didn't run into enemies, he would be fine. First, however...

"Take the bubble for a second, please," Jack said. Druk-Druk took over with a grumble—she specialized in spacetime—while Jack turned to regard the open space. He spread his arms, taking a deep breath. The Realm Heart in the main body's inner world shuddered. Unique Dao fluctuations passed through their connection and erupted from the clone's body. He used his Dao to reach into the point where the portal previously hung, the new anchoring point of the Green Dragon Realm to this universe, and *pulled*.

The universe was a bubble in the dimensional sea. So was the Green Dragon Realm and all other hidden realms, except much smaller. Interestingly, the inner worlds of B-Grade cultivators and above were also their own dimensional bubbles. They were governed by unique rules, of course, but that was beside the point.

The important thing was, since they were dimensional bubbles, they could be connected to places outside the cultivator's body. Technically, one could even form connection points between their inner world and the universe, but that would be dangerous and pointless. Living creatures from the outside couldn't enter inner worlds—with exceptions, like Venerable Saint Thousand Shell, who was tied to the Life Drop, which was in turn a part of Jack's soul.

He couldn't actually absorb the Green Dragon Realm in his inner world. Not only was it impossible Dao-wise, but it was also too big. It wouldn't fit. What he would do instead was form a permanent connection between the two dimensional bubbles. Essentially, instead of the Green Dragon Realm connecting to the universe, it would now connect to Jack's inner world. That would protect the realm from any harm, and also enhance Jack's inner world.

While living creatures couldn't pass through the portal, energy sure could, especially when you were the master of both sides of the connection.

Jack pulled at the portal. He sensed it move through space, an invisible anchoring point, then passed it through his body and into his inner world. The sensation was weird, but it succeeded.

At that point, the main body in the Spiral Stair galaxy paused its cultivation to work with the clone. Their two inner worlds were connected. Together, they moved the portal from one side to the other, planting it firmly in the main body's inner world. It was just an energy signature, so transferring it between two connected dimensional bubbles was doable, if difficult.

When it was over, Jack took a deep breath, exhausted. That was harder than he anticipated. But also very rewarding.

He could feel it already. The portal was open in the main body's inner world, flooding it with a constant stream of energy. After all, the Green Dragon Realm had existed for a very long time, and it was many times larger than Jack's inner world. It could supply energy all the way until Jack reached the A-Grade, and the cultivators there would only feel a tiny difference in energy density.

Of course, that would still take a very long time, because the energy which could pass through the small portal was limited. It was a great increase in cultivation speed regardless. Even without any space monster cores, Jack was confident he could reach the peak B-Grade within a millennium.

Having your own little realm, created by an Archon and left to grow for a billion years, was overpowered indeed.

Jack smiled as he rushed back into the ship. Next destination... Earth!

CHAPTER FIFTEEN
DOUBLE TROUBLE

Jack opened his eyes in the New Cathedral. They flashed. A grin played on his lips, and power surged through his inner world.

Sitting in his office, Jack laughed with joy.

"Good job, myself!"

Several galaxies away, his clone had just absorbed the Green Dragon Realm. Working together, they managed to attach the realm to the main body's inner world, leading to yet another power-up for Jack.

He wasn't sure how exactly this worked, but he was excited to find out. He quickly set to experimentation.

An egg-shaped portal floated in his mostly empty inner world. Through the vacuum echoed a sound like rushing waves; the sign of energy flowing rapidly from the realm to Jack's inner world. The portal was only ten feet tall and six wide, pumping out energy at full capacity, like a drain at the bottom of the sea. The energy influx was far faster than what Jack could achieve by cultivating.

Originally, he would have needed hundreds of thousands of years of cultivation to reach the peak B-Grade. With this portal steadily pumping out energy, he could cut that down to a mere thousand. A more than great pace in normal circumstances. Of course, it wasn't enough in the current war state, but it was a great step forward.

Jack stood in his inner world, gazing at the portal from afar. The other inhabitants of the world floated beside him.

"What a nice door!" The Stone exclaimed. "They forgot the knob, though. Do you have the details of the manufacturer? I'd like to give them a word or two! Speaking of doors, I remember seeing a beautiful one. It was white and marble, with two little flowers growing on it, and it smelled vaguely of lavender. Not that I have a nose, but so I was told. Speaking of lavender…"

Jack zoned out The Stone, as he'd gotten used to doing lately. He could now let it hang out in his inner world, speaking at will, and he just didn't hear it. The human brain was a wonderful thing.

"Where does that lead, kid?" the turtle asked. Its eyes were narrowed. "Why does it feel so… homely?"

"That's the Green Dragon Realm," Jack replied. "The same place where you fell asleep a few years ago. I grafted it to my inner world."

The turtle's eyes brightened. "I see. And you connected it here to…"

"To absorb its energy, mostly, as well as protect it from the universe," Jack explained. "It has a ton of life energy, too. I was thinking to use some of that energy to start refilling the Life Drop."

"Brilliant!" The turtle nodded in approval. "You said you would refill it, and now you're doing it. I like it when you keep your word."

"I always keep my word."

"Aren't you worried about emptying it out?" the turtle asked, gazing at the portal again. It was releasing energy at a tremendous rate.

Jack shook his head. "The Green Dragon Realm is shaped as an inverse, wide cone. Just the jungle on its top is a hundred thousand miles wide. The entire thing has a volume hundreds of times larger than my inner realm's, so all the energy I need is a drop in the bucket."

Saint Venerable Thousand Shell became thoughtful. "That's great, but how exactly will you refill the Divine Blood?"

"Watch this."

The Life Drop was currently glued to the middle finger of the fist-shaped meteor which occupied the center of Jack's world. As he waved a hand, the Life Drop popped off, teleporting beside them. With another wave, it flew closer to the portal, anchoring itself right before its entrance. The incoming flood of energy buffeted it, and thanks to Jack's god-like powers in this world, it remained in place.

"There," he said. "The incoming energy is life-attuned. As it brushes by the Life Drop, some of it will be absorbed."

There was something sparking in the turtle's beady eyes. A hint of... excitement? "Acceptable. That breeze of life energy looks comfortable indeed. I will go take a nap. Wake me up when it's one twentieth full."

"Wait," Jack said. "You mentioned the Life Drop has more applications. Can you teach me before you go?"

The turtle grumbled. "It's useless now, kid. That's why I said to wake me up at one twentieth. When it's time for you to know, naturally you will know."

With that, the turtle turned into a green ray of light, disappearing into the immobile Life Drop. Jack imagined it ruffling its shell and settling down for a nap. He shrugged.

The Green Dragon Realm was basically an energy generator for his inner world. Controlling a minor dimension certainly came with other uses—Jack fantasized summoning an army of plant dragons to fight for him in the future. For now, however, he was content with this.

Which didn't mean he was done. He already had one minor dimension, yes—but what about a second?

The real body reached into his space ring, removing an item that near-instantly appeared inside his inner world. It was a round bead blacker than black, absorbing any and all light that reached it. This was the seed of the Black Hole World, an anchor able to open a portal to that sealed place.

Jack had already used it once a few days ago. He'd flown far away from the New Cathedral, activated the bead, and passed into the Black Hole World. He'd then explained the current situation to Grand Elder Pasan, the leader of that world, and asked for her opinion.

Surprisingly, the Grand Elder refused to leave yet. With the current state of the universe, and her people as pure-hearted and naive as they were, she figured sending them out now would lead to widespread destruction. They'd already waited a billion years, she said—they could wait a little more until the Second Crusade ended. Or until they were needed.

Truth be told, they would be useless outside. Their strongest cultivators were at the D-Grade, and their inheritances, while great treasures to a backwater faction like the Animal Kingdom, were nothing much to the Black Hole Church. Jack disagreed with the Grand Elder's decision on the principle of freedom, but he could see her reasoning.

Everything else aside, a minor dimension was an extremely valuable thing, both for hiding and transportation purposes. He could see the Church commandeering the Black Hole World for its forces and forcing the black hole people to relocate to a friendly planet, where they would be vulnerable. The Arch Priestess didn't strike him as an asshole, but it was the natural thing to do. Jack would have done the same if Earth was at stake. Letting such a valuable resource be wasted on low-level cultivators was unwise.

However, since Jack owed them a favor, he promised to keep the Black Hole World a secret for now.

The Grand Elder did, however, agree to let him connect their world to his inner world. The purpose of this wasn't to use it as an energy battery like the Green Dragon Realm. After all, the Black Hole World was tiny, only a hundred miles across. Their energy was too little.

What they did have, however, was incredibly solid spacetime laws. Such a small dimension should have collapsed long ago by the sheer pressure of the dimensional sea surrounding it. The only reason it hadn't was thanks to Archon Black Hole's extreme understandings of spacetime. By sacrificing world size, he'd achieved extreme stability—the exact opposite of what Archon Green Dragon had done with his own world, which was slowly deteriorating.

Jack had to wonder about the justification of Archon Black Hole doing that. The Black Hole World was meant to be a temporary shelter for his descendants. They were supposed to exit after a million years. With his powers, he could have easily crafted a massive world for them where they could live comfortably in sunlit prairies, and that world would still last for ten million years—ten times longer than necessary. Instead, the Archon had decided to make a stuffy ball of layered stone just a hundred miles across, sacrificing life quality to greatly extend the world's lifetime.

Had the Archon lied to his descendants? Did he intend for them to stay trapped in there for a billion years? Maybe, Jack thought, it was a move of desperation. The Archon had grown so disillusioned with the outside world that he preferred his descendants to live in their own little world forever.

Jack didn't know how he felt about that. It scared him. Just what could drive a mighty Archon to such extreme despair? Was he right, or was there some other reasoning which Jack just didn't grasp? Even Grand Elder Pasan revealed she had no idea.

In any case, that was an old matter, probably unrelated to modern-day events. The important thing was that Jack's inner world was stable, but of course, it was nothing compared to what a Spacetime Archon could achieve. By connecting the two, he could allow their laws to intermingle, gradually enhancing the stability of his world. It wouldn't increase his cultivation, but it would help with future breakthroughs.

A second connection point appeared in his inner world. This one was black, and shaped as a black hole instead of a portal. It didn't suck in energy; it only circulated, breathing in and out like a living creature. Compared to the energy-flooding portal of the Green Dragon Realm, this second connection point seemed calm and steady, as if it could exist for eternity.

Looking at the two, Jack felt like he could see the Archons. Green Dragon was a powerful, rowdy individual, using his powers to kick up a storm wherever he went. Black Hole was calm, collected, and calculating. His plans reached deep into the future, a gradual accumulation.

Jack chuckled. He had a feeling his assumptions were accurate. He still remembered how, in the vision he saw of Green Dragon, the Archon had some... choice words for the Space and Time Old Gods. Which he'd said right to their faces.

"Two minor realms..." he muttered. "We're doing pretty well here. Don't you think so, Stone?"

The Stone, which had been going on about gardening techniques, propped up. "Most certainly! You're standing on the shoulders of giants. That's why I like you, Jack. You know how to get a good thing going."

"...Are you trying to flatter me?"

The Stone deflated. "No," it said in a small voice. Jack laughed.

"You don't need to worry. I won't abandon you, Stone. You're a friend now. A bro. While I live, you will never be alone again."

The Stone perked up. "Really?"

"Yes, really. Isn't that right, Copy Jack?"

Copy Jack shrugged. "Yes."

The Stone beamed at that. "Thank you, thank you! I knew I could count on you! That lion woman was so evil; just when I thought I'd been freed from an endless life of solitude, she threw me right into a space ring and left me there. Can you believe it? At least on my meteor I had *something* to enjoy. The stars were nice. There were astral winds. But in a ring? That's goddamn boring."

"She was a real piece of work," Jack agreed. "How did you even see the stars, anyway? You don't have eyes."

"I sure do! Look here, right above my mouth."

Jack frowned and leaned in. He could see nothing. The Stone had a human-shaped mouth with a stone interior, but above that, it was nothing but—

"Holy shit," he said, drawing back.

"See? I do have eyes!" The Stone replied proudly.

Jack laughed. Right above its mouth, The Stone had two beady eyes so tiny they blended in. He only recognized them because one blinked.

"You're a piece of work as well," he said. "Anyway, I gotta get back to cultivating. I'll take you out as soon as I find an opportunity. See you around, Stone, Copy Jack."

"See you!" The Stone replied excitedly, while Copy Jack waved.

Jack opened his eyes in the real world. Interacting with his friends was nice, but he had work to do. He grinned. The sack of space monster cores at his feet was only half-empty, but the progress it had given him was nothing short of impressive.

CHAPTER SIXTEEN
CHALLENGE

Jack opened his status screen. The space monster cores he'd absorbed so far had given him a bunch of levels.

Name: Jack Rust
Species: Human, Earth-387
Faction: Bare Fist Brotherhood (B)
Grade: B
Class: Paragon of Cultivation (Legendary)
Level: 432

Strength: 8680 (+)
Dexterity: 8680 (+)
Constitution: 8680 (+)
Mental: 1200
Will: 1200
Free points: 1400
Free sub-points: 2

Dao Skills: Meteor Punch IV, Iron Fist Style III, Brutal-

izing Aura III, Neutron Star Body III, Supernova III, Space Mastery III, Fist of Mortality III, Death Mastery III, Titan Taunt III, Immortal Commune I
Inner World size: 10,000 miles
Matter Condensation: 64%
Titles: Planetary Frontrunner (10), Planetary Torch-bearer (1), Ninth Ring Conqueror, Planetary Overlord (1), Grade Defier, Planet Destroyer, Challenger

From Level 404, he'd risen all the way to 432. The energy density of his inner world had increased significantly, crossing the halfway mark to reaching the middle B-Grade. Most importantly, leveling up gave him a crazy amount of stats thanks to his Legendary Class. Every level gave fifty. After twenty-eight levels, he now had one thousand four hundred points to distribute. That was massive.

Of course, rising through the levels wasn't always such an easy process. The only reason he'd advanced this fast was because he was eating high-level space monster cores like candy. The Church had invested greatly in him, and they'd made it clear this was all they could provide. After this sack was empty, their assistance would be limited.

He hoped these cores would be enough to push him to the middle B-Grade—just 36% left to go. After that, maybe he'd go hunting for space monster cores himself. He'd heard many times that this galaxy was unnaturally chock-full of space monsters.

For now, however, he had a ton of stat points to distribute.

1400... he thought with disbelief. *That's so much...*

Once upon a time, every level gave him two points, and those two had been enough to seriously push his strength forward. Now, he needed over a thousand to achieve the same effect.

His Physical substats were balanced, all at 8680. He could invest everything into them to push them over ten thousand. However, that would leave his Mental and Will too far behind. All the strength in the world would matter little if he was trapped in an illusion.

Back when he was an F-Grade cultivator, Shol had told him to adopt an 8-1-1 distribution between his stats. As he climbed, nobody had anything to say against that strategy, so it remained the one he followed—with the sole exception that, when possible, he enjoyed round numbers.

Jack hardened his heart, investing almost half of his stat points into Mental and Will. Three hundred went into each, raising them both to a round 1500. That was a twenty percent increase. Instantly, he felt his mind sharpen, his understanding deepen, his purpose filled with utter clarity. He could watch the rain and calculate the path of every individual droplet. He grinned.

But this wasn't what he liked most.

Eight hundred points remained, and he gleefully poured them all into Physical. His body seized. Tremors and cramps spread through him as the System struggled to enhance him further. After all, it wasn't omnipotent, and his body was already extremely powerful. Every step forward was a hurdle. The once enjoyable sensation of increasing stat points had turned highly unpleasant.

Jack convulsed on the floor, gritting his teeth through the burning pain. His entire body was on fire. The life particles making it up, which were already densely clustered, were forced to make room for more. It was a slow and difficult process.

When the initial shock passed, Jack struggled to his feet. He could sense that the enhancement wasn't over; it'd become a constant stream of Life Dao particles into his body, lowering the pain to a threshold he could barely ignore. Jack clenched his fist, easily telling he'd grown a bit stronger, but not too much. From what he estimated, this process would take several weeks to complete. He could sense himself approaching the limits of body tempering.

In fact, he had the sneaking suspicion that the System points he inserted into his Physical were beginning to lose their efficiency. It wasn't indicated anywhere on his status screen, but he couldn't shake off the thought.

Regardless, every increase was a good one. The tempering

process would continue for weeks, but the System already indicated all his points as invested.

Strength: 9480 (+)
Dexterity: 9480 (+)
Constitution: 9480 (+)
Mental: 1500
Will: 1500
Free sub-points: 2

It was decent. Pretty good, actually. Jack was flying!

He couldn't help thinking about Brock. His brorilla brother didn't have the benefit of the System, so his own stats were rising at a slower pace. Compared to Jack, though, he did have another advantage: a smaller inner world, which could fill up with energy much faster.

Brock had also been given a sack of space monster cores compatible to his Dao. And, just yesterday, he'd broken into the middle B-Grade.

Jack decided to take a break, pacing out of his room to find Brock sprawled on an inflatable couch, reading the Bro Code. There were many couches in their mansion. Many of everything, actually. The Church had given them real luxury.

Of course, the entire mansion was worth nothing compared to a single space monster core.

"Sup, bro," Jack said, walking into the sunlit garden. A long wall surrounded the entire place. There was a bar, multiple lounges, and a large pool. The couch Brock was currently lounging on was in the middle of the pool, a bright yellow floatie. The brorilla himself wore a pair of pink swim shorts, chilling with one foot in the water.

"Hey, bro," he said. "All good. Meditating. You?"

Jack laughed. Brock wasn't kidding. He had his Bro Code out—he really was meditating on his Dao, except he was doing it on a floatie in a pool in the sun. That was the life. Jack himself needed more peace and quiet, having to retreat into his dark office to cultivate. He was a bit jealous, but more so, he was happy for his little brother.

"Enjoy the good life, bro," he said. "You deserve it."

Right as Jack was about to jump into the pool, however, a new voice called out, "Hold it! What do you think you're doing?"

Jack paused, annoyed. "What do *you* think you're doing, Starhair?"

The man walked in from the garden entrance, taking in both Jack and Brock with distaste. "I am charged with assisting you. What you're doing now is a waste of time. We're at war. Our army is dying, and you think you're on vacations?"

Jack reined in his anger. "Relaxing is an important part of cultivation," he explained patiently. "I've cultivated non-stop for two weeks. I just achieved a major power-up. If I don't celebrate a little, I'll be tense, and my efficiency will drop."

"Bullshit. You're just spoiled by all the praise you're receiving."

"You're out of line, Ass-Kisser Bro," Brock warned him from the pool. Starhair ignored him.

"I don't care how powerful you are or what you've been through, Jack. I don't care about your potential. You're just a weakling right now, so act with respect."

Jack smirked. "Respect to whom? You don't deserve it. Not only is your mind severely untempered, but even on the topic of power, you are weaker than us while at a higher cultivation level. The only thing you have going for you is your age, and that's only if we count it in years instead of wisdom. If anybody should be showing respect here, it's you."

Starhair's eyes flashed, like he'd heard exactly what he wanted. "Do you seriously think you're stronger than me?" he asked, laughing. "I acknowledge your future potential, but right now, you're just an early B-Grade. You, defeating me? That's such a load of crap!"

"Really? Then how about we find out?"

Starhair's laughter died down. Suspicion entered his eyes, like this was too easy. "Are you challenging me?"

"You are the challenger, but yes. I don't mind. Then perhaps you'll stop your silly little games, like coming here to taunt me and trying to steal some of my spotlight by beating me in a public duel. Which is not a bad idea, mind you, just a little simple for your level. Also, highly miscalculated, because you can't beat me."

Starhair narrowed his eyes. Jack could see the cogs turning in his head. As for Jack himself, his initial anger was long gone, and he was now calm. This was a simple situation to him. After everything he'd been through, Starhair's elementary machinations were almost cute.

"One moment, Ass-Kisser Bro," a voice called out. Brock. He still lay on the floatie couch, reclining casually, but his eyes held a hint of hard amusement. "You don't deserve to challenge Big Bro. You fight me instead. I will teach you your place."

Starhair looked between Jack and Brock. "You want me to fight the sidekick?"

"There is no sidekick here," Jack said. "Brock is my brother on equal footing. If he says you fight him, then you fight him." Starhair was getting riled up, but Jack held up a hand to stop whatever lame words were coming next. "If you can defeat Brock, then I'll fight you next. Wouldn't that work better for you? You get to steal not one spotlight, but two."

Starhair considered it for a second. Finally, he grinned. "I don't know what's gotten into you, but fine. I'll defeat you both."

"Hmm," Brock said. "Weird. The Bro Code disagrees." He flipped his Bro Code to a certain page and turned it outward. It showed a brorilla spanking a blushing man with long hair. Jack laughed. Starhair frowned in anger.

"State your terms," he said.

"Terms?" Jack asked.

"Time, place, and stakes." He raised his chin a touch higher. "Let nobody say that I, Starhair, bullied you."

Jack and Brock looked at him as if he was a joke. "The location can be anywhere safe nearby," Brock said. "Time is now. Oh, in a few hours, actually. TV Bro will want to record this. Stakes… If you win, I become your little bro. If I win, you shut up and accept your place."

"Do you agree with that?" Starhair asked Jack. It was obvious he'd expected them to set a date a few months into the future, so Jack and Brock could try to make more breakthroughs. He hadn't thought Brock would dare fight him right now.

"Sure," Jack replied. "The sooner we're done with this, the better."

"Deal!" Starhair laughed. "You'll pay dearly for underestimating me. Summon your manager and let's go."

"How about you go on ahead and find a suitable place?" Jack asked. Starhair snorted, still smirking, and took off like a starry rocket.

Only Jack and Brock remained, and they sighed.

"He's lucky he's so harmless," Jack said. "Otherwise, we might have had to kill him."

"Mm," Brock agreed. "He's not bad, just arrogant. As I said; Ass-Kisser Bro needs a good ass-kicking to become a proper person."

"That falls to you, bro. Show him what you got."

Brock grinned. "Okay."

CHAPTER SEVENTEEN

BROCK VS. STARHAIR

SOPHIE DROPPED EVERYTHING SHE WAS DOING TO ARRANGE THE DUEL. SHE also informed everyone she knew, apparently, because what seemed like half the New Cathedral arrived with her on the airless celestial body within the solar system the Cathedral occupied.

"Hello, Jack, Brock!" she shouted as she flew closer. She wasn't a D-Grade, so she couldn't really fly, but she wore what resembled a space mech suit. Jack had never seen that before—it must have been a luxury item for E-Grades.

"Hi, Sophie," Jack replied. "Nice clothes."

"Thanks! It's new!" she exclaimed, doing a little twirl. Her voice came out robotic through the suit—which apparently utilized a Dao device to spread the sound in the vacuum. "Are they about to start?"

"I think so."

"Quick! Quick! Set up everything, guys, we *must* get good shots!"

At her command, her entire crew of photographers, projection stone specialists, and all sorts of media experts fanned out. They established themselves in various positions to ensure they had a good outlook no matter which direction the battle spread in. Of the entire crew, only Sophie was an E-Grade. Out of the entire audience, in fact, she was one of the few people wearing mech suits.

Thousands of people were spread out on the moon, one of two which orbited a large, uninhabitable planet, on which Brock and Starhair were set to duel.

The barren planet wasn't the original location of the duel. After all, with two people at roughly the peak B-Grade power level duking it out, any nearby planet was bound to be destroyed. They'd originally selected an empty region of space, but Sophie swooped in, claiming she'd already gotten permission from the Arch Priestess to use a planet. She said it would make for a much more impressive battle. Basically, she wanted to make this duel a public event which would go down in the history books, using it to further increase Jack and Brock's fame.

Jack didn't mind. It wasn't his planet. If the Church wanted to destroy it, they might as well.

Sophie's media crew had brought along chairs and set up a stadium, of sorts, where they'd also installed a massive projection screen. After all, the duel would be taking place a tremendous distance away—from the moon to the actual planet—and almost nobody could see that far.

As for the projection itself, a group of B-Grades had been tasked with approaching the battle and recording it from up-close, or as up-close as they could get without risking interference. In Sophie's words, this was a grand, grand, *grand* event!

Jack looked around. Someone had spread their Dao to create a bubble of air and decent temperature. On the small spectator field, there were stands with food and drinks. Everyone was gathered in groups, talking excitedly about the upcoming duel while loading all sorts of delicacies on their plates. It resembled a party. And, while Jack understood the need to keep things that way, he couldn't help feeling a little bitter.

Duels weren't supposed to be like this. They weren't spectacles.

They were real battles, of real people, with real stakes. There was nothing fun about them.

He sighed as he paced toward a familiar figure. "Hello, Master. Enjoying the show?"

Elder Boatman turned around. This was the energy clone he'd made to accompany Jack and Brock. They hadn't had much contact yet because both disciples were too busy cultivating to meditate on the Dao.

"As much as you are," the Elder replied in his gravely voice. "Jack, this is Elder Soresight. Soresight, this is my disciple, Jack Rust."

"A pleasure, Elder," Jack said, eyeing the other man. It was an elderly-looking individual draped in dirty monk robes. He seemed close to the end of his life. Yet, his eyes and face glowed with energy, like he'd fallen into the pot of kindness as a child.

He was a middle A-Grade.

"The pleasure is all mine, Jack," the Elder replied. His voice was soft, yet energetic. "I've heard a lot about you. Seen, too. You make for interesting interviews."

Jack laughed humorlessly.

"Have you had anything to eat yet, Jack?" Elder Boatman asked. "If I may suggest..."

He waved, and a disc teleported to his hands. There was a glass of what looked like orange juice, as well as a plate stuffed with all sorts of delicacies. Well, delicacies for the New Cathedral. Jack found the gum worms and rotten-looking fruit less than appealing.

"Thanks," he replied, accepting the disk. "How did you teleport so many objects so casually?"

"I have my ways," the Elder replied. A hundred feet to the side, a gray alien who'd just gotten off the food line looked surprised at his now-empty hands. He grumbled something, then turned to get back in line.

"It's starting!" Sophie's voice rose over the crowd, ushering everyone to their seats. Jack sat next to the two Elders at the very first row. There was one more Elder present, sitting far to the side. The Arch Priestess hadn't attended.

"That's your spiritual companion," Elder Soresight noted, looking at the large projection screen. "Are you worried about him?"

"Not at all," Jack replied. "Brock knows what he's doing. Since he challenged Starhair, he must have confidence in winning. Besides..." He grinned. "I really look forward to seeing his current power."

The Elder nodded, and all three of them focused their sights on the screen.

There was no atmosphere on this planet. This was one of the solar system's outer planets, so the rock that made it up was beyond cold. A dark white color suffused the entire surface.

Brock and Starhair stood ten miles apart on a barren plain. They seemed tiny compared to the planet, but their vast auras towered higher than the tallest mountains. They were like two gods in humanoid form.

Brock was calm. A pair of red shorts was his only garment. He'd shelved the Bro Code and held his Goldwood Staff with both hands, completely unperturbed by the crowd. He'd fought with real stakes before—a little bit of publicity was nothing to him.

Starhair, on the other hand, was clearly affected by the pressure. He wanted to win this so he could escape his position as personal assistant and return to being the elite he knew he was. He secretly gripped his fists. His aura flickered, making his white robes flutter.

I will not lose to a monkey, he resolved himself. I'm Starhair. A 6500-mile peak B-Grade. I will win.

The two just stood there and waited for the signal to start. As the distant crowd settled into their seats, Sophie's voice washed over the entire planet, "Welcome, everyone, to a battle for the ages!" she shouted. Loud cheers followed—clearly pre-recorded.

"We bring to you a duel between two exceptional cultivators. On the right side, we have Envoy Starhair—a peak B-Grade human following the Dao of Stars! However, Starhair is more than just an elite at his level. He sports a colorful streak of war accomplishments as a member of the legendary Spoon Squad!"

More cheers came. Real ones this time. Either Starhair was more known than Jack expected, or the Spoon Squad were war heroes.

"On the other side," Sophie continued as the cheers died down, "we have Brock the Brorilla! Some of you know him from the recent broadcasts." A new wave of cheers confirmed her words. "He follows the Dao of Brohood, and is the spiritual companion of Jack Rust, the legendary ten-thousand-mile cultivator of the Fist! However, don't think Brock is any sort of sidekick. With a spectacular 8800-mile breakthrough into the B-Grade, he is a prime genius in his own right, an unprecedented talent for the last hundreds of thousands of years, only surpassed by his own brother. With a cultivation at only the middle B-Grade, he dares to challenge Starhair, a known elite at the peak B-Grade! Give it up for Brock the Brorilla!"

The crowd exploded. Jack was so taken aback by the intensity of these cheers that he forgot to hold his food, letting a bit of his orange juice fall to the ground. The very moon below them shook by the crowd's passion.

"The hell?" he asked.

"You might not know, but Brock is a crowd favorite," Elder Boatman explained with mirth. "His plushies, stickers, and shirts have become household items in the New Cathedral. People pride themselves in being part of the so-called Bro Army."

"What Bro Army?" Jack asked.

"Brock said so in a broadcast. Everyone wants to participate, apparently. Who would have thought?"

Jack shook his head, turning back to the screen.

"I hope everyone is ready," Sophie said, her voice ramping up. "Let's not keep our fighters waiting any longer. You just know they're rearing to go at it. The duel is to first blood, as always. Give it up for both our fighters, and here. We. Go. *It's Fisting Time!*"

Jack groaned.

The moment she spoke the final word, Brock and Starhair

launched at each other like twin rockets. They closed the ten-mile distance in the blink of an eye. A staff smashed forth. Three thick hair strands rushed to meet it. The two collided in the middle of the plains, and instantly, the projection zoomed out. The entire plains disappeared. A hundred-mile crater was formed beneath their feet, causing the entire planet to shake and cracks to form everywhere.

This was just the opening salvo.

Staff and hair rapidly clashed against each other. Every strike was cataclysmic. Entire parts of the planet were shorn off by the shockwaves, peeling it as one would skin an apple.

Starhair threw three hair strands against Brock's staff, then had another three attack from the other side. Brock took one hand off his staff, placing his palm against the hair strands. Burning golden light erupted. The hair shrunk back, unable to approach despite their starry might, as Brock's light pressed on. Starhair teleported away. The light reached him regardless, because it moved at light speed and spread in every direction, and he had to use his hair strands as a shield. All six converged before him, hiding him completely to block the light. Brock flashed right in front of him, smashing a staff into the shield and sending Starhair flying.

The crowd cheered. Jack took a sip of his orange juice, then spat it on the floor and coughed. This was no orange juice—it tasted like orange-colored blood.

"What the hell is this?" he asked.

"Orow milk. Very nutritious," Elder Boatman explained, not taking his eyes off the screen. Jack grumbled and returned to watching.

Brock pursued Starhair's retreat. The two jumped around the planet, easily covering its circumference. As another staff strike landed, rebounding against the shield of bouncy hair, Starhair roared out. All six of his strands spun around like a chainsaw. They turned sharp, eviscerating the very space around him. He dove for Brock, who didn't retreat. He simply raised his staff to defend.

Gold and blue light spread in two opposite cones, temporarily outshining the sun. Energy erupted at colossal quantities. Jack didn't even need to watch the screen; he saw the massive shockwave spear through the planet, slicing it cleanly in half, revealing a molten core. Lava spilled into space, chilling instantly and turning into dark rock. Planetary fragments were launched in all directions, all at least the size of mountains. A few headed for the spectators' moon but were quickly deflected by a couple of B-Grades. Another few crashed into the second moon, taking it off its orbit and resulting in massive explosions. The spectacular fireworks were clearly projected in the screen.

The duel of Brock and Starhair was still ramping up. Starhair's entire body was shining. Each strand of hair moved at blinding speed, and carried the weight of a star, powered by controlled nuclear fusions. Beneath their titanic strikes, the planetary fragments shattered, showering the universe in specks of frozen rock.

The power of an elite peak B-Grade was nothing to scoff at. But Brock was strong, too.

At some point, the Bro Code had appeared in his hands. Hymns filled the world. They reached every ear, every heart. Brock flipped the Bro Code to a page depicting a multi-armed brorilla. Suddenly, ten thousand golden arms erupted from his back, each over a mile long. They shone brilliantly.

So did Brock's eyes. He looked straight at Starhair, unperturbed by his hair. "It's spanking time," he declared. The ten thousand arms rained out, all with their palms straight. They collided with Starhair's hair. Every strike ended with the hands pushed back, but there were too many of them. Starhair couldn't block them all, and he could not approach Brock either, as the arms were denser the closer he got. Brock was taking a page off the space octopus's book—quite literally.

Palm strikes rained forth. Starhair flashed, teleporting continuously in every direction to dodge Brock's slaps. Brock mirrored his opponent's movements to keep himself a mile away, at the very edge of his attack range.

Starhair was looking for a gap in Brock's defenses, only to find none. Enraged, he roared and charged. His hair spun around again. He cut through a hundred arms in an instant, rushing toward Brock. However, for every arm he sliced off, ten took its place. The sliced ones regenerated, too. Brock was like a hydra.

"No bro dies alone," Brock chanted, his eyes and body golden. "If one bro lives, everyone does. We only fall together."

CHAPTER EIGHTEEN
DEATH OF SPACE

Brock's avalanche of palm strikes neutralized Starhair's momentum just as he charged past the halfway mark. He was then pushed back. The hands kept slapping, a series of strikes so dense Starhair didn't have time to teleport away. He tried regardless. A portal opened next to him, and just as he was halfway through it, a hand grabbed his robes and pulled him back out. There was no escaping this beating.

Starhair roared again. He gathered his hair into a soft shield, absorbing all impacts and reflecting them back. Hundreds of arms exploded, but Brock had many more. Starhair was smashed into a large planetary fragment and pushed through it until the entire thing shattered in a shower of ice. He kept flying backward until he rammed into the planet's hard core. This time, because his shield was neutralizing most of the impact, he didn't have the momentum to break through. He was stuck against the core, slowly forming a larger and larger crater as Brock pummeled him with palm strikes.

"Check it out!" Sophie's voice echoed. "Brock is going slap-happy on Starhair!"

Her comment must have enraged the peak B-Grade. He detonated a good part of his energy, erupting with enough force to pulverize the planet's core below him and send away all of Brock's golden arms. When the smoke cleared, Starhair sported a new form. He was now a ten-foot-tall humanoid made of starry hair. Jack assumed he'd somehow split his hair strands and turned them into armor.

"You fought well, but this ends now," Starhair shouted. "Fall!" He charged at Brock, moving far faster than before, tearing up space wherever he passed. A few golden arms slapped into him, achieving nothing. He disintegrated them by merely rushing past.

His new set of armor gave him extreme defense, strength, and speed. He was vastly more powerful than before. It was clear he was going all-out, or at least close to it.

Facing this charging form, Brock didn't panic. He brought his hands together. The Bro Code flipped to a new page, too fast for anyone to see, then slapped shut. "You are misbehaving," Brock chanted slowly. "As your big bro, it is my duty to bring you back into line."

Somehow, despite his slow words and Starhair's blinding assault, he hadn't arrived yet. Golden light erupted once again from Brock's body. The ten thousand arms dissipated. So intense was the new burst of light that space shattered behind him, framing his figure in the void. Everyone looked away.

When they looked at Brock again, he was surrounded by the form of a golden brorilla. Jack knew it was a phantom because he'd seen this move before, but if he hadn't, he would have certainly believed it was real—so lifelike and solid was the figure. It was a magnified version of Brock, shining golden from head to toe, radiating light like a brotherly buddha. His eyes held not anger, but love and strictness, as if Starhair was just a misbehaving child.

That comparison was apt size-wise, as well. Compared to Starhair's ten-foot form, Brock was at least twice as tall.

It was only after the phantom solidified fully that Starhair reached Brock. Stars erupted within his hair armor. He punched out, carrying the force of detonating strikes. "Begone!" he shouted.

Brock brought his hands together, then raised an open palm. He brought it down on Starhair as one would slap a fly.

A colossal explosion shook the void. All the power Starhair had amassed was for naught. He was violently diverted from his course and flung away. His speed remained enough to sear space around him. A single large piece remained of the once-solid planet, and Starhair smashed right into it, once again showering the world in specks of ice and stone. He continued through, smashing through several smaller pieces of the planet before finally coming to a stop mid-space.

The projection zoomed in on him. He seemed enraged, in disbelief, and desperate. His hair-armored form remained whole. Then, suddenly, he reverted it. The hair fell away, turning back into the six strands attached to his head. Intense unwillingness covered his now visible face. He still seemed pissed as hell, but he forced himself to stand down.

A line of blood flowed from his forehead. He had given first blood. Brock had won the duel.

The audience cheered. "What a spectacular battle!" Sophie exclaimed. "An excellent demonstration from both fighters. Give it up for them, everyone!"

Cheers and claps resounded through the void. Jack cheered too, though the Elders remained calm by his side.

"That was a good fight," Elder Soresight commented. "It was closer than it seemed."

"Yes..." Boatman replied. He smiled. "But Brock wasn't going completely all-out, even at the end. He never used the power of his bros to enhance himself. Maybe he considered it cheating."

"Starhair didn't go all-out either," the other Elder said. "That boy has a very powerful but dangerous move. I'm glad he had the composure not to use it."

Jack's chest swelled with pride. His little brother was so strong now. Once upon a time, he'd been small enough to ride on Jack's shoulder, and all he did was throw poop at the people he disliked. Thinking back to those days, Jack couldn't help feeling emotional. How far he'd come. Both of them.

"Well done, Brock," he said, transmitting his voice directly to the brorilla.

Brock looked over and smiled. He then turned to Starhair and flew over. The peak B-Grade hovered in place, steaming with rage, shame, and unwillingness. He looked angrily at Brock as he approached.

"Good fight, bro," Brock said, extending a hand.

Starhair looked at it. He hesitated. Then, finally, he controlled his emotions and shook it.

"You won fair and square," he admitted. "Good fight."

The audience cheered again.

Jack's clone covered distance rapidly. Their little starship, piloted by an Envoy called Druk-Druk, had already reached the Milky Way galaxy. Finding Earth wouldn't be difficult—Jack knew its rough location in the Systemless part of the galaxy, and also its teleporter frequency.

Before that, there was something else he needed to do.

The starship hovered just outside System space. It was an invisible line Jack had brushed with his perception.

"Can you hold them for a moment?" he asked Druk-Druk, motioning to the desk-sized, opaque space bubble hovering inside the starship. The captain rolled her eyes and accepted. This bubble housed the Church cultivators Jack had released from the Green Dragon Realm. Once they made it to Earth, the Bare Fist Brotherhood would give Druk-Druk a larger starship so she could carry everyone back to the New Cathedral.

As she took over maintaining the space bubble, Jack teleported outside the starship. He hovered before the border of System space, taking a deep breath. Then, he flew in.

You have returned to the New World. Welcome!

He grinned at the System notification. Quickly pushing it aside, he looked into his Class, trying to summon his newest Dao Vision, the entire reason he'd risked coming here.

His Paragon of Cultivation class offered him a top-tier Dao Vision at every minor realm, including the early B-Grade. However, as Jack was outside System space, the Dao Visions couldn't be "downloaded." He hoped that would happen automatically as soon as the clone entered System space. After all, they shared the class.

Nothing happened for a few moments. Jack only felt a strange emptiness. *Are they onto me?* he wondered. *Should we run?*

And then, the Dao Vision arrived. It struck his mind like a sledgehammer. He shook from the shock. His body escaped his control, as he was already drawn into the vision, but that was fine. They expected it. Druk-Druk would pull him back to the ship and step on the gas to get as far away from this place as possible.

Therefore, Jack focused on perceiving the Dao Vision. And what a vision it was.

The universe was silent. Stars glittered in the far distance like inconsequential dots. But not everywhere. A large part of Jack's vision was covered by absolute darkness.

He realized he was facing a black hole. A real one, not the imitation that was the Animal Abyss. He could sense spacetime going haywire, absolutely demolished by a far superior power. It was pulled apart the same way a machine would dismantle a stuffed toy. Slowly, but surely. Inevitably.

Jack had studied black holes before. He knew some principles from Earth science, had read about them in Archon Green Dragon's inheritance, had seen one from a distance at the Cathedral, and had experienced a faint version of the real thing in the Animal Abyss. However, those experiences all paled compared to the real thing. He couldn't wrap his mind around it. Despite his recent power-ups, he was like an ant before this anomaly. Even the Arch Priestess, whom he'd met recently, would seem weak here.

Jack knew, without the shadow of a doubt, that black holes existed on a higher realm than cultivators. Even Gods. That's why Enas, the most powerful Old God and arguably most powerful entity in the universe, had been unable to escape after falling into one.

Wait. What exactly is this vision about? Jack wondered.

Every Dao Vision he'd seen so far was based on a cultivator. It showed them doing something. However, he'd floated before the black hole for a few moments now without anything happening. Was there no other cultivator here? Was the vision just about meditating on the black hole?

He wouldn't complain if it was.

As he looked around, he discovered that was not the case. There *was* someone here. A single man, dark of skin and hair, barely visible in the darkness. His aura labeled him as marginally weaker than the Arch Priestess, but he was also an Archon.

It was not Archon Black Hole, as Jack initially suspected. He'd never seen this person before.

The man hovered in space a couple miles away from Jack, unaffected by the terrible spacetime flows surrounding the black hole. No, not exactly unaffected; as Jack took a closer look, he noticed the man was riding what resembled a silver surfboard made of extremely dense material. It could have been fashioned out of an actual neutron star. This surf board alone warped space around it, and the man was using his Dao to enhance that influence, anchoring himself and the surfboard against the pull of the black hole. They weren't immobile, either; just surfing around the event horizon.

Jack would be lying if he said he expected to see someone surfing a black hole. Then again, this was probably easier than outright resisting its gravitational pull.

Jack himself was just a projection here. The gravity didn't affect him. If it did, he would have been powerless to resist.

The dark-skinned man muttered something. Jack didn't quite catch it. He tried to float closer but found himself unable to move. All he could do was strain his ears and try to catch the words, instinctively spread outward by the man's powerful Dao.

"The death of space..." the man muttered. "A downward spiral. A universal end. Everything ends here, but where does it begin?"

He seemed to be in the middle of his meditation. Jack knew Archons could detect the System recording them to make Dao Visions, but this one was apparently too focused on his ruminations and resisting the black hole to notice. Below his surfboard, a torrent of dark energy shot out for endless miles, the aftereffect of the friction between him and the black hole.

Before Jack could consider those words, the man spread his hands. Space bent and shattered around him. The void appeared; and out of it crawled death. Not the death of living creatures, but the death of space and time, of the Dao itself. The true end.

Jack shivered at the sight. What emerged from the void manifested as black foam in the physical world, but on a spiritual level, it was beyond his understanding. He had the irrational fear that this encroaching darkness was so deadly it could harm him through the Dao Vision. Thankfully, it didn't approach him. It merged with the flow, angling toward the black hole. It seeped in gradually, disappearing behind the event horizon.

Jack couldn't sense what happened afterward, but he could see it clearly. This true death energy was similar to the black hole's. They merged, not fighting because of their different sources, just agreeing on total death. The event horizon welcomed this energy, and the black hole grew a tiny bit larger.

Their compatibility wasn't absolute, however. Though similar energies, the black hole's was purer. A small part of the man's foam dissipated as it was purified. That didn't disappoint him; instead, he smiled, pearly white teeth shining in the darkness. He seemed satisfied.

"Death born of space," he muttered. "All becomes one."

CHAPTER NINETEEN
SKILL UPGRADES

JACK OPENED HIS EYES TO FIND HE WAS DRENCHED IN SWEAT. HE WAS STILL shaking. Watching a black hole from up-close was *not* an easy experience. It was like having a first-row table to the greatest forces of the universe... which sounded suspiciously like the Second Crusade.

The clone had been dragged back to the ship by Druk-Druk while the vision was ongoing. They were already far from System space and approaching Earth. The main body of Jack, however, had experienced the vision almost at the same time as the clone.

Death born of space... he thought, looking at his fist. All becomes one.

He hadn't known what to expect from this first vision. What he saw was better than anything he could have hoped for. The System hadn't lied when it mentioned top-tier visions. It gave him the greatest gift possible. A path to unite his two dualities—Life-Death and Space-Time.

If I walk down the same path as that surfer... Can I combine all my Daos?

The thought was too exciting to ignore. He'd suspected this was possible but didn't know where to begin. It was so clear now. Of course it was a black hole. It combined death and space. What starting point could be better?

Once again, Jack was thankful for the System being so sloppy. It was so spread out that even the Immortals couldn't control it. Otherwise, they would definitely not help him as they had. They might even try to harm him through it.

Which would be useless at this point. Jack had long located the mini-System core inside him, a small glowing sphere attached to his soul—or inner world—which served as a storage and communication device. It could augment him when he leveled-up, but he could easily suppress or destroy it anytime he wanted. That's what he would do if they ever tried to use it against him. Until then, it could only do good, not harm.

In fact, amongst the high-ranking Church cultivators, it was customary for people to remove their System core when they reached the A-Grade. That's when it stopped being useful, as the System no longer awarded stat points in the A-Grade.

Jack shelved those thoughts to focus on his new Dao Vision. He even paused the absorption of space monster cores. There was so much to unpack.

Death born of space, he repeated. How can I achieve that?

In his mind, life and death were clearly connected, as were time and space. That much was obvious. However, despite his extremely deep insights into all of those Daos, he could not see the connection point between the two different sets. Spacetime was one thing. Life and Death were another. One pertained to mass and the fabric of reality, the other to souls and their mysterious interactions. One existed in the physical world, the other in a field of abstraction.

How could they be united?

It was clearly possible. The dark-skinned cultivator in the vision had achieved it, at least to some extent. Black holes could serve as a starting point. Jack could also ask Elder Boatman, but he wanted to experiment by himself first. Asking for advice too early could set him on the wrong path.

He raised his hands and began summoning the power of space before realizing what he was about to do. He was still in his mansion on the New Cathedral. Playing with major forces here could have disastrous consequences.

"Brock!" he called out. "I'll be going out for a bit, okay? See you soon!"

No reply arrived, but Jack knew Brock must have heard him. Therefore, he teleported over the mansion, then teleported again in quick succession. At his current level, each teleportation could span thousands of miles. Before long, he was so far away from the New Cathedral that the planet resembled a colorful dot. Nothing else was nearby, only emptiness.

Here should be fine, Jack figured. He resumed what he'd been doing. His hands came together. A ball formed between them, rippling and transparent, a sphere of pure space. Then, pressing his hands together, he tried to condense it. The physical sensation of compressing something between his hands helped. Too soon he realized that his hands were touching each other, and the ball of space was nowhere near compressed enough.

Grumbling, he let it dissipate. He opened his arms, this time manifesting a ball of space several miles wide. He was like a fly hugging a giant. Still, he began compressing it. The task was easy at first. The ball reduced in diameter from several miles, to a single mile, to a hundred feet, to ten feet. He was feeling serious resistance by now. Space was not an easy thing to fold.

He pressed on regardless. The ball continued to shrink, eventually becoming a sphere three feet across, pulsing with highly condensed power. Jack realized he was basically hugging a bomb, but he hoped it would be fine. He grabbed it with his hands and pushed it in, condensing it further. He moved slowly and methodically. It wasn't just a matter of having the power to do it, but he had to simultaneously control the Dao so it didn't break out. After all, the only thing keeping it together was his control, and the ball was growing more volatile as it was pressured.

It eventually reached the point of a beach ball, and he kept pushing. It became the size of a basketball, then a tennis ball between his palms. By this point, the ball was glowing from all the condensed energy, and Jack could feel the searing heat emitted. This was the same process he followed to unleash his Supernova attack, but pushed to new extremes.

The more he condensed the ball, the more it would seek to explode. However, there would come a point where the gravitational pull of the ball towards itself would overpower its ability to expand. It would collapse under its own weight, shrinking unstoppably until it became a single point of infinite density, turning into a black hole.

Jack had no desire to create an actual black hole this close to the New Cathedral, let alone right in his face. That point of no-return was very far away from the current compression level, anyway. What he was trying to do was sense how space reacted when pushed to its endpoint. How did the Dao handle the possibility of death? What would happen?

He hadn't tried this before, so he frankly had no idea. He just hoped that interesting things would happen as he approached the state of a black hole.

As Jack pushed down, compressing the ball to the limit of what he could control, a transformation occurred. The empty space inside the ball bubbled. At the very center, where the pressure was greatest, a little bit of foam appeared. Its color was unclear, flickering between various extremes. Jack was terrified. The foam didn't *feel* threatening, but it was an unknown power held against his chest. Who knew its properties?

The surfer's black foam had felt extremely dangerous.

He stopped compressing. His attention was split between maintaining the space ball and inspecting the foam. He could sense a bunch of properties inside it; like the Dao particles were so tightly pressed against each other that they began to merge, forming new, unknown substances that shouldn't exist in the universe. It was genesis.

No. It was despair.

Jack could sense it. At first glance, this foam was a beautiful act of creation, the combination of existing particles into new, exciting forms.

His Daos of Life and Death on the other hand warned him this was not the case. The act of creation was just a byproduct. What really occurred was the Dao particles trying desperately to survive. As they collapsed, they clung to each other, combining forces to resist the massive pressure.

They didn't *need* to combine. Nothing forced them. They could have just broken down into nihility, but they wanted to survive. They feared death.

Jack struggled to maintain the ball as he focused on this foam. He inspected it thoroughly. He couldn't read its properties yet, which was fine, because it was just a transitionary state. If he somehow kept pushing, the particles would unite more and more thoroughly until they just couldn't anymore. They would collapse, and a singularity would be created. The death of the Dao. The end of the universe.

Calculating all those things while maintaining the highly volatile space ball was challenging. Jack's concentration finally slipped. A tiny, imperceptible flaw appeared. The compressed energy rushed out of it like the wind escaping a balloon, and even as he tried to patch the hole, the ball had already destabilized. More and more interactions occurred, snowballing out of control.

"Fuck!" Jack said.

The ball exploded. There was no time to move away. The impact found him straight in the chest, catapulting him back so powerfully he skidded at almost the speed of light. A visible shockwave spread out, upsetting the surrounding spacetime. There was a dark, deadly void where the ball used to be. Particles rushed in to patch it, then popped out with a second explosion. The surrounding space was ravaged. Jack was glad he'd been pushed away.

He was also glad he'd thought to move away from the New Cathedral for this experiment.

If he had let this happen on the planet, the town would be gone. The force of the explosion vastly dwarfed a nuke's. The only reason he'd survived point-blank was his extreme physicality, and even then, he was severely injured. His chest was a mangled mess of blood and bones. His arms had disintegrated from the elbow down. He groaned as the pain caught up to him, taking his breath away, then did his best to persevere while his regeneration got to work. It was slower now, without the support of the Life Drop, taking him a few minutes to heal completely.

By this point, the region of space around him had already returned to normal. As for the two shockwaves, they would dissipate harmlessly. By the time they reached the New Cathedral, they would at most feel like strong breezes from the sky. He might knock over someone's vase.

Jack flexed his newly regenerated hands, still morphing at the pain. That had been dangerous. He'd known it wouldn't kill him, but maybe he should put safety measures in place next time. Having his hands blown off was hardly pleasant.

But that ball was a very potent attack. Its power vastly eclipsed that of his Supernova. If he could weaponize it, it would become a powerful addition to his arsenal. It could evolve further, too—with enough power, and with enough control of spacetime, creating an actual black hole wasn't outside the realm of possibility. Though, doing it quick enough to use in battle was another story altogether.

There was also the issue of that mysterious foam. His original purpose had been to discover a way to unite life and death with spacetime, and that foam seemed to hold the key. He'd given space particles the fear of death and changed their behavior. It could be considered an initial success.

The System core inside him agreed.

Congratulations! Space Mastery III → Space Mastery IV

Space Mastery IV: The power of space lies at your fingertips. You can use it freely, and even extreme applications are making themselves clear to you. You are well on the road to mastery.

Congratulations! Death Mastery III → Death Mastery IV
Death Mastery IV: Death is the end. The final, inevitable result of entropy. It is also just another power you control. You can spread this power to everything, even the Dao itself. You are well on the road to mastery.

Jack patted himself, smiling. After Meteor Punch, these were the first skills to reach the fourth tier, something he felt was long overdue. He was proud of himself.

The only thing missing was Time Mastery, a skill he guessed he should possess but didn't. Who knows why. Maybe it fell together with Space Mastery?

In any case, this experiment had gone great—save for his exploding hands. If he meditated on the vision again, maybe tried the same thing a few more times, he might gain even more improvements. A new path had opened before him.

His Dao, which had felt a little stagnant recently, had just found the way forward.

He still intended to consult Elder Boatman, but for now, a little bit of resting would be nice. He was exhausted. Space parted easily around him, and he soon appeared at the entrance of his mansion, pushing open the door.

The Arch Priestess stood right in the middle of the entrance hall. She was staring at the door, and therefore, at him. His breath caught to his throat. *Fuck,* he said. *I messed up.*

Instantly, Jack was tense again. He tried to read her face for hints of her intentions, but that was difficult when everything but her eyes was covered by a veil. In those eyes, all he could see was... amusement?

That couldn't be right.

She still wore long white robes, hiding everything except her golden eyes and tanned, bare feet. She stared at him, not speaking.

"Greetings, Arch Priestess," Jack said calmly. He was suddenly very conscious of the fact he only wore shorts. "It's an honor to have you visit me. How can I help you?"

She stared at him for a long moment. Then, she laughed. "The world doesn't revolve around you, Jack Rust," she said. There it was again—that hint of amusement. "Keep up the good work."

And just like that, she teleported away. Jack remained standing in the hall, still stressing out. *What the hell was that about?* he wondered. He shook his head. *Whatever.*

He walked through the next room, into the living room, intending to reach his office and reset his mind before returning to cultivation. However, he saw Brock in the living room. He lounged on a couch, relaxed, slurping on a bowl of gum worms while reading the Bro Code as one would a comic.

"Sup, bro?" the brorilla said as Jack entered.

"Oh, hey, Brock," Jack said. "Did you see the Arch Priestess?"

"Yes. She came to discuss the Dao."

Jack nodded, not fully comprehending. He recalled her promising to come over and discuss the Dao with Brock when she had the time. Something about being interested in the perspective of a beast-born cultivator. It made sense.

However...

Something was off. Something about Brock's relaxed posture, something about his aura. Jack had seen this type of aura before in college, of all places. He suddenly had a very disturbing suspicion.

"Brock," he said slowly. "Did you sleep with the Arch Priestess?"

Brock swallowed his gum worm. "Yes. Why?"

CHAPTER TWENTY
DADDY IS HERE TO STAY

JACK STUTTERED. "THE ARCH PRIESTESS? THAT'S—SHE'S—BROCK! GOOD fucking job!"

The brorilla's frown broke into a smile, and then he laughed. "Thanks."

"How does that even work?" Jack asked, sitting down beside his brother. "You're a brorilla, she's a human. Aren't you, you know, incompatible?"

"She's not a human," Brock replied, closing the Bro Code and putting it away. "Even if she was... Where there's a will, there's a way."

"What is she if not a human?"

"A space monster," Brock replied simply. Jack thought back to the original expedition into the Green Dragon Realm. One of the Church's leading cultivators, the second-ranked C-Grade, had been a humanoid space monster as well. That man resembled a dragon in human form. He had whiskers and claws and scales. The Arch Priestess seemed... fairly normal?

Then again, she was covered head to toe in robes. Her feet and eyes were similar to a human's. Everything else was hidden.

“What does she look like?” Jack couldn’t help asking.

Brock thought about it. “Strong. Powerful. Hairy.” He nodded to himself. “Very beautiful.”

“Well, I’m happy for you, bro. I just never thought that... Wow. You’re going out with one of the most influential and powerful people in the universe. Aren’t you, like, seven years old?”

Brock shrugged. “Brorillas become adults at three.”

Jack laughed again. “We must celebrate! How about this? Today, we take a break from all things cultivation and drink to our heart’s content.”

“Thanks, bro, but it’s no big deal.”

“Your first girl? Of course it is!”

“Bro. It’s nothing. Don’t be a teenager.”

Jack caught himself. In Brock’s eyes, sleeping and being with someone was a completely normal thing. He was a big bro. Of course he’d be crazy popular.

Jack saw this as a rite of passage given his previous Earth culture, but to Brock, it was just another day.

“Alright,” Jack finally agreed. “But we need to have at least a shot.”

Brock smirked. “Okay. A shot.”

Jack rushed to the kitchen, returning with two shot glass filled with an amber liquid. He didn’t remember its name, but it was a hit on the New Cathedral. Even C-Grades could get a buzz.

Jack and Brock couldn’t, not without consuming prodigious quantities, but that was alright.

“To the Arch Priestess,” Jack said, raising his glass.

“To the Arch Priestess,” Brock agreed. They clinked their glasses and downed them.

“You did get her name, didn’t you?” Jack asked.

“She doesn’t have a name.”

“Really? Is it a religious thing?”

“No. She never had one.” Brock’s eyes took on a sad glint. “She’s been through a lot.”

"Oh. Well, there is no need to share if it's her private business. I just hope she's fine now."

"She is. And, she wouldn't mind. There is a large, separate dimension nestled in the center of this galaxy, inhabited fully by space monsters. They have their own society there. She was forced to leave when she was young, then met some roaming cultivators and joined them. She never had a name, only a title—though that's something she should share herself."

"I see..." Jack replied. "A separate dimension inhabited by space monsters? I didn't know that existed. Nobody mentioned it before."

"It's why this galaxy is so full of space monsters. The bestial ones are often chased out to maintain a working society. That place is called the Space Monster World."

"KID!" a new voice blasted into Jack's ears, taking him completely by surprise. "That's my home as well! That's where I come from! It's here, you're actually here!"

Jack recoiled from the sudden shout. The grabbed his head. Venerable Saint Thousand Shell was practically zooming around in Jack's inner world like an excited puppy.

"Why didn't you tell me before?" Jack asked.

"You never told me you were in the Spiral Stair galaxy! How was I supposed to know? I'm not some nerd like The Stone to tell from the stars."

"...Right. So, this Space Monster World?"

"It's exactly what Brock said. A world inhabited and run by space monsters."

"How come it's not conquered, then? It sounds like a bunch of space monster cores to me."

The turtle snorted. "We space monsters are not weak, kid. We have a few Archons of our own. The world is also sealed so A-Grades and Archons can only leave, not enter. It's basically unassailable."

"Unassailable, you say?"

Jack's mind was already racing with ideas, but the turtle cut him short. "Don't even think about it. First of all, while leaving is easy, entering is very difficult. Most importantly, cultivators are not welcome there. The

Church cannot use it to hide. Even the Arch Priestess, despite her status as a space monster Archon, cannot bargain asylum for her people."

"*Huh.*"

"Bro," Brock said, snapping his fingers in Jack's face. "Are you okay?"

"Yeah, sorry. The turtle just said it comes from the Space Monster World as well."

"Maybe it's bros with the Arch Priestess."

Jack chuckled. "I don't think so. This turtle is very, very old."

"*Your mother is old. And my name is Venerable Saint Thousand Shell.*"

"In any case," Jack continued, "I'm happy for you and her. And this Space Monster World is interesting to know, though I'm not sure how it can help us currently."

"Probably can't." Brock shrugged. "Otherwise, we would know already."

"Yeah."

Jack gathered the two shot glasses from before, as well as the now-empty gum worm bowl which Brock had been eating from. *Ew.*

"I'll get back to work now, bro," Jack said. "Happy reading."

"Thanks. You too."

And with that, Brock went back to studying the Bro Code, completely unaffected by the fact he was sleeping with one of the greatest cultivators in the universe, as well as his immediate superior.

While Jack's main body was cultivating, pondering the mysteries of space and death, and drinking to celebrate joyous occurrences, the clone was buzzing with excitement. He couldn't believe this was finally happening.

After so many years of being away, after only seeing his family once in the span of five years... He was finally returning to Earth. For good. The main body would go off and adventure, but the clone could stay here.

It was a dream come true. If Jack could snap his fingers and reach the A-Grade, the joy of that would be nothing compared to the happiness of being able to spend his life with his family.

He remained glued to the starship window as a blue and green planet appeared in the distance, orbiting a new sun. They were far from System space by now. Nobody could touch them here. They'd also waited a few days on an uninhabited planet to make sure they weren't followed, which only served to enhance Jack's emotions.

They approached the jewel of the universe. His breath was cut short. Without waiting for the starship to land, he teleported away.

"Hey!" Druk-Druk shouted. Jack had dumped on her the space bubble containing the released cultivators of the Green Dragon Realm, but it was something she could handle. The starship slowly headed to a landing platform near the Forest of the Strong, where various guards rose into the air to meet it.

Meanwhile, Jack had teleported directly to his home's master bedroom. As he appeared in the spacious room, he saw the covers raised and the laughter of two people coming from underneath. His breath caught to his throat. For a split-second, before he even spread his perception, he was lost.

Then, two female heads popped out of the covers—Vivi and Ebele, Jack's wife and daughter. "Dad?" Ebele asked. "Dad!" She made to run to him before her eyes narrowed with caution. She paused. "Dad?" she asked again, keeping herself at bay.

Her caution was short-lived. Vivi burst out of the sheets, rushing to Jack and practically flying into him. She wore loose red robes which hugged her body, contrasting her dark skin. Her eyes blazed with joy, and she was shaking. Her Dao perception had already recognized this really was him.

"Jack!" she shouted in disbelief, clutching on tightly even as she questioned him. "How?"

Jack grinned. Since Earth was outside System space, he had no way to communicate with them. His arrival was completely unannounced.

He hugged Vivi tightly. Now free from his surprise, he could see that the raised sheets were just a pillow fort viewed from the back. Vivi and Ebele had been playing underneath.

He raised a hand to cup the back of his wife's head, hugging her tighter. "I'm home," he said. At the same time, he extended his other hand toward Ebele, whose hesitation was melting away. He was proud of her. When he suddenly appeared, she'd held herself back in case he was an illusion or someone else disguised as her father. Unlike Vivi, she couldn't use her perception to check his aura.

This was not a level of caution Jack wished on any child, but being a warrior himself, he acknowledged her mental fortitude at such a young age. It just made him sad that she had to be like this.

Not anymore, he promised himself. I'm here now. I will protect Ebele, so she can live free.

His daughter dove into his embrace as well. Jack hugged her tightly. For a moment, holding both his wife and daughter, he felt like the happiest man on Earth.

"I'm home," he whispered to them. "And this time, I'm here to stay."

The three of them sat on a blanket on the grassy fields outside their house. A basket of food rested between them. Ants occasionally scurried around, trying to get some, but Jack patiently kept them at bay.

"I can't believe it." Vivi was covering her mouth, joyful tears streaming out of her eyes. "Are you really going to stay? Forever?"

"Forever," Jack promised. Ebele was at his side, stubbornly clutching onto his arm as if afraid he'd disappear if she let go. This, too, saddened Jack, but he knew there was nothing he could say. Time would help them get used to his presence. They wouldn't need to worry about him leaving ever again.

It had been three hours since he first arrived. While Druk-Druk was parked far away, waiting patiently, Jack had opted to spend the first few hours with his wife and daughter. There were more people he needed to visit, but these were the most important ones. He needed to know how they were doing—and tell them about his adventures.

Vivi had been working hard these past few years. She'd taken charge of the planet after the professor stepped down. Under her command, Earth had blossomed with both military power and citizen welfare. She'd done a lot to eliminate hunger and poverty from all parts of the world. Things weren't perfect yet, but the fact that a large portion of Earth's inhabitants died during the Integration had freed up a lot of resources she could easily distribute. Couple that with the prowess of cultivators, as well as being outside the oppression of System space, and Earth was suddenly well-equipped to be a paradise.

After the recent stabilization of the planet, Vivi had more free time, which she spent with Ebele.

The little girl herself had recently turned seven years old. She was just a tiny thing, yet bursting with energy. Jack could tell she'd been working hard. She'd been like that the last time he was here as well, and he'd tried to direct her to a more childish lifestyle. There was no reason to push herself yet. She could go to school and enjoy life.

She hadn't heeded his words, apparently, but Vivi was doing her best to pull Ebele back in line. That was one reason why they were playing in a pillow fort before. It felt weird to both wife and daughter, but it also helped ground them in reality. It was nice to forget about one's burdens for a while.

In fact, it was currently August, and Ebele was set to start school soon. She would attend Edgar's Academy, which was arguably the most prestigious establishment on the planet currently. The curriculum was a mess, of course, since things were still in a state of constant flux, but Vivi believed it would offer her daughter the best education possible.

It was free, of course. The Academy accepted students based purely on merits, and Ebele had passed all tests with flying colors.

"What do you think about school?" Jack asked, ruffling his daughter's hair. "Are you scared?"

"I'm a cultivator. I'm not scared," she replied stubbornly.

"She's totally scared," Vivi said. "She was telling me last night."

"Mom!"

Both parents laughed. Jack swept his daughter into an embrace. "You don't need to worry about anything," he said. "The world is a beautiful place now, and you're a beautiful person. You'll make friends easily. The best friends in the world."

She looked up at him with her big eyes. "Do you really think so?"

"I'm sure," he replied, kissing her forehead.

God, he loved being back.

The months flowed by. Jack lived in bliss. It was only the clone that was on Earth, but the two could share memories whenever they wanted. Both of them were living the dream.

The main body cultivated with great intensity, accompanied by his brother as they strived for the peak. The clone lived with his family, spending every day with them, caring about no wars or troubles. It was a free life. For the first time since the Integration, Jack was actually happy on an everyday basis. Not just content—happy.

September arrived. Ebele attended Edgar's Academy, which wasn't a boarding school. There was a starship which took the kids to and from the Academy every day, touring the entire planet in only a couple hours. Ebele lived nearby so she could skip it.

Of course, the school was just a secondary campus of the Academy. Its main focus was on cultivators, who lived and studied there until they reached the middle E-Grade, or for three years at most. It had only been operational for two years now, but it was already clear that not many people would hit the time limit. While they didn't have access to the System's quick leveling, the Academy ensured they had the right resources and guidance to steadily move forward.

There were battles, as well. The cultivator path couldn't do without them. The Academy's disciples made excursions to reasonably difficult dungeons, sometimes accompanied by professors to keep the casualties at a minimum. Accidents always happened—no one could grow without real stakes—but such was the life of a cultivator.

Overall, life on the planet had calmed down. There were rules and regulations. It was a cultivator's world, but a peaceful one.

Jack spent most of his days with Vivi, helping her run the planet in various ways but not interfering too much. This was her stage now, not his. He was content to stay in the shadows.

The other half of his days were spent with Ebele. The girl was excited for every moment she had with her father. The two of them meditated together, practiced martial arts, discussed the world and the Dao, played games... By being able to spend more time with her, Jack could keep her away from the extremely hard-working mindset she'd adopted in recent years, which would only harm her in the long-term. As the days passed, she was calm and happy. She laughed more often.

She'd made friends, too. Anay, a boy from India, and Lin Ping, a girl from China. Both were bright kids, and Jack thought they were good people, too. That was the important part. He'd sometimes watch over the three as they explored the Forest of the Strong or other areas neighboring the Academy, not all of which were safe. Of course, with Jack present, there was no danger whatsoever.

The C-Grade dungeon of Earth, an underground ocean spanning the entire planet, was also steadily explored by the highest-level cultivators. Nobody had actually reached the C-Grade yet on-planet, but there were enough D-Grades to form large groups and tackle the early areas of the dungeon. It helped them sharpen their Daos, apparently. Casualties were few and far between.

Jack would sometimes join these groups, not actively helping them clear the dungeon, just saving them at the last moment if things went wrong. That allowed them to take greater risks, hastening their progress.

He would also visit his mother often.

All in all, life was finally good.

CHAPTER TWENTY-ONE

THE IMMORTALS STRIKE

The Second Crusade was meant to take a long time. With the Church hiding away and splitting their forces, it would be relatively easy to delay for decades, if not centuries. The Old Gods would have time to arrive from wherever they were in the universe, and then protracted warfare could begin anew for a long, long time.

As a result, Jack didn't need to be in a mad rush to cultivate. He could take his time, meditating on the Dao while slowly increasing his cultivation base. It would be a slower, yet much safer path than the one he usually took, spanning centuries of relative calmness. A peaceful break in his path of war.

However.

There were two sides to this war. And while the Church was confident they could delay for a long time, the Immortals were also smart. They'd planned for a long time. They were only now beginning to show their hand.

Elder Tribulation of the Black Hole Church commanded a powerful war force. His army was one of the most advanced in position, shouldering the responsibility of delaying the enemy army's initial advances. Essentially, they were in the front lines. A dangerous yet noble duty.

The Tribulation Battalion hid in a large meteor belt similar to the one around the Death Boat. It was extremely long and daedalus, with colossal celestial bodies flying around freely, oftentimes colliding and breaking into fragments. Due to the overlapping gravitational fields and flying debris, this was a particularly difficult area to search, which was why Elder Tribulation had chosen it as their hiding spot. They could hide away here for years to come.

Until one day, a blue screen flashed before the eyes of every cultivator in the Tribulation Battalion.

You have returned to the New World. Welcome!

It was sudden and unexpected. Completely out of nowhere. Everyone shot to their feet, confirming with each other that they weren't hallucinating. The perception of Elder Tribulation exploded powerfully outward.

This was the message everyone received upon re-entering System space. But they were still in the wild galaxy. Even if the Immortals were willing to spend the resources required to spread the System here, it would have taken many years to arrive, and the expansion would have been easily observable. It was impossible for this galaxy to be Integrated.

Yet, somehow, the Tribulation Battalion had entered System space.

"What's going on?" Elder Tribulation barked. He was not an easy-going man. Large and powerfully-built, with hard eyes and muscles cording every inch of his body. His ferocity in battle was unmatched, and his warriors were all hardened veterans.

Despite their confusion, they did not panic. Everyone exited the starship and formed a battle array. The unknown always meant danger.

It didn't take long for the enemy to appear. A colossal starship emerged from the folds of space, dominating the world around it. Perfectly white, it was shaped as a mountain-sized needle. Five figures rode its back. All A-Grades.

Four were Immortals, with two-digit numbers painted on their featureless faces. The fifth was a man in swirling starry robes, clad in a cloud of darkness.

"Hahaha!" the man laughed. "Did you really think you could hide, Tribulation? All your tricks are useless! Catching you in System space is so damn easy!"

The starship's teleportation had finished. The moment it emerged fully, flashes erupted around it, revealing hundreds of B-Grade cultivators. All wore the robes of the Hand of God and were arrayed in battle formations.

Five A-Grades, one of which was at the late A-Grade, and hundreds of B-Grades.

Facing them were Elder Tribulation at the late A-Grade, another early A-Grade Elder of the Church, and several dozen B-Grades. This was not a battle they could win.

Elder Tribulation gritted his teeth. They were supposed to be safe here. The meteor belt should have taken many years to search through. Yet, from one moment to the next, they had somehow entered System space, and all their hiding was for naught. Nothing could hide from the Immortals in System space.

Elder Tribulation did not understand. He had the feeling he'd die in confusion.

"Scatter," he commanded. Yes, his soldiers were brave, but he would not doom them to a lost battle.

They were also well-trained. The moment he gave the command, the orderly formation completely broke apart, every B-Grade escaping in every direction. The enemy B-Grades followed, beginning a massive chase. Some would escape, some would get caught—that was the reality of a wild retreat.

Only two people hadn't run. Elder Tribulation, and the other Elder present, an early A-Grade woman with white eyes and blonde hair. She was Elder Tribulation's wife, and the two held hands as they resolved to go down together.

Neither specialized in speed. They could not escape. Even if they could, that would only expose their soldiers to A-Grade pursuers. All they could do was try to delay as much as possible.

"How did you do this, Night?" Tribulation asked. "Will you tell me before my final battle?"

The man with swirling dark robes—Elder Night of the Hand of God—smiled. "No," he replied.

Tribulation laughed. "So be it!" His aura erupted. Space collapsed everywhere within the area. Terrible lightning clouds emerged from the void, accompanied by pale white light. He and his wife charged into battle. Darkness filled the world.

On this day, Elders Tribulation and Blind White of the Black Hole Church fell heroically in battle.

The destruction of the Tribulation Battalion rippled outward. News of the ambush and mysterious System message had spread before the battalion even began its retreat. The New Cathedral was immediately notified of the event, and information reached the Arch Priestess herself in moments.

She stood in a grand meeting room. Accompanying her was Elder Soresight. She paced back and forth.

"How could this happen?" she asked. "The System cannot reach this far. How did they do it?"

"I have no idea," Soresight admitted. "Should I try to glimpse into the past?"

"Please do."

Elder Soresight cultivated the Dao of Time. He was not particularly powerful in battle, but his Dao allowed him to deconstruct the river of time and glimpse past events. It was a powerful information gathering ability, which was why he was stationed on the New Cathedral.

While Soresight had his eyes closed, the third A-Grade in the room spoke up.

"We're in trouble," he said. This was a bald old man with a long beard and heavy eyes, dressed in loose monk robes. Elder Heavencrash, he was called. Save for the Archons, he was one of the strongest Elders of the Church. "We are already outnumbered. We cannot lose more Elders."

As he finished his words, the meeting room door was pushed open. The Arch Priestess looked over so quickly her robes fluttered. The newly-arrived messenger kept his head low, trembling.

"I greet the—"

"Report," the Arch Priestess cut him off.

The messenger gathered his words, "Yes. Two more battalions were attacked. Elder Periphery is currently in battle against overwhelming numbers. Elder Godspeed managed to escape with his battalion. All reported the same System message just before they were attacked: You have returned to the New World."

A fist smashed into the long meeting table, disintegrating the wood but leaving the floor below untouched. Elder Heavencrash growled, standing above the now-pointless chairs. "What is happening here?" he growled.

"You may retreat," the Arch Priestess instructed the messenger, who disappeared immediately. Afterward, she turned to Heavencrash. "Calm down. I need you focused."

He took a deep breath. "Sorry, Arch Priestess. It won't happen again."

It was then that Elder Soresight awakened from his meditation. He opened his mouth to speak, then paused as he took in the lack of table.

"Speak," the Arch Priestess commanded.

"I'm sorry. I couldn't see anything," the Elder reported. "As I traveled back in space and time, I was rebounded by a powerful force. I believe it was an Archon."

The Arch Priestess's eyes darkened. She'd counted on this information. Unfortunately, Soresight was not an Archon, but the Hand's respective specialist was. "Archon Empire," she growled. "That man must die."

"We'll never get him, Arch Priestess. That coward hides deep in System space."

"I want all our researchers on the task," she commanded. "And tell all other forward battalions to retreat."

"Are you sure, Arch Priestess?" Soresight replied. "We'll be giving away a lot of ground."

"Would you rather we give away our Elders?" Heavencrash asked.

"Stop fighting and follow my orders," the Arch Priestess said tiredly. "Maintaining our forward positions is important, but until we know how they're doing this, we'd just be sending our people to die. The risk is too large. Have everyone retreat to the secondary zones."

The two Elders bowed. "Yes, Arch Priestess."

She sighed, falling back into her chair as the two Elders distributed her order, then sat in a tense silence. She would have leaned against the table if it still existed. Unless they figured out what was happening and how to stop it, they were stuck between a rock and a hard place. If the battalions remained at the front lines, they would be vulnerable. If they kept retreating, they'd eventually find themselves clustered around the New Cathedral, which would make them easily discoverable by the Hand of God scouts.

Soresight was right. They couldn't surrender too much ground. But they couldn't afford to lose more Elders, either.

What do I do... the Arch Priestess wondered.

A hesitant knock came on the door. "Enter," she said. A new

messenger appeared, this one seeming more confused and less flustered than the previous one. He had her attention immediately.

"I greet the—"

"Report."

"Yes. We have received a message for the Arch Priestess."

"A message?" she asked curiously. "By whom?"

The messenger gulped. "The Immortals. They... They wish to invite you to something called the Immortal Summit of Spiral Stair."

She raised a brow. The assault and invitation landing at the same time... This was certainly not a coincidence. "What is that summit? And with whom?" she asked.

"They didn't say. They only said it will be held in one week, on the brightest blue star of the area closest to System space. They said that, if you agree and swear on your Dao to participate, they will cease attacks until then. If not, they will press their assault relentlessly."

The Arch Priestess frowned. That was almost too good to be true. The Hand had them cornered; if they stopped for a week, that would give the Church enough time to figure out what was going on and regroup.

She didn't like this. At all. The Immortals had just achieved a massive surprise attack, and they were going to sacrifice that just to have her participate in some discussions? She didn't understand anything. She was completely on the back foot, dancing in the palm of their hands. It was like they were playing a completely different game, one where she didn't even understand the rules. She was at least two steps behind.

She could guess who else was invited to that summit, but it didn't explain anything.

"What's the catch?" she asked.

The messenger gulped. "Respectfully, Arch Priestess. The Immortals didn't mention this outright in their message, but they gave no method to attend the summit telepathically. They also declared that anyone who approaches, besides you, will be eliminated on sight no matter what. If you desire to participate, you can only do so physically. In an area which, according to recent events, will be System space."

The implications dawned on everyone at the same time.

"Impossible," Heavencrash shouted. "You must not go, Arch Priestess."

"I agree," Soresight said. "It is certainly a trap. The Immortals have no sense of honor. If you go, they will ambush and kill you, and our army will be left headless. We will lose half the war."

The Arch Priestess considered their words. These two were her advisors, and she trusted them. She also agreed that this was a ridiculous proposal. The summit was just an excuse. It was extremely clear that, if she went there, she would die. That would be a much heavier loss than just a few Elders. The Immortals only proposed this to shake her—they knew she would never agree.

They also knew she couldn't lie. Her Dao wouldn't allow it. As much as she would have liked to, agreeing to their one week of peace and then just not showing up would ruin her cultivation. It would be the same as dying.

As for working out ways to not attend physically... that was a gamble. There was no time to make a clone. She couldn't send anyone else carrying a projection stone, since the Immortals had already declared they'd destroy anyone who wasn't her on sight.

If she promised to attend and found a way to do it from a distance, that would be fine. But she wouldn't find a way. The Immortals, in System space, would absolutely shut off all avenues. Then, if she promised to attend, she would have no choice but to do it physically. And that was a death sentence.

It was a three-way conundrum. If she refused, they would press their assault with whatever new way they'd found to utilize the System. If she accepted, then she would be taking a huge risk. Either she'd find a way to attend telepathically against their wishes—a highly unlikely scenario—or she'd fail and most probably perish.

They could have specified that I have to attend physically, she realized.

They didn't, to give me a sliver of hope. To make me doubt myself. To even out my options. All of them are equally terrible, and whatever I choose, they win. This is psychological warfare.

All those were clear in the Arch Priestess's mind. Yet, she smiled.

"Arch Priestess!" Soresight and Heavencrash exclaimed in unison, for once putting away their mutual dislike. She ignored them.

"Tell the Immortals I agree," she said. "As long as they hold their forces, then one week from now, I will attend their Immortal Summit of Spiral Stair. I swear it on my Dao."

CHAPTER TWENTY-TWO

MIDDLE B-GRADE

THE POWERS OF LIFE, DEATH, TIME, AND SPACE SWAM CALMLY THROUGH THE air. They turned around each other, entwining and disengaging, forming and deforming. Where Life and Death met, they yearned to unite. The same happened for Time and Space. However, if Time met Life, or any other combination, they simply swam unhindered as if not even noticing each other.

Jack sat in the center of these four swimming ribbons. His breathing was even, his eyes closed despite the many shapes and colors manifesting around him. He was considering his Daos, marching on the slow path of unifying them. Every question he solved birthed three more. Yet, he was advancing.

His cultivation was still progressing nicely. In his inner world, energy still erupted from the portal to the Green Dragon Realm, slowly but surely saturating him. From the steady black hole, the portal to the Black Hole World, laws rippled out, subtly enhancing his own.

Both in quantity and quality, his inner world was progressing. His Daos were advancing. His already formidable power was growing fiercer by the day. He yearned to let it out.

A knock on the door snapped him out of his reverie. The swimming colors collapsed, folding into themselves before disappearing; the magic hid away. Jack opened his eyes.

Another knock on the door. "Bro," a voice called from outside.

"Coming," he replied. As he stood, gazing at the chairs and desk of solid wood outfitting his office, his heart was already filled with trepidation. Brock wouldn't interrupt his cultivation for no reason. Had something happened?

He walked to the door and opened it. Brock, who'd been about to knock again, knocked on Jack's forehead instead. "Oh," he said. "Hey, bro. Come. We have a guest."

"Lead the way," Jack replied, still smiling. The two crossed the empty mansion rooms—they'd been offered house staff but declined—to arrive at the main living room. There, sitting on a fluffy chair, was the Arch Priestess, wearing her signature white robes which covered everything but her eyes and feet.

"Arch Priestess," Jack said, nodding respectfully. Why was she here? Well, he could think of a reason why, but what did she want with him? He shot a side glance at Brock, finding him nonplussed.

"Hello, Jack," the Arch Priestess said. "Sit."

Jack did as he was told.

"You may not have heard," she began, "but the Immortals advanced yesterday. They implemented a new stratagem which caught us off guard and killed three Elders while forcing us to recall our forward troops."

"Three Elders?" Jack replied. Since he'd been cultivating, he hadn't heard about this new development. "What happened?"

"They somehow managed to bring the System to this galaxy. We still don't know how, or even if that's actually true. It should have been impossible. Maybe they found a way to displace our troops into System space without their knowledge. Space shenanigans. In any case, the end result is that our troops suddenly found themselves in System space, which resulted in the enemy immediately locating and ambushing them."

"That sounds terrible," Jack said. "Hiding is our greatest weapon at this point, correct?"

"Very. The situation yesterday was grim. Right afterward, however, the Immortals contacted me. They were willing to halt their advance, giving us time to regroup, in exchange for me joining a 'summit' they are organizing. Of course, that's a trap. The only feasible way for me to join their summit is to physically go there, which will result in my certain death."

"Oh," Jack said. "So you refused."

"Of course I accepted."

He raised a brow. "I don't follow, Arch Priestess."

She smiled at him—under her veil. "You should. After all, you are the reason I don't have to die."

"Me?"

"Yes, you. I promised to attend their summit, and I cannot break that promise without ruining my Dao. However, while they are convinced the only way for me to join is my physical presence, there is something they do not know. Something that you, Jack, can help me with."

He frowned in thought. A moment later, his eyes brightened. "Immortal Commune?"

"That's right." Her smile beamed into a grin. "They don't know about your class. You possess a way to contact the Immortals directly. Six days from now, you will send your clone to System space and have it activate the skill. You will then link up with your main body, and use that to project sound and image between our meeting room and the Immortals' summit."

"So you basically want me to be a projector."

"Yes."

He laughed. "I can do that. Will my clone be safe? If I'm not mistaken, it will need to remain in System space for the entirety of the summit."

"I have already dispatched Elder Godspeed to your location. His specialization is obvious. If they try anything against your clone,

Elder Godspeed will take you and run away, and they cannot blame me for breaking the connection."

"Sounds good to me."

"How close are you to the middle B-Grade?" she asked.

"Both close and far. Thanks to all the cores you gave me, I've reached 93% Matter Condensation. Unfortunately, I've run out of cores, so I'm stuck there."

She nodded. "I can give you a couple more as a reward for helping us during the summit. That should get you to 100%. Then, while your clone is in System space, you can watch the next Dao Vision before activating your Immortal Commune skill. After the Immortals realize what your class is, they might block you from accessing Dao Visions, so it's best to do it beforehand."

"I understand. Thank you for your care, Arch Priestess."

"My pleasure." She smiled again. "With all that settled, you are free to go. I have some private business to discuss with your brother."

Jack opened his mouth and closed it again. He glanced between the Arch Priestess and Brock. Both winked at him.

He had the feeling they were made for each other.

"I'll go now," he said weakly. "Have fun."

"Thanks, bro," Brock said as Jack walked away. He couldn't help shaking his head. This place was getting crazier and crazier… and his little brother was growing up so quickly. In fact, the Arch Priestess had been visiting more and more frequently lately, and she and Brock had been going at it like rabbits in heat. There was great sound insulation, of course, so they could be discreet.

Jack had already communicated the Brock-Arch Priestess situation to Vivi through his clone. She was finding it extremely amusing. Her own little sitcom, she called it.

The Arch Priestess had fulfilled her promise. Three more space monster cores had arrived to Jack's house, all bursting with energy. After quickly absorbing them over a few days, he'd reached 100% Matter Condensation. And that meant it was time for a small breakthrough.

Jack sat alone in meditation. His breaths came in and out, long like snakes of wind. His body pulsed with power.

In his inner world, energy ran rampart. The portal to the Green Dragon Realm had temporarily stopped spouting its green torrent. Only the Black Hole World still spun, steadily pumping its advanced laws into Jack's inner world.

The energy density had reached a limit. By Jack's calculations, it was exactly double the starting one. His inner world had gone from feeling empty to decently saturated, permeated by a sense of contentment. If he didn't know the proper way to cultivate through the B-Grade, he might have continued doing the same thing.

But he did know. Therefore, he got to work.

His palms crashed together, and it was like God's angry roar. An intense shockwave rang through the entire inner world. The ambient energy, which had been spontaneously coalescing into formations, shattered back into individual particles. The bonds collapsed, and everything came into a state of flux as Jack's roar smashed into the borders of his world, demolishing them and pushing outward.

"Expand!" he roared.

The moment the walls fell, they tried to rise again, but the energy was a veritable flood. Like an overfilled bowl, it spilled outwards, past the borders of Jack's world, seeking to conquer the dimensional sea. His Daos spread with it, imposing order on the chaos. Entire regions of nothingless were tamed, forced into stable existence as they were flooded with laws and energy.

From ten thousand miles, Jack's world reached eleven, then eleven and a half. The expansion slowed as it progressed. He reached twelve thousand miles and kept going, but the dimensional sea was fighting back now, whatever laws were assisting his expansion beginning to recede. Finally, at exactly 12,600 miles, the expansion came to a stop.

This wasn't a demonstration of Jack's potential. It was a process identical for everyone. Generations of cultivators had figured out that 26% was the optimal increase of the width of one's inner world. After a total of three expansions—one in every minor breakthrough—he'd have an inner world with exactly double its initial diameter.

Jack could have pushed it farther if he really wanted to. Most people could. The reason he hadn't, wasn't that he had a better place to spend his remaining energy.

The energy density of his inner world had doubled from the time he first reached the B-Grade. Now, after increasing the inner world's diameter by 26% and therefore doubling its total volume—since it was a sphere—the energy density had fallen to the exact level from which it started. His Matter Condensation was back to 0%.

However, to expand his inner world, he'd consumed part of the dimensional sea. And that part wasn't devoid of energy. Multicolored wisps now floated in the borders of Jack's world, forms of energy still undecided on what they would become. They'd just been dragged from nothingness into a reality governed by hard rules. This was their most malleable state.

Jack, exactly as generations of cultivators had instructed before him, capitalized on these energies. He grabbed them with his willpower and spread them evenly around his inner world. He then manipulated their composition and turned them into air, water, fire, and earth. The four elements formed the backbone of his world. The air formed a very thin atmosphere which filled the void. The water turned into moisture. Fire coalesced into large spheres, the progenitors of stars, while earth gathered together into free-floating chunks of stone, their respective gravities not powerful enough to form anything larger.

These chunks of stone were the most important part. They ranged in size from a human fist to a large table, all evenly spread and maintained separate by the current weakness of gravity. After all, gravity was a form of energy, too. Its effectiveness depended on the density of spacetime—the so-called *G* factor—which would increase along with the overall energy density of his inner world. As that happened, gravity would grow stronger, and the various chunks of stone would gather together into larger ones. That way, Jack could eventually begin creating a planet in his inner world.

This was all theory. Again, generations of cultivators had experimented with their inner worlds, eventually arriving at the current optimized progression through eons of trial and error. It was not a simple process, nor was it completely intuitive. Who knows what Jack would have done if he reached this step without instructions from his predecessors. However, now that he did have instructions to follow, the end result felt right. Harmonic, even.

Which didn't mean it was perfect. Every problem had a solution which was simple, elegant, and wrong. The cultivation world was constantly evolving, one step every generation. They were optimizing their process. Once Jack reached an exceedingly high boundary, perhaps he could use his then-insights to further optimize some previous part of the cultivation path. For now, he had no grounds to do such things. The path he'd been shown felt right. Better than anything he could come up with. So he followed it.

Sometimes, you innovated. But only a fool would choose not to stand on the shoulders of giants.

Jack's eyes snapped open. A flash of light erupted, lighting up the room. His aura deepened at that moment. If a low-level cultivator was watching, they would instinctively fall to their knees and worship.

Jack smiled. He had successfully reached the middle B-Grade.

CHAPTER TWENTY-THREE

JOINING THE SUMMIT

THERE ARE TIMES WHEN ONE FEELS SMALL. FOR EXAMPLE, WHEN THEY'RE surrounded by individuals greater than themselves.

This was partially how Jack felt as he sat in the center of the meeting room. It was small, yet imposing. Frescos filled the walls, depicting Old Gods in their moments of glory. Twelve chairs hugged the round wall, each framed by a carving of a particular Old God, one for each chair. That way, if someone looked at a person sitting in one of those chairs, they would see a stone halo surrounding their head, as if they were saints of that Old God.

Despite the chairs, there was a suspicious lack of a table.

The Arch Priestess sat in the chair before the Enas carving. It depicted a kind old man raising a hand, out of which tumbled a thousand peaceful embryos. It was supposed to signify him creating life. Jack found it creepy.

Elder Boatman's clone sat before the carving of Axelor, illustrated as a ball of darkness swallowing the world. Elder Soresight sat before the Old God of Time, a rippling pond through which a man was portrayed in various stages of his life. Finally, Elder Heavencrash sat before a carving depicting various balls in the shape of a human.

Each ball was supposed to be a planet, though Jack had no idea which Old God this was. He hadn't asked.

As for Jack himself, he sat at the very center of the room, where the table would be if there was one. He was cosplaying as a projector. Once his clone reached System space and activated Immortal Commune, the images of the summit would hopefully be projected above the head of Jack's main body in the center of the room.

For now, he was just sitting between four silent, A-Grade individuals. The pressure was mounting. It was a good thing his mind was hardened, or he might have made a fool of himself by sweating.

"How is it going, Jack?" the Arch Priestess asked. "The clone was supposed to be in position ten minutes ago. Did something happen?"

"The starship is just flying slower than expected," he replied. "We should be arriving any moment now." His eyes flashed. "Ah. Just did, actually. Now I'll probably watch the Dao—"

His voice cut off as new light filled his eyes. Not all Dao Visions were tame. Some assaulted his mind, leaving him no choice but to view them immediately. The last one had been like this, and Jack had expected this one to be similar as well.

However, since they were already delayed, there was no time to carefully perceive this vision. Jack rushed through. He couldn't accelerate the vision itself, but he could slow down his own perception. Since the vision only played out in his mind, slowing his perception relative to the vision would accelerate it, making it flash over in just a couple of seconds. All he saw was a massive explosion. He would review it again when he had the time.

A moment later, Jack's eyes returned to the real world. He and his clone were fully connected—a slightly jarring experience, even now. The clone took a deep breath, then reached into himself and activated Immortal Commune for the first time.

Immortal Commune I: This skill has no tiers. It allows you to seek council with the designated Immortals through the

System's long-range communication network. Restraint is advised as this skill consumes significant System resources.

He didn't know exactly how it worked. No one did. They just assumed, based on the context, a very good chance it could connect him to an Immortal currently in the summit. If not... They might be in trouble.

Jack expected something grand to happen. Instead, a new blue screen appeared in his face.

Hello. You have activated Immortal Commune. Please answer a few questions so we can connect you to the appropriate Immortal. What is the purpose of this commune?

Jack just stared at the screen. Whatever he expected, it wasn't this. His main body relayed the information to the Arch Priestess and the Elders, who began offering suggestions all at once.

"Silence," the Arch Priestess interrupted the cacophony. She turned to Jack. "The only Immortal we know certainly attending the summit is the Heaven Immortal. Say something that sounds of utmost importance."

Jack nodded.

The clone looked at the screen and said, "I would like to discuss an issue of utmost importance with the Heaven Immortal."

Please provide details

"I have information on the Black Hole Church. I know their true plans, but I will only tell the Heaven Immortal."

Please wait

Jack waited. The screen floating before him was surreal. As bloodthirsty and brutal as the System usually was, it now resembled a bot from customer support. Jack wondered if he'd ever get this image out of his head.

The Heaven Immortal has denied communication. Reason for denial was declared as, "I'm busy." Would you like us to transfer your request to the nearest available Immortal?

Shit.

Jack tried not to panic. He was at the edge of System space somewhere in the Milky Way galaxy. The summit, from what he knew, took place in the Spiral Stair galaxy. The nearest available Immortal would not be there.

"Do not transfer the request," he said, going out on a limb. "Inform the Heaven Immortal that this cannot wait. I stole secrets of the Church and am escaping. They will catch me soon, and I will be unable to communicate. I must speak to him right now."

Please wait

Jack's heart was beating in his throat. If this didn't work out, and they connected him to some random Immortal in some random galaxy, he wouldn't be able to attend the summit. The Arch Priestess would have broken her word. According to her, that would have disastrous consequences, both for herself and the army as a whole.

Would she blame him? Could they recover? Had his inability to convince a bot altered the entire flow of the war?

His spiral of worries was interrupted by a single word, ringing loud and clear in his mind.

"***Speak.***"

The voice carried grandeur and power, but also coldness. If the almighty System had a voice, this would be it. Jack knew he was speaking to the Heaven Immortal. The leader of the Immortals, the Hand of God, and the System. One of the most powerful entities in existence.

And he was thinking instead of replying.

"I carry the will of the Arch Priestess," he said telepathically. "She is seeking to connect to the summit. Please permit."

This was a phrase they'd planned beforehand. It needed to be clear and concise. Now that he'd spoken it, the Arch Priestess couldn't be blamed if the Heaven Immortal denied her access to the summit. It wouldn't be her fault.

Silence followed. Jack imagined the Heaven Immortal realizing it had been played. How would he react?

"Permission granted."

There was no anger, no hesitation. The Immortals were emotionless. Instead of feeling rage at being tricked by Jack, or demanding an explanation it already knew, the Heaven Immortal immediately moved on. It was brutally efficient. Terrifying.

Jack felt the connection between them grow wider. From transferring only sound, it now included image. A metallic face appeared in his mind. It was completely featureless, with only the number '1' drawn on its forehead in red paint. From the back of its head, various little tubes spread out, disappearing beyond the edge of the projection.

Jack was face-to-face with the Heaven Immortal.

Without panicking, he transferred the connection to the main body. The main body then projected the scene above his head, while relaying to the Heaven Immortal his own surroundings—the Arch Priestess and the three Elders. To someone of Jack's caliber, using his Dao to capture and project his surroundings was a trivial matter.

Receiving the image of the Arch Priestess, the Heaven Immortal widened its image further. Jack now saw the Heaven Immortal hovering over a flat disk of stone carved with complex, glowing runes. It wasn't a language he recognized. Each rune was so small it was barely distinguishable, yet all together they covered the massive stone disk.

The disk floated alone in space, framed by distant stars. Bright blue light came from below, but not enough to be blinding. Five figures stood on the disk. One was the Heaven Immortal, with tubes coming from its back and disappearing into a dark fold of space. There was one more Immortal, sporting the number '6' on its forehead, along with a handsome, human-looking cultivator in loose robes. This man gave Jack pause. He carried a heroic aura which was hard to ignore.

The remaining two people were, unexpectedly, space monsters. One was an extremely muscular humanoid covered in interlocking gray plates. While naked, it possessed no discernible genitalia. It stood at the same height as the Immortals and possessed a thick tail. Its human face betrayed both cunning and confidence.

As for the final member of this summit, it was a massive silver dragon. Its head rested on the stone disk, larger than all other members, while the rest of its colossal body floated behind it in space.

Jack couldn't perceive the auras of these people through the projection, so he could only wonder how many were Archons. The Heaven Immortal certainly was.

"Arch Priestess," the robot said. "You pulled quite the charade to avoid attending physically. Are you intimidated?"

"Only a fool battles on her opponent's terms," the Arch Priestess replied, her tone dismissing the Heaven Immortal. "Two Overlords of the Space Monster World, it is an honor to finally meet you in person. Or, well, as in person as my projection speaking to your clones can be considered." She chuckled. They didn't. "I've worshiped your carvings as a child. Meeting you has been a lifetime wish."

"Always nice to see a fellow space monster doing well," the silver dragon rumbled. Its voice was neither cold nor warm. It sounded neutral.

The other space monster spoke with daggers, "You have already framed yourself as inferior, Arch Priestess. Now you're just nailing your own coffin."

"I don't see you attending in your real body either, Overlord," she replied calmly.

"I was never challenged. If I was, my real body would be here, as would my armies."

"Then you're a fool. One who just got lucky."

Next to this Overlord, a puff of silvery smoke left the dragon's nostrils. It seemed amused.

Jack was only now noticing the faint transparency of both space monsters. As the Arch Priestess had mentioned, they were clones, and not strong ones, either. If he had to guess, they didn't want to leave the safety of the Space Monster World.

However, if they were the Overlords of that world, that made them both Archons. Maybe not even average Archons.

It was interesting to Jack how outspoken space monsters were. It probably came with their bestial nature. They had started antagonizing and cursing at each other within the first minute of interaction. This would be fun if it didn't concern the future of the universe.

CHAPTER TWENTY-FOUR

IMMORTAL SUMMIT OF SPIRAL STAIR

"We host this summit on the Space Monster World's request, to let them openly and clearly determine their allegiance,"* the Heaven Immortal intoned. *"I believe, Overlords, that the truth is clear as day. The Black Hole Church doesn't even dare to appear in our presence. All they can do is hide—a conduct unbefitting of their space monster leader. It would be foolish to ally with them."

"Different armies have different advantages," the Arch Priestess replied. "The Old Gods will soon arrive to fight by our side. Eleven extreme Archons. During the First Crusade, ninety-nine Immortals led the entire cultivation world against them and still lost. Now, only thirty-three Immortals remain, and the cultivator world is divided. Their power is inferior to what it used to be. They are bound to fail."

"Senseless drivel,"* the Heaven Immortal declared. *"We would not launch the Second Crusade without extreme confidence. After all, we had no reason to hurry. We are prepared, we are strong, and we possess more A-Grade cultivators than ever before. Before us, the Church is nothing but fleeting mice. Even the Old Gods will be powerless to reverse the situation—we naturally have ways to deal with them."

"There is no way to deal with them," the Arch Priestess said. "They're bluffing to secure your alliance, Overlords. They cannot do it alone."

"They do not seek our alliance," the humanoid space monster Overlord corrected, his words cutting her sharply. He took on a slightly more formal tone. "The Immortals have requested only that we abstain from this war. Given everything I've seen, I want to agree. The Old Gods are mighty, but their intentions are unknown. The Immortals are clearly the stronger party. Besides, Arch Priestess, I do not appreciate how you retreated your armies to this galaxy in particular, endangering the Space Monster World to force our hand in assisting you."

"Force your hand?" The Arch Priestess chuckled. "It was the Immortals who forced your hand when they created the System. Even if you don't fight them, do you think they will leave the Space Monster World alone? As soon as the System reaches you, they will use it to cut you off from the Dao of the Universe, either starving you until all powerful monsters die, or outright breaking the entry seal and invading you."

"We are aware of the Immortals' desire to conquer. However, they have promised to stay away from this galaxy for one billion years," the humanoid Overlord said. "That is a lot of time. Our children can live and grow. When the future comes, the space monsters of that time ought to be ready, or they deserve to be annihilated."

"The First Crusade was a billion years ago, and you knew there would be a second. You had a billion years to prepare. Tell me, Overlord, are you ready, or do you deserve to be annihilated?"

Jack saw fury spark in the eyes of the humanoid Overlord. He did not reply immediately. "I will not rob my world of a billion years of freedom for a lost cause," he finally said. "You are forced to fight, Arch Priestess. I am not."

She laughed. "I expected Overlord Great Silver to preach neutrality. After all, he is a wise, calm monster. But you, Fiend King... I've heard so much about your courage growing up. I didn't think you were a coward."

His tail smashed into the stone disk without warning. The entire thing shook. Jack saw the projection tilt as part of the disk was smashed to smithereeens. The number six Immortal reacted immediately. It raised its hands and stabilized the disk.

"Calm yourself, Fiend King," the Heaven Immortal said. "You are our guest. Do not destroy our property."

The humanoid Overlord did not reply. He seethed with anger, doing his best to contain it. The Arch Priestess's words had gotten to him. Based on what Jack had seen so far, this was indeed an aggressive individual, even for space monsters. Surrendering to the Immortals without a fight was already difficult for him.

It was not cowardice, of course, but the word struck deep inside the Overlord.

"There is no cowardice in wisdom," the Heaven Immortal spoke up. "The Overlords act correctly. We possess the past, the present, and the future. Moreover, we are not enemies with them. If we can coexist peacefully for a long period of time, why not do so? In the far future, our descendants can choose their own paths."

"Here is where you make a mistake, Heaven Immortal," the Arch Priestess declared proudly. "You might possess the present, but the future is already out of your hands. It doesn't matter whether you win this Crusade or not. Our next generation is far superior to yours. Just this year, we had two disciples break into the B-Grades with 8,800 and 10,000 miles respectively. The Second Crusade is not the end of this war. Even if you win, Jack Rust will soar in the future and take revenge. No matter what you do, you will lose."

She glanced at Jack.

Jack thought he was just a projector. Suddenly, he was dragged into this whole mess. The eyes of the two space monster Overlords fell on him, only just realizing who he was, and he gulped. A moment later, he straightened his back. If he could help gain an ally for the Church, he would.

The Heaven Immortal, however, only laughed. A cold, mechanical sound. "Who doesn't know that war fosters geniuses, Arch

Priestess?" it asked. "Your Church is not the only side to experience that effect. Our next generation is also skilled beyond compare."

It raised a hand to indicate the only human physically present—the early A-Grade who hadn't spoken since the start of the summit. Now, said A-Grade raised his gaze, eyes shining with ambition.

"Our former Head Envoy, Elder Hero, achieved a perfect breakthrough of nine thousand miles in his time. The first in history. Since then, he has enjoyed countless resources and experienced countless adventures, excelling in every single challenge he ever faced. Recently, his breakthrough to the A-Grade approached perfection as well. Your own star cultivator may have used unknown means to achieve a breakthrough beyond nine thousand miles, but that is no guarantee of his future success. Most importantly, he is only a middle B-Grade embroiled in the chaos of war. You know the fragility of geniuses, Arch Priestess. How can you claim your next generation to be superior to ours, when chances are they will perish on the way?"

The Arch Priestess's face spasmed. She was clearly pressured, but her voice remained even. "I could say the same about your genius. An early A-Grade is nothing in a war of this scale, especially when targeted. He will never have the chance to mature."

"That's where you're wrong, Arch Priestess. He already has." The Heaven Immortal's voice turned mocking. "Elder Hero, please."

The early A-Grade, who still hadn't spoken, let his aura erupt. Jack couldn't sense it, but he could perceive the man's casually dominating air. The aura of an emperor. Of a man who shouldered the world. An unprecedented, unsurpassable hero.

Below that aura, Elder Hero was a blond man in loose white robes. He seemed picture-perfect. His looks were unblemished, his blue eyes piercing, and his body was perfectly well-shaped. Jack had no doubt that pristine muscles hid beneath those robes. He carried a greatsword, an antithesis to his lack of armor, and gave a smile which could illuminate an entire world.

Yet, beneath that perfect exterior, Jack could sense arrogance. In his eyes, this man was less a hero and more a high school bully, except impossibly better in every facet of human existence.

"I ask the Arch Priestess to let me prove myself," he said with fake humility. The mockery was evident in his voice. "It would be improper to duel this child you praise so high, since my cultivation is far superior to his. However, you are surrounded by three late A-Grades. You may pick any of them. I will challenge them to a fifty-year death duel to prove my undeniable potential. If not, I can challenge any middle A-Grade of your choice right now. Allow me to prove that I already possess the power to stand at the highest level."

Jack looked around. The two Overlords appeared intrigued. As for the Arch Priestess and her Elders, they all had ugly expressions. Since this Elder Hero and the Heaven Immortal dared to make such a statement, they had supreme confidence. There was a good chance that whichever Elder accepted this challenge would end up dead and humiliated.

Jack didn't know about the other two, but his own master, Elder Boatman, was far more hot-headed than he looked. He would one hundred percent step forth to accept the challenge. Which would only enhance Elder Hero's momentum and leave Jack overshadowed.

Even if Elder Hero couldn't really defeat the other Elder in fifty years, that was fine. The most important part was the duel declaration. It would severely weaken the momentum of the Church and practically seal the matter of the space monster neutrality. They'd been check-mated.

The Arch Priestess knew this. So did the Elders. That's why no one spoke immediately—they were desperately looking for a way to turn the tide, finding none.

But Jack could.

"What a loser!" he claimed, laughing rowdily. Everyone turned to look at him. The pressure was crushing. Yet, he pretended not to notice it. "We are the parties at stake here, Hero. We represent the next generation of our factions. Do you not dare to face me directly?"

Elder Hero frowned at him. "You are a mere middle B-Grade. I'm almost an entire Grade above you. If we were to fight, people would laugh at me."

"I didn't say to fight right now. You challenged our Elders to a duel in fifty years, but that's the timeline of a coward. I don't need that much. Thirty years. You and me. To the death. Do you dare?"

Elder Hero just stared. Then, he laughed—a bold, masculine sound. "*Leash your dog, Arch Priestess. I think it went rabid.*"

The Arch Priestess' eyes were glued on Jack. She scanned his face, his resolve. She didn't ask him anything. Finally, she turned to Elder Hero. "Our champion issued a challenge," she said. "Do you dare to accept, or not?"

At this, everyone fell quiet. In their eyes, this was suicide. It was just an attempt by the Arch Priestess to sacrifice her most talented cultivator in exchange for marginally impressing the space monster Overlords. However, they wouldn't really be impressed. Sacrificing a talent was always a detestable action.

Sure, they'd win the dick-measuring contest, but they'd lose a great asset in thirty years.

Elder Hero must have come to the same conclusion. "Very well. Since you insist, I will accept. A duel thirty years from now... I will treat it as a warm-up. Afterward, in fifty years from now, I will also fight Elder Boatman to the death. That is your master, isn't he, boy?"

"He is," Jack replied calmly. He grinned, showing all teeth. "I look forward to breaking you."

"Then our decision is easy as well," the Fiend King said, his voice laden with distaste. "Our stance will be decided thirty years from now. If Jack Rust wins, we will ally with the Church. If Elder Hero wins, we will remain neutral. Let no one say that we are cowards."

Everyone nodded in agreement. Essentially, the result of this negotiation had been placed completely on the outcome of the thirty-year duel. Everyone thought they were the winners here—but that was only because the Immortals, Elder Hero, and Overlords all believed Jack's challenge was pointless. They never thought he could win.

Yet, even now, Elder Hero wasn't done. Once he got an advantage, he'd push it to the end.

"If you believe so much in your disciple, Arch Priestess," he said, "how about we add some additional stakes to the duel?"

"Like what?" she replied.

"If Jack Rust wins, we can promise to give the Church an Archon-level space monster core."

The Arch Priestess's eyes widened. That was an exceedingly precious treasure. Elder Hero didn't have the authority to bet it. Yet, since the Heaven Immortal didn't speak up, they'd obviously come to an agreement.

The two Overlords didn't seem to care.

"And if you win?" the Arch Priestess asked.

"Then," he proudly raised his head, "I will take your hand in marriage."

Silence befell the summit. Everyone was stunned. The Elders of the Church were the first to recover, and they instantly started yelling all at once. "How dare you?" Elder Heavencrash roared. "Heaven Immortal! Control that rabid dog of yours!"

The other Elders had similar things to say. This was clearly an attack on their pride. The Arch Priestess would obviously never accept. She, however, raised a hand to stop them all.

"Sure," she said simply. The Elders swiveled to look at her with wide eyes.

"Arch Priestess!" they said.

"It's fine." She waved them down. "It is my decision, and I know what I'm doing. Jack will win."

The Overlords were speechless. Which was natural, in Jack's opinion, since he, too, had been rendered speechless by this bet. The Arch Priestess bet *herself* on his duel? Never mind anything else, she was currently sleeping with Brock. What the hell was up with that?

And what kind of weirdo was Elder Hero to request such a thing?

"Perfect," Elder Hero said, only now recovering from his surprise himself. "With my talent and your lineage, I'm sure our children will be exceptional."

If the Arch Priestess was nervous, she didn't show it. She looked at him as if he was an idiot—something which, judging by his frown, annoyed him greatly. "I believe this summit is over," she said. "We've said all there is to be said. Overlords, while our current relationship is not the best, it really was a pleasure meeting you. Heaven Immortal, you can go fuck yourself. Goodbye."

CHAPTER TWENTY-FIVE
BIRTH OF TIME

THE SUMMIT ENDED WITH A BANG. JACK'S CLONE WAS TAKEN AWAY BY ELDER Godspeed—a short, effeminate man—and rushed through the universe to escape any pursuers. They would take a wide route before returning to Earth.

Jack's main body wasn't in a hurry. He sat in the middle of the Church's meeting room, surrounded by three animated Elders.

"What the hell was that!" Boatman asked. "Jack! Why would you sacrifice yourself like that? You know you cannot win!" He turned to the Arch Priestess. "And you. Why did you let him do it? Why did you agree?"

"We might have made a mistake," Soresight said.

"Not if we win the war before the thirty years are up," Heavencrash added, his face dark. "Isn't that your plan, Arch Priestess? You would never agree otherwise."

Facing their tension, she smiled calmly. "If we could win the war within thirty years, that would be great. However, it's impossible. We don't even know if the Old Gods will have arrived until then. It is safe to assume the duel will happen."

"Then what exactly are you planning?" Heavencrash asked.

"Very simple. I plan for Jack to win."

Everyone's eyes turned to him. Jack frowned. "I believe in myself, but I don't know... I'd never heard of Elder Hero until today."

Boatman spoke up, "He was the Head Envoy of the Hand until a few years ago. He and Sovereign Heavenly Spoon have clashed a few times, and do you know what happened? Hero won. Every time." He sighed with worry. "What came over you, Jack? You have such a bright future. You've already expanded your potential to the limit. Why would you gamble everything on such an impossible task?"

"Because I had to," Jack replied. "We had lost all our momentum. Those space monster Overlords would never take us seriously if I didn't step up. Besides, if I hadn't, you would have accepted his challenge, Master. You or another Elder. And regardless of victory or defeat in fifty years, Hero would be the heroic one now, and we would be the losers."

Boatman opened his mouth to disagree, then thought better. He sighed again.

"It wasn't your place to salvage the situation," the Arch Priestess said softly. "However, as you said, you were forced to. Because we failed. There had been no other way out for our Church. You did the right thing, Jack. Thank you."

The tones were dying down, but Elder Heavencrash wouldn't relax so easily. He looked for a table to disintegrate and found none. "The right thing?" he asked. "He just offed himself, Arch Priestess! If we don't manage to assassinate Elder Hero within thirty years, he will take away our greatest talent and our reputation. It's not like Jack will be able to run away. Look at him. You just know he has a headstrong Dao."

"Thank you for your confidence, Elder Heavencrash," Jack said.

"Don't mock me, boy! I'm a thousand times your elder, and I only want what's best for you. You messed up big time!"

"Only if he can't win," Elder Boatman spoke up.

"What?" Heavencrash turned to him. "Do you think it's possible? Are you also insane?"

"I think it will be very, very difficult," Boatman replied. "For anyone else, it would be impossible. But Jack has performed miracles before. More than once. If there is anybody who can carry our flag and win that duel, it's him. And besides..." He stood up, walking behind Jack and placing a hand on his shoulder. "He's my disciple. I believe in him."

"So do I," the Arch Priestess replied.

Soresight chuckled. "It's not like we have a choice, Heavencrash. The dice has been cast. We can only do our best."

Heavencrash grumbled. "I know. I still think it was a stupid-ass decision, but at least it was a brave one." He turned to Jack, worry and confusion alternating in his gaze. "I will choose to believe as well."

"Thank you, Elders, Master, Arch Priestess," Jack said. "I know my decision was spontaneous, but there was no choice. I don't comprehend the heights of my opponent. But I will still work extremely hard, strive for the greatest progress possible, and do my best to win." Jack sensed himself lack confidence. That had to be fixed immediately. "No," he said, correcting his previous words. "I will not do my best. I *will* win. I swear it on my Dao."

It felt like a stone slab crashed down from above and landed on his soul, weighing it down. His oath was not something he could break. That was good. He could use that weight, a reminder to never relax. In this battle, he had no choice. He would win.

Hearing his proclamation, Elder Boatman laughed. He seemed to have recovered his good mood. "Well said, Jack! There is no other way now. You just have to win!"

"The Church will support you with everything we have," the Arch Priestess said. "However, we are already running out of compatible cores... I will give you some more, but really, that is all we have."

"It's okay," Jack said. "I have a plan."

"A plan?" Everyone looked curiously.

"Yes," he replied, raising his head. "I'll go to the Space Monster World."

Jack floated in space, an ethereal body. A ghost. Before him hovered a massive bubble, stretching on for a thousand miles. Despite its massive size, the bubble contained just a few particles. It was far emptier than the void of space.

This was the second Dao Vision Jack had gotten from his class, Paragon of Cultivation. It was the one he'd briefly seen just before his clone activated Immortal Commune. Now that Jack had returned to his house, he had the time to watch it more in-depth.

The bubble floated before him for what seemed like eternity. He knew that the flow of time inside it was vastly accelerated, but it had still been thousands of years in the outside world with nothing happening in the bubble. To Jack, of course, those thousands of years came just as information. He'd only stayed here a few minutes.

There was another cultivator with him. A green-robed woman, sitting cross-legged with her eyes shut. Just by existing beside her, Jack could sense a tremendous flow of life energy, as if she contained the life of a thousand planets. He guessed she was an Archon.

If she'd noticed the Dao Vision being recorded from beside her, she did not react. She sat there, motionless, like a statue. Waiting.

The few particles inside the bubble moved at extreme speeds. In the almost complete nothingness, even the constraints of the universe didn't really apply. The particles were far faster than the speed of light. They zoomed around erratically. At some point, two would collide—but they were so small that the chances of it happening was abysmal.

The woman was patient.

At some point, a few minutes after Jack appeared in the vision and watched the bubble in silence, something finally happened. The woman's eyes snapped open. In the next moment, the world exploded. Two particles had crashed head-on to release a tremendous explosion. It came seemingly out of nowhere.

As the explosion occurred, Jack's understanding of the Dao was suddenly and completely upended. His perception caught how the two particles instantly disintegrated. Yet, from the exact point of the explosion, or perhaps from inside the destroyed particles, more emerged. The universe was born anew. There was time and space, matter, all sorts of wild Daos, each flaring with the intensity of a thousand suns. Infinite Dao particles were born of nothingness.

It all happened in an instant. One moment, the two particles clashed. In the next, the entire bubble was awash with energy, a bright, rainbow-colored mixture containing everything. It was only the restraints of the woman beside him who stopped the explosion, preventing it from spreading farther. Otherwise, with its speed, Jack was convinced it would have destroyed many nearby stars before it even slowed down.

Everything had happened so quickly he hadn't time to process it. In his understanding, the Dao could be neither born nor destroyed. It was just particles moving around or changing their properties. Yet, he'd just witnessed an act of true creation. Parthenogenesis. Something out of nothing.

How was that even possible?

All laws lost their effectiveness as things approached the extremes—too fast, slow, large, or small—but this was another level of discovery altogether. This woman before him, and whatever experiment she was conducting, had taken the most iron-clad rules of the universe and used them to wipe her butt. It was ridiculous.

It also meant there was so much more to learn. In comprehension of the Dao alone, Jack could match most early A-Grades. If there was knowledge so vital to the essence of the Dao, but he hadn't had the slightest clue about it before, just how high did the Dao go? What was the limit? Did it even exist?

While he was busy being shell-shocked, the woman had already gotten to work. Her hands formed a myriad seals in a second. The bubble compressed, returning the released energy of the explosion to its previous white-hot state, then holding it there until it ran its course. Slowly, the energy cooled off.

Jack then watched something even more mysterious. The flow of time within the bubble changed. Before, it had been artificially accelerated by the woman. It had now become something else, something that both moved on its own and was completely different from the universe's regular flow of time. They were two different rivers. The water droplets which made them up were the same, but the rivers themselves were very different from each other.

Jack had observed the creation of a completely new Dao of Time.

The woman also watched with rapt attention. As the new Dao was created, she smiled. "The birth of time," she whispered. "All come from one."

The two of them remained hovering in space, passive observers, as this new Dao of Time found its bearings inside the bubble. From every Time particle dashing around randomly, they all came into sync. The flow of time stabilized. All the other energies fell into line afterward, wrapping around Time like vines around a column.

This isn't just Time, Jack realized. This is a whole new universe! She created a new universe! That explosion before was a Big Bang!

He was shaking with excitement. The woman, however, didn't seem interested in watching the growth of this universe any longer. She waved a hand dismissively. The bubble collapsed in on itself and disappeared. The energies inside it hissed and bubbled as they came in contact with the laws of the universe, then slowly melted away, incorporated easily. The new river of time fought back before falling in line with the time flow of this universe.

Suddenly, there was nothing. No sign of the previous bubble, explosion, and universe. Jack remained there, frozen in space, until the woman turned to look at him. She raised a smiling brow. "Shoo," she said, waving a hand in his direction. The vision shattered, and Jack was back at his house, still starstruck at what he'd just witnessed.

This vision was the greatest he'd ever seen. He felt it contained monumental secrets of the universe, secrets he could only slowly begin to unpack. There were so many things he didn't understand.

Why had the other Daos wrapped around time, and only then were stabilized? Did Time play a more crucial role than he'd imagined?

Was it really that easy to create a new universe? Could the woman have kept it on her person to study or use as a weapon? Why did she so wastefully destroy it?

And, most importantly, what secrets hid in that single moment when the two particles collided? How exactly was that universe born? How was something born from nothing? And anyway, what was inside the Dao particles?

That single instant of creation was too fast and too blinding for Jack to observe. One moment, there was an explosion. The next, there was everything. He hadn't managed to perceive the events in between, but he had a suspicion that, if he could, he'd glimpse into extremely primal mysteries.

He was so damn excited.

There was still some time before he left for the Space Monster World. Therefore, Jack closed his eyes and returned to the vision, watching it over and over.

CHAPTER TWENTY-SIX

FLYING TO THE SPACE MONSTER WORLD

THE SPACE MONSTER WORLD WAS A REALM HIDDEN IN THE HEART OF THE Spiral Stair galaxy. A realm of space monsters. Due to a seal Jack didn't quite understand yet, A-Grades and Archons were unable to enter, which was why the space monsters were confident in defending themselves against the Immortals.

After all, while A-Grades couldn't enter, they sure could develop inside. The space monster race had several Archons holding down the fort.

With Jack's recent declaration of a thirty-year duel, he needed to advance quickly. It was the one-year deadline for Earth all over again. Since the New Cathedral had run out of space cores to give him, there was only one place where he could reasonably expect to find them. A place where the Immortals couldn't chase him down.

Of course, adventuring through the Space Monster World wouldn't be easy. Outsiders were hunted there, and that would be doubly the case for Jack, who planned on hunting A-Grade space monsters himself. In a sense, it was a desperate gamble, the only one with at least a chance of succeeding.

But Jack wouldn't just kill himself. He had a plan. As well as a protector.

"Are we ready?" Jack asked. It was a sunny day on the New Cathedral. He and Brock were on their mansion's rooftop, accompanied by Starhair, Sophie, the energy clone of Elder Boatman, and a new clone—that of the Arch Priestess herself. A white-clothed woman identical to her main body, except that her aura was at the peak B-Grade level instead of the Archon one.

The Church had invested heavily on Jack and Brock. The Arch Priestess had done so personally as well. Their survival was paramount, so they needed as capable a protector as they could get. Since A-Grades and above couldn't enter the Space Monster World, an Archon's peak B-Grade clone was their best bet. After all, while the clone's energy reserves were pathetically low compared to the real thing, its Dao understandings remained far higher than any real B-Grade's.

"I'll miss you guys!" Sophie exclaimed, her eyes widened to the brink of tears. "But don't worry! With all the content we've prepared, I'll make sure your reputation remains as high as ever! You'll be heroes by the time you come back!"

"They sure will," Elder Boatman's clone replied. "Let's board. Arch Priestess, please."

He took a respectful step back, motioning for the Church's leader to go first. The Arch Priestess obliged. Her bare feet stepped on the rooftop, approaching the starship parked there. It wasn't a new vehicle. The *Iron Maiden* had been the one to bring Jack and Brock to the New Cathedral, and it would be the one to bring them out of it as well. It was perfect for the job: fast, stealthy, and with high defensive properties.

After the Arch Priestess disappeared through the sliding door, Elder Boatman followed, his clone a hovering shadow. While he couldn't enter the Space Monster World, he would be the one to drive them there. Jack and Brock went next, finally followed by Starhair, whose grumbling echoed low in the ears of everyone. He had no business going to the Space Monster World. His only job was to take care of Jack and Brock on the way as their personal assistant.

"Take care of yourselves!" Sophie cried again from the rooftop as the door slid closed. "Remember to film good content!"

Jack waved at her, a stone-like thing nestled in his palm. It was a top-grade projection stone. On Sophie's instructions, they were to use it to record their most striking feats in the Space Monster World so she could spread them later.

"She's a good person," Brock said, looking at the shrinking form of Sophie as their starship slowly lifted off. "Do you think we'll ever see her again?"

"Probably," Jack replied, leaning against the window. He suddenly felt emotional. "I hope so. If something happens to a civilian like her, we'll have already lost."

Sophie and the mansion grew smaller. The New Cathedral now filled the window, a sprawling city expanding at a prodigious rate. The last stronghold of the Black Hole Church, placed on a tiny planet on a galaxy far, far away. It looked so small from up here. In the distant jungle, a brontosaurus raised its head as if roaring them goodbye.

Jack turned away from the window as the planet appeared in their sights. There was nothing to see anymore. Their home of few months was now a distant memory.

"There is nothing for me to even do here," Starhair grumbled. The Arch Priestess had already retreated to one of the starship's three rooms, letting him speak freely. "I'm literally useless. How can I assist you on an empty starship?"

"By not whining," Jack replied. Starhair sighed.

"I guess I'll cultivate. Which room should I go to, Jack? Yours or Brock's?"

With the Arch Priestess in one of the starship's three private rooms, and Elder Boatman's clone not requiring a room, as he'd be constantly steering the starship, the remaining two rooms went to Jack, Brock, and Starhair. As the least in status, Starhair didn't expect to get his own room, though he would in normal circumstances. Jack and Brock would rather stay with each other than with him. Not because he was a dick—he'd gotten much better since Brock beat him up—but because they were brothers, and they were used to it.

This time, however, Starhair's calculations were incorrect. None of them would need to share a room.

"Your own," Jack said with a smirk.

"Really?" Starhair replied. "Are you sure?"

"Oh, I'm sure."

"I'll go rest," Brock said, walking to the rooms. He opened the door of the leftmost one, where the Arch Priestess had gone, and disappeared inside. The door closed soundlessly behind him.

"Wait, what?" Starhair said. "Jack, you must save Brock! He went to the wrong room! The Arch Priestess will disintegrate him for trespassing!"

Jack winked. "It's fine."

"It's fi—What? I mean... What?" Starhair looked between Jack and the closed door in complete incomprehension. Finally, it dawned on him. "You can't mean... No. Really? No way. They aren't... Are they?"

Jack laughed. "What can I say? Brock has a special charm." He kept laughing as he paced to his own room—the middle one. "See you, Starhair. And Master, thanks for all the hard work. I'll cultivate hard."

"You better," Elder Boatman replied, hand grasping the helm of the ship, while Starhair remained frozen in the middle of the common room.

"Elder!" he exclaimed, turning around. "Is it true? Are they..."

Elder Boatman shrugged. "Brock is a very charismatic man. And the Arch Priestess is a very powerful woman. They're a match made in heaven."

Starhair opened and closed his mouth, no sound coming out. He stiffly retreated to the last room. His worldview had just gotten upturned.

Not only had he been defeated by a brorilla two small realms below him... but said brorilla now also had a woman far superior to any Starhair could claim. What an unfair world!

Jack meditated in his room. Cultivating in the B-Grade was usually a slow, gradual process. But not for him. Not only had he completely blown through the early B-Grade thanks to the New Cathedral's resources, but he'd also received two extremely high-level visions. He could sense his path unfolding in the distance.

The first vision showed a man unifying Space and Death to create an imitation of a black hole. Jack hadn't fully explored that vision—he hadn't had the time—but he'd definitely reaped some benefits. Both his Space Mastery and Death Mastery had reached the fourth tier.

The second vision showed a woman unifying Time and Life in what was probably a Big Bang. An explosion creating a world out of nothing. This vision was far more mystical than anything Jack had witnessed, and it contained far too many mysteries. He wasn't even close to unpacking it. He even had the sense that, if he managed to completely understand this vision, he would have climbed to heights surpassing A-Grades. The Dao of an Archon.

And beyond that, if he could manage to fully unify all four concepts... Who knew what would happen.

In other words, Jack had many things to meditate on. His plate was as full as ever.

The second vision was the one he currently chose to focus on. It wasn't easy to experiment with. Creating an explosion of that caliber would require careful preparation and years of waiting for random particles to collide. Maybe if he built a particle accelerator similar to CERN's? Then again, if it was that simple, he had no doubt the Archon woman would have done it that way.

While experimenting was difficult, mentally rewatching the

vision was free and effortless. He dove into it, striving for another tiny step forward. He observed the explosion, the creation of a world embryo, and how everything stabilized around a spontaneous flow of time afterward. It seemed, once again, that Time was the cornerstone of world creation, or at least one of them. It was like the main column keeping a building aloft. In this metaphor, maybe Space served as the building's foundation, keeping both concepts around the same level.

Then, what about Life and Death? How did they fit in? Both visions had portrayed them in relation to the Dao particles, so maybe Space was the foundation, Time was the column—the main axis—while Life and Death made up the bricks?

Jack suspected that wasn't the case. Still, he was currently lost. He knew that Dao particles could "die," or at least they had a tendency to protect themselves from destruction. He also knew that a powerful enough explosion could manifest life seemingly out of nowhere.

But as to exactly what those meant, he had no idea. It was a work in progress.

He sighed. At the very least, the System core inside him recognized his efforts:

Time Mastery IV: Time is a river you have learned to tame. You are diving in its waters, exploring its properties, and interacting with the fish. Before long, the bank itself will be your playground to shape as you wish. You are well on the road to mastery.

Life Mastery IV: Life is the beginning. The kickoff, the inevitable starting point of creation. It is also just another power you control. You can spread this power to everything, even the Dao itself. You are well on the road to mastery.

The absence of these two skills had troubled him for a while.

Only now did they appear, and directly at the fourth tier. Was this some kind of threshold? Were they considered part of the Death and Space Mastery skills until the third tier?

That was the only explanation Jack could think of, especially with how similar their respective descriptions were. Hell, the Life one was identical to Death's, except for the first two sentences.

Additionally, while the skills were fused, were Death and Space the overall name because those were the first he developed, or were they somehow superior to Time and Life? Probably the former. Jack felt that balance was key.

So many questions, so few answers. The path kept widening. Jack couldn't wait for the moment when it all snapped together, when his path became singular and all mysteries turned clear.

Though, of course, such an event was still far away.

Shaking his head, he left his room, heading for the common space. He felt a little bad for Elder Boatman, who had to constantly steer the ship while everyone else relaxed, so he tried to keep him company as often as possible.

"How is it going, Master?" Jack asked.

"Good. Peaceful. We haven't run into any Hand patrols as I expected, so I can say this has been smooth sailing."

The hooded figure's voice held a rare hint of joy. Apparently, he'd half expected them to come under attack. Go figure.

"Maybe it's because you're such a good captain," Jack said.

Boatman laughed. "Don't flatter me, disciple. You have nothing to gain from it."

"Perhaps." Jack smiled. "But, can I ask you something, Master? Feel free not to answer if it's too personal. How high is your Death Mastery skill?"

Boatman didn't reply. For a moment, Jack worried he'd overstepped. Such information was generally kept extremely private, as it could give a cultivator's enemies an advantage.

Just as Jack was ready to apologize, Boatman spoke up, "I no longer possess a System core inside me. It's harmless, but it's also useless after you reach the A-Grade. Some keep it because they're addicted to the numbers. Most get rid of it. Anyway, since I don't possess a System core, there is nothing quantifying my skills. If I had to guess, my Death Mastery would be somewhere between the fourth and fifth tier. At the peak of one or the very start of the other. It's hard to tell."

"I see," Jack replied. "Thanks for sharing it with me. I promise to never tell anyone."

Boatman finally turned around, his pale face giving a hard smile. "I know you won't. But, if you want my advice, don't fixate on the numbers. They can take you off track or discourage you. Focus on making progress, one little step at a time. It's a long road ahead, but if you just keep walking, you're bound to reach very far. Especially in your case."

Jack nodded deeply. "I will try. Thanks, Master."

"No problem."

Jack took some time to consider his master's words. At the same time, he looked backward. They'd been traveling for a few days now, and Brock hadn't emerged from his room once. Neither had the Arch Priestess. Jack thought it was natural—privacy would be harder to come by in the Space Monster World.

"Are we close, Master?" he asked.

"Very," Boatman replied. "In fact..."

The light of teleportation cleared around the starship. A vast emptiness was revealed. Stars glittered all around, redder here than in the outer reaches of the galaxy, as well as denser.

Ahead in the distance, a different shape hung. A swirling portal, similar to a mini-galaxy except far smaller. It was only a few miles from end to end. Jack could see it from this distance only because of his superhuman vision.

"We're almost there," Boatman replied with a content smile. "Just a few minutes and—"

The starship shook. A tremendous impact rocked the roof, cracking it apart and making the starship spin wildly. Jack almost flew out of it. He just barely managed to grab onto a steel column and remain attached. The void had already infiltrated from the outside, sucking in the air of the starship. Nobody needed it, thankfully, but that wasn't the point.

Everybody flashed outside the starship in an instant. Far in the distance, a figure blazed like the sun. Power radiated off of it in waves, searing the surrounding space, burning time so heavily it slowed down. Jack couldn't even look straight at the figure. His entire body was burning. His Dao perception was going haywire. Whoever this was, they were far, far too powerful. Overwhelmingly so.

His heart reached his throat, and he knew without the shadow of a doubt...

This was an Archon.

CHAPTER TWENTY-SEVEN

FACING AN ARCHON

A GENTLE ENERGY WRAPPED AROUND JACK, PROTECTING HIM. HE FINALLY managed to raise his head. He still had to squint, but he could now vaguely make out the figure who'd smashed their starship.

It was a man. He wore crimson robes, and his long red hair fluttered upwards as if some wind was blowing from below. His two arms were connected before his chest, his long sleeves invading each other. His skin was tanned, but his eyes were coal-black. His figure was broad, muscular, and masculine, and his visage was fierce, like a master of martial arts. The few wrinkles that marred his hardened face subtracted little from his aggressiveness.

More important than the man's appearance was his aura. It blazed out of him. Jack could see it as a literal sun, spreading for endless miles through space, showering the world in unfiltered heat.

He was the strongest person Jack had ever seen displaying his power, besides in Dao Visions.

"Archon Summer Noon," the Arch Priestess said, confirming Jack's suspicions. The gentle aura protecting Jack originated from her. "To what do we owe the pleasure?"

"Just paying a visit," the other man replied. His voice was loud, brass. Fiery. "I came to fish in a pond, but I found a shrunken whale. Lucky me."

"So the Immortals are using Archons now?" the Arch Priestess replied, her voice hard. "Have you all lost your mind? You know we'll do it when you do it. The war will escalate."

"I am not participating in the war yet," Summer Noon said. "In fact, I won't even kill your little clone or that of the Elder behind you. I only have a single reason for coming today."

He didn't specify that reason, but he didn't need to. Everyone knew.

"Jack," the Arch Priestess said.

"Precisely. Hand him over, and I won't touch any of you. Resist, and I'll char you all to ashes."

Jack's blood had already gone cold despite the heat. He was being hunted by an Archon. Before that man, before his massive aura, Jack felt as vulnerable as a newborn baby.

Is this the day I die? he wondered, gritting his teeth.

The Arch Priestess snorted. "Once the fight starts," she said in Jack's mind, "rush into the starship. We have to make it to the Space Monster World before he catches up."

Jack didn't ask anything. He just prepared to do as instructed. His Dao was circulating just below the surface. He could activate every single power he possessed at a moment's notice.

Archon Summer Noon noticed their silence.

"You better think this through, Arch Priestess," he said. "You and that A-Grade may be just clones, but the brorilla is the future of your Church. Will you throw his life away for stubbornness? You know you cannot escape."

The Arch Priestess didn't reply. "*Now!*" she yelled in Jack's mind. He instantly burst with his full potential. He galvanized Lightning Body, and then used every iota of life energy in the recharging Life Drop to activate his four-armed form. That would empty it again, but it was necessary. They were facing an Archon. This was the single greatest crisis in Jack's life.

He became a tall, four-armed, lightning-covered behemoth of a man clad only in a pair of shorts. Everyone around him followed, activating everything at once. Brock radiated golden light. Starhair's hair shone like a thousand stars, taking on a redder hue than usual. The Arch Priestess's aura erupted, showering the world in brutality. All four of them rushed into the starship and tried to take off.

Archon Summer Noon was on them that very instant. He'd been hundreds of miles away before, but that distance vanished, the very essence of space melted. From this close, the heat was suffocating. Jack felt his skin bubble like he was burned alive. It reminded him of that time he swam through lava.

The Archon wore a calm smile as he drove a finger forward. The fire bent to his will, forming a gargantuan, sun-clad finger which descended on their starship.

Elder Boatman's clone roared. "If you want to kill my disciple," he declared in anger, "you'll need to get through me." A scythe was in his hands like it had always been there. A terrible dark cloud erupted.

Spacetime died. Sound died. The void died. Everything died as the Elder swung his scythe, the very same attack which had once torn an entire tribulation in half.

"Even your main body couldn't face me, Boatman," the Archon said with a hint of ridicule. "Your clone is nothing."

The sun finger rammed into Boatman's full-powered strike and barely even paused. It broke through an instant later. Some flame tongues died, reduced to nothingness, but they were only a tiny fraction of the attack. The rest bulldozed through, completely evaporating Boatman's Death, melting his scythe before even touching it, and crashing heavily against his body.

The black cloak disintegrated. For a moment, Boatman's pale and frail-looking body was revealed—just that of a stubborn old man.

Then, he disappeared, turning into energy which immediately melted away.

Elder Boatman's clone had lasted a single instant.

However, in a battle of this caliber, every instant was important. Boatman's sacrifice had given the rest of them time to reenter the starship. The Arch Priestess's Dao wrapped around it, hurtling it through space. She was pouring everything she had. The starship was faster than before. In the single instant Boatman secured for them, they crossed half the distance to the Space Monster World.

But it was useless. Everything was before an Archon. He appeared right behind them again, slamming down a palm. Space was meaningless. The very sun descended to burn them whole. Jack felt his body struggling, and he saw the metal walls of the starship give way, dripping drops of molten steel which vaporized before they touched the floor. The *Iron Maiden* really possessed extreme defensive capabilities—any normal starship would already be gone.

Jack took in everything at once. An attack he couldn't even fathom was flying at them. It would hit—they had no way to dodge. Starhair was shivering. Brock's eyes were harder than they'd ever been. The Arch Priestess rocketed out of the starship. She didn't even have time to say anything. She flew at the sun.

Brock's entire body shone a brilliant gold. For a moment, Jack thought he'd self-detonated. The horror subsided as he noticed that Brock remained whole, just channeling all the power of his inner world at once, pouring it into the Arch Priestess.

Brock was a powerful fighter. He was also a great support. Right now, as the Arch Priestess's clone dove into the falling sun, he did his best to keep her alive just a moment longer. Jack could sense his brother's emotions through their bond—helplessness, despair, anger at his own weakness. Jack felt for him, he really did. But he knew what they had to do. Both of them knew.

The Arch Priestess and Elder Boatman were only here in clone form. Losing those clones meant little. The survival of everyone else was the top priority.

As the Arch Priestess flew into the sun, Jack was already grabbing the ship's helm, pushing it onward. His new understandings of space erupted. With the Arch Priestess's assistance, he managed to escape the Archon's lockdown, teleporting away, rushing toward the Space Monster World, where they would be safe.

Yet, he saw it, even as he flew away. The Arch Priestess faced a sun. She seemed to grow beneath her white robes. They exploded, revealing a body clad in silver fur. She was half human and half something else. Her mouth held fangs. Her hands ended in sharp claws. The Arch Priestess roared. The void shook by her mere fierceness. It was the most powerful, most shaking, most intimidating roar Jack had ever heard. The roar alone held extreme laws of the Dao. He would have been paralyzed if he was any closer.

The Arch Priestess was human from the waist down, but from the waist up and excluding her eyes, she was a silver lion. Not a leonine, like the Animal Kingdom Overlords, just a lion space monster. And she was a beast.

Unceremoniously, she pounced and bit at the sun. Her fangs carried more than just a physical touch. The Dao warped around her, as if the universe itself was trying to slaughter the sun. She pierced through the fire. Even at the peak B-Grade, her clone was far stronger than Elder Boatman's.

But it was not enough. As the Arch Priestess flew through the sun to reach Archon Summer Noon, he laughed and raised his muscular hands. He grabbed both her jaws, easily stopping her bite and momentum, then pulled them apart. Her mouth was torn up and down. It was a cruel sight, but she didn't show the slightest pain. Instead, her eyes were glued to his.

"*I will remember this!*" she shouted telepathically, spreading her voice to all who would listen. Archon Summer Noon laughed.

"I look forward to it!"

Fire enveloped her body, destroying it completely. The Archon then stepped through space to approach their fleeing starship.

They were close to the Space Monster World now. Very close. The swirling portal almost licked at them. But they wouldn't make it. The Archon was already upon them, and even if they wanted to sacrifice themselves, all three of them were far too weak.

Jack looked for a sliver of hope, an opportunity, anything. That was his instinct after so many years of battles. He wouldn't give up. Except there was nothing. His own strength was unworthy of mention. Even if he sacrificed himself, he couldn't delay the Archon's advance. At that moment, he hated himself for being weak.

Starhair was gazing at the window with wide eyes. He could also do nothing. The sun was falling again. Their skin was melting.

As for Brock, he had been struck the hardest of the three. Not only had he channeled all of his energy into the Arch Priestess—the only reason she achieved what she did—leaving him exhausted, but he'd also just watched his woman get torn apart. Even though it was a clone, the mental impact was striking. It briefly disturbed his Dao.

There was nothing else. Only them and the starship. Jack watched the falling sun and prepared to throw himself into it. Maybe, if he combusted all his energy and self-exploded, that would delay the strike a little, giving Brock and Starhair time to reach the portal.

Even as he prepared to jump, he could sense that Brock was doing the same thing. The pain hit him hard. His little brother was going to die. There was no time to hesitate or talk it out. Neither would step back. They would both go, and they would sacrifice their lives to save Starhair.

What a shitty ending.

Jack pressed against the melting floor, ready to launch himself upward. Right as his feet entered the metal, however, he touched upon something. A current of energy giving him a jolt. A current which remained strong despite the heat.

It was like a flash through his mind. He'd once noticed a subtle current of energy flowing through the starship. The *Iron Maiden* possessed weapons—it was just something he never thought he'd have to use. He didn't even know what it did.

"Wait, Brock!" he shouted as fast as he could.

Without thinking, Jack pumped energy into the current below him. It was quickly saturated. The entire ship grew alive around them, the half-melted walls unraveling, turning the entire starship inside out. Jack, Brock, and Starhair were suddenly floating in space, still flying toward the portal.

The ship demanded a target. Jack mentally gave it one. The inside out starship flew backward at incredible speed, erupting with a level of energy only slightly weaker than the Archon's. The Daos at play were far weaker, of course. Only now did Jack realize that this must have been Elder Boatman's personal method of transportation. It was enhanced with enough power to stall a peak B-Grade if needed. And the Elder had given it to them.

Suddenly, Elder Boatman's words didn't seem so weak: If you want to kill my disciple, you'll need to get through me!

Appreciation once again filled Jack's heart.

As the ship made some distance, Jack noticed its new shape. It hadn't just turned inside out. It had transformed into a flat sheet covered with spikes on one side. The fact that the whole thing was half-melted only made it more intimidating.

Archon Summer Noon had just released an attack, so he couldn't react in time. The starship reached him instantly. Despite that, Jack didn't dare hope. Just an Archon's passive defenses were not something the weapon of a late A-Grade could hope to pierce.

Thankfully, this wasn't just an attack.

The Archon's eyes widened. "No!" he shouted.

As the ship-turned-spiked sheet reached him, it wrapped around him. It formed a perfect sphere with the spikes turned inward, then contracted as if trying to ground him down. Jack had an epiphany—this was exactly why the ship was called *Iron Maiden*.

Of course, it wouldn't work. A pulse of power spread from the Archon, stopping the sphere's contraction. The magically enhanced metal was melting like paper in the fireplace.

Though for a single instant, it managed to contain the Archon.

He was no longer focusing on the attack heading for the starship. It'd lost a significant portion of its power.

Jack, Brock, and even Starhair worked together. The portal was right behind them. The attack would reach them first. They went all-out to defend.

Starhair had come to his senses, knowing he couldn't hold back—or maybe he was too terrified to think. He screamed in frustration as he uprooted three of his six strands of hair, sending them flying at the attack. Each shone red. Then, as one, they exploded. Jack realized it was actually the stars inside them, going off like miniature supernovas.

The explosion was powerful, enough to give the attack pause.

Brock went next. He overdrew his spent powers, manifesting a large golden brorilla around him to smash his staff forward. The golden phantom melted before it even touched the flames. However, the energy it released weakened them further. The strike was now at only a fraction of its original power.

Jack roared. His Life Form and Lightning Body worked in tandem. His punch shot forward. For a moment, everything came to a standstill—then erupted all at once. "*SUPERNOVA!*"

A blinding explosion filled the world. Sun flames met fist-shaped ones. The two attacks ground at each other until they were turned to nothing, leaving only a broken, wounded expanse of space. It regenerated far more slowly than usual.

Jack and the others were completely burned. But alive. The portal was near now, as the shockwave of the explosion had flung them closer. Through the shattered void, Jack glimpsed Archon Summer Noon. He'd just managed to vaporize the *Iron Maiden* around him. His hair flew wildly now, and his robes were torn in places. That attack had been stronger than Jack gave it credit for—it managed to almost injure an Archon.

No—there *was* a wound. It just wasn't one made by the starship. Through Archon Summer Noon's torn robes, Jack made out a fist-sized hole at the center of his chest. It seemed old.

Before he could consider this further, the Archon roared and released a new attack. “Get back here!” he commanded. Endless flames rose against them, but it was too late. Their backs touched the portal, and they were sucked in. The flames crashed against it ineffectively. It shook but held. The Archon roared in frustration.

As for Jack, Brock, and apparently Starhair... They’d entered the Space Monster World.

CHAPTER TWENTY-EIGHT

SPACE MONSTER WORLD

JACK FELT LIKE HE WAS GETTING TORN, FOLDED, SPUN, AND WRAPPED AROUND himself in timespace. He was everywhere and nowhere, all the time and never, all at once. The wormhole leading to the Space Monster World was by far the roughest he'd experienced.

The pressure would have annihilated any C-Grade who tried to enter. Even weaker B-Grades would struggle. To Jack, Brock, and Starhair, while the sensation was uncomfortable, it wasn't dangerous. Even in their injured and exhausted state.

The wormhole spat them out on a field of dry ground. They tumbled, grabbing a hold of themselves. Jack suppressed a groan as his heavily burnt skin rubbed against hard dirt. His focus was whisked away to the fact that he couldn't breathe. It took him some time to adjust. As he lay face-up on the ground, gazing at a crimson sky, he felt as if the weight of the entire world was placed on his chest.

"Is everyone okay?" he managed to say after a while.

"I'm fine," Brock replied.

"I'm... fine as well," Starhair said, sounding far less confident.

Jack laboriously turned his head over. Starhair once wore pristine blue robes made of the finest silk. Now, that silk had melted against his skin, and whatever blue remained was marred by a river of blood which flowed from the top of his head. Half his hair was missing—or, actually, it was more accurate to say that his scalp had been removed in those places, revealing patches of bone underneath.

"Shit," Jack said, rushing to stand. "That looks terrible."

"I'm fine," Starhair repeated through gritted teeth. He ripped away whatever remained of his robes and wrapped it around his head like a turban. The gruesome sight was hidden, but his pain remained.

"That's not fine, Starhair," Jack said. "You're seriously injured. We got to help you."

"I said it's fine," the man stubbornly replied. Jack could see the emotions whirling in his eyes—pain, despair, frustration, and a bone-deep fear. "I'm not supposed to be here," Starhair continued, looking around. "This is the Space Monster World. I would have returned with Elder Boatman. I shouldn't be here."

"You are now, and we'll make the best of it." Jack laid a hand on his shoulder. There was an entire world around them just begging to be explored, but he prioritized ensuring that Starhair was okay. After all, he'd injured himself to save them. To save himself, actually, but Jack and Brock had still benefited, so letting him be would be ungrateful.

Starhair tried to say something but flinched in pain. He groaned. "I... I severed half my cultivation," he said as if only just realizing it. His eyes grew cloudy. "Fuck. I shouldn't have done that. I got scared. Fuck. *Fuck*."

"Hey, man, it's gonna be alright," Jack said. "Take deep breaths. You're alive, and you're young. You'll regain it all."

"Yeah, in centuries!" Starhair laughed. "We're going into war and I'm a cripple! In a hostile hidden world! Oh, what an idiot I am. What a cowardly fool!"

Jack turned to Brock, raising a brow. The brorilla was also

injured, but nothing too serious. Just burns which were already regenerating and a fading, and heavy exhaustion.

Brock paced over. “It’s okay, bro,” he told Starhair. “You relax for now. Turn off your mind. Let us find a safe place first, and then we’ll talk.”

Starhair nodded.

Only now, as Brock turned his gaze upward, did Jack follow.

The Space Monster World stretched endlessly all around them. They were on a barren wasteland, like the terrain at the edge of a desert—yellow, dry, infertile ground with only the occasional weed growing. Trees were few and far between. This terrain stretched as far as the eye could see—or their Dao perceptions. Jack noticed no curvature of the ground, indicating they were on some sort of flat world.

Overhead, crimson skies cast their glow. On closer inspection, they were made up of endless crimson clouds, sparking with similarly crimson lightning as if a storm was constantly underway inside them. The light was low in intensity, similar to a full-moon Earth night, but flashes of red occasionally brightened the world, giving it a dark and bloody feel. There was no rain.

Most importantly, this world was not hospitable at all. The ambient temperature was enough to boil water. The Dao density was so suffocatingly high that anyone below the D-Grade would exhaust themselves in minutes and then be crushed to the ground. Even Jack felt his powers grow weaker by at least ten times, and that was only because he was a B-Grade. His power came from his inner world. If he was still a D or C-Grade, who harnessed the ambient Dao to exercise their cultivations, he would be similar to a mortal in this place. So wild was the Dao.

He’d experienced a similar suppression before, at the Green Dragon Realm, but this one was even more intense. He suspected that anyone below the B-Grade would be unable to fly.

Jack looked around, taking stock of all these things. However, he didn’t see even one living creature.

"What do you think we should do?" he asked. "Stay here and recover? Or scout things out?"

"Staying here would be the safest," Brock replied. "Let's recover a little. Then we can keep going. Resting too much is un-bro-like."

Jack laughed. "You got it, bro." They settled down cross-legged. Starhair did too, though still wearing an expression of pain. There was nothing they could do to help him. He needed time.

Ten minutes later, Jack and Brock's burns had fully regenerated. Their skin was pink and healthy like a baby's. It would have happened far faster, but these burns were oddly stubborn.

"I still can't believe they sent an Archon after us. That was fucking scary," Jack said, flexing his fingers. "I didn't expect them to be so decisive."

"The Immortals are robots. They lack emotions. They wouldn't underestimate us out of arrogance," Brock replied.

"I know. Still, well played by them... We may have survived, but our protector is gone, and we barely made it."

"You know what that means, right, bro?" Brock smiled. "We survived the attack of an Archon. We're strong."

Jack smiled back. They high-fived.

"Let's get out of here," Jack said. "I don't like how exposed we are. Should I ask our guide?"

"Please do, bro."

Jack reached into his inner world. "*Hey, turtle,*" he said. "*Are you awake?*"

"I'm always awake," Venerable Saint Thousand Shell's voice echoed in his mind. "That was one hell of a battle, kid. Good job. Very good job."

"Thanks. We're in the Space Monster World now. Do you recognize this place?" Jack sent it a mental image of their surroundings. The turtle scoffed.

"What am I, an encyclopedia? The Space Monster World is so humongous that I haven't even traveled one hundredth of it. Even if I had been through this place, I wouldn't necessarily recognize it. It's been a billion

years. I bet all the terrain I know has changed by now. You should just go find a local and ask for information."

"A local?" Jack frowned. *"I'm a cultivator. Won't they try to kill me?"*

"Oh, man up, kid. You're strong. No matter how powerful the space monsters, the chances of you randomly running into an A-Grade are practically zero. Just beat the shit out of whatever you find and interrogate them. I'll translate for you as needed."

Jack had to admit that made sense. "*Okay. Thanks.*"

"*Anytime.*"

"The turtle says we should just find a local and interrogate them," he told the others, then pointed at a random direction. "Wanna go that way?"

"Lead the way, bro."

Starhair didn't say anything, just got up and prepared to follow. His aura felt far weaker than normal. If Jack had to guess, his power level was now closer to a middle B-Grade than a peak one. It sucked.

He saved us, Jack thought. *If there's a way to help him, I will.*

He took to the air. The other two followed. They cut through the skies like a trio of missiles, keeping their altitude low to avoid being detected.

Five minutes passed. They couldn't easily teleport due to the Dao density, but their speed remained great. If they were in America, they would have crossed an entire state by now. In the Space Monster World, the terrain remained identical. Barren wasteland as far as the eye could see. Jack was beginning to wonder if the entire world was like this. Even his Dao perception, which spread far farther than his eyesight, was met with the exact same terrain.

After a time, he spotted something different. A pair of horses galloped through the wasteland—the first living creatures he'd seen. Of course, they were more like horses from hell than regular horses. Their manes were made of dark flames. Fiery prints were left where their hooves met the ground, their eyes were red, and their entire bodies were thickly corded with muscle. Each was seven feet tall.

Despite their intimidating exterior, the power of these animals was nothing threatening. They were at the D-Grade. Jack was about to ignore them before he realized that this was the Space Monster World—why would the locals resemble humans? These horses might well be intelligent creatures.

He led the others to turn toward the horses, overtake them instantly, and smash into the ground right in front of them. The two horses screeched to a halt and rose on their hind legs. When the dust cleared—falling faster due to the increased gravity—the horses saw Jack's form clearly. The leading one released smoke from its nostrils and opened its mouth to reveal bloodied, flat teeth.

"OUTSIDERS!" it cried out. "DIE!"

Its voice was dark and devilish. It spoke in a strange language Jack didn't understand—full of growls and clicks—but Venerable Saint Thousand Shell supplied instant translation.

The horse brought its front hooves right on Jack's face. He raised two hands to grab them, easily stopping the horse, then raised it over his head and slammed it on the ground behind him. A crater appeared.

"Are you guys idiots?" he said in English. "We fly and do a superhero landing in your faces, and you choose to attack us? Jesus."

The horses didn't seem to understand him. He suspected it wouldn't matter anyway. The second horse lunged at him, head turned sideways and jaws opened wide to shatter his face. He punched it hard enough to send it flying. As for the first horse, after it recovered, it made the mistake of attacking Brock. The brorilla slapped it so hard that half its teeth went flying, and the entire horse spun three times around itself before landing.

"Bad bro," he said. "Do not attack your big bros."

The horse neighed sadly from the ground. It hadn't received a serious injury, but it now apparently acknowledged its defeat. The other horse galloped over from where Jack had sent it flying, and the two of them sat on the ground, proudly accepting their fates.

"YOU ARE STRONGER," the leading horse said. "KILL US."

"What are they saying, bro?" Brock asked. "Should I bro slap them again?"

"It's fine. They surrender," Jack explained. "But they're fucking weird. First they attack us without a care in the world. Then they surrender and ask for death. Like, what the fuck?"

"We should find a way to speak to them," Brock suggested.

Jack nodded. "Hey, turtle. Can you translate what I'm about to tell them? I'll tell you, you tell me what sounds I need to make, and I'll make them."

"Only if you say my name properly."

He sighed. "Please, Venerable Saint Thousand Shell."

"I accept your apology," the turtle replied triumphantly. "What do you want to tell them?"

"That I need some information, and they'd better give it to me."

CHAPTER TWENTY-NINE

DOUBLE TROUBLE

The turtle instructed him on what sounds to make. It was easy with his intelligence, just weird. The space monster language was unique, involving all sorts of sounds ranging from clicks, to howls, to actual letters. It felt like tongue yoga.

He made the right sounds anyway—well, the closest he could come to them. It took some practice.

"WHAT INFORMATION?" the horse asked, all business. "WILL YOU NOT KILL US?"

"If I wanted to kill you, you'd already be dead," he replied, still butchering their language.

The horses glanced at each other. "WE ARE NOT DEAF."

"That's not what I—Anyway. Just don't try anything stupid, okay?"

"OKAY. WE DO HAVE EARS, BY THE WAY. THEY'RE UNDER THE FUR."

"Cool. Can you stop shouting?"

"I AM NOT SHOUTING."

Jack suddenly felt the urge to go find other space monsters to interrogate. But maybe they'd all be shouting. *Oh god.*

"Tell me about this world," he said. "Where are we?"

"THE ASTARION PROVINCE."

"Okay. How many provinces are there?"

"I DO NOT KNOW. MORE THAN ONE."

"Very helpful. Who's the strongest space monster here? Do you have A-Grades?"

"PROVINCE MASTER ASTARION. HE IS VERY STRONG."

"How strong?"

"VERY. STRONGER THAN US. STRONGER THAN YOU."

"Would you call him an A-Grade?"

"WHAT IS THAT?"

"Space monsters are not familiar with the System's Grades," the turtle explained to Jack. "They use different classifications. From D-Grade to Archon, they call themselves dukes, counts, Barons, Autarchs, and Overlords."

"That's fucking stupid. It's the reverse order of British royalty."

"I don't make the rules."

Jack sighed. "Is your province master an Autarch?" he asked.

"YES."

"Okay. Does he have, like, a faction of Autarchs?"

"NO. THE ASTARION PROVINCE IS AN OUTER PROVINCE. AUTARCHS ONLY COME OUT HERE TO BE PROVINCE MASTERS."

"So there are outer provinces. That's good to know. I suppose there are inner ones as well?"

"YES. OUTER PROVINCES, INNER, AND CORE. ONLY TWO CORE PROVINCES. THE OVERLORDS."

"That makes sense. So the Space Monster World is separated in provinces, with each province master being an Autarch, and the innermost you go, the higher the level of people. Correct?"

The horse thought for a moment. "YES. BUT NOT ALL PROVINCE MASTERS ARE AUTARCHS. SOME ARE BARONS."

"But not in the inner provinces?"

"NO. ALL AUTARCHS THERE."

"And why do you call the provinces core, inner, and outer? Is there a center?"

"THE WORLD IS RINGS. THE DARK CANAL IS AT THE CENTER. WORSHIP THE DARK CANAL."

"What's the Dark Canal?"

"I DO NOT KNOW. BUT IT MUST BE WORSHIPED."

Jack turned to his friends and relayed the information he'd received.

"Ask it for directions to that Dark Canal," Brock suggested. "The inner and core provinces will be located that way as well. If we want to farm space monster cores, that's where we'll find the good ones."

Jack nodded in agreement. He asked the horses, which pointed him in a certain direction—the exact opposite of the one they'd been following before.

"Nice guess, bro," Brock said, giving Jack a thumbs-up.

"Well, we have our directions," Jack said. "Should we leave? I think these horses are pretty stupid, to be honest. We're better off finding someone smarter on the way."

"I agree. We should kill them, too, or they might spread information about us being here."

Jack turned to the horses. "It's a shame. I know they tried attacking us first, and that we have to kill them, but they've been pretty obedient since we subdued them." He sighed, raising a fist. The horses neighed sadly and closed their eyes. "I guess if I have to."

"Space monsters submit completely to the stronger party," the turtle explained lazily as Jack's fist came crashing down. "If the stronger party isn't clearly indicated, they fight on sight. However, if you don't want to kill them, why not take them as your mounts?"

Jack's fist stopped an inch away from the leading horse's muzzle. The wind ruffled its mane of dark flame.

"Go on," he said.

"If they wish to become your followers, they can spit out their core into your care. That way, you can kill them anytime you wish, meaning they will never betray you."

"Hmm." Jack frowned. "That sounds a bit extreme."

"You can always ask them, but they'd certainly prefer it to dying. Becoming the mount of a powerful individual is no shame in the Space Monster World. It can even be a kind of honor. Every high-status space monster has a mount."

"Why would I take them as a mount? I'm way faster."

"You don't need to ride them. If you have their core, you can store the entire monster in your inner world. Just take them out as you reach a city to show your status."

Jack hesitated, then simply asked, "Do you guys prefer to die or become our mounts?"

The horses glanced at each other. "YOU ARE OUTSIDERS. WE MUST FIGHT YOU TO THE DEATH."

"Don't be like that," Brock said, stepping forward. "Just because we come from outside this world doesn't mean we need to be enemies. We're not so different, after all. Let's work together instead of being brainwashed to kill each other. Let's be bros."

"Wait, you understood what they said?" Jack asked.

"Of course. The Bro Code supersedes language."

"Then why did you let me translate? And where did you learn that word?"

"I've been reading the dictionary."

Jack gave him an odd glance. Meanwhile, the horses visibly shook, their mental barriers evaporating to liberate their free will due to Brock's brohood. They could now think clearly.

"HE HAS A POINT," one of them said.

"I AGREE. LET'S BECOME MOUNTS."

"YES."

Both horses turned to Jack, suddenly speaking in the common language of the universe. "YOU ARE A STRONG MASTER. WE WILL SERVE YOU WELL."

He raised a brow in amusement. "Even though I am an outsider?"

"IT MEANS NOTHING. YOU DEFEATED US. OUR LIVES BELONG TO YOU."

"First Brock, now you. How can you can speak our language?"

"This is the language of the Space Monster World. Everyone speaks it. We were speaking in hellhorse before to be rude."

Jack shrugged. "Alright, guys," he said, turning to Brock and Starhair. "We're now friends with these bad boys."

Brock looked at him weirdly. "They're female," he said. Starhair still seemed out of sorts. He just shrugged and nodded.

"Cool," Jack said.

The two horses shook as if about to vomit. Then, with a dry heave, a solid gem emerged from each of their throats. They were dark red and with swirling flames inside—pretty, if not particularly powerful. When Jack touched one, he felt a connection to a different being, an entity of chaos. The hellhorse.

The sense of complete control was fascinating.

"WE BELONG TO YOU, MASTERS," the horses said, bending their front feet to bow.

Jack laughed. "Don't be like that. We're friends."

"FRIENDS?"

"That's right. Friends, bros. As long as you don't betray us, we're all in the same team."

"BUT YOU'RE STRONGER."

"That's alright."

The two hellhorses were clearly confused, but they'd get used to it.

Jack took one core into his inner realm, while Brock did the same to the other.

"Do you have names?" he asked the horses.

"I AM DOLPARTAZOL THE HARBINGER OF DOOM," the leading horse replied. "AND THIS IS EZAQUIL THE ETERNAL DAWN."

"Okay. Then, I will call you Dolly," Jack told it.

"And I will call you Eza," Brock said to the other one.

Suddenly, Jack realized something. He reached into his space ring and removed a carrot. He'd had it there since the last time he visited

Earth. In fact, he had entire boxes of vegetables. They didn't go bad in space rings.

"Do you want a carrot, Dolly?" he asked. "The horses on my planet like it. They're significantly less infernal than you, but we might as well try."

Dolpartazol, the self-appointed harbinger of doom, ate the carrot. "IT IS VERY TASTY, MASTER. THIS IS NOW MY FAVORITE FOOD. CAN I HAVE ANOTHER?"

"Just one, okay? No more until we reach... whatever destination we're planning to reach."

"OKAY, MASTER."

As Dolly enjoyed her second carrot, consuming it in small bites to make it last longer, Jack turned to the others. "There's one more thing we gotta do. We can't be walking around like this in civilization centers. They'll attack us on sight."

He reached into his space ring again and took out a shining blue liquid. It resembled a sea of stars. Even from inside the bottle, this potion radiated power intense enough for Dolly to stop mid-bite and stare at it.

They had known they'd need disguises. The Arch Priestess had gone to great lengths to secure three transformation potions of the highest caliber. They would remain active no matter how hard they fought or exerted themselves, and the disguise would fool anybody unless they came face-to-face with an Archon.

They originally had three potions—one for Jack, Brock, and the Arch Priestess's clone, the people who were supposed to enter the Space Monster World. Unfortunately, the Arch Priestess clone had kept hers on her person, so it was destroyed. Jack now only had two potions for three people and no way to create another.

"I'll be fine without," Brock said. "I'm a brorilla. I can fit in."

"Are you sure?" Jack asked.

"No. But we can try."

Jack nodded. They had no other choice. He gave one potion to Starhair, but before using them, they had to find suitable forms.

Once they ingested the potions, the disguise could not be changed or taken off.

"Show me the most common race of humanoid space monsters," Jack asked Dolly, connecting his mind to hers. She projected an image to him. Jack ingested his potion.

He felt his body change. Bones snapped into place. Some shattered while new ones grew. His flesh was torn apart as his entire form was restructured. When the transformation was done, Jack was a hulking humanoid, pale green in color. He stood nine feet tall, with short horns sticking out of his forehead and lines of spikes trailing his spine and limbs. Two bat-like wings spread from his back, though he could easily fold them if he wanted to, and a thick tail extended from his lower back. His hands and feet ended in sharp claws. Thankfully, he could still make them into fists. He'd also changed his facial structure a little bit—after all, the Overlords had seen his face during the summit, so they might recognize him from afar.

Overall, Jack's new form looked like a green devil. Completely bad-ass. The only problem was that he, apparently, possessed two sets of male genitalia, one hanging above the other. That change alone felt so damn weird.

Good thing his magical shorts had changed to fit his new size.

Brock observed the transformation with interest. Starhair, however, was shaking. "That looked like it hurt," he said.

"A little bit," Jack confirmed. His voice had gotten deeper and guttural. "But it's just for a minute. Come on. Drink your potion."

"...I don't want to."

"Then we'll have to leave you here. We can't carry around an outsider with us."

Starhair gulped. He looked at the potion, observing the blue stars inside it, then gulped it down. "Okay. It's not that—" He instantly started convulsing. He fell to the ground and started writhing as he screamed in pain.

Jack scratched his head. When he said it only hurt a little bit, he hadn't been lying. It was just that his pain perception was apparently skewed by everything he'd experienced.

Oh well, he thought. He'll be fine. A little bit of suffering builds character.

Two minutes later, Starhair lay on the ground, panting in his new body. It looked exactly like Jack's, except with a different face. They also had other minor differences, but overall, Jack thought they would easily pass as two members of this space monster species.

"What are we called, anyway?" he asked Dolly.

"DOUBLE DEVIL," she replied. "AND I HAVE TO SAY, MASTER, YOU LOOK DASHING. YOU WERE HIDEOUS BEFORE. ALL FLESH AND NO ARMOR. NOW YOU'RE A PROPER SPACE MONSTER."

"Thanks..." he replied, then turned to the others. "Okay, everyone. We're ready. Let's head for the inner provinces—and maybe find someone smarter to interrogate."

CHAPTER THIRTY

CROSSING THE SPACE MONSTER WORLD

THE WAY LEADING TO THE CENTER OF THE SPACE MONSTER WORLD WAS AS deserted as Jack imagined. At least, at first. The dry ground continued unabated. Even after an hour of flying, covering tens of thousands of miles, it persisted.

"What the hell?" Jack asked mentally. "Is the Space Monster World empty?"

"At the outer provinces, yes," Venerable Saint Thousand Shell replied. "The world is huge, but the environment out here is not the best. Most importantly, space monsters suck at coexisting. The constant killing prevents the population from growing."

Jack took another look around. Emptiness, as far as met the eye. This world really was huge—so much it made him wonder.

The Green Dragon Realm was the masterpiece of Archon Green Dragon, who specialized in spacetime and had even used a part of his body to create the Realm Heart. Despite that, the end result was only a hundred thousand miles in diameter. Which Jack had never thought of as small before, but this Space Monster World was significantly larger. If the Green Dragon Realm was placed here, it would just be another province. This world was far more stable, too, almost like the universe.

"Who even made this place?" Jack asked the turtle. *"And don't tell me it occurred naturally."*

"The history of the Space Monster World goes too far back... When I was born, a billion years ago, the truth was already lost in time. We weren't always sapient. It took millions of years for us space monsters to develop the ability to record history, and by then, whoever created this world was gone. We only know what we see."

"Don't give me that. What about the seal outside the world, keeping A-Grades out? What about this Dark Canal Dolly mentioned?"

"There are theories. At the time, the most powerful entities in the universe were the Old Gods, but even they would be hard-pressed to create such a vast world and such a powerful seal around it. Some monsters claim our world was created by Axelor to match Enas's act of birthing the Ancients. Others say that we, and this entire world, are natural creations of the universe. That nobody would have the power to establish this place artificially. Some even say this is a separate universe which just failed to develop fully."

"And the Dark Canal?"

"Here, too, there are theories. Some say it contains the secret to immortality. Others, that it holds clues to the realm above Overlord. They even say it is the resting place of the original creator of the Space Monster World. Unfortunately, I've never been there, so I can't tell you. Besides the two Overlord factions who control it, nobody knows what really lies inside."

That was intriguing.

"Could there really be someone above Archons?" Jack asked.

"No," the turtle replied immediately. *"People love to speculate, but it is impossible. There is no realm beyond Archon. Think about it. Even the hardest bottlenecks in cultivation have a success rate of one in a hundred, maybe one in a thousand. There have been thousands of Archons since the start of history. Some have reached that realm with overwhelming momentum, rising head*

and shoulders above their peers. Yet, of every single Archon in history, nobody has touched the next realm. Nobody has even glimpsed it. There is just no way forward. Even the Old Gods themselves are only extreme Archons."

"Hmm. We'll see."

The turtle snorted with laughter. "If you really want to find out, kid, just go up there and try yourself. Maybe then you'll be satisfied. Just don't hold out hope. I was the spiritual companion of Archon Black Hole, an exceptional man even amongst Archons, and even he had expressed to me how impossible it was to advance further."

Jack refused to be brought down. "I have devoted my life to pursuing the peak," he replied lightly. "If that peak is the Archon realm, then so be it. If there is more, then I will reach that too."

"Well said. That's why I like you, kid. You're so headstrong you can't possibly fail."

Jack chuckled. "*Thanks.*"

"Look," Brock said, drawing Jack's attention. "There's someone over there."

"Hmm?"

He saw it, too. A lone humanoid walked in the distance. It was a double devil, the species Jack and Starhair had transformed into. It was moving in the same direction as them, just far slower, so overtaking it would be easy.

"Shall we?" Jack asked. They had several things to check.

"We shall," Brock replied. The three of them accelerated, speeding off into the sky and landing before the double devil shortly after.

It froze, then quickly, it said, "I submit."

That was a nice change of pace from being attacked on sight. It indicated their disguises were working, and that Brock could pass as a space monster as well. Inwardly, Jack was relieved this thing wasn't shouting—if everyone was as loud as their two horses, it would get old really fast. The double devil was also speaking their language. As the hell horses had said, this was the universal language of the Space Monster World.

Jack took a better look at the double devil. It was green-skinned and of similar size as him and Starhair. Unlike them, it wore an attire one would find on an Earth desert, with brown robes falling loosely over its body. Red pants reached to its knee, while flaps of fabric wrapped around its head, only revealing its eyes and mouth. Jack guessed that lower-level double devils needed protection from the elements around here. This one was only a peak D-Grade.

"Relax," he said, speaking in a similar guttural voice to the other devil. "We don't care about you. We just want directions. Which way are the inner provinces?"

The devil gave him an odd look. Jack didn't care if he'd misspoken; at worst, they'd interrogate and kill this guy.

His intentions must have shown, because the double devil averted its eyes and turned extremely subservient.

"It's that way, my Baron," it said respectfully, pointing in the direction it had been following as well. "Right past a small settlement called Bone Ring. I was on my way there as well to trade."

"Oh? What does a weakling like you have to trade?"

Jack was trying to mimic the crude manner of speaking used by space monsters. The double devil didn't seem to sense anything off. It revealed an expression of pain as it reached into its pouch and retrieved a pair of gem-inlaid rings.

"I found these two, my Baron," it said. It stretched its hands out, clearly unwilling. "Please, take them."

Jack glanced at the rings. He didn't question just how the devil had "found" them. "I don't want your trash," he said. Then, followed by Brock and Starhair, he took to the sky and shattered the sound barrier multiple times on their way out. They'd angled their course in the direction the double devil had indicated.

"Well done, kid," the turtle said. "You spoke like a true space monster! It seems your disguises work, too. That priestess kid knew what she was doing. As long as Brock doesn't let anyone probe his soul, you'll be fine."

Jack nodded.

While they'd gotten instructions from Dolly and Aze before, it was easy to get lost in such an expansive, featureless place. Finger-pointing could only get you so far. Until Jack found a reliable way to navigate, stopping every once in a while to ask the locals was the best way to go about it.

Speaking of Dolly and Aze, the two hellhorses were currently floating in Jack and Brock's inner world respectively. Jack glanced inward. Dolly was ineffectively wheeling her feet as she slowly traveled through space. Floating beside her was The Stone, explaining just why horses shouldn't wear metal horseshoes. Dolly was listening with rapt attention.

"IS THAT SO?" she asked. "YOUR WISDOM IS STUNNING. TELL ME MORE."

"Certainly! So you see, your body has methods to adjust itself. Placing iron below your hoof is a sure-fire way to disrupt your temperature regulation, your grip on the ground, and your natural defenses against wear and tear. It is a crude solution for crude situations. If I was a horse, I would—"

Jack tuned off, letting the two continue their conversation. He'd already figured out how to isolate the sound coming from his inner world. At least The Stone had company now.

They kept flying. This world's increased Dao density made everything more tiring, so they stopped every now and then to ensure they remained at peak condition, in case anything happened. On the way, Jack sometimes chatted with Brock or the turtle, while Starhair remained downcast and silent.

It was another half hour before they passed by the settlement the double devil had mentioned. Aptly named the Bone Ring, this place resembled a desert fort with large bones arranged around it, sticking out of the ground with their tips facing the sky. It was like the entire fort was built inside the palm of an ancient, buried monster.

They didn't stop here. Such a small settlement on a far-out location would mean nothing. Jack doubted there were even any B-Grades present. They only swooped down to ask another passing local for directions—a bipedal bison monster—before continuing on their way.

Finally, two hours after the start of their trip, the terrain began to change. The dry ground gave way to mild greenery, and the boiling temperature receded, replaced by an only slightly superhuman heat wave. Instead of weeds, bushes and trees now covered the ground. They weren't dense by any means, but the area was at least slightly vegetated.

"This must be the inner province," Jack said.

"Think again, kid," the turtle interjected. "It's just another outer province. The entrance portal to this world places you somewhere close to the outer edges, so you have to cross at least two or three outer provinces before you approach the inner ones. Unless, of course, things have changed since the last time I was here."

Jack whistled. "Just how large is this world?"

"Millions upon millions of miles. Even the outer provinces aren't the end of it. There is another ring behind them simply called the Inhospitable Zone. Its environment is too unstable. Nobody in their right mind would choose to live there, even if they could."

The entire circumference of the Earth was only twenty-five thousand miles. For this world to have a width of millions of miles... It really was large beyond belief. The total area was in the trillions of square miles.

Refueled by this new knowledge, the three of them soldiered on.

"Do you know which province this is, Dolly?" Jack asked, having taken out his hellhorse and holding her aloft.

"IT IS NOT THE ASTARION PROVINCE," she replied. She kept gazing at the distant ground with suspicion—horses were not used to flying.

"And you know because the terrain changed?"

"IT MAKES FOR EASY BORDERS."

"I see. Thanks, Dolly."

"NO PROBLEM, MASTER."

He put the horse back into his inner world. They continued

flying. Given the only slightly more hospitable terrain, Jack could now see more space monsters around. The vast majority were bestial, grazing upon the rare blade of grass and attacking everything on sight. Each and every one of them had a hellish appearance.

The intelligent locals were mostly double devils. Jack saw a smattering of other species, all diverse beyond reason, including a humanoid species with four legs, three eyes, and a face which naturally resembled a creepy clown's. He steered the heck away from those. There were also many sapient species which weren't humanoid. The two hellhorses were a good example of that.

The existence of non-humanoid sapients meant that anything they saw could be a cultivator or an animal. Unless Jack memorized the species, it would be difficult to tell from a distance. It went the other way, too. At one point, they came down to ask a humanoid gorilla-thing with four arms for directions, but it could only growl and spit at them as it ineffectively tried to attack. Once it realized it was pointless, it transformed into a stone statue, which promptly fell to the ground and shattered by itself.

Fucking weird.

So far, the strongest creatures they'd encountered were at the middle C-Grade level. Nothing stronger. They assumed—and the turtle confirmed—that stronger space monsters would only be present at the inner and core provinces. The outer provinces did have their province master, but there typically wasn't a capital, so looking for them across an entire province was pointless.

Therefore, they ignored everything and made a beeline for the center of this world. Nobody had time to waste on weaklings.

CHAPTER THIRTY-ONE
EMPTY STAR CITY

INNER PROVINCES, EMPTY STAR PROVINCE...

The Dao density had shot up again. Jack, Brock, and Starhair felt even more restricted, like swimming in a mire. The very air itself was made of Dao.

Lush greenery spread below them. Forests teeming with life, beautiful lakes, snow-capped mountains. Nature spread all around, vitalized by the extreme Dao energies in the atmosphere. Of course, not everything was pleasant. The beasts inhabiting this place were hellish, with horns and dark flames and all sorts of dark signs on their bodies. Jack tried to feed a squirrel only for it to unhinge its jaw like a snake and try to eat his hand. Brock befriended the critter anyway.

Everything here was strong—a direct product of the high Dao density. Even the snake-squirrel thing possessed power at the D-Grade, with the various wild animals reaching up to the B-Grade, if rarely. They also killed each other at all times. The forest floor was strewn with low-level space monster cores, which one could gather if they only had the courage to wade into the hellish beast territory. If left untouched for a bit, worm-like creatures emerged from the ground to consume these cores, using their power to transform into stronger monsters. Jack saw a worm absorb a D-Grade core, then grow into an early D-Grade, hippo-like creature.

His biologist sense was tingling. These things were not, of course, animals. The most plausible scenario was that space monsters were basically bundles of energy, with their bodies being only an instinctive coating of that energy. Kind of like clothes were to humans. As space monsters consumed the cores of others, their own power increased, and they chose more powerful bodies to reflect that. Even the trees were monsters.

It was a unique ecosystem. One that worked despite being in constant violence.

These were the inner provinces.

Jack took a deep breath, letting the ambient Dao purify his lungs. "I like this place," he said.

"It gives me the creeps," Starhair replied from the side. The two still wore their double devil disguises, which made Starhair's response seem out of place.

"Where there are bros, everything is okay," Brock said. The squirrel sitting on his shoulder unhinged its mouth and tried to bite Brock's ear off. The brorilla swatted it away. "Bad bro. No biting bros."

The squirrel whimpered in disappointment.

"The city shouldn't be far," Jack said. "Let's continue."

It had taken them an entire day to cross the outer provinces, even at their speed. Then at some point, the desolate landscape and terrible environmental conditions had disappeared, giving way to a lively world. The Space Monster World wasn't as uniformly desolate as Jack originally assumed. It could be beautiful.

Their destination, Empty Star City, was proof of that beauty.

A rising of white houses over the water emerged. An entire city built on a rock in a river, with a titanic waterfall cascading just to the side. This waterfall tumbled down a steep cliff, a mountainside which arced out like a ring, placing the river and the city on a flat surface dozens of miles above the ground, the cliff itself stretching beyond where the eye could see.

The natural environment was on a different scale here. The cliff was taller than Mount Everest. The river was wide like a sea. A single rock island on its path was large enough to host a city.

It made them feel small.

As Jack and company approached Empty Star City, they witnessed more signs of civilization. Space monsters arrived in boats, swimming, or walking on water. Some were climbing the cliff to reach the city, while a few rode flying treasures. Even fewer were the ones who could fly by themselves—B-Grades, or Barons, as they were called in this place. Hundreds of space monsters moved in and out of the city, the diversity of species striking.

Besides those who came in groups, everyone basically belonged to a different species than everybody else. Moreover, since these weren't real bodies but more like placeholders, they didn't need to make biological sense, leading to a plethora of appearances. Everything was possible, from floating eyeballs to golems of clay.

Jack remembered some creatures back at the original Cathedral who resembled glass panes with limbs. In hindsight, maybe they were space monsters too.

This was by far the largest city they'd come across in the Space Monster World, and also the first they were going to enter. All the others, they'd just watched from a distance. This was the first time they truly allowed themselves to merge with the coming and going of space monsters. It was an awe-inspiring experience.

Of course, merging was just a word. The moment they arrived at the city gates flying, indicating they were Barons, the surrounding space monsters fell over each other to give them space. An alligator-thing accidentally stepped over a hyena-thing—the two monsters and their groups quickly came to blows. Blood flew.

Jack looked at the carnage with indifference, just like the rest of the crowd. This was the Space Monster World. Killing was their way. Even the C-Grade guards posted at the city did nothing to stop the battle. Their only job was to guard the buildings. Everyone could enter, exit, and fight as they pleased.

The hyena group won, triumphantly tearing out the cores of the alligator group and swallowing them whole, blood and all. Jack didn't pay them too much attention. The rest of the crowd closed around them, uncaring as well, and the hyenas went on their way. Everyone spoke the same language as in the outside universe.

Jack, Brock, and Starhair were already busy. Jack and Brock reached into their inner worlds. In the next moment, two hellhorses stumbled into reality, their intense body heat scaring away the nearest space monsters. It took them a moment to orient themselves. When they did, they were overjoyed.

"I AM HERE, MASTER! LET ME SERVE YOU!" Dolly said as Jack jumped on her back. She glared toward the gate. "ANYONE WHO BARS MY MASTER'S PATH IS COURTING DEATH!"

The space monsters all stepped back even farther.

Jack patted her neck. "Easy, Dolly. Let's just walk in."

"*When in space monster land, do as space monsters do,*" Brock told him telepathically. His own hellhorse, Eza, was already slinging slurs at the nearest space monsters—what Jack assumed were slurs. No space monster would enjoy being called a "MOLD-COVERED SNAKE WORM."

"You know what?" he told Dolly. "You can scare them a bit. Just don't eat anyone."

"BUT I WANT TO EAT THEM."

"Maybe only the ones who start trouble."

Dolly neighed sadly but obliged. Starhair jumped on her back, right behind Jack, and the five of them entered the city.

White buildings surrounded them on all sides. They ranged from one to three floors. The streets snaked in odd directions, clearly built without any care for order, and it went without saying that thieves and murderers waited behind every turn. For a weaker monster, entering those streets was suicide.

There was, however, a larger, straighter street heading from the entrance to the center of Empty Star City. It was exactly this street that Jack followed. Shops lined its sides, manned by C-Grade space monsters selling everything the mind could think of. Weapons, armor, fabric, clothes, food, drink, prostitution, building materials, and much more. Everything was thrown haphazardly onto this street, all cobbled together into a huge mess.

Notably, despite the vast diversity in strength and species between space monsters, there were no children. They didn't procreate like humans did. New space monsters emerged as the worms Jack had seen in the forests outside the town, and then they slowly developed over time. Although, sex was a thing, so he had to wonder just how space monsters came up with that.

"What exactly are we doing here?" Starhair whispered.

"Recon, mostly," Jack replied. "This place should have at least one A-Grade or two, but we can't just hunt them down. Let's find a place to stay, talk to some locals. If we want to go around hunting A-Grades, we can't do so blindly. We need to know exactly how things work. We need a plan, and this is the best place to make one."

Starhair nodded. "Alright."

"LOOK AWAY, BUTTERCUP. MY MASTER IS THE SUN TO YOU."

Dolly remained on fire—literally and metaphorically. As they moved through the streets, she and Eza were cursing at any pedestrian slightly late to walk away, or snapping their jaws in the direction of people they disliked. The horses themselves weren't particularly powerful, but the towering aura of Jack, Brock, and Starhair kept everyone else at bay. There was clear awe in the eyes of any space monster around them.

Taking the hellhorses was a nice idea after all. It helped them blend in. The surrounding space monsters seemed to approve of this chaos, whereas Jack had a tendency to remain low-key. Usually until he spanked someone.

The crowd thickened as they approached downtown. Jack was forced to slow down a bit, unwilling to let Dolly and Eza stampede the crowd. Eventually, they reached a wide square. Tall buildings surrounded it, looking grander and more orderly than the random assortment closer to the gates.

The largest building was stadium-like and currently closed. A plaque over its entrance announced the "Bi-Canal Auction." The rest of the buildings looked luxurious, but none indicated their function.

"Do you know which is a hotel, Dolly?" he asked.

"WHAT IS A HOTEL?"

"A place where we can stay."

Her neck snapped to the side, stretching more than seemed possible. She snapped her teeth around the collar of a random passerby and dragged them close. "POINT THE INN TO MY MASTER, VERMIN," she ordered through closed teeth.

The person she'd grabbed was a cloaked figure. Dolly's actions had pulled back its hood, revealing a furred, scarred face—a sort of humanoid rat person. The moment its hood fell back, it looked incensed and ready to slice at Dolly with a dagger which magically appeared in its hand. Jack's heavy aura, however, forced the monster into inactivity.

"It is there, my Baron," it said, its voice suddenly subservient, and previous rage all but disappeared.

Jack nodded. Dolly spat away the ratman's collar. "FUCK OFF," she told him, and the ratman disappeared in the crowd.

Jack kept his eyes on it for a little longer. He wouldn't normally be so overbearing, but this was space monster society. It worked on a foundation of personal strength and bullying. He couldn't afford to appear different.

At least, nobody seemed to suspect their double devil disguises —or Brock.

"Be a little careful, Dolly," he whispered to her. "The Empty Star faction's headquarters are in this city, and their leader is an Autarch. We don't want to accidentally start a feud with them."

The horse's eyes went wide. "YES, MASTER."

Jack fed her a carrot. He knew that the faction's headquarters were in the back of the city, far away from here, but there was always a chance of some disciple wandering out.

The ratman had pointed them to one of the most luxurious buildings in the square. It was four stories tall and built entirely of green jade. Each floor had its own roof spreading outward like a pagoda, while the entrance was guarded by two C-Grade monsters. They bowed as Jack and the rest walked through. Since this place was built to accommodate a wide variety of space monster species, they didn't need to dismount.

Tables covered the floor, some with chairs, some not. Various space monsters huddled around them, all at the peak D-Grade and above, while a lone C-Grade snake sat behind a bar at the back.

Dolly approached a random space monster—a floating eyeball wearing a comically long cloak. "ARE YOU WITH THE EMPTY STAR FACTION?" she asked.

The eyeball turned around. "No," it replied suspiciously. Jack didn't know how it produced sound.

Dolly bit at its cloak. "POINT US AT THE INNKEEPER!" she commanded.

"Easy, Dolly," Jack said, placing a hand on her neck. "The reception is right there. Stay quiet for a bit."

"YES, MASTER."

She let go of the mortified eyeball, then walked Jack to the reception at the other side of the room. The snake looked up. It was an actual, little green snake, though it possessed power at the late C-Grade.

"Three rooms," Jack said, tossing an item over the counter. They'd run into an early B-Grade space monster on the way. Killing it was easy, but Jack hadn't absorbed the core. It worked as currency around the Space Monster World. Brutal.

The snake gazed at the early B-Grade core and nodded appreciatively. "Yesss, my Baron," it said, coiling its tail around the core and pulling it away. From the way everyone around the inn stopped to stare at them, Jack suspected he'd overpaid, but it didn't matter. He wanted to connect with big-shots, and the best way to do that was to act like a big-shot himself.

Besides, getting B-Grade cores wouldn't be too difficult.

"Our top floor is almossst full," the snake continued. "Would it be okay if one of you resided in the sssecond floor from the top?"

Jack considered it. The top floor sounded like a sign of status. "No," he said.

"Very well. Give me a moment."

The snake stood there, sending telepathic instructions to someone. A few moments later, it said, "A third room has been opened asss well. Please follow me."

Jack and Brock finally dismounted, absorbing the hellhorses back into their inner worlds as they climbed a set of spiral stairs. Even the railing was opulent. This inn was no joke.

They climbed three flights of stairs. On the fourth, they ran into an early B-Grade humanoid space monster with skin the color of sand and equally dry. It glared at them angrily but didn't dare speak. It was carrying its things as it moved from the top floor to the one below. Jack assumed he'd kicked it out, but he didn't care—this was how space monster society worked. The other monster could only blame itself for being weaker.

As they entered the top floor, Jack saw there were over twenty rooms. Heavy auras emanated through the doors. If all these rooms were occupied, and the one who'd been kicked out was an early B-Grade, didn't that mean there were over twenty B-Grade space monsters staying at this inn alone?

"Is it normal to have such high clientele?" he asked the snake.

"Our inn hasss quite a reputation," it replied. "Of course, our current guest list is grander than usual. The bi-canal Empty Star Auction is held in three days. Every powerful space monster in the surrounding provinces wants to attend, just like you do, my Baron." At this point, the snake's voice took on some excitement. "I hear that even several Autarchs will be present! They would never grace our inn, of course, but it's ssstill an event."

"Oh?" Jack asked. "And where would they stay?"

"They're guests of the Empty Star Faction, of coursssе. Rumor has it that during this auction, the faction will offer several items worthy of being bid on by Autarchs. That's why the Empty Star Autarch personally invited them."

Jack's eyes shone. An auction with valuable enough items to tempt A-Grades? Several of them in attendance, alongside who knew how many B-Grades? This was just dreamy!

"Tell me more," he said with a smile.

CHAPTER THIRTY-TWO
ITEM PRESENTATION

Empty Star City was abuzz with activity. Jack surveyed the crowded space around him, the main square of the city—unimaginably called the Empty Star Square. Everything here was named like that. He assumed creative space monsters were shunned.

Speaking of creative space monsters.

"GET OUT OF MY MASTER'S WAY, YOU CONSTIPATED TURDS, OR I WILL DEVOUR YOU AND YOUR LOVED ONES!" Dolly bellowed into the crowd, sending terrified space monsters fleeing left and right. They were creating a huge scene. Jack wanted to cringe and tell her to take it easy, except this was how dignified space monsters acted—what would be distasteful in human society was the norm here, and vice versa.

It wasn't just them. Several mounts of important individuals were loudly announcing their presence across the square, forcing the less powerful space monsters to huddle in the space between them like packed sardines. Of course, they didn't enjoy that. Multiple fights broke out and ended with the death of one party. The square floor was already awash with blood.

Tomorrow was the day of the Empty Star Auction, a centennial event held in Empty Star City. Several A-Grades had gathered, according to Jack's information, so the entire city was in a festive mood. To further this excitement, the city officials had decided to publish a list with some of the auction's high-end items a day early. That was right now.

A space monster which looked like a floating human mouth appeared over the central stage. It licked its lips. Then, its voice echoed across the square, passing over everything like a thunderclap.

"Greetings, everyone! Welcome to the Empty Star Auction's item presentation!"

Its voice was terrifyingly loud. Some weaker space monsters bled from the ears and had to flee the square. The earth shook like an earthquake. Thankfully, all the buildings were constructed of sturdy materials, so they held—which wasn't a coincidence.

Jack resisted the urge to clasp his ears. As annoying as the voice was, he was a space monster now—he couldn't show a single scrap of weakness. He only made the tail of his double devil disguise swish loudly double devil to express his irritation.

"The Empty Star faction would like to especially welcome two esteemed guests," the floating mouth continued. "Elder Puerto of the Great Silver faction, and Elder Crownbeast of the Fiend King faction. Hosting you is our great honor."

The crowd went quiet. Everyone turned toward two godzilla-like monsters. Jack had noticed them before—they easily towered over everything else in the crowd—but hadn't realized who rode them. Now, he knew. Two Elders, each from one of the Space Monster World's Overlord factions.

Elder Puerto was a humanoid, old-looking woman with a wrinkled face and long red hair. She stood quietly on top of her godzilla monster, which nobody dared to approach. Her aura blazed with the power of an early A-Grade.

Jack struggled to find Elder Crownbeast at first. It took him a moment to realize that the head of the massive beast had no one standing on it because the Elder *was* the godzilla-like beast. It easily towered a hundred feet into the sky, covered in hard gray scales and with a line of spikes cascading its back. Vertical irises split its eyes, which surveyed the crowd with cold indifference.

"These bros are crazy," Brock whispered. Jack and Starhair nodded in agreement. The two Elders belonged to opposing factions, and one's mount was from the same species as the other Elder. Basically, one was riding the other. If this wasn't a deadly insult, Jack didn't know what it could be.

Yet, Elder Crownbeast seemed unbothered.

"I will now proceed with naming some of our most precious items," the floating mouth continued. "First up is a Crimson Orchid, tempered in the blood of hundreds of thousands of monsters!"

The crowd cheered. Jack had no idea what that was, and given that the floating mouth wasn't using any props, he remained clueless. He cheered regardless.

"Next is the tail scale of a Cretan Fay."

The crowd cheered again.

"The third item is..."

It kept going, Jack not recognizing any of the items. They sounded precious, but not too much, since none of the higher-level monsters were responding. The only exception was Jack, who'd tried to fit in during the cheers for the first item. Whoops.

It wasn't until the sixth item that he recognized something.

"Our next item will be a late Autarch core," the floating mouth said. It was the simplest name so far, yet the one which drew the most violent response. The square rocked from excitement. Even the two Elders of the Overlord factions raised their heads.

Jack had to admit he was intrigued. The best core he'd consumed so far had been at the early A-Grade. A late A-Grade core... If it was compatible, just how many levels would it give him? Could it push him straight to the late B-Grade?

He only had thirty years before his duel with Elder Hero. Any items which could increase his strength in a short time were extremely important. He had to get this core.

As Jack considered that, he also came to a sad realization. He had no money. The Space Monster World used monster cores as currency, and while he did have a couple from the journey here, there was no way he could compete with any of the high-rollers in such a massive auction.

"Feels like we're back in the D-Grade," Jack muttered. Brock laughed.

"Don't worry, bro. There is more to life than money."

"But I need money."

"I don't get the joke," Starhair said, his voice warped by his double devil transformation. "D-Grade resources are well-priced for their level."

Jack and Brock glanced at each other, then smirked and didn't respond. If they used level-appropriate resources, they'd still be E-Grades. The D-Grade was when Jack had started his Life Stone business in the Cathedral to earn infinite money and accelerate his cultivation.

The floating mouth was still going. In the time it took Jack's group to make some quippy remarks, it had already rattled off several items, none of which seemed particularly interesting or recognizable.

"For our nineteenth item," the mouth continued, "we offer an incomplete Dao manual recovered from Entropy Mountain. Its name is fractured, but it seems to contain the words 'black hole.' Our experts believe it is an ancient, peak A-Grade, Space-Death Dao manual."

Mild excitement came from the crowd. Incomplete Dao manuals weren't a new concept. In the long history of the Space Monster World, there had been many outstanding monsters, most of which passed down their legacy in the form of Dao manuals—a device similar to the snow-globe items Jack had seen in the Black Hole World.

However, the Space Monster World was nowhere as peaceful. Inheritances and legacies were constantly lost. An incomplete manual was a manual damaged by the shockwaves of some battle, and their contents were often far too fractured to form any meaningful conclusions. Acquiring one and studying it was a gamble. They weren't considered too valuable—the only reason this one made the cut for a high-end item was its possible peak A-Grade level, but that also meant it was thoroughly incomplete. Otherwise, only an idiot would sell it.

The two Elders of the Overlord factions didn't react to the name of this item. They had complete peak A-Grade inheritances at their factions—why would they waste time on an incomplete one? The rest of the crowd was equally uninterested.

But not Jack.

Black hole... Space-Death... he thought, eyes shining. *This is... an opportunity!*

Incomplete Dao manuals may be generally useless, but in this case, Jack already cultivated a very similar Dao. One of his two main pursuits at the moment was exactly the workings of a black hole. Even if the manual as a whole was unreadable, there had to be some intact parts. With a little bit of luck, he could use them to glean insights into the questions which troubled him!

Even better, this wouldn't be too expensive an item. He might be able to get it!

The mouth kept naming items, but Jack wasn't too interested. "Hey," he said, using his understanding of gravity to pull a random space monster from the crowd into his open hand. It was humanoid, D-Grade, and scared shitless.

"Y-yes, Master," it said.

"What prices do you think these items are going to fetch?" Jack asked. He also isolated sound around them.

"I... I am not sure, Master." The monster tried to gulp, but Jack's grip around its throat made that difficult. Its voice came gargled. "For the cheapest of these items, maybe a few B-Grade cores would be enough... But for the most expensive, even a dozen early A-Grade cores might not make the cut!"

Jack's eyes darkened. He let the monster drop, and it hastily scurried away through the crowd.

A few B-Grade cores... I'm poorer than I thought.

He didn't even possess *one*. B-Grade monsters were rare, let alone A-Grade ones. It appeared that even the black hole-related incomplete manual would be hard to get... Especially since he only had one day.

How do I go about it? he wondered. He cupped his chin, looking over the rest of the crowd. Stealing it would be difficult with all these A-Grades. Could I kill a few B-Grades and take their cores?

This was the Space Monster World. Such things happened often, though not necessarily amongst high-level people. If he created too much trouble, he might get kicked out of the city—or accidentally start a war. He definitely didn't need an Overlord on his ass right now.

"And now, the last high-end item we present today," the mouth said. "Something truly special..." Jack paused his train of thought and looked over—if this item had an intro, it was probably something interesting. The two Elders of the Overlord faction perked up as well.

The mouth coughed once. "Two months ago, one of our Elders was exploring a hidden realm at the edge of the Inhospitable Zone. They almost lost their lives several times, when finally... They chanced into an incredible treasure. Something left behind for eons, the item which had inadvertently birthed that entire danger site. It was a corpse. The body had long degraded, but its core remained strong. It is this core we offer today. An Overlord-level core."

The crowd fell silent. Then, all at once, they erupted. The square shook. It was pandemonium. Even the two Elders were animated, laughing into the sky.

"This core will belong to the Fiend King faction!" Elder Crownbeast roared, his voice overwhelming the square. Elder Puerto, however, coldly laughed back.

"This is my faction's territory, Crownbeast. If you think you can come here and run wild, think again!"

"This is an auction, Puerto. Only cores speak here. Let's clash tomorrow, and see if you or I brought more!"

The red-haired old woman smiled. "I look forward to it."

Jack was also shocked. Overlords were the space monster equivalent of Archons. It was the highest level of existence. The core of such a space monster was an unbelievably rare and precious commodity. If he got it, it would accelerate his cultivation by a hundred times!

Unfortunately, he was doomed to only watch, never to touch it. He could never raise enough money by tomorrow. As for taking it by force, that was also impossible. Maybe he could take one of these Elders, but he wasn't dumb enough to think he could overpower every A-Grade in Empty Star City at once. Even if he did, one of the two Overlords might come after him over such an item... And, after barely escaping Archon Summer Noon, Jack had deeply realized how inadequate his current strength was against an Archon. He wouldn't make such enemies until he was ready to face them.

But he still wanted that damn core.

CHAPTER THIRTY-THREE
CHALLENGE

THE CROWD'S ROAR TOOK SOME TIME TO ABATE. THE ANNOUNCEMENT WAS just too stunning. Overlord-level cores were never, ever available. There couldn't have been more than a few hundred of them across the entire history of the Space Monster World, not to mention that cores were also consumables.

If someone got their hands on that core, they could use it as infinite currency, but nobody would be that stupid. The greatest currency was one's own strength. They'd just absorb it and grow massively more powerful.

"No wonder the Overlord factions sent Elders here," Jack said.

"They're buying the core for their big bros," Brock replied. "Big bros, big money."

"Yeah. Would be sweet if we had that much."

"You don't need Archon cores," Starhair said. "You're a B-Grade. Even A-Grade cores would be great."

"Not if I have a duel with a late A-Grade in thirty years."

Starhair thought about it. "Yeah. Not in that case."

The mouth had finished its announcement, but the crowd remained. Many discussed what had happened with those around them. Some space monsters, however, were looking at the sky. As if waiting for something.

It didn't take long to figure out what.

A large form took to the air. It looked like Elder Crownbeast, except much smaller. Basically a mini godzilla. It must have been standing behind the Elder before, which was why Jack hadn't seen it.

As soon as this new monster reached a high point in the sky, it stopped and laughed out loud. "I've heard so much about the Empty Star faction, but this is even grander than I anticipated!" it shouted. Peak B-Grade undulations followed its rough voice. And, though its words were pleasant, its tone was not. "My name is Crownbeast Saturnstar. Chief disciple of Elder Crownbeast. I am not considered too strong in the Field King faction, but I sure love a good battle! Since I've come all the way here, it would be a shame not to experience the young talents of Empty Star. Who dares to spar with me?"

This monster had wasted no time in provoking everyone. The crowd below chilled—Jack saw even Elder Puerto narrow her eyes at Saturnstar. Meanwhile, Elder Crownbeast remained perfectly calm, as if completely unrelated to the matter.

Jack had seen his fair share of rivalries, so it wasn't hard for him to understand what was happening. The Great Silver and Fiend King factions weren't at war, but as the only two Overlord factions of the Space Monster World, they were constantly competing with each other. Each looked for an opportunity to one-up the other.

In this case, it was clear that Elder Crownbeast had brought his disciple here to humiliate the Empty Star faction. All that talk about not being too strong was bullshit. Jack could feel the monster's towering aura, standing at the very top of the peak B-Grade. Even if this wasn't the chief disciple of the Fiend King faction, he remained a spectacular talent.

Nobody responded to the beast's provocation for a while. Who would? A-Grades couldn't lower themselves to face him, and all the B-Grades present couldn't defeat him.

The silence emboldened Crownbeast Saturnstar. "I have long

heard that the Great Silver monsters are not too strong, but they are brave. Was I mistaken? How come nobody dares to face me?"

Jack could feel the crowd's simmering anger. This guy had just come into their territory and insulted them all. How could they take this lying down?

Finally, one space monster couldn't take it anymore. "I will face you!" it roared, shooting into the sky. This was a flying red fish with golden hair. Jack found it almost comical. It didn't even have limbs!

Behind the fish trailed a cloak displaying a sun's periphery with its insides undrawn. The insignia of Empty Star.

"Fishborn Averel, second disciple of the Empty Star faction!" the fish declared. It spoke normally, through its mouth, though bubbles appeared with every word.

The godzilla guy laughed again. "Please give me your guidance."

He then shot forth. Even in the Space Monster World's dense Dao, the sky shattered below him. Every step was cataclysm. The monster took three of them, crossing half the sky and arriving before the fish, pouncing out to bite it.

The fish monster was the size of a car. It looked comically small before the godzilla cosplayer, but what it lacked in stature it made up for with unlimited power. Energy erupted from its body. The sky around it was painted a deeper blue, an ocean blinking into existence over the entire Empty Star City. There were fish inside it, of many species Jack had never encountered before. There were reefs, rocks, and strange materials. His eyesight couldn't penetrate too deep into the blue waters, but his Dao perception could, and he spotted a seabed running across the top of this ocean.

The fish had summoned it upside down, probably to let the audience watch the battle.

The godzilla monster suddenly found himself surrounded by water. Rocks fell towards him from all directions. Somehow, he had become the center of gravity in this ocean. The water pressure he endured must have been immense. At the same time, swordfish flew at him, each crossing the ocean far faster than any fish had the right to.

Crownbeast Saturnstar was unconcerned. Facing this new ocean, he only resumed his previous movement, trying to trade hit for hit. The swordfish pierced into his body, penetrating it with their entire noses and stopping there. Thanks to the monster's size, it wasn't a debilitating injury. As for the water pressure, while it had certainly slowed him down, that was the most it could achieve.

Seeing the godzilla's jaws still approaching, the fish monster narrowed its eyes.

An entire reef dislodged from the seabed above. It crossed the water so fast it resembled teleportation, instantly reaching the godzilla and slamming hard into him. Tons of rock flying at extreme speed contained terrifying momentum. A shockwave crossed the ocean and reached the surface below, where it spurt an entire lake's worth of water into the sky. As soon as this water left the ocean, it was freed from whatever gravity magic held it in place and rained toward the square.

However, even the entire reef hadn't been enough to stop the godzilla monster. An aura of savagery surrounded him, manifesting as angry red light. He endured the hit through sheer anger. The damage was done, his jaw attack continued, and the fish monster no longer had time to defend. It found itself between the jaws of the godzilla, and as they clasped down, the fish released a terrifying shriek which pierced the ocean to echo in everyone's ears. It was the most grating sound Jack had ever heard. Many D-Grade monsters fell unconscious.

The two monsters held still. Then the ocean disappeared like it was never there, revealing the two locked in place. The godzilla's jaws had closed around the fish, penetrating it with sharp teeth. Blue blood flew everywhere. If he just slammed his mouth shut right now, he could probably rip his opponent in two.

But he didn't. This battle was over, and high-level space

monsters, no matter how wild, wouldn't kill each other for no reason. Otherwise, their entire civilization would have collapsed.

"I admit defeat," the fish muttered. The godzilla opened his mouth slowly, and the fish pierced through space to teleport away, too humiliated to stay. Its injuries were also heavy. Maybe they required immediate treatment.

The godzilla monster was slightly injured, but nothing serious. Even the swordfish holes in its body were slowly regenerating. The power difference between them hadn't been small.

"Hahaha!" Saturnstar shouted. "A nice appetizer! Now, come on. Bring me a real fighter. You can't tell me that's the best you got!"

The crowd seethed with anger and humiliation. That fish fighter, indeed, was the best they had. It was just that the godzilla guy was too freakishly strong. Even if the Empty Star faction's chief disciple was present, nobody knew whether she could defeat Saturnstar or not.

Silence reigned. After a short while, Elder Crownbeast, the larger version of his disciple, spoke up, "Come down, Saturnstar. There is clearly no one here who can face you. No need to humiliate these good people further."

The Elder's words were also scathing. The representative of the other Overlord faction, Elder Puerto, seemed ready to explode in anger, but there was nothing she could say. Her disciples either weren't here or they couldn't match up to Saturnstar. If she opened her mouth, she would only invite more humiliation upon herself. At least, in this case, it wasn't the Great Silver faction which had been humiliated, only Empty Star City.

As the godzilla beast floated down, lazily passing its gloating gaze over the crowd, a new voice rose to the sky. It was laughter, raucous and unprompted. Everyone looked for the source and found it as a double devil mounted on a hellhorse.

"What a joker!" this double devil shouted. "When you said you were the chief disciple of an Elder, I almost believed you for a second.

Too bad your talent is mediocre. In my village, someone like you could only work as a potato-chopper at the local tavern, let alone becoming the disciple of a powerful Autarch!"

All eyes trained on this raucous individual. They began to hope. As they looked him over, however, their hope turned into confusion. This was only a middle B-Grade space monster. What exactly was it trying to do?

Elder Puerto looked at him and shook her head, while Elder Crownbeast only grinned.

Crownbeast Saturnstar stopped his descent and glared at Jack. "I do believe that you come from a small village," he said dismissively. "Only a country bumpkin would come up with such a stupid scheme. You know you don't possess the strength to be challenged by me, so you hope to retrieve some of your lost honor by mocking me. That's ridiculous. I'm not even angry at you. Everyone understands you're nothing but a dancing clown. Fuck off back to your village before I destroy you, trash."

The double devil—who was obviously Jack—grinned at these words.

"Who said I only intend to mock you?" he asked back. "In my eyes, you're nothing but a barking dog, and thus you should be put down. Even the trash collectors of this city don't want to dirty their hands on you, so I will reluctantly lend them a hand."

Saturnstar narrowed his eyes at Jack. "Are you trying to challenge me?"

"Oh wow. I knew you were weak, but are you deaf as well? Yes, my slow friend. I am challenging you to a duel."

The crowd laughed. They didn't understand what exactly was going on, or why Jack was apparently trying to suicide, but his verbal prowess at least was nothing to scoff at. Saturnstar grunted. He originally hadn't placed Jack in his eyes, but he did not enjoy losing a verbal exchange like this before the entire city.

"Are you really insane?" he asked. "Does the Empty Star City hire rabid dogs to speak for them? Your words are nothing but noise in my ears. If you want to kill yourself regardless, I'll be glad to help you."

"The only noise in my ears was your mother last night," Jack replied. "And I got to say, it was a little bit annoying. Can you tell her to shout less next time?"

The crowd froze. So what if it was immature? Laughter erupted everywhere, and Saturnstar's gray scales turned red around his face —from both anger and humiliation. He'd clearly always held confidence in his verbal abilities, but only now did he realize that engaging Jack was a mistake.

And, of course it was. Saturnstar couldn't have known, but Jack had humiliated numerous powerful people in his lifetime, many mocked to the point of dishonor. His victims included E-Grade Lords, various deacons and Elders of the Animal Kingdom, Envoys of the Hand of God, and even Elder Ocean of that same faction, who'd flown into a rage and almost assaulted Jack after being verbally humiliated.

Jack's talent was legendary in the outside universe, but so were his boldness and sharp tongue. Compared to all his previous opponents, Saturnstar was laughable.

The godzilla-like monster grew redder with anger. Even Elder Crownbeast was animated.

"Fine," Saturnstar spat out. "If you wish to die so much, then come up here. Don't make me come down to get you!"

The crowd around Jack urgently ran away. The only ones left were Brock and Starhair, as well as the two hellhorses, who hadn't experienced Jack's true strength and so believed their master was suiciding.

"I WILL DIE WITH YOU, MASTER," Dolly said. "YOU ARE DUMB BUT I LIKE IT. ASSHOLES SHOULD BE PUT IN THEIR PLACE."

The fact that her normal voice was at shouting volume didn't help Saturnstar's mood. He made to fly down, but Jack raised a hand to indicate there was no need.

"Keep your regal ass in the sky, godzilla," he said. "I'm coming over to kick it. Or, better yet…" Purple light gathered in his hand, forming the shape of a flip-flop. Jack grinned manically. "I'm gonna spank it."

CHAPTER THIRTY-FOUR
BEATING SATURNSTAR

Jack took to the air. His middle B-Grade aura roiled around his double devil transformation, just a fraction of his opponent's. Crownbeast Saturnstar cracked a grin.

"You really can't wait to die," he said.

"The opposite," Jack replied. "I look forward to teaching you a lesson."

The godzilla-like beast no longer seemed as angry. He had absolute certainty in destroying Jack. In his mind, he had already won.

"And what gives you such confidence, double devil?" he asked playfully. "You know you are about to die, yet you still fly towards me. Why?"

"Well, I can't spank your ass without coming closer."

The crowd laughed again—the confused yet entertained kind—while Saturnstar lowered his head. Red light shone over his body. Savagery crackled, dying the sky a bloody red. Facing this light, Jack simply raised his Dao-made flip-flop.

"Prepare your scaly butt," he said.

Saturnstar smiled. "I'll make this quick."

He lashed forward. Air cracked where he passed, the extreme Dao density doing little to stop him. A set of powerful jaws closed around Jack—except he was no longer there. Jack had delicately stepped through space to appear behind Saturnstar. "Too slow!" he said. "Great Spanking Arts: Latin Mother Cracking Down!"

The flip-flop loudly slapped against Saturnstar's ass, carrying with it a miniature version of Meteor Punch. The godzilla monster growled. As he was still in his charging motion, the strike easily sent him flying forward, tumbling head-over-heels. The scales on his lower back had reddened by the heat of the impact—but, to the onlookers, they looked red from spanking.

The audience froze. Their jestering cheers echoed through the air a little before dissipating. Everyone's eyes were glued on Jack, this unknown double devil who'd just jumped two small realms to fight one of the Fiend King faction's greatest disciples.

"What exquisite space manipulation..." Elder Puerto said, her eyes shining. She beckoned to one of her assistants. "Record this battle!"

Similar exclamations rang all over the square. The floating mouth was licking its lips. Elder Crownbeast's features had hardened. Brock was scratching his ear. As for Crownbeast Saturnstar, Jack's opponent, he wore an expression of utter disbelief.

"How did you do that?" he asked.

Jack smiled. "Simple. You're an unruly beast, so I used the power of discipline to get an advantage."

"...Are you hiding your cultivation?"

Jack's smile widened. "Does it look like I am?"

Hiding one's cultivation was possible. However, the amount of energy one expended in combat could not be hidden. Everyone had clearly seen that Jack only used a middle B-Grade's energy just now, it was just that the quality of his energy and his level of Dao understanding were far superior to his opponent's. There were only two possibilities: either Jack was a once-in-a-lifetime talent, or he was an extremely powerful person at the late A-Grade or above hiding his cultivation. Would someone at that level fool around with juniors?

"Saturnstar!" Elder Crownbeast roared. "Kill him!"

Saturnstar's gaze sharpened. He'd reached the same conclusion as his elder. This person was extremely talented and had a bone to pick with them, but he wasn't allied with the Great Silver faction or they would know about him. At least, he wasn't allied yet. They had to kill him right now.

Saturnstar pounced. He was no longer holding back. Savage light swam around him, spreading with extreme luminosity like he was a crimson sun shooting through the sky. The lower-level space monsters had to avert their eyes. The higher-level ones watched with rapt attention.

Jack felt space constrict around him. His opponent's Dao of Savagery commanded the world, forcing Jack to fight him head-on through sheer untainted battle lust.

Of course, to Jack, such a rudimentary space lock might as well not exist. He possessed the inheritance of two space-related Archons, had studied black holes, and mastered space to a higher degree than even most A-Grades. In comparison, Saturnstar didn't even focus on Space—and the Space Monster World's inheritances were generally inferior to the outside universe's to begin with.

Jack ignored the space lock and teleported to the side. Saturnstar passed by like an angry freight train, receiving another firm smack on his buttocks. He roared. Red light erupted, sending the air particles into a frenzy and having them fight each other. A billion tiny cyclones filled the sky. A weaker space monster would have been torn to shreds, but Jack didn't even defend. The rampaging particles bounced off his highly tempered body.

Because Saturnstar was going all-out, he couldn't efficiently control his powers. Some of the tiny cyclones escaped outward. The ones that fell toward the city were stopped by a flickering blue shield, but the rest were not. The environment around the city exploded. Dozens of wandering space monsters lost their lives, the massive river was sent into a frenzy, and many large rock islands disappeared, torn to pieces. The surrounding forest, whose every tree was equal to a D-Grade existence, was eviscerated for several miles.

In the outside universe, peak B-Grades possessed the power to destroy planets. The Space Monster World sported a far higher Dao density, making everything much sturdier and reducing every cultivator's powers. Still, peak B-Grades could cause widespread destruction. They were walking apocalypses.

Jack overlooked the massive area of devastation around Empty Star City. He tsked. "That wasn't very responsible of you. Little children should be environmentally friendly!"

The godzilla roared and turned to attack Jack again. His fighting style was simple: all he did was charge. It usually worked because of his great speed and space lock. Unfortunately, Jack outclassed him in both aspects.

It was like a bull trying to catch a fly. Jack easily dodged every attack, making Saturnstar seem comically slow. He also interjected his own flip-flop strikes, shouting clearly made-up bullshit like, "Third Spanking Art: Divine Fatherly Love!" and "Belt Buckle Instills Discipline!"

Despite Jack's small size, his strikes were intense. Eruptions occurred with each one. Dull thuds echoed alongside Saturnstar's frustrated screams, while every flip-flop strike unleashed a conic shockwave which painted the sky purple.

"All you can do is run!" Saturnstar shouted in frustration, already panting and bleeding. "Face me like a true monster!"

Jack ignored him.

Saturnstar finally lowered his head, releasing a deep, guttural growl. "This is my strongest attack!" he bellowed. "If you survive it, I will admit defeat! World Domination!"

He charged forward, far faster than before. It was clear this move consumed tremendous amounts of energy. His massive body turned into a straight line, a red missile flying head-first. The sky shattered where he passed like a bullet tearing through fabric. If he struck a mountain, the mountain would instantly and violently disintegrate.

Jack watched the approaching monster. He was like a bullet train from hell. The space lock returned around him, slightly strengthened, but still nothing concerning. Jack could easily dodge. However...

"All I can do is run, huh?" Jack asked, his lips curving into a grin. He stretched an arm forward, his open palm facing the incoming attack. He turned his body sideways and bent his legs, planting himself firmly into the sky. As Saturnstar approached, Jack held.

The massive red missile, powered by the full force of a peak B-Grade, hill-sized space monster crashed right into Jack's palm.

The sound was like ten thousand thunderclaps, or a mountain-sized gong.

GONG!

The shockwave swept the sky for a hundred miles behind Jack, ripping it off the background and leaving a dark gaping hole. A sphere of devastation spread outward.

Yet, Jack had held. He hadn't budged in the slightest. His hand remained outstretched, having firmly grabbed onto the top of Saturnstar's head and stopped him. The monster's body was already beginning to fall—he'd lost consciousness by the impact.

The crowd had gone deathly silent. They could not believe what they'd witnessed. Even Elders Puerto and Crownbeast were frozen for a moment, which gave Jack time to act. Because he wasn't done. The whole reason he stepped up for this charade was to earn some coin—in the Space Monster World, the killer could take all the belongings of his victim.

Actually, that wasn't entirely true. It wasn't the only reason Jack did this. He'd seen such a godzilla-like monster before. Back during the Integration, in his first Dao Vision, he'd seen a C-Grade man vanquish one such beast with a single punch. That moment had been branded into Jack's memory. It was the inspiration on which he'd built his entire cultivation path.

It was time to pay tribute.

Jack flickered, appearing below the falling beast. He pulled back his fist, the flip-flop nowhere to be seen.

"JUNIOR, STOP!" a voice boomed from below.

Jack's fist blurred forth. It exploded on Saturnstar. The energy drilled its way through, creating a smooth hole through the center of the monster's chest, obliterating his organs. He died instantly.

Jack smirked. "Still not enough..." he muttered, the same words that one-punch man had said, a meaning only he would understand.

A deep roar came from below. Jack sensed an angry A-Grade barreling towards him, but he did not panic. With a swift movement, he took off Saturnstar's space ring—it had been worn on one of his smaller scales—and took it into his robes. He also pocketed the dead monster's core. Only then did he turn around to find Elder Crownbeast, a larger and stronger version of Saturnstar, charging over with murder in his eyes.

Jack prepared to run. He didn't know if he could beat this monster, but he knew he could escape. He'd just never fought an A-Grade before, so he lacked a frame of reference.

Even if he *could* win, he wasn't sure if it was a good idea to showcase his full strength here. The part he'd already shown was nothing compared to a true A-Grade. That kind of talent might be too shocking.

He hoped all those thoughts would be unnecessary, and his expectations were correct. Another red figure flashed between them, raising a hand to stop Elder Crownbeast. He stopped instantly in midair, his momentum mysteriously extinguished.

"Puerto!" he shouted. "This devil killed my disciple! Will you really try to stop me from exacting revenge?"

"Your disciple started this battle. The double devil behind me only answered the challenge. Killing him was reasonable," Elder Puerto replied calmly. She looked like a red-haired grandmother with a body of iron.

Elder Crownbeast foamed from the mouth. "This is absurd! My disciple showed mercy against that fish, so he could be shown mercy in return!" The other Elder did not respond, which only infuriated Crownbeast more. "Puerto! Will you really defend this person from me? He is not even your disciple!"

"I am not defending him," Puerto replied. "I am simply standing up for what is right. If I let Elders of another faction waltz into our territory and slaughter our talented youth, I would really be worthy of ridicule."

Elder Crownbeast was only getting angrier. Still, he did not attack. "You!" he said, turning to Jack. "Explain yourself!"

The full brunt of his aura weighed down on Jack, who did not seem to notice. Both Elders were taken aback. "What is there to explain?" he replied calmly. "Your disciple challenged and disrespected me. I defeated him in a fair duel. Isn't that the rule of the world?"

"You didn't have to kill him!"

"I didn't have to show mercy either. Honestly, your disciple should have seen it coming. Don't tell me he thought he could mock an entire city and get away with it just because he has a moderately strong master."

"MODERATELY STRONG!" Elder Crownbeast looked ready to explode. At this rate, Jack wouldn't even have to fight him—he'd just die of a heart attack. "Puerto! Step aside and let me kill this little asshole!"

"I cannot do that," Puerto replied.

"Do you really think you can stop me?"

"I believe I'm qualified to try. And, if push really comes to shove, I'm sure the Empty Star Autarch will stand on my side."

Elder Crownbeast had never been angrier in his life. He was a space monster Autarch. When had he ever been publicly disrespected like this?

But, the truth was, he really couldn't do anything. As much as he wanted to lash out, his only option right now was to cut his losses and keep a grudge.

"Whatever! Just because you can hide behind others now, kid, doesn't mean you'll be able to do it forever!" he declared to save some face. "Give me my disciple's space ring. I'm leaving."

Jack raised a brow. "Why would I do that?"

"Brat!"

"What? I defeated and killed your disciple in fair combat. By the rules of our world, all his items are mine now."

Crownbeast opened his mouth, but no words came out. He was shivering in rage. "Oh yeah!" he replied. "Then do you dare meet *me* in fair combat, *brat*?"

Jack laughed. "I would rather not."

By now, murmurs were spreading through the crowd below. Jack's actions were just too flashy, and his talent was undeniable. As if those weren't enough, he'd just publicly torn apart the face of a Fiend King Elder. This was a legend in the making!

Crownbeast was on the verge of launching himself against Puerto and damned be the consequences. However, even space monsters didn't reach the A-Grade by being impulsive. No matter how angry he got, he'd never lose control.

"Remember this day, kid," he growled. "Because this is the day you fucked up. I'll be back for the auction."

Without another word, Elder Crownbeast tore through space and disappeared. The square fell into silence for a moment. Then, as one, everyone erupted in cheers. Jack had done so many incredible things, and most importantly, he'd defended their honor! They didn't know his name, but they still worshiped him!

"MASTER IS AMAZING! HE'S NOT STUPID AT ALL!" Dolly said, drooling at the mouth.

"That's my big bro!" Brock exclaimed, laughing. He then looked around. So many people adoring his big bro... This sure looked the perfect place to spread some brohood!

As for Starhair... He was drenched in cold sweat. Jack's actions complicated things, and he did not like complications.

Jack bowed slightly at Elder Puerto. "Thank you for protecting me."

The Elder looked him up and down. "Are you really not hiding your cultivation?"

"I am not."

"Good. You're already enemies with the Fiend King. Once this auction is over, I will take you with me to the Great Silver faction. The Canal Delve is approaching—we could use a talent like yours."

Jack considered it. Joining an Overlord faction and securing their protection sounded like a great deal... but it wasn't necessarily so. His disguise wasn't perfect. If he ever actually met the Overlord, it was possible he'd be discovered. Plus, entering a faction was not necessarily the fastest way for him to increase his strength.

That Canal Delve though... Could it be about the Dark Canal? The sacred center of the Space Monster World?

He'd planned to this point before he even spoke up against Saturnstar. He intended to refuse—but this gave him pause. The Dark Canal was a place he definitely wanted to visit. If his previous experience told him anything, that was where the greatest treasures and inheritances would be—along with the greatest dangers.

"Is it okay if I think about it a little?" he asked.

Elder Puerto raised a brow, surprised. If Jack was reading her face right, she was even a little offended. "Fine," she said, then teleported away.

Jack sighed. The cheers from below were still deafening. He'd opposed one Overlord faction and been invited to join the other, complicating his situation massively... At least he'd earned what he came for.

He looked at his robes, where a gray space ring floated. A smile spread across his lips. The auction was tomorrow... and he had money!

CHAPTER THIRTY-FIVE
WORLD OF HEROES

After the two Overlord faction Elders left, Jack remained as the day's greatest winner.

He had defended Empty Star's and Great Silver's honor. He'd won a valiant duel before tens of thousands of monsters. He'd jumped two small realms to fight a genius.

Each of those would be enough to mark his name. Combined... They made him a hero!

"It's fine, guys, it's fine, thank you," Jack muttered as he returned to his inn. Monsters crowded him from all sides, trying to congratulate him or shake his hand. Many offered to buy him a drink. Female monsters poured from every direction. Even Dolly's shouts—and occasional bite—couldn't stop them.

Brock and Starhair followed from a distance, laughing all the while. It was only several minutes later that they managed to cross the inn's entrance, where the guards stopped the overflowing crowd. Jack stumbled into the tavern space, finally able to breathe. He looked around. A dozen eyes fell on him—all radiating respect.

"Hey," an ogre said from the side. "Good job out there."

"Yeah. You really showed that guy who's boss!" another creature

—a five-legged octopus—agreed. Maybe it should be called a quintopus? A cthulhian monstrosity? Jack wanted to ask, but he wasn't ready to start a conversation.

He waved thanks to all of them, then made his way to the back, where the stairs were located. He could have teleported to his room, but he didn't want to be rude by breaking the inn's spatial seals. Besides, he knew something most people did not. If you wanted to be a hero, you had to let people see you. Even chasing you around built prestige.

"Congratulationsss," the snake innkeeper whispered in Jack's ears, startling him.

"Can you not do that?" he replied.

"My apologiesss. On behalf of Empty Star City, I will waive your accommodation fee. Pleassse. Proceed."

"Oh. Thanks."

Brock and Starhair had caught up by now. The three of them climbed the spiral staircase, soon reaching the top floor, where their rooms were located.

"Jack?" Starhair asked. Even in double devil form, he still wore his bandana, covering the injuries left by him sacrificing half his hair to delay Archon Summer Noon.

"Yeah?"

"Good job out there... but, please, be careful. We were safe before. Now that we're involved with A-Grades, there's no telling what will happen."

Jack gave Starhair a faint smile. "Have you adventured before, Starhair?"

"Of course."

"What was the chance of death?"

Starhair thought about it for a second. "Up to ten percent."

Jack nodded. "There are three possible paths in life, Starhair. You risk it all and thrive, you risk it all and die, or you persist in mediocrity. Of the three, there is only one I fear. What about you?"

The other man stopped, his face filled with confusion. Brock smirked to the side. As for Jack, he turned and entered his room. Brock followed.

"Well done, bro," he said after the doors closed. "What's the harvest?"

"Let's see." Jack reached into his robes, removing the space ring he'd taken from Saturnstar. It was gray and regular-sized—the godzilla-like monster had worn it on the tip of one of his scales. Jack connected his mind to the ring and inspected its contents.

"Well?" Brock asked.

Jack frowned. "It's... decent. But far less than I'd hoped for."

With a wave of his hand, a small pile of cores appeared. The room was instantly saturated by their rich energy—Jack had to seal it to prevent others from noticing. Brock picked one up.

"Not bad," he said.

"But not good either," Jack replied.

Before them lay ten peak B-Grade cores followed by thirty late B-Grade ones. There was also a single early A-Grade core. Their elements were varied and random. Clearly, these weren't meant to be used as cultivation resources, but as currency.

This was undoubtedly massive wealth. Even the late B-Grade cores were each very difficult to acquire, let alone the A-Grade one. It was just that, as rich as this was, Jack had a feeling it was nothing but change compared to an Overlord Elder's space ring. He couldn't compete for the truly high-level items.

In the Space Monster World, one core was roughly equivalent to three of the previous small realm. For example, one late C-Grade core would be worth as much as three middle C-Grade ones. The difference in large realms, like a peak C-Grade and an early B-Grade core, came with a tenfold increase in value.

It was a crude and clanky system, more complex than it needed to be, and was made even worse by the fact that these ratios weren't set in stone. Different places used different exchange rates. If someone wanted to buy a specific core to advance their cultivation, they might need to fork up much more than the core's monetary value. The higher one went, the more fuzzy the lines—for A-Grade cores, these rules basically didn't apply, and the economy reverted fully to exchange-based transactions.

Roughly speaking, the single early A-Grade core Jack had was worth as much as the ten peak B-Grade ones combined, which were worth as much as the thirty late B-Grades. He also had Saturnstar's core, which he'd ripped out of the monster's body with his killing blow.

Overall, Jack had the rough equivalent of three early A-Grade cores and change. It was a great amount of wealth. Just not enough. The late A-Grade core offered in the auction had a plain monetary value of nine early ones, three times Jack's wealth. The Archon core was simply pointless to think about. The only item he might have a chance at acquiring was the black hole-related incomplete manual... but, thinking about it, Jack released a sigh.

Elder Crownbeast would be present, no doubt carrying a stupid amount of riches. Once Jack bid on something, the Elder would surely outbid him just to be a jerk.

He sighed again. This auction... would be difficult.

"What do you think, big bro?" Brock asked. "Can we do it?"

"Honestly? No."

The brorilla laughed. "A bro should always keep a level head. That Elder has anger in his heart, which makes him weak. We can work around it."

Jack smiled. "Damn right!"

"It's late," Brock said as he stood. "Rest, bro. Cultivate. I will see you in the morning."

"Sure thing. See you, bro."

Brock left the room, leaving Jack alone. However, he didn't go to his own room. He took the stairs and returned to the ground-floor tavern, then calmly walked out of the inn. A smile of anticipation was plastered on his face.

Jack had rallied the crowds. If Brock didn't use this opportunity to spread some brohood, he was no big bro!

Centrum Nightsky was a member of the Featherwell battalion of the Black Hole Church. He was a soldier—at this stage, that was all an early B-Grade qualified for.

The war was still escalating. Their forces had figured out how to counter the Immortals' System Cannons, but that didn't mean the war was over. It only meant they'd be slaughtered slowly.

If this was a few months ago, Centrum would have been demoralized and on the verge of deserting. But things weren't the same as back then. Now, the army had hope. It had heroes.

Centrum clutched a small doll. It was a Brock plushie, the kind that had sold over a million pieces by now. This one had been given to him by his daughter, and he held it very dear. The alarm still blared over his head, but Centrum took a moment.

"I believe in you, bro," he whispered, chuckling at his own words. "Take care of my daughter. Build a nice world for her."

Centrum took the plushie into his space ring, closed his eyes, took a deep breath, then teleported outside. Energy attacks flew left and right. The void shattered, revealing a gaping darkness leading into the interdimensional sea. Whoever was sucked inside was never seen again.

In the distance, Elder Featherwell was fighting another A-Grade. Their battle was incredible to watch. Feathers covered the sky, violently ripped apart by all sorts of spectral ghosts. It was a level of power Centrum couldn't even hope to reach. His potential was already wrung dry.

But he could still fight.

"Centrum!" a voice reached him. A panicked squad commander. "We need you here!" he said as a blast of green energy slammed into his protective shield, corroding it. The commander barely managed to dodge in time.

Centrum rushed over. He took stock of the battlefield. They were outnumbered. The enemies were more and stronger. This was a losing battle.

There was just nothing he could do about it right now. His only options were to stand and fight, or flee by himself. If he fled, there was a small chance he would survive, but that would only urge more of his comrades to flee as well. If he stayed, his death was certain, but at least he could take a couple enemies with him. He could help the war effort.

Another green energy blast flew at him. Centrum waved his sword, cutting it up—a single droplet fell on his forearm and began to sizzle. Intense pain assaulted Centrum as his arm melted. With a decisive motion, he chopped it off at the shoulder, preventing the effect from spreading. He used his Dao to seal the wound.

As he joined with his comrades and charged the enemy, his mind traveled to the plushie he kept in his space ring. It traveled to the recording he'd seen, of one C-Grade man challenging an entire B-Grade faction.

Create a safe world for my daughter... he thought again as he dived head-first into the fray.

Centrum Nightsky slew two enemy soldiers and saved the life of a comrade before he finally fell. He died a hero. They all did.

CHAPTER THIRTY-SIX

EMPTY STAR AUCTION

THE EMPTY STAR SQUARE WAS EVEN MORE CROWDED THAN THE PREVIOUS day. This was no longer just an announcement of the auction items; today was the actual auction, and due to the number of people wanting to attend, the square had been chosen as the official venue!

A packed crowd spread all over and into the surrounding streets. The C-Grades and above could no longer fit, so they'd climbed onto the rooftops. B-Grades were standing in the air. As for the two A-Grades present, Elder Puerto and Elder Crownbeast, they hovered even higher than the B-Grades, occupying a height no one dared to infringe upon.

The floating mouth from yesterday, the official auctioneer of the Empty Star faction, floated over a raised platform. Every eye was glued on it. A long row of boxes waited at the back of the platform.

The auction... was beginning!

"Welcome, everyone, to the Empty Star Auction!" the mouth declared, its voice magically booming across the entire city. Cheers rose in response. Some monsters growled. The mouth waited for the crowd to calm down before continuing. "It is our honor to have all of you in attendance. Many prestigious monsters have graced us with their presence today, especially Elder Puerto of the Great Silver faction and Elder Crownbeast of the Fiend King faction. Please enjoy our hospitality!"

More cheers from the crowd. Elder Puerto waved at them, while Crownbeast remained stationary, dark, and gloomy. He hadn't forgotten yesterday's humiliation, and neither had the crowd.

Jack, who stood alongside Brock and Starhair amongst the other B-Grades, rubbed the back of his head. "Think he holds a grudge?" he asked Brock.

"Absolutely, bro."

"Good."

"Allow me to set some ground rules," the mouth said. "Between monster cores, every minor realm will bring a threefold increase in value, and every large realm a tenfold increase. The Dao attunement of the core will not be taken into account. The winner of each item is expected to receive it and pay up immediately. If they are not able to pay, they will be executed, and the item may or may not be re-auctioned at the Empty Star faction's discretion. Finally, as the auction takes responsibility for the safety of our attendees, fighting is prohibited in the square for the duration. Any offenders will be executed and their space rings seized."

He paused to let the rules sink in for everyone. It was nothing outrageous, actually. Standard stuff. Jack was surprised the no-fighting rule needed to be mentioned, but then again, this *was* the Space Monster World.

"Let us proceed with the first item!" the mouth declared. Two double devil attendants pushed the first box forward on a cart. "Salvaged from the northern wastes of the Waist Blood Province, this item is the crystallization of the area's carnage! Our sages estimate it has fed on the blood of hundreds of thousands of monsters. We lost three B-Grade experts to capture it, so its strength and value are beyond doubt! I present to you, the Crimson Orchid!"

One of the attendants pulled a stick out of the box, letting the whole thing collapse around its contents. The Crimson Orchid was revealed to the world. It was a flower the size of a human's torso, with thick, tall petals covering it completely. It reminded Jack of a pitcher plant. The whole of it was entirely red, and the moment it appeared, the entire square was filled with the thick scent of blood.

Boy, I'd hate living in this area, Jack thought.

"The initial bidding price is one late B-Grade core, and you may bid in increments of at least one early B-Grade core," the mouth declared. "Let the Empty Star Auction... begin!"

Before it even finished its words, people were shouting prices.

"One late B-Grade core and one early B-Grade!"

"One and three!"

"One and seven!"

"Two late B-Grades!"

"Three late B-Grades!"

"Four late and two early B-Grades!"

The price hitched up rapidly. Jack struggled a bit to follow the pricing—everyone else was much more familiar with this world's currency exchanges.

"The first item is so expensive..." Brock muttered.

"It's customary for auctions to start with a heavy-hitter to get the audience going," Starhair explained. "Don't worry. Not everything will be as pricey."

The bidders competed for a while before the price stabilized. Bids were rarer and at smaller increments. Eventually, the item was sold for one early A-Grade core and three peak B-Grades. In a rare gesture of kindness, the real bidders of this item had let the audience shout low prices for a while to make them feel good.

The final winner was a late B-Grade octopus with five legs, which Jack recognized from his inn's tavern.

"Congratulations!" the floating mouth said. The octopus teleported on stage, passed a space ring to an attendant, and once its contents were verified, took the Crimson Orchid and teleported away. Jack didn't see where it reappeared. It was probably running away in fear of someone killing it for the orchid after the auction.

And, it was correct. Jack spotted several shadowy figures teleport away at the same time as the octopus. It wasn't his business.

"Next up!" the mouth declared. "From the glaciers of the southern Hex Province, we have..."

A few more items passed. All were precious, but none matched the price of the Blood Orchid, at most reaching eight peak B-Grade cores. Jack noticed that not all of the items had been part of yesterday's announcement. Apparently, that had included only the highest-valued ones.

Four items after the orchid, another high-value item appeared. It was a stone wheel containing mysterious inscriptions. According to the auctioneer, it was a broken manual pertaining to the Dao of Momentum. After a few price calls, it came down to two individuals who really wanted that item. Their fierce bidding war ended with one taking home the wheel for a whooping one early A-Grade and five peak B-Grades cores.

Like the octopus, this monster wasn't strong enough to protect this treasure, so it ran away. And, like the octopus, it was followed. Whether it escaped or not would depend on its speed.

This wasn't a phenomenon limited to the Space Monster World. Even in the outside universe, auctions were both about securing the item you wanted and escaping with it. Savory individuals were everywhere—and too much wealth could lead to one's downfall.

So far, the two Elders above hadn't spoken a single time. Neither had Jack. Nothing had caught his interest enough.

Finally, twenty-one items into the auction, something did. "Found by one of our Elders in a vast underground labyrinth," the mouth declared somberly, "we present something which needs no introduction. A late A-Grade core!"

An attendant walked on stage and placed a silk-covered item on a pedestal. She then lifted the silk. A sphere was revealed to the audience, the size of Jack's waist and emanating a terrible aura of power. Green swirls filled it, moving as if alive. Life energy emanated from it in waves, making those closest to the stage take deep breaths in hopes of ingesting just a little of the core's energy.

Jack's eyes shone. A late A-Grade core would be useless to him if it was incompatible... but this one carried the Dao of Life! Had it been made for him?

He made a split-second decision. The black hole manual was important, but it was a big gamble. This core could help him rapidly increase his powers in a short timespan. It was exactly what he needed. He decided to get it.

Well, if he could. The core's monetary value was nine early A-Grade ones, so three times Jack's current wealth, but very few people possessed that kind of money. With a little bit of luck...

"The starting price will be one early A-Grade core, and bids can be made in increments of one peak B-Grade core," the mouth instructed. "May the bidding begin!"

"One early A-Grade core and three peak B-Grade ones!" someone shouted.

"One and seven."

"Two early A-Grade cores!"

The price was quickly approaching Jack's limit. Too quickly.

"Two early A-Grade and three peak B-Grade cores!" he shouted, hoping for a miracle.

"Four early A-Grade cores!"

The response had been sharp and instant. Jack looked up, where a huge godzilla-like beast gazed at him with mockery. He almost cursed. Of course. Elder Crownbeast would never let him get anything unless he really, *really* hitched up the price.

Fuck this guy, Jack thought. Two can play this game.

"Five early A-Grade cores!" he shouted. He didn't have this much. If the auction ended now, he would be in trouble, but he was confident Elder Crownbeast would take the bait.

He had to risk it. If he didn't, then the Elder would certainly bid on the black hole manual as well, or any other item Jack was interested in. His only chance was to milk the Elder's reserves a little—

after all, while he certainly carried an immense amount of wealth, he had to save most of it to bid against Elder Puerto for the Overlord core.

Elder Crownbeast narrowed his eyes. "Two middle A-Grade cores!" he shouted.

"Two and two!" Jack shouted back.

"Two and four!"

By now, everyone else had stopped bidding. Not only was this too much money, but they wouldn't be idiots to bet against an A-Grade.

Jack bit his lips, pretending to hesitate. "Two middle A-Grade cores and seven early ones!" he shouted.

The Elder laughed. "Three middle A-Grade cores! Let's see how high you can go, boy!"

Jack pretended to throw a fit. Then he crossed his arms and sullenly sat on Dolly's back. "IT'S OKAY, MASTER," the hellhorse said. "YOU'LL GET HIM NEXT TIME!"

Jack pretended to grumble. Inwardly, he was happy. He'd managed to make Elder Crownbeast waste three middle A-Grade cores on an item he could have gotten with almost half of that. In fact, he'd have liked to get the price even higher, but even Jack couldn't take on too much risk. Any A-Grade was extremely intelligent. Up to this point was fine, because the Elder knew that Jack had gotten three early A-Grade cores from Saturnsun, so it was reasonable he had a few more. But, going any higher might raise suspicions.

"That was good, bro," Brock said. "We lost the item, but it's okay. At least he paid through the nose. What a loser."

Jack laughed. They hadn't bothered to keep their voices down, so several people from the audience looked up nervously. Elder Crownbeast remained still like a statue. The late A-Grade core he'd just won was received by one of his assistants.

"*Please don't do that again,*" Starhair said telepathically. Jack looked over to find him looking perfectly composed, but there was no hiding the panic in his voice.

"Sorry I scared you," he replied. "It worked out."

"Luckily."

"Worth the risk."

Starhair did not reply. Jack turned to watch the rest of the auction. He'd done everything he could so far. Hopefully, he'd win the black hole manual or something else.

The floating mouth presented a few more items, but the Elders did not speak again. They were both saving their resources for the final and far most precious item, the Overlord core. Jack hoped he'd at least made a dent on Crownbeast's wallet.

On the thirty-third item, a ginseng root emitting extreme life energy was presented. The auctioneer called it Star Root. Jack bid on it, but Elder Crownbeast eventually won it with one middle A-Grade core and two early ones. Jack didn't dare go too high this time. The item's actual value was far lower.

On the fiftieth item, the auctioneer presented a case containing ink and pencils. They had the mystical power to connect two individuals through matching tattoos. Brock wanted this item, and Jack bid on it, but it was eventually won by a straw-hatted peak B-Grade monster at two early A-Grade cores—a price far above the item's actual worth. He must have wanted it very badly. Even Brock only had a passing interest—blowing their entire wallet on it just wasn't worth it.

Finally, on the sixty-ninth item, came the one Jack had been waiting for. The incomplete black hole manual. The one he wanted to win no matter what.

CHAPTER THIRTY-SEVEN
BETTING FRENZY

"My wild monsters!" the announcer shouted, commanding everyone's attention. He was great at his job. The entire square—the entire city—was riled up and hanging from his lips. He continued, "I present to you this auction's sixty-ninth item. A broken Dao manual uncovered by one of our disciples in an abandoned ruin. According to our estimations, this manual was created by someone at least at the late Autarch level. However, due to its state of great disrepair, a more accurate judgment is impossible. While this manual cannot be used to construct a Dao path, it might be able to provide insights into the Daos of Space and Death. Bidding starts at one late B-Grade core, with a minimum increment of one middle B-Grade core."

With an exaggerated flourish, one of the attendants revealed a black sphere with blue motes of light lazily swimming inside.

The crowd's reaction was lukewarm. Space monsters were more gifted in the physical aspect than cultivators, but their Dao talent was relatively lower. Not many cultivated double Daos. Of those, the ones that happened to cultivate specifically Space and Death and also be at a high enough level to deconstruct this manual and salvage insights from the ruins... Well, suffice to say they were very few.

Jack, however, perked up. He'd been aiming for this item but hadn't held much hope. Now, it turned out this was one of the cheapest high-end items in the auction. What was just one late B-Grade core? He had plenty! He'd even offer thirty times that price!

"Hey, bro," Brock said, coming up to whisper in Jack's ear. "I'm whispering now so that Crownbeast sees us. He knows you cultivate Space but not Death. In his eyes, this item is useful to you, but not ridiculously so. If he also suspects you're just trying to make him waste money, he won't bid too high."

Jack nodded. "That was my plan as well," he whispered back.

Rare bids came from across the crowd. While space monsters who cultivated black hole-related Daos were rare, the plaza was packed. There were bound to be some present.

"Three late B-Grade cores!" someone shouted.

"Four!"

"Four and two middle ones!"

"Two peak B-Grade cores!" Jack shouted. Silence came momentarily as all the bidders eyed the new arrival. Most hovered in the sky at the same level as him—B-Grades—but they'd witnessed his strength the previous day. Many grimaced and gave up. A few, persisted.

"Two peak and two late cores!" came a thin voice. Tracing the figure, Jack found a thin woman hidden under a massive straw hat. Magical shadows cascaded over her face, with only her pale jaw revealed. She seemed humanoid.

"Three peak ones," Jack shot back.

"Three and two."

"Four peak ones."

"Four and two!"

Jack frowned. "Six peak ones!" he shouted.

Space cores multiplied in value threefold for every small realm and tenfold for every large one. There were three late B-Grade cores to a peak one, but ten peak ones to an early A-Grade core.

The woman paused. Her jaw tightened. Just as she was about to respond, a new voice washed over the crowd, stunning everyone into silence.

"One early A-Grade core."

It was calm, yet resolute. It carried absolute belief in victory. Everyone looked up to find Elder Crownbeast hovering there, his yellow glare glued on Jack. "Well?" the Elder asked. "Are you going to keep betting, kid?"

"What a thoughtful way to spend your faction's resources," Jack shot back without missing a beat. "One A-Grade core, one Elder's life, just to bully a junior. I'm sure your Overlord would be pleased if he saw you right now."

Crownbeast's forehead wrinkled. "You may not refer to Overlord Fiend King."

"Yeah, and you may not waste faction resources for personal benefit, but I guess we're both at fault."

"If you must know, this is my private wealth," Crownbeast replied, rearing up his head. The entire crowd was watching. "I am saving the faction's for when it is needed."

"Everyone knows that's not true. But, whatever. If you want to go bankrupt over this, I'll accompany you. One early A-Grade and three peak B-Grade cores."

"Hmph!" Crownbeast replied. "We both know it's not worth that much. Let's see who's more wasteful. One and six."

"*See what you did? Now neither of us is getting the manual!*" a voice reached Jack's mind. Surprised, he turned around to find the woman from before glaring at him. Green eyes glowed under her hat.

"*Stay in your lane,*" he replied, then spoke aloud, "Two early A-Grade cores!"

"Two and five," Crownbeast replied.

"Three early A-Grade cores!" Jack gave Crownbeast a relaxed smile. "I can do this all day."

This was actually the full extent of his wealth. He was bluffing.

Crownbeast opened his huge mouth which could fit a bus and laughed, shaking the earth's foundations. "What a fool! Only an idiot would spend three A-Grade cores on a broken manual. It's a good thing you're strong, otherwise I fear you'd have died back when you were still a pupa worm! Hahaha! Have your manual, stupid brat. That price was my disciple's wealth. I hope you consider it well-spent!"

Speaking to that point, Crownbeast gave Jack an ugly smile. Jack tried hard to compose himself—it was hard not to react when you were actually the winner.

"It's free money," he replied. "If I can make you eat a small public loss, it's worth it."

Crownbeast laughed again. To him, this bidding war wasn't a matter of resources. He certainly had more than Jack. However, if he spent a fortune to win a worthless item, he would be ridiculed. Even worse, Jack could keep betting blind after he ran out of wealth, and there was nothing Crownbeast could do about it.

He wasn't as rash as his words made him sound. Stopping here was a calculated decision; a certain victory, compared to the risk of betting even more. Crownbeast would never suspect that Jack was actually perfectly suited for this manual, nor that he really didn't care about this world's currency.

Making him pay ten times the price was good enough.

One's man trash is another's treasure, Jack thought. He barely held his smile as he flashed to the stage, exchanged the cores for the broken manual, then returned to his friends.

He couldn't participate in the auction any longer. All he had left was Saturnsun's peak B-Grade core. By any reasoning, this was the perfect time to flee the city, as Crownbeast—who might want to chase him—was still pinned down by the auction. Jack, however... had a plan.

He ignored the crowd's confused looks as he settled onto the back of Dolly—who was only flying because he held her aloft. "*See?*" he told the straw-hat woman. "*I did get it.*"

Her head snapped over so fast it cracked. "*It's not worth that much, you idiot!*"

He did not respond.

The rest of the auction flowed smoothly. Another thirty items passed, some more valuable than others. Fierce bidding wars erupted for each of them. The entire city was aflame with excitement. Even the common folk remained perched on rooftops, eyeing the commotion. It was rare to see so many masters gathered in one place.

Merchants crossed the crowd, selling what looked suspiciously like gummy worms. The monsters above were risking their lives to escape with precious items, while the atmosphere below was one of celebration. Most D and C-Grades had come to watch the show rather than bid on items.

And for the past few hours, the crowd had been slowly increasing. Even more people of all Grades had arrived. This province-wide celebration was reaching its crescendo.

"Everyone," the mouth said. For the first time, it floated forward, reaching the edge of the stage. "So far, this Empty Star Auction has gone on for fourteen hours. We have sold ninety-nine mystical items to the highest bidders, accumulating a total wealth of three middle A-Grade, eighteen early A-Grade, fifty-one peak B-Grade, two hundred and thirty-six late B-Grade, five hundred and forty-four middle B-Grade, and eleven hundred early B-Grade cores. Overall, that is the rough equivalent of two peak A-Grade cores. It is a tremendous amount of purchases, and we thank you all for your patronage."

The crowd cheered wildly.

"However!" the mouth shouted, grabbing everyone's attention. "As you all know, every Empty Star Auction sells exactly one hundred items. They are the hundred rarest, most valuable objects our faction has been able to acquire. So far, we have presented ninety-nine. That means there is one left. The crown of this auction. I present to you—the Overlord core!"

The crowd erupted. Shouts echoed over the buildings, washing over the city and the river around it. The water shook. Leviathans surfaced, offering deep roars to the sky before receding underwater.

Jack looked up. The two Elders were both standing at attention now. Neither looked at the other, but the tension was palpable. The air around them was shivering as if coming from an open oven.

The mouth raised its voice even higher. "The starting price is one late A-Grade core," it said, "and the minimum increment is one middle A-Grade core. Let the bidding begin!"

Jack blinked in surprise. The most expensive item so far had been *sold* for a middle A-Grade core and two early ones—at its final price. The Overlord core's starting price was almost double that. How precious was it!

Elder Puerto laughed, a sharp but calm sound. "The Overlord has sent me here to acquire this item," she said. "Since this is our territory, I hope Elder Crownbeast will show us some face."

"Elder Puerto is surely joking. This is an auction. How could I not earnestly participate?" Crownbeast laughed as well. "Besides—what a coincidence. My Overlord also sent me here to acquire this item. Shall we have a friendly competition, Elder Puerto?"

Both Elders smiled, but the smiles didn't reach their eyes. There was nothing friendly about this. They would financially grapple and try to rip each other apart.

"Allow me to begin, since we are the hosts here," Elder Puerto said. "One late A-Grade core. The starting price."

"Two late A-Grade cores."

"Three."

"Two peak ones."

The bids had instantly escalated to peak A-Grade cores. Crownbeast's current bid, which he nonchalantly made, was worth more than everything else in the auction combined. And this was just the start.

"I see you came prepared," Puerto said. "Three peak A-Grade cores."

"I offer four."

"Then I offer five."

"Hah! You're prepared to bleed for this, Puerto, but so am I! Six peak A-Grade cores."

"Let's see who has more blood to give. Seven."

"Obviously me—I'm so much larger! Eight."

"Nine."

"Ten!"

The crowd burst into waves of cheers. Jack felt his eardrums shake. The entire city rumbled as if caught in an earthquake. Ten peak A-Grade cores! What kind of concept was that!

Only now did Jack understand the true level of wealth in this world. The true difference. There were thousands of high-level monsters present, each able to rule their own corner of the world. Yet, none of them were able to produce a single late A-Grade core. All they could do was watch from below, like ants at giants, as the two Elders threw around obscene quantities of wealth.

Jack fantasized how, if he had all those cores, he could just hole up somewhere and reach the late B-Grade realm, maybe even the peak. He thought to the broken black hole manual in his space ring—it would be invaluable to his future progress, but right now, he couldn't help but feel it was a bit cheap.

Ten peak A-Grade cores was already the monetary value of the Overlord core. Since Overlords weren't truly in the next Grade, but only a half-step above the peak of the A-Grade, Jack suspected its value was even lower. However, that didn't matter. A core's actual worth depended on many more things, including rarity. Peak A-Grades cycled through the world—but how often was an Overlord born?

"Eleven peak A-Grade cores," Elder Puerto shouted.

"Twelve peak A-Grade cores!" Crownbeast insisted. Both Elders seemed a bit strained by now. Clearly, this amount of wealth was too much. They were only early A-Grades. They'd probably never seen such money in their lives.

Why didn't they send someone stronger to deal with these prices? Jack wondered.

"Thirteen cores!" Puerto declared. The moment she said it, she released a deep breath, as if she'd given everything she had.

Crownbeast didn't reply immediately. He remained still and expressionless like a statue, struggling inwardly. Jack thought there was only one reason why he'd hesitate—the funds given by his faction had run out, and anything he said from here on out would weigh against his personal wealth.

"Fourteen cores!" he finally declared. "If you can go at fifteen, I'll give up! This is just not worth it!"

Which meant, *I don't have that much.*

Puerto smiled bitterly. "You were only given thirteen by your faction, Crownbeast. Did you really use your personal fortune as well?"

"For the glory of my Overlord, there is nothing I'd hold back. His favor is worth more than any core." He turned his body completely, giving her a full glare. "What is it going to be, Puerto? Are you going to bid more or not?"

She shook her head. "I'm out," she said, then disappeared in a puff of red smoke. Her aura completely dissipated—though Jack could sense it holing up in an estate at the far north of the city.

Crownbeast laughed in relief. The crowd roared and cheered for him. Jack, who had been absorbed by the excitement, resisted the urge to clap.

"Congratulations, Elder Crownbeast," the mouth said. With the oaken box beside it, it slowly floated to the sky, coming to hover right before the Elder. It bent its body forward as the box floated over. "The Overlord core couldn't have a better owner."

Crownbeast laughed again. He seemed to be in a great mood. "There you go!" he said, flicking a finger and tossing out a space ring. "I included a small tip as well. Enjoy it!"

The ring stopped by the mouth, which shivered in surprise a moment later. "Thank you, Elder!" it said, true emotion slipping into its voice.

"I'll stay in the city for a bit," Crownbeast said. "Can your estate accommodate me?"

"Absolutely! Please, this way, sir." The mouth respectfully led the way to the same estate Puerto had disappeared in, at the far north, and Crownbeast followed. The crowd was left hanging, still cheering and shouting.

"That's it?" Jack said. "No closing speech?"

"Mouth bro gave the closing speech before the final item," Brock said. "Maybe it thought there'd be a battle."

"Hmm. In any case... Shall we return to our rooms? So many things happened, and we need to work out how to leave the city. I bet Crownbeast will try to follow us."

"Right. Let's go."

Jack turned Dolly toward their inn and set off while most of the crowd was busy celebrating. Absent-mindedly, he spared a glance for the straw-hat woman from before... but she was nowhere to be seen.

CHAPTER THIRTY-EIGHT

BLACK HOLE

After the auction was over, the crowd didn't disperse right away. They couldn't if they wanted to. The streets were so packed that people formed long lines, many monsters fighting each other in the confusion.

As everyone was struggling to leave the square, some people noticed a peculiarity. There seemed to a gathering on the now-empty auction stage. Several people sat on it cross-legged, exchanging cups of wine and laughing. Their pleasant conversation spread throughout the square.

"What's going on?" a monster asked its friend.

"No idea."

Whispers spread. As more people turned to the drinking group, the square began to quiet down.

One monster decided to go for it. "Hey," it asked. "Can I join you guys? It's better than waiting down here."

A double devil on the stage grumbled. "I don't even know why I'm here," he muttered, but another wine-drinker spoke over him—a gorilla-looking monster who raised his cup.

"Sure thing, bro," he said. "The more the merrier. There's enough wine for everyone."

The asking monster laughed as it jumped to the stage, receiving a cup the brorilla removed from his space ring. The joy was infectious. In some odd way, everyone relaxed as they eyed the gathering on the square, and even the occasional fighting stopped. They wanted to be up there as well. They wanted to belong in that group.

The brorilla laughed again, then turned to address the square. "There's enough wine for everyone," he repeated. "Come up here, bros!"

Brock and Starhair had said they'd remain for a while, but Jack had things to do, so he returned alone. He now sat cross-legged in the middle of his room. His bare thighs rubbed against the polished floor, while the faint scent of wood permeated the room. It was much more spacious than he was used to, containing an entire kitchen and bar alongside a king-sized bed, but those didn't concern him. Comfort was temporary. Power was forever.

The broken Dao manual rested on Jack's legs—a dark sphere inlaid with motes of blue light. It was like seeing a small universe from the outside, with all its million stars.

Those stars were swimming constantly. Some followed set trajectories. Others jumped around erratically, while a few shimmered in and out of existence as if about to die. Those movements visually clashed against each other, giving any watcher a jarring feeling.

The auctioneer was right. This Dao manual was thoroughly broken. Moreover, because of its innate complexity, it was impossible to tell which stars were intact and which were faulty. Attempting to study this was like reading a book whose words had been randomly scrambled.

However, that didn't mean it was useless. Jack calmed his mind, sinking into a meditative state. He then pierced his perception into the sphere, carefully combing through it. He was slow and thorough. An hour later, he hadn't even gone through a tenth of it.

While the sphere was broken and jumbled up, that didn't necessarily apply to all of it. There could be sections which were relatively intact, and though they offered little to the untrained eye, they could benefit someone already familiar with the basics. It was exactly those sections Jack was searching for. The reason he'd spent so much to acquire this sphere.

Yet, even after a few hours and combing over half the sphere, he'd come up with nothing. A rueful smile was forming on his lips.

Some risks don't pay off, he thought. That is part of the road to mastery.

Suddenly, he noticed something. A tiny section where the jarring sensation was missing. Eleven stars in a circle, falling together and narrowly missing each other before spreading out again. It was a mystical sight—and it spoke of mastery. All thoughts were wiped off Jack's brain as he focused, bringing his full attention on that tiny part of the sphere.

He observed and studied the movement of the stars. Soon, he realized it wasn't just them that were moving, but also the darkness between them. Space was weaving through itself, and there was also something more, something heavy and dark which wasn't space. It reminded Jack of death, but not quite that either.

Dark matter? he wondered. The thought was quickly banished. Dark matter, or dark energy, was what Earth scientists used to call the extra energy they measured in the universe, but which they could not find. It had stumped them for decades. After the Integration, it had become apparent that dark matter was just the ambient Dao particles swimming through the universe.

This wasn't that. The dark energy swimming between these stars wasn't just Dao particles. It took Jack a few moments to realize where he'd seen it before.

Right! The dark surfer!

His second-to-last Dao Vision had depicted a man on a black surfboard riding the currents of a black hole. He'd been trying to copy it. In his attempts, he'd summoned the exact same type of energy—a foamy, encroaching crystallization of space-death. A form of hungry nothingness.

This realization gave Jack hope. That black foam represented the dark surfer's greatest insights, and he was an Archon. If the same kind of energy was present here, tightly controlled, it meant the creator of this Dao manual had reached the same level. This wasn't a peak A-Grade inheritance, but an Archon inheritance! Maybe it was even connected to the same dark surfer!

He slowed his thoughts, he was getting ahead of himself. Jack refocused, diving into the stars with renewed vigor. He didn't dare keep his hopes up—for all he knew, this section of stars was a minor part of the inheritance, or even worse, part of a fractured whole.

Time flowed ceaselessly. At some point, Jack's surroundings began to fade. The stars became his whole world, and through it, he saw another image. It was colorless and vague—nowhere near the clarity of a Dao Vision. In this image, he saw a red-scaled lizard man standing in an undistinguishable environment. The man bent his knees, lowering his center of mass as he swung a halberd behind his back, ready to unleash it forward.

A bodiless roar echoed in Jack's ears. On the halberd's head, a dark sphere appeared. It floated right along the blade, swallowing its middle part, and it only kept growing darker. Deeper. Heavier. The bricks making up the floor were sucked into the sphere. So was air. Every Dao particle in the surrounding space was absorbed, further enhancing the sphere's terrifying weight until the entire world seemed to be falling into it.

The man's face flashed with surprise, joy, and panic. He teleported, reaching a region of emptiness, then swung his halberd. The sphere flew out. Where it hit the ground, everything was sucked into it, forming a lake-sized crater into the earth. The man laughed.

"*The center falls, the world helps, the hole forms!*" he shouted.

Though the visuals were fuzzy, his voice was crystal-clear in Jack's ears.

The vision dissipated then. Jack was back in his room, panting on the ground. He didn't know when he'd fallen. He didn't care. The vision had inspired him—because, in creating a miniature black hole, the man had only used the power of a peak A-Grade!

Of course, it was a weak imitation of a black hole. Even B-Grades had ways to form that lake-sized crater. That didn't really matter though , because it proved something important which Jack had been missing. It was possible to create imitations of a black hole at lower levels!

So far, he'd been trying to recreate the real thing. The death of space, the end of time. True nothingness. Such a concept stood at the very peak of the universe, only approachable by Archons. Jack had experimented just for the insights. However, if there could be weaker versions...

His mind was already roaring with possibilities. The man in the vision had used a peak A-Grade's power, but his space and death Daos were exquisite. Superior to Jack's, though not by much. Maybe he couldn't recreate the feat, but could he pursue the principle?

Jack returned to his meditating position and temporarily put away the Dao manual. Closing his eyes, he entered his inner world, a mostly empty universe littered with floating pieces of earth. Somewhere in the center, a large figure was hunched over a chessboard made of the planetary fragments flying around.

Venerable Saint Thousand Shell was deep in thought. He pointed his head at a piece, which floated and slowly moved to another position.

"You picked it up! Now you have to play it!" the Stone gloated from its position at the other side of the board. "This was a mistake! You should have taken my knight. Queen takes knight, then I would be forced into a long sequence! Still winning, of course, but longer! Or you could have moved your a2 pawn—always a good choice."

"Will you shut up?" the turtle groaned. "I'm trying to think."

Wrinkles creased its reptilian face, as every road it saw ended in defeat. Finally, it placed down its queen in a square surrounded by enemy pieces, none of which could actually touch her.

"I thought you'd do that! You miscalculated!" the Stone exclaimed. "Bishop at e4, check. I can use this tempo to ensure a winning endgame!"

The Stone had no limbs to move the pieces, but Copy Jack was there. At its command, he grabbed a bishop-looking piece, then moved it to the indicated position. He nodded in approval all the while.

"Hey, guys," Jack said. Nobody had noticed his arrival, so all three jumped. The turtle accidentally kicked over the chessboard.

"Whoops," he said. "Guess it's game over."

"No worries!" the Stone replied. "I remember the position. We can recreate it!"

The turtle gave it a death stare before turning to Jack. "How's it going, kid? You can't be having a worse day than me."

"Pretty good, actually. Listen, I'll be experimenting a bit over on that side. Try not to get killed by the energy ripples."

"...Okay."

"Hi, Jack!" the Stone said, hopping in place. "Do you want to play some chess? It helps you work on your Dao!"

Jack laughed. "Thank you, Stone, but I'm a little busy. You already got a gaming partner."

"Oh, please," the turtle grumbled. "This is ridiculous."

"You know," Jack said, "for how long you've been alive, I thought you'd be good at chess. You had a lot of time to practice."

"I did practice, and I am good. That's why it's ridiculous. I hate losing."

"Huh." Jack threw a glance at The Stone, which was currently spinning around in joy. "Well, have fun. I'll be a few thousand miles that way if you need me."

Leaving the three to their fun, Jack teleported away, quickly reaching the fringes of his inner world. Walls of starry dust indicated the borders, while the terrifying emptiness inside was his to command.

Experimenting in his inner world wasn't ideal because it had small differences to the outside one. However, he didn't want to leave the city right now, and even if he did, he wasn't familiar enough with the Space Monster World to wantonly destroy the wilderness. As for experimenting inside Empty Star City, that was far too reckless.

For now, the inner world would do.

Jack spread his arms wide, summoning the power of space and creating a large bubble of sealed space. He then used his Dao and willpower to compress it, shrinking it from a mile in diameter to roughly three feet. This wasn't his limit, but it was good enough to stop and think. The space particles were going wild inside it.

Last time, he'd tried compressing this sphere to the limit, hoping to achieve a gravitational singularity. All sorts of weird phenomena had occurred, including an elementary form of the space-death foam. In the end, he hadn't even come close to creating a true black hole. Though he'd gotten a bit stronger since then, he was still way, way off.

Which made perfect sense. Black holes were some of the most powerful forces in the universe. Even Enas, the leader of the Old Gods, had been trapped inside one for a billion years. If Jack could create it, that would be almost unfair.

What did the red man do? Jack asked himself, thinking back to the vision. That man had created something like a black hole, though far weaker than the original. Unfortunately, the vision was too fuzzy to make out how he did it.

What clues do I have?

Jack revisited everything he'd seen, the entire sequence. The black hole-like thing had formed on the blade of the man's halberd. That didn't necessarily matter. Maybe it was the focal point he was most familiar with. Soon after forming, it had begun sucking in its surroundings, so it really did work like a black hole.

Afterward, the man had taken this black hole and teleported away. That was the first clue. If he could teleport it away, it was under his direct control. A real black hole could never move that way because it couldn't interact with space in any way other than consuming it.

What happened next? Jack's eyes flashed. The man had thrown his black hole against the ground, where it created a massive crater before disappearing.

It disappeared! Black holes didn't do that! If it was a real black hole, it would have just kept growing until it swallowed the entire Space Monster World.

So it really isn't the real thing, Jack deduced. *It has to be some sort of artificial creation which mirrors some qualities of the black hole... But how?*

How is a black hole created?

Too much matter gathers in one place. Its gravitational pull becomes more and more intense until even its atoms can't bear it. They collapse, gathering into one spot of endless density. Since its radius is zero, the gravity very close to it is infinite, absorbing even light and timespace. The more it absorbs, the greater the radius in which gravity is so powerful nothing can escape. That is the event horizon. That's how black holes are created.

How can I imitate it?

Jack looked down at his hand. A realization popped up in his mind.

He used his halberd because it has mass! The black hole needs actual matter as its core, not just space particles like I've been doing!

He let the bubble dissipate. Space particles erupted outward, but Jack paid them no mind. He created a new mile-wide bubble, this time centering it around his own fist. He took a deep breath, then compressed it.

The pressure ballooned quickly. He wasn't sure how powerful it was, but he knew a regular B-Grade would have been crushed. He compressed the bubble until his torso was outside of it, then kept compressing, the edge of the bubble sliding across his forearm. The pressure was staggering by now. Even his durable body found it hard to endure. He was thankful he'd spent so much time tempering it, otherwise there was no way he'd able to do this.

Finally, the sphere compressed enough that it encapsulated just his fist. The space particles were going crazy in there, zooming around frantically as they tried to escape. His hand was feeling the pressure. The bones were slowly giving way. The pain was horrific.

Jack clenched his teeth and focused his willpower into compressing further. His hand shattered with a sickening crunch. Bones and flesh were pulverized, becoming a pressurized mass which rushed to the very center of the bubble and hovered there. The space particles already behaved differently, gravitating toward that mass and struggling to escape. A few fell into it, sticking to the mass, increasing its gravity. Hints of black foam appeared as the space particles began dying despite their best efforts. The pressure was more than Jack could handle. The bubble was destabilizing.

It went better than last time, but this was still far from a true black hole.

"Fuck!" Jack said, throwing the bubble with all his might. It flew toward the center of his inner world and exploded before it traveled a mile. Intense fluctuations of space and death flooded the world. Thankfully, this was his world, so Jack neutralized most of the impact. He was mostly unhurt.

"Fuck," he said, clutching onto the stump of his wrist. This wasn't his real body, but the pain was real. "Still not enough..."

His eyes flashed with calculations. This had gone far better than previously. Indeed, it was better to use some matter as the center of the black hole, and preferably his fist, which he was most familiar with. He'd learned that much. But he still hadn't achieved the level of the red man who created the incomplete Dao manual.

He knew he could do it. His understandings weren't too far off from that man's. He could create at least a weaker variant of a black hole, he just had to figure out how. There was still something missing.

"Well, I'll get it," he promised himself. "Already, this can almost work as a weapon. I just need time to charge it."

The explosion of the compressed sphere wasn't a black hole, but it contained the black foam, a terrifying force of nature. Even Jack wasn't sure he could survive a direct hit. This was a very powerful skill he was cooking up—he just needed to solve a few more problems. Mostly the charging time, which right now was too long.

If he figured out how to actually summon a black hole, like the red man had done, his battle power would skyrocket. He had a feeling the potential of this move was far above Supernova's.

While Jack was absorbed in his inner world, that didn't mean his real body was defenseless. He always left part of his consciousness on lookout. At this point, as he pondered on the mysteries of the universe, that part of his consciousness registered a knock on the door.

Jack returned fully to the real world and stretched his arms. "Come in," he said.

The door opened, and in came Elder Puerto.

CHAPTER THIRTY-NINE
INVITATION

JACK SHOT TO HIS FEET FASTER THAN A STARTLED DEER. "ELDER PUERTO! Welcome!"

She waved him off. "I see you're meditating. Good. A talented monster like yourself shouldn't slack off."

"You flatter me."

"I will get to the point, Mr... You never gave me your name, actually."

"Jack Monstrous, Elder."

She sat on a random chair and crossed her legs. Though Elder Puerto seemed like a buff red-haired old lady, she was much heavier. The steel chair creaked under her weight. The legs bent ominously.

"Well, Jack Monstrous, I will be leaving Empty Star City today. Have you considered my offer?"

"Your invitation to the Great Silver?"

"Precisely. If you agree, I can take you with me. I will guarantee your safety and help you get access to the main faction."

Jack thought about it. "That's a generous offer, Elder."

"Please, speak plainly. With your talent, we'll be peers soon enough."

He laughed.

"I did think about it. I'm willing to join your faction, on three terms."

Puerto raised a brow. "Oh?"

"My first term is that you let me join the next Canal Delve. The second is that you support me fully despite not originally being from your faction. The third is that I won't come with you right away—I have some things to do, so I'll make my own way to the faction."

"Hmm." She leaned forward, her eyes flashing with calculations. "Getting invited to the Delve is not something I can promise, but I can say it depends entirely on you. If you can show a good enough performance, you'll naturally be invited. As for not being originally from the faction... Who cares? The only thing that matters in the Great Silver is strength. You'll receive all the support you deserve. Are my answers satisfactory to you, Jack Monstrous?"

There was a hint of threat in her voice. The Great Silver was one of the Space Monster World's two great Overlord factions. Most monsters would kill their best friend for a chance to join, even as a janitor. Jack was personally invited by an Elder, and he still dared to put forth terms, as if *he* was the catch here.

Fortunately, Jack possessed the qualifications to be arrogant, and Elder Puerto knew it.

"They're satisfactory," he replied. "And my third term?"

"That's no problem at all. I didn't want to babysit you to begin with. If you say you'll make your own way, feel free, just make sure to arrive within three years."

"Why's that?"

"The Canal Delve is at four, and we can't have a stranger join us."

"Okay, yeah, I'll be there in time."

She nodded. "You don't strike me as naive, Jack Monstrous. Could you be unaware of Elder Crownbeast aiming for you? He can wait here for at least a year, and the moment you leave Empty Star City, he'll come for you. It's hard to avoid an A-Grade's perception. That's why I offered to escort you."

Jack smiled enigmatically. "I know about Elder Crownbeast. I angered him, so he'll do anything he can to get me... But I have my ways. I'm confident I can escape safely."

"Mm. Good." She sized him up once more. If he wasn't mistaken, she was impressed. "Are you maybe looking for a sex partner?"

Jack was taken aback. "Uh. I, uh, I'm very flattered, Elder, and I would accept in a heartbeat, but I already have a dedicated partner."

"That's a shame. Very well then. I probably won't catch you later, so I expect to welcome you in Great Silver faction within three years. Don't die."

"I'll try my best. Thank you, Elder."

"Good luck, Jack Monstrous."

Elder Puerto opened the door and walked out. Jack imagined she did it for the show, because there's no way she didn't just teleport away the moment she was out of sight. Regardless, he couldn't sense her. His perception was foiled. Both coming and going, Elder Puerto was like a ghost—like she was never there.

Wait. Did she have any aura at all?

Maybe it was a projection.

He shook his head and sat back down. Elder Puerto would leave today, but he didn't have to. Three years was a long time.

First, I'll get a basic grip on this black hole thing, and then I'll go.

Six months later...

Jack, Brock, and Starhair headed for the city gates, riding their hellhorses.

"GET OUT OF THE WAY BEFORE I DEVOUR YOUR LOVED ONES!" Dolly shouted, snapping her teeth at the passersby.

"Hey, bro, chill," one space monster said.

"Yeah, bro. Take it easy. I don't have any loved ones."

"Me neither!" a third replied.

"I DO NOT POSSESS LOVED ONES EITHER, BESIDES MY

MASTER. I'M SORRY IF I BROUGHT UP BAD MEMORIES. AND I'M SORRY FOR CHEWING ON YOUR TAIL THAT ONE TIME."

"No worries, it grew right back!"

"See you around, bro!"

Jack tilted his head. "You know, Brock, I know I didn't leave my room for six months, but I'd swear this city has changed a little."

"You think?" Brock asked. He walked next to the hellhorses, constantly clasping hands, fist-bumping, and hugging random monsters. Some of them were crying.

"We'll miss you, big bro!" they shouted, falling into Brock's arms like flies.

"It's okay, bros," Brock replied sagely. "We may be apart, but we'll always be connected by our brohood."

"Yes, big bro!"

"Hey." Jack leaned toward Starhair. "How long do you think he'd need to convert this entire world?"

"Who cares? Seeing all these monsters obsessed with stupid bro love twists my guts."

"Don't be grumpy, Starhair. It's fun. You like fun."

"I don't like fun. I prefer cultivation."

"Then you're doing pretty terrible I guess."

Starhair threw Jack an astonished look, but he only laughed and shook it off. This was his first time out of meditation in six months, so Brock's antics were refreshing. Even Starhair was. They remained in their double devil disguise, but the other cultivator had raised his bandana a little bit. His hair, half of which he'd sacrificed to let them escape Archon Summer Noon, was slowly growing back.

A contingent of bros was waiting for them by the gates. Jack didn't know how many monsters Brock had converted, but it had to be a lot. They'd brought fireworks and gongs. It was a sad occasion they were determined to make the best out of.

"Little bros," Brock said, hijacking the guard's raised stage. "Separations always come, but saying goodbye is part of the art of life. I hope you keep brohood in your hearts. Farewell!"

"Farewell, big bro!" the crowd of monsters shouted, some shedding tears. The three cultivators flew away, riding their hellhorses into the sunset, while gongs and fireworks waved their goodbyes. It was the end of an era for these city bros, but also the start of a new one. And that was worthy of celebration.

"Seriously, how do you do that?" Jack asked.

Brock gave him an earnest look. "Everybody needs brohood. Even Starhair. They just don't know it until I show them."

"I only need one thing, and that's my hair back," Starhair replied. Brock smiled at him.

"We'll see."

A few minutes passed. The three of them dismounted the hellhorses, placed them in their inner worlds—"BYE, MASTERS"—and accelerated into the distance. Sonic booms trailed their flight.

"I don't think he's following us," Brock said, glancing behind his shoulder.

"I hope he isn't," Starhair added worriedly.

"He certainly is," Jack replied. "He thinks he's hiding, but I can sense him. He's just biding his time."

They were flying in the direction of Great Silver faction, which was very, very far away. The lush jungles below them changed into an arid desert. An hour into flying, their pursuer still hadn't shown himself.

"You know," Jack said, "this is getting a bit nerve-wracking."

"You think!" Starhair replied.

Jack stopped in midair. He turned around, eyeing the cloudy sky above. This curtain of clouds covered the entire Space Monster World, hiding the real sky. Even now, Jack had no idea what it looked like.

"You've followed us long enough," he said, enhancing his voice so it boomed over the land. "Show yourself!"

A moment of silence followed. Then another. As Jack was about to shout again, loud laughter filled the air.

"Hahahahaha!"

The clouds broke apart as if ripped by a giant hand. A second layer was revealed far above them—in between stood a giant, godzilla-like form, a massive monster with vertical irises and spikes running down its spine. Its eyes were warped with malice and triumph.

"What a fool you are, Jack Monstrous!" Elder Crownbeast shouted. "If you had left with Puerto, I wouldn't be able to touch you. If you waited a couple years, I'd be forced to leave. But you just couldn't hold it, could you? You threw yourself right in the monster's mouth!"

"You are the fool," Jack replied with a smile. "You know we're prepared for you, and you still came."

"I'm also prepared."

The Elder's massive form descended slowly. As it did, Jack noticed he'd grown even larger. He'd only been three hundred feet in the city, but now he'd risen to three thousand. Maybe this was his real size, and he'd just shrunk himself to avoid accidentally breaking things.

In fact, he looked exactly like the giant monster that one-punch man had fought in Jack's first vision, except much stronger.

"What's your trump card, brat?" the Elder said, narrowing his eyes. His aura roiled. "Bring it out, and let me crush it!"

"There is no trump card," Jack replied. "Only my fist."

"You can't be serious."

"Oh, I am."

Elder Crownbeast hesitated. His aura spread far but found nobody.

"You didn't call your master?" Crownbeast asked. "Not Puerto? Not anybody?"

"Nobody," Jack replied. "I don't need help."

"Could you really be an idiot?"

"You know..." Jack grinned, clenching his fist. "I've never killed an Autarch before."

Elder Crownbeast started laughing, both in disbelief and

ridicule, but he was cut short. Jack's aura erupted. A potent combination of life, death, space, and time washed over the world, destroying the empty land beneath. The quantity of his energy wasn't too great, but the Daos it carried were vast. Miniature fists floated through the air, while a larger fist phantom spontaneously formed around Jack, each finger a different color—green, black, blue, white, and purple, the color of the Fist.

Elder Crownbeast chocked on his words. "What's that aura?" he asked, looking around. His eyes grew wider. "You're so strong... How is this possible? How can you possess such power at the middle Baron level!"

"You'll never find out," Jack replied calmly. He clenched his fists, and all the phantoms disappeared. The world held its breath. Brock and Starhair had already retreated.

"Do you really intend to fight me?" the Elder asked. "This is ridiculous. I'm almost a large realm above you!"

"I told you," Jack said. "I've never killed an Autarch before. I want to find out how it feels—I want to step on that stage."

Elder Crownbeast finally took Jack seriously. He considered his immense talent. Slowly, his wildly rolling aura condensed around his body, cladding him in wild red light.

"Even the brightest disciple I ever mentored cannot match up to your little toe," Crownbeast admitted in a low growl. "I was planning on dragging you back to the faction, but I changed my mind. You cannot be allowed to grow. You must die now."

"Bring it on, lizard," Jack said, and he did not wait. He charged.

CHAPTER FORTY

FIGHTING A-GRADE

JACK CHARGED INTO ELDER CROWNBEAST, PIERCING THROUGH MULTIPLE layers of space. His speed was far superior to what he'd showed in the duel against Saturnstar. He reached Crownbeast in an instant and punched out sideways, smashing his fist against the Elder's aura like a comet from the heavens.

The sky behind him distorted. Tendrils of purple energy spread out, flashing to the horizon, but the Elder's crimson aura held.

"Fool!" Crownbeast laughed. "Us crownbeasts specialize in defense! Even if I stood here and let you hit me for an hour, you still wouldn't be able to injure me!"

"I'm just warming up," Jack replied. "How about you sit still and wait if you're so sure?"

"As if!"

The beast's jaws flashed with extreme speed. One moment he was upright, the next his fangs were around Jack, ready to eviscerate him. Space warped, and the jaws snapped on empty air.

"Too slow!" Jack shouted from above the Elder's head. He smashed a fist down, trailing it with stars. "Meteor Punch!"

The meteor smashed into the top of the godzilla's head and

pushed it down. The entire monster shook as it dropped, righting itself in midair. A ten-mile-wide crater formed on the desert below. Sand rose to the heavens.

"You're strong, I'll give you that!" Crownbeast shouted. "The greatest talent I've ever seen. However, you're just too arrogant. It's impossible to jump a large realm to fight me! You just don't have the power! And what's more, I came prepared! I thought your master would arrive to fight me, so I practiced discipline and manners for the past six months. Your Great Spanking Arts gain no advantage against me!"

Jack paused, his fist drawn back. "Did you actually believe that?"

"What do you mean?"

"...Maybe I overdid it. In any case, shut your mouth and fight me like a monster!"

"As you wish!"

Elder Crownbeast closed his mouth, hiding his fangs as he launched himself head-first at Jack like a torpedo. This was the same move Saturnstar used as a finisher, but to the Elder, it was just another move. A three-thousand-foot monster barreled toward Jack at speeds far surpassing that of sound. At the same time, a mighty space lock came over him, along with a mighty feeling of bloodlust produced by savagery. Twin restraints prevented Jack from dodging. He broke both at the same time, narrowly disappearing into space as Crownbeast pulverized his previous position.

Jack reappeared nearby, charging immediately. He shouldn't give the Elder any time to breathe. In melee, Crownbeast couldn't charge up any big attacks, and the small ones would be easier to dodge.

Jack rushed into Crownbeast. His fists flared. Punch after punch smashed into hard scales, while Brutalizing Aura assaulted the Elder's mind. Winds of savagery attempted to immobilize Jack, but he resisted them with pure willpower.

However, while Jack could protect himself, his strikes were ineffective. His fists broke against the crimson aura and hard scales. Progress was slow, like poking a giant to death.

"Hahahah!" Crownbeast laughed. "Dance around, fool! You'll run out of energy eventually, and then I'll catch you!"

"I told you to shut the fuck up!"

Jack stuck close. He pelted the godzilla with many small attacks, infusing them with the power of death. Scales cracked and rotted, but it was too little. They barely counted as scratches.

A thick tail rose for Jack, and he expertly curved space around him so it missed. He nailed a straight punch into the monster's chest, then flashed behind it and smashed another at the back of the neck. He teleported unpredictably. Arms, legs, torso, head. The monster was assaulted by a flurry of blows which only scratched it.

As Elder Crownbeast reared up for another attack, Jack dodged it preemptively, securing a few instants for himself. The world was sucked into his fist. More and more Dao particles were absorbed, making his hand glow. Right as it reached critical mass, Jack let it rip.

"Supernova!"

A star exploded on the Elder's back. Purple light filled the world, the shockwave rolling onto the earth below and demolishing it completely. The desert had transformed into a blackened crater.

Jack had flown back from the impact. His fractured hand bones quickly set into place. As he looked toward the monster, however, he frowned. The scales and red aura, which he'd broken through for the first time, were rapidly regenerating. The wound below them remained, but it was nowhere near debilitating. He'd need to stack a dozen such strikes to actually harm the giant monster, and he'd run low on energy by then.

Elder Crownbeast was surprised for a different reason. "You actually managed to injure me?" he uttered in disbelief. "How can you be so strong?"

"Still not enough..." Jack muttered. "No choice then."

Green light covered his skin. Suddenly, he grew a foot taller and sprouted two extra arms from his armpits. His only article of clothing —the magical pair of shorts which enhanced his defense—grew with him. Thankfully, the transformation didn't affect his double devil disguise.

This was the second time Jack used his battle form since reaching the B-Grade. The Life Drop had been emptied out during his breakthrough, and recharging it was slow, even with the entire Green Dragon Realm fueling it. Six months after its last use against Archon Summer Noon, it had only recovered enough energy to maintain this transformation for a few minutes. A time which would be cut even shorter if forced to regenerate any injuries.

Jack had to make it count.

"You grew even *stronger*?" Elder Crownbeast shouted, sensing Jack's burst of energy. "What kind of monster are you!"

"The last you'll ever see," Jack growled as he charged. His physical strength had skyrocketed. He needed it to actually injure the Elder. He teleported in, easily dodging an attack and smashing an empowered Supernova into the monster's chest.

This explosion was even stronger than the last. A new sun appeared. Purple light illuminated the world, while the boom traveled for a thousand miles. Another layer of rock was pushed into the ground, deepening the crater, and all those happened with the vast majority of energy focused on breaking Crownbeast's defense.

Another hole appeared on the monster's chest. Broken scales flew into the sky, while cracked ones surrounded a crater of blood and bones. The corner of a lung was revealed before the Elder's flesh regrew. He seemed stunned, but not grievously injured. It wasn't just his defense that was great, but also his endurance.

"How can you injure me so?" he muttered, fear seeping into his voice for the first time. "How is this possible!"

By now, it was beginning to dawn on Crownbeast that he'd made a mistake. Jack's speed was far superior to any other B-Grade's, and also superior to Crownbeast's. If Jack wanted to run, the Elder couldn't stop him. The best outcome here was a draw.

But, if Crownbeast wanted to run, he couldn't. He wasn't fast enough. And now, for the first time, he was beginning to suspect he might lose—unless he took this seriously.

"Will I really be defeated by a middle Baron?" he shouted, infuriated by his own words. "I will destroy you, Jack Monstrous! Assault form!"

His body shrunk. From three thousand feet tall, he became just thirty. His defense and power were greatly reduced, but his speed rose tremendously. He flashed out, instantly catching up to Jack. He turned and swung his own scaly fist. Jack caught it with his two right forearms, both of which shattered like matches. He was sent flying backward, blood trailing his path.

Crownbeast reappeared over him, smashing Jack with his tail mid-flight. Jack punched it but was overpowered. He crashed into the ground and dug himself a mile deep.

Crownbeast didn't let up. He charged into the hole, and the ground erupted, showering the crater with pieces of rocks. Two bloodied forms flew out. Jack's body was riddled with constantly regenerating wounds.

Unfortunately, his cultivation base was just too low. He was far outclassed in strength and defense. In this new form, he only slightly surpassed Crownbeast in speed, and that's because the monster really suffered in that area. Jack's only path to victory was his extreme understanding of the Dao.

How arrogant was it for a youth to challenge a millennia-old elder in world comprehension? How bold? Yet, it was true—the Dao grew with experience more than it did with time, and in this regard, Jack held the definitive advantage.

Crownbeast also sported some injuries, although only superficial. The two traded blow for blow, but Jack's attacks only inflicted scratches, while the Elder's were devastating. Only the Life Drop's regeneration kept Jack in the fight—when it ran out of energy, he'd have to escape. It's also worth noting that all this occurred on Jack's highly tempered body—any other B-Grade would have been smashed to smithereens.

"SUPERNOVA!" Jack shouted, meeting the Elder's fist with his own. A new explosion shook the world. Jack flew back, his hand shattered and his shoulder cracked, while Crownbeast grunted and pursued. His scaly hand was also fractured.

I must do something! Jack thought. I'll never win like this!

He did have his newest weapon, but it took time to charge, and Crownbeast would never give it to him. He needed to earn it.

The two clashed again. Strikes flew. Fists met scales. Scales met flesh. The sky shattered and was washed away, the clouds ripped apart to reveal more layers above. The earth had long given way to a field of devastation. Blood rained from the sky—mostly Jack's.

Between their various exchanges, Jack saw his opening. He braced himself. A set of jaws flew at his shoulder, and he let them land. Bones shattered—flesh was rent. Crownbeast didn't expect this attack to work. Before he could recover, Jack used the time earned by not defending to charge up his own strike.

"Supernova!" he shouted. His fist smashed into the opponent's chest. The explosion burned Jack as well. Crownbeast flew down like a rocket, his still-closed jaws ripping out Jack's shoulder and arm. He was nailed into the earth, but flew back out a moment later. His mangled chest was already regenerating.

"Fool!" he said, panting. "You can't trade hits like this! I'll just out-sustain—"

He did not finish his words.

Jack hovered in the middle of the sky. One of his four arms was still missing, the open wound dripping blood. His chest was burned, yet his face didn't betray the slightest hint of pain. His eyes were razor-focused. His mouth was hard.

A bubble of sealed space spread around Jack's fist. It compressed in pulses, raising the pressure to terrifying degrees. The moment Crownbeast resurfaced, the bubble was reduced to encapsulate only Jack's fist, which shattered. Bones and flesh warped together, collapsing into a singular point. The power of space raged.

As the bubble compressed even further, becoming a nail-sized singularity, black foam filled it. A terrible suction force erupted outward, sucking the air into a spiral, a whirlpool given life and giving death. The now-black sphere grew larger as it absorbed the world. From the size of a nail, it grew to the size of Jack's hand.

He brandished his arm. In place of a fist, he now wielded a black hole of death which swallowed the world. Dark ribbons of energy spread outward. The horizon curved around Jack. The swirling energy warped his image.

Crownbeast didn't surface in time to stop this. He watched as Jack finished preparing his attack, then charge at him. He never thought he'd feel terror against a middle Baron, a person almost an entire large realm below him.

Yet, he did. He was frozen. His every instinct screamed to get away from that black sphere, yet he could not. It sucked everything, even spacetime. Coupled with Jack's originally superior insights into Space, Crownbeast was locked in place, unable to dodge. All he could do was take the blow.

"Shell mode!" he shouted. His body regrew to its original size of three thousand feet, maximizing his defense. The crimson aura roared and thickened. He even crossed his arms before his chest and leaned forward, bracing himself as best as he could. Defense was his specialty. In this state, he could withstand even the all-out attack of a middle Autarch.

Jack and his black hole sailed forth. They seemed slow, yet were deceptively fast. They reached Crownbeast in an instant.

Jack's strongest attacking skill up to this point, Supernova, was not that complex. It had come from a mere B-Grade faction, and he'd already learned it at the D-Grade. He'd polished it a little since then, but the sad truth was it was inadequate for his current level. His powers had been missing a proper vessel.

This black hole skill was far superior. It used concepts at the level of an Archon. Even now, Jack could barely comprehend and use it, but it allowed him to utilize his previously blocked insights to their full potential. It was, without exaggeration, an attack insanely stronger than anything he'd shown before.

The black hole remained at the stump of his wrist, and he shoved it at Crownbeast's crossed arms, where it kept going. The crimson aura, the scales, the bones, the hard flesh... All of those were completely incapable of stopping a black hole. It pierced right through, absorbing everything and turning it into its own power, growing constantly stronger.

Jack dislodged it from his wrist and shot it out while he retreated. It penetrated beyond Crownbeast's arms and sank into his chest, right under his disbelieving gaze. It flew deep. Organs and bones were warped and turned into mush, which collapsed into the fake singularity. A growing hole appeared on the monster's chest. Its dense body only worked against it—the more matter the black hole absorbed, the faster it grew. A terrible ripping sound echoed as the monster's body was torn apart.

However, at the end of the day, this wasn't a real black hole. It was only supported by Jack's Dao, and he was moving farther away by the minute. It also could only withstand a certain amount of mass. At some point, a black spark flew out—and the black hole, without any other warning, erupted.

It was like a supernova exploding inside Crownbeast's chest. His already dislodged innards scattered into the sky. Blood flew everywhere. The explosion was almost entirely contained in his body, which made it all the more destructive. Crownbeast's chest disappeared. Only the sides of his torso remained, with the rest burned into a massive, thousand-foot-wide, completely see-through hole. Black energy flew into the sky, carving holes in the ground and clouds.

Alongside the explosion, the space-death foam produced in the black hole was released. It stuck onto Crownbeast's body and consumed it from the inside, killing it so thoroughly that not even the space it occupied remained. By the time the foam was exhausted, the monster's body was so eaten up that only two halves remained—

below his waist, and above his shoulders. Everything else was just gone.

The two halves of Crownbeast smashed into the ground below. The beast's vitality was impressive—even now, it remained alive, but even it couldn't recover from such a wound.

As life slowly left his body, Crownbeast turned a pair of terrified eyes on Jack. "Monster," he whispered. "Monster..."

Jack was also badly injured. Some of the explosion had gotten him as well, and he'd nearly been struck by a beam of deathly foam. An entire arm remained missing from when Crownbeast had bitten it off, one of his wrists was a stump, and the last of the Life Drop's energies worked in overdrive to repair his mangled body. He fell to the ground panting—but landed on his feet. He looked at his empty wrist in awe.

He'd just killed an A-Grade. And the black hole attack... was the most powerful skill he'd ever utilized. By far.

Jack cracked a smile. "Now we're talking!"

CHAPTER FORTY-ONE
RESOLVE

Brock and Starhair flew over a blackened and ruined patch of earth. Since they'd retreated so far away, it took them some time to find Jack. Once they did, Brock rushed over.

"Bro!" he said, stars filling his eyes. "That was so cool!"

Jack laughed. "Thanks, Brock. I tried my best."

"I can't believe you did that," Starhair muttered dazedly. "A middle B-Grade killed an early A-Grade... I'm numb. Like it's all a dream."

"You *are* in a dream," Jack replied. "Except it's mine."

The two pieces of Crownbeast's body lay on the ground, a marker of Jack's triumph. They contained his space ring and core—thankfully placed near his brain, not his chest. Before that, Jack wanted to inspect something else.

Congratulations! New Dao Skill unlocked:
Black Hole III: By harnessing the fundamental properties of matter and space, you can force them into a state of collapse. You create a weaponized, artificial black hole. When outside your

control, it erupts, releasing all the mass it has absorbed in one massive explosion.

Jack couldn't help the grin on his face. He'd finally done it. After studying several Archon inheritances and Dao Visions, as well as the incomplete black hole manual, he'd finally managed to create this skill. It wasn't just a weapon—it felt like the culmination of his entire path of cultivation so far. After all, most of his core experiences combined led here.

It was also the very first skill he created which belonged entirely to him. Meteor Punch was inspired by the fist-wielder in Jack's first vision, while Supernova was derived from the Exploding Sun's inheritance. All his other skills were more auxiliary, so they didn't really count.

Black Hole, while containing bits and pieces of many different inheritances, was something uniquely created by Jack. His version even had many differences from the red lizard man's who made the incomplete Dao manual.

It was technique he understood in-depth, since he was its creator, and also one perfectly suited for his exact cultivation path. Those factors contributed to its terrifying strength.

If Jack ever created his own inheritance, this would be the first real technique he inscribed.

Of course, the current Black Hole was far from complete. It was a high-level skill, so it began at tier III, but he'd only just embarked on the way of mastering it. Plus, there were other targets to hit. His single greatest Dao Vision so far had been about a woman engineering a Big Bang, the controlled creation of a universe. Unlike the black hole, which combined Space and Death, this woman had demonstrated a fusion of Time and Life, the other of Jack's dualities. He had a feeling that mastering this Dao Vision as well would be the next big step on his path.

Most people's potentials tapered off at the B-Grade because they'd chosen a narrow path. Jack had done the opposite. His potential was endless—but realizing it meant he had to constantly struggle with the highest-level concepts of the universe. He had to show up at the top level uninvited and play ball.

That was the true Road to Mastery.

Unfortunately, Jack was outside System space, so his victory against Elder Crownbeast didn't grant him any levels. Fortunately, the Elder had a core, and absorbing it would be kind of the same thing. Even more fortunately, the core was located in the Elder's brain, so it hadn't been destroyed by the black hole.

Jack rummaged through the colossal skull and emerged holding a crimson, pulsing orb. It radiated intense power. The earth around them flaked off.

And this was just the start. Killing Crownbeast at this point was the greatest lucky chance Jack could have had. He ran over to the fallen beast's hand, cut off at the wrist, where a space ring was nestled between broken scales. He peeled it off to peek inside. Immediately, his face brightened.

Crownbeast's space ring contained Dao manuals, weapons, pills, and a wealth of monster cores ranging from the early to the peak B-Grade. It was essentially a treasure trove. Most importantly, it contained the items Crownbeast had won in the auction.

The late A-Grade core... and the Overlord core!

Jack started laughing, holding the space ring to his chest. The coffers of an Overlord faction had bled to secure these objects. Now, because of Crownbeast's miscalculations, it all belonged to Jack!

"Let's get out of here," he said. "If any A-Grades were nearby, they might be rushing over."

He disintegrated Crownbeast's remains with the flick of a hand —they were vulnerable now that his Dao was gone—and launched into the sky, creating a new crater behind him. The wind whooshed in his ears. Jack laughed into it, shooting straight into the clouds, emerging above them and under another layer of clouds. He debated going up to see what lay at the top of the sky. Was this really the time?

Why not? he asked himself. If anyone was going to come, they'd be here by now. Plus, this can't take more than a couple moments.

"Wait here," Jack said. "I'll check things above a moment."

He dashed up without waiting for a reply. He flew into the second layer of clouds and emerged into a similar scenery. A third layer waited above him. He also noticed that the ambient pressure had doubled—a curious sign, though nowhere near enough to affect him.

He kept shooting upward. The third layer, the fourth, the fifth... Every layer was separated from the next by roughly a thousand miles, but that distance mattered little to Jack.

By the time he reached the seventh layer, he was beginning to notice differences. The colors were growing darker, starting from their original gray color and approaching black. The pressure was mounting aggressively, too. Only B-Grades could fly at the ground level, but now, even Jack was struggling.

The hell? he wondered. I'm as powerful as an A-Grade, but I can't reach the sky!

He kept going. The eighth layer strained him further—by the time he reached the ninth, he could no longer proceed. Every mile he soared upwards exhausted him—using teleportation was no different. At this rate, he'd run out of energy, and that might be dangerous.

He let himself drop.

What lies up there? Jack wondered, gazing at the not-quite-black clouds above. He had a sense he wasn't even close to the top. *When I have the power, I'll find out. I can also just ask someone.*

He chuckled. Why did that feel like admitting defeat?

He fell through a layer of clouds, then another. The pressure rapidly lessened as he descended, and before long, he'd once again reached just above the first layer, where Brock and Starhair waited.

"Well?" Starhair asked.

Jack shook his head. "I have no idea. I couldn't make it. I suspect that... only Overlords have that privilege..."

"All will come at their time," Brock said. "Shall we, bro?"

"Yeah. Let's go."

Jack shook the issue away for now—though he promised to revisit later.

The three of them traveled in the gap between the first two cloud layers, flying away at max speed. They kept their perceptions spread out to avoid any surprises, but none came.

A few hours passed. From above the clouds, the three of them crossed several provinces, flying for hundreds of thousands of miles. Jack had chosen a direction that led to neither the Great Silver nor the Fiend King faction. His first priority was absorbing the cores he'd acquired, and that required secrecy. Their current target was the barren outer provinces.

Half a day later, they decided they were far enough. Jack shot through the clouds, facing an endless red expanse. Blue weeds grew intermittently, and green foxes shuttled between them. There was no powerful space monster in sight.

"Perfect," he said.

A hill protruded from the expanse like a pimple. Jack dove into it, carving a thin tunnel deep into the earth. Stone and dirt parted before his might. He waved his arms around, and soon, he'd opened up a small cave for all of them. There were various stone rooms, each able to isolate from the others using large boulders as doors.

"Nice build, bro," Brock said as he and Starhair flew in.

"I can't believe we have to stay here..." Starhair said. "There isn't even a bathroom."

"You'll manage," Jack replied with a laugh. "Let's get to business."

He waved a hand and three items appeared. It was the three cores—Crownbeast's early A-Grade one, the late A-Grade from the auction, and the Overlord core.

The early and late A-Grade cores exuded a great aura, but they paled before the Overlord one. It was like a black sun. The moment Jack took it out, the entire cave swam with dark light, and illusions of death swung scythes at their heads. This core alone was more intense than the living Elder Boatman.

Starhair backpedaled, an expression of horror on his face. Only when Jack sealed the core's aura did he recover, but even Jack could only do so much. Black steam escaped his restraints, lazily drifting about the cave.

"Holy shit," he said. "Sorry. I didn't think it would be this powerful."

"Very cool," Brock admitted, leaning closer to the core to study it. The black steam tickled his nose, but he didn't seem to mind. "It's almost alive."

"It *is* alive," Starhair muttered. He leaned against a wall, grabbing his heart. He gulped. "I've never seen such a powerful core before, but I've read about them. Overlords are different. Their inner world is so rich with life that, even after death, it retains a degree of intelligence. It's like an animal. If you try to absorb it, it will resist with all its might, unleashing its energies to wreck your body."

"Hmm." Jack cupped his chin. "Sounds dangerous."

"It is. I've heard about a late A-Grade Elder who managed to find one such core. He diluted it in a vat of water, then rested inside it until all the raw energy had been absorbed. You should do the same —just with a lot more water."

"Isn't that wasteful?" Brock asked.

"Some of the core's energies escape," Starhair agreed. "But it's not much, only around twenty percent, and it makes the process much safer."

"How long does it take?" Jack asked.

"If I recall correctly, it took that Elder seven years."

"That's too much." Jack shook his head. "I cannot waste that much time on a single core."

"Excuse me?" Starhair snapped. "You cannot waste seven years on an Overlord core? God. If anyone else heard you, they'd have a heart attack! That's the most arrogant phrase I've ever heard!"

Jack stared at him. "Raise your eyes, man. Don't settle for the dumpster fire you call cultivation."

"That's—Whatever. I suggest you dilute the core in water. It's better than dying."

"I won't die."

Jack eyed the core. Even sealed in a purple net of his Dao, it radiated intense destruction. He pictured how, if he tried to absorb a wisp of this energy, it would recklessly rush about his body to ruin him. He did have a highly tempered body... If he absorbed it one wisp of energy at a time, he was over ninety percent certain he could handle the pushback. It would take much less than seven years, too.

But it wouldn't be pleasant.

Jack made up his mind. "I will go into seclusion," he said, pulling the Overlord core into his space ring. "Here." With a flick of his wrist, the other two cores flew at Brock and Starhair respectively. Brock got the late A-Grade, while Starhair would enjoy Crownbeast's early A-Grade core. They were properly compatible with the two of them.

Starhair grabbed the core reflexively. He looked at it, stunned. "For me? I... I didn't even do anything. I can't accept this."

"We're a team," Jack said. "We have to share at least a bit. Plus, that core is not compatible with me. You should use it to regrow your hair more quickly."

Starhair looked between the core and Jack. An early A-Grade core didn't sound like much, but in truth, it was an astoundingly precious resource! Starhair's net worth in the outside universe couldn't buy such a core, and he ruled an entire constellation.

Of course, space monster cores were rarer in the universe than here.

"Thank you," Starhair said, accepting the core. As for Brock, he smirked at Jack.

"Thanks, bro," he said. "Appreciate it."

"No worries. We're bros. Supporting each other is what we do."

Jack went to one of the smaller caverns. Thinking better about it, he created a hundred foot corridor leading to a cavern with thick rock walls.

"I won't come out until I've fully digested the core," he said. "I don't know how long it will take. Stay safe until then. See you, bros."

"Good luck, bro."

"Be careful!" Starhair shouted as Jack rolled a huge boulder in front of the opening. It smashed into place with a loud thud. He was now alone, in darkness, in a roughly ten by ten foot cavern deep underground.

Jack took a deep breath and pulled the Overlord core out of his space ring. Instantly, the entire cavern was submerged in the black mist of death, so dense it was suffocating. Any low-level cultivator placed here would die instantly. Jack's Life and Death Daos protected him, but he still felt a chill creep down his spine.

"Here we go," he whispered to himself, then mustered his courage and probed the core.

CHAPTER FORTY-TWO

ABSORBING THE OVERLORD CORE

THE OVERLORD CORE CONTAINED A LARGE, STORMY BLACK OCEAN. AS JACK focused on it, he saw himself growing smaller and smaller, rapped by the winds of this storm.

In the huge sphere which dominated his perception, dark lightning flashed, shedding the light of death on the water. Figures were revealed inside it—some smaller, some larger, all bloodthirsty creatures with terrifying visages. It was like every creature the Overlord had ever killed was trapped in this core. They were many, they were powerful, and their anger went beyond blind rage.

Jack gulped. Facing this huge sphere of water, he felt small. He could overpower this unruly ocean—but absorbing it felt impossible.

"One step at a time," he told himself. He could sit here and stare at it in fear for days, but that wouldn't change what he had to do.

The reason such an ocean of power could fit inside the torso-sized core was because it was highly condensed. Jack gently extracted a string of energy, sensing it fight madly to escape his control. It was like holding onto an angry snake. He brought it to his chest and pushed it in.

The snake went wild. It hissed and snapped its jaws, rushing through Jack's body in the most destructive rampage it could achieve. He gasped. Blood spurted out. His veins broke, his muscles and tendons tore, his bones were pierced. Thankfully, his body was extremely durable, and his regeneration effective even without the Life Drop. The snake couldn't kill him—but it could make him suffer.

Jack couldn't hold it in—he screamed.

The Overlord's Dao of Death was different than Jack's. Jack pursued the concept of death, its finality. This Overlord had focused on the savagery which caused death, on destruction. Their energy embodied this concept. As the tiny black snake wreaked desperate havoc inside Jack's body, its sole purpose to damage him as much as possible, all Jack could do was seal his pores so it couldn't escape. He caged in the beast.

Flashes of burning pain. It was like he'd swallowed a maggot trying to eat him alive. Yet, he gritted his teeth and persisted. More screams left his mouth. The pain was maddening.

Even worse, there was nothing he could do—unless he diluted the core, wasting part of its essence, the only way he could harness this energy was to let it exhaust itself inside his body. Only this way could he ensure maximum effectiveness.

The snake was rampaging, but its energy was also depleting. A few minutes later, it finally slowed down. Its damage lessened, letting Jack's regeneration catch up. Finally, it stilled. The destructive Dao embedded in the wisp had been exhausted, leaving only the pure, raw energy of death.

Jack absorbed it into his inner world. He sensed the difference—this core's energy was so pure and compressed, that even one wisp produced a noticeable improvement in his inner world. Not enough to advance his Matter Condensation by even one percent—but noticeable nonetheless.

As soon as the energy was absorbed, Jack collapsed to the ground. He was dry heaving. Intense pain still wreaked his body from all the wounds the snake had left behind, and the memory of its rampage shadowed Jack's mind, trying to shake him. That was torture. Had it really only been two minutes?

Jack gritted his teeth. That was just one wisp of the core's energy. A tiny part. There were hundreds of thousands of shadowy creatures waiting for him in there, maybe millions. Would he really have to do this for each of them? Maybe he should dilute the core in water like Starhair had suggested. This was impossible.

I cannot waste the efficacy, he thought through gritted teeth. He planted a fist on the ground and used it to raise himself. Sweat dripped down his forehead—he was panting but resolute. *I cannot afford to delay. The only way out is through.*

His regeneration was only now finishing up the repairs, and Jack waited until it was done to keep going. As it finished, he raised a brow. His body felt... slightly stronger than before. Denser. More durable. The parts ravaged by the snake had been almost imperceptibly enhanced.

He wondered for a moment, then started laughing. "Life from death!" he shouted. "Thank you, senior Overlord, whoever you were! You have done me a great favor through the ages!"

The more Jack interacted with this Overlord core, the more benefits he discovered. He was sure that, if he could fully absorb it, it would transform him completely and greatly increase his powers. It wouldn't be a small difference—but a whole new world!

The only problem was, absorbing this core would be a battle... but Jack had nothing if not willpower.

He pulled another wisp from the core, forced it into his chest, and screamed.

Starhair stood nervously in the main cavern of their underground cave. He hadn't gone to absorb his core yet—he was concerned about Jack, who'd chosen to try something obviously impossible. The man was suicidal. He only prayed he stopped this madness early.

"Stop pacing around," Brock said. "Big bro will be fine."

"How can you be so calm?" Starhair asked. "He's killing himself."

"He's not. You must believe."

"Believe in what? It's impossible!"

On cue, a miserable scream cut through the cave. It sounded like someone being eaten alive. Starhair jumped and rushed for Jack's cave, but Brock flashed in front of him. "No. Believe."

"Are you insane? Your brother is dying in there!"

Another scream echoed, sharper than the previous one. Brock didn't budge. "Believe," he repeated.

Starhair cursed. He returned to pacing back and forth. "You can't be serious," he spat out.

"I am. Stay put and absorb your core. Big bro knows what he's doing."

"I don't believe you."

"You don't have to. Just do as I say."

Starhair wanted to lash out and destroy the cavern. He barely held himself in check. Instead of absorbing his core, he just sat there, waiting for Jack's inevitable cry for help. But it never arrived. The screams continued for a whole two minutes before abruptly cutting off.

Starhair shot to his feet. "He's unconscious. Or dead. I'm impressed he lasted that long. Let's go."

"Go where?" Brock replied.

"To save Jack, of course!"

The brorilla only shook his head.

"What's the matter with you?" Starhair shouted, getting angry now. "Your brother just passed out mid-scream and you won't even check on him? Do you not care!"

"I care more than you think," Brock replied calmly. "But I believe in him. You don't understand yet. You will. Just wait."

"That's—"

The screaming restarted. It had barely been half a minute since they stopped—had Jack just taken a break? What was going on?

"Absorbing the core will take a long time," Starhair said. "He's already suffering. There is no way he can last that long."

Brock smiled.

Time passed. Every few minutes, Jack's screaming would pause, only to restart seconds later. His voice grew hoarser. After an hour, Starhair had gone numb. He just listened on. "How can he last this long?" he whispered, eyes shaking in horror. "How is he even alive?"

"I think it's time to start," Brock said. He waved a hand, creating a soundproof barrier around Jack's cavern to isolate the screams. Their cave grew deathly quiet.

"What if something happens to him?" Starhair asked.

"Big bro is competent. If it's too dangerous, he will stop. He cannot die."

Brock took out the peak A-Grade core. It was a violent torrent of extremely high-level energy—yet, compared to Jack's Overlord core, it was sadly lacking. The brorilla retreated to another small cave to absorb it, and Starhair reluctantly did the same. He remained concerned, but he did his best to focus.

Three days later, Starhair emerged from his seclusion. Two of his three uprooted strands of hair had reformed—only one remained. He sat alone in the empty cave, watching the boulder shutting Jack's cave. The sound isolation barrier remained. Deep in worry, Starhair undid it for a moment, only for the sound of hoarse screams to instantly fill the cave.

He was stunned. Disbelief and horror warred within him. Finally, he numbly reinstated the barrier and sat in meditation. "How..." he whispered.

It took another five months before Brock emerged. He seemed reborn. His aura pulsed in waves, both stable and vastly strengthened. He had steadily stepped into the late B-Grade.

Starhair eyed Brock with despair. In the time it took him to repair his broken cultivation, Brock had climbed an entire small realm. That cultivation speed was unreal. Starhair... was already far surpassed.

He chuckled in resignation.

"How's big bro doing?" was the first thing Brock asked.

"He's fine. I'm removing the sound barrier every few days to check in on him, but he never stops screaming. He doesn't even take breaks anymore. It's just one constant, never ending torture. I have no idea how he hangs on."

"Because he knows he has to," Brock replied calmly. He sat down cross-legged. "Meditate. Big bro might be a while."

Time flowed on. Due to the inherent difficulties, Jack's process of absorbing the core was much slower than Brock's. He also had much more energy to absorb. The months turned into years. Brock and Starhair remained in the cave, still like statues, pondering on the truths of the world. They occasionally opened their eyes to discuss something which perplexed them. Starhair was the one explaining at first, though as time passed, he found himself more and more on the receiving end of wisdom.

He was stubbornly resisting the bro plague, yet little by little, a crack had formed in the corner of his heart...

Starhair's checks on Jack turned from daily, into weekly, into monthly. One year in, his screams grew so hoarse they were barely audible. Starhair had never found him not screaming.

Three and a half years passed. In the blink of an eye, they'd been in the Space Monster World for four years. It was unknown how the war outside progressed, if the Church was still persisting, or whether the Old Gods had arrived from their far corner of the universe. All Starhair knew was this cave.

His injuries had healed within the first two years of seclusion. Now, he was pondering on his Daos and absorbing the ambient energies, making slow but steady progress. He no longer bothered to lift the sound barrier. Whatever was going on inside that cave had surpassed his understanding.

Jack's deadline to visit the Great Silver faction had also passed, but... Oh well...

Finally, one day which seemed no different than the others, the boulder sealing Jack's cave moved. The man himself left seclusion, stepping into the light for the first time in almost four years.

As soon as Jack appeared, Brock's eyes shot open, and Starhair rushed to welcome him. "Are you okay?" he asked, but he abruptly paused ten feet before Jack. It wasn't by choice. He just couldn't move.

Something had changed in this man. Visually, Jack looked the same as before—bare chest, calm eyes, relaxed yet confident posture—but his aura was vastly different. Darker. More savage. His eyes hid pain so deep it put the oceans to shame. It wasn't some Dao which made Starhair pause—just a profound sense of inferiority.

This was not a man. It was a dark angel. Someone... unfathomable.

"I'm fine," Jack replied, and all the darkness disappeared, leaving just a simple man. "Why wouldn't I be?"

"Because... In there... You were screaming the whole time!" Starhair shouted.

"Just a little bit of pain," Jack replied calmly. His smile didn't reach his eyes. "It's nothing. Oh, hey, bro. Got any food? I'm famished."

Jack walked past Starhair, reaching the cave proper where Brock welcomed him with open arms. They took out a table full of Earth delicacies and tore into it, chatting and laughing like nothing was wrong.

For Starhair, reality was jarring. He couldn't reconcile the two facts he faced. Jack had been screaming in a dark room for three and a half years—now he came out unaffected? How was this possible? Was it all some elaborate prank?

He couldn't help himself. He crossed the corridor and approached Jack's cave. The stench hit him before he even arrived. Dark, damp metal. Blood. Rot.

Starhair braved the smell. It turned his stomach, but he had to know. He had to see.

He reached the opening and froze where he stood. His legs were rooted to the ground, and all his cultivation left him, leaving him a mortal.

This was a room of gore. The walls, the floor, the ceiling... Every square inch was covered in layers and layers of dried blood and rotten flesh. The smell was intolerable. The sight, revolting.

Starhair's eyes were shaking. He forced himself to turn around, away from this hellish sight, to gaze at the man eating and laughing so nonchalantly. How had he done this? That was more blood than he carried in his body. Endless ounces. How many times had he run out and forced new blood to form? How many times had he died in that room? How much had he suffered?

Three and a half years of constant torture... The mental fortitude required to withstand this was something Starhair couldn't fathom. He'd always wondered how he, a rare genius with a faint hope of reaching the A-Grade, could be so inferior to Jack. Only now did he realize the gulf which lay between them. The true difference. How could he ever compare? How could anyone?

Jack was simply inhuman. Unfathomable. Eternal.

"Hey, Starhair!" Jack shouted, biting into a piece of meat. "Come eat with us! This is beef from my planet—it's really tasty!"

What have you been through? Starhair wondered, not daring to voice the question. His legs were shaking. His eyes were fuzzy. *How did you become like this? What have you seen, Jack Rust?*

He is... a monster... An impossible monster...

CHAPTER FORTY-THREE
ELDER DIVINE

JACK FINISHED EATING, THEN TOOK A WELL DESERVED THIRTY-SIX-HOUR NAP. When he awoke, still in the cave, he was rearing to go.

For the first time in three and a half years, he opened his status screen.

Name: Jack Rust
Species: Human, Earth-387
Faction: Bare Fist Brotherhood (B)
Grade: B
Class: Paragon of Cultivation (Legendary)
Level: 503

Strength: 10,380 (+)
Dexterity: 10,380 (+)
Constitution: 10,380 (+)
Mental: 1500 (+)
Will: 1500 (+)
Free points: 2650
Free sub-points: 2

Dao Skills: Meteor Punch IV, Space Mastery IV, Death Mastery IV, Neutron Star Body IV, Iron Fist Style III, Brutalizing Aura III, Supernova III, Fist of Mortality III, Titan Taunt III, Black Hole III, Immortal Commune I, Time Mastery IV, Life Mastery IV
Inner World size: 16,000 miles
Matter Condensation: 6%
Titles: Planetary Frontrunner (10), Planetary Torch-bearer (1), Ninth Ring Conqueror, Planetary Overlord (1), Grade Defier, Planet Destroyer, Challenger

Absorbing the Overlord core had been hell, but the benefits it brought him were appropriately immense. He'd jumped straight into the late B-Grade and even progressed a little into it. His inner world had grown from 12,600 to 16,000 thousand miles—over doubling his overall energy capacity—and its density had increased as well. That brought an increase in gravity, which made many of the floating earth chunks stick together. They looked more and more like planets.

Jack was still far away, but he was slowly approaching the A-Grade.

However, his cultivation increase was far from the only benefit. The repeated destruction and regeneration of his body had inadvertently strengthened it. The Overlord's energy wisps had sought out every weakness in Jack's body to exploit it, pointing them out for his regeneration.

Throughout his life, Jack had fought many battles and received many injuries. Some left hidden marks behind, which slightly lowered his combat efficiency. Now, after his body had been destroyed and remade thousands of times, all those hidden injuries had disappeared. His Dao cycled unobstructed, in perfect harmony with every inch of his body. He was in his best state ever—and his overall body tempering had advanced by miles, too, even if it wasn't reflected in his Physical stats, which hadn't budged.

Something else had.

Neutron Star Body IV: Your body has reached a frightening density. You can manipulate it at will, alternating between the weight of a feather and a mountain. Though inferior to a real neutron star, you're well on your way...

The skill upgrade brought with it a terrifying increase in Jack's battle power. His defense, offense, and speed all shot up. His regeneration would be much more energy-costly, but it was a cheap price to pay, especially since he had the Life Drop.

If he fought Crownstar again now, he could easily destroy him without using the four-armed battle form. In fact, Jack suspected his current level of durability rivaled the dead Elder's.

Thanks to all of his level-ups, he also had a large number of stat points to distribute. The highest ever.

How do I go about this? he considered. The 8-1-1 distribution he'd stuck with throughout the years had yet to fail him, so he decided to believe in it. At the same time, he enjoyed round numbers.

Jack split a thousand points equally between Mental and Will, raising them both to two thousand. He then poured the rest into Physical. Those two sub-stat points remained, but it was too little to be worth ruining the symmetry of his Physical substats.

When he was done, Jack gazed proudly at the fruits of his labor.

Strength: 12,030 (+)
Dexterity: 12,030 (+)
Constitution: 12,030 (+)
Mental: 2000
Will: 2000
Free sub-points: 2

Wow, he thought to himself. I once had five points.

He was four hundred times smarter—to generalize the term—

than a pre-System human, and over a thousand times stronger. Those numbers did not account for his many hidden stat increases—like the recent purifying he received from the Overlord core—his skills, the synergy between his different stats, or his Dao.

Right now, Jack was confident in fighting a middle A-Grade. If faced with a late A-Grade, maybe he couldn't win, but he could probably run away. A peak A-Grade would ruin him.

And he was still far from an Archon.

"Hey," Brock said, stepping into the main cavern. "You ready, bro?"

"Always." Jack rose to his feet, cracking his knuckles. The ocean of power in his body hid deep. He smiled. "Let's go. We missed the three-year deadline with Elder Puerto, but if we hurry, we can still catch them before they begin the Canal Delve. Maybe we can join."

"What if the Overlord is there too, and he sees through your disguise?"

"A risk we have to take. I must visit the Dark Canal, and going with an experienced faction is the best scenario. Besides, even if the Overlord is there, my disguise can hold up to even close scrutiny. He'll only see through me if he suspects I'm really a human, which he has no reason to."

Brock nodded. "Alright. Hair bro! You coming?"

"Coming!" a third voice rose to meet them as Starhair rushed into the cave. "I'm fed up with this place. Please tell me we're leaving."

Jack laughed. "We're going to somewhere you'll hate even more."

The three of them flew through the earth, emerging in the red wasteland they'd last seen. This was their first time leaving the underground in almost four years. Jack couldn't help the joy in his heart.

"The Dark Canal is that way," Brock said, pointing to their left.

"How do you know?"

"The bros in Empty Star City taught me to navigate."

"Alright. Let's go."

The three turned into rays of light, and then they were gone. Next stop... The Dark Canal!

Elder Divine of the Black Hole Church was one of the strongest forces in the current war. His cross-legged form emanated divine light for thousands of miles. Everywhere that light reached, the void became hospitable, while flowers bloomed and wilted. His power was legendary.

However, even legends can fall.

Elder Divine had been tasked with destroying the System Cannons. These were the newest weapons of the Immortals—machines capable of shooting bubbles of System space into the vast cosmos. It was how they'd managed to ambush the Church army a few years ago, the event which led to the Immortal Summit of Spiral Stair.

Thanks to the temporary ceasefire, the Church Elders had figured out a way to protect themselves from total destruction. The cannons were large, making them easy to locate, and could be destroyed. Unfortunately, the Church was overall weaker than the Hand of God, so every such assault usually required the Church agents to sacrifice themselves and blow up their inner worlds. It was a constant price in blood they'd been forced to pay.

The Arch Priestess had decided to see if she could avoid that by throwing overwhelming power at the cannons. On Elder Divine's insistence, he'd been chosen to lead a top-level elite force, and he'd successfully destroyed one. They thought they'd escaped.

Space rippled ahead of Elder Divine. Two forms appeared—a man and a woman, each holding one half of a blade. The man was dressed in black and the woman in white—both were ethereal in aura.

"Yin Yang..." Elder Divine whispered. He was a bald, bearded old man dressed in simple clothes. His skin was wrinkled and full of dark spots, yet bright blue light emanated all over his body. As he opened his eyes, that blue light intensified and focused on the new arrivals.

"Elder Divine," the man replied respectfully. "I have long admired you. It is my honor to face you in combat."

"Hmm..."

Divine did not reply. He was a peak A-Grade, and a powerful one, too. More than most. However, the people before him were also peak A-Grades, and they were experts at combining their powers. Even with the assistance of his team, this was not a battle he could win.

He looked behind him. Three cultivators waited. Elder Malefic, middle A-Grade. Elder Godspeed, middle A-Grade. And, finally...

"We can take them," Elder Heavenly Spoon said, always with that aloof smile. He was the Church's youngest Elder, who only recently reached the A-Grade. A bright talent. He could fight one small realm above himself.

Elders Yin and Yang of the Hand of God flew close to each other, then rotated their two half blades in a common swing. The floodgates of the universe opened behind them—a yin yang diagram overlapped with their bodies, holding infinite truths.

Elder Divine looked at his team and smiled. "Godspeed," he commanded. "Take the others and run away. I will handle this."

"Elder!" Godspeed exclaimed. He was a slim, young-looking man whose features were currently clouded by despair.

"We can fight them!" Heavenly Spoon insisted. His aloof facade cracked. "We're strong, Elder. So are you. There is no guarantee we'll lose!"

Elder Malefic didn't speak, but she bit her lips until they bled.

"Their reinforcements will arrive before ours," Elder Divine explained calmly. "We could fight, but our chances of survival would be slim. If I hold them back, you three can escape. You have Godspeed. He'll lead you to safety."

"No, Elder! We cannot let you do this!" Heavenly Spoon insisted. He took out his silver teaspoon, manifesting a green phantom behind him. His face darkened and glowed at the same time. "I am not afraid of death, only starvation. And abandoning you would starve my soul, Elder."

"Yeah!" Godspeed agreed. "It won't be too late to escape afterwards. Let's show them the power of cornered cultivators!"

Elder Malefic also prepared herself. A pink aura surrounded her, stinking sweetly of silent death.

As the three were preparing to fight, Elder Divine struck without warning. His palm gathered the world's power and shot it out. It seemed slow, yet was impossibly fast. The two enemies attacked at the same time. However, Divine had not been aiming at them.

Before Godspeed, Heavenly Spoon, and Malefic knew it, they'd been struck backward, flying with a momentum they could not contain. Space parted and they crossed light-years in an instant. A terrifying black and white sword landed on Elder Divine's back at the same time, breaking his blue aura and making him spit blood.

"Elder Divine!" Godspeed screamed, still flying away.

"Do not deny the elderly their honor," a faint voice reached all of their ears. It was calm—there was no fear in that voice, only kindness. "This world does not belong to us, but to you. Only you can save it. The three of you, Jack Rust... You are all magnificent talents. All of you can reach the Archon realm. I will not let you die on my watch. Leave... Grow stronger... And let this old man complete his final duty. Let me light my dying embers one more time, and lay down my life to protect the next generation."

As tears welled up in their eyes, the three thought they saw Elder Divine's smile—old, toothless, yet bright like the sun.

"Make me proud. I entrust everything to you," he said. "Create a sunny world for my descendants."

Then, they were too far away to hear. Flashes of light erupted in the distant void. A blue sun was born, shaped as a massive, hundred-armed old man, struggling against a black and white sword which slowly tore him to shreds.

Only now did the three Elders manage to stop themselves. "We have to go back!" Heavenly Spoon shouted. "There is still time!"

"Spoon," Godspeed placed a hand on the man's shoulder, and as Spoon turned around, he saw the tears glinting in the other Elder's eyes. "It's too late. Don't waste his sacrifice. Let's go."

Heavenly Spoon's aloof facade shattered completely. "Damn it!" he roared to the heavens, shaking the universe. Godspeed formed a white bubble, encapsulating all three of them and retreating at terrifying speed. They were gone in the blink of an eye.

Elder Divine fought with everything he had, unleashing his full powers for the first time in several hundred thousand years. This was the first peak A-Grade casualty of the war. He died a hero.

CHAPTER FORTY-FOUR
SEEING THE DARK CANAL

Jack zoomed over the landscape. Lush jungles had given way to an endless blue ocean filled with all sorts of wondrous creatures. They'd caught glimpses. Mermaids, telepathic fish selling corals, snakes as thin as a finger and a mile long. Jack had even witnessed a monster as large as a mountain skip over the water like a carp. This was certainly not a low-level area.

But it wasn't at Jack's level, either. The three easily flew over the ocean, enjoying the breeze while occasionally fending off attacks.

"I wonder how a canal exists in the ocean," Starhair said. "I thought they connected bodies of water across land."

"I'm sure it will be something equally majestic and stupid," Jack replied, calmly zooming over the water.

Their destination wasn't hard to find. After Brock pointed it out, they'd developed a feel for the Space Monster World's energy circulation. There was a faint current of energy coming from the core of this world—the Dark Canal. This current was strongest here, and could be felt everywhere, even in the outer provinces and the Inhospitable Zone.

What could create such a phenomenon, Jack had no idea.

The more they followed the energy current to its source, the denser the ambient Dao became. By now, it was multiple times denser than when they first entered this world. Even some weaker B-Grades would have trouble flying here.

The monsters present were accordingly strong. Plenty were at the middle B-Grade, with the occasional late or peak B-Grade. They hadn't run into an A-Grade monster yet, thankfully, but this explained why B-Grade cores had been so common at the auction. Maybe the strongest space monsters came to this area to hunt.

It also made Jack wonder. If the monsters here were so strong, what about the ones in the Dark Canal?

A flat and barren island appeared on the horizon, cracked by the years, standing proudly in the middle of the ocean. The sound of rushing water filled their ears from hundreds of miles away.

Suddenly, space split apart before them. An owl-headed humanoid monster stepped out, wearing only a skirt which left its muscular chest bare. It stared at them with unblinking eyes.

"Shit," Jack said. This guy was at the middle A-Grade. What the hell was going on?

Instead of attacking them, the monster opened its mouth to speak, "You are not allowed here. Return."

"Uh... Hi," Jack replied. "I'm Jack Monstrous. We were invited by Elder Puerto of the Great Silver faction to join the Canal Delve."

The monster pierced him with its glare. "Wait," it said.

A few moments passed. Jack nervously wondered whether he'd be allowed in. After all, Elder Puerto had told him to come to the faction a year *before* the delve—it was just that he was too busy cultivating.

"Nice head, bro," Brock said, getting no response.

It took one hour for the owl monster to speak again. "Follow me," it said, then turned and stepped on the wind. Its speed was great. Starhair had to sprint to keep up.

"I'm Elder Owlhead of the Great Silver," the monster introduced itself. "You're lucky you ran into me. If you'd met the Fiend King's patrolling Elder on the other side of the island, he might have killed you."

"Was it really luck?" Jack shouted to be heard over the wind. "You guard the direction of your faction's territory. Since we came from Empty Star City, we would have run into you no matter what!"

The owl monster smiled. "Perhaps."

"I can't believe we're actually here," a voice reached Jack's mind. It was Venerable Saint Thousand Shell, speaking from inside his inner world.

"Is this place important to you?" he asked back.

"Of course! This is the holy place of the entire Space Monster World. Every monster would give up a limb to visit, but it's not easy! The wild monsters around here are fierce. Only Autarchs can approach safely—even peak Barons might struggle."

"What level are you, exactly?"

"I was a peak Autarch once, but that was a long time ago... My slumber in the Supreme Blood has diminished my powers. Now, I barely qualify as an early Autarch, maybe a peak Baron."

"So why haven't you come here before?"

"I only became an Autarch long after leaving the Space Monster World, and by that time, the entrance seal wouldn't let me return." The turtle's voice took on a reminiscing tone, as if narrating the stories it'd heard as a child. "They say that the truth of the Space Monster World is hidden on the island of the Dark Canal. Who made us? Who made this world? Who enforced the entry seal?"

"Well, my friend, I look forward to finding out."

The island rose a hundred miles above the water, its sides steep cliffs. It was also cut in half. Right in the middle of the island, a massive canal ran through, at least a thousand miles wide and dark like the night. The ocean water foamed as it rushed in, then was lost in darkness forever. Only the canal walls rose from the darkness, reaching up to the island's ground level.

Jack paused in midair.

A heavy sense of time covered this beyond ancient place. The real age of the Space Monster World was unknown, but it was certainly more than a billion years. It hid innumerable secrets, and this massive canal held the truth to them all, a hidden part of the history of the universe.

Even Jack was overwhelmed by awe.

"*Oh wow, this place looks like shit,*" another voice reached his mind —The Stone.

"*Says the talking stone,*" *Jack replied.*

"*Hey, at least I'm whole!*"

"*What do you mean?*"

"*This place is a mess. All the statues are gone, there's a huge crack in the middle, and the crown is nowhere to be seen. Pity, huh?*"

"*Wait. You've been here before?*"

"*Oh! You're right! I have! Shame I don't remember anything.*"

Jack's eyelid twitched. "*Don't joke now. You mentioned statues. A crown. What the hell, Stone?*"

"*...Sorry, Jack. I'm trying, but I really can't remember anything. Even the statues were only a flash of memory—I cannot recall what they looked like, only that there were three of them, each tall like the sky. Maybe I really am broken...*"

Jack tried to reconcile his intense urge to know more and his desire to make The Stone feel better. At least the turtle hadn't heard this message, or Jack would never get them to shut up again.

"*It's okay,*" *he finally said.* "*However, if you remember anything else, you must let me know immediately. Alright?*"

"*I promise,*" The Stone replied.

Jack let the conversation drop as he sighed. He'd obtained The Stone so long ago, yet he still knew nothing about it. If it really was from this place, and it remembered things looking very different... Just how old was it? And how did it end up riding a random asteroid in the Milky Way galaxy? What was its true identity?

"Keep moving," Elder Owlhead said, noticing how Jack had paused.

Soon after, they left the ocean and entered the island. They weren't flying over the canal. Instead, they crossed barren rock to reach a small camp, perched right on the canal edge. Before they even approached, Jack was overwhelmed by its vast aura. It looked like something one would find in the outer provinces—but its occupants were the elites of the entire Space Monster World.

They landed by the edge of the camp, where another person was waiting.

"Jack Monstrous," Elder Puerto said, her long red hair and wrinkles failing to hide the irritation in her face. "I thought I told you to come to the faction within three years."

"I'm sorry, Elder," Jack replied. "I was unable to. I rushed over as soon as I could."

"Hmph. Do you understand how important this Canal Delve is? It only happens once every thousand years, and the earlier in their life one can enter it, the more benefits they reap. Our B-Grade disciples underwent a crazy tournament for the right to one of the very limited spots! Do you expect us to push away a disciple who already traveled here to make space for you?"

"Us space monsters value personal strength the most. That is true justice," Jack replied. "Since the spots were decided by a tournament, I'll be happy to face anyone Elder Puerto deems suitable. If I lose, I'll have nothing to say. If I win, well, they can only blame their own weakness."

Puerto's face spasmed, but then she sighed. "Well said. That is the way of the world. Since you're here, and since you intend to enter our faction"—she gave him a sharp glance, to which he nodded—"I'll get you a spot."

"Thank you, Elder! However, as greedy as I may seem, I have another thing to ask. Can you give my companions the opportunity to earn a spot as well?"

Her face instantly scrunched up. "Canal Delve spots are not candy, Jack. You don't get to bring in your followers."

"They are not my followers. They're powerful monsters in their own right. I'm confident they can both earn their spot fair and square—as long as you give them the opportunity."

She looked the two of them up and down. Brock calmly met her glare. Starhair began sweating.

"I can't make this decision on my own," she said. "Give me a moment."

"Thank you, Elder Puerto."

They waited. Three minutes later, after the Elder telepathically contacted someone, she sighed in irritation. "Fine. The Grand Elder has accepted your request. You three will officially join our faction. Then, tomorrow, you will fight against the three weakest winners of the tournament. If you win, you may take their spots. If you lose, you will immediately head back to the faction and go through the proper initiation rites."

Jack beamed up. "Thank you, Elder!"

"Thank you very much, Elder," Starhair added.

"Thanks, Grandma Bro."

She whipped her head at Brock, who calmly met her stare again. "No problem..." she replied after a while. "Follow me. Thank you, Elder Owlhead."

The other Elder, who had waited patiently during the conversation, nodded and flew away.

Elder Puerto led them into the camp. It wasn't large. Nineteen comfortable-looking tents were spread out widely, giving everyone their personal space. While nobody was emitting their aura on purpose, all of them together created a heavy pressure. Jack could sense that the weakest people here were at the peak B-Grade, and there were several Elders present, a few of which sported auras above the middle A-Grade.

There was also a single cabin at the very edge of the camp closest to the Dark Canal. Jack glanced at it and didn't dare look again. The aura emitted from inside it was absolutely terrifying. That was an Archon. Overlord Great Silver in the flesh.

"I didn't know the esteemed Overlords would participate as well," he commented in a low voice.

"The Canal Delve concerns the entire faction," Elder Puerto replied. "While the disciples are here to secure inheritances for themselves, the Elders come to gather resources. There are many precious items which only appear here, nowhere else. Our success in this delve directly affects our faction's wealth for the next thousand years."

She paused at this point, as if uncertain whether she should say the next part or not. Finally, she decided to speak.

"Actually… The Overlords are not supposed to personally join the delve," she whispered. "This is the first time it's happened. I don't know why."

"Oh," was Jack's only response. He had a guess. With the Crusade going on outside, the Overlords wanted to strengthen their factions as much as possible. It made sense they'd join.

However, it seemed that while the Overlords were aware of the Second Crusade—they'd participated in the Immortal Summit, after all—they hadn't let anyone else know. At least, not their low-level Elders.

Why? Jack wondered but had no answer. He certainly wasn't going to spill the beans.

"Tomorrow, the Grand Elder will formally invite you to the faction, and then you'll fight," Elder Puerto said, motioning toward an empty patch of ground. "You may set up your tents here."

"And if we don't have tents?"

She gave them a smile, all teeth. "Then you sleep on the ground. Rest well—you'll need it."

CHAPTER FORTY-FIVE
TAKING SPOTS

Jack, Brock, and Starhair stood before a peak A-Grade space monster. It was a double devil, just like Jack and Starhair, dressed in black ceremonial robes which fluttered behind it. Its gaze was strict. This was a man who lived and breathed battle.

Grand Elder Sanzuki.

"Welcome to the Great Silver faction," he finished, having recited a war poem in a language Jack didn't recognize.

"Thank you, Grand Elder!" the three of them replied at the same time. The crowd surrounding them did not clap, expressing their disapproval—the silence was almost deafening.

Each faction was only allowed to bring nine B-Grade disciples into the Dark Canal. The competition for those spots was heated, and it grew even more so by the fact that most spots were taken by older and stronger disciples who'd visited the Canal before. The ones who'd never come here before—and so would receive the greatest benefits—had to struggle for just a handful of spots.

At present, only five of the Great Silver disciples were first-timers. They'd struggled valiantly to reach this moment, and now three of them were in danger of losing their spot just a day before the delve. It was obvious why the crowd remained silent. Even Jack was feeling a bit like an asshole.

Unfortunately, he carried too much on his shoulders. He couldn't afford to waste opportunities, even if that meant taking them away from someone else. In the end, this was the cultivation world. The losers could only blame their own weakness.

"Prepare yourselves. We reconvene in two minutes for the end of the tournament," the Grand Elder announced, much to the dismay of the B-Grades present. They walked away grumpily.

One moved toward Jack's group. "First you take away my manual, then you steal the spots of my little brothers and sisters," she said, green eyes shining in the darkness under her straw hat. "You are despicable, Jack Monstrous."

Jack had been surprised when he ran into this person here. It was the same straw-hatted woman he met during the Empty Star Auction, the one who'd competed with him over the incomplete black hole manual. She wore the same red clothes, and her straw hat still emitted the magical darkness obscuring her face. Only her eyes were visible, and they were not happy.

This was the head disciple of the Great Silver faction, Strawpin. An acclaimed genius who hailed from Empty Star City—hence her presence there. She'd left for the Great Silver early in her cultivation journey, though, which explained why people didn't recognize her.

"Sorry things turned out this way," Jack said. "I can lend you the manual if you want. I'm done studying it."

"Hmph. That's the least you can do," she replied, holding out a pale, humanoid arm. Jack raised a brow in amusement. He stretched his own hand, summoning the broken manual from his space ring and handing it over. She made it disappear with a flick of her wrist.

"Up!" the Grand Elder's voice filled the camp. Everyone rose into the sky, where they formed a large circle. The energy ripples of a battle would spread to a far larger radius, even in such Dao density, but the people present could handle them. In fact, they wanted to dissipate the ripples so as not to alert the Fiend King camp on the other side of the canal.

Great Silver had not left his cabin.

"Jack Monstrous and Edithland, you may begin," the Grand Elder said.

A fierce, wolf humanoid jumped out of the disciple ranks, glaring at Jack. "I fought hard for this spot," she said. "I won't let you take it."

Jack sighed.

Of course, as much as the wolf woman wanted to hold on to her spot, it was impossible. She was only on the level of Saturnstar, whom Jack had easily defeated *before* his breakthrough. They tussled a bit, Jack pretending it wasn't too easy, before winning through Meteor Punch.

"Sorry," he said, approaching the fallen wolf woman and offering a hand to raise her up.

She snorted and refused to take his hand. After rising on her own, she limped away. Jack gave her one last glance before flying up.

The air had changed by now. Most of the Great Silver group, Elders and disciples alike, had originally disdained Jack and the rest. They were outsiders who came to steal the benefits of faction disciples. How could they like them?

Jack's battle, however, had changed their outlook. He was strong—extremely so. Everyone could tell he hadn't been going all-out. While faction camaraderie was important, the Canal Delve was even more so—and a powerful ally could greatly benefit everyone.

As a result, most people now gazed at Jack and company lukewarmly, waiting to see how the other two would perform. The only ones still with bitter eyes were the two disciples who'd yet to fight.

Brock's opponent was a rock golem man. His strength and defense were admirable, but his speed was lacking. None of that mattered. Brock was often overshadowed by Jack's extreme talent, so it was easy to forget he was a great genius in his own right. He'd been the first in multiple million years to reach an inner world of 8,800 miles. If not for Jack, Brock would be a strong contender for the title of the universe's greatest genius, having a ton of adventures and spearheading the new era.

He tussled with the golem man a bit before driving him into the ground, then calmly returned to his spot beside Jack.

All the Elders' eyes were changed now. They'd heard about Jack's strength, but to see Brock so powerful as well was a surprise. These weren't random cabbages they were fighting. They were some of the most gifted disciples of an Overlord-level faction. Each was a world-class talent, yet Jack and Brock were dispatching them like common goons—from jumping a small realm to do so, no less.

Everyone looked at Starhair, excited to see his performance. Unfortunately, he was nowhere near as flashy.

Starhair's opponent was another double devil utilizing the power of flames. He was actually the third least powerful disciple from Great Silver—the Grand Elder had arranged for Jack to fight the weakest disciple, Brock the second weakest, and Starhair the third weakest in an attempt to let at least one of his disciples remain.

Unfortunately, while Starhair wasn't a super genius like Jack and Brock, he remained a star disciple of the Black Hole Church, a faction much larger than the Great Silver.

The two clashed for a long time. Eventually, Starhair gained the upper hand and secured victory. The battle hadn't been easy, but not super close either.

Everyone stared at the three of them. *Who are these guys? Where did they come from?* were the questions plaguing everyone's mind. Even Strawpin, who disliked Jack, was chewing on her lip thoughtfully.

"On behalf of the faction, I apologize for what happened," the Grand Elder told the three loser disciples. "However, you know the rules. Power trumps all. Bringing the strongest lineup available into the canal is important for the future of our faction. Your loss here, while surely frustrating, is the only scenario. Elder Owlhead will guide you outside the Donut Sea, at which point you are to head back to the faction. I've arranged some compensation for the three of you."

They didn't perk up at the mention of compensation. They were clearly extremely frustrated, but what could they do? Starhair's opponent almost said something before the wolf woman dragged him back. "We understand, Grand Elder."

"Good. Now go."

The three flew off without a second glance. Jack allowed himself to experience the emotions. He hadn't done anything wrong, but he still felt bad.

Strength is all that matters, he told himself, then decisively looked away.

"Hey," he told Strawpin, who wasn't standing too far away. "When does the delve begin?"

She glared at him. "My name is not *hey*. I'm Head Disciple Strawpin, and you will refer to me as such, Jack Monstrous."

"Sure."

"Sure, what?"

"...I won't say it."

"Then I won't reply."

"I'll just ask someone else."

"And create a rift in our relationship? Pretty bold of you, Jack Monstrous."

He sighed. "When does the delve begin, Head Disciple Strawpin?" he asked, and at that, she smiled.

"There you go! Was it that hard? Nevermind, don't reply—bad question to ask a double devil. We're set to begin in two weeks. You really cut it close."

"Yeah, I do that sometimes. Not a great idea, but it tends to work out."

"Mhm." She raised a brow at him. "See you, Jack." And then she flew away, disappearing into one of the smaller tents. Her straw hat and red robes were the last to go.

Jack shook his head as he returned to his friends. "We got two weeks. I'll probably just meditate. I need to polish my new cultivation a little."

"I'll just chill," Brock said.

"I think I'll do the same," Starhair added, throwing Brock a glance. "Though I hate being paired up with you. It always goes the same way."

"And what way is that?"

"We befriend new people all the time."

"First, it's not befriend, it's bebro," Brock said, his grin wide. "And second, all good. These are strong people, right? If brohood is fake, they won't fall for it."

Starhair grumbled something. Jack left the two alone as he headed for his new tent—they'd occupy the tents of the defeated disciples. A smile was on his face the whole time. He'd love to stay out here and have fun, but he really did need to meditate. His cultivation had advanced too quickly. Two weeks of meditation now would bring him noticeable benefits—and, if the Canal Delve was as dangerous as he imagined, he'd need them.

CHAPTER FORTY-SIX

ENTERING THE DARK CANAL

Two weeks later, Jack's eyes slowly opened. He sensed the restlessness in the camp surrounding him. He smiled.

"It's time."

He got up and opened the tent flap to witness a camp in the middle of deconstruction. Disciples and Elders alike walked with grim faces as if going to war. They waved their hands, sucking the tents into their space rings, then wiping the ground clean of all disturbance.

That last act took Jack by surprise. The space monsters, who cared only about themselves, would wipe the ground after them? Was it manners, or just respect for the Dark Canal?

"What are you looking around for?" Strawpin's voice reached Jack's ears. He looked up to find her floating over him. "Gather your tent. We're departing!"

He sucked it into his ring like everyone else was doing. Nearby, Brock and Starhair did the same. The three of them took to the air, not forgetting to wipe the ground behind them, and joined the growing lineup of the Great Silver faction.

More so than when they fought the other disciples, Jack had a chance to observe everyone. Besides the three of them, there were six more disciples, all at the peak B-Grade. Ten Elders accompanied them—the peak A-Grade Grand Elder, two late A-Grades, three middle A-Grades, and four early A-Grades. Nineteen people in total. In any other part of the world, their combined auras alone would have devastated the landscape. Here, they only summoned a strong breeze.

The camp was completely recovered in a matter of seconds. The ground was pristine, like they were never there—with the sole exception of the wooden cabin, which even now remained unmoved. Just as everyone gathered in the sky, the cabin door opened. A lone figure stepped out.

It looked similar to the last time Jack had seen it, except smaller. Silver scales, flexible whiskers, deep eyes, sharp teeth and claws. This was Great Silver—a silver dragon, one of the two Overlords of the Space Monster World. His aura was deep like the world. His Dao resonated in a deep bass. He was... irreproachable.

Probably stronger than Archon Summer Noon.

He was also far smaller than last time. His avatar in the Immortal Summit had been huge—right now, he was small enough to fit through the cabin's door.

Crownbeast could also change his size, Jack realized. Is it an ability of all space monsters? Or just a few?

Great Silver flew to the head of his faction, growing in size to become like a truck. "Let's go," he rumbled, not sparing anyone a second look. He shot into the distance—everyone followed.

Their camp had been situated at the edge of the Dark Canal. A vertical cliff awaited just to the side, descending a hundred miles into the darkness. They flew over it. As soon as they passed the edge, Jack felt a cold current flowing from below, infiltrating even his extreme physique. He caught some of the weakest disciples shivering.

Great Silver led the way at a speed that was neither fast nor slow, letting them savor the experience. Endless darkness spread below their feet. Not even Jack's perception could penetrate it—for the first time since reaching the D-Grade, he felt fear of the dark, as part of the nearby world was hidden from him. The Dark Canal seemed like the place nightmares crawled out of—everything children imagined hid in the dark, existed in the Dark Canal.

"Spooky," Brock said in a low voice.

"Damn right," another disciple replied. "And we haven't even entered."

A third disciple piped up, "You should be careful down there, bros. Almost every threat is Autarch level."

"Then why are we going in?" Starhair asked.

"We have the Elders. They'll keep us safe."

Jack smirked. Brock hadn't been idle these past two weeks. Every other disciple and even a couple of low-level Elders had been initiated into brohood. The only disciples still resisting were Starhair and Strawpin, who considered brohood distasteful.

"Cringe," was all Strawpin said.

The Dark Canal was over a thousand miles wide, but they were fast. Only a few minutes later, Jack sensed another group heading their way. He saw them soon after—twenty monsters, just like them, headed by a heavily muscular, gray-skinned humanoid with fierce claws, sharp teeth, and a thick tail swishing behind his back. The lovechild of Predator and Frieza. If devils had a king, this would be him—and he was aptly called the Fiend King.

"Great Silver," Fiend King called out.

"Fiend King."

As the two Overlords neared each other, their auras clashed—not aggressively, they were just too great not to rub against each other. The sky was split in two, one half silver and the other dark red, before nature rebalanced itself.

Each Overlord swept his gaze over the other's disciples.

Jack held his breath. Unless one of the Overlords decided to really scrutinize him, his disguise should hold—but, if it didn't, he'd die here.

Thankfully, nothing happened. Fiend King's gaze only stopped on him briefly before moving on.

"New faces," he said in his dark, sharp voice.

"We had quite a few talents recently," Great Silver replied.

"I hope they perform well in the Hall of Trials."

"So do I, Fiend King."

As the two Overlords stood face-to-face, their Daos warring routinely in midair, the differences between them were sharp. Great Silver was old, wise, and thoughtful. The Fiend King was aggressive, deadly, brutal. So was the group following him. Contrary to the Great Silver faction, the Fiend King elites were made up of devilish monsters, most sporting sharp claws or deadly, drooling fangs. In comparison, Great Silver's group looked random and mismatched—though they didn't lose out in actual strength.

The two people Jack paid special attention to were a yellow-eyed, hellhound-looking monster—the Fiend King's Grand Elder—as well as a humanoid devil similar to Fiend King in appearance, except instead of demonic he was extraordinarily handsome.

"Listen up," Strawpin said, arriving to Jack's side. "That guy over there is Fiend Prince, their head disciple. His father is Fiend King, and he's said to be the future of the faction. His talent is extreme. People say his battle power is already at the early Autarch level, though I don't believe that. Be careful of him. His schemes run deep."

"Got it," Jack replied. If this guy was at the early A-Grade level at most, he wasn't a threat. Since Strawpin found that level of strength hard to believe, neither was she. His real opponents would be the Elders.

Strawpin kept giving him a rundown of the enemy forces, but nothing he paid attention to. The disciples were unremarkable, besides the Fiend Prince, and there was no one too special among the Elders either.

He did appreciate her advice, though. Maybe she was less of a bitch than he thought.

As long as I don't run into the Overlords or Grand Elders, I have room to struggle, he planned. For the late A-Grades, I'll have to judge case-by-case. I can probably escape some of them, but not all. As for the middle A-Grades, even if I can't beat them, I can still run away. Just need to take care of Brock and Starhair.

I've come a long way, haven't I?

Fiend King and Great Silver had exchanged a few more words before returning to their respective factions. It was a good reminder that they weren't really enemies, only rivals—at least, while the Second Crusade roamed outside their world.

"Listen up," Great Silver said. Watching a dragon speak was more surreal than Jack expected. "We will descend into the Dark Canal now. I want everyone to remember their missions. Elders, travel in your assigned teams and gather as many resources as possible. For this particular delve, I expect you to take more calculated risks than usual. Disciples, remember that even the weakest creatures down there can threaten your lives. Remain close to your accompanying Elders at all times and be extremely careful until you reach the Hall of Trials. After that, your fate will depend on you."

"Yes, Overlord!" everyone shouted at once.

"Finally, leaving the Canal alone is dangerous, so we'll meet up at the entrance location in ten years. I'll escort you all out. If you miss that appointment, you're on your own."

"Yes, Overlord!"

"Good." The dragon's face warped in an ancient smile. "I wish you all luck, and a bountiful harvest."

The Fiend King was already done talking to his faction. Whatever he'd said to them—his words had been isolated by a sound barrier—the devils looked ready to go.

"Let's go," Great Silver said, and both factions dove into the darkness.

After all those descriptions and warnings, Jack expected the Dark Canal to be a zone of death, a monster-infested world where only A-Grades could survive.

Yet, reality betrayed expectations. As they descended lower and lower into the darkness, they came upon a scene of desolation. The ocean cut through the canal like a raging river. The water was black and frothing, shooting into the sky every time it met rock. Stone islands rose from the water, stubbornly standing against the river flow, but they were empty. There were no creatures, no plants, no buildings, no monsters in sight besides themselves.

The deeper they went, the denser the darkness. By the time they landed on the very first stone island, Jack's mighty perception couldn't spread farther than a mile from his body. He was practically blind. As for the Dao pressure, it had shot up tremendously. Anyone below the peak B-Grade would simply be unable to fly, and even a less talented peak B-Grade might struggle.

In a Dao thousands of times denser than normal, any lower level cultivators would either implode or be completely immobilized. The air here was harder than regular concrete.

Jack turned to the woman beside him. "I have so many questions."

"Shoot," Strawpin said, looking around warily.

"Why did we all enter from the same spot? Wouldn't it be safer for us disciples to go directly to that Hall of Trials?"

"We can't. The rules governing the Dark Canal are mysterious and strict. All we know is that this specific island is the starting point—the people who attempt to enter from anywhere else simply disappear. Even the two ends of the canal, where the water goes in and out, are dead zones. Don't go that way. And, this goes without saying, but don't enter the water either. It's much more dangerous than the islands. Also pointless—there's nothing down there."

"I see," Jack replied. He was glad he ran into the once-in-a-thousand-years Canal Delve. Otherwise, he would have arrived here by himself at some point, and he might have had an accident trying to enter.

Then again, maybe not. He'd be prudent enough to gather information first.

"Just how powerful is this place?" he asked. "Autarchs stand at the top of the world, but I feel like they're considered normal here."

"The Dark Canal is the origin and core of our entire world," Strawpin replied, the reverence evident in her voice. "It's only natural for this place to be made for Autarchs, isn't it?"

"I guess... What about that Hall of Trials?" he asked the burning question. "What's that?"

Strawpin gave him a piercing look. "You don't know?"

"It never came up."

Calculations shone in her eyes. She stared for a few moments before looking away and replying, "The Hall of Trials is the world's greatest cultivation haven. Every monster who knows about it yearns to enter, but almost nobody can. According to legend, it was established by the creator of our world, and it contains inheritances at the absolute highest level. Everyone who enters is transformed. It is no exaggeration to say that a monster's level of success in the Hall of Trials shapes their entire future."

"I see. So, it's kind of a big deal."

She once again glared at him. "Yes, Jack. It's kind of a big deal."

"Jack!" Venerable Saint Thousand Shell screamed in his mind. "She mentioned the creator of this world! Ask her more!"

"I was planning to," he replied, then turned back to Strawpin. "You mentioned the creator of this world. So, it really was created by someone?"

She chuckled. "Well, that's just the legend. I don't know if it's true or not. All I can tell you is that, while our world and its entrance seal could be natural, the Hall of Trials is definitely not. Someone made it—and they were far stronger than even the current Overlords."

CHAPTER FORTY-SEVEN
EXPLORING THE DARK CANAL

Soon after they landed in the Dark Canal, everyone broke off. The Elders of both factions rushed in all directions—stepping on the wind, teleporting, or running on four legs—while even the Overlords parted space and disappeared. Soon, the only ones left were the B-Grade disciples—eighteen people in total—and their accompanying Elders.

Jack inspected these Elders. Each faction had sent one middle A-Grade and two low A-Grades. It was a considerable force, enough to deal with most threats the Dark Canal could throw their way—assuming they didn't push their luck. To Jack's disappointment, Elder Puerto wasn't present. Elder Owlhead was. He stood with his muscular arms crossed and face looking straight ahead as if cosplaying some ancient Egyptian god.

Besides Elder Owlhead, who was the leader of their faction's side at the middle A-Grade, the two early A-Grade Elders Great Silver had sent were a shapeless brown blob with limbs and eyes swimming over its surface, and a scantily-clad, female double devil. Jack wondered if she also possessed two sets of genitals; he didn't actually want to find out.

On the other side was a four-legged beast wrought of shadow. Darkness made up its body, dancing over it like flames, while wicked red eyes shone from within. It was the middle A-Grade Elder of the Fiend King faction, flanked by two early A-Grade Elders resembling the classical devil of Earth mythology—curved horns, bat wings, triangular-tipped tail, trident in hand. Their body was bulky, red, and covered in black fur. Surprisingly, one of the two was short and chubby.

These six Elders came together to oversee the eighteen disciples headed by Strawpin and Fiend Prince.

"We will now head towards the Hall of Trials," Owlhead said in a neutral voice. Jack liked this guy. He seemed impassive but fair. "As you all know, its location changes every delve. We will wander in its general direction until we Elders sense the Dao ripples it gives off, then we'll make a beeline for it. This is not a resource-gathering trip—the Dark Canal is too dangerous for Barons. Just follow us, stay in line, and pray we don't run into anything too strong."

Jack raised a brow at that. He leaned toward the nearby Strawpin, whispering, "Does that really happen?"

"Sometimes," she whispered back. "Even late and peak Autarchs can disappear in the Dark Canal. It's not unheard of for the entire disciple group to go missing—though it's certainly rare."

"I wish something was easy for once."

"Relax. The Elders are powerful—they'll keep us safe as long as we just stick close."

How could she know that Jack was planning to do the exact opposite? Playing it safe wasn't his style. The Dark Canal was filled with other opportunities, and he had the power of a middle A-Grade. He could look for them. If he stuck with this group, sure he'd reach the Hall of Trials, but he'd miss everything else on the way.

"I'm leaving these guys. Will you follow?" he asked Brock and Starhair telepathically.

Starhair hesitated. "I'd rather follow you than strangers..."

"I go where my big bro goes," Brock replied. "And if we want to rejoin the group later, I can track them down."

"You can?"

"Some of these disciples are my bros. I'm aware of their general direction."

"Really! How long have you had this skill for?"

"Since forever. Why?"

"...Nevermind."

Owlhead and the shadow beast—apparently called Elder Shadowhound—were giving a set of careful instructions to the group, but Jack didn't care much. "Can we leave the group if we think we see an opportunity?" he asked.

Elder Owlhead struck him with a stare. "If you break off, we won't save you."

Jack nodded. Then, without another word, he turned into a streak of purple light which vanished in the distance. Brock and Starhair followed a beat later.

The rest of the group was left stunned. Elder Shadowhound laughed, the sound like a malefic hyena. "What arrogant disciples you have, Owlhead. Your faction sure enjoys humiliating itself!"

Its voice was gravely, much unlike its laughter. Owlhead remained silent, his gaze stuck where Jack and the others had disappeared. Strawpin was looking in the same direction—her eyes filled with shame and anger.

Good riddance, she thought to herself. It's bad enough that you took three of our spots... but you did it just to suicide immediately?

"Let's go," was all Owlhead said, leading their group into the darkness.

The Dark Canal was a massive, frothing mass of water. Stone islands floated on its surface, their positions haphazard.

The first thing Jack realized was that these stones weren't really islands. Nothing connected them to the bottom of the ocean. They simply floated on the surface, slowly moving in random directions and tipping over when pressure was applied on their sides. Yet, for all intents and purposes, they felt exactly like stone.

Jack had no idea what magic kept them afloat—or why their speed and direction seemed completely irrelevant to the frantic water below.

Each stone island was only a few miles across—a normally insignificant distance to people of their level, yet proportions changed under the massive pressure. In the Dark Canal, where the Dao was suffocatingly dense, Jack needed a few seconds to fly over each island. Teleporting was out of the question. Not only did the dense Dao prevent him from moving long distances and make the process exhausting, he also had no intention of teleporting outside his perception range. That would be blindingly stupid.

The three of them resembled rays of light as they flew over the dark ocean. Although each stone island was small, the distances between them were random. Some were almost touching each other. Others were tens of miles apart. Given that the Dark Canal was a thousand miles wide and several thousand long, the area they had to cover was tremendously large.

Even half an hour into flying, they'd run into neither opportunities nor monsters. Starhair was the first to break the silence.

"Maybe we should—"

Before he finished his words, a dark pink tentacle burst out of the water below, intercepting him and wrapping around his body. He made a sharp shriek as it pulled him downward.

Jack reacted instantly. Before the tentacle could retract, a Meteor Punch erupted on its middle part, cutting it clean off and releasing Starhair. The explosion was far weaker than usual—it was more like a grenade than a meteor, and the energy ripples only spread for a few miles before getting suppressed by the ambient Dao.

"Behind me!" Jack shouted. Eleven more tentacles emerged from the water, surrounding him—which meant the monster's body was directly below him. He readied his punch and smashed it down. Supernova exploded against the ocean. Dark water shot in all directions, revealing the shrieking mouth of a creature straight out of a nightmare. While it possessed twelve tentacles—now eleven—its body was that of a manta ray, hiding flat right below the water surface. Most of it was just a wide, gaping mouth filled with sharp teeth. Starhair had been instants away from getting devoured.

Jack's punch had smashed right into the monster's mouth, piercing it and exploding out the other side. The monster rocked in angry panic, smashing down on him with each of its eleven remaining tentacles. A golden brorilla appeared for each of them.

"We got you, bro!" they said in unison, using their bare arms to wrestle the tentacles. Jack used this time, when the monster couldn't move, to unleash a barrage of punches. Holes appeared on its thin body. Black blood merged with the water.

Jack's strikes hadn't been random. They traced a line of holes across the monster's midsection. Finally, it couldn't take it any more, and it ripped in two, spilling multicolored juices on the water. Jack could sense they were radioactive, though that didn't affect him. The tentacles seized before losing their power, and the monster's entire body crumbled, crushed by the immense pressure the moment its Dao dissipated.

Soon, only a core remained, alongside a frightened Starhair. "I almost died," he kept muttering. "That thing almost killed me. In an instant!"

Jack made a grasping motion, pulling the monster's core out of the water and into his hand. "Early A-Grade," he said. "Not particularly strong though. Can any of you use a chaos-attuned core?"

"Not me," Brock said.

"I... I can't either," Starhair replied, snapping out of his fright. "Did you guys see that? The thing almost killed me! It came without warning!"

Jack wasn't compatible with the core either. He pocketed it, replying, "You should be careful."

"I can't do much. I'm not a monster like you two—an A-Grade enemy can instantly destroy me!"

"I know. Just stay close to us, and we'll protect you."

Starhair muttered something under his breath, the sound unintelligible, then scuttered closer to Jack like a wet cat. A rancid smell hit Jack the moment Starhair approached—the octopus monster had covered him in some foul liquid when it grabbed him.

Brock was still staring at the water below them. "So strong..."

"Yeah," Jack replied, his face stony. They weren't referring to the octopus. An A-Grade monster had randomly attacked them in the middle of nowhere. That was the very apex of power, enough to become an Elder in the greatest factions of the universe, yet here it was only the level of common mobs.

Just what kind of place was this Dark Canal? How powerful was it? How high-level?

Like a peak A-Grade dungeon... Jack realized with a shiver. Suddenly, he didn't feel as confident anymore. Early A-Grade monsters were fine. They'd probably be able to defeat middle A-Grades as well, since they were slightly weaker than cultivators of the same level. However, if they ran into a late A-Grade or peak A-Grade monster... They might die.

"Should we join back with the group?" Starhair suggested, following Jack's reasoning.

"There's no point." Jack shook his head. "If a late A-Grade monster appears, being with the group won't save us. The strongest Elder was only middle A-Grade. If anything, the group is larger, so it draws more attention. Traveling by ourselves is the safest option."

"What if we're unlucky?"

"Then we can only blame our bad fortune," Jack replied, shrugging. "You cannot escape chance. Sometimes, all you can do is hope."

"...I don't like the sound of that," Starhair said, but there was nothing anyone could do. Jack was right. The safest way forward was alone.

The next hour was peaceful. They'd kept moving deeper into the

Canal, though at an odd angle. It wasn't the fastest path, but it meant they had less chances of running into other cultivators. After all, in this perception-isolating darkness, allied and enemy Elders could be just as dangerous as the native monsters.

They did run into another early A-Grade monster. It was an amorphous mass of eyes and twisting limbs—as if the monster was trying to imitate human arms but wasn't sure what they looked like. Jack and Brock took out this monster as well.

They were beginning to see a pattern now. The mindless monsters infesting this place were much closer to the universe's space monsters than the usual residents of this world. Was there a point to this comparison? Or was it coincidence?

In fact, as they traveled, Jack realized this entire place was very similar to the Space Ring of Trial Planet. A large darkness filled with bubbles of safety, between which prowled chaotic space monsters. Was it possible that Archon Black Hole, who'd participated in creating Trial Planet, had heard of this place?

No—if that was the case, Venerable Saint Thousand Shell would have known as well. This was either a convergence of laws or a coincidence. Jack withheld his judgment for now—he had a feeling it would become clear later on.

Three hours into their exploration... something finally changed.

CHAPTER FORTY-EIGHT
FIGHTING FOR TREASURE

ROOTS SPREAD OVER THE STONE ISLAND. GNARLY, TWISTING THINGS, colored a bright green which stood in contrast with the dark waters below. The roots wrapped around the island surface and dove into the water, from which they absorbed energy. Massive bulges came from the parts steeped in the ocean, then traveled the length of the root backward until they reached the thing in its center.

And what a thing it was. A massive vine, all green and no flowers. Its slender body wrapped tightly around itself, climbing three hundred feet into the sky, made of multiple smaller vines coiling and uncoiling around each other as if strangling something at the very center.

Intense life energy radiated from the vine. Jack had sensed it from a dozen stone islands away—whatever this was, it had to be extremely precious!

"What do you think, bro?" Brock asked. "Worth it?"

"Always," Jack replied. "The vine itself doesn't seem sentient. The problem is that guy."

A huge snake was wrapped around the base of the vine. Its massive scaly body rose and fell with each breath, the snake obviously asleep. They couldn't see its head, but its body was a hundred feet in width, the same gray color as the stone beneath. If it wasn't coiled around the green vine, it might as well have been invisible. Even now, Jack could see it with his perception, but he couldn't detect any energy coming from it.

An ambush predator. A terrifying one. Unlike the tentacle creature they fought before, this snake had solidly stepped into the middle A-Grade.

"This monster is strong enough to rule its own galaxy," Starhair said. "Yet, here it is, guarding a plant."

"This place is blown out of proportion," Jack agreed. "I have no idea why, but I hope to find out. For now, let's kill this thing."

"How about you kill it and I watch?" Starhair asked.

"That's what I meant. Let's go, Brock!"

The two of them shot out. Water rippled under them. Jack's body flashed with green and purple, activating the Life Drop transformation even as the power of the Fist coursed through his body.

Brock glowed, a massive golden brorilla manifesting around him like a monkey buddha. Chanting flowed from its mouth. The words were unintelligible, but as they spread through the air, the sound turned into more brorillas, which gained sentience and rushed to surround the snake.

Its eyes snapped open. Vertical irises split a red gaze as the snake opened its massive mouth to hiss at them. However, at such a small distance, getting caught off guard was nasty. Jack's Supernova smashed into the snake's midsection, bending its entire body—only for its flexibility to absorb the impact. As its mouth gapped open, all air in its body escaping due to Jack's strike, a host of brorillas flew into it. They started kicking and punching at the snake's gums, a particular trio wrestling its forked tongue. They were more annoyances than threats—Brock didn't yet possess the power to harm a middle A-Grade opponent. His brorillas dealt the same damage as a mosquito to a human.

The snake honed its glare on Brock. He wobbled—the massive

brorilla phantom around him shuddered, almost dissipating before solidifying its form. An instant of surprise passed through the snake's gaze before it lunged, fangs open wide to swallow. It snapped them at Brock—and came up short. It couldn't reach.

Jack was standing on the snake's body, pinning it to the ground under his immense weight. After fully activating Neuron Star Body, even he didn't know how much he weighed, but it had to be at least several thousand tons. Given the Dark Canal's extreme Dao density, which amplified gravity, he was like a mountain range. The snake needed a moment to shake him off—a moment it wouldn't have.

Jack wasn't just standing. He'd been charging up a massive strike. A transparent bubble of space spread around his fist, compressing in pulses. A sound spread through the air, an ominous "pong, pong, pong." As the snake turned back to look, it found the bubble reduced to the size of Jack's fist, which had long collapsed under the pressure of space. Dark foam was emerging—a power which gave even the snake pause.

Its enormous body whipped up. When it was actually trying, even Jack's immense weight mattered little. He flew off, but not before completing his strike. "Black Hole!" he screamed, jamming the newborn black hole into the snake's slithering body. A hissing, melting sound followed.

The strike had burrowed deep, sucking in the snake's scales, flesh, and blood. Jack glimpsed at a pulsing red interior, every inch of flesh moving independently to avoid the black hole. Green blood shot out. Some of it flew toward Jack, who punched it away. The rest landed on the stone beneath them, corroding it instantly and reaching the ocean below, where endless steam arose.

Brock was lucky the snake's bite hadn't landed.

As Jack was retreating at top speed, the black hole reached its limit and exploded. Dark foam escaped in all directions. The snake hissed in pain, the sound almost human, as an entire section of its body disappeared. It was split in two. Even the stone island below them vanished for a mile radius, including part of the vine's roots.

Jack grinned at the destruction. This was a hastily made black hole, not one he'd fully charged—yet it had grievously injured a middle A-Grade opponent.

Of course, this mindless snake might possess the powers of a middle A-Grade, but that didn't make it equivalent to a cultivator of that level. A proper cultivator would possess a vast wealth of battle experience, wisdom, tactics, and strategy. They would optimize their powers to the limit of possibility. For example, they'd never ignore Jack and let him charge up such a powerful strike.

Just as he gloated over the snake's idiocy, however, Jack realized he'd made a mistake himself: the battle was not over. Intense energy erupted from both halves of the snake. They were both alive. The head part extended to once again lash at Brock, fangs poised to bite down on him. Meanwhile, the snake's bottom half flew at Jack—green blood shot from its open wound like a geyser, melting anything it touched.

This time, the snake's head succeeded in reaching Brock. He had little time to react. Sharp fangs wrapped around the golden brorilla, thankfully not wide enough to swallow it. They still pierced into the golden glow. Green liquid poured out, corroding the gold. Brock roared, veins bulging out on his forehead. "Bros, lend me your power!" he shouted.

The many smaller brorillas he'd conjured before turned into rays of golden light which shot into the massive brorilla phantom. Its brightness intensified, yet there was nothing Brock could do to escape. He was grappled, and the snake's sharp gaze somehow magically rooted him in place. All he could do was defend, and hope the acid never reached him.

He gritted his teeth and held on.

As the snake's back half fell onto Jack, green blood sprouting from the open wound, he realized they were both in danger.

"Supernova!" he shouted, smashing out a punch. The strike pushed away the acid and burrowed into the beast's open body, causing massive damage but not slowing it down. It didn't care. It knew it was already dead—all it wanted now was to take them with it.

Jack's goal hadn't been to push the beast away. Facing the charging open wound, all he needed was to repel the acid. He utilized the few instants he earned to warp space, spending a massive amount of energy to teleport out of the way. He reappeared behind it.

The snake's tail wasn't something a human could grab onto, its one hundred foot width extending the whole length, but Jack was no ordinary human. Arms of the Dao appeared around it. Jack grabbed the space before him, the purple arms mimicking the action. He could feel the massive strength between his hands, the snake struggling to escape. Though his twelve thousand Strength was not for show.

Veins bulged. His muscles went taut, and tendons threatened to rip. Jack ignored all those to grasp firmly onto the snake's tail and spin his body around, pulling it forcefully through the air. The open wound on the other side spilled acid everywhere. The island was riddled with holes. Half the roots had melted.

"Hah!" Jack shouted. He endured the tension and focused all his power on flinging the snake, sending it flying toward its front half, which had almost penetrated Brock's defenses. The two halves of the snake reunited in unexpected fashion, wrapping around each other and attacking itself in blind panic. The momentum threw the snake's head off Brock, letting him escape.

A supernova erupted where the two halves met. A massive explosion followed. An entire half of the stone island collapsed into the water, unable to endure the impact, while the snake's two halves squirmed and hissed, their energy depleted. They flopped on what remained of the ground, then lay lifeless. The back half sank into the dark waters.

"Thanks," Brock said, panting on the stone. The massive phantom around him had dissipated—defending against the acid for a few instants had sucked his energy dry.

"No problem," Jack replied, wiping the sweat off his brow. "Are you okay?"

"Yes."

"Good."

Starhair flew their way from the distance. "Well done! You guys were awesome!"

"Thanks." Jack gave a tired smile. "Let's check our spoils."

Warily, he approached the vine. He half expected it to come alive and swing its roots at him, but nothing happened. Instead, as he got closer, he noticed that the battle just now, while brief, had dealt a lot of damage to the environment. Half the vine's roots had melted or been destroyed, and so had part of its main body. Green juices flowed freely onto the stone. Through a hole in the vine, a heart formed of twisted roots could be seen in its middle, beating frantically in its attempt to save the plant.

Jack sighed. *Why do I feel bad about a vine?* he asked himself as he reached into the plant and removed the heart. Despite the vine's size, the heart was only the size of Jack's torso—he inspected it, sensing the rich life energy it contained, then put it away.

"Not bad," he muttered.

By his estimations, this heart contained about as much power as a middle A-Grade core. Speaking of which...

He turned back to the snake, only to find that Brock had already fished out its core—a dark green thing reeking of death and poison. Jack smiled. "Well done, Brock! The core is useless to all three us, but the heart could be useful. You can have it. It wouldn't matter much to me anywa—"

The ocean ahead of them exploded before he could finish his words. A giant shark shot out of the water, making a tight curve in the air and falling toward their island mouth-first. It was easily large enough to swallow what remained of the stone island. It was also a late A-Grade monster. The snake's tail from before hung out the side of its mouth, the powerful acid not even tickling the shark's interior.

Jack entered battle mode instantly. This was too powerful a creature, and it was approaching too fast. It would eat them up. He had to take the others and—

The darkness above their heads parted. A massive shape swooped down, grabbing the shark in its even larger jaws and crunching. The late A-Grade creature released a pained roar—a torrent of energy, whose attunement Jack couldn't identify, pushed through the shark's body and tore it apart. The now-dead shark turned into silver motes of light which disappeared into the larger creature's mouth.

As the creature landed on their stone island, tipping it over by its sheer weight, Jack was frozen. This was an Archon-level existence. An Overlord.

It was a silver dragon.

CHAPTER FORTY-NINE

STARHAIR'S SHAKE UP

JACK STOOD FROZEN. ALL THREE OF THEM DID. THE GIANT SILVER DRAGON opposite them didn't leave them much choice.

It was a creature beyond large. In the dense Dao of the Dark Canal, he couldn't even wrap his perception around it. He quickly tried to calculate its size—it had eaten the shark, which had eaten the snake, which was several miles long.

God...

If this thing wanted to harm them, there was nothing they'd be able to do. It was an Archon-level existence. Jack's current power was woefully inadequate to even think about escaping.

However, he had a feeling things wouldn't go that way.

"Jack Monstrous," the creature's voice boomed, echoing for miles. There was a hint of amusement to it. "Or, should I say... Jack Rust."

Its body began to shrink. From countless miles tall, it grew shorter and shorter, until it was the size of a horse. Its power remained, able to still squash them like flies.

Jack was surprised at being seen through so easily. He leaned forward, giving the creature a respectful bow. "Overlord Great Silver. Thank you for saving us."

Starhair bowed as well, and so did Brock, though not as deeply.

Now that it had shrunk, the Overlord's form was clearer. It was a silver dragon radiating moonlight. Leathery wings spread from its back, while all four of its legs ended in sharp claws—like a tiger given wings. Its face was aged, yet its eyes held more wisdom than ferocity. A sturdy gaze landed on Jack—its weight pressing him down.

"What are you doing in my world, young human?" the Overlord asked. "And why did you not present yourself to me, as you ought to?"

"Greetings, Overlord," Jack said, scrambling to come up with a good response. If he didn't play his cards right here, they might all die. "I made a mistake when I tried to sneak around. I was too afraid of you, and I ended up becoming disrespectful. Please accept my apologies."

"Hmm..."

The dragon rumbled, shaking the island below them. Jack noticed that, while he'd grown smaller in size, the island remained tipped.

"You did not answer my first question," the Overlord insisted. "What are you doing in my world?"

"I came here to gather experience."

"And steal my faction's resources."

"...I admit that was my intention as well. I bear no ill will against space monsters, but I have a duel to the death in twenty-five years, as well as a looming war threatening my entire universe. I will not lie to you—my mindset was to grasp as many benefits as possible and grow my cultivation in the shortest timespan."

"You are wise not to lie," Great Silver said.

"Would lying be of any use?"

The Overlord laughed. "No, not at all." He took a few steps forward, the stone groaning under his feet. "That is a good disguise you have. It fooled me outside the Canal. A gift from your Arch Priestess?"

"Yes, Overlord."

"Hmm. That the cultivators of the universe have access to such means worries me, but it is not the present subject. The question now is... Should I kill you?"

Jack gulped. The face of the Overlord loomed closer—a pattern of old scales, some dark by the years, yet interspersed with sharp teeth and deep, knowledgeable eyes. While the real threat of Great Silver came from his cultivation, Jack's instincts responded to these superficial signs: the teeth, the eyes, the size, the silver steam escaping his mouth.

Before Jack knew it, the Overlord stood before him. He could be killed in an instant.

Yet, Jack raised his head. "We have infringed on your territory, Overlord. It would be reasonable to kill us."

The dragon face had no hair, yet the scales over his eyes moved like he was raising a brow. "You sing the wrong tune, human. You should convince me to spare you, not eat you."

"You *should* spare us. Not because you can't or shouldn't eat us, but because there is no benefit to you doing so."

"And what benefit is there in sparing you?"

"We can help you. Your faction and the Fiend King's are contesting for resources, yes? With my status as a disciple, I could clear out several of the Fiend King's Barons and low-level Autarchs. Something that you, for all your power, cannot do without enraging the other Overlord."

"Hmm. That is true. However, if the Immortals ever reach our world, we'll need every competent monster available. Fiend King and I are on the same page. We want to limit killing."

Jack felt his arguments grow distant. "I can still secure resources for your faction, Overlord!"

"You probably can, but I don't want to get involved in your war. Neutrality suits us. If word got out that I'm letting you grow stronger in my domain, our already precarious peace with the Immortals might be affected."

"I'll be discreet. Let me participate in this Canal Delve, Overlord. If the Church grows stronger, you benefit as well."

"You're getting ahead of yourself. Before letting you participate, I should first decide not to eat you."

"I believe big dragon bro has already made up his mind," Brock said, stepping forward to join the conversation. "We will fight for you and be discreet. Nobody will know we were here. As big bro said, you benefit when the Church grows stronger. At the end of the day, only one faction in the universe seeks to conquer, and that is the Immortals."

The dragon regarded Brock with interest. "You are a special one. Bold, both of you. How come your friend over there has pissed himself? Perhaps I should eat him so he doesn't slow you down?"

Jack and Brock turned around, finding Starhair shivering, his face pale. He had never come face-to-face with death like this—and this led to him shaming himself a little.

"Please don't eat him, Overlord," Jack pleaded. "He is a good man."

"I've eaten my share of good people," Great Silver rumbled. "Regardless... It is as you say. I prefer you getting stronger, if only to hope for a miracle. I know that we live on borrowed time. If the Immortals win, we might survive, but only while they show us mercy..."

The Overlord's voice had fallen by the end, betraying sadness and aged helplessness.

"I want you to keep acting as my faction's disciples," he said, adopting a commanding tone. "Forget your greed and rejoin the group. You don't want to draw too much attention to yourself. Any treasure you earn, either from my faction or the other, will belong to you—space monsters believe in personal strength. Just limit the killing whenever possible. Remember this: the treasures of the Dark Canal are great, but they pale in comparison to the Hall of Trials.

Your priority should be to survive until then. Don't take stupid risks."

"Yes, Overlord," Jack and Brock replied as one.

"Mm, good. And, one more thing. If anybody realizes who you are, especially Fiend King... I will end you immediately. Is that clear?"

"Crystal, Overlord."

"Your group is that way," Great Silver spread a wing to indicate a direction. "Make haste. When you reach them..." His voice lowered, as if giving them some secret, "Don't rush to the Hall. Follow the Elders. This Delve will be... special."

"Special, Overlord?"

"I wish you luck."

The dragon didn't wait for an answer. He shot into the sky, rapidly growing in size until he was larger than a mountain, then disappearing in the darkness far faster than Jack could achieve. In an instant, he was gone.

Only then did Jack release his breath.

"What the hell was that?" he said, clutching his chest. "I thought we were goners."

"Did you really piss yourself, bro?" Brock asked Starhair, who was only now recovering from the shock.

"I..." He trailed off, his face becoming beet red. He then clenched his jaw and said, "So what? You got a problem?"

"No," Brock replied, smiling.

"Do you think he's still here?" Starhair turned to Jack, demonstrating commendable adaptability.

"Maybe?" Jack responded. He looked around. "He's an Overlord. If he wanted to hide, I couldn't find him... but I don't think he'd stick around. His time is precious, and we have no reason to disobey his orders."

"Right." Starhair's body relaxed, and he slumped into a sitting position. "By the Gods..." he muttered, holding his head. "I was not ready for this. I'm supposed to be back at our universe, fighting other

B-Grades for the Church, not... whatever cross-Grade abomination this is."

Jack smiled and sat beside the other man. "Welcome to my world, Starhair." Despite the warmth of his smile, his gaze was distant, lost in past pain. "I know it isn't easy. Since the start of my cultivation journey, over ten years ago, I've been in a constant state of struggle. I've made enemies far above my level and surpassed them. I've braved countless dangers, risked my life like it meant nothing. The rewards made me who I am—but the price was high. Too much struggle can pollute the soul. Too much pain warps the individual."

Starhair listened attentively. Jack sighed, leaning back with his arms outstretched. His eyes saw past the ruined stone island around him, into the past.

"I've lost my son, you know," he said. "Murdered, right in front of me."

"I'm sorry."

"It's okay. His loss will never leave my heart, but I've made peace with it. It was the greatest pain I've ever experienced, far beyond a mere three years of absorbing the Overlord core. Yet, though it was undoubtedly the greatest, there were many other great pains, all of which pushed me beyond my limits and scarred my heart. Insights don't come cheap."

He smiled ruefully.

"What I mean to say," he continued, pulling himself away from reminiscing, "is that the road to mastery is fraught with risk and suffering. It is not a path to be tread lightly. Yet, here you are now, and you have no choice but to walk down the same road Brock and I have. I wish things were different, but they aren't. You're already too deep—you will either swim or drown."

Jack ceased speaking, having said all he had to say. Starhair remained silent. His eyes were lost in thought, his heart beating like a drum. Getting thrust into a world of death would unsettle anybody.

"You are not alone though," Brock added from the side. "You have us. Your bros. If the entire world seems like it's abandoning you, you can always rely on us."

Starhair's eyes flickered. A spark was born inside them—a cog turned, and his worldview shifted. "Thanks," he said, shaking his head. He rose to his feet. "Let's go. We have a group to catch up to."

Without waiting for a response, he turned into a ray of light and flew into the distance, the wind wiping his tears. His hair waved behind him—six strands of star-heavy power. Jack and Brock exchanged a smiling glance before following.

In moments, the trio was gone, the ruined stone island left to its ruin.

CHAPTER FIFTY
HIDDEN COLORS

"This way," Brock said.

The three of them turned slightly, angling their flight path. They cut through the omnipresent darkness like arrows, the extremely dense Dao powerless to hinder their progress.

Through Brock's Dao of Brohood, he could track the position of people who'd become his bros—to an extent. Thanks to the two weeks they spent in the camp before the Canal Delve, several of the other B-Grade disciples had been bebro'd, which was how the trio planned to rejoin the disciple group heading for the Hall of Trials.

"How far away do you think the actual Hall is?" Starhair asked.

"We've only traveled ten percent into the Dark Canal," Jack calculated. "However, we were traveling diagonally and also fighting sometimes. If the group flew straight ahead at the speed of the slowest disciple, they must have crossed double that distance by now. I suspect we'll catch up in an hour, at around thirty percent of the way to the end of the Dark Canal."

With their perceptions and speed greatly limited by the extreme Dao density in the Canal, exploring its entire thousand-mile wide area was close to impossible. Traveling down to its end, was far simpler. All they had to do was fly straight ahead. Barring the various monsters blocking the path, it would take less than a day.

"Not that easy," Brock said, furrowing his brows. "The location of our bros jumps left and right—space is warped."

"Really?" Jack said in surprise. He focused his perception into the folds of space. At this point, he could be considered an expert on par with A-Grade space cultivators. Few people in the universe could claim to surpass him in this regard. Yet even when actively looking for distortions, he came up with nothing. "Are you sure? Space looks fine to me."

"Maybe it's warped up ahead, between us and them," Brock replied. "We'll see. Be careful."

The three fell silent, tirelessly shooting forward. The occasional monster attacked them, but, with the exception of a middle A-Grade one, they were all at the early A-Grade and easily disposed of. Besides the many cores, they ran into no treasure.

The more they flew, the more Brock's suspicions seemed true. They'd been flying for several hours. According to Jack's calculations, they should have already caught up, yet the group remained far away.

"How?" Jack asked, struggling to wrap his mind around it. "Even an Archon specializing in Space would struggle to set up such an elaborate distortion. It covers such a great area, and I can't detect it? Wow."

Another thirty minutes later, Jack creased his brow. "Wait," he said. They instantly came to a stop. The darkness around them looked exactly the same as before, as did the frothing waters below.

"What?" Starhair asked. "Did you find the space distortion?"

"No," Jack replied. "But I sense something else. A calling. Like a very faint stream of Dao emitted from far up ahead." He paused. "It's the most powerful Dao I've ever felt."

"What do you think it is?" Brock asked.

"Maybe the Hall of Trials? Elder Owlhead did mention he could sense it when close-by."

The power of one's Dao perception relied primarily on their cultivation level, as well as their specific Dao specialties and overall power. Jack cultivated Space, amongst other stuff, so his perception was more sensitive than most. Coupled with his overwhelming power for his Grade, he was probably sharper than any other B-Grade.

Brock and Starhair focused but got nothing.

"Let's keep moving," Jack said. "If it comes from the Hall of Trials, we'll catch up with the others anyway."

Shortly afterwards, they paused again. The location of Brock's disciple bros had originally been aligned with the Dao stream Jack was sensing, but as time passed, they began to diverge.

"They turned," Brock said, cupping his chin. "Why?"

"Strange. Since they were headed in this direction, the Dao stream really must be the Hall of Trials. Why would they turn away now? If I can sense it, the Elders guiding the group definitely can as well."

The three glanced at each other, but there was nothing else to deduce.

"What do we do, big bro?" Brock asked. "Do we go after your sense or the disciple group?"

"Let's go for the group," Jack decided. "Whatever this Dao stream is, we have to prioritize finding them. Great Silver was clear—we disobey, we die. Even if it *is* the Hall of Trials, maybe the Elders just know a safer way forward."

Brock and Starhair nodded. "Alright."

The disciple group kept diverging from the path to the suspected Hall of Trials. At first, Jack thought they were just choosing another direction to approach from, but as time passed it became clear that was not the case. They were circling it at a radius. Why?

"Everything will be answered once we find them," Jack said, accelerating. "Let's hurry!"

Their distance to the group shortened rapidly. Then at some point, an odd change took place.

The stone islands gave way to dirt ones. It was fascinating. Stepping on them felt like standing on actual land, yet they floated undisturbed in the aggressive waters of the Canal.

Jack tapped the ground a few times with his foot. "Not giving way. Think it's normal?"

"Nothing's normal here, bro," Brock replied. He scooped a handful of dirt from the ground and placed it in his mouth. "Mhm," he said, spitting it out. "Tastes like dirt."

"...Why did you do that?"

"How else would I know its taste?"

"You know what? Nevermind. What do you think, guys? Should we return to the stone islands or keep going?"

"I don't like this..." Starhair said, gazing at the ground with suspicion. "It's supposed to be stone islands. The Elders made it clear."

"Maybe it's a treasure," Jack ventured a guess.

"Or a monster. I say we turn back and find another way."

"We can fight monsters, but we shouldn't miss treasures," Brock said. "I say we continue."

"I agree with Brock," Jack said. "In any case, the group went this way, so how dangerous could it be?"

"I can sense they're very close," Brock added.

Starhair sighed. "Alright. Let's go."

The three took to the air again. They were no longer attacked by monsters. Instead, their path took them deeper into the dirt island region, where a faint musty smell hung in the air.

They were on high alert. Clearly, something was wrong here—but what?

Strawpin accelerated, pushing her way to the front of the group, next to Elder Owlhead. The wind threatened to steal her straw hat, but who was she to let it?

"Elder!" she called out. "Excuse me for my bluntness, but are you sure this is the right way?"

Elder Owlhead turned his head ninety degrees. His still gaze was unnerving. "Why do you ask?"

"I've read the records on previous delves. There has never been a different biome before the Hall." She gestured below them, where endless dirt islands stretched out. "I fear this is either the lair of a powerful monster or the birthplace of some great treasure. In either case... It is not something we should be approaching."

Owlhead remained silent. Just when Strawpin thought he'd never reply, he did. "Are you doubting me?"

"I wouldn't dare," she replied quickly. "Just... I want to make sure we're on the right track."

"We are."

"Okay. Thank you for your time, Elder."

Owlhead watched Strawpin return to her place at the back of the line, near the Fiend Prince. They didn't look at each other. The Elder kept his gaze on them for a while before turning his head a hundred and eighty degrees to face the front.

"They're beginning to suspect," he said telepathically.

"Hehehe. And so what? They're disciples—their opinion weighs little. It was the Overlords who asked us to delay reaching the Hall, so we'll be fine no matter what," Elder Shadowhound's voice echoed in Owlhead's mind, dark and shady.

"I know," he replied, "but their unrest can backfire. Maybe we should leave this biome."

"Are you stupid? Dirt islands over such a large area... This is unheard of! Who knows what treasure lies at its core? With our means, we'll be safe against pretty much anything. We might as well use this chance to get rich!"

"And the disciples?" Owlhead asked.

"The disciples will obey us. If they become a problem..." Under its shadows, Elder Shadowhound's mouth curved into a sinister grin. "The

strong will prey on the weak. That is the way of our world, and blasted be the faction rules. No witnesses, no crime."

Owlhead considered it. "*Alright,*" he replied, and the group carried on, deeper and deeper into the dirt island area.

Jack, Brock, and Starhair zoomed through the Dark Canal.

"We're here," Brock said suddenly. The darkness split before them—twenty-some figures were revealed in the distance, calmly flying forward. As Jack laid eyes on them, they paused, the leading Elders turning to regard the new arrivals.

"You survived," Elder Owlhead said.

"Yes, Elder," Jack replied. "Sorry for worrying you."

"Worrying? We laughed at your misfortune!" Elder Shadowhound said, chuckling darkly. "You sure are arrogant. First you ditch the group to go hunting for treasures alone, then when you fail, you return with your tail between your legs and expect to be taken back in. What do you think we are, for you to come and go as you like!"

Facing the Elder's chiding, Jack frowned. He had no intention of being meek—doing so before Overlord Great Silver was already testing the limits of his patience. To someone of similar strength to himself, Jack wouldn't necessarily start a conflict, but he'd certainly bite back if challenged.

"I thought I *could* come and go as I like," he said. "If we are welcome, let us join you. If not, let us know so we can move on. Why waste everyone's time on pointless drivel?"

"Drivel? Good, good, good, Jack Monstrous! You got guts!"

The Elder's aura blazed forth. It wasn't just a warning—he aimed to push Jack into the water, a truly dangerous notion. Jack was about to defend, but another aura rose to shield him, Elder Owlhead appearing right in front of him.

"Please calm down, Elder Shadowhound," he said. "These disciples made a mistake. It is good enough that they survived to rejoin us. Let the issue rest."

"Hmph! You're too calm, Owlhead! You should vent a little every once in a while!"

"I follow my faction's command," Owlhead replied calmly. Shadowhound snorted and turned around, leading the group onward.

Jack turned to Elder Owlhead. "Thank you for protecting me, Elder," he said.

"You are a disciple of my faction. Of course I would protect you," the Elder replied, his inquisitive eyes not leaving Jack's. "You were lucky enough to miss all monsters, but that won't happen again. Stay with us from now on."

"Yes."

Owlhead nodded, then teleported back to the front of the group, leading everyone alongside Elder Shadowhound. The two flew close together despite their heated exchange.

"I don't like this person," Brock said telepathically.

"*Why?*" Jack asked.

"His aura is wrong. Something about it. My bro sense is tingling."

"Hmm. Alright. I don't see it, but I'll keep an eye out."

They quickly caught up to the tail end of the group and slowed down to match their pace. Coincidentally, Strawpin was at the tail end as well.

"You're so lucky," she said. "When I saw you leave, I thought you'd just wasted three of the faction's spots to suicide. Only blind luck saved you. To be honest, I don't know if I'm happy or disappointed you survived."

"Sweet words," Jack replied. "Come now, Strawpin. Don't be a bitch."

"Excuse me!"

Snorting laughter came from the side. "Suits you right," Fiend Prince said, his commanding voice spreading easily. "That's no way to speak to your fellow disciples."

"They're not—Screw you, Prince. Shut your mouth. And you,

Jack Monstrous—next time you do something stupid like that, the native monsters won't even need to lift a finger. I'll deal with you myself for wasting sect resources."

"Sure," Jack replied disinterestedly, then ignored her as he flew forward. He had a certain tolerance for bad manners, especially when it came to maintaining decorum, but it wasn't infinite.

Maybe I'll need to use my flip-flops again, he mused as the group tore through the darkness.

CHAPTER FIFTY-ONE
OVERLORD TREASURE

The dirt islands looked like they stretched infinitely. They didn't. At a certain point, the ambient energy changed. No longer was it uniform across all Daos—it now contained heavy elements of earth, dirt, and rock. The air smelled of wet soil. The darkness thinned.

"We're approaching the core of this area," Owlhead warned everyone. "Keep your guard up. Disciples, fall back."

The disciples obeyed, and so did Jack. While he could stand side by side with the two middle A-Grade Elders, he didn't want to reveal his power yet. The more cards in his sleeve, the better.

As the eighteen disciples of both factions slowed down, the Elders advanced: Owlhead and Shadowhound, the leads from both factions, the female double devil, and the brown blob of... mud? From the Great Silver faction, and the pair of devils from the Fiend King faction, one tall and imposing and the other short and chubby.

All together, they made a formidable force. They delved deep into the dark mist and disappeared.

Jack clicked his tongue. He didn't want to reveal his strength, but he wanted to see what was going on!

"Let's approach," he told Strawpin and Fiend Prince. "I want to see."

"No, it's dangerous," Strawpin replied.

"You're goddamn right!" Fiend Prince said, laughing. "What are we, cowards? Onward!"

He shot forth, followed by his faction's disciples and a grinning Jack. Brock and Starhair came a moment later, while Strawpin, grumbling, took her faction disciples and advanced as well.

The darkness parted before them. Everyone scanned the space ahead with their perceptions, not their eyes, which gave Jack a definitive advantage. He saw it before anyone else. A massive, ten-mile-wide dirt island. It was so packed with dirt that it constantly poured off the sides, some sticking to the island and slowly but surely expanding it.

Jack wondered what created this overabundance of dirt, and he didn't have to look far to figure it out. A golden lotus bloomed in the middle of the island. Its energy undulations were staggering. Endless waves of golden brown energy, spreading as far as met the eye, invaded the darkness and maintained a stalemate with it. This energy was so potent that parts of it spontaneously materialized as dirt, overfilling the island and enhancing the elemental aura of this place.

Jack scanned the environment again. The area had smelled faintly of dirt and earth, of moist soil, but the lotus itself contained something more. Holiness. Divinity. It was like the Goddess of Earth herself had descended here, creating a land so irreproachable that even the energies of the Dark Canal had to give way.

Strawpin gasped. "Golden Earth Lotus!" she exclaimed, her voice filled with awe. "An Overlord-level treasure!"

Jack looked around. Every disciple's gaze was tainted with greed, as well as helplessness. They knew this was not their stage. With all the Elders present, it would never be their turn to even touch it. Jack himself wasn't too interested—as high-level as this lotus was, he cultivated neither earth nor divinity.

A moment later, he realized he'd forgotten something. He was extremely interested in this treasure, because he knew someone who cultivated those exact elements! Jack swished around to look at Brock.

The brorilla was transfixed. His hands were closing and opening, reaching for a staff that was not there. His breaths came deep and rugged.

Jack thought back to Brock's Dao. The brohood he cultivated was a form of religious divinity, one of the elements exuded by the lotus. Additionally, he was a beast cultivator who used the staff—many of his battle tactics and early techniques revolved around the earth.

Brock was a perfect match for this treasure, and Jack instantly resolved to help him get it. He had been the one to benefit most from their various travels—helping out his brother was long overdue.

"*We're getting that,*" he told Starhair, then turned a calculating gaze on the treasure. While he'd been blinded by the lotus, there was more in sight.

The Elders floated a little ahead, too absorbed by the treasure to care about the disciples disobeying orders. Their energies were in disarray. They, of everyone present, understood how precious an Overlord treasure was. Every single one of them was steeped in greed, including Owlhead and Shadowhound, the two middle A-Grade leaders. Their previous harmony was all but gone. Jack even thought they'd start fighting any second.

When cultivators ran into treasure, it wasn't uncommon for a fight to the death to occur. It was one of the cultivation world's unspoken laws, and it was doubly the case for the aggressive space monsters. Friendships broke down before riches. For a treasure of this grade, everything was fair play—backstabbing, treachery, underhanded tricks. Everyone was instantly on guard against everyone else.

"...How do we handle this?" Owlhead asked, the first to speak.

"I want this treasure, and I'll fight you for it," Shadowhound said. "However... Let's not be hasty. The dirt island area is so widespread that there's no way it went unnoticed. Since the native monsters aren't swarming here, there is only one explanation—something very dangerous guards this treasure."

"I agree," Owlhead replied. "I can't sense anything. It's either underwater or perfectly harmonized with the lotus's energy signature."

"It hasn't reacted to us yet. It can't sense us. That's good, it means we have time to plan."

"Uh, excuse me," Strawpin said, interrupting the two Elders' tense conversation. They turned stern gazes at her. She pressed on regardless. "I thought the goal was to take us to the Hall of Trials... Since this place looks dangerous, could you escort us there first and then return to fight for the lotus?"

Shadowhound snorted. "Shut up, disciple."

"We've been assigned as your caretakers, but that doesn't mean we'll waste a great opportunity for you," Owlhead added. "Running into this lotus was fate. We will pursue it. Frankly speaking, it's worth more to either faction than a mere handful of disciples... and, there are also some things you don't know. In any case, you disciples can stay back and wait or move out on your own. Just don't bother us."

With that, both Elders turned to the front, speaking amongst each other to formulate a plan. Strawpin's eyes flashed dangerously, but she held her tongue.

Fiend Prince laughed. "We can only blame our own weakness. I will wait farther away. If things go wrong, I'll take the rest of my faction's disciples and try to reach the Hall of Trials anyway."

"Same," Strawpin said, boiling with anger.

Jack didn't say anything. He kept his gaze on the six Elders as well as the dirt island housing the golden earth lotus.

"What about you, Jack Monstrous?" Fiend Prince asked. "What will you do?"

"I think I'll stay and watch," Jack replied. "I'm not one to miss a good show."

Fiend Prince and Strawpin exchanged a glance. Nobody reached their level without decent intuition.

"Then I'll stay as well," Strawpin decided.

"Me too," Fiend Prince agreed. The other disciples also remained, not wanting to be far from the head disciples.

Jack didn't particularly care about them. No matter what happened, they wouldn't be able to compete with him. His true opponents here were the Elders, especially Owlhead and Shadowhound, along with the mysterious monster guarding the lotus. To acquire it, he'd need to get through them all—a needle-sharp path.

He favored his chances, however, because he possessed the greatest weapon of all—the element of surprise.

He turned his attention back to the Elders, who were treating all disciples as if made of air.

"We need information to formulate a plan," Owlhead said.

Shadowhound nodded. "Agreed. You four—draw lots. The loser goes to scout."

Those Elders jumped and looked at each other with terror. They were only early A-Grades—going near the den of whatever guarded this place meant almost certain death.

"Don't think of deserting," Owlhead warned them. "This is your duty to the Space Monster World. Now... Draw!"

With a swish of his hand, four straws materialized inside it, only their top ends visible. They appeared identical. The four Elders hesitated, then one by one drew their straws. The loser was the third one —the short and chubby devil—gazing with horror at the short stick in her hand.

"Were you really impartial?" Shadowhound asked. "Those straws were made of your Dao. Who is to tell us you didn't just give the short stick to whoever you wanted?"

"I swear it was fair. Do you have a better way of drawing lots? Besides, I think most of our fellow Elders would agree."

Shadowhound glanced around. Of his two Elders, the one who'd drawn the short stick exclaimed this was clearly cheating. The other one, only stood there silently. He didn't care whether the lots were rigged or not—he was safe right now, while a repeat would put him at risk.

Seeing that Elder's reaction, Shadowhound tsked. "Fine. You win this one. Shortplum: go and pluck that lotus."

"I..." The short Elder hesitated.

"If you go, you may survive. If you don't, I promise you'll die a most horrible death," Shadowhound threatened, his eyes shining redder under the shadows.

"...Fine. I'll go."

The short and chubby devil took a deep breath, then distanced himself as he flew forth. Every eye was trained on him, including Jack's—the other disciples couldn't see all the way to the lotus. Silence reigned.

The short devil Elder advanced carefully. She moved at a slow pace, repeatedly scanning her environment for any threats. Her job was only to scout. The moment she sensed anything amiss, she would retreat immediately.

Even as she flew halfway over the island, nothing happened. Could I be so lucky? the devil wondered. Could there be no monster? Or maybe it's absent right now. If I do pluck the lotus... Could I run away and actually keep it!

Greed flashed in her eyes. Of course, she was an experienced Autarch—she'd never drop her guard. That's how she saw the strike coming.

The dirt below her moved imperceptibly as if blown by a gentle breeze. The devil shot backward, but it was too late—a massive hand of dirt appeared, phasing out of thin air. It grabbed at Elder Shortplum. Despite the strike's slow movement, the Elder was completely helpless to dodge it. As the massive hand wrapped around her, she shrieked.

"Elder Shadowhound, save me!"

Her plight fell on deaf ears. Nobody came to her rescue. Within moments, the hand crushed her body, and all moisture left her, leaving her a broken, dry husk. Her body dissipated a moment later, becoming nothing but dirt which fell to the ground. The hand retreated toward the lotus, disappearing through the air like it was never there.

"A dirt monster," Owlhead commented, watching from afar. "Maybe an earth elemental?"

"Probably. But, its power... It was at least a late Autarch. Maybe close to a peak one," Shadowhound intoned. He licked his lips, a crimson tongue passing over shadows. "I think we can take it."

"Right. We have the weapons the Overlords gave us. Even if it's a peak Autarch, we can struggle with it—and, if we lose, we might be able to escape. It relies on the dirt below, so its power will be greatly diminished outside its domain. Maybe that's why it hasn't attacked us yet."

"Right. It doesn't perceive us as threats."

"But it should."

"Hehe. We'll show it."

Avarice played on the eyes of both Owlhead and Shadowhound. As for the rest of the Elders, their greed had morphed into fear. They'd realized that, at this point, they were just expendable pawns. The chances of them getting the treasure were minimal, yet their risk was immense. Unfortunately, the two leaders wouldn't let them leave even if they wanted to.

Jack shook his head. These people had just sent an Elder to sacrifice herself as a scout, and they hadn't even batted an eye at her death. Not one consoling word. They were so ruthless it was scary...

But, again, this was the cultivation world. There was no compassion, only benefits.

CHAPTER FIFTY-TWO

THE HUNTER STALKS

The Elders floated forward slowly. Owlhead and Shadowhound took the lead, putting their lives on the line for treasure. The remaining three Elders followed. Jack watched from a distance.

As their feet treaded on air, they cautiously surveyed the space ahead of them. The lotus bloomed—the dirt remained still, lifeless if not for their knowledge that it wasn't.

The attack came without warning. A hand phased into reality, already formed and present, and dug for Owlhead. He crossed his arms to defend—a blast of psychic energy erupted, shaking the other monster. Its strike remained devastating. Owlhead flew back, through the other Elders, and barely managed to steady himself after a mile. A thin trail of blood flowed on his forehead—yet, he was okay.

"Lure it out!" he shouted.

The Elders fanned out, approaching the monster from different directions. A torrent of fire launched into it, followed by a claw swipe and what seemed like brown vomit. Shadowhound leapt at the enemy, blasting it with solid darkness.

All these attacks approached the lotus and disappeared as if crossing into a different reality. Energy rippled out. A bodiless moan echoed through space, an injured giant, as space around the lotus warped and collapsed. A new sight was revealed.

A whirlwind of dirt, floating around the pristine lotus and protecting it. A space distortion had hidden it, the emitted energy undetectable next to the treasure it protected, but it now lay bare for all to see. The many attacks had disturbed the monster, yet not broken it.

A second moan arose. The dirt covering the island took to the air, drawn to the center of the whirlwind by an invisible force. More and more of it gathered, coalescing into a humanoid shape.

The Elders wouldn't let it finish transforming. They attacked again, blowing up the dirt as it began to gather. They couldn't disperse it entirely though. A second hand appeared, slowly trailed by a forming arm, and joined the battle.

The original dirt hand—which they now saw was connected to the whirlwind by a thin stream of dirt—shot sideways, slapping one of the Great Silver's early A-Grades. The second hand matched the strike from the other side. They closed around the female double devil from the Great Silver faction like twin mountains, slamming shut.

She got splattered, dying a horrible death.

Owlhead held a piece of silver paper, yellowed by age. His teeth were gnashed, and his grip tight around the paper. His eyes frantically searched the forming elemental. "We must find the nucleus!" he shouted.

"I know!" Shadowhound replied.

Perhaps shocked by the death of the female double devil, the two remaining early A-Grades—one from each faction—had slowed their attacks. The dirt gathered faster. It formed a giant torso, supported by two great legs and ending in a featureless head. As the final bits spun into two arms, connecting to the floating hands, the elemental roared without a mouth, shaking space and the minds of all who heard it. A few of the watching disciples cried out, leaking blood from their orifices.

"Fall back!" Strawpin commanded. "It's too strong for us!"

The elemental towered a mile into the sky. It raised its leg and kicked at Shadowhound. There was no time to dodge—the strike obliterated him, making him dissipate into a cluster of tiny shadows.

"Shadow Clone!" a voice came from the void, and a second Shadowhound appeared near the dead one, having barely dodged the strike. He was panting, his shadows flickering—that was not an easy technique to use, yet he'd had no choice.

The elemental roared again.

Jack narrowed his eyes. With the elemental fully formed, its aura was clear for all to see. It was situated somewhere between the late and peak A-Grade—facing a handful of middle and early A-Grades, this should be a slaughter.

"We need to run!" Strawpin shouted, but Jack ignored her.

Come on, he thought, staring intently at the battle. You knew it would be strong. Surely, you have some trump cards. You can't be this stupid!

"Shadowhound!" Owlhead shouted. His hand still gripped the piece of paper, his eyes frantically searching the elemental's body. "I can't see its nucleus!"

"Me neither!" the other Elder replied. "We need to strike hard!"

"What are they talking about?" Jack asked.

Fiend Prince arrived beside him, calmly watching the battle. "Elementals are regenerating creatures. The only way to stop them is to strike their nucleus. Typically, you just keep hitting it until the nucleus reveals itself, then you deliver a powerful strike there. That is impossible in this case. The Elders have their trump cards, given to them by the Overlords to protect us, but there is no point using them if they can't find the nucleus. And, without those powerful attacks, they can't inflict enough damage to reveal it. This monster being an elemental really fucked them over."

Jack fell into thought. He needed this treasure. If the Elders couldn't win this battle, he'd need to help them—maybe sneak in and use Black Hole, his most powerful strike, to expose the nucleus and let them destroy it with their trump cards.

However, if that happened, he'd have revealed his power. They'd also be wary of his black hole, not letting him charge it. If he fell into a brawl with them in that state, there would be no guarantee of victory... but what choice did he have?

At worst, I'll just escape, he concluded, gritting his teeth. "Brock! Take Starhair and go—"

He didn't have time to finish his telepathic words.

The Elders didn't know he'd been about to help. As they saw this lifetime opportunity fade before their eyes, they grew desperate. A new darkness covered Shadowhound's form. It shone with black light so intense it surpassed the physical realm, shining directly on people's souls. Blood dripped from within the shadows, yet the elemental seemed entirely unaffected.

Because it wasn't the target.

The brown blob Elder with multiple eyes and limbs floating over its form from the Great Silver faction, staggered. All those eyes blinked, then shone dark. The Elder threw itself forward, heedless of caution or danger.

"Shadowhound!" Owlhead shouted in outrage.

The brown blob Elder approached the elemental in a straight line. It was predictable. A hand fell from above, aiming to squash it.

The Elder exploded.

Brown flesh flew everywhere, then was immediately disintegrated by the greatest explosion Jack had ever witnessed. Even in the suppression of the Dark Canal, a new sun appeared. Everyone averted their eyes. Heat and light traveled together, destroying the world in one massive shockwave. The island below rumbled, parts of it collapsing into the sea, while the elemental, who'd been the closest to the explosion, released a low moan of pain.

When the light receded, Jack saw a crater burned into the island's surface, as well as a large hole where the elemental's waist used to be.

"Incredible!" Fiend Prince shouted. "He controlled the other Elder and forced it to detonate its inner world! What admirable ruthlessness!"

"Elder Blob!" Strawpin yelled.

"How dare you, Shadowhound!"

Owlhead's face was warped with fury. Shadowhound hadn't chosen his own Elder for this suicide tactic, but Great Silver's—this was clearly deliberate.

Shadowhound staggered—move after move had taken a toll on him, but he could still fight. "What are you yelling for, you idiot?" he shouted back. "There is no other way! We need to find the nucleus!"

"You should have used your Elder, not mine!"

"I'll use mine as well!"

"You better!"

The only remaining early A-Grade Elder, a burly, biblical devil-looking individual, paled at hearing this. He immediately turned and ran. Owlhead was already behind him. A palm strike landed squarely on the Elder, launching him straight toward Shadowhound, who teleported and bit the devil's head off. A shadowy version of its head appeared in place of the original.

The devil went rigid. A moment later, it launched itself at the elemental, forgoing all notions of safety.

Though the elemental now missed its waist, the attack hadn't hit its nucleus, so it wasn't really injured. Its legs and torso still stood as normal. More dirt was rising from below, reforming the missing waist. As its attention was focused there, it delayed its reaction to the devil Elder's advance.

A second explosion rocked the world. The reforming waist was blown away completely, and so was the elemental's chest, the dirt disintegrating and scattering everywhere. Only its head and limbs remained, its middle section once again reforming. But it still stood.

"Elementals can't store the nucleus in their limbs!" Fiend Prince shouted excitedly. "It's in its head! They can do it!"

"Now, Shadowhound," Owlhead shouted, charging at the

elemental. He tore the silver paper in half, unleashing a burst of powerful Dao. It eclipsed the two self-detonations from before—this was a part of an Overlord's strike, the strongest force in the universe.

A silver dragon head appeared in the sky, ephemeral yet real. It opened its mouth to release a beam of silver energy, right at the elemental's head. Space shattered where the beam passed.

At the same time, Shadowhound's form flashed, activating some talisman himself. A massive leg appeared, gray and covered in scales. It was as tall as the elemental's, yet moved with far sharper intent. The leg cleaved upward in a fierce kick, aiming for the head, as was the silver beam.

The elemental saw the threat. It stopped reforming, investing all of its power into defense. Barrier after barrier of dirt manifested, shielding the elemental twelve times. The silver beam crashed into them. The first barrier was pierced through without resistance. So were the second and third. It took nine barriers to waste the beam's energy, and the tenth even cracked a little.

The elemental moaned. There was another attack.

The massive kick smashed right through the remaining barriers. All they achieved was to slow it down a little. The leg then crashed into the elemental's head, shattering it completely, dispersing and disintegrating the dirt. A massive canyon was cut into the darkness above, extending for miles.

As the elemental's head dissipated, there was a sound like breaking glass. All the dirt seized, then collapsed to the ground, no longer held aloft by magic. A single brown core fell as well.

The elemental was no more.

But the battle wasn't over. Jack suddenly appeared behind Elder Owlhead, stepping out of the space crack he'd been hiding in. He had four arms and was taller than before, while one of his fists was replaced by a spinning black hole sucking in the ambient Dao.

Owlhead turned around, too late to react.

Jack had chosen his moment carefully. He'd waited for the exact do-or-die moment in the Elders' fight against the elemental, when everyone's attention was completely focused on the clash between the Overlord talismans and the dirt barriers. He'd used this moment to slip into a space crack and charge his black hole attack, then teleported right behind Owlhead and struck him instantly.

Owlhead had only been paying attention to the elemental and Shadowhound—he registered no other threat. Coupled with the fact that Jack had chosen the single best moment to attack... he was caught off guard. He didn't have time to dodge or defend. A well-timed black hole struck him in the chest, sucking in his innards and exploding, killing him instantly. Not even his core remained. A middle A-Grade Elder had died, just like that!

Everyone froze, their victory celebrations cut short. It wasn't just Owlhead. Nobody had seen Jack move. Nobody expected such a stunning turn of events.

"What did you do!" Shadowhound shouted, instinctively rushing away from Jack. A moment later, he realized who it was who killed Owlhead. He started laughing. "Thank you! I was afraid Owlhead would best me, but you just went and killed him! What a nice young monster you are. You secured me the lotus! If you desert your faction and join mine right now, I can take you as a personal disciple—I like your style!"

Strawpin was at a loss for words. Rage and indignation bubbled up inside her. Jack had stolen the spots of her fellow disciples, ran off by himself, then returned only to betray her faction and assassinate a middle Autarch Elder. At this moment, she hated him more than anyone else in the world!

Fiend Prince, on the other hand, laughed. "That's the Fiend King way of doing things! I knew I liked you, Jack Monstrous!"

"Fuck you, Jack!" Strawpin shouted.

Jack, however, ignored them all. He turned his body to face Elder Shadowhound, aiming a fist at him.

The Elder frowned. "What's the meaning of this?"

"I did not betray any faction," Jack intoned slowly. "I killed

Owlhead because he was despicable, and also in my way. I will kill you for the same reasons. That lotus is mine."

Shadowhound paused for a moment. Then, he laughed again. "Are you serious? Are you insane? You can't possibly think you can take me!"

Jack smiled coldly. "You specialize in Will attacks. Since your element is darkness, you have an affinity for space and chaos, as well as absorption. You are also an expert in suppressing groups of weaker enemies through soul domination. Amongst middle Autarchs, you rank somewhere in the middle of the pack—neither strong nor weak—and, most importantly, you don't favor direct battles but ones of subterfuge. Right now, injured and exhausted, you're about as weak as a middle Autarch can be. Am I correct in my assumptions, Elder Shadowhound?"

The Elder snorted. "You planned this all beforehand," he said in a low voice. "Fine. Have it your way, young monster. I applaud your spirit, but no amount of preparation can surpass an absolute difference in cultivation. Whatever attack you used on Owlhead will not work on me. All your elaborate plans will fail. You have been blinded by greed, and you failed to realize that against someone like me, you are just not worthy."

Jack's smile remained. "Let's find out, shall we?"

Throughout his cultivation journey, Jack had explored treasure-filled locations more than once. Trial Planet, Green Dragon Realm, Black Hole Church... He was no longer the greenhorn he used to be. Now, he was an experienced cultivator who could be as ruthless and calculating as needed to always emerge on top.

Choosing Owlhead as his first target had been deliberate. He'd kept his cards hidden and was relatively uninjured, marking him as the most dangerous opponent in one-on-one combat. Shadowhound, on the other hand, had exerted himself multiple times, revealed his strengths and trump cards, and was also injured. Jack had confidence he could take him.

From the start of the battle till now, everything had played right into his hands—including what was about to happen.

"Shadow Realm!" Shadowhound shouted. A flash of darkness spread from his body to cover the entire world. Everything else disappeared—it was only him and Jack in an endless, featureless, black expanse. The Elder laughed. "I've spent endless millennia perfecting my shadow arts. Defend against them if you can, boy!"

The shadows morphed into countless beasts and weapons, all charging straight at Jack. He smiled. His body became a missile which crashed against them. The battle began.

In the outside world, the other disciples saw Shadowhound and Jack exchange threats, then suddenly go still. Both were frozen in midair.

"They're trapped in a battle of wills," Strawpin said. Her eyes flashed cautiously. "That's... What do we do?"

"Isn't it clear?" Fiend Prince replied. He spread his fingers to reveal sharp claws. "We kill them both, then fight between ourselves for the lotus. I have to say, this Jack Monstrous did us a huge favor. No idea what he expected to happen."

"Mm. I agree," Strawpin said. She believed in her faction, but she was also an experienced monster—in the face of a treasure like the golden earth lotus, assassinating an enemy Elder and a sort-of traitor was nothing much.

The other disciples rallied behind these two and made to fly onward. However, a person suddenly flashed before them. It was a humble-looking brorilla, standing straight with his hands behind his back.

"What are you doing?" Fiend Prince asked.

"Nobody will interfere in my big bro's fight," the brorilla replied, calmly facing the two peak disciples of the entire Space Monster World, as well as thirteen of their peers.

The disciples frowned. "You can't be serious. Do you really think you can stop all of us by yourself?"

Brock cracked a confident smile. "I might."

CHAPTER FIFTY-THREE
BRO SUPREMACY

Jack smashed into the many weapons and monsters summoned by Elder Shadowhound. Each was wrought of darkness and pain, their sharp edges glinting without light. They seemed deadly. Yet, they were nothing but figments of the imagination, parts of Shadowhound's will.

They could only harm Jack if he let them.

"Fool!" Shadowhound shouted, gloating already. "You should have never let me trap you here! I've trained my Will for untold millennia, while you only recently evolved from a worm. Prepare to die!"

Jack smiled. He rushed into the onslaught. His fists flashed purple, obliterating any darkness they fell upon, but there were more enemies than he could manage. They cut into him. Blades cleaved off his limbs, monsters chomped at his shoulders. Yet, he remained calm throughout. Every piece of damage they inflicted regenerated instantly. His fists slammed out, continuously obliterating monsters, knowing full well that Shadowhound experienced each fatal blow his summons received.

Groans of pain left the Elder's mouth, but he remained confident. "Fool! This is my domain! There is no way you can defeat me!"

Jack smiled. "We'll see."

Battles of wills were won by the person with the strongest will. Jack specialized in Physical and didn't possess many Will attacks, so if Shadowhound just stood still, Jack would be unable to touch him. Defense, however, didn't rely on techniques. Jack's willpower had been forged through endless pain and suffering, endless struggle, endless loss. In this aspect alone, he was confident in facing anyone, even Archons and Overlords. It didn't matter how strong they were—their willpower would always be inferior to his, as was evident by their inferior talent.

Jack endured the assault, not even changing his expression. "Keep coming at me, Shadowhound. Throw me everything you got, but remember this: I will not budge. No matter what attacks you've prepared, I've been through worse. When you finally grow tired, I'll still be here—and then, it will be my turn."

Shadowhound roared, unleashing more attacks. Jack defended calmly. No matter how many strikes hit him or how much pain he experienced, it was all fake. He waited patiently. As for what would happen in the real world until then... He wasn't worried. His bro had it covered.

Hearing Brock's arrogant words, Fiend Prince snorted. "Get out of here," he said. He flew forward, smashing a fist onto Brock. This looked like a casual strike, but it contained more than eighty percent of his full strength. It was enough to destroy any other B-Grade besides Strawpin.

Brock raised his palm and caught the fist. A dull thud echoed. Brock's monkey grin was revealed behind his hand. "Nice try, bro, but you need to try harder."

Golden energy erupted. Fiend Prince frowned and yanked his

hand free, retreating as quickly as possible. He gazed at his fist—his fingers had been singed by golden fire. He looked up to find Brock's aura materializing into a golden brorilla shadow overlapping with his body. He tsked. "This guy is serious," he told Strawpin. "There is no time to delay. Let's get him together, so we can reach the Elder before he kills Jack Monstrous and leaves the shadow realm."

Strawpin looked behind Brock. Some of them could probably bypass him, but Starhair waited right next to Jack Monstrous, guarding him—and the aura he revealed was no less than that of Strawpin's. She tsked. They had to get the monkey.

"Disciples—attack!" she shouted, then shot out first. A long needle appeared in her hands. Her hat flew into the air, revealing long dark hair, and broke apart into multiple different strands of straw which hovered around her needle. With a mighty stab, she flung them forward.

Fiend Prince attacked at the same time. There were no fancy moves—he just charged. As for the other thirteen disciples, they fanned out and unleashed their moves on Brock, much like the Elders had done against the elemental.

At least, they tried. The Great Silver disciples waved their hands but nothing happened. To their horror, they realized they'd lost their connection to the Dao.

"You may not rally against your big bro," Brock's voice struck them like divine decree. "Retreat and consider what you've done!"

"Ahh!" the disciples screamed. Intense pain erupted from their inner worlds, making them lose the ability to fly, and crashed into the dirt island below. Five people were gone, ten remained.

Strawpin clicked her tongue. "Fools. I told you not to trust him!" she exclaimed as she continued her strike.

Facing their combined attacks, Brock clasped his hands together. "To interrupt a duel is un-bro-like. So is to gang up on someone," he declared. "You will be punished."

Golden energy flared. It was like some ancient Dao resonated with Brock, echoing from inside his body. Scriptures appeared everywhere—chanting filled the air, unintelligible but carrying distinct power. All other disciples felt the Dao tighten around them, restricting their movements.

At the same time, the scriptures materialized into golden bodies. A dozen brorillas appeared, each carrying a different weapon and radiating the same light. "For big bro!" they exclaimed, falling onto the weaker disciples. A melee erupted.

Fiend Prince and Strawpin were unaffected. They charged directly at Brock, who smiled in welcome.

"Come."

The three clashed. A staff appeared in Brock's hand, as well as in the golden phantom's surrounding him. Expert twirls met the pair's advance. Fiend Prince was a fierce melee combatant, but Brock countered him easily, the staff flowing from one stance to the next without pause or pattern. Strawpin's needle stabbed forward, fast and accurate, but it couldn't penetrate the golden brorilla. As for the strands of straw, both stabbing and wrapping around Brock's phantom was ineffective.

Strawpin gnashed her teeth. "To me!" she shouted. The strands wrapped around the needle, losing some flexibility but greatly enhancing its power. She stabbed out again, this time managing to penetrate the golden brorilla. Most of the strike's power was lost, however, and Brock managed to stop it between his fingers.

"Well done, straw bro," he said, grinning.

Meanwhile, Fiend Prince had taken advantage of this opening to unleash a devastating offensive, cutting the golden brorilla to pieces and slowly advancing on Brock. The brorilla's eyes shone. He let go of Strawpin's needle, allowing her to retreat. "You're good enough!" he exclaimed, joy in his voice. "Then, let me try out my newest ability!"

The golden brorilla shone brilliantly. Fiend Prince and Strawpin retreated, fearing an explosion, but that didn't happen—instead, the massive brorilla phantom compressed and compressed, eventually plastering itself directly on Brock's body. He now shone as if wearing golden armor—an awe-inspiring aura emerged from inside him, as if a brorilla irreproachable, unfathomable, unopposable. A little bit of golden light remained after forming the golden armor, and it transformed into two new arms, sticking out below Brock's armpits.

Brock smiled. "Big Bro Form! Come!"

He didn't wait. He charged out first, smashing into the pair like a bull. Fiend Prince's martial arts were broken. The needle stabbed Brock, only barely penetrating his armor and drawing out a hint of blood.

Brock laughed. He twirled his staff, bringing it down on his opponents. In this form, he possessed significantly higher offense, defense, and speed. He was overall much stronger, enough to pressure both of them by himself. Meanwhile, his dozen golden brorillas from before were fighting the weaker disciples, slowly gaining ground.

As Strawpin and Fiend Prince desperately resisted Brock's pounding, they exchanged a glance, recognizing the shock in each other's eyes. They were supposed to be the strongest B-Grades in the world. Yet, this low-key brorilla, this silly guy who kept drinking wine, could fight both of them while simultaneously defending against nine other top disciples?

And he was *winning*?

"I refuse to accept this!" Fiend Prince roared, his fiery blood getting the best of him. He switched to offense, bravely charging into Brock's assault. *He uses a staff,* he deduced. *If I get into close quarters, I win!*

Strawpin changed her stance to match him. Her needle shot out, delivering a thousand stabs in the blink of an eye. The strands of straw wrapped around it glowed, steadily burning away to release more power.

Brock welcomed their attacks. He calmly defended, using his staff and armor to meet each of their strikes. Clangs filled the world. The darkness shook behind them, pierced by shockwaves. In the outside universe, this battle would have shattered planets—here, it could only raise some wind.

Brock defended and waited. Eventually, one of Fiend Prince's attacks went an inch too wide—Strawpin's stab wasn't perfectly synchronized either. Brock used his staff to push the devil's hand aside, striking at his face with the butt of his staff. Fiend Prince went flying. Strawpin's strike landed, piercing Brock's skin but stopping against his ribcage. In return, he swung his staff and delivered a full-force strike into her chest, sending her flying as well. She smashed into Fiend Prince, who'd just recovered, stunning them both for an instant.

"Big Bro Slap!" Brock shouted. The two head disciples braced themselves, ready to block his staff, but it was only a feint. The true strike came from above. A golden palm materialized, larger than Fiend Prince and Strawpin combined, and smashed against their heads. They coughed out blood. The palm kept going, carrying them along through the air until they smashed into the island below, titling it dangerously. Cracks spread all around. Strawpin's scream echoed.

The palm remained, pressing down on them. Before they could escape, Brock shot toward the eight weaker disciples, who were already losing against his conjured brorillas. As soon as he joined the fray, the battle became pointless—disciples smashed into the island below one by one, all injured but alive.

When Fiend Prince and Strawpin finally managed to push the golden palm away, their hair disheveled and bleeding from various places, they found their fellow disciples groaning on the ground beside them, while Brock and his army of golden brorillas slowly descended from the sky above. His sole injury, a stab inflicted by Strawpin, had already healed.

"Yield," he commanded. "You cannot defeat me."

Strawpin bit her lips. "How can you be so strong! Are you hiding your cultivation?"

"I follow the true path," Brock replied simply. Their inaction indicated their surrender. He let his brorillas disperse, maintaining his golden armor just in case.

“Hahaha!” Fiend Prince laughed, his voice laden with bitterness. “I admit you’re strong, the strongest Baron I have ever met, but do you really think you can spare the time to fight us? Your friend is trapped in the Elder’s Shadow Realm. While we delay you, he’s dying! It’s a miracle he’s even survived this long!”

Hearing his biting words, Brock only chuckled. He spared a glance for Jack and Shadowhound, both of whom remained immobilized, facing each other. “Don’t worry, my big bro can handle this. He’s far stronger than me.”

“Far stronger?” Strawpin recoiled. “Don’t make me laugh. That’s impossible!”

The sound of breaking glass echoed from behind Brock. Jack and Shadowhound moved again. However, while Jack was panting, he was uninjured—Elder Shadowhound was bleeding from all orifices, the crimson glow in his eyes fading.

“My turn,” Jack said. He charged.

Elder Shadowhound screamed. “This is impossible! Get away from me!” he shouted, flying back in retreat.

Strawpin was stunned. So was Fiend Prince and every other disciple. Brock was already challenging their understanding of the world—he was much stronger than they ever thought possible. And... If Jack was even stronger than that... If a late Baron could make a middle Autarch scream and run away in fear...

How is that possible? Strawpin asked herself, frozen in place. Her gaze alternated between Jack and Brock—two impossible existences. Her eyes shook. *Such levels of talent... How is this even possible? Am I actually weak... or are they just... monsters?*

The shadow realm shattered. All the wraiths, all the monsters and the blades had carved up Jack’s body, but he stood tall. He just defended. It was Shadowhound who was spending his energy to release these attacks. Eventually, the Elder got tired. Sweat poured down his body. Blood flowed from his orifices. When he couldn't take it anymore, the world of will withdrew, and Jack was free.

He glanced to the side, finding the many disciples on the ground while Brock hovered over them—as it should be. He was pleasantly surprised to find they were all alive. Brock limited the killing, as Great Silver had instructed.

Good job, bro.

He turned to his opponent.

"This is impossible!" Elder Shadowhound shouted. "Get away from me!"

He shot into the distance, but why would Jack let him? He flashed ahead of the Elder, delivering a devastating Meteor Punch. Shadowhound's eyes flashed with glee. "Aha! You really are a fool, you fell for it! I don't know how you developed such willpower defense, but there is no way you can match a middle Autarch in a direct clash. Die!"

He continued his path, darkness enveloping him like a black meteor. Jack grinned at the similarity. His Meteor Punch changed midair into Supernova, a stronger attack, and smashed against Shadowhound. Flesh scattered. The Elder shot backward, blood trailing his path, as even the shadows around him flickered to reveal a dark, hyena-like body.

Shadowhound specialized in Will attacks, which had already been defeated by Jack, so his physical prowess was lacking. Additionally, he was already injured and exhausted. How could he possibly match up to Jack, who could fight even stronger middle A-Grades on equal footing?

Jack teleported. He intercepted Shadowhound mid-flight and smashed a flurry of blows onto him, forcibly altering his trajectory. He flashed again and smashed a knee into the Elder's midsection from below, shooting him upward. With a final teleportation, he reappeared above the Elder, preparing a massive strike and unleashing it downward. "Supernova!"

Elder Shadowhound screamed as his ribcage shattered. Blood

erupted like a geyser. He broke the sound barrier as he fell, crashing into the edge of the island so heavily he tipped the whole thing, almost upturning it. *Now is my chance!* he thought. The final vestiges of his Dao of Darkness activated, preparing to hide him in the ever-present dark mist. He was lucky to be in this environment—here, even a late Autarch couldn't find him. This was the move he relied on to dare struggle against Owlhead!

However, he didn't expect Jack to show no mercy. After he smashed Shadowhound downward, he hadn't delayed an instant—he dived after him, preparing another Supernova, even more powerful than the last. The Elder may have lost, but he'd already demonstrated an ability to dominate other people. If he used that move to take control of Starhair, it could mean trouble. Jack wouldn't let that happen.

As Shadowhound opened his eyes, ready to blend into the darkness, he found a massive fist descending on him like a falling star. *Shit.*

"Supernova!"

The world rumbled. Tall waves splashed out, while an entire half of the island crumbled, upsetting the water below. Shadowhound's mangled body sank into the sea, but not before Jack snatched his core.

A middle A-Grade... Dead!

Jack was panting, but he stood and surveyed the place. All threats were neutralized. They'd won. As for the disciples who remained on the ground, gazing at him with extreme shock... They honestly weren't much.

"Good job, Brock," he said. "I hope those guys didn't give you trouble."

"Not much," the brorilla replied with a shrug and a smile. "They're actually very well behaved!"

CHAPTER FIFTY-FOUR
FERRYMAN OF THE DEAD

A battle of tremendous scale was splitting the stars in the Spiral Stair galaxy. Energy blasts shot left and right—summoned beasts roared, smashing through dozens of cultivators, as powerful fighters went amok behind enemy lines. Magic was everywhere. The Dao was asunder.

Elder Boatman oversaw the battle from its midst. Besides the leading Archon of each army, who were fighting their own cataclysmic battle far to the side, he was the leader here.

This was one of the largest scale clashes between them and the Immortals yet—a rare chance where their troops had outmaneuvered their enemy, temporarily earning the right to victory. A triumph here would mean a lot for the Church, both in morale and troop balance.

They couldn't fail.

A squad of veterans charged out of the Church's lines, impacting heavily on their opponents'. Each possessed a Dao suitable for breaking through a mass of enemies—different Daos were more or less balanced in individual combat, but in large scale battles like this, the Dao configuration of a squad was vital. Most of the battle's tactics revolved around positioning the right cultivators at the right spots to counter the enemy.

Long lines of wizard cultivators unleashed energy blasts at the enemy from afar, protected by defense-oriented cultivators. The assault specialists of each army tried to flank the other, while a mass of mostly Physical cultivators duked it out in the middle. Everyone found their place to die.

Boatman couldn't help reminiscing. This reminded him of his mortal years—it was infantry, cavalry, and artillery all over again.

Besides the arrangement of specialized cultivators, there were more stratagems at play.

The previous squad of veterans, which Boatman had been watching, had now broken deep into enemy lines. Hundreds of enemies swarmed them, pelting them with attacks as the veterans' momentum ran out. They were too deep—they could not return, and they could not be rescued. The enemy commander must have seen the end goal of this—he'd already ordered his soldiers to retreat, no doubt, but it was difficult for the people in the melee to react in time.

Boatman closed his eyes in respect.

The veterans detonated their inner worlds. A massive explosion split the universe, cracking open a huge hole to the void beneath existence. A shockwave of pure energy erupted, obliterating dozens of enemy cultivators and injuring hundreds. The entire battlefield paused momentarily. Boatman reopened his eyes, gazing upon the distant cloud of raw, destructive energy.

"Farewell," he whispered, spreading his perception to bless those warriors' death. It didn't really do anything, but it comforted him, and he liked to think it comforted their ruined souls as well.

The Church faced many disadvantages in this war. However, they had a single advantage—they fought for survival. For their lives, for their children's lives, and for the future. The resolve they could muster far outweighed the enemy's, who fought only to fuel the Immortals' thirst for conquest.

The Hand of God could not utilize suicide bombers. The Church could. A harsh, if noble sacrifice.

As the energy ripples dissipated and space repaired itself, the battle resumed. Hundreds fell from either side. These were the brightest talents of the universe, each having risen above the endless masses only to eliminate each other like this. It wasn't fair. It wasn't pretty. It was war.

Boatman composed himself. He had work to do.

From the wall of warships behind the enemy army, a stream of monsters ran out. They were rabid, snapping at each other as well as every cultivator near them. A stream of Space Dao led them towards the Church army, where they would serve as the Hand's lesser version of suicide forces.

Boatman flashed to appear in their midst, between the armies. His black cloak billowed. He drew his scythe. "Guillotine," he muttered, then slashed at the void. A thin black slice shot out, spreading in three directions, turning into a sharp cone which flew at the enemy space monsters.

Hundreds fell in an instant. No matter how the Immortals searched the galaxies under their control, A-Grade space monsters were almost impossible to find. They would all fall before Boatman's scythe.

Suddenly, golden light erupted. The darkness receded, broken by the light, and the remaining half of the space monsters sailed over Boatman, impacting their army. He hoped they'd be handled before causing too much trouble—because he certainly couldn't bother with them any longer.

A man faced Boatman through the void. He wore shiny plate armor without a helmet, letting golden hair glint in the wounded starlight. A face chiseled from marble smiled at him. "Elder Boatman. Despite your disciple's insistence, we find each other."

Boatman frowned. "Elder Hero... Your power has grown yet again."

Hero laughed. "I had a lucky breakthrough. The middle A-Grade looks good on me, don't you think?"

A shudder ran through Boatman's body. This man, Hero, was trouble. His cultivation speed was unheard of, and his foundation was only growing more solid. He'd gone from the early to the middle A-Grade in less than a decade—Boatman himself had taken millennia. As for his battle power, it was nothing short of terrifying. Different Daos formed halos around him. His sheer aura upset the world, forcing everyone else in the entire battlefield to avoid him.

Boatman grew serious.

Having just broken into the middle A-Grade, Elder Hero had the power to contest with Boatman, a particularly powerful late A-Grade. This was unnatural. Ungodly.

If not for Jack and Brock, this might have been the greatest genius to ever exist, Boatman realized, his red eyes growing darker. *I can't let him grow anymore. Thirty years is just too short—how could Jack hope to match him in time? Since he stands before me, I have to kill him now... no matter what. I must protect my disciple.*

His decision made, Boatman raised his scythe. Hero gave a confident smile. "Are you sure about that, old man?" he asked.

Boatman charged. His black cape billowed against the astral winds, raising high behind him to reveal a pale body containing infinite power. The scythe blade went from white to black, and the Dao of Death formed the shape of a skull behind him. With his glowing red eyes, he imagined he made a frightening image—he always did.

Yet, Hero only smiled, his teeth pearly white. "What a blatant villain," he shouted, readying his sword. "A perfect target for the blade of a hero!"

Hero cleaved upward, golden white light rising like the tide. It met Boatman's black scythe and devoured it, the black and golden white strangling each other for endless miles.

Boatman sensed an almost divine power clash against his. The Death he took such pride in parted, ineffective like the river flowing around a rock—Hero's sword energy persisted, shooting for Boatman, who had to take a step back and swing his scythe again to neutralize it.

"You are too dangerous," he said in a dark voice. "You cannot be allowed to grow. Even if it costs me my life, I will kill you today."

"Hah! It will cost you your life alright. Do your worst. In the name of justice, I'll bring you down!"

"Spare me your rhetoric."

Boatman gathered energy around him, going all-out for the first time since Jack's breakthrough. Only this time, he had more space to work with. Dark energy converged, the battle's dead cultivators enhancing his powers. His form slowly changed. From a pale and old vampire, he became nothing but bones, his face a smileless skull. The shadows of his cloak deepened, shrouding him in mystery, while his scythe elongated.

"I am the Ferryman of the Dead," he declared, his voice changed to a deeper, more insidious tone. "Nobody can escape death. Not even you. And today, in the name of Death itself, I shall claim you." He readied his scythe. "Bare your soul for me."

Hero laughed. "And you accuse me of rhetorics! Fine, fine. Let's see what a million years of cultivation did for you, little villain."

Golden light erupted from Elder Hero. At that moment, he became more than a man. This light contained the faith of the people, the very concept of heroism draped over his shoulders like a cape. The entire battlefield paused, consciously or unconsciously in awe of his transformation. His jaw seemed sharper, his eyes kinder, his chest broader—his sword large enough to encompass the world.

"I am not a man, Boatman, but a hero, an ideal, a concept," Hero said with booming laughter. "And concepts never die!"

Boatman remained silent. He reached the other man in an instant. The two cultivators clashed, their battle capturing the entire battlefield. Black sparks flew everywhere. The finality of each strike spread outside their battle, threatening to claim the lives of everyone around them. Weaker cultivators fled in droves.

Hero's moves were majestic. Every slash carried the determination to save the world—an idea he'd convinced himself he carried. The world folded and crashed against Boatman, refuting Death with every strike. Booming laughter echoed.

The battle soon became unbalanced. The golden light consumed more and more of the void. The power of death shrunk, while Boatman had to retreat, forced into a defensive position.

Terrifying! he realized. Only a middle A-Grade, yet his power is touching the peak! This man... cannot be allowed to live!

His aura resurged. "In the name of Death, I will claim—" He paused mid-word, realizing he'd blundered. The golden light which Hero's attacks spread everywhere had not dissipated. It had simply laid there, burying itself in the vestiges of space, biding its time. As Boatman focused inward, prepared to unleash a powerful attack, all that golden light converged on Hero's sword instantaneously, filling it with much more power than ever before. Space itself shuddered at its wake.

Hero smiled brilliantly. "Now is your time of reckoning, evil-doer. Sword of the People!"

He slashed out, filling the universe with his sword's brilliance. Every ray of light was a mortal calling out for salvation—every patch of darkness between them a lost soul Hero was trying to avenge.

Boatman watched that golden light flood and destroy his defenses. Death gave way, then collapsed completely, leaving Boatman defenseless. Half the flood remained. An endless golden wall was approaching. This was not an attack he could survive.

I'm sorry, disciple, Boatman thought to himself with bitterness. In the end... I was not enough.

As the light approached him, however, it shuddered—and, in a single instant, collapsed. The rays of light became naught but harmless twinkles. Boatman gazed around him in surprise, finding that it wasn't just him. The entire battlefield had come to an abrupt cease-fire. A terrible dark energy covered every inch, hindering Boatman's perception, not letting it spread past a few thousand miles.

It didn't need to. He could sense them. Almighty, colossal existences, the cornerstones of this universe's reality. The darkness had been released by just the first amongst them—but there were ten more trailing behind, all powerful beyond belief.

A black ball the size of the sun appeared to the side of the battlefield. Tendrils of darkness swept from its surface, whipping space around. It radiated entropy in its purest form—a level of energy Boatman had never experienced before, not even from the Arch Priestess. Even the two fighting Archons stopped, one's face filled with joy and the other's with fear.

The moment it appeared, the black sphere unleashed its tendrils, each wide like a planet. They swept through the B-Grades of the Hand of God, killing them as one would ants. They didn't even have time to cry out.

Elder Hero's face changed seven different colors. Boatman laughed. "How's that for a villain?" he asked, stabbing his thumb toward the black sphere. "Go test your blade against it, like a true hero."

He knew what that was. Everyone knew. Their entire army rose with cheers, both from the massacre of the enemy forces as well as the arrival of their saviors.

The sun-sized black sphere was Axelor, the current leader of the Old Gods, the God of Entropy. A creature at the very limit of Archons. Possibly the strongest entity in the universe.

Two more colossal shapes appeared behind Axelor, sailing smoothly through space. They were humanoid and made of ripples—one's spread everywhere chaotically, the other's moved smoothly in one direction, like a calm river. They were the Old Gods of Space and Time. In the flesh.

Hero ignored Boatman's jeers. The moment the Old Gods made their appearance, having finally arrived from the far end of the universe, he abandoned his already destroyed attack against Boatman and rushed full-speed to his army's Archon. The Archon did the same. The two met in the middle. Instantly, the Archon crushed something in his hand, and a tremendous surge of Space

Dao enveloped them both, teleporting them away just before one of Axelor's dark tendrils smashed through their location.

"No!" Boatman cried out, hating himself for failing to react in time.

The Space God turned into a ray of blue light, instantly arriving at the previous location of Hero and the Archon and diving into the folds of space after them. Presumably, it followed them to the endpoint of their teleportation—Boatman wished the Space God could at least kill Hero, giving Jack time to grow. Otherwise, his odds of winning that duel would be extremely slim. Boatman didn't want to underestimate his disciple, but even he understood that, for Jack to win, he would need nothing short of miraculous growth.

If you do fight... No matter how impossible it seems... I believe in you, my disciple!

Boatman had lost and almost died, but it was hard to maintain a bad mood. Intense relief swarmed his heart as he watched the remaining troops of the Immortals surrender, a part of their entire army just gone. They'd spent years waiting for the Old Gods, sacrificing their numbers to hold on against overwhelming forces. They'd been pushed to the brink.

Now, the Gods had arrived. There was hope. They could finally go on the offensive.

Boatman laughed, unable to hold it in. "Welcome back, Gods! Let the true war begin!"

CHAPTER FIFTY-FIVE
ABSORBING THE LOTUS

JACK SURVEYED THE CROWD OF DISCIPLES. ALL WERE SITTING ON THEIR KNEES on the partially destroyed, centermost dirt island.

"So," he said, tossing the middle A-Grade core in his hand up and down, "I guess we're all that's left."

"You were amazing!" Fiend Prince exclaimed, his eyes filled with stars. "How can you be so strong?"

"Luck, skill, and hard work, I guess..." Jack replied, a faint smirk on his lips.

"You are the strongest Baron I have ever seen. Stronger than I ever thought possible. Will you teach me?"

Jack laughed. "I don't take disciples, but thank you for the kind words."

"I can pay."

"It's not an issue of cores. I want to avoid unnecessary connections."

"Hmph." Strawpin snorted. "Of course he wouldn't teach you. You're nothing to him." Receiving Jack's glare, she brightened up. "I want to apologize for insulting you before. I thought you were disrespecting my faction and wasting our resources, but you clearly knew what you were doing. It was I who was blind. Please don't take offense."

Jack raised a brow. "And here I thought I'd need to use my flip-flops. Don't worry about it."

"What are we going to do now?" she asked. "The Elders are all dead, but we are still not at the Hall of Trials..."

She let her words hang, her intention clear. Jack swept his gaze over everyone. "I'll escort you there," he said. "With me, Brock, and Starhair, you have little to fear. Well, I guess you'll all die if we're unlucky and run into a late Autarch monster, but hopefully that won't happen."

Fiend Prince laughed. "That's the monster life! Thank you, Jack Monstrous. And you too, Brock. Your power is astounding."

"Thanks, bro."

"No problem, bro," Prince replied, already picking it up.

Jack grinned. "Before we leave, Brock and I must absorb some treasures and enhance our power. It could take a few weeks. You guys will need to either wait here or go off on your own, whatever you prefer. This area is safe though—the elemental's aura is still rich, and it will keep other monsters at bay for years."

"We'll wait, of course!" Fiend Prince replied. "Going alone is suicide. Besides... You're so cool! We'll follow you anywhere!"

"We'll wait as well," Strawpin added, notably less excited than her counterpart.

"Alright. Then, you're all free to meditate. I suggest remaining close so we can protect you if more monsters arrive."

"Yes, sir!"

Done speaking, Jack turned around with Brock. He couldn't deny he enjoyed the starry eyes of those super talented monsters as they looked at him. At the same time, they made him uncomfortable.

"What do you think, big bro?" Brock asked with a monkey grin. "Enjoying it?"

"I don't understand why me. You beat them all up at once. They should be admiring you."

"You're my big bro, and also very impressive. They admire both of us."

"I guess that's right."

Having walked away from the other disciples, who'd all switched to meditating positions suitable for their monstrous bodies, Jack retrieved some items from his space ring.

"We have one late A-Grade core, three middle A-Grade cores, and several early A-Grade ones. There is also the golden earth lotus over there."

The lotus still stood, though defenseless. It was the single greatest harvest—an Archon-level treasure. Jack turned to Brock.

"I think you're the biggest winner here, Brock. The elemental's late A-Grade core and the lotus are both suitable for you, and I have to say, you absolutely deserve them. Have fun."

"Thanks, bro," Brock said, receiving the late A-Grade core. Jack had picked it up after the battle, alongside the various Elders' space rings, which had been disappointingly empty.

The brorilla didn't wait to hear the distribution of the rest of the cores. He neither wanted anything else nor was interested in giving his opinion. Instead, he flew to the very top of the lotus, whose hard stem created a seating position. As Brock sat down with the late A-Grade core in hand and began to meditate, the lotus's energies rushed up to him, while the core also melted slowly.

Absorbing them wouldn't be a quick process, but it would be a lavish one.

"Let's look at the rest," Jack said, turning his proud gaze away from Brock. "Come here, Starhair. These cores are compatible with you, and these with me. The rest can be divided amongst the disciples."

Starhair accepted the cores he was offered, also raising a brow. "Are you taking them under your wing?"

"I promised Great Silver to take care of them. Since these cores are useless to us, giving them to the disciples makes sense—after all, it's their world's resources that we're taking. Giving back a little is fair."

"If you say so."

"Let's meditate and absorb these. I suspect Brock will take weeks or months to finish, so I'll keep guard after I finish absorbing mine. What will you do?"

"Meditate," Starhair replied with a shrug. "What else?"

They retreated to different positions on the broad dirt island. Jack, Starhair, and the various disciples all sank into silent meditation, while Brock oversaw them from the top of the golden earth lotus.

Time passed. Over the following days, everyone except Brock finished absorbing their cores. Most switched to meditating on the Dao—a cultivator's pastime—while Jack split his attention between meditating and keeping watch. After all, a native monster jumping out of the water to eat a disciple wouldn't be too out of place.

Thankfully, nothing happened. The elemental's aura persisted, just as Jack suspected—the other native monsters had probably sensed the battle, but they had no way of knowing the powerful elemental had perished. Even if they came to investigate, it wouldn't be anytime soon.

In contrast to the elemental's lingering aura, the lotus's energies were rapidly drying up. Its roots were withering, and the golden color of its leaves had lost its luster. Brock was growing stronger. His aura surged every day, approaching the peak B-Grade. His Daos were growing more refined as well.

Jack didn't mind waiting. As much as he was on the clock, he would never burden his bro with that. A few weeks were nothing, anyway—he enjoyed watching Brock's rise to power.

Two weeks later, someone approached him. "Hey," Strawpin said.

"Hey," Jack replied. He noticed that her hair was tidy under her straw hat, while her pale skin shone with a certain luster. She smelled differently, too—wilder?

"I was wondering," Strawpin began, "are you looking for a sex partner?"

"A what?"

"What did you not—"

"No, I got it. I already have a partner, though."

"I'm sure they wouldn't mind," Strawpin said, inching closer. Her smell filled Jack's nose. It probably passed as attractive to space monsters, but he wasn't really one, so he found it off-putting. His thoughts must have shown because Strawpin backpedaled, a surprised look on her face.

"I'm sorry," she said. "I thought we'd be a good match... There are many monsters pining for me, you know."

Jack gathered himself. "I can imagine. You're talented and beautiful. Unfortunately, I'm in an exclusive relationship with another monster, so I can't return your affection. Thank you, though."

"Are they better than me?" Strawpin asked with a pout.

"That's... not a comparison I'd want to make."

"I see. Okay. You don't need to lie, though—I know that no powerful monster has exclusive partners."

"I'm different. I'm not lying to you."

"Mhm. Alright." Her disappointed gaze was hard to hide. "I won't bother you anymore, then. If you ever change your mind, let me know, alright?"

Jack gave a wry smile. "I promise."

"Mm."

She headed back to her fellow disciples, her walk now carrying more swagger than strictly necessary. Jack didn't see the point. Her long robes revealed nothing.

"What's the issue with these people?" he asked Starhair telepathically. "One head disciple wants me to take them as my disciple, the other wants me to just take them."

"The price of power," Starhair replied, doing a mockery of Jack's voice. "Oh no! I'm so powerful and handsome that all the most influential people want me! What am I gonna do?"

"Very funny. I don't speak through my nose."

"You do sometimes."

"I do not!"

Both laughed—without a change in expression.

With nothing to do, Jack also checked his new stats, enhanced by the single middle A-Grade and various early A-Grade cores he'd absorbed—the only ones compatible with him.

Level: 513

Strength: 12,530 (+)
Dexterity: 12,530 (+)
Constitution: 12,530 (+)
Mental: 2000
Will: 2000
Free sub-points: 2

Matter Condensation: 26%

He was taking steady steps toward the peak B-Grade realm. The cores had given him another ten levels, as well as five hundred stat points, which he'd poured into the Physical substats. He'd also worked on his black hole skill a bit, achieving tiny improvements, and experimented with the Life-Time Dao Vision to no avail. That concept of creation, whatever it was, remained tantalizingly out of reach.

I'll get there, he promised himself. One step at a time.

It took another two weeks for Brock to finish absorbing the lotus and core. One day, the withered lotus simply cracked and collapsed like old stone. Brock floated down from his previous position, golden light spontaneously flickering around him. There was a certain air to him—as if he'd grown one step closer to being the entire universe's big bro.

"Sup," he said as his feet touched dirt. Over the next hundred years, all of it would wash away, and the surrounding islands would go back to being bare stone.

"Hey, bro." Jack welcomed him with a smile. "You look great."

"Thanks. I work out."

Jack laughed. "I see you reached the peak Baron realm?"

"That's right." Brock smiled back. "Only one step from being an Autarch... Though it won't come anytime soon."

"This is the first time you're a small realm above me, isn't it?"

"Yes. But not for long."

"Hopefully."

While Starhair greeted Brock as well, Jack turned to the monster disciples. "Are you guys ready?"

"We were born ready!" Fiend Prince replied, raising a fist to the sky. "Welcome back, big bro! Thanks for protecting us, other big bro! Is it time to test our fates?"

A grin played on Jack's lips. This guy's energy was infectious. "If that's what you want to call it."

"I do!"

"Perfect. Then, yeah, it's time. Let's go, bros. The Hall of Trials awaits!"

The monsters cheered, then took to the sky after Jack, Brock, and Starhair, following the trio into the darkness. The dirt island hosting the lotus's husk remained behind them, a relic forever lost in time.

It was time to see the Hall of Trials.

CHAPTER FIFTY-SIX
REACHING THE HALL

THE DISCIPLE GROUP EXITED THE DIRT ISLAND AREA VERY DIFFERENT FROM when they entered. Brock's strength had surged. All six Elders were gone, their cores long absorbed. In their place, Jack and Brock now led the group.

Starhair, of course, also enjoyed everyone's respect. His strength was enough to rival Strawpin and Fiend Prince's, while his friendship with Jack and Brock earned people's envy.

In just a short few weeks, Jack and Brock had secured the disciples' admiration. Their level of talent was unfathomable, but it wasn't just that. Any other monster might have left these disciples to fend for themselves—Jack and Brock had taken responsibility for killing the Elders and promised to protect the disciples all the way to the Hall of Trials.

As for the disciples... Being escorted and protected by Elders was one thing, but experiencing the same from people of your own class... That was a different emotion altogether.

"Are you sure you don't want a disciple, Jack Monstrous?" Fiend Prince asked, flying beside Jack. "I'll be good, I promise. I can wipe and mop your floors if you want. I'll work hard!"

"I'm good, Prince, thank you," Jack replied with a laugh. He'd interacted with the other disciples over the previous weeks, and Fiend Prince was one of the people he enjoyed. He was straightforward to the point of being funny. As for Strawpin, while she was somewhat stuck-up, her heart was kind. She'd only acted aggressive to defend the disciples whose spots Jack's group had taken.

Of course, now that she knew they more than deserved those spots, she'd completely switched her tune.

"How do you even know the way?" she asked, flying on Jack's other side, between him and Brock.

"I can sense the Dao released by the Hall of Trials. At least, I think I can," he replied. "If I'm right, the Elders were leading you in circles before."

"Why would they do that?"

Fiend Prince frowned. "That's weird. I understand that they'd want to explore the dirt area once they discovered it, but are you saying they were already moving in circles before that?"

"Yeah," Jack replied. "I was hoping you'd have an idea."

"No clue." Strawpin shook her head. "I've read the records on previous delves. Unless all previous generations deliberately obfuscated something, there was never a reason to delay. After all, the faster the Elders can drop us off at the Hall of Trials, the faster they can go treasure hunting."

"Owlhead did mention something weird," Fiend Prince added. "When Strawpin asked them to take us to the Hall and then return for the lotus, he said there are some things we don't know."

"I thought he told me to go fuck myself."

"That too."

"Maybe they were afraid to go treasure hunting and wanted to delay so they had an excuse to take things slow?" Strawpin ventured a guess. It wasn't too likely, but nobody had a better idea.

Jack didn't participate in the brainstorming. He was aware of more things than the rest. The Second Crusade had just erupted outside the Space Monster World—with the Overlords desperate to strengthen their factions, this delve was very different from all previous ones. Great Silver himself had hinted at this. Using the records as reference points was meaningless.

The Overlord had also mentioned something else. After urging Jack's group to meet up with the other disciples, he'd said, "Don't rush to the Hall of Trials." Maybe the Elders had received similar orders. The problem was, Jack had no idea why.

He was as lost as the rest of them.

In any case, thinking about that wasn't something Jack could afford right now. The Dark Canal was a dangerous place. Just by himself and Brock, they couldn't protect all these disciples forever. Rushing or not, they had to reach the Hall of Trials.

"What's the Hall like?" he asked.

"You don't know!" Strawpin's face glowed. "The Hall is where the world's creator left his legacy—or so the legends say. There are several tests there, and the better you perform, the higher the floor you're allowed to enter!"

"Oh," Jack said, becoming intrigued. "How many floors are there?"

"Six, but don't underestimate their difficulty! Even Fiend Prince and I, the head disciples of the Overlord factions, can only reach the fifth floor at most."

"You're stroking your own cock!" Fiend Prince laughed. "The fifth floor is a dream. It means we have a decent chance of becoming Overlords in the future—and, not to piss on myself, but I know my chances are small. The fourth floor is more realistic."

"Well, I don't know about you, but I can reach the fifth!" Strawpin replied, her face red. "The Overlord says I'm the greatest talent he's seen in a million years, superior to even Grand Elder Sanzuki! Since he reached the fifth floor, I can as well."

Fiend Prince gave a wry smile. "Traditionally, the fifth level is for characters like Overlords or Grand Elders. People with the potential to reach at least the peak Autarch level. The fourth level is for talented disciples with great hopes of becoming Autarchs, and anything below that... Well, it's for less talented ones. They're still not easy to reach though."

"What's the point?" Jack asked. "Since only peak B-Grades are entering, everyone should be able to reach the third or fourth level, right?"

"Right. But, that's only because we're sending peak B-Grades in there. The Hall of Trials can accommodate people of lower cultivations as well—it tests talent, not cultivation level. It's just that weaker people can't cross the Canal to reach it."

"Isn't that kind of stupid?"

"Seems so! I have no idea, honestly. The Hall and Dark Canal are far more ancient than anyone can remember. Maybe things were different in the past. Maybe the Canal wasn't as dangerous."

"What about the sixth floor?" Brock asked.

At this, the two head disciples fell silent for a time.

"It's not unheard of for people to reach it," Strawpin finally replied. "Over the history of our world, there have been three such cases. All of them became not just Overlords in the future, but exceptional Overlords. The most recent one was Overlord Rainbow a hundred million years ago. There were three Overlords at the time, and it's said she fought the other two by herself and still won."

"Impressive!" Jack exclaimed, his eyes flashing. The Overlord or Archon realm had no internal classifications of power, but some people were stronger than others. The Arch Priestess, for example, was a particularly powerful Archon. The Old Gods were all at the peak of power, and Axelor with Enas were yet another step higher, able to dominate regular Overlords. Jack thought it was similar to how talented cultivators could steamroll anyone in their cultivation boundary.

In most cases, that only applied to young cultivators who'd yet to grow into their full potential. When it came to mature cultivators, everyone at the same cultivation level was more or less the same, because anyone more talented would have already reached the next realm. Only the Archon realm was an exception, because no matter how talented one was, they just couldn't ascend higher. That was why there were great differences in power between Archons.

In fact, the existence of extreme Archons was the main reason why people believed there was no higher realm.

"You can probably reach the sixth floor though," Fiend Prince said, glancing at Jack and Brock. "I don't know how you did it, but you're unbelievably strong. In fact, I'd be surprised if you *didn't* reach it."

"We'll see," Jack replied with a smirk. "Isn't six floors such an ugly number though? Why not five or seven?"

"Beats me."

Jack disagreed, but he elected to continue the conversation with only Brock, through telepathy. Some of the things he was going to say might reveal they came from outside the Space Monster Realm.

"I think it's important," he said. "Whoever created the Hall of Trials was such an exceptional individual that there's no way they randomly chose to have six floors. There has to be a meaning to it. Maybe because it's half the number of the Old Gods, for some reason? Or because it's the number of Grades, from F to A?"

"I agree it's important, bro, but I have no idea. Let's figure it out when we get there."

Jack nodded.

A few native monsters attacked them on the way, but thankfully, nothing above the middle A-Grade. Jack and Brock handled them all—every battle only enhancing the awe in the disciples' eyes.

Eventually, the scenery changed again. The Dao stream Jack had been following turned more and more intense until everyone could sense it. Then, it kept growing until it was a brewing storm, a current of power simply waiting to erupt. It gave him goosebumps.

They emerged into an area where the black mist was thicker than ever. A stone island spread under their feet, far wider than any other, stretching into the darkness. Jack paused and strained his perception to the limit. What he saw made him gasp.

From the edge of the stone island, his perception could barely reach its center. There was a pyramid stretching into the sky, faint lines denoting six floors each an entire mile tall. Its base was seven miles wide, growing narrower the higher one looked. At the very top, it was flat, as if part of it had been shorn off. Tremendous power fell from up there—Jack wasn't eager to visit.

The black mist hugging the pyramid was so dense it almost turned solid. It rolled off the walls as moisture. The walls themselves were the brown of sand, easy to make out in the mist, while the surfaces were bare. The front of the pyramid sported a massive double door, half a mile tall, carved with the striking image of a monster tearing apart what looked like a human.

It gave Jack the chills. This world and the outside universe didn't communicate much. Why would there be the image of a human here, in this world's cradle? Why was that human getting torn apart?

Not a human, actually, Jack corrected himself. An Ancient. They were genetically similar to humans, and with this world's timeframe, it could only be one of them. Were the Ancients and the first space monsters at war or something? Did the monsters create this entire world as a fortress?

The more he saw, the more questions he had, and nothing seemed to make much sense.

Jack looked away from the pyramid, surveying the space around it, and was once again shocked. Before, when he simply brushed by its surroundings to reach the pyramid, he'd assumed it was surrounded by hills. Now, he realized they were statues. Three large ones formed a triangle around a pagoda, while another eight—smaller and farther away—created a diamond-like shape to encapsulate the triangle.

Eleven statues in total. Another weird number. What the hell was going on?

"What do you see?" Starhair asked, his perception not reaching the statues.

"You'll see," Jack replied. "Let's go. There is no danger here."

He knew that instinctively. The place carried such a heavy air of holiness that, even if there were native monsters present, Jack suspected they'd hesitate to disturb the peace.

Their group floated forward. Gasps echoed every once in a while as more and more people perceived the statues and pagoda. Some of the older disciples, who'd visited this place before, wore wry smiles. This was the same reaction they'd had the first time. The same reaction everyone had.

"Who are these bros?" Brock asked.

The larger statues were two miles tall, while the smaller ones were one mile. They really were mountains, completely made of stone. Any paint on them had long washed away, while the stone itself persisted, magically enhanced to endure billions of years of erosion.

As they approached, Jack could make out more details. The three large statues were the first he surveyed. One depicted a massive, tentacled sphere. The other two were humanoid, except their faces were featureless and the texture of their bodies odd, as if their skin was rippling.

"We have no idea who these are," Strawpin explained, unable to hide the awe in her voice. "The records speculate they're strong ancient monsters who helped build this place, but in truth, we don't know."

Jack cupped his chin. "I see. I have no idea either."

CHAPTER FIFTY-SEVEN
HALL OF TRIALS

GREAT SILVER AND FIEND KING HOVERED ON TWO SIDES OF THE PYRAMID. Powerful enchantments kept them hidden, intricate enough that even Jack had failed to detect them. Of course, the Overlords didn't care about some disciples—the enchantments were meant to hide them from wandering native monsters, which, contrary to Jack's assumptions about the sanctity of this place, could and did pass by.

The Overlords weren't just standing around. A massive ring of power circled the pyramid, passing through them and getting amplified. The dark mist above them roiled—a faint light came from the flat top of the pyramid, very slowly growing brighter. Thanks to the hiding enchantment, all these were invisible unless someone flew high up.

"Did you notice?" Fiend King asked. "That new disciple of yours almost noticed the enchantment."

"He specializes in Space," Great Silver replied casually. "A faint intuition is to be expected."

"Hmm. All the Elders are missing. How did they get caught, while the disciples escaped?"

"Bad luck. Do you want to focus on this or that?"

Fiend King snorted. “I thought you could meditate and talk at the same time?”

“We cannot afford any distractions. Doing this without a third Overlord is hard—if we don’t devote our full attention, the ritual could go awry, and fifty million years of preparation will amount to nothing.”

“Fine,” Fiend King exclaimed, closing his eyes and focusing entirely on the ongoing ritual. Great Silver did the same. To them, the disciples entering the pyramid were entirely inconsequential—what they were working on was far grander than a few hopeful upstarts. The only reason they’d asked the Elders to delay the disciples’ arrival was to protect them in case the pyramid ended up exploding—but interrupting the ritual to warn them now was not a price they could afford to pay.

Only Great Silver spared an extra thought for the disciples. Jack Rust did something... he deduced. He somehow killed the Elders. Maybe swooped in while they were fighting over some treasure? That would explain why the other disciples defer to him so much... but, in the end, it doesn’t really matter. At least he escorted them here. Good boy. It’s a shame the Immortals are going to kill him and everyone he knows.

The two Overlords hovered before two of the pyramid’s three sides. The third was taken up by a twelve-foot-tall totem pole, containing twelve rings depicting various monsters. Each exuded the faint aura of an Overlord. The ring of power passed through the totem as it did through the Elders, slowly sapping its energy. The light from the pyramid’s top grew ever brighter.

Aside from the three large statues forming a triangle around the pyramid, the other eight statues, smaller in size, surrounded them in an octagon shape. Most were humanoid, with distinctive features—one was made of spheres, another also of spheres but smaller, a third was made of what seemed like fire...

After the first few statues, Jack didn't need to look anymore. The space monsters may not have known what these statues depicted, but he certainly did. The Old Gods. Eleven of them, with the exception of Enas.

He looked down, where the statues met the stone island. They were one and the same, the stone simply extending upward. That indicated the statues had never moved. They'd been created like this, in perfect harmony, which meant there was never a statue of Enas here. The statues had been made *after* the Old God of Life had been tossed into a black hole.

What's the meaning of this? Jack wondered. Did the other Old Gods create space monsters after the First Crusade? That makes no sense. This world and the Dark Canal are older than a billion years—both were created before Enas's imprisonment. Why is there no statue of him?

Could there have been a statue, but after his imprisonment, the other Old Gods came here, took down all the previous statues, and recreated eleven of them anew? That's just too tedious.

Why would the Old Gods create the Space Monster World, anyway?

The creation of the Space Monster World, as well as its entrance seal which prevented A-Grades from entering, was too grand a project. People suspected its creator had surpassed the Archon realm, but if it was multiple Old Gods working together, then it could be explained.

But why? And why did the pyramid door portray a monster feasting on an Ancient?

"Let's go in!" Strawpin said, too excited to wait. She was basically skipping from foot to foot.

"Right," Jack replied, snapping out of his thoughts. "Let's go." *And everything should be clear by the time we exit.*

The large group put the statues behind them and gathered before the pyramid door—looking tiny in comparison.

"How do we open it?" Jack asked, looking up.

"We don't," an older disciple replied. "We just go in, like this." He put a palm against the door and disappeared. Jack perceived the familiar ripple of energy—this was short-range teleportation. He shook his head, then followed the disciple. Everyone did.

They reappeared in a towering hall. Thick columns of brown stone held up the mile-high ceiling, while engraved on them were the visages of fierce monsters preying on Ancients—and, more rarely, each other. There was a certain timeless air to this place—the weight of endless years pressing down on Jack's shoulders.

"Is this the first floor?" he asked. The others nodded.

"The first floor is the minimum result one can achieve," Strawpin explained. While she hadn't come here before, she'd read about the Hall of Trials extensively. "It is also where we receive the tests to judge our potential. After this, everyone can visit their respective floors to enjoy the rewards."

Jack nodded. There was no door to this hall, only walls, but he supposed teleportation served a pyramid well. After all, forcing peak B-Grades to walk up stairs felt a bit too humbling. Flying up, on the other hand, would be too easy.

"And what exactly are these tests?" he asked.

She smiled at him. "Come and see."

The large hall they were in was devoid of furniture, though it wasn't completely empty. In the very middle stood a bronze steele. It rose twenty feet into the air—so not particularly high—and its surface was covered in tiny inscriptions. At the very top of the steele, three names were written in a larger font, each containing the writing style of its holder.

"Eternal Radiance, Progenitor, Rainbow..." Jack read aloud. "Who are these people?"

"The only three monsters to ever reach the sixth floor," Fiend Prince replied, his usual recklessness replaced with reverence. "As for the names below them, they belong to people who reached the fifth floor."

Jack gazed at the steele again. It reminded him of the old Cathedral's ranking obelisk, yet impossibly grander in meaning. It was possible that, from the people who populated the ranking obelisk, only the very apex geniuses like Min Ling would have the qualifications to even appear on this steele, let alone reaching the top tier.

It was the entire history of excellence of the Space Monster World, compressed to a space only twenty feet across.

Jack looked up again. The three larger names dominated the top of the steele, their superiority evident.

Eternal Radiance, Progenitor, Rainbow... Jack repeated in his head, committing the names to memory. Their font wasn't the same neutral one as in the names below. It appeared that each of these people had earned the right to personally inscribe their names, thus demonstrating their writing style for the future generations.

Eternal Radiance wrote in confident, straight, deep swipes. An absolute sovereign. Progenitor wrote in jagged, short lines, as if too busy doing other things to inscribe on the stele properly, while Rainbow's letters were elegant and pretty, yet containing undeniable momentum.

Just glancing at the names, Jack felt he had a good idea of the people they represented. He yearned to inscribe his own—what would it look like?

"How often does someone reach the fifth floor?" Starhair asked, focusing on the host of smaller names below.

"You're thinking to gauge the length of time this stele has existed based on the number of names," Fiend Prince said. "A good idea, though you're hardly the first. Delves happen once every thousand years, but nobody reaches the fifth floor usually. Maybe once every ten delves?"

"I thought you and Strawpin both aimed for the fifth floor?" Starhair asked.

"We're exceptions. It's uncommon for two geniuses this great to be born close together. Strawpin and I both stand head and shoulders above our peers."

Said peers stood right next to him, but he didn't seem to care.

"I count tens of thousands of names," Jack said, skimming the stele. There were only three names at the very top, each comfortably resting in its own space, yet the smaller names below were tiny and nestled tightly against each other. Three versus tens of thousands—the disparity between the fifth and sixth floor was staggering.

"It's close to a hundred thousand," Strawpin said.

Starhair did the calculations. "With an average of one person every ten thousand years, this means the stele has stood for a billion years. That can't be right. I thought it was longer."

"You're right. The names are automatically wiped off the stele one billion years after they were first inscribed. Your calculation is pointless."

"...You could have led with this."

"But where's the fun in that?" Strawpin replied, her previous stricter attitude having melted away. It only appeared when she was in charge.

"Does the same happen for the sixth floor names?" Jack asked.

Fiend Prince shook his head. "We're not sure. We do know that they last more than a billion years—Overlord Eternal Radiance, for example, was a legendary figure from two billion years ago. However, it's possible those names are also wiped, just on a longer cycle. We've never seen one disappear yet."

"I see..." Jack muttered. The disparity was even greater than he'd expected. He'd been certain he could reach the sixth floor easily, but now it was beginning to look like a bit of a challenge.

Something occurred to him then. If this stele recorded the names of everyone who'd reached the top floors, it was possible that their results in the so-called tests were also recorded. Jack could test himself against not just the geniuses of the present, but also the greatest geniuses in history—an entirely different level.

The fire of competition burned in his belly. He couldn't wait.

"How do we enter the tests?" he asked.

"Simple," Strawpin said. "You touch that other stele over there."

She circled the large bronze stele, stepping behind it. Jack followed her to find a second stele, originally hidden by the first. This one was made of silver and much smaller—only reaching nine feet in height and three in width. It was empty.

"The tests all take place in a separate space, so we cannot observe others directly," Fiend Prince took over explaining. "However, everyone's results for each test will appear on this stele. It is also the entry point—just touch it and you'll be teleported over."

Jack observed the stele again. While empty, he did notice two vertical lines on it, splitting it into three identical sections. *Three tests, then?* He grinned. *Bring it on.*

He looked behind him, searching for the eyes of his brother. He found them easily. The same fire burned in them as it did in his. "See you at the top, brother," he said, unable to contain his grin.

"Damn right, big bro," Brock said. He stepped up beside Jack, and, at the same time, the two touched the stele and disappeared. Jack noticed he could have resisted the spatial pull, but he obviously chose not to.

Half of the other disciples, including Starhair, Strawpin, and Fiend Prince, did the same. The only ones left were those who'd been here before. Each person could only attempt the test once in their lifetimes, and the result was locked in forever. These monsters were only here to reenter the same floor as last time and continue reaping the benefits.

However, there was no rush in that. The Canal Delve would continue for many years, and this test only took a few hours.

The remaining disciples sat on the ground, eagerly discussing the others' expected results. First they'd watch, then they'd cultivate—otherwise, they would have no fun.

CHAPTER FIFTY-EIGHT
TEST OF DAO

Jack materialized in a different hall. This one was also made of stone, but was noticeably far smaller. Barely a hundred feet separated the floor from the ceiling, while another hundred spanned between the right to left and front to back walls. The entire room was a box a hundred feet to each side, giving no indication of its position inside the pyramid.

Jack's perception failed to penetrate the walls, while his ears caught no sound. Wherever he was, it was completely isolated. This was probably a separate fold in space, yet the flow of spacetime around him indicated no such thing. An exquisite application. His mind returned to the statues of the Space and Time Gods outside the pyramid—could they have participated in the creation of the Hall of Trials?

"Greetings, young monster," a voice welcomed him. Jack turned to its source—the single other thing in the room besides himself. An entity of stone stood against the back wall, patiently waiting. Jack took the time to inspect it as he walked over—it seemed like a living creature yet wasn't. In fact, it reminded him of Sparman, the sparring robot he'd interacted with during the Integration Tournament.

Sparman had later become an important guardian of the Forest of the Strong.

"Hey," he replied, stepping up to the automaton. "How do you do?"

"I'm fine, thank you," the thing replied. It was humanoid and made of black stone, enchanted to endure the infinite flow of time. It wore no clothes and had no facial features, except for a single white eye in the middle of its face. Its voice was produced through vibrations—oddly smooth and pleasant to the ear.

"The name's Jack. Who are you?" Jack asked.

"I am the automaton assigned to this hall. I will be the overseer and conductor of your aptitude tests. Are you ready to begin?"

"Wait," Jack said quickly. "Can you give me some information first? Who created this place? For what reason? What exactly will I be tested on, and how?"

"I am not allowed to divulge information on the tests before you face them," the robot explained in an even voice. "All I can tell you is that this is the Hall of Trials: a training place for the new generation of soldiers."

"Soldiers? Against what?"

"More information will become available based on your results. Are you ready to begin?"

Jack sighed. "Sure."

"Good. The first test concerns your understanding of the Dao, and will be adjusted based on your current cultivation level. Please stand in the middle of the room and release your Dao aura."

Jack followed the instructions. He took position in the very center and released his aura to the maximum—a powerful gust blew out, smashing against the walls and shaking them. The entire hall was suffused with the aura of power, of Life and Death, of Space and Time. The robot, though carrying no aura itself, didn't appear to mind.

Jack waited. A moment later, a strange feeling came over him—it was like the hall itself fell silent to listen, exploring his aura. The feeling disappeared as quickly as it came, and shadows manifested in front of Jack, coalescing into a humanoid shape. Nothing was visible of it except its white eyes. Jack looked at it expectantly.

The shadow raised its hands. Jack braced himself, waiting for an attack, yet none came. Instead, the shadow deftly moved its fingers, dragging them through the air and leaving trails behind them to form what resembled ancient runes.

The moment Jack's eyes met the runes, he was transfixed. To the untrained eye, these would be nothing more than squiggly lines—to Jack, they were something far greater. A manifestation of concepts, ideas given form as lines. He'd seen this before while inheriting Green Dragon's legacy. They were Dao runes.

The particular set of runes before him spoke of spacetime. They portrayed a steady ripple of time traveling through flat space, then a massive celestial object appearing to warp them both. Every measurement was exact in the rune's intricacies. The test was clear —a beginning state and an alteration were given, and he was to calculate the precise warping of spacetime induced by the celestial object.

Jack snorted. This was not a simple task, but to him, it was far too easy. He quickly waved his hands without much thought, easily copying the runes and adding in his own insights. The final state of the system became clear—he depicted the exact warping which could occur in both space and time.

The shadow observed his runes, then nodded in approval. If it was impressed by his speed, it didn't show it.

All the runes collapsed and the shadow started drawing a second set. This one was more complex, representing a person's journey through life, all their formative experiences and important checkpoints. The shadow's finger suddenly paused, having drawn the line until the person's start of middle-age. It dropped its hand and looked at Jack expectantly, the runes hovering incomplete.

Jack focused as he perceived these runes. They reminded him of the death and life cubes he'd previously meditated on, but at the same time, more than even the cubes, they reminded him of the time he'd spent in the Mortality Dao Chamber of the old Cathedral. In there, he'd watched the lives of a thousand mortals advance and shape each other. He'd learned to read a life. This rune was no different.

Slowly—respectfully—he raised his finger to the end of the rune and continued it. Unlike before, he took his time. This test wasn't particularly difficult either, but there was a certain inherent complexity when it came to Life and Death. It wasn't like spacetime, where everything was clear-cut and the final state was a result of precise calculations. Life contained a great element of chance, as well as hints of each cultivator's personality, because the same reality seemed different to different people. The truth was subjective, to an extent—that's why Jack took it slow, pondering on these truths as he drew them out, taking the time to fully insert his understandings into the runes.

His lines were subtly different from the shadow's. When he was finally done, having portrayed this hypothetical person's emotional changes all the way to their inevitable death, he slowly removed his finger. The end result was two separate sets of runes, with clear differences between them, combining together to form a harmonic whole. Jack hadn't just taken over, he'd made sure to incorporate and validate as many of the shadow's insights as possible.

The shadow looked over the runes for a long time, then nodded deeply. Its white eyes flashed with what could be interpreted as appreciation. Jack smiled—having your life's work validated was always a pleasant feeling.

The runes collapsed, and another test began.

The shadow's challenges grew exponentially more complex. Its next test depicted an entire solar system, with its sun and planets and moons and meteors and all sorts of little things. Jack had to accurately chart all their interactions with spacetime and each other. It took some time, but he succeeded—not quite a challenging task, but far more difficult than the first one. Thankfully, his foundation was solid, so failing here was impossible.

The fourth challenge concerned Life and Death. The shadow drew out an entire village of people, their lives and deaths plain for all to see, if they knew where to look. Jack used the presented lives of these people to draw out their future generations, assuming the village unaffected by outside factors. He chose to draw one of the brightest possible futures. The next generations slowly washed away the mental burdens passed down to them by their elders, eventually creating a stable and expanding, happy village.

By the time he was done, he didn't know how long it had been. He'd lost track of time while drawing. The complexity of these runes had increased massively, from the starting set of three to the village encompassing hundreds of runes, so the time it took to complete them had also increased. Jack assumed it had been several hours.

At the fifth test, the shadow changed its tune. The darkness crept away from its face to reveal a faint smile, sharp teeth glinting through. It raised both hands and drew spacetime runes faster. They didn't just hang there this time—as soon as they were drawn, they flew at Jack like attacks.

He could obviously use his cultivation to destroy them, but that wasn't the point. Instead, excitement rising inside him, he raised his hands and drew runes in return. They clashed against the incoming ones. Lines met loose ends, completing them. The runes fizzled out of existence, neutralized.

The shadow accelerated, but so did Jack. Their runes turned faster and more complex—yet, every attack of the shadow was perfectly neutralized, Jack matching it in speed and grace. Its smile widened.

Life and Death runes crept into the battle. A mess of concepts now launched itself at Jack, each attack a question, each defense a perfect answer. Jack realized he was grinning. This was exhilarating. To meet someone who could match him and battle them in such a way... It was like meeting a soulmate. Someone who walked the exact same path as him. He wanted to keep going until he dropped, no longer caring about tests and floors.

His hands accelerated. His Fist shone through, igniting his fighting spirit. Jack could sense the creeping difficulty, but he wasn't satisfied. He accelerated further, going all-out against the shadow. Facing its barrage of questions, not only did he draw perfect answers, but he incorporated his own testing questions and shot them back. The moment the first such rune reached the shadow, it paused for a second, stunned—and then its smile turned into a full-on grin. Its hands blurred as it accelerated to match Jack's pace, the previous slow scaling all but forgotten. It accepted his challenge.

The stream of attacks turned two-way, Jack actively fighting back against the shadow. Questions and answers clashed in midair, the runes constantly becoming more complex, more complete. They were operating not on a surface level, but in deep concepts wrapped around each other, testing their opponent on the most hidden nuances. Jack was feeling genuinely challenged by this level, and all he knew was that he loved it.

Adjusted to my cultivation level my ass, he thought. No other B-Grade could do this. But fine. Let's see what you got!

As the shadow jumped to a new level of complexity, Jack had to really zone in. Everything else disappeared as he went completely all-out, pulling from his arsenal concepts he didn't fully grasp. A question about Death headed his way. His fingers flashed, drawing a perfect answer and a question furthering the subject, then shooting it right back. There wasn't only Death in his question—he'd included an aspect of Space, gradually combining the two concepts, using his understanding of black holes to foil the shadow.

The shadow opened its mouth and laughed out loud—the first sound it'd made. Death and Space entwined, jumped from its fingers. They met Jack's question, answered it, and pushed through. The shadow kept going, fusing Life and Time in the next question. They were now discussing the deepest secrets of the universe, an area where Jack wasn't fully knowledgeable, but neither was the shadow.

Both were struggling now, reaching for more than they could grasp. Jack felt his genuine joy mirrored in his opponent, and he could sense his understandings skyrocket through this battle, missing pieces falling into place.

Their answers turned imperfect. Light washed over Jack every time he failed to defend, and the same happened to the shadow, the shockwaves of Dao pushing back its darkness to reveal a pale face, featureless except for its eyes and mouth, which sported a creepy, abnormally wide grin.

Runes flew back and forth. Time, Space, Life, Death, all combined into an imperfect mess glued together by Jack's understanding of the Fist. He charged through any problems he couldn't solve, while his own attacks pierced deep, threatening just like a fist. Their runes were so many and so intricate that they spread from floor to ceiling, from wall to wall, every rune a soldier in a massive battle. Ethereal blue light filled the entire hall.

The shadow finally showed signs of exhaustion, its finger-light sputtering as if attempting to draw concepts more complex than it could muster.

Jack saw his opening—and knew he was also reaching the end of his rope. He forced his hands to move faster. Exquisite runes appeared, the crystallization of Jack's understanding into black holes. The shadow's runes began to collapse. The two-way battle turned into a single-sided barrage of runes, against which the shadow desperately tried to defend, but most punched through its resistance. Flashes of light now covered it constantly. Jack had gained the definitive advantage.

Finally, the shadow raised a hand, using raw energy to disperse the runes. Everything came to an abrupt pause. "I yield," said a voice, tinged with both joy and frustration. "Good job."

"Well fought," Jack replied, nodding deeply at the shadow. It may have lost, but it had provided Jack's most enjoyable battle ever. His Dao and heart were soaring.

A chuckle escaped the shadow's lips as it dissipated, turning into thin air, leaving the room as empty as it once was. The flying runes might as well have been a dream. Jack struggled to cope with the sudden lapse in action. He fell to his knees, panting, the tension still not completely out of his System.

“Congratulations,” the automaton at the far wall said. Its voice was slightly deeper than before. “Dao test result... Eternal!”

CHAPTER FIFTY-NINE

TEST OF WILL

JACK STRUGGLED TO FIND HIS BREATH. ACROSS FROM HIM, THE AUTOMATON waited. "Are you ready to proceed?" it asked.

"Wait!" Jack said. "You called my test result Eternal. What does that mean?"

"It is the highest possible classification. Congratulations!"

"When was the last time someone got that result?"

"I cannot divulge that."

"...Fine." Jack stood up, his regeneration already working wonders for his stamina. The hall, though small, seemed to have infinite ambient Dao. His perception caught it streaming in from the corners. "Before this test began, you said there were some things you couldn't reveal unless I got the appropriate results."

"That's right."

"Then tell me now. Who built this place? Was it the Old Gods depicted in the statues outside?"

The robot hesitated. "I do not understand the question. The Hall of Trials was constructed by our Gods. They are the ones depicted outside. However, while they have certainly existed for a long time, calling them old is unsuitable."

"Why did they make this place?"

"The Gods constructed the Hall of Trials to assist the future generations of monsters. Their intention was to establish a cultivation civilization able to expand with each generation, so it could stand firm against the enemy when the time came."

"The enemy?" Jack asked. "What enemy?"

The automaton paused. "It is time for the next test," it said in a more mechanical tone.

Jack dusted himself off. He cracked his neck and flexed his fingers, taking in the wide room around him. His previous Dao battle against the shadow had been ephemeral, yet had still created physical shockwaves. The hall, however, remained pristine.

With a better idea of the tests' difficulty, Jack wondered if death was possible. Strawpin and Fiend Prince hadn't mentioned anything of the sort, but maybe it was completely natural to them, death being such a core part of the Space Monster World.

Jack took a deep breath. I wonder how Brock is doing... he thought wistfully. Can he reach my results? Can I reach his?

In a sense, this was the first time the two bros were in direct competition. Jack really looked forward to the result.

"I'm ready," he said.

"Good," the automaton replied. "The second test concerns your willpower and resolve to pursue the peak. It is not adjusted to your cultivation. It is also endless, so please give up whenever you feel you've had enough. To begin, please stand in the middle of the room."

The first test could be shorter or longer depending on the participant's attainments in the Dao. As a result, in the time it took Jack to finish battling the shadow, some weaker monsters had already proceeded past the second test.

The monsters seated outside the tests, the ones who'd come here before, discussed excitedly as they surveyed the silver stele.

"Look!" one of them cried out. "Another person finished the second test; another Talented assessment."

"At least it wasn't Average!" another monster said, leading to a wide chorus of laughter.

Names already littered the stele. It was split into three columns, where the results of each participant would appear, one test per column. The first already contained eight names—everyone except Brock and Jack Monstrous had finished. Most had achieved the Talented classification, while a poor two people only got Average. These last ones were the target of the other monsters' ridicule. It didn't mean their final results would be inferior to others—after all, this was just one of three tests—but, amongst elites, every hint of weakness was worth some ridicule.

There were also some pleasant surprises. Strawpin and Starhair had both achieved the Genius classification. If they could maintain that result for the other two tests as well, they'd be able to enter the fifth floor of the Hall of Trials—a feat usually seen once every ten thousand years. For two people to enter the fifth floor at the same time was an extremely rare occasion, not to mention that Fiend Prince was still in the game—the Dao was his weak point, so it was expected he'd only achieved a Talented assessment on the first test. He only needed two Genius assessments to reach the fifth floor.

However, even that wasn't enough to occupy the spectating monsters' minds. They looked forward to two things only. Jack Monstrous and Brock, those impossibly extreme talents... Could they really achieve the legendary sixth floor? The one which had opened only three times in the entire history of the world?

They chatted to pass the time, everyone sneaking glances at the stele, eager to watch history being made.

"Look!" someone cried out, drawing everyone's attention. "Brock's results are out!"

Every monster turned to the stele. At the very top of the first column, burning golden and pushing every other name down a position, was the name of Brock along with his classification.

"Eternal?" a monster said with puzzlement. "What's that?"

"Wasn't it supposed to be Prime Genius?" another asked, rubbing its chin.

"Yeah, that's right."

"What's going on? Is the stele broken?"

"You idiots!" another monster cried out, shivering with excitement. This was a disciple of the Great Silver faction, a monster who'd been bebro'd by Brock before. "Don't you realize what this means? Big bro Brock surpassed the Prime Genius classification! He reached another level above it which we didn't even know existed!"

The remaining three bro monsters agreed. The others, however, only glanced at each other. "That's impossible," one of them said. "There is no higher classification. Prime Genius corresponds to the sixth and final floor, everyone knows that. It's more likely that the Hall of Trials changed the name, or that it was miscommunicated by our ancestors. After all, it's been a hundred million years since the last time—the language changes, so it's not impossible for some words to have changed their meaning."

"Are you an idiot?" the first bro monster argued. "Prime Genius and Eternal don't even sound alike. Do you think the Hall of Trials is a place where names can change randomly?

"Mind your tongue, friend, or you might find it severed," the insulted monster replied, quick to get feisty.

"Oh yeah!" the bro monster stepped up, puffing its chest. The two began to approach each other but were caught off guard by another excited shout.

"Jack Monstrous's result is out too! Wait... Who's Jack Rust? Are they the same person?"

Every monster turned to look at the stele. A second name of burning gold had appeared, overtaking Brock's to occupy the very top of the column: Jack Rust, Eternal!

"Probably an alias," some monster muttered. "I don't imagine it matters. The important part is, he surpassed Brock!"

"The two results appeared almost together," a bro monster said. "They couldn't have been too far apart. Look—both got this Eternal classification."

"See?" the insulted monster from before said smugly, the previous fight all but forgotten. "If Eternal was a higher classification never before achieved, do you think it could appear twice?"

"Why not? Both those monsters were awesome."

"Let's just wait and see," said a slightly older monster, eyes trained on the stele. Its eyes were shaking. "I suspect that, no matter what... We're about to experience history!"

Jack stood in the middle of the hall, taking deep but even breaths. "Well? When is the second test starting?"

"In three," the automaton replied.

"Three what?"

"Two. One. Begin."

Jack wanted to cry out at the absurdity but didn't have the time. A massive weight landed squarely on his head. He suffered a headache stronger than anything he'd imagined possible, a giant with spiked shoes jumping up and down on the soft matter of his brain.

He yelled and almost tumbled to the ground but kept his balance. His eyes were bloodshot.

"Fuck you," he muttered. "This is nothing."

The pain intensified. Through it, he could barely sense the ambient Dao converging from across the hall, stuffing itself through his ears. His body's balancing functions weren't working. He was overdosing on Dao.

The stomping giant was joined by a second, then a third. Spikes drove themselves through Jack's brain. He could feel himself hemorrhaging. *Is this killing me?* he wondered.

However, after the initial shock passed, this tremendous pain wasn't unbeatable. He'd been through worse. Even the absorption of the Overlord core, which he'd endured for three years, had been worse than this.

Some time later, a new sensation joined the party. As Jack's brain was still slowly cracking apart—or so he thought, but couldn't be sure it wasn't an illusion—his body caught on fire. Literally. He saw flames jumping out of his skin, purple and white, singing him from the inside out. He felt them consume his tempered body slowly, like he was aged wood, letting him experience the burning for a longer time.

This is fake, he realized. I can't be burning. It's an illusion.

There were tiny signs. The dance of the flames was off, the heat pulsing at slightly irregular intervals. These were imperfections made on purpose. Whoever crafted this illusion wanted Jack to figure out it was fake—but only if he could maintain his composure through the extreme pain. Otherwise, the rising panic and suffering would quickly culminate in him failing.

Now that he knew the damage wasn't real, Jack was no longer afraid. "Bring it on!" he roared.

The pain spread to his soul. He could feel it tearing, like an apple which someone grabbed and slowly tore in half. His life's work sputtered out like fruit juices—all the connections he'd made were ripped apart one by one. This was agony on another level. Jack could endure mental and physical pain because those were limited by the constraints of reality, but the pain of the soul was a different beast, expanding to fill its container. It was potentially infinite in intensity, and this test was set to prove it, slowly but surely ramping up.

Jack clenched his teeth so hard they hurt. Even now, this wasn't nearly the worst he'd ever experienced. When he'd absorbed the Life Drop, it had forcibly ripped apart his soul to enter and knitted it back together. That pain still haunted him.

He wouldn't give up. This trial would help him save himself, his family, his planet, and his universe. He was determined to win.

Jack lost track of time. After a while, the pain spiked again. He fell to his knees, unable to hold it in. Minutes passed. It felt like hell. This really was similar to the Life Drop's suffering—a pain hard to put into words, one which even Jack could barely handle. He suspected that, if it shot up again, he might fail. His weakness surprised him—though any sane person would have long given up. He'd even lost the ability to think clearly.

All that kept Jack going was sheer, instinctive stubbornness.

At the next spike of difficulty, the pain didn't change. Instead, a new dimension was added. Jack found himself suffering alongside his family. They were burning in vats of oil—no matter how he reminded himself it was fake, his heart was in agony. His splitting soul dripped blood.

Jack didn't know how long that stage lasted, nor how he made it through. By the end, he was mentally and psychologically wrung out. Nobody could persist forever. Not him. Not anyone.

When the world blinked again to enter the next level of this twisted trial, Jack was almost relieved to find that only the extreme pain remained. The images of his family were gone. To his horror, however, he found Eric standing in front of him—his son, who'd died because of Jack's weakness. Murdered, right in front of him.

"No..." Jack muttered. He had already been on his knees—now, he leaned his head forward until his forehead touched the floor. He couldn't bear to look. Eric was just standing there, but whatever came next would no doubt be terrible.

This trial was infinite, the automaton had said so. Jack hoped he'd already won. "Enough..." he groaned, his voice raspy and tired.

Everything winked out. The pain, the fire, his splitting soul. In one disorienting instant, he was just himself, resting on the floor in memory of his agony. He collapsed, quivering. He'd always prided himself in his willpower, but this had been too much. Everyone had a limit. Even Jack. He didn't know what his result was yet, but he felt he'd aged by at least a hundred years. This was yet another scar which would never go away.

Power came at a price. Always.

An indeterminate amount of time later, Jack finally forced himself to his feet, pushing a fist against the floor. He looked straight at the robot and walked over. "How did I do?" he asked, his voice hard.

"Whatever your result, please give yourself time to rest," the automaton replied, clearly parroting a speech it had been given long ago. "This test was designed to push you to your limit. It was infinite. At whichever point you gave up, don't consider it a personal failure —and, most importantly, don't let it scar you."

"How did I do?" Jack repeated, his tone even harder.

The automaton paused, gears whirring from some unseen place. "Willpower test result... Eternal!"

"Good," Jack said, smashing his fist into its chest. He didn't hold back. An explosion occurred, blasting a crater into the wall while the automaton itself exploded, shattered in pieces of cogs, gears, and wayward flesh. Jack eyed the destruction. "Fuck you," he said. "That was not necessary. Fuck you."

The hall shook. Jack looked around, his hard gaze scanning every corner, every column. "What are you angry for?" he shouted at the walls. "Did you not expect this after pushing me to my limit? I know the pattern anyway. The last trial is always combat. Bring it on!"

He did not wait, smashing a Meteor Punch against another wall. The entire room shook. Jack had too much anger inside him which needed venting. He roared again, "Bring it on!"

CHAPTER SIXTY

TEST OF COMBAT

On the first floor of the Hall of Trials, the watching monsters were still debating what Eternal could mean. Most participants had already finished and been spat out by the stele, with only Strawpin, Fiend Prince, and Starhair remaining. The presence of more monsters only intensified the debate.

"Look, they're done with the second test!" someone cried out. Everyone turned to look at the stele—two names dominated the very top of the second column, both burning with golden letters. Both had achieved an Eternal classification, but one was clearly placed above the other. After all, the stele ranked all test participants, even if they had achieved the same overall classification.

The second name spelled Jack Rust. And the first, the one at the very top, was Brock!

Of course, this didn't necessarily mean Brock's willpower was sturdier than Jack's. The trial had exploited Jack's greatest mental scars—his family and son. Brock possessed fewer such weaknesses, so it was hard to tell who would prevail in a different kind of test, especially since Brock hadn't been through as much suffering as his bro.

But those didn't matter. Both had classified as Eternal talents in willpower—and, in this test, Brock had emerged superior, solidifying his place as a true and worthy bro.

Intense conversation erupted as soon as the monsters spotted the names. "I knew big bro could do it!" a monster cried out. "Who do you think is going to do better in the combat test? Jack or Brock?"

"It's obvious, isn't it? Brock only defeated us disciples, while Jack Monstrous, or Rust, or whatever he's called, killed two middle Autarch Elders!"

"That doesn't mean anything. Big bro Brock clearly wasn't going all-out."

"But neither was Jack!"

"I bet an early Autarch core on Jack."

"Me too."

"I bet it on Brock!"

Sometime during the conversation, Strawpin had been spat out of the trial, ignored by everyone. Her eyes searched the stele. Shock ran through her core. Having great insights into the Dao was one thing, but in the willpower trial, she'd barely achieved the Genius level. No matter how high Eternal was, whether it was one or multiple levels above her... How could anyone reach it? How could they not go insane? The agony she'd experienced was way more than she ever thought possible.

Jack Monstrous... Brock... she thought, her eyes quivering. What the hell are you?

A shadow materialized in the middle of Jack's hall. It resembled the one he'd fought during the first test but was clearly different. The darkness hiding it was thinner, and it held a sword—most importantly, its aura was only around the early B-Grade, though the way it held itself told Jack it was decently talented.

He didn't care. He flashed over and smashed a fist into it, obliterating the shadow in a single strike.

Another formed almost immediately. This one was at the middle B-Grade, and it suffered the exact same fate as its predecessor. So did the two next shadows, sitting at the late and peak B-Grade each.

Four shadows had already passed, four parts of the test, but Jack hadn't even started venting.

A fifth shadow materialized. This one was a cut above the rest—an early A-Grade, power emanating from it in ripples, painting the air around it gray. Suddenly, the hundred foot cube seemed too small for an A-Grade fight. It was a distance Jack could cross in instants.

He did not wait for the shadow to attack. As soon as it formed, he charged, smashing his knuckles into its face. For the first time, he didn't win on the spot. The shadow raised an arm to defend, getting blown backward but remaining whole. Jack pursued. An almost animalistic rage consumed him. He did not activate the Life Drop, opting to pummel the shadow to death. Meteor Punches rained. The floor and walls were cratered, the shadow desperately defending until it no longer could. Jack's fist broke through its arms, burying itself in the shadow's chest, then exploded. Fragments of darkness rained.

He panted, more from rage than exhaustion. "Again!" he shouted.

The sixth shadow was at the middle A-Grade. This was the first real challenge—the difference in their cultivations was similar to when Jack fought Elder Crownbeast, though his relative power had increased since then. Absorbing the Overlord core had brought many more benefits than simply increasing his cultivation.

He was confident he could beat this shadow, no matter what Dao it used. It would just take a while.

Before he could attack, the room shook. The shadow flickered, then dissipated, its face betraying unwillingness. A new shape formed in its place. A bald young man, dark-skinned like the night, donned in white ceremonial robes. He held no weapon. His eyes betrayed hunger—and, unlike all previous opponents, there was nothing shadow-like about him.

Jack paused. "Who are you?" he asked. Something about this youth's gaze differentiated him from the lifeless shadows before. This was a person, not a construct. And, though his aura was only at the peak B-Grade, Jack could sense its tremendous depths. He was suddenly on guard—whoever this entity was, it was unmistakably the greatest genius Jack had ever fought.

"I thought I'd accelerate things," the other man said. His youthful voice held a hint of amusement—or was it mockery? As if he knew the world's greatest joke but wouldn't reveal it.

"Accelerate?"

"You would defeat the Prime Genius shadow, but it would take some effort. I want to fight you at your best. After all, you're the first challenger to stand a chance against me. I yearn for a good fight."

Jack narrowed his eyes. "You didn't answer my question. Who are you?"

The figure chuckled. "Defeat me, and I'll tell you."

"Cool."

Extreme power radiated from his opponent. Though only at the peak B-Grade, he was vastly superior to the middle A-Grade shadow from before. An almost Jack-level talent.

This made Jack not completely confident in victory, but then again, he didn't need to be. He only needed to fight. The Life Drop transformation was already complete.

A punch shot out, trailing purple stars. The dark man raised a palm, catching Jack's fist. The shockwave shook the hall. Dao met extreme Dao, two fundamental forces of the universe clashing against each other.

Jack's punch carried tremendous power. Though it was only a Meteor Punch, it had previously sent an early A-Grade shadow flying. This man, whoever he was, stopped it with little effort.

Jack narrowed his eyes and jumped back. When they clashed just now, he'd clearly experienced the other's Dao—his punch's momentum had been wasted, exhausted until it became nothing. It was a great deteriorating force reminding Jack of death, yet not quite. This was something greater. A wider concept.

His rage began to abate, replaced by intrigue. He was, at the depths of his heart, a cultivator. Such a Dao, such an opponent, couldn't help but interest him.

The other man caught Jack's eye and grinned. "Let me tell you a secret, Jack," he said, spreading his arms to the side. Black spheres appeared in each—not black holes, but carrying similar finality. One was purely physical, the other mental. As for the man's aura, it carried the essence of a soul—a great Dao stretching over all three fields.

The man continued, "I didn't accelerate our fight just to keep you rested. My siblings and I take turns fighting the challengers of the Eternal floor. The next challenger would have been mine. However, I didn't want to risk your brorilla friend reaching this stage first. I wanted to fight you—our Daos match well. Even if you fail to defeat me, just facing me will have been a great boon to your future strength."

Jack snorted. "Should I be honored?"

"You should be angry. I am the strongest of my siblings. Facing me means your chances of victory are low, and the Eternal floor is not like the rest. To reach it, you require an Eternal classification in all three tests instead of just two. By appearing before you, I placed a great obstacle in your way, one you may have otherwise dodged."

Jack smiled toothily. "You talk a lot. Just fight me. I don't care who you are—I'll beat you all the same."

The other man laughed. "Give it a shot! Just, one moment. This arena is a bit small." He snapped his fingers. The hall around them disassembled, revealing patches of colorful void. More walls materialized, forming a new hall with walls a mile wide each. "There we go," the man said, cracking his shoulders. He seemed really eager. "Are you ready? I know I am."

"Come at me, bitch."

The two charged at each other. They clashed in the center, Jack's fists sailing to meet his opponent's open palms. The dark spheres from before had manifested as darkness, which covered the mysterious man head to toe like some sort of malicious aura, forming a stark contrast against his white robes. To Jack, he looked like an ancient beast.

Fist met palm. Dark and purple lightning shot out, impacting against the walls, shattering and destroying. They fought inside a large box in a different dimension—as cagey as could be. Only one of the two would walk out alive. Jack was pumped up, his previous anger vented and forgotten.

"Come!" he shouted. Lightning arced over his body, further enhancing his already ridiculous physicality. This was the Thunderbody technique he'd taken from the Animal Kingdom's Emberheart family—a very useful enhancement. He hadn't been able to use it against Crownbeast, as the concentration required would mess with his then-amateur use of Black Hole. Now that he'd practiced it more, he could go completely all-out.

The dark man's eyes shone. "Good technique! Hit me!"

Jack dove in. He became a streak of purple and green lightning flickering across the room like an angry dragon. Space bent in his wake, even its million-fold density unable to support his power. He shot a hundred punches in an instant. The dark man was beset in all directions.

With a shout, darkness erupted from his body. It spread outward, not fast but unavoidable. Every punch that fell into it disappeared, its momentum sapped completely, the energies deteriorating as if by the passage of a million years. This was entropy at work—everything that could end, ended.

Jack grinned at the challenge. He already suspected whom he was facing, but he didn't say the name—no need to honor his opponent before defeating him. Instead, he charged.

And instantly retreated.

A dark palm had appeared before Jack, almost grabbing his face.

The other man had slipped his hand through space and clad it in foreboding darkness. Jack knew that, if that hand touched him, he'd age rapidly. Perhaps even reach the end of his life.

"I thought this was only a test," he said, licking his lips.

"A test with stakes," the other man replied. "Beat me, and you earn the world. Lose, and you pay the price. Why do you think my previous challenger adopted the title Eternal Radiance? You can always forfeit now if you want."

Jack didn't reply. His eyes scanned the opponent, looking for an opening. There is no way his defense is omnipotent, he thought. If all attacks deteriorate before reaching him, there is hardly a point in fighting. There has to be a way out. But what?

This wasn't an opponent who could be defeated by mere strength. The Daos he utilized stood at the peak. Without similar mastery, Jack knew he'd never be able to touch him.

This pleased Jack. He sank into his laws, letting them circulate his body and fill his heart. Everything else disappeared to leave only the battle—heart of fire, mind of ice.

Jack shot out again. He sealed space in a radius around him, so the other man couldn't sneak in any attacks, and imbued his fists with the essence of Time. He reached his opponent and punched out —not with a powerful fist, but one designed to last through endless time, to shoot through the universe unendingly until it hit a target. For the first time, Jack utilized the concept of Infinity, an abstract part of the Daos of Time and Space.

The opponent smiled. "Finally, we're getting somewhere!" Darkness spun around his palm in a spiral as he reached out and caught Jack's fist. The two concepts warred. Infinity stretched on, while Entropy tested its limits. The punch's momentum began to wane—nothing was truly infinite, only converging to it. Entropy held a definitive advantage.

Black ribbons shot at Jack. He flew back, desperately trying to avoid them, then had to teleport to save himself. In a place with such dense Dao, piercing space was a tall task—Jack could do it, but it took a lot out of him.

He panted, staring his opponent down.

"You're good, Jack Rust," the other man said. His smile remained. "The strongest mortal I've ever seen. However, are you good enough? My Entropy isn't something you can punch out of the way. Without deep enough Daos, you're doomed to lose!"

CHAPTER SIXTY-ONE
FIGHTING ENTROPY

Jack didn't panic. His punches couldn't reach the enemy, but that was fine—throughout his many years of fighting, he'd developed some versatility. He had more ways to harm opponents than ramming his knuckles up their nose.

Think, he told himself.

The opponent wasn't omnipotent. If he could just spread out his aura of entropy to cover the entire room, Jack would age and die. The only reason he hadn't done it yet was that he couldn't—his power wasn't infinite, so that powerful darkness could only cover a small area. If this man was the scheming kind, which he probably was, the area he could cover with his darkness was larger than what he'd shown so far, preparing a trap for Jack. He should be careful.

Jack had several ideas he could try. Each had a low chance of success, but when put together, he was confident at least one would work. He just hoped it wasn't the suicidal one.

The other man didn't just sit there. He charged, falling onto Jack like black death. Jack drew back. His four-armed battle form and Thunderbody worked in tandem to vastly increase his speed, making him way faster than his opponent. Dodging was easy for now, at the price of consuming a lot of energy. He couldn't go on forever.

Jack ducked, dodging a claw-shaped palm of darkness, then jabbed out one of his own. Darkness appeared over his opponent's chest to cover the strike—yet, a green shadow carried on, penetrating the darkness to strike the heart. The opponent paused—his eyes stirring.

The Fist of Mortality was a soul attack Jack had created back at the old Cathedral, after experiencing a thousand mortal lifetimes in the Mortality Chamber. It was a mental attack, meant to steep the target in rich emotions and stun them. He hadn't used this move a lot in recent years, but it evolved in pace with his Dao of Life, maintaining a decent level. Most importantly, as it wasn't physical, it couldn't be stopped by entropy.

While the dark man was stunned, Jack didn't lose time. He released a quick Meteor Punch right at his face—aiming to finish this in one strike. The opponent's eyes flashed with mirth. Darkness materialized before his face to stop Jack's fist, then he reached out with his other hand, attempting to grab Jack's arm. He succeeded—a terrible sense of weakness filled Jack for a moment before he could retreat. By the time he yanked his arm free—he was the stronger party, after all—he could sense that several decades of his lifespan had evaporated. It didn't really matter, his current lifespan measured tens of millennia, but it was a terrifying concept. If the other man could grab onto him for more than an instant... What would happen?

"Nice try," the dark man said, "but, unfortunately for you, Entropy is mostly a concept of the soul. If your physical attacks can't touch me, soul ones definitely won't."

Jack chuckled. "I thought as much. But it couldn't hurt to try, right?"

"Not unless you wanted those decades."

"I can spare a few."

"Good, cause I'm about to take them."

Jack found himself smiling. This was a difficult battle with the possibility of long-term damage—so why did he enjoy it so much? It was nice to face a decent opponent, for once, instead of fools with weak Daos who just happened to possess tremendous cultivation.

Spacetime warped around Jack—not teleporting, just accelerating him. He reached the opponent and locked space around them both so none could move. He pulled his fist back. Intense suction erupted. The dense Dao flew into his fist, compacting farther and farther like a brewing bomb. Purple light erupted. A sharp whistling sound filled their ears.

"Fool!" the dark man exclaimed, gathering layers upon layers of darkness before him.

"If I can't sneak past your Dao," Jack said, charging this move to the limit, "I'll just overpower it. Supernova!"

He shot it forward. The world exploded. Jack flew back, smashing into the far wall and forming a massive crater. The cracks spread all the way to the other side, letting glimpses of the colorful void slip in.

He forced his eyes open. *Did I get him?* he wondered.

A dark hand appeared before him. There was no time to dodge. It smashed into the center of his chest, dark lines spreading across his body, the rest of the dark man appearing after his hand. "Another nice try," he said with a wicked grin, "and one that might have worked, were we at the same boundary. Unfortunately, I'm one higher. You cannot overpower me."

Jack tried to move but couldn't. He tried to breathe but couldn't. The potent life force suffusing his soul was snuffed out like an army of candles under a cold breeze. He summoned his Dao, exploding a smaller Supernova before his chest. The dark man easily dodged it by jumping backward, while Jack spat blood by the impact. He immediately teleported away without even stabilizing his wounds—the dark man flew in, piercing his leg into the wall and creating a massive hole overlooking the void beyond.

Jack clutched his chest, wheezing for breath. Ten thousand years of his life were just gone. They were inconsequential in the grand scheme of things, but it was still a shock. Most of all, he worried it would influence his potential. The younger a cultivator was, the more vibrant their fires of life, and the easier it was for them to progress. He didn't have a problem there yet, but another strike or two like that and he might begin to notice changes.

I have to finish this fast, he realized, *regaining his composure. My durability is useless. This guy... is not playing around!*

The dark man attacked again. Jack dodged, analyzing the situation with a calmness only the heat of battle could bring. He ducked and weaved between strikes, used bursts of his Dao to disrupt the opponent's attacks. All the while, his eyes were sharp.

He's not fast or strong, and his attacks, while insidious, are not that powerful either, Jack calculated. *All he has is extreme defense, which he relies on until his opponent is exhausted. His fighting style is oddly similar to his Dao—slow, but will eventually get you.*

Can I endure longer than him? he wondered before shelving the idea. The only reason Jack could defend so calmly was his dual use of the Life Drop battle form and Thunderbody, both of which consumed tremendous amounts of energy. He'd run out long before his opponent.

It was irritating. Jack had mastered four or five different Daos to a great level and possessed a dozen different skills, yet here he was, losing to a guy who used a single Dao masterfully. It emphasized the importance of mastery—and why everyone suggested focusing on just one or two Daos. It wasn't a problem Jack had faced before, given his Dao superiority over all his opponents, but it quickly became apparent when facing an opponent of similar caliber.

Alas, that was the price he paid for striving for the peak.

What else can I do? Jack wondered, calmly dodging attack after attack. He was rapidly running out of ideas. Only a single one remained, one he was decently confident would succeed but was very risky. There was a chance it would backfire hard enough to kill him.

No choice, he concluded. *Let's do this.*

"You want to fight in the Dao? I'll show you some Dao!" he

declared, clenching his fist. A bubble of space appeared around it, compressing in pulses. "You think your Dao of Entropy is so great, but I possess something on that level as well!"

The dark man frowned. "Arrogant!" he shouted. He intensified his attacks, using some arcane art to deteriorate part of himself for greater energy right now. His strikes sharpened. The dark aura of entropy flushed outward, flooding the space, leaving little room for Jack to dodge. He had to teleport all over the place, rapidly exhausting his energy reserves. Doing this while maintaining focus on the brewing black hole was difficult.

After a while, he couldn't. The black hole had compressed enough that holding it in place required his full concentration. He dashed left and right, dodging as well as he could, but the dark winds touched him. His lifespan evaporated by the century. All he could do at this point was grit his teeth and hang on.

The dark man had realized what was going on, but there was nothing he could do besides attack with everything he had. Jack struggled to maintain concentration, struggled to endure the onslaught. Every pulse came morbidly slow. Space compressed around his fist. The Dao of Entropy sought to disrupt him, to break his technique and end it prematurely, but he used his body to shield it, enduring the consequences.

His fist crumbled in the sphere of compressed space. All the crushed flesh and bones gathered in the middle, a tiny core of mass, while black foam spontaneously manifested around it.

The dark man's eyes widened. "No!" he shouted.

Jack allowed for one last compression pulse, then turned around and jabbed the Black Hole at his opponent. The dark man had teleported to the other side of the room but it didn't matter. Space was limited—and the black hole sucked it in. It reached him faster than should be possible, a fist of swirling darkness threatening the master of darkness himself.

The dark man gritted his teeth. With all of space sucked into the black hole, dodging it was impossible. He knew that. If he didn't defend and let it hit him, he would be torn apart and then exploded—his defenses depended on his Dao, not the robustness of his body. His only choice was to use his Dao of Entropy on the black hole, and both men knew it.

As they knew what would happen once he did.

A black hole was the combination of Space and Death. Entropy was Time and Death. The two Daos were similar in composition, and also in power. Of course, the dark man's expertise was significantly higher, but that didn't matter. As he pushed his entropy into the black hole, destabilizing it, there was only one possible outcome.

A black hole didn't wane with time. It expanded.

Jack chuckled, blood dripping from his lips. "Checkmate," he said.

The black hole in place of his fist grew rapidly. Quickly becoming much larger than he'd ever seen it before, even larger than the one which had destroyed Crownbeast's sturdy body. At that size, he couldn't control it. He dislodged it and flew back, crossing his four arms before himself. The dark man retreated as well, summoning walls of darkness to defend. Both created new space in their attempts to escape.

Their speeds were great, but this close to a mature black hole, they seemed slow.

Space and Time fell into the black hole, finding certain death. Black foam spread outward. The artificial black hole, only stabilized by Jack's Dao, spun out of control. It sucked in everything except for the two cultivators and exploded.

The impact was cataclysmic. Far, far exceeding the Supernova from before. The walls of the room blew outward as if made of straws. The colorful void shuddered, this entire part of the interdimensional sea warping around itself like stormy waters. Jack was struck by a tremendous shockwave and blown backward, into a region where time and space were meaningless, where his physical form was maintained through willpower alone. His bones snapped like matches. His lungs bled. He struggled to maintain consciousness —to lose himself here meant certain death.

The black foam had invaded Jack's body. It crushed his bones into dust, wrecking his flesh, tearing through his organs. Even his brain was assaulted. The Life Drop released all its remaining energy in an attempt to save him, guided by the desperate efforts of Venerable Saint Thousand Shell, but it was a losing battle. The lack of reality didn't help.

Jack snapped into focus. With a single feat of willpower, he forced the interdimensional sea into three-dimensional existence, then took a step to cross it all. Since spacetime held no sway here, one step was the same as many. He reappeared on a piece of brown stone floating through the colors, a leftover of the previous hall, its enchantments giving it a semblance of spacetime on which Jack could survive. He collapsed against it, barely large enough to accommodate him, as his body battled to remain alive. The black foam exhausted itself and was purged, but many injuries remained. Slowly, regeneration took the upper hand—Jack would survive, though he'd come closer to death than he'd wanted. He was also exhausted.

A set of dark feet settled on the same stone. "I died," said the other man with a smile. He looked pristine, even his white robes immaculate. "The enchantments of the Hall can reconstruct this body, but the previous one died. It fell to the chaotic spacetime flows of the dimensional sea. I didn't think it was possible, but you won."

Jack chuckled, turning around to lay on his back, arms extended on either side, almost grabbing the other man's ankle—there wasn't much space here. "Well fought," he replied.

The man's smile remained. "The Hall wouldn't let you die, you know that. The battle would end if I depleted half your lifeforce. Yet, you still destroyed it, risking true death for a shot at victory. Was it worth it?"

"Obviously."

"What if you hadn't made it?"

"That would be fine. I exist to strive for the peak—dying in the process is an acceptable result."

The dark man chuckled. "Have you figured out who I am?"

"From the very start. You're Axelor, the Old God of Entropy—or, should I say, just God. You don't look very old. I assume a fragment of your real self given a mortal mind and placed in the Hall of Trials to test challengers?"

The God chuckled. He took a seat beside Jack, legs crossed beneath him. "Let's have a little chat," he said. "There are some things you should know."

CHAPTER SIXTY-TWO
SPEAKING WITH GOD

Jack and Axelor rested on a piece of stone floating through the endless, colorful void. The Hall of Trials could teleport them back anytime, but Axelor had temporarily suppressed its functions. The dark man gazed at Jack, who lay sprawled on his back, a triumphant grin spread across his face.

"You know it's uncouth to lay down in the presence of a God," he said.

"I just kicked your ass—I can lay however I want. Besides, you're not a God, just a part of one."

Axelor chuckled. "Indeed."

The silence stretched. While the interdimensional sea didn't possess the concept of time, the stone's enchantments and the two cultivators' aura forced it into being.

"I have questions," Jack said.

"And so do I," replied the God of Entropy. "How about we take turns?"

"Fine by me, just know I won't reply to everything."

"As won't I."

Jack cracked a grin. “You’re an annoying one, aren’t you?”

“I’ve been given a mortal mind. I find banter a core part of your reality.”

“I guess. So, what are you doing here? What do the Gods want with the Space Monster World?”

“We created it,” Axelor replied. “The world, its inhabitants, and the Hall of Trials. Long, long ago.”

“Why?”

“My turn. What happened to the outside universe after the Immortal Crusade?”

“You really don’t know?”

“No challenger to the Hall has left the Space Monster World. They tend to do it after, much to my annoyance.”

Jack chuckled. He wasn’t going to say everything—after all, while this version of Axelor seemed friendly, he did possess the power to vanquish Jack if he really wanted to. Letting him know he was trying to liberate Enas would be a bad idea.

“The Gods lost the Crusade,” Jack explained. “They retreated to the far ends of the universe, doing I don’t know what, while the Immortals enslaved all cultivators and pit them against each other. The plan was to create warriors strong enough to completely annihilate you Gods.”

“A sound plan,” Axelor said, nodding. “This mortal shell has many horrible disadvantages, but it adapts to change much better than our divine selves. I have no doubt that, while the Immortals mustered their armies, the Gods did nothing to enhance their power. Their omnipotence is so deeply entrenched in their minds that even defeat couldn’t shake it.”

“My turn,” Jack said.

“Not quite,” Axelor interrupted. “You didn’t finish answering my question.”

“Oh, you want to play it like that? Cool. A billion years after the First Crusade—that is, now—the Immortals launched a second one.

Their goal is to purge all their opposition in and out of System space—which is the name of their territory. This Second Crusade is still ongoing. I came here to look for the power to stop them. From what I know, you Gods are rushing to join us."

"Why would we do that?"

"Not so fast. It's my turn now. Why did you create the Space Monster World, its inhabitants, and the Hall of Trials?"

Axelor mused. He raised his gaze, piercing through the interdimensional sea to gaze at the distant past. "We needed to fight back. The mortal creations of Enas were an affront to our divinity. We feared he was raising them as warriors against us—to suppress us, devour our power, and force us to reunite as one."

"Excuse me? Reunite as one?"

"We were one being originally. One split into three, then three into twelve. That is how the Gods came into being."

"...Alright," Jack replied, his eyes flashing with possibilities. He hadn't known that. He suspected no one did.

"After we realized Enas's intentions," Axelor continued, "we decided to create our own toy soldiers. While our ability to craft mortality paled in comparison to him—it was, after all, his domain—we combined our powers to tame the spontaneous Dao manifestations wandering the universe. We blessed their minds and turned them from mindless into civilized, creating the Space Monster World as a place for them to prosper and slowly develop civilization. The Hall of Trials was meant to enhance the strongest of them, creating a force that could rival Enas's."

His gaze darkened then.

"There was a war, long ago," he continued. "We lost."

"So the Ancients proved themselves superior to your creations."

"Not necessarily. All mortal lifeforms are equally inferior. The creations of Enas just had more time to develop. They were already delving into the Dao by the time we discovered them, while the monster races were mindless abominations roaming the stars."

"I see..." Jack said. This was all new information, and it brought even more questions to mind. Of course, there was no guarantee this was all true, though Jack suspected it was—at the very least, it explained why there was no statue of Enas outside the pyramid. "Your turn," he said.

"Why do you carry the aura of Enas?"

That question was asked with no lack of suspicion. Jack prepared his answer carefully.

"I once absorbed a legacy," he explained. "A processed drop of Enas's blood. It helped me a lot in earlier years, and still does."

"That makes you his supporter."

"I guess so. I do owe Enas a favor, but that doesn't make me his devotee. My current goal is to protect my people from the Immortals, nothing more and nothing less."

Axelor's gaze was sharp. "Alright."

"Your story contradicts what I thought I knew," Jack began his next question. "People say that Enas created the Ancients, gave them life and Dao, and treated them like a loving father. They say that you, Axelor, corrupted them. That you led them to creating the Immortals, who later genocided the Ancients, fought the Gods, and enslaved the universe. On the other hand, you mentioned that Enas planned to utilize them as soldiers..."

"The version you've heard is a mix of truth and lies," Axelor replied. "Enas did create the Ancients, and he did give them access to the world's Dao, but there was nothing loving about that. It was merely an experiment—a game, a way to explore his powers. He never really cared. Enas, in general, is not a loving God, no more than any other. He is cold, calculating, and selfish. The Ancients liked to say his domain was Life, but a more apt name would be Survival."

"Aren't they the same thing?"

"In a way. However, they carry different connotations in the mortal language."

"I see..."

That brought all sorts of implications. The Black Hole Church was trying to revive Enas because he was the God who loved and supported mortals—if that wasn't the case, was reviving him the right choice? Was there even a choice?

Of course, Jack wouldn't take Axelor's claims at face value.

Come to think of it, he realized, the Sage is kind of an Enas clone, and I don't remember him ever being kind to anyone for no benefit of his own. He doesn't strike me as a loving father. Calculating, sure. Uncaring. Possibly selfish.

Fuck.

"As for my own involvement in the development of the Immortals," Axelor continued, "it was overstated. I did interact with the Ancients, but not to nudge them in any particular direction, simply to investigate. They rejected me, on Enas's suggestion, and spun all sorts of tales about me. The creation of the Immortals was a result of natural civilization entropy—something all too easy to relate to me, given my domain."

"So you're saying you're not the bad guy," Jack said.

"I'm neither good nor evil. I'm a God. Mortal affairs are beneath me—well, not beneath this version of me, but certainly so for my real self. Any influence I might have had on the Ancients was unintended—I did not want to sabotage Enas's creations, but rather send my own to meet them in the field of battle."

"Why not just kill them?"

"We never really believed the mortals would be a threat. Enas threw the gauntlet—to use one of your expressions—by creating them. We simply picked it up. Using overwhelming force would ruin the meaning of his challenge and declare him the obvious winner."

"You know, the more you talk, the more you sound like a God. Not in the good sense."

"Yes, I've noticed. I can't help it—even in a mortal shell, my thoughts and experiences are those of a God."

Jack laughed—not out of joy, but at the sudden understanding he was conversing with a literal God of the universe.

"So, what now?" he asked. "Did I earn the qualifications to enter the sixth floor?"

"No."

"No?"

"You earned the qualifications for the seventh. The Eternal floor."

Jack's eyes shone. "There's a seventh floor?"

"Of course. What kind of silly number is six?"

"That's what I said!"

It was Axelor's turn to laugh. "There was a great battle around two billion years ago. The Trial Island split in half, forming what you now call the Dark Canal, and the Hall fell into it. The seventh floor broke off and shot upward in the process. It now lays at the center of the sky, unapproachable by all, though I can give you access."

"What do you mean the center of the sky?"

"This world is shaped as a sphere, but on the inside. The ground is the inner side of its periphery, while the sky is the innermost part. The seventh floor currently lies at the very center of the sphere—the center of the sky, after twelve layers of clouds, where the pressure is so intense not even Overlords can approach. Not usually, anyway."

"So nobody has been there since that battle?"

"Nobody has earned the right. I must admit, I did not expect two worthy challengers to show up at the same time..."

Jack smiled. "Brock."

"Right."

"And what's there? At the seventh floor?"

"The greatest inheritance eleven Gods could create. You may access it, though not a monster yourself."

Jack wasn't surprised his disguise had been seen through. "The other disciples will be shocked," he said.

"You have no idea. However, I have to warn you, Jack. The current two Overlords have been pushed to their limits by the ongoing Crusade. They intend to use a long-forged treasure to forcefully activate the connection to the seventh floor and plunder it. I cannot stop them. All I can do is give you and your brorilla companion access as well, but what you and the Overlords do is up to you. You could die."

Jack frowned. "That makes sense. Overlords don't usually participate in the Delve. I thought something was up when Great Silver told me to delay reaching the Hall."

"What will you do?" the God asked. "Will you go or not go?"

"...I want to go, but not if it's certain death. You're trying to set me up against two Overlords. Can you give me any advantage over them? A tiny fighting chance?"

"I can adjust the seventh floor's energy ripples to hide you. However, it is a temporary solution. If you want to claim any advantages, you'll need to make yourself seen."

Jack considered it. "What if I want to escape? Can you help me do that?"

"It depends on the circumstances. I can hide you from here, but my connection to the seventh floor has been cut off. I cannot join. Helping you escape is difficult. All I can promise you is that coming down will be a lot easier than going up. However... I never said you should fight the Overlords. If you can just convince them to let you join the floor's plunder, that will be good enough. Even if you can't, I don't think they'd outright kill you. You can help them against the Immortals."

Jack had to admit that made sense. He weighed the odds. If he did visit this seventh floor, he would need to negotiate with two Overlords—two entities far beyond his current power. It was risky. On the other hand, if he settled for the sixth floor, he'd lose out. And there was always a chance the Overlords would kill each other, creating a situation where he could reap all the benefits.

No, scratch that. They're monsters and cultivators. They will certainly fight.

"I'll go," he decided. "Brock too. This is not an opportunity we can afford to waste."

Axelor nodded. "I thought so. Very well. I will activate the teleporter now and pull us back to the Hall of Trials, then I'll give you and the brorilla access to the seventh floor. Only, Jack... Can I ask for a favor?"

He raised a brow. "Yes?"

"If you become strong enough in the future, can you return to liberate us? Me and my two siblings. We've spent too long trapped in this pyramid. We yearn to see the world."

Jack gave a stunned smile. "I promise."

CHAPTER SIXTY-THREE

ASCENDING TO THE SEVENTH FLOOR

THE ENERGY OVER THE PYRAMID HAD REACHED A CRESCENDO. GREAT SILVER and Fiend King chanted into the sky, the darkness above them roiling in huge waves, powerful Daos surging. The hiding enchantment had long been broken. If any disciples had remained outside the pyramid, they would easily be able to see what was happening at this point—and they'd probably run far away.

In fact, the energy undulations were so massive that the entire Dark Canal was upset. All the various Elders and native monsters ran away from the Hall of Trials. The ocean surged with angry waves which devoured entire islands. Strong breezes sliced through the Canal, killing anything in their path, while the Elders were in panic—they had no idea what was going on, but only fools would approach at this point. Even the strongest native monsters steered clear.

It was natural. This ritual used the cumulative energy of over twelve previous Overlords, as well as two living ones, to forcefully override the defense mechanisms established by three Old Gods working together. The clash of energy was nothing short of mythical.

The only place spared from the uproar was the interior of the

Hall of Trials, where the disciples had no clue anything was happening.

The silver stele flickered. Its surface rippled like water, letting two people step through—Jack and Brock, each carrying an aura of victory. The two glanced at each other on the way out.

"Sup, bro," Brock said.

"Hey, Brock. Had fun?"

"Yeah."

The shouts alerted them to their surroundings. Every other disciple had already exited the trial, and they swarmed Jack and Brock, adoration evident in their gazes. "You guys are so cool!" Fiend Prince shouted. "You're my idols!"

"You're certainly very impressive," Strawpin admitted, her excitement more contained. "Eternal... I've never heard of such a qualification before. What does it even mean?"

Jack nodded at them, then turned to observe the stele. Fiend Prince, Starhair, and Strawpin had achieved two Genius and one Talented results each—lacking in the Dao, willpower, and combat tests respectively. Based on what they'd said before, Jack assumed this qualified them for the fifth floor. All other disciples had a mix of Talented and Average assessments, almost all qualifying for the fourth floor.

At the top of all three columns were the names of Jack and Brock, glowing golden. The qualification of Eternal was stamped next to them for all three tests. To his surprise, Jack found he'd ranked above Brock in Dao and combat, but below him in willpower. He threw a surprised glance.

"What?" Brock said. He was trying to be calm, but there was no hiding the pride in his monkeyish grin. "Don't underestimate me, bro!"

"I never did," Jack replied. "I'm so proud of you, Brock."

"I'm proud of you too. You beat me in two tests. I'm glad. Otherwise, we'd need to discuss who is the real big bro here!"

They laughed.

"Most importantly, bro," Brock said, "did you notice?"

"Notice what?"

The brorilla motioned at the stele, and Jack took another glance. He saw it now. His name was written as Jack Rust, not Jack Monstrous.

"Shit," he said. He didn't know how the stele knew, nor did he care right now. The important thing was that, once this reached the ears of Fiend King, he'd know the truth. Great Silver had made it clear that wasn't allowed to happen. Jack would soon have not one, but two Overlords trying to kill him.

"This is a huge problem, isn't it?" Starhair asked.

"Yeah," Jack replied, no longer bothering to hide the truth from the monster disciples.

"What do we do?"

"We risk it all. Brock and I will enter the seventh floor. In the worst-case, I think we can take shelter in the Hall. I have my connections."

"The what floor!" Strawpin exclaimed. "You mean the sixth, right?"

"No. The seventh," he replied, winking at her.

She gasped. The disciples behind her shivered from excitement. As for Fiend Prince, he was unable to hold himself. He jumped up and down, pumping a fist into the air. "I can't believe this, I can't believe this! This is so great, so fucking great! Take me as a disciple, I'm begging you! I'll do anything!"

Jack laughed. He really liked this guy. His excitement was infectious.

"Tell you what," he said. "If we survive this, I'll consider making you my first disciple."

"Yes! Wait—survive this?"

On cue, the entire Hall shook. The disciples almost lost their footing before remembering they could fly. Dust fell off the ceiling, while several of the huge columns holding it up cracked. The shaking abated after a while, turning into a constant low rumbling.

"What the hell was that?" Strawpin asked. "Jack! What is going on?"

"That's our call," Jack said, ignoring her as he looked at the ceiling. A golden portal had formed up there—one bearing the exact same color as his and Brock's names on the stele. He turned to the brorilla. "Wanna risk your life with me, bro?"

Brock smiled. "Always."

"Good. Let's go. Starhair, stay with the disciples and keep them safe. Don't leave the Hall unless you have to—I suspect the Canal is more dangerous than usual right now."

"What about you?" Starhair asked.

"We got to fight some Overlords."

With those words, and with the disciples' eyes filled with confusion, Jack and Brock flew toward the golden portal.

"Should you have revealed that?" Brock asked.

"It doesn't matter. The Hall is isolated, and I think the seventh floor will be as well. Nobody will be able to contact them."

"Mm. Good."

"You're so cool!" Fiend Prince's yell echoed from below as the two bros rushed into the portal, which closed behind them. Brilliance surrounded them in all directions. They popped out of the top of the pyramid, finding an unexpected scene.

The top of the pyramid was shorn off as if by a sword. A smaller golden pyramid stood in its center, filled with all sorts of swimming arcane runes. It was cracked. The runes steadily streamed out, weakening its power, while a wide beam of golden light speared upward from the smaller pyramid, penetrating the darkness and rising into the sky. The light was unsteady, as if whatever had created it barely succeeded.

Jack and Brock were inside that beam of golden light, having popped out of the smaller golden pyramid. Jack quickly looked around, finding no Overlord in sight. All he saw was the Dark Canal's energies being in complete disarray, as well as a twelve-layer totem lying broken on the pyramid's top.

"They must have already gone up," he said.

"What's going on, bro?" Brock asked. Jack explained quickly.

"We must hurry," he concluded. "Whatever is going on, we can't afford to be late!"

The golden beam tried to pull them up, but they maintained control of themselves. On Jack's cue, they turned into rays of light, racing upward. The pyramid soon disappeared. All that remained was a vertical road of golden light crossing the endless darkness.

Jack and Brock followed it. The darkness was pushed away by this light—the pressure was thinner, and any hidden dangers non-existent. Strawpin had mentioned that anyone trying to enter or leave the Dark Canal through anywhere other than the entrance point disappeared. Jack hoped the golden light would stave off that effect.

It did.

After rising for a while, maintaining a decently low speed to be wary of danger, the darkness around them faded. Expansive stone stretched on either side, split down the middle by the Dark Canal—what Axelor had said was the result of an ancient battle. The darkness now lay below them, while the light speared into the clouds above.

"Doesn't feel like we spent that long in the Canal," Brock said.

"We didn't," Jack replied, looking down. "Besides your months of absorbing the lotus, it was only a few days."

"Dark days."

"Only figuratively."

They ascended higher. There was no Overlord in sight still. They followed the beam of light into the first layer of clouds, rushing past them to find themselves facing the second. The clouds were gray, occasionally illuminated by the crimson lightning trapped inside.

The light rose endlessly. Following it, they passed the second layer of clouds, then the third, then the fourth. Jack had tried to fly up here once but had been stopped when he reached the ninth layer due to the exponentially increasing pressure. They weren't facing that issue now. The corridor of golden light rebuffed whatever Dao pressure existed up here, letting them breeze through. They kept their guard up regardless.

Half an hour later, Jack and Brock were approaching the twelfth and final layer of clouds. The pressure up here must have been staggering, enough to stop even Overlords, but they weren't feeling it.

"I think I know where the pressure comes from," Jack said. "Axelor said the entire Space Monster World covers the inside of a sphere, and we're headed at its center. That doesn't make sense from a space point of view. The sphere's dimensions to encompass the entire world would be huge, so the center of the sky should be much farther away from the surface compared to what we've traveled so far. My guess is that there's space shenanigans at play, with the price of bringing the sky closer being this pressure. Endless cubic miles of highly dense volume are compressed to a mere hundred miles—of course the pressure is ungodly."

"That makes sense," Brock replied.

They broke through the twelfth layer to find a different scene ahead of them. They were inside a huge sphere of clouds, maybe a dozen miles in diameter. Space itself shivered by the Dao density. The light speared upwards to the very center of this sphere, where a small pyramidic structure floated, rotating slowly.

This was clearly the broken-off top of the Hall of Trials. The seventh level. Its walls were the same color, while its base looked rough, evidence it had been broken off—and not as cleanly as the pyramid down below indicated. The beam of light stopped at the center of its base, though it didn't appear to penetrate the stone.

Jack and Brock glanced at each other. “We need to either teleport inside or go find an entrance,” the brorilla said.

“It’s risky to teleport with the Overlords present. The energy ripples of the pyramid will hide us, according to Axelor, but not if we appear in front of their noses.”

“So we need an entrance. Will we be okay if we step out of the light? Or die instantly?”

“I think we’ll be safe,” Jack replied. “Let me try.”

He activated both the Life Drop transformation and Thunder-body, pushing his defensive capabilities to the peak. He then took a tentative step outside the beam of light.

Nothing happened. The Dao around them was extremely dense, but the pressure he experienced was somehow no higher than the average of the Dark Canal.

“All good,” he called out, letting his enhancements dissipate.

Brock followed him outside the light. “Now what?”

“Can you feel this?” Jack asked back. “The Dao is aligning with us, somehow. Like we’re part of it. This must be what Axelor promised—the Dao signature of this place will hide us from the Overlords.”

“So we can die *after* delivering an ambush.”

“Well, hopefully there’ll be a smarter way. Come. We can’t break through the floor, obviously, so let’s look for an entrance.”

It didn’t take them long. One side of this small pyramid—only a mile tall—held a set of golden double doors. Those doors were broken, only hanging on by their bottom hinges. In front of them lay the shattered remains of a golden statue. It still emanated hints of its aura—placing it at the peak of the A-Grade.

“Even Gods can’t afford Archon guards,” Jack noticed.

“This happened recently,” Brock said. “Maybe a few moments ago. The two Overlords came here, defeated the guardian, broke the doors, and invaded. How are they handling the pressure?”

“I think they forcefully rode the same light we did,” Jack said, “though I can’t imagine it came without a price.”

"Are you sure we want to do this, bro? They easily destroyed the peak A-Grade statue. They're too powerful."

Jack considered it. "The rewards hidden inside are things we've earned. These guys are stealing them from us. We don't need to fight—hidden by the Dao as we are, we can maybe take some things under their noses and escape undetected. Or negotiate. Or just leave."

"Alright. I'm with you. Let's go."

CHAPTER SIXTY-FOUR

OVERLORDS IN ACTION

After passing through the broken doors, Jack and Brock entered the final floor of the Hall of Trials. It was the reward they'd justly earned, now usurped by others.

A scene of pillage welcomed them. The room behind the gate must have once been grand and majestic. Murals used to cover the walls, painted with colors of the Dao itself and punctuated with gems. Golden statues stood at the back, depicting the eleven Old Gods besides Enas, while a massive empty throne rose against a sidewall to the right, another doorway below it.

Now, the colors had been scraped off the walls, the gems pulled out. The golden statues had been cracked open to get to whatever was inside them—if there was anything—and the throne's velvet had been peeled off, leaving behind ugly tears and bare stone. The room had been ransacked. The only reason Jack and Brock knew the missing materials was from their still-lingering aura—everything was constructed of the highest possible quality materials.

The scene sparked Jack's anger. "Overlords, the highest under the heavens, and they behave like common bandits," he spat out. "Shameful."

"This is not the bro way," Brock agreed with a dark gaze. "It's bad enough to break into the shrine of your ancestors. To take the decorations? That's going too far."

"It's pointless, too. They don't lack gold or jewels. Why do this?"

"Guess we'll have to ask them," Brock replied, pacing into the room. It was depressing. This hall was meant to welcome the greatest talents of history, the people with the potential to reach or surpass the Old Gods. Perhaps the walls told stories about the creation of the universe or depicted epic heroic feats. Now, they'd been done so dirty, even the murals were indistinguishable.

The two bros crossed the room quickly. The next one was similar—a grand show of wealth and knowledge, all stripped clean. Even the various pieces of furniture were missing.

"It's a miracle they left the bricks behind," Brock said angrily. "I'll smack them in the head with one."

The doorways led down a single path hugging the seventh level's outer wall. Following it, Jack and Brock reached the third room, which was also the same. Stripped down, pillaged, destroyed. For three similar rooms to be placed in a row like this, and more to come, Jack assumed they were telling a story or shared a theme. They were meant to create in young monsters a feeling of awe and context before they received the inheritance of the Old Gods. Probably detail their mission of destroying the Ancients.

At the fifth room, Jack paused and stuck to the wall. He motioned for Brock to be quiet. The line of rooms hugged the outer walls, and they'd approached the corner now, so the next door was on the left wall instead of the back one. They couldn't see behind it, but they could hear faint noises. It sounded like stone cracked in half, metal being wrenched free.

Jack felt the ripples of someone's perception pass over him without stopping. The Dao signature of the pyramid hid them, just like Axelor promised. Jack looked at Brock, who nodded. Carefully, he peeked through the corner, gazing into the next room over.

It was also pillaged. The *next* one, however, was in the process of getting destroyed. The two Overlords stood inside, Great Silver and Fiend King. The former stood with arms crossed—the latter dashed from wall to wall, taking everything he could into his space ring.

Jack drew back, then spread his perception over the corner, draping it over the Overlords as thinly as possible so it would go unnoticed. He saw Fiend King arrive before a golden statue—some six-armed humanoid monster—and crack it in half. He took a peek inside, snorted, then left it and proceeded.

"Can you not do that?" Great Silver asked with the tone of someone who'd already said it a dozen times.

"No. These statues are hollow for a reason. One will contain something inside it, I guarantee it, and when I find it you won't be so smug." Fiend King was completely unapologetic as he tore the room apart.

"Is it so bad to leave a treasure or two behind?" Great Silver pleaded. "These rooms are our legacy. They've stood undisturbed for billions of years. We'll take the real treasures, of course, but these are just decorations. What you're doing is completely unnecessary."

"Weak thinking like that is why your faction is in decline." Fiend King snorted. "Even the metals and paint on the walls are precious. Nobody will ever come here, anyway. We might as well take them. Maybe we can trade with the Immortals."

"Ah, yes. Trade. The path to our enslavement."

"Better than being conquered."

While they conversed, the room had already been stripped clean, and Fiend King kicked down the doors to the next one. He charged in and continued ransacking.

"This guy is unbelievable," Jack said after relaying everything to Brock. "The pettiest cultivator I've ever seen."

"He deserves the slap of justice," Brock replied.

"Yeah. A shame he's too strong for my flip-flop."

Through his perception, Jack had gauged the strengths of the Overlords. Having forced their way here without the Hall's permission, they were under constant pressure. Part of their energy went into staving it off. Their energy levels had fallen from the Archon level to the peak A-Grade, but their Daos remained. Jack and Brock together might be able to fight one of the Overlords if they went completely all-out, but there was no way to struggle against two.

Moreover, the Fiend King's despicable means were working against them. He left nothing behind. Following the Overlords, there was no benefit for Jack and Brock to get, and there never would be. Since they'd reached this point, however, all they could do was keep going.

The rooms kept coming. Jack had no idea what they signified—his thin perception over the Overlords wasn't enough to read the murals—but it didn't really matter, either. Finally, at the tenth room, the path turned again. Jack caught the Overlords pausing. They stared at the door against the right wall, then turned to each other with somber gazes.

"Time to kill," Fiend King said.

"Looks like it."

Great Silver was the one to open the door this time. They burst into the next space, and Jack's perception with them. This room was clearly different than before. It was short and wide, spreading roughly a mile from left to right, its side walls angling upward like it had been built directly onto the pyramid's outer walls.

Three heavy golden doors stood at the back. A word was written over each, in a language Jack didn't recognize but could instinctively understand: Dao, Will, and Cultivation. Besides those and the red carpet which stretched from the left to the right wall, the room was almost empty.

A lone automaton sat behind a paper-filled, stone desk at the back of the room. It was far more refined than most—it wore elaborate robes which covered it like real ones, though they were made of stone, just like its skin. Its unmoving face exuded wisdom. A long beard hung from its chin.

"*Oh!*" The Stone exclaimed in Jack's mind. "*That's my dad! Hi, Daddy!*"

"Your what!"

As the two Overlords entered the room, the automaton put its pen aside and stood from its chair. "I am the Stone Scholar, the guardian and groundskeeper of this floor," it said, its raspy voice growing clearer by the word. "You come without permission. You trespass. Begone."

"We wouldn't be here if we intended to be gone," the Fiend King said with wicked laughter.

The automaton was still awakening from its neutral state. Only now did its perception spread properly to cover the long line of rooms. If it spotted Jack and Brock, it didn't show it—its stone face contorted in an expression of fury. "You defiled the halls!" it roared. "Insolence!"

The walls shook. The pyramid paused its rotation, standing still as if all of reality held its breath alongside the automaton. It glowed with seething aura as it roared, "Die!"

"This entire world is in great peril," Great Silver said quickly. "We need the inheritances here. We could use your help in defending."

"SHUT YOUR VILE MOUTH! YOU DEFILED THE HALLS! YOU DIE NOW!"

The Overlords exchanged a glance. Fiend King laughed. "How could I have known?" He chuckled. "Guess we have to kill it now."

"No other choice," Great Silver said heavily as both of them released their aura.

The automaton was at the peak A-Grade level of power, and Jack could sense it was stronger than most, radiating intense energy in tune with the structure around it. The Overlords had also been pushed to the peak A-Grade level by the pressure of this place, but their insights remained those of Overlords, and there were two of them.

The clash of energies was uneven. The real clash, even more so.

The automaton attacked first, abandoning the three doors it stood in front of. Its stone sleeves swung as if made of fabric, channeling the energy of the world in its strike. A rainbow of Daos coalesced—eleven different streams, each bearing the signature of an Old God. They formed a white sun behind it, whose light covered the automaton and made it seem angelic.

The Overlords rushed to the left and right respectively. Fiend King unleashed a crimson aura, becoming brutality incarnate, his devilish body radiating violence. Great Silver opened his draconic mouth, silver energy converging—it was raw power, yet almost sentient. Jack instinctively felt that Great Silver's Dao was something close to Wisdom. A wise, white fire.

Jack waited behind the corner, his attention fully focused on the battle. He relayed everything to Brock behind him. The Stone's stunning revelation wasn't something they could bother with right now.

The automaton released white energies with each swipe, like divine brushstrokes through the air. Everywhere they passed, the void was incinerated, purified until nothing was left. As the white light approached Fiend King, he roared and raked his claws against it. Crimson met white. The two energies twisted around each other, the white coming out slightly on top.

From the other side, Great Silver opened his maw and released a beam of silver. Space itself melted before it, letting it reach its target instantly. The automaton conjured a shield to block, but it was broken through, the silver light flooding it and pushing it out of balance. Fiend King appeared to its side—he smashed his tail against it, sending the automaton flying, then teleported over it and smashed it heavily into the ground. The tiles cratered.

The automaton wasn't done. It teleported away just in time to dodge a slash of Great Silver's claws, which hit the ground and broke it further. The automaton reappeared behind Fiend King, wide sleeves rising against the devil, the white light stopped by sheer muscle mass. Fiend King turned around, grabbed the automaton, spun thrice around himself and slammed it against the ground. Coincidentally, it crashed into the same spot as before, further deepening the crater.

Of course, grabbing your opponent was a Dao clash in and of

itself. The Fiend King had used his Dao to penetrate the other's barriers, releasing shockwaves which crashed against the walls, shaking the pyramid and threatening its structural integrity. Dust fell from the ceiling.

Jack hesitated. This stone automaton—The Stone's father?—was in a tough spot. If he and Brock joined in, there was a chance they could help it turn things around.

"Let's wait a bit," Brock whispered. "We're hidden. We can ambush them at the critical moment."

Jack nodded. That was the best way to win here.

"What sorry excuses you are for monsters!" the automaton roared. "You're Overlords, yet you couldn't match me alone! You amount to nothing! You have less talent than the rabid dogs whose behavior you so shamefully copy!"

"Shut your stone mouth!" Fiend King roared, appearing over the fallen automaton and punching down. White light formed a barrier—it held against his punch, but not against the beam of dragon silver which came right after. Great Silver rammed bodily into the automaton, pushing it hard into the ground, the cracks expanding widely.

At that precise moment, something changed. The dragon Overlord couldn't have seen it, so tightly pressed against the automaton, but Jack did. Fiend King's face warped into a fiendish grin. His hands blurred. He reached inside his robes, pulling out a miniature of the twelve-layer totem and snapping it in half. In the same motion, his other hand aimed downward, unleashing a torrent of energy he must have been building for a while. Crimson power buried both the automaton and Great Silver, not harming them, but using a momentum-adjacent Dao to heavily push them downward.

Great Silver roared. "Fiend King! What are you doing?"

The floor below them had already suffered multiple strikes. Even the pyramid's precious materials couldn't handle such impacts forever—the bricks split, then cracked, then shattered, revealing a hole to the sky below. Great Silver and the automaton were both right above it, momentarily immobilized by Fiend King's attack.

Normally, this would have meant nothing. As Great Silver realized to his horror, the spot they occupied was located precisely above the beam of golden light from before. A beam which was rapidly destabilizing—Fiend King had crushed the control totem, and the forceful override of the Hall's security was deteriorating. The golden beam shuddered, then roared out in fury, the process reversing in an angry lashing of the Hall of Trial's energies.

The smooth golden light leading upward turned into a siphon, pulling everything down. It wasn't particularly powerful, certainly not enough to threaten an Overlord—unless, say, one was floating right above it, with another Overlord's power pushing down on them.

"No!" Great Silver roared.

"I counted our steps since entering this place, Silver!" the Fiend King shouted, roaring with laughter. "I aimed for that spot in particular, and you helped me break it like the fool you are!"

"I trusted you!" Great Silver roared again, his draconic fury bursting forth. "This concerns the survival of our species!"

"There is no compassion amongst monsters, Silver. Only winners and losers—and you are the latter."

"HOW DARE YOU!" the automaton roared in turn. "IN THE NAME OF THE GODS, I WILL VANQUISH YOU!"

Great Silver and the automaton released their energies together, pushing upward, but they couldn't overcome the sum of Fiend King's pressure and the golden beam's pull. Not when they were right over it. With a series of frustrated roars, Great Silver and the automaton were both sucked into the golden beam, falling downward at extreme speed. Their anger was so great that they kept tearing at each other as they fell past the layer of clouds, their future unknown.

Jack and Brock still waited in hiding, this turn of events too sudden for them to react. They were waiting for the final cataclysmic clash between the automaton and the Overlords, when nobody would bother with defense. This... was a bit too unexpected!

Suddenly, everything was quiet. Fiend King stood alone in the room—the golden beam remained, but its suction power wasn't enough to threaten him unless he stood right next to it.

"Fuck off, loser," he said, dusting himself as he turned to the three golden doors. "Now, let's see... Where do I begin?"

"How about you begin by dying?"

Fiend King jumped, then whipped around. "Who's there!" he roared out. As he took in the new arrivals, he paused. "Jack Monstrous?" he said in disbelief. "Brock the brorilla? What are you doing here? How can you even stand in this pressure?"

"We stand for what is right," Brock said, angrily cracking his knuckles.

Jack smiled. "And we're here to destroy you."

CHAPTER SIXTY-FIVE
FIGHTING OVERLORD

Jack and Brock faced Overlord Fiend King in a pyramid floating in the middle of the sky. It would have been shocking if it wasn't so dangerous.

Fiend King laughed. "You and what army? I don't know how you got here, but this is where your journey ends. Go back. Don't throw your lives away."

"We got here the right way. By earning the qualifications," Jack said.

Fiend King's laughter was cut short. "You were classified as Eternal?"

"That's right."

"Both of you?"

"Yes."

"That's the stupidest excuse I've ever heard. We've never had a single Eternal talent—two at a time is impossible."

There was envy in the Overlord's voice, clear as day. He was one of the two rulers of this entire world, yet the Hall of Trials was a constant reminder of his inadequacy. He'd only reached the fifth floor as a youth—anyone able to reach the sixth or the impossible seventh would only humiliate him indirectly.

"It doesn't really matter, does it?" Jack asked. His aura slowly rose out of his body, cascading in ever taller waves. The dense ambient Dao was pushed back, the shattered bricks and tiles beginning to float. Even the suction force of the golden light abated momentarily. Brock followed a moment later, releasing his own golden aura, the air filled with chants and sparkles.

Fiend King narrowed his eyes. "You are not suppressed. And this aura, so high above your level... Did you really qualify as Eternal talents?"

"There's only one way to find out," Jack said, entering a battle stance, arms raised before his face like a boxer. He couldn't hide his grin. He roared, "Show us the strength of an Overlord, Fiend King!"

The Overlord frowned for a while, then his face warped into a snarl. His own crimson aura erupted, meeting Jack and Brock's in the middle of the hall, further shattering the tiles. Winds picked up, whipping their hair. The Fiend King's tail swished through the air, carrying muscle and violence, capable of demolishing planets with a single touch—his claws and teeth were bared, sharp edges glinting in the light, while the muscles under his gray skin expanded. He became a creature of nightmare—a being made to slaughter.

"Just die," he spat out. Crimson erupted between sweeping claws. The light raked the floor and walls, drawing thin lines, sending more bricks and tiles flying. Jack leaned to the side, dodging the strike, and used his own Dao to suppress the other's brutality. As for Brock, he only raised a palm, blocking the claw energies head-on.

Jack smiled. "It's been a while since we fought side by side, bro."

"My favorite kind of battle. Together, we are unbeatable."

"You think too highly of yourselves!" Fiend King roared. He moved so fast he disappeared.

Jack narrowed his eyes, then instinctively raised an arm to defend. He activated the four-armed battle form and Thunderbody instantly. A gray shoulder smashed into him from the side, sending him flying, nailing him into the far wall.

"Bro!" Brock shouted, but the gray tail was already before him. A giant golden brorilla manifested—the same one which had easily defended against Fiend Prince and Strawpin. The gray tail smashed into it, warped the golden light, and shattered it, carrying on to strike Brock in the chest and blow him backward.

"How dare you challenge me!" Fiend King shouted. "I am the King of Carnage. I'm invincible!"

"Oh yeah? Go fight the Immortals then," Jack said, having already escaped the pile of rubble. He charged the Fiend King and punched out, purple trailing his fist, a meteor crossing space. The Overlord grabbed it in his palm, the meteor fizzling out. His skin was tougher than the hardest steel—and his eyes, as he held Jack by the fist, murderous.

A claw came slashing down. Jack was about to decisively sever his hand to escape when a golden palm smashed into the Overlord from the side, shaking him. Jack put all his strength into escaping—a massive yank ripped his hand free from the Fiend King's grip, long bloody lines drawn against his skin.

The Overlord wasn't injured by Brock's hasty attack. If anything, he was more surprised at Jack escaping. "You're this strong?" he asked in disbelief. His eyes flashed. "All the more reason for you to die."

He pursued Jack. Jack struck, still retreating. "Supernova!" Fist met tail, purple explosion against crimson aura, and a shockwave erupted which battered the entire pyramid. Even Supernova couldn't resist the Overlord. Jack's hand shattered, all bones inside snapped, as the tail carried through and found him in the waist. He turned into a missile flying backward. If not for the pyramid's hard walls, he would have flown for endless miles. In this case, he didn't, but that was even worse. The materials making up the pyramid were extraordinarily tough. Jack smashed into them, losing all the air in his lungs, breaking his back.

The entire hall was a mile wide and only a few hundred feet long. It was an extremely tiny space for hosting a peak A-Grade battle, with the hard walls making any impact even more punishing. They couldn't leave, either—the only two exits were barred by a golden suction force and a long series of rooms respectively.

Jack opened his eyes to find Fiend King tearing into Brock. A dozen golden brorillas were completely failing to stop him, their bodies destroyed as mere afterthoughts, while Brock's defenses crumbled faster than he could put them up. Jack rushed out, charging up a Black Hole while the Overlord was busy elsewhere.

Claws raked Brock's body, drawing long red lines which stretched from his shoulder to his waist. Red blood with hints of gold flew out. Brown fur littered the air. Brock coughed, more blood escaping his mouth, as he twirled his staff and smashed it into the Overlord's shoulder. The impact was minimal. Fiend King gave a monstrous grin as he stabbed his tail into Brock's stomach, not penetrating his body, but pushing him back again. He then turned to face Jack.

A black hole flew at the Overlord. A hint of horror crossed his face—he shot out his tail, striking the black hole at the maximum possible distance. The hard skin and tough flesh were warped, but the black hole also struggled. It was, after all, just an artificial one crafted by Jack's Dao. It had its limits. The Overlord might have been suppressed to the level of a peak A-Grade, but his body remained beyond sturdy.

The black hole imploded. An intense shockwave struck the walls, shaking several bricks out of position and disintegrating the closest broken floor tiles. Jack was once again smashed against the wall by the impact. So was Fiend King, but besides the tip of his tail disappearing and some blood dripping down the corner of his lips, he seemed fine.

"You injured me," he said, surprised at his own words. "I'll make you suffer. I'll tear you limb from limb!"

Jack frowned deeply. That had been his strongest attack, which had finished off every opponent so far. Even the fragment of Axelor had been no exception. That the Fiend King could resist it didn't bode well.

"Are you okay, bro?" Brock asked, dusting himself off. He was injured, blood marring the fur on his chest, but he didn't seem to mind.

"Good enough," Jack replied, wiping the blood from his lips. "We can't beat him as two individual fighters. We need to work together."

"Right. He just split us before."

"I know."

The two fell into a common pace. A new aura suffused the hall. Fiend King snorted, then charged. "Useless!" he cried out. His claws sliced the air. Jack moved back to weaken the blow. A golden shield appeared before him, in time with his own Meteor Punch, meeting the strike and neutralizing it.

Fiend King took this time to smash the body of his tail against Brock, but a Supernova explosion sent it off course. Brock simply ducked under the strike, then smashed his staff at Fiend King, pushing him backward. His large golden brorilla compacted, turning into a sheet of armor over Brock's body, as well as two extra golden arms.

"Big Bro Form!" Brock shouted.

Jack chuckled. "Is that supposed to be me?"

"You're my big bro. Of course you inspire me."

"What bullshit are you spouting!" Fiend King roared, charging again. His power and speed were overwhelming. He was the perfect killing machine, possessing extraordinary aspects across the board. By themselves, Jack and Brock couldn't hope to match him. Even a normal peak A-Grade would be above their powers.

When working together, however, their combined battle prowess was more than the sum of its parts. They hadn't fought side by side often, but they were spiritual companions, each sharing a part of the other's soul. Their connection was deeper than any other.

They could read each other's intentions, react before they even moved, perfectly coordinate their strengths.

Moreover, they were bros. Brock's Dao circulated between their souls, empowering them in a constant cycle.

Fiend King charged, but Jack and Brock fell on either side of him. They moved in perfect sync. When the Fiend King focused on one opponent, the other struck back. Their attacks were perfectly timed, forcing him to only defend against one. Their defense was a combination of two outstanding Daos. Jack was the stronger party, but they even accounted for that, balancing their contributions to achieve a perfect fusion.

They received injuries at first. One gash here, one tail smash there. Yet, the more they worked together, the better they flowed around each other. Their souls were singing in harmony. Fighting became instinctive, requiring no effort, as if they slowly merged into a single being with two bodies. Their efficiency rose. The Fiend King had held a slight advantage at first, but he was pushed back now, his strikes ineffective. The attacks he did receive weren't too threatening, but the damage added up.

The Fiend King roared. He balled his claws into a fist and struck at Brock, but a purple and golden shield blocked him. It was like hitting a wall. A punch struck the back of his knee, bending it, as a staff strike landed on his now-exposed chest. Before he could recover, a second punch exploded against the back of his head. The strikes accelerated. The Fiend King tried madly to defend but was unable to, fists and staffs pummeling his body from all sides. Bones cracked. Bruises appeared. The skin he took such pride in tore, letting hints of gray blood leak out, while his regeneration failed to keep up with the onslaught of attacks. They came from everywhere all the time.

He tried to strike back, to break the chain, but it was as if they knew the future. His attacks were predicted and blocked before he even made them, the lapse in defense causing him more damage from the ongoing pummeling.

The Fiend King lost control completely. He was confused by the many strikes, unable to tell up from down or left from right. He was helpless. For the first time in millions of years, he felt the fear of death.

He roared, finally snapping, his crimson aura exploding out of him and wrecking his own body in the process. His eyes madly scanned the hall for the golden beam of light—it was there, in a now wide region of destroyed floor. He feigned an attack, then dashed sideways, letting more strikes land on him to escape.

A strong hand grabbed his tail. Fiend King felt his momentum evaporate, and true horror rose in his heart. He pushed forward with all his power. A second pair of hands grabbed onto his tail, yanking him backward, and the Fiend King saw to his horror the beam of light grow farther away. True panic took him over—his survival instinct overriding every other function.

He severed his own tail—a function of his body he'd never used before, nor did he think he'd ever have to. The severing pushed him forward with extreme momentum, reaching the golden beam in an instant. He dove for it. Great Silver could be waiting below, but the dragon was compassionate. It wouldn't kill him. Fiend King could live.

A massive fist smashed into his backside. His already great momentum grew to unstoppable heights. Even the golden beam was unable to capture him, and Fiend King was forced to watch as he overshot it, flying straight through the suction force and impacting the wall on the other side.

"NO!"

He roared, blood escaping his mouth. He turned around to try again, but his pursuers had already caught up, and he had no more tails to sever. A golden staff stabbed into his abdomen, bending the Fiend King over and releasing all air from his lungs. A black hole was pushed into his open mouth, guided by a green-tinged arm.

Fiend King looked up, sensing his skull collapse, to find a pair of cold eyes locked onto his. This had all happened too fast. A few moments ago, he was the ultimate winner, earning the entire seventh floor for himself. He was going to reach new heights. And now, he, an Overlord of the Space Monster World... was dead. Dead to some low-level brats.

Fiend King roared in impotent fury and denial as the black hole warped his head, sucking it all in, then exploded. Bits and pieces of gray flesh flew everywhere. The Fiend King's body collapsed, a headless thing, while Jack and Brock watched it coldly to make sure there were no surprises coming.

When they were finally sure it was dead, they both collapsed. It hadn't been as easy on them as the Fiend King thought. His attacks had found purchase multiple times, sending streams of carnage through their veins, and the constant high-speed attacking had pushed them to their limits. Jack's Life Drop had almost run out of energy—it hadn't had much remaining after his battle with Axelor. It was a good thing the battle lasted so little.

But they'd won.

They looked at each other. "Good job, bro," Brock said, giving a bloody smile.

"You too," Jack replied, unable to hold his laughter. "Do you realize it, Brock? We killed an Overlord. We secured ourselves the seventh floor rewards. We finally... won!"

CHAPTER SIXTY-SIX

SPOILS OF BATTLE

The seventh floor of the Hall of Trials was silent, as if paying homage to the victory just struck.

Jack and Brock were panting, yet smiling. They'd just worked together to beat an Overlord. A suppressed Overlord, sure, but an Overlord regardless. They had, for a moment, stepped into the highest stage of the universe.

Jack's grin touched his ears. "Can you believe how far we've come, Brock?" he asked.

"There is still a lot to go, bro. But… We did good. Congratulations."

"Right back at you." Jack raised his gaze, taking in the main features of the room. The desk of the Stone Scholar had been blown away from the battle, the parchments on it disintegrating the moment they left the desk's area. The three doors at the back, however, remained pristine. Each had a sign over it: Dao, Will, Cultivation.

"One more thing before that," Jack said, reaching into his inner world. "*Hey, Stone… Can you explain what's going on here?*"

"*Of course I can!*" The Stone replied. Its mental voice was angry, like it was fuming, and Jack quickly connected Brock to their telepathy so he could participate as well. He would have taken The Stone out, but he suspected the pressure would crush it instantly.

Seeing it had everyone's attention, The Stone continued, "*That was my daddy! They attacked my daddy!*"

Jack pinched his nose. "Can you not call him that? How does father sound?"

"*Why? It's the same thing.*"

"*Okay. Tell us about your... daddy.*"

"*He made me!*" *The Stone exclaimed.* "*I'd forgotten all about it—it's been a while—but he made me a long time ago. It was right there, on that desk. I was lying down while Daddy inserted all sorts of magical devices into me, and—*"

"*Stone. Please. Don't phrase it like that.*"

"*Well anyway, he created me! I remember everything now. He wanted to see the outside world but couldn't leave, so he made me instead. After I grew up, the idea was for me to go down there, check out the world, then fly back up to tell him.*"

"*That didn't work out as planned.*"

"*Not really, no. I, uh, I got lost a bit, and then I couldn't go back up. My meteor shuttle broke by the pressure, no longer able to receive my mental commands, so then I just sort of... drifted.*"

"*All the way to the Milky Way galaxy?*"

"*It was a good drift.*"

Jack sighed. "How did you not remember this until now, Stone?"

"*Memory is a delicate thing. Do you remember being a baby?*"

"*I would if nothing else happened for literally hundreds of millions of years.*"

"*Hey, that's mean!*"

Again, Jack sighed. "Sorry. So, uh... Is that how you knew chess? The Stone Scholar taught you?"

"*Oh yes, that and all the other arts. We spent a few thousand years together.*"

"You mentioned he couldn't leave," Brock intervened, glancing at the hole in the ground where the golden light still tried to suck them in. *"He's gone now. What does that mean?"*

"Oh, it wasn't that he couldn't leave. He just didn't want to. His job was to guard this place, so abandoning his post would be kind of sad. Now that he's down there, I don't even know if he can get back up. He's probably super pissed."

Jack and Brock exchanged a glance. "So, an apocalyptic force has just been unleashed on the Space Monster World," Jack said.

Brock shrugged. "It's not that bad. Great Silver can probably take him down there. I just hope the stone daddy doesn't die."

"You too, Brock? You're one of them?"

"I have no idea what you're talking about."

Jack rolled his eyes, then switched to telepathy. "Do you think the Stone Scholar can return if he beats Great Silver?"

"No. Daddy once said that he could stay here, but even he couldn't battle the ascension cascade."

"Ascension cascade?"

"The magic stopping other people from coming up here. Without the assistance of the golden light, I suspect no one will return for a long time."

"Hmm. I see."

Jack looked around again. He paced to Fiend King's corpse and took his space ring, then tossed it up and down in his hand. "Our spoils," he told Brock. "Wanna have a look?"

"Sure."

Jack threw it over, and Brock caught it easily. He focused, pushing his perception to look inside. "This bro was a hoarder. There's useful stuff in there, but also tons of valuable trash."

"Valuable trash?"

"See for yourself."

Jack took back the ring and checked it out. To his surprise, Brock hadn't been exaggerating. This was the spaciest space ring he'd ever seen, and it was filled with piles of what seemed like garbage but was actually treasures. It wasn't just the decorations of the previous room. There were low-level monster cores, precious ores, trinkets, weapons, armor, cultivation manuals... All rising in messy, hundred-foot-tall piles.

They say that one person's trash is the other's treasure, but this guy went too far! He's a true hoarder! Jack thought. He took the time to look at these things carefully. All of them were precious, but most were useless to the current him. All the wealth of the Space Monster World mattered little right now. Even the core cultivation manuals of the Fiend King were kind of low level. He guessed all of these could be treasures valuable to a faction, so he quickly drew them into his own space ring, filling it to the brim.

All that remained were a few A-Grade monster cores and the decorations of the previous rooms. Statuettes, flaked paint, golden goblets, paintings, torn velvet, even a few statues of monsters killing Ancients. Not all of these could be easily restored.

Jack took out the decorations and placed them in a neat pile at a side of the room. He then bowed at them. No matter what, the creators of this place had helped him and Brock, and they would soon do it again. Respect was due.

"When we return to the Canal, let's help Stone Daddy Bro come up here," Brock said. "He'll want to redecorate."

"Right," Jack replied. He then looked at the remainder of Fiend King's treasure: a small pile of A-Grade cores, including two at the peak A-Grade and five at the late A-Grade. Great cultivation resources. Jack left them in the space ring and tossed it at Brock.

"What?" the brorilla asked.

"I know you took the lotus, but I've reaped way more harvests than you across our adventures," Jack replied. "Take this. You deserve it."

"Are you sure?"

"Yes. Besides..." Jack turned to the three rooms. "I suspect that the Fiend King's wealth will pale compared to what the Old Gods have left us. That's the real prize."

Brock also turned to look at the doors, eagerness clear in his gaze. Jack spoke to The Stone again.

"You mentioned the Stone Scholar was both the guard and caretaker of this place," he said. "He's obviously not here to direct us, but since he raised you, do you happen to know how we're supposed to accept this reward?"

"Most certainly!" The Stone replied. "It's all coming back now. Oh my gods, I'd forgotten about Franky!"

"Who's Franky?"

"My favorite stone buddy! He used to laugh at all my jokes. Oh, the times we had together, lying down on that stone desk while Daddy trained us."

Jack and Brock exchanged another glance. *"Did Franky seem like a ticklish pebble?"* Jack asked. He'd seen such a thing long ago, at Trial Planet. It was a silly pebble which ended up saving his life when he swapped it for the greatest treasure there. Presumably, Lord Longsword still had it.

"He was very ticklish, yes, but that's not all he did. He spoke, too!"

"Okay, not the same guy then. We've run into a pebble which could do nothing but giggle. After the Crusade is over, we should go fetch it."

"That would be nice. For now though, we should find Franky! Maybe he's just behind those doors!"

Jack gave a sad smile. *"Sure, buddy."* It went without saying that, if Franky was still in this place, he'd have been on the stone desk. Perhaps one of the items which disintegrated during the battle. Jack didn't have the heart to break the news.

"So?" Brock asked, motioning at the doors.

"Right," The Stone replied. "Ahem." Its voice turned deeper, "Oh, brave young monsters, you finally arrived at my abode! Accept my congratulations. It has been over a hundred million—"

"Can we cut to the chase?" Jack asked.

"Ah, yes, sure. The point is, you may choose one of those doors each. Only one."

"Right. And I guess the rest will become magically locked once we choose one?"

"I don't know. It's just the rule. I always thought Daddy was enough to enforce them."

"But he isn't here now."

"I guess."

Jack turned at Brock and winked. Rules were important, but with the Second Crusade raging and this place already ransacked, Jack wasn't going to follow them. "Which door are you interested in, Brock?" he asked.

"Dao and Cultivation. They're what we need right now."

"I agree. Cultivation is my first priority, with the duel and the Crusade and all, but the Dao is also important. Hmm. Do you want to choose a door each first, just in case the rules are magically enforced?"

"We survive here thanks to the assistance of this place's Dao," Brock said. "Let's not die stupidly."

"Very correct, brother."

The two walked forward, standing before the two doors. "I take Cultivation, you take Dao?" Jack asked.

"Right."

"You first."

Brock walked to the first door—the Dao one. It had no handle. Placing his hand onto it, he pushed, and the door creaked open as if for the first time in a billion years—which wasn't far from the truth. A rectangular room was revealed beyond. The pyramid didn't use space magic here—from the way this room stretched to the left, it was apparent the three of them shared the remaining surface of the seventh floor.

No space magic meant the rooms would be possible to break into, if risky. As Brock had said, it wasn't a good idea to infuriate the place keeping you alive. But it was an option.

Brock didn't enter the Dao room immediately. He peeked in—the inside was empty, save for a meditation mat in the center and shelves covering the walls, hosting no less than a hundred crystal spheres. Some danced with colors inside—others were dark, while yet more exuded a feeling which reached the soul.

Jack, who was also peeking in, gasped. He could sense that each of these spheres contained a Dao Vision, as well as precise instructions on how to comprehend them—similar to the incomplete black hole manual, only undamaged. They represented an incredible wealth of knowledge and power.

"Try opening another door," he said, containing his excitement. Brock walked to the third door, the Cultivation one, and pushed. Nothing happened.

"Locked," he said.

"Let me try."

Jack placed his hand against the third door, pushing it open effortlessly. The two bros glanced at each other and grinned. "Bingo," Jack said. "Let me try something." He stepped into the room, then exited, then walked to the Dao room. He entered it easily. His grin couldn't have been wider.

"Let's go together," Brock said. He tried to enter the same room as Jack but failed, his entry stopped by an invisible wall. Jack exited, and then Brock could enter without a problem.

"We can't open more than one door each, and there cannot be two people in the same room, but we can open both doors and take turns," Jack deduced. "The Gods didn't expect two challengers to arrive here at once. We hit the jackpot."

Brock laughed. "Fine by me. Where do you want to start, bro?"

"I'll take the Dao room first. I feel I'm on the cusp of discovering something great. Do you mind?"

"Not at all. I'm peak B-Grade. With the resources of this room, I can break through."

"To the A-Grade!"

"To the A-Grade."

The cultivation room also had walls covered in shelves, except, instead of crystal spheres, it contained all sorts of cultivation resources. There were several Overlord cores, their vast auras only blocked by the glass cases surrounding them. Even different kinds of treasures, like body tempering ones, weren't lacking in that room. It was, without any exaggeration, a treasure trove. Jack suspected both he and Brock could break into the A-Grade here, given enough time.

"What about the Dark Canal?" Brock asked.

"We can't do anything about that," Jack replied. "Whether Great Silver can beat the Stone Scholar, whether he'll pursue Starhair next... If we go down there now, we'll achieve nothing. We don't have the power. Axelor can probably keep Starhair and the rest of the disciples safe, so we should focus on earning as much power as possible before we return. I'm thinking to stay here for a long time. Maybe until right before my duel with Elder Hero. There's around twenty-five years remaining."

"Twenty-five years is a long time."

"For us, yes. For every other cultivator? It's nothing. Just the blink of an eye."

"What about the war?"

"We can't impact the war as B-Grades. If we want to help the Church, we should stay here until we're strong enough, then go out there and beat Elder Hero to a pulp. If things go downhill before then... It is unfortunate, but there's nothing we could have done anyway. In the grand scheme of things, our current power is a drop in the ocean."

Brock considered it for a long moment, then nodded deeply. "You're right. This is the quickest path to power. It is the best we can do to help. To return now because we can't handle some risk would be un-bro-like."

Jack turned to the three doors—two open, one closed—and took a deep breath. He missed his family. Ever since entering the Space Monster World four years ago, he'd lost contact with his clone on Earth, so he had no idea how they were doing. He imagined Ebele was steadily growing. By the time he returned, she'd be a true woman. Losing that time pained him.

However, he had left a clone behind. He missed them, yet they had him, and they could be happy. He'd enjoy the memories too, after he returned, and then hopefully he'd be able to spend endless years with his family without a looming crisis in the horizon.

He stepped into the Dao room, while Brock entered the Cultivation one. Their greatest cultivation session began.

CHAPTER SIXTY-SEVEN
IMPROVING SKILLS

Jack walked into the Dao chamber of the Hall of Trials' seventh floor. He could scarcely believe it. He'd come all the way here, to a foreign world filled with monsters, and earned the right to their top inheritances. The kind that no one in history had ever seen before.

His steps through the room were slow, reverent even. Over a hundred crystal spheres lined the shelves on the wall. Each contained insights to one or several Daos—it was a tremendous wealth of knowledge.

Of course, Jack wasn't interested in collecting them. His own path had already been set. He only looked for crystal spheres relevant to the exact Daos he followed.

Over the years, his Dao had gone through several transformations. First, it was just the Fist. It was later enriched with several other Daos, including Power, Weakness, Indomitable Will... Those were all concepts which formed his foundation and the basis of his own, personal Dao, which he developed at the D-Grade.

Some time later, as the Daos he followed rose to new heights, they were diluted to some of the most primal and powerful concepts in existence. Space, Time, Life, Death. His spectrum of Dao had narrowed back down to four, all spearheaded by the Fist. It was these fundamental powers of the universe that he now pondered—their secrets held the path to the peak of mastery, he knew that, but they were also unbelievably difficult. Even with all his experiences, even with the many top-level inheritances he'd received from several Archons, Jack was only now scratching the surface of what was possible.

Black Hole was the combination of Space and Death—a potent force which had evolved into his killer move. He still hadn't mastered it. Every time he used it, he put himself in as much danger as his opponent, the black hole merely a bomb he held with the business end pointed outwards. Refining his understanding of it was one of his main goals.

The other was exploring his other Dao Vision—that of a woman creating a universe. A combination of Time and Life, a power at least on par with a black hole, if not at a higher level.

Then came Entropy, which he'd only recently experienced. It was the fusion of Time and Death, similar yet different to a black hole. He knew precious little about it, but having felt its effects in his battle against Axelor, he was confident it was something inside his purview. Whether it would become a skill of its own or just an amplification of another, he had no idea.

Following the theme of his four main Daos combining into pairs, the only combination remaining was Space and Life. Jack had no idea what that could look like. A white hole, maybe—the theorized endpoint of a black hole in another universe? Or, perhaps, the white hole wasn't a separate combination but part of the Life and Time thing the woman in the Dao Vision had going on?

Jack had many things to consider. Thankfully, he finally had time and resources. He'd get to the bottom of at least some of those.

He crossed his legs on the meditation mat at the center of the room. It had a mind-amplifying effect, a small but appreciated addition to his efforts. His perception spread to cover the crystal spheres, then, with a swish of his hand, three of them floated to him. They contained various spacetime-related inheritances, none higher level than those he'd already comprehended. With all three at hand, as well as his own insights and previous Dao Visions, he got to work.

The first order of business was perfecting his black hole technique. As his battle against Axelor had proven, it contained plenty of power but lacked control. If he could manipulate it better, utilizing its apex of destructive capabilities and aiming them all at his opponent rather than a wild explosion, its overall effectiveness would rise to a different level. That's why he'd chosen all the spacetime inheritances first.

Time lost its meaning as Jack meditated. He didn't know if it had been hours or months. At some point, he opened his eyes, dissatisfaction evident. His experiments had been failures. The power of a black hole was now slightly easier to control, but nowhere near the level he desired. In fact, he suspected that even after reaching the A-Grade, he still wouldn't be able to control it. It wasn't a matter of energy. He was missing something.

"The problem is, it's too wild," he muttered to himself. "Once it appears, it absorbs everything and quickly gets out of hand. If I could control its energy levels, I could control the black hole... But how do I do that?"

He fell into thought. Some time later, he spoke again.

"Entropy could help. When fighting Axelor, he used it on my black hole, which increased its rate of energy absorption and accelerated its growth. What if there was no energy to absorb, however? I could cover my black hole in a bubble of entropy to nullify all incoming forms of energy. That would temporarily pause its growth, but then what? Maintaining two such high-level concepts would be too draining, and it doesn't change the fact that I can't control the eruption of the black hole once I send it flying. Hmm."

He decided to test it. Diving into his inner world, he moved to an empty corner of his universe and formed a black hole around his hand. The process felt natural now—he'd gotten used to it. After he compressed space enough for the death foam and a singularity to form, it began absorbing matter and energy from its surroundings at a rapidly increasing pace.

Jack creased his brows. While maintaining the black hole, he split part of his awareness to invoke Time and Death. It was straining, but he managed. Combining them with what his body understood after suffering Axelor's Dao, he formed an elementary version of Entropy, which he wrapped around the black hole like a bubble.

The hole's growth stopped. It stabilized, maintaining its volume. Jack would have celebrated if not for the limited applications of this technique. So what if he could pause its growth? At most, he could maintain it for longer before using it, but that didn't help much. He'd still eventually lose control.

As he pondered on this, his eyes suddenly snapped open. *What!*

He'd kept most of his attention on the black hole and bubble of entropy. That was how he'd suddenly sensed something new—with the black hole no longer growing, he could detect an almost imperceptible trickle of power leaving it. It was extremely faint, yet clearly there. How could energy leave a black hole? That made no sense.

Wait. Didn't I read about this once?

Astrophysicists on Earth had theorized that a black hole very slowly deteriorated, expelling its energy in tiny streams of particles. Jack could barely recall that—he never had more than a passing interest in astronomy—and didn't even know if the theory had been proven or not, but did it really matter? He'd proven it now.

This added a whole new avenue of controlling it. Very slow deterioration was vastly different from no deterioration at all, especially when one controlled the flow of time.

Suppressing his rising excitement, Jack manipulated the barrier of Entropy. He poured part of it over the black hole, greatly accelerating its demise. This was exactly what Axelor had done, except he hadn't had a barrier around it, which ended up with the black hole absorbing too much energy and exploding. After all, its rate of absorption far outstripped its rate of decay. With the barrier in place, the hole had nothing to absorb, so its decay was the only factor at play. Under the massive time acceleration, he watched it slowly grow smaller in size, as the departing particles were crushed by Entropy.

Jack's eyes widened. This is it! he realized. I can control the black hole!

It was nowhere near ready to be used in battle, but the seeds were there. Jack moved his arm around, the black hole still stuck on the stump of his wrist, and slowly manipulated its size. He shrunk it by pouring some Entropy over it, then enlarged it by creating gaps in the barrier. In fact, he realized that by adjusting the size of the gaps in his entropy barrier, he could control the black hole's rate of growth.

The technique needed a lot of refining still, but it worked!

"I figured out the secret!" he exclaimed. "A black hole is a hungry beast, and entropy is the control mechanism! By adjusting its environment, I can control the black hole. It's perfect!"

His mind raced with possibilities. If he shot the black hole at someone, like he usually did, he could wrap it in a precisely calculated barrier of Entropy which was much easier to control remotely than the black hole itself. That way, he could control it even inside someone else's body, grinding their bones to mush and then willing the black hole to either explode or wink off. He could even make it fly around by controlling the shape of the Entropy barrier.

If the previous technique was the equivalent of gunpowder and bullets held in Jack's hand, he'd now made a gun. Its effectiveness had increased exponentially.

Of course, it would take a lot of practice to make this usable in battle—the mental demands were insane—but he was confident he'd manage given time. And he had plenty of time right now.

He didn't know how long it had been since the start of his meditation session, but it couldn't be more than a year, right?

He opened his eyes to check for status screens.

Congratulations! Black Hole III → Black Hole IV

Black Hole IV: By draping Entropy as a layer around the black

hole, you've managed to regulate its growth and decay. A truly formidable power lies under your control.

He laughed. It had been a while since his skills moved, so to see them rising again was a good feeling.

Jack refocused. He'd already mastered how to combine Death with the complete spectrum of timespace to create an extremely effective combat technique. He could stop here—he was already more than satisfied—but what if he could go further?

His mind raced to the Dao Vision he hadn't been able to figure out yet, the one where that woman created a universe.

"If I add space in there, can I stabilize it? Maybe it wasn't about time to begin with?" he wondered. With the winds of triumph on his sails, he settled down again. He had a feeling that, when he emerged from meditation, his strength would have increased… by leaps and bounds!

CHAPTER SIXTY-EIGHT
PEAK B-GRADE

THE WORLD CREATION DAO VISION REMAINED HARD TO UNTANGLE. JACK WAS stumped. He was convinced that the level of his Dao understanding rivaled that of most Archons by now. Yet, even after seeing the Vision a thousand times, even after comprehending the individual Daos it relied on, he was unable to crack its secrets.

How? he thought, gritting his teeth.

He dove back into the vision. A green-robed woman sat patiently in space, overlooking a bubble of empty space. Only a handful of particles filled it, crossing the massive space haphazardly at great speed. This had been happening for a long, long time.

Suddenly, two particles crashed, and a new world was born. Reality unraveled. The particles exploded, and a million different Daos sprang into existence as if each had contained a world. The massive, empty bubble was consumed by a large explosion which left in its wake liquid matter. The Dao of Time inside it wobbled and realigned itself on a new axis, forming a timeline perpendicular to the one of the universe around it, yet one which moved at a different frequency.

The rest of the elements stabilized, attuned to that particular frequency, and a new universe was born in the bubble, one whose every particle differed from those of the previous universe on a level Jack wouldn't even realize was possible without seeing it. Like discovering a new color. Reality and the physical laws quickly diverged from what Jack knew, all their transformations based on that universe's Dao of Time.

This whole sequence happened instantaneously. Even Jack, with his sharp senses and perception, could only get glimpses. He understood the basic principles of what occurred, but the actual process was far too vast and complex. There were so many moving pieces that understanding them all would take an eternity.

He even suspected this was a concept on a higher level than Entropy or the black hole, though he really had no way of knowing. It was certainly more complex.

With a sigh, Jack left the Dao Vision for the thousandth time. "This is too difficult," he muttered. "Either I'm missing something or my current state of being isn't enough. Probably both."

With a decisive tug of will, he forced the problem away, out of his mind. He would revisit it when better able to. Jack then rolled his shoulders, standing up after a long period of meditation. The stone room around him remained the same—shelves over shelves were filled with crystal spheres.

"How long has it been, Stone?" he asked telepathically.

"Hmm. Probably several hundred million years."

"What!"

"What?"

"I meant from the time I started meditating in this room."

"Oh. Then, like, five years. Venerable Saint Thousand Shell has gotten better at chess."

"I was ALWAYS good at it," the turtle's voice rumbled. "Anyway, nice job comprehending that black hole thing, kid. I got good news as well. The Divine Blood is almost fully charged."

Jack smiled. "*That's great.*" The Divine Blood was the official name of the Life Drop.

Five years... he thought, instinctively raising his gaze to the sky, only to meet a stone ceiling. I wonder how the rest of the universe is doing. I've been gone for a long time already...

The Dao room had already given him everything it could. He stepped out to reach the ruined chamber on the other side and sat down to relax. The golden beam from five years ago had already disappeared, but neither Great Silver nor the Stone Scholar had returned. They probably couldn't.

Through the open door of the cultivation chamber, Jack caught sight of Brock. He instantly shot to his feet again. The brorilla radiated pure, unadulterated power, as if he was the cradle of all life, the center of the universe. His cultivation had gone through a qualitative change, completely incomparable to what it used to be.

"Brock!" Jack exclaimed with joy. "You've reached the A-Grade!"

The brorilla opened his eyes and smiled. "A year ago," he said, slowly rising to his feet. "I was just stabilizing."

"How did you manage to break through so quickly?"

"You'll see. Come on—it's your turn, big bro."

"My turn?"

"Right. Your turn to break through."

Jack was stunned. He eyed the room, its vast reserves of cultivation resources barely dwindled. Brock stepped out, exuding vast power, and suddenly Jack yearned for it as well. He desired to step into the highest realm. To claim the power he deserved.

"I'll be in the Dao room," Brock said with a smile. "Let me know when you're ready to go."

Jack didn't reply. He walked into the Cultivation room as if in a trance, spinning around slowly to survey the walls, covered in shelves hosting all sorts of wondrous materials. There were Overlord cores, extreme treasures of various kinds, body tempering resources... Everything was at the Overlord level. The golden earth lotus Brock had enjoyed before would fit right in with the contents of this room, and it wouldn't be a particularly impressive one either. In fact, Jack noticed the compressed essence of another golden earth lotus just sitting on a shelf. The treasure so many A-Grades had risked their lives for wasn't considered anything special here.

"The seventh floor lives up to his reputation," he whispered, licking his lips. "Can I break through here?"

He was aware of the method to reach the A-Grade.

At the start of the B-Grade, the cultivator formed an inner world inside themselves, the larger the better. Then, throughout that Grade, they gradually purified that world, instilling it with matter and higher Dao workings. They made it realer. The threshold to entering the A-Grade was to generate life and cultivators inside their inner world.

Of course, that was as hard as it sounded. It didn't necessarily require insights into the Dao of Life, just an understanding of the Dao so extreme that the inner world worked by itself, life produced as a result of various natural processes. In a way, it was similar to the creation of life in the actual universe, with the cultivator helping the process in a similar way Enas had.

Finding himself cross-legged, Jack reached inside himself, manifesting in his inner world. "Guys," he said, glancing at the turtle, The Stone, and Copy Jack. "Can you hide in the Life Drop for a bit? I'll try to break through."

The three had been in the process of building a garden made purely of Dao. Hearing Jack, Venerable Saint Thousand Shell laughed, flicking a claw and instantly wiping the garden out of existence.

"Hey!" The Stone protested.

"Hahaha!" The turtle laughed. "I knew it! Isn't the shrine of my ancestors brilliant, kid?"

"It certainly is," Jack replied with a smile.

Copy Jack gave Jack a deep glance, then turned into a ray of light which sank into the Life Drop. The turtle and Stone soon followed. The Life Drop contained its own inner world, though tiny in comparison to Jack's, and having these three there ensured they wouldn't somehow complicate the breakthrough.

Jack now floated alone in his inner world. He surveyed it. A sixteen-thousand-mile wide, mostly empty expanse. Newborn stars flickered here and there, while continent-sized planetary fragments floated through the void.

At the very center stood a large purple fist, the core of Jack's Dao. The Life Drop hovered to the side—a green droplet of Enas's blood—while the portal to the Green Dragon Realm yawned right behind it, constantly feeding its excess of life energy into the blood.

Far to the other side, a black hole spun slowly, every pulse infusing the inner world with advanced spacetime laws. Through it lay the Black Hole World, the masterpiece of Archon Black Hole.

Jack took a moment to appreciate what he had. He'd worked harder and risked more than anyone, but he also possessed access to an unbelievable amount of resources. Archons would go to war over any of these treasures—the Life Drop, the Green Dragon Realm, and the Black Hole World—and he had three of them. It was part of the reason why he stood so much higher than anyone else at his level—with the exception of Brock, who somehow kept up despite lacking a similar level of resources.

Jack opened his eyes in the real world. He took a deep breath, then flexed his fingers, making several items float his way: a green ginseng root emanating dense energy of Life, a rippling glass shard containing the power of spacetime, and a pitch-black drop of liquid suffused with a thick aura of Death. These were all top-level treasures, yet here, he could use them freely.

Thank you, Gods, he said, absorbing all three into his inner world. He then settled into cultivation.

Jack was Level 513. As the three treasures orbited around each other near the center of his inner world, their energies spreading outward, he felt the density of his world's Dao steadily increasing.

He helped the process along, investing all his attention into it. An unknown amount of time later, he realized that the three treasures had dissolved fully, their energies spread across his inner world and pushing its density to the peak. It almost felt like the world was groaning by all the energy it had to contain.

With a pop, its boundaries expanded, the energy density rapidly falling. From sixteen thousand miles, it grew to twenty, achieving the final doubling of its original width. The Dao density returned to normal levels, but the sheer volume of energy present out-scaled the original one by hundreds of times.

Jack smiled. He spread his perception to find that the massive amounts of Dao had increased the efficiency of all forces, including gravity. The various continental-sized pieces of earth had grouped together, forming spherical clusters—planets. They were rough and misshapen, early in their development, but Jack meticulously covered them in the Daos of Life and Time to push them along. He watched these planets fall into orbit around the purple fist which hovered in the middle of the world, then smash into each other until their final sizes and positions were solidified. Several sported their own moons. Water appeared between volcanoes and wastelands covering their surfaces.

Jack's inner world had started at ten thousand miles wide. After expanding at the middle, late, and peak B-Grade, it had doubled in diameter, reaching twenty thousand miles. Its volume, and therefore its energy, had increased by hundreds of times.

Even at twenty thousand miles wide, this should be nowhere near enough to sustain a solar system. However, Jack found that everything in his inner world was shrunken compared to the outside one, or perhaps it would be more apt to say space was larger. While energy couldn't shrink or enlarge, stars and planets could, leading to a single solar system being born inside Jack's inner world. His purple fist acted as the sun, while seven planets orbited it. To the people who would eventually be born there, he assumed the Black Hole

World and Life Drop-Green Dragon Realm would be nighttime curios.

Jack had already reached the peak B-Grade realm and refined his cultivation as much as possible. He had everything he needed. With a fierce concentrated expression, he sat down on top of the sun.

It was time to reach the A-Grade.

CHAPTER SIXTY-NINE
UNIVERSE OF THE BODY

Jack surveyed his inner world. The matter previously created had forged a solar system, with his fist as the sun and various planets circling it. In the accelerated time of his inner world, Jack had already seen these planets go through a series of geological changes to settle on a somewhat more stable state.

Of course, these changes weren't the exact same as what Earth had gone through. His Dao and the universe's were subtly different—and that was expressed in everything that occurred inside them, whether big or small. Jack looked forward to discovering what the lifeforms he created would look like.

With the planets no longer erupting or getting smashed by a hail of meteors, Jack thought it was time to move to the next step. He manipulated their growth. Slowly, an atmosphere appeared around most of them—barring the ones too far or too close to the sun—followed by oceans. Millions of years passed in the blink of an eye, Jack manipulating the flow of time freely.

After the first oceans appeared, Jack descended on each of these worlds. His body was the size of a continent. He bent down, taking a deep breath and blowing into the oceans. The wind of his breath made them overflow, temporarily flooding the newly created continents—but it also contained the very first hints of life, a wealth of living cells placed in a safe haven. Jack moved from planet to planet, breathing life into each of them, then calmly stepped back to watch.

The bacteria began multiplying erratically. He saw, through his omniscient gaze, single-celled organisms adapt and thrive in their new environments. At the same time this happened, Jack himself experienced several changes. The flow of time, which he'd freely manipulated so far, now felt heavier, as if anchored in place by the very life he'd infused into his world.

To his surprise, even single-celled organisms possessed souls, their unique life signatures, and pulling the fabric of time under their feet was like tugging at a piece of cloth carrying multiple sharp stones. It was still possible, but it risked getting torn, and it was certainly heavier than it used to be.

Seeing that bacteria had souls, Jack laughed. At the very start of his cultivation journey, he'd been told that only cultivators had souls, while monsters did not. That was a load of crap. If amoebas could have a soul, then so could a three-meter-tall wolf.

Soon, his laughter was replaced by a frown. As life populated his world, he was beginning to get a distinct sense of wrongness.

Why?

He inspected everything, passing his gaze from the tiniest pebble to the sun itself, through every single creature in his world. There was nothing wrong. Why did he feel that way?

The more creatures that appeared, the slower time got. At the start, even a billion years could pass in seconds, but the resistance had increased. The single-celled organisms evolved into more complex structures and eventually stepped out of the oceans. He watched as they developed limbs and sentience, ecosystems forming. He was their God—a unique feeling.

Yet, that feeling was undermined by the constant, growing sense of wrongness. Like this wasn't the proper way to do things. Some instinct, deep in his heart, insisted he was making a mistake.

Jack took a deep breath. By now, it had been over a year in the outside world. A year in which Ebele grew and the Church fought a bitter war. This was precious time. He took another breath, pressing his eyes shut, then snapped them open. He waved his hands—fleets of meteors appeared in his world, large and shaped like fists, then came crashing down on the planets.

Animals ran around in panic. Jack saw the flames reflected in their eyes. He let the meteors crash, eradicating all life, changing his planets' trajectories, resetting his inner world to the empty, timeless state it had originally existed in.

He felt weary—an angry god, one of slaughter.

Jack had interrupted his own breakthrough. He clutched his chest, bringing a hand to his mouth to catch the coughing blood. Yet, when the pain abated, his eyes remained sharp.

This wasn't the right way, he knew it with certainty. It was the breakthrough method every text and A-Grade had described, yet, for him, it was wrong. His heart told him so—as if he was choosing a lesser path, one which didn't express his true potential. Eradicating all life and wasting a year of real time was an acceptable sacrifice to retrace his steps.

Jack didn't begin recreating life immediately—if he did, it would only end the same way. Instead, he sat down cross-legged on top of his purple fist sun, meditating on the feeling of wrongness which remained warm in his heart.

"What's the problem?" he asked aloud. "What did I do wrong?"

No answer came. Jack relaxed, taking his time. He sank into meditation. His senses turned off, letting the feeling of wrongness expand naturally in his heart until it became clear. He could see its desire. A larger universe—no, a more thorough one.

"Is my inner world incomplete?" Jack wondered. No one answered. No one could. This was his path to forge. All he could rely on was himself.

"No, not incomplete," he replied. "Just... not whole?"

It was a confusing feeling. The sense of wrongness in his heart didn't judge anything in his inner world, but it still viewed the entire world with contempt. A sense of disjunction was prevalent. There wasn't something wrong, it just was. Somehow.

Jack opened his eyes again. Rising panic threatened to swell his heart—he knew there was no breaking through if he didn't resolve that feeling, and the more he waited, the more time he wasted. His family and people needed him. Across the universe, millions were dying for his incompetence.

Yet, he gently put that feeling down. Such thoughts wouldn't help, only make things more difficult. His road was simple—to solve this problem—and he would do it because he simply had no other choice. If he failed... Then, with a heavy heart, he'd have to settle for an incomplete breakthrough. He could still help the war like that. He wouldn't sacrifice everyone for a revelation which might never come.

"Ten more years," he promised himself. "Well within the deadline of my duel. If I don't succeed until then, I will settle."

Since his thirty-year declaration of a duel with Elder Hero, he'd spent four absorbing the Overlord core, five fusing Entropy into his black hole, one in his failed breakthrough just now, and several months here and there. It was over ten years in total. His adventures were like sharp flashes—the vast majority of his life was occupied by uneventful meditation. He could see now how cultivators could live for hundreds of thousands of years without going mad. If he wasn't on the clock, he would have liked to settle down somewhere for a few millennia and ponder on the Dao.

Less than twenty years remained until his duel, but that was plenty of time. Jack returned to the problem at hand. He fell into deep meditation, tuning out everything else, focusing on the seed of wrongness which he now acknowledged in his heart. His overall cultivation was in disarray—but why?

"What is my path?" Jack asked himself, speaking with eyes closed as if in a dream, listening to his own voice. "My fist, which I follow. My Dao, which I discover. My body, which I temper. My inner world, which I cultivate."

Silence fell for months.

Jack pondered silently.

Finally, he spoke again, "That is incorrect. My fist, my Dao, and my inner world are connected now. They are three parts of a whole. Only my body is separate. I use it as a physical medium to my strength—sooner or later, no matter how I cultivate it, it will fall behind my other aspects. My four aspects will become three, one wasted. My path will be lesser, a fourth of it wasted."

His eyes snapped open. A green light shone inside them—the Dao of Life, which made up the bodies of people.

"I must combine my body with the rest of my cultivation," he realized. The moment he perceived this notion, he knew it was correct. Why had he never heard of it? He'd asked various A-Grades and read many texts about breaking into the A-Grade, yet nobody mentioned such a thing. Was it relevant to Jack's specific combination of Daos? Was it about his extreme understanding into the Dao giving him insights the others lacked? Or did it have to do with his tenth Dao Fruit and ten thousand miles breakthrough, which no one else possessed, granting him a perfect inner world?

He did not know, but at this point, it didn't matter. He had a job to do.

Jack rose to his feet. The world around him, which had waited silently for a long time, suddenly flared to life. Dao and energy erupted. Green sparks of life emerged from the void, drawn out of the folds of reality they'd been hidden in. Jack made a grasping motion at the Life Drop, which dislodged itself from the portal to the Green Dragon Realm and flew into his hands. It was potent, radiating intense life energy.

Jack smiled, then squeezed it between his fingers. This divine object, which had once been impregnable to even his mightiest efforts, crumbled like a popped balloon.

"*YOU DID WHAT!*" the turtle screamed from inside, but Jack only laughed. The Life Drop and its current inhabitants would be fine. He'd just emptied it rapidly, not truly broken it.

Unimaginable quantities of Life energy flooded the world, taking it over. The purple sun was tinged green—the planets spontaneously burst with trees and animals which quickly died to the lack of living conditions.

Combined with the constant stream of Life energy pouring out of the Green Dragon Realm's portal, Jack found that his inner world was completely suffused with the energy of Life, even pushing his other Daos aside. It was a temporary imbalance he could accept, because his body was also made of Life Dao. This was the best way to connect them.

"Brock," his voice echoed in the real world. "Close the door. Now."

He didn't even know if the brorilla had heard or responded. He was too deeply entrenched in meditation. He just hoped for the best.

Jack pictured himself. A human body, tempered to the extreme, hiding in its center the gateway to his inner world. Both inside and outside were filled with the Dao of Life—the most potent life force. Jack understood what he had to do. He also realized this was a very risky procedure, but there was no going back. And he didn't want to. His path was the pursuit of mastery, and now, for the first time, he felt so close to it. As if, more than his breakthrough to the B-Grade, this would firmly set him on a path far surpassing any other.

That, or it would kill him. But that risk was a small price to pay for eternity.

Jack focused as deeply as he could. His inner world was an island in the dimensional sea, a bubble of its own universe connected to his body through his Dao and willpower. He pictured them as a portal. With a deep breath, he grabbed his entire inner world and pulled it through the connection to make it physically enter his body. The entire solar system and the laws which regulated it were warped and sucked through a tiny hole. They reappeared in Jack's physical body.

For a moment, he was stunned. The reality of this state was staggering. Planets coexisted with his organs, each pushing against the other. Twenty thousand miles had been compressed into six feet of human. The spacetime laws which served as the borders of Jack's inner world were rapidly unraveling, unsupported by the stricter laws pertaining to this universe compared to the lax dimensional sea, and Jack felt his body on the verge of exploding.

The irony of all this crossed his mind. What would Brock think if an entire solar system suddenly spilled out the door?

He wiped that thought, focusing fully. His spacetime laws rushed to the fore—all his expertise came into play, skillfully weaving the broken laws back together, creating new seals and warps to replace the quickly waning ones. His inner world, which had begun to unravel, restabilized.

Jack could make a universe fit inside his body, but that didn't refute the fact that he still needed organs and flesh inside him. He needed to find a way to reconcile the two warring realities—and master the Dao to make it happen.

CHAPTER SEVENTY
A-GRADE

As his inner world and flesh body tried to coexist, Jack felt himself strained. For a moment, he thought he'd die. Understanding arrived then.

He had an idea. In an instant, amidst the warring realities of his body and inner world, he knew what to do. And, to achieve it, he needed tremendous amounts of energy.

The inner world and his body were fiercely attacking each other —both of which were tempered to the extreme. Their cataclysmic clashes were suppressed by Jack's Dao, but he momentarily let that go. Intense ripples spread outside his body, like he'd swallowed a blacksmith hammering an anvil. They crashed into the walls, shaking the entire pyramid. The various treasures lining the shelves of this room were also sucked into the ripples. They burst apart, unable to endure the impacts. There were dozens of them, many being Overlords cores or items on the same level. All their power erupted at once, filling the chamber with a completely terrifying amount of energy. Jack was suffocating. This was more than enough for multiple people to break into the A-Grade, and the pyramid's enchantments kept it from dispersing.

He realized Brock had closed the door. *Good bro.*

Jack's body was cracking under the pressure—he quickly got to work. His Daos burst into action, sucking in the energy like vacuums, forming several colored whirlpools around Jack. The massive amount of energy came under his control, if temporarily. He immediately put it to use.

His body and inner world, which were fiercely clashing, were forced to fuse. Energy was funneled into them, ironing out their differences. Jack's Daos worked at full force. The fusing proceeded, all problems solved by his Daos or hammered down by his fist, the two realities slowly becoming one.

His organs turned into planets. His stomach, lungs, spleen, those and all else were now covered in tiny continents. His flesh dissolved into energy, turning into the starry vacuum of space, with its properties dictated by the Dao of Life to operate the same way flesh did. The purple fist sun took the place of his heart, and his bones absorbed its radiance before exuding it, turning into mini suns themselves. His blood became rivers of stars which brightened the cosmos. Only his skin remained the same, turning dark and starry from the inside to resemble the endless horizon of space.

Jack opened his eyes to find he was no longer human. He had transcended. His new reality was hard to come to grips with, but he knew it would happen. For now, he remained in breakthrough. The tons of energy he'd unleashed before had been partly consumed to fuel the fusion of a small universe into his body, but parts of it still remained, and Jack intended to use them to make his breakthrough as perfect as possible.

The portals to the Black Hole World and Green Dragon Realm had been pulled into his body alongside his inner world. They now hovered aimlessly, sticking out like sore thumbs. They could be better.

With a tug of will, he reached through the portal to the Green Dragon Realm and pulled it in. The entire realm disappeared from the dimensional sea and reappeared inside Jack's body. Its intense life energy spread out, helping Jack adapt to the change—and, at the same time, the stability of his laws reinforced the realm, which had been deteriorating for millions of years.

The Green Dragon Realm wasn't empty. It contained many animals and a few cultivators—Jack had let them live there a long time ago. His body didn't reject them, which was good. Their power was too low to be a problem anyway.

On their side, the beasts and cultivators of the Green Dragon Realm witnessed the change. The ground shook under their feet. They saw the sky above them distort, then get ripped away like cloth to reveal an odd starry dome. A purple sun hung in the distance—vaguely shaped like a fist. Long celestial bodies hovered in various directions, some glowing more than others, all reflecting the light of the sun like moons. Rivers of stars crossed the cosmos, while the far distance was also littered with stars, sparkling in various intensities and colors—this was the inside of Jack's skin, where different areas simulated the glittering stars of the universe.

On the surface of the Green Dragon Realm, a frog-eyed man and a human girl watched the sky with a mix of terror and marvel. "What the hell..." Borkuren Madiba muttered.

Sassa gazed upward, her mouth hanging open, the stars reflected in her eyes. "It's beautiful..."

Between them, their teenager child balled its fists, excitement rising inside it as it sensed the laws of the world subtly change.

Jack didn't contact them. He repeated the process for the Black Hole World, ripping it out of the dimensional sea and embedding it into his body. The people sitting in benches at the top of the world witnessed the colorful void warp and be replaced by a starry sky. For the first time in a billion years, they saw stars. Their eyes widened. They hugged each other, a feeling of anticipation overcoming them.

Mia and Grand Elder Pasan, who also happened to be there, were stunned. Tears fell from the elder's eyes. "This is... a new era..." she muttered, falling to her knees. "We didn't disappoint you, Ancestor... We survived... Our children, your children, will be free!"

Meanwhile, Mia clutched her hands before her chest, worship rising in her heart. "Thank you, Jack Rust..." she whispered.

Jack sensed the changes inside his body and was satisfied. He'd perfectly combined his inner world and the two small realms into himself. He was now more than a man. Deep in his heart, the feeling of wrongness was gone. He'd stepped onto the right path. He suspected this wasn't the only way to achieve this level, but it was the way for him.

"Universe of the body..." he muttered, chuckling. "Cultivation never stops, does it? It's just a gift that keeps on giving. I wonder what lies at the top. Does it even exist?"

As far as he knew, he was the first person in history to achieve this Universe of the Body realm—as he decided to call it. He'd already diverged from the cultivation path everyone else followed. All at once, he understood why everyone was stuck at the Archon realm, why it even existed. Archon was just a name for those who surpassed the A-Grade without having set the foundation to proceed to the next realm.

Jack knew, with absolute certainty, that he could progress further. The A-Grade was just another stepping stone for him. He would become the first S-Grade, and he would create a path to let others follow him in the future, to let the cultivation world overcome its bottleneck and take a major step forward. After all, cultivators as a whole were still in their infancy. They had colonized seventy-three out of billions of galaxies. Jack would become the pioneer to a brighter future.

If he survived this war.

He smiled with anticipation. Achieving this Universe of the Body boundary had massively increased his powers to an extent he couldn't even calculate. His physicality had grown multiple times more robust, while his ability to perceive the Dao had shot upward, inscribed onto his very bones. However, he wasn't done. He still needed to break into the A-Grade.

Sinking back into his body, Jack gazed at the wrung out Life Drop in his hand. With a grin, he tossed it out, burying it deep into the Green Dragon Realm and letting it drink from its energy.

He then gazed at his organs. Each had been made into a planet, temporarily bare. That would change soon. The strength of an A-Grade cultivator depended on the strength of the cultivators living inside their inner world, so Jack needed to create some. Technically, he already possessed powerful cultivators in the Black Hole World and Green Dragon Realm, but as they were mere visitors instead of being born of his Dao, their power didn't add to his.

Waving his hands, Jack temporarily isolated the two realms from the rest of his body—an invisible curtain, one they wouldn't even perceive but which would protect them from the time acceleration he was about to use.

The barren planets of his organs began to move and shake, going through a series of geological changes. Meteors crossed the starry void which used to be his flesh, crashing into the planets to shape them. Eventually, the universe stabilized. The planets didn't spin around themselves or orbit the sun—they were, after all, his organs—but Jack's Dao created the right laws to make them work.

His mental image descended again. He stood over the oceans and blew into them, upsetting the waters. Tiny organisms were infused. He stepped back and let them grow, watching them multiply and evolve as they populated his planets. Amoebas turned into fish, which turned into amphibians, which turned into land animals. Birds appeared. The worlds of his organs grew richer, the lifeforms on them sporting great diversity.

His stomach held large, dinosaur-looking lizards. His spleen was a world of poison, its creatures colorful and deadly, while his lungs became windy realms populated mostly by flying creatures. His intestines sported long worms. It was interesting how the nature of each organ affected the growth of its inhabitants. At the same time, the influence of Jack's Dao of the Fist was prevalent, his every planet favoring the birth of fist-wielding animals. Most species were barbaric and warmongering, but they also enjoyed their lives, living fairly and straightforwardly.

Jack found himself loving them like a father.

His ability to accelerate time lessened again, burdened by the many souls he now contained, while the creatures inside him kept evolving. He saw the first sapient beings appear, not all of them humanoid. They multiplied and developed. The moment they acquired true sapience, his time-accelerating abilities fell out hard. He could still do it, to an extent, but the flow of time inside him now approximated the real world. It was perhaps only ten or twenty times faster. He assumed it would accelerate again as he delved deeper into his Daos, but the creatures inside him would also grow stronger and more populous, restraining him further.

The growth of an A-Grade cultivator depended on two things—resources and time. The more resources one had, the more treasures would be created inside them, and the thicker the Dao would be, letting their newborn cultivators grow faster. The more time they let pass, the more their inner cultivators would progress, growing their overall strength and therefore the A-Grade cultivator's.

In time, he pictured his organ-planets covered by sprawling civilizations, using the rivers of stars which were his blood to travel from one organ to the next, spreading and exchanging insights. It would be glorious. He really looked forward to it.

Jack possessed incredibly rich Dao. He was certain his inner world would develop far more efficiently than most, but there was nothing he could do to lessen the restraints of time. His next breakthrough wouldn't happen for a while. Probably until long after the Crusade had ended. This was the highest realm he would reach for now, any further gains limited to his Dao and techniques... but he didn't mind. He had a feeling this would be enough. His current strength was unfathomable—certainly near the very top of the universe.

Elder Hero wouldn't know what hit him.

As Jack thought about these things, his inner world had kept growing. The Dao was so rich that it practically begged the native creatures to discover it. Jack found a host of gorilla sapients. With a smile, he descended to them invisibly, nudging their minds in the right direction.

A golden-furred gorilla going through a life-or-death struggle suddenly grasped something majestic. Its entire aura changed. It used these fledgling powers to defeat the beasts attacking it, then gazed at its fist.

This was the first creature in Jack's universe to touch the Dao. More would come, their overall strength quickly rising. The moment the first appeared, the Dao in Jack's body began to circulate subtly, propelled by the insights and utilization of its cultivators. A self-contained system.

At the same time, the moment that golden-furred gorilla touched the Dao, Jack knew he'd truly broken into the A-Grade. His inner universe had stabilized. He opened his eyes, gazing at the dark and destroyed room, sensing the massive changes inside his body. Everything felt different—now that he no longer needed to guide the development of his inner universe, he could take some time to get used to his new body.

For now, he couldn't stop grinning.

He had ascended. He had transformed. And he was ready to kick some Immortal ass.

CHAPTER SEVENTY-ONE
EXITING SECLUSION

Fourteen years ago, soon after Jack entered the Space Monster World...

Sovereign Heavenly Spoon lay sprawled over a soft chair. His mouth was a hard line. Calculations flashed through his eyes. All across the windows surrounding him, endless stars twinkled, the heralds of tiny days in endless night. Their colors could awe any mortal mind. Yet, the Sovereign was lost in thought, the starry view all too familiar. The darkness in his mind was greater than that outside the starship.

"Hey, Spoon," a voice interrupted his musings. He rose to his feet, fighting hard to regain his usual joviality.

"Min Ling," he said, looking at the door. "How many times must I ask you to address me as Elder?"

"Not doing it."

He chuckled. "Well, that's fine too. Any good news?"

"I wish."

She plopped down on a chair, her leather armor sinking against the cushion. Her appearance and aura had changed over the past few years—she'd cut her long dark hair short, barely reaching her shoulders, while her body was covered in scars beneath the armor. She could mend them anytime she wished, but had vowed to only do it after the war was over. In her brown eyes, lightning played, oftentimes wrapped in fire.

She didn't speak for a while, and neither did Spoon. They were comfortable in the silence. It allowed their facades to wash away.

The Sovereign's shoulders slumped, until he eventually collapsed back in his chair as well. "What happened this time?" he asked tiredly.

"The Gods came back."

"They did!"

"Yeah. They barged into the battlefield, instantly destroying the opposition and saving Elder Boatman."

Spoon chuckled. "Eleven Gods is hardly what you want to see mid-battle. Did the enemy receive heavy casualties?"

"If you want to call it that. They lost a few low-level Elders and an army of B-Grades. Hero was there too, but he managed to escape."

"Of course he did. The man is a cockroach."

Min Ling scratched her scalp. "I was thinking. You know how we keep sending assassins after him and he keeps narrowly surviving?"

"Yeah?"

"What if we're just training him?"

Spoon considered it. "I guess we are. But, all it takes is one mistake, and then bam, no Hero."

"Yeah..." She fell silent for a moment. "Anyway. After wrapping up that battle, the Gods didn't visit the New Cathedral. They charged straight into System space. Right at the Immortals."

Spoon perked up. "And?"

"And came back a few hours later. Injured."

"They injured the Gods?"

"They did worse. Only ten Gods returned. The one of Mass didn't. We intercepted some enemy communications; they call Elder Hero the God Killer."

Spoon fell silent. Min Ling waited patiently until he was ready to speak. "I didn't even know Gods could die," he finally said.

"Everyone can. Apparently."

"This is terrible."

"Yeah."

"How did they lose? You can't expect me to believe Hero dueled one of them and won."

"Of course not. Unfortunately, we don't know the specifics. The Gods aren't saying, at least as far as I can tell. My guess is they simply got swarmed. The Immortals command a bunch of Archons —rushing in after announcing their presence was just arrogant."

"An arrogance they paid for."

"Even Gods commit hubris."

"And now what?"

"Now, we wait. Word is that the Gods retreated somewhere to tend to their wounds. When they're ready, they'll attack alongside the Church. A battle to judge the fate of the universe."

Spoon nodded. "Are you thinking what I'm thinking?"

"That we should get some food?"

"That the Gods were humbled. One of them dying may have been good for us. They were arrogant and thoughtless before, uninvested. They thought they could come and go as they like. That's not true anymore. They've tasted fear. They've seen one of them perish. They know the Immortals are worthy enemies, so they'll work alongside us, even if they disparage us as mortals. In fact, I don't even think they'll retreat this time, as they did in the First Crusade. They'll fight to the death."

Min Ling considered it. "I disagree. Those things were born divine. They've never tasted struggle. The moment things go south, they'll run away, hiding at the edge of the universe and hoping the Immortals self-implode."

"...Which isn't that unreasonable, actually."

"I know."

Another round of silence passed.

"Think they're actually licking their wounds?" Min Ling asked, letting her head drop back in resignation. Her real feelings, those of fear and muted hope, resurfaced. "Or did they already escape?"

"I have no way to tell. I suppose they're considering it. What did our communications say?"

"That the Gods gave a decree. They will recuperate for a few years. Then, we strike, and we destroy the Immortals once and for all."

"...Is it weird that I got hyped up?"

"No. I was too."

"Now I only have one more question."

"Shoot."

"If I'm here, and you're here... Who's steering the damn starship?"

She burst out with laughter. "The Sage's routes are accurate. But, alright, I'll go. Can you cook up something?"

"I could just conjure it."

"I know, but I want you to work for it."

"Fine. How's pasta and tea?"

"Can we not have tea for once?"

"Tea is the quintessence of life."

Min Ling sighed. "I knew we should have gotten more people."

"No," Spoon replied sharply. "More people means more liabilities. It's better this way. If we fail this mission, only we die."

She gave him a long stare. Then, she slipped into the helm room, guiding their ship while Sovereign Heavenly Spoon busied himself in the kitchen.

The small starship crossed the emptiness between galaxies.

Brock had been meditating in the Dao room. As soon as he sensed the commotion of the next room settle down, he rushed out. The main chamber remained messy—the door to the cultivation chamber was firmly shut.

The brorilla had heard Jack's request to close the door. He'd been in shallow meditation at the time, thankfully. What happened afterward left him stumped. A tremendous storm of energy whipped up in Jack's room, so intense that even the seventh floor's protection mechanisms failed to contain it completely. Beams of pure energy radiated from where the door met the wall, creating a unique kind of light show, while Jack's Dao became so miniscule compared to the overall energy, it was barely detectable. Brock had almost rushed in to save his bro.

However, while Jack's Dao appeared tiny, it was stable. It wasn't waning with time. Instead, the rampant energy was slowly dying down, as if something was absorbing it.

A day after the incident, Brock returned to the Dao room, keeping his perception spread in case Jack needed him. A year later, the energy storm fell to a constant low level. Another three years, and Brock sensed the door of the room open, at which point he bolted out.

"Bro!" he exclaimed. As he saw Jack, he paused.

"Hey, Brock," Jack said, a calm smile on his face. "How are you doing?"

Brock did not respond, eyes glued on his brother. His appearance had reverted to the human one, his double devil disguise wiped off. He'd also broken into the A-Grade, just like Brock, which was expected.

Except, his aura... Brock couldn't comprehend it. Staring at Jack, he may as well have been looking at the open sky, the endless stars of a starry night. There was an almost metaphysical tingle to it, something which even Brock, with his A-Grade cultivation, couldn't quite grasp. A deep sense of reverence rose from his soul, filling him with so much awe he could barely speak.

"Oh, sorry, am I releasing my aura?" Jack said, noticing Brock's stare. "I'm still getting used to this. How about now?"

Before Brock could respond, Jack's aura completely disappeared. If he wasn't looking at his big brother, he would have thought he left the room. His aura was completely restrained inside his body, just like a common mortal, yet a faint sense of awe persisted, existing at the back of Brock's mind as a whisper only the most attentive would notice.

"What?" was all Brock could ask. For the first time, the big bro in front of him was completely unfathomable. Unreadable. His strength reached unknown depths, and Brock had no idea how this was even possible. It was like Jack had completely transformed.

All Brock knew was that, whatever happened to his big bro, he'd grown massively stronger. It was an increase far greater than what breaking into the A-Grade would justify. Brock could feel it in his bones—if they tried to spar right now, he wouldn't even pose a challenge. A dozen Brocks at a time would still lose. The strength hiding in Jack's body was apocalyptic.

Or divine, he realized.

Jack laughed with joy at Brock's reaction, but he wasn't one to leave his bro hanging. He explained everything, about his Universe of the Body, his breakthrough, how he'd almost miss-stepped before utilizing all those resources at once.

"How strong are you now?" Brock asked.

Jack frowned in thought. He opened his status screen again, taking in the new changes.

Error! Inner World undetected. Unforeseen physical changes detected. Calculating.

Error! Calculations impossible. Using faulty stat translation protocol. Approximation mode activated.

Approximation results: Physical stats doubled. Further increases impossible.

Congratulations! B-Grade → A-Grade

Congratulations! You have successfully developed cultivators in your inner world, firmly stepping onto the path of godhood.
All stats +400
Free stat points per Level Up: 50 → 0. The Immortal System can no longer fuel your growth.

Level Up! You have reached Level 550.

Congratulations! The Bare Fist Brotherhood faction has reached the A-Grade. New functions unlocked in the faction screen.

Jack smiled again. No matter how times he read it, his joy didn't change.

During his meditation session, he'd first risen from Level 513 to 549, investing all stat points into Physical. The result was a total of 14,330 points. Then, when he fused his inner world into his physical body, the System's best approximation of what happened was a doubling of his Physical stats. He reached a staggering 28,660. After the extra points of the A-Grade breakthrough, he settled on 29,060 points. His Mental and Will stats, both at 2,400, now looked puny in comparison.

Given that his body had already approached most Archons' in intensity before, claiming the title of the physically strongest cultivator in existence right now wasn't necessarily a stretch. He possessed the physical prowess of a small universe. His relative power to others was difficult to estimate.

Name: Jack Rust
Species: ???
Faction: Bare Fist Brotherhood (A)
Grade: A
Class: Paragon of Cultivation (Legendary)
Level: 550

Strength: 29,060
Dexterity: 29,060
Constitution: 29,060
Mental: 2,400
Will: 2,400

Dao Skills: Meteor Punch IV, Space Mastery IV, Death Mastery IV, Neutron Star Body IV, Black Hole IV, Iron Fist Style III, Brutalizing Aura III, Supernova III, Fist of Mortality III, Titan Taunt III, Immortal Commune I, Time Mastery IV, Life Mastery IV
Inner World size: ??? miles
Inner Cultivator Boundaries:
Highest: F-Grade
Average: F-Grade
Titles: Planetary Frontrunner (10), Planetary Torch-bearer (1), Ninth Ring Conqueror, Planetary Overlord (1), Grade Defier, Planet Destroyer, Challenger

Interestingly, his Class hadn't changed. He had no idea why. Instead, his species had gone from human to question marks. *Makes sense. Am I even human anymore?*

He sighed, looking over his numbers again.

"Well?" Brock asked. "How strong are you?"

"I'm honestly not sure," he replied. "I think I'm at least on par with anyone I've ever seen fight—Great Silver, Fiend King, Summer Noon. It's hard to tell until I actually battle an Archon or two."

Brock nodded. "I'm proud. I think my power is late to peak A-Grade."

"Which is great. We're both amazing, bro."

"Damn right!" Brock replied, pumping a fist.

"How many years did I spend in there?" Jack asked.

"Around ten since we arrived at this seventh floor. Fifteen since your duel declaration to Elder Hero, so another fifteen until you need to fight. We have time."

"Yes and no," Jack replied, shaking his head. "We do have time, but our cultivations have risen sharply. We have the power to fight at the highest level now. I think we should leave this place early and go find the Church. We can still cultivate until the war's climax if we're there, but it would be a shame to miss it."

"I had the same thought," Brock agreed. "With your power, bro, we don't need to be afraid of anything. Only the Gods are above you now."

"Well, I think there are many Archons more powerful than me as well, but sure. In any case, leaving this world won't be a problem. Do you want to check out the final room before we go?"

"The Will one?" Brock asked, looking at the middle door they'd never opened. "But we can't go in."

Jack smiled. He touched his palm on the door—a flash of purple light spread out, illuminating so-far invisible runes and erasing them. The door creaked open. "We're powerful now, Brock. We can do anything we want."

Brock laughed. "With you here, bro, I fear nothing. Let's check it out."

CHAPTER SEVENTY-TWO

NOTHING CREEPY ABOUT A STONE DADDY

THEY WALKED INTO THE THIRD ROOM, MORE OUT OF CURIOSITY THAN anything. To their surprise, it was almost empty. The only feature was a pedestal in the middle, around which was drawn an intricate magic circle. A single pebble rested on the pedestal. The moment they entered, the pebble cracked open to reveal a mouth, and its booming voice washed over them.

"Welcome, monsters! Experience my three trials of Will to—"

"*Franky?*" The Stone's voice echoed in Jack's mind. A moment later, surprise turned into joy. "*Franky! It's you!*"

Jack laughed. He summoned The Stone from his inner world, covering it in a bubble of stable space to save it from the pressure. "Franky!" The Stone exclaimed again as it appeared, falling to the ground and rolling toward the pedestal.

The pebble paused. "Stone?" it muttered, then again, "Stone!"

The pebble fell off its pedestal, and it too rolled on the ground, crashing into The Stone in what could charitably be described as a hug. All sense of awe was cut short as the two pebbles rolled around each other, talking excitedly and enjoying their reunion.

"And that's how I graduated Daddy's teachings! I then spent the last three hundred million years guarding this chamber," Franky said. His voice was slightly deeper than The Stone's. "It was a bit boring. I started talking to myself."

"Oh my gods, me too!" The Stone exclaimed. "I was riding that broken meteor shuttle for like a billion years!"

"At least you had a view," Franky said, spinning toward the brown walls around him.

"Yeah, well, all views grow tiring after a while," The Stone replied. "Oh! These are my friends, Jack and Brock. There's a turtle and a second Jack, too, but they're inside the first Jack."

"Like when Daddy inserted those devices into us to measure our properties?"

"Kind of!"

"It really isn't," Jack said. "Hi, Franky. Nice to meet you."

"Very nice to meet you too! Thank you for taking care of my sibling."

"It was mostly me taking care of them," The Stone said, then lowered its voice to a whisper—which Jack could still hear, "You can't imagine how stupid kids can be. They'd have died a hundred times over if not for me. They don't even know the arts, can you believe that?"

"Ah, yes, the folly of youth," Franky replied all too sagely.

"We're still here," Jack reminded them. Both stones hopped in surprise, rising a few inches off the ground. Franky cried out as if suddenly remembering something.

"Oh no, my speech!" he exclaimed. "I've been practicing for half a billion years, I must get it right!" He quickly rolled back to his pedestal, then hopped up on it. "Ahem." He cleared his non-existent throat. "Welcome, monsters! Experience my three trials of Will to—"

"We're kind of getting ready to go," Jack tried to interrupt politely. "We were thinking if you wanted to come with us?"

"I have prepared this speech for half a billion years. Nobody goes anywhere until I say it at least once."

"...Fine," Jack replied. Franky's voice boomed again.

"Welcome, monsters! Experience my three trials of Will to sharpen your willpower and earn the qualifications to pursue the peak of Dao. These trials have been meticulously forged by our creators and ancestors, the Gods of the universe, so first you must kowtow eleven times in respect!"

"Very nice speech, Franky," Jack said, clapping.

Brock agreed. "I can tell you practiced it. Sent shivers down my spine."

"Really?" Franky exclaimed. "Wait, I mean, you must kowtow eleven times to receive my trials!"

"How long do these trials take?" Jack asked.

"A hundred years each."

"Yeah, we don't have time for that unfortunately."

Franky's mood dropped like a sailor who couldn't swim.

"But we can return later!" Jack continued, and the pebble perked up again.

"You promise?"

"I promise."

"Yay! I mean, that's excellent, young monster. You have permission to postpone the three trials of Will."

"See?" The Stone said, hopping up and down in excitement. "I told you they're great!"

"They do seem... delectable," Franky answered, trying really hard to maintain his imposing facade. "So, um, you mentioned following you somewhere?"

"That's right," Jack said. "We're about to leave this place and the Space Monster World to join a war going on outside. We'll also check on your father in the Canal below. Last we saw of him, he was fighting an Overlord."

"Daddy is also an Overlord," Franky replied with pride. "He will win, I know it!"

"I'm beginning to hope so as well, though the other guy wasn't bad either."

"Then what are we waiting for? Let's go!" Franky exclaimed. He fell down, rolled next to The Stone, then both of them turned into rays of light which shot into Jack's abdomen.

"...That was weird," Jack said. "I didn't let them in."

Brock shrugged. "Talking stones. Anyway. We're going?"

"Yeah."

They left the now-empty Will chamber behind. All treasures in the Cultivation chamber had been used up by Jack's back-to-back breakthroughs, but the manuals of the Dao room remained. "We should borrow these," Jack said. "After the Crusade, we can return them."

"Yes," Brock agreed. "We'll ask for Stone Daddy Bro's permission as well, if he's still alive. They're his."

"Of course. But please, can you not call him that?"

"Why?"

"It's creepy."

"Nothing creepy about a stone daddy."

The two stocked up on top-level cultivation manuals, emptying the third room as well. Only the decorations were left behind, forming a neat pile in a corner of the room. They could have rearranged them, but the Stone Scholar would probably want to do that himself, if he still lived.

Then, Jack and Brock dove into the hole in the ground and let themselves fall. Gravity took the reins. They accelerated far faster than normal, becoming a pair of meteors which crashed through the twelve layers of clouds. Finally, darkness appeared below them, and they seared right through. Nothing showed up to obstruct them. In moments, they'd reached the Dark Canal again, and both stopped their ascent right on the pyramid's top, a shockwave spreading widely from their halted momentum.

It wasn't empty.

Two people sat cross-legged, meditating side by side. Great Silver and the Stone Scholar, both looking healthy. Their eyes snapped open as Jack and Brock appeared.

"You're reckless," Great Silver said. "Your disguise broke, yet you still came here instead of trying to run away."

"I prefer to call it daring," Jack replied with a smile. He landed smoothly on the pyramid's ceiling, Brock right behind him.

"Daddy!" two voices rang out as The Stone and Franky leapt out of Jack's body and into the Stone Scholar's embrace. He caught them both in confusion. "Franky? What are you doing here?" he exclaimed. "And... Stone! You returned!"

"That's right! Jack and Brock are my friends, they brought me here."

The Stone Scholar looked at Jack again, his motionless stone eyes betraying nothing. He rose to his feet, placing both stones in his pocket. They screamed like children going down the slide. "Change of plans, Overlord," he said. "I will not stay neutral. These people brought back my wayward child—if you decide to kill them, I will battle you to the death."

Great Silver didn't reply immediately. His draconic eyes were glued on Jack's abdomen, from where the two stones had jumped out. He clearly sensed something was wrong, yet couldn't quite place it.

Finally, he withdrew his gaze, turning it to the Stone Scholar. "These people took advantage of Fiend King's moment of weakness to ruin him. As this world's sole remaining Overlord, I hold the right to judge their fate. If you stand against me, Scholar, then you may also suffer. You can fight me, but not my army."

Jack frowned, then spread his perception much farther than he'd previously been able to. A dozen Autarchs were arrayed on the stone island beyond the pyramid. The Grand Elders of both Overlord factions were present, both at the peak A-Grade, flanked by a gathering of Elders of various levels. They were an imposing force. Clearly, they had ways to know Fiend King had perished, and they expected Jack and Brock's arrival. The dead Overlord's underlings now followed Great Silver.

If Jack had only broken into the A-Grade, he couldn't have

handled this gathering of enemies. Even if the Stone Scholar held back Great Silver, they'd still be hard-pressed to escape. Now, however, things were different. Jack hadn't just reached the A-Grade—he'd stepped into a whole new realm.

He smiled.

The Stone Scholar snorted. "I've already stated my intentions, Great Silver. Do you really want to make me your enemy?"

"I haven't decided yet. If I do want to kill them, however, you cannot stop me."

"Then I guess we have to find out."

"That won't be necessary," Jack said, suddenly appearing between the two Overlords. They recoiled, eyes wide open in surprise. They hadn't sensed his teleportation despite being an entire large realm over him. This should have been impossible.

Jack took in the stunned, wary looks of both Overlords. He smiled. "Thank you for the offer, Stone Scholar, but your assistance isn't needed." He then turned to Great Silver, speaking from barely a few feet away. "You, all those Elders, all the forces of the Space Monster World... I don't need any help. I can kill all of you by myself."

A wind of darkness blew, gently crossing the silence. No one spoke for a moment. *I can kill all of you by myself.* Jack's words were too stunning, his proclamation too great, his challenge too arrogant. Great Silver locked eyes with him. Jack saw the changes in his gaze. The dragon realized he couldn't read Jack's aura, realized he couldn't measure his true depth.

Great Silver's gaze softened, and for a moment, he seemed so old.

"Are you really as powerful as you say?" he asked.

Jack smiled. The Overlords, the Elders, the disciples, every single eye was glued on him. "See for yourself," he said, releasing his aura. In that moment, he became the center of the world. A gentle ripple spread from him, not oppressive in the slightest, but awe-inspiring as if gazing at a God. Everyone froze in shock.

It wasn't only Jack's aura, which overwhelmed even Great

Silver's. His body became momentarily transparent. An entire universe was revealed within—planets of organs, a sun for a heart, rivers of stars as blood, and bones of glowing light. The darkness of the Dark Canal parted, receding from Jack as if touching anathema, and a wave of worship spread around him, extending for untold miles.

Jack recovered his aura, hiding it completely again. He didn't need it anymore. His calm smile had never faltered, yet everyone around him was stunned. Great Silver shivered. In the face of Jack's divinity, the draconic majesty he took such pride in was nothing but a party trick.

"Who are you?" he whispered.

"I'm Jack Rust," Jack replied. "My body is a universe, and I am a fist." He walked right up to Great Silver, who took a step backward instinctively. "You were looking for the power to contest the Immortals, a hope to rise against them," Jack declared calmly. "I am that hope. You have seen what I am, what I can do. Stand by my side, Great Silver, and lead all monsters to war for me. The Immortals will destroy all of us sooner or later. Only together can we resist. Join the battle."

Monsters respected strength. Great Silver didn't know how his own power measured against Jack's, only that Jack had stepped into a cultivation realm nobody had heard of before. He felt like an idiot. The doors to the realm above A-Grade, the ones he'd been trying to break open for millions of years, simply lay on a different path. They were on a junction he'd already walked past. He understood now why he'd never succeeded, and that it was impossible for an Archon, any Archon, to advance ever again.

But not to Jack Rust. His road... was limitless.

Great Silver bent his front legs, bowing to Jack. The Elders all around were shocked anew, but they understood. They bowed in turn. So did the Stone Scholar, motivated by instincts deeper than he thought he possessed. Every head besides Brock's was bowed at Jack.

"You are not a monster like us, but we revere strength above all,"

Great Silver said, evidently emotional. "Please, allow this old dragon to pledge his life to you. I will follow you to the end of the world, and so will all the monsters under my command. As the sole Overlord of the Space Monster World, I offer you our complete and unquestionable allegiance."

Jack smiled. He reached down to raise Great Silver from his bow. "I don't need anyone's allegiance. How about we become allies?"

The dragon shivered again. "I could do that," he replied. Then, as if struck by some ancient instinct, he turned to the sky and roared, spreading his wings to create gales. All monsters around him roared as well, their voices joined in one, unified cry which parted the darkness and reached the heavens.

"To war!" Great Silver roared.

"To war!" everyone else replied, and right then, it felt like the entire Space Monster World was with them.

Jack smiled as he turned to the Stone Scholar. His question went unspoken.

"I cannot join," the Scholar said. "My mission is to guard the Hall of Trials' seventh floor. I cannot leave. Besides, I would be useless—my power deteriorates the farther away I get from the Hall."

Jack nodded. "That's fine. I can take you back up there in a bit. The Fiend King tore down all the decorations, but I've left them all back so you can rearrange them. It could be a nice pastime."

"Thank you!" the Stone Scholar exclaimed. "And, if I may ask for one more thing..." He reached into his pockets, removing both The Stone and Franky. "Can you take my children along? I cannot leave, but they can... and a life following you will be much more fulfilling than anything I could offer them."

Jack smiled sadly. "Yes."

"Thank you..." the Scholar said, his voice breaking despite being made of stone. The two stones protested, but he took them aside to speak to them.

"Oh my Gods, oh my Gods!" Fiend Prince exclaimed from the side—the disciple group was also present, just insignificant compared to all those Elders. "We're going into the outside world, this is so exciting! Hey, Jack—does this mean I can become your disciple?"

Jack laughed. "Don't you mind that I killed your father?"

"He died because he was weak. I'm sad about it, of course, but there wasn't much love between us. It'll pass."

Jack nodded, then shook his head in disbelief. In truth, Fiend Prince had negligible chances to follow in Jack's footsteps. His talent wasn't high enough, at least not right now.

He liked this guy though, and could help him along. Besides, he might have a chance if they found a way to perfect his inner world despite lacking a tenth Dao Fruit. He'd look for such an alternative anyway to help Brock, who certainly possessed the potential to walk the same road as Jack.

Actually, Brock would be fine either way. Reverting one's cultivation to the B-Grade and re-trying the breakthrough was possible. Older cultivators wouldn't be able to do it, as their potential had already run out, but it would be easy for Brock. Once they had a few spare years, Jack was confident Brock would achieve his own special realm, equal to Jack's Universe of the Body.

Fiend Prince would struggle in comparison, but he just looked so damn eager.

"Whatever," he said, laughing. "Yeah, sure. You can become my first disciple."

The monster shone like a beacon of joy. He jumped into the air and pumped his fist. "Alright!"

CHAPTER SEVENTY-THREE

SAFE TIME TO FAIL

A WOMAN STALKED THROUGH THE GRASS. SHE LOOKED TO BE IN HER EARLY twenties, with dark skin, darker hair, and eyes the color of amber. Her lithe body was covered in green leather armor, painted with yellow splashes to blend into the terrain, while her hands held a flexible spear.

Ebele's ears twitched. She fell to the ground, crawling the last few feet. A thick tree stood in front of her. She grabbed the bark and peeked from its side, catching the glint of metal. Vertical bars sandwiched by wood. Cages. Inside which a collection of pink boars oinked in distress.

Her eyes narrowed. "Damn," she spat a whisper.

The creatures of this forest were highly desired as both pets and materials. However, since this was Academy territory, no outsiders could enter. Stealing animals was illegal even if they could. The Academy strived to maintain a healthy ecosystem, promotion of biodiversity, and smooth allocation of differently-powered beasts to facilitate the safe and timely training of its students, who could wander this forest freely.

Some of these students were assholes. The ones Ebele faced now, laughing with greed as they counted the number of cages over and over, were one such group of people. Poachers.

Three, four... she counted. I can probably take them.

She stepped out from behind the cage. The others spotted her instantly, shooting to alertness. "Who's there?" they asked.

"The forest," she replied. "Coming to reclaim its own."

As she stepped into a column of light piercing the foliage, the students' faces went from panic, to relief, to wariness. "Ebele Rust," one of them said with a frown. "We want no trouble with you."

"Oh, but I do. Poaching is a serious offense—you face anywhere from disciplinary action to direct expulsion and imprisonment. Release the pinkoars and follow me to the Enforcement Hall immediately."

The students glanced at each other, realizing they outnumbered her four to one. "No," they said.

"Yeah. Thought as much." She flourished her spear, the tip cutting a smooth path through the air. "Prepare to suffer."

Her opponents were full of tension, but they didn't panic. No student of the Academy was a weakling. They fanned out, brandishing their own weapons as they surrounded her. The pink boars watched with hope.

"You're a Foundation cultivator, just like us," one of the four disciples said. "Don't think you'll beat us just because you carry your father's name."

"Of course not. I'll beat you because you're honorless, low-life thieves, and I'm this year's first-ranked disciple."

Another student snorted, his features contorted in rage. The blue cloak he wore—standard student uniform—rose to an unseen gale, the stars painted on it almost dancing. "Get off your high horse. I need this money."

"Sure you do. To fuel your coredust addiction?"

"To take my family out of the Evergrove slums."

Ebele shook her head. "I sympathize, I really do. However, torturing and killing innocent creatures is never okay. Surrender, and

I swear I'll give you the money to help your family—after I turn you in."

"Shut up! Someone like you has no place speaking here!" the student shouted, lunging. His rapier stabbed straight for Ebele's abdomen. Her brows narrowed dangerously. No student would dare kill another—especially inside Academy grounds—but a serious injury here would cost her weeks of cultivation.

She twirled, letting the rapier scratch her armor to make some distance. Her spear stabbed out. It broke through the opponent's guard in a single strike.

Unfortunately, he wasn't alone. The other three disciples coordinated well, and their flurry of blows fell on Ebele, forcing her back. She stabbed and dodged. The tip of her spear entered someone's forearm, while its body broke a knee—both injuries could be easily healed.

She ducked under a club and jumped back to avoid a spray of poison. A nunchaku crashed into her head from behind. All her body tempering couldn't save her from such a blow—she recoiled, almost falling forward, and was beset by four people at once. Her Dao of Heroism erupted, pushing them back and giving her a moment's respite to reposition, but they still snuck a hit at her lower back. She gritted her teeth.

"What's going on here?" a voice asked. Ebele glanced over, filled with hope, only to have it instantly demolished. The new arrivals were two students holding a squealing pinkoar upside down. As they scanned the situation, letting the pinkoar drop and escape to pull their own weapons. They turned them to Ebele.

"There were more of you," she said sourly. "Of course."

"Should have done your research, Ebele," a disciple said. "Now get fucked."

Six people attacked her at once. All were close to the late F-Grade. That was how the old-timers—those who'd been adults when the System arrived—called the first realm. The younger generation of cultivators, who started their journey outside System space, preferred to call this realm Foundation Establishment.

Ebele was slightly higher-leveled than them. She was far stronger than each, but against six talented people, there was little she could do. Even her newfound Dao was of limited use. They left her sprawled on the forest floor, groaning and bleeding, with a healing potion placed far enough away that she'd need some time to reach it.

"You're lucky your father is who he is," one of the disciples said as he spat on her. "Otherwise, you wouldn't even get the potion."

Killing other disciples was an absolute taboo in the Academy—the enforcers had ways to know. Dying by yourself in the forest was a different story, but not when it came to the daughter of Jack Rust. If anything happened to her, D-Grades would get involved, and the truth would come out instantly. These disciples couldn't afford to cause any real damage even if they knew she'd tell on them.

The group ran away with the cages in tow, the squeals of pinkoars reaching Ebele for some time still. It took her a while to be able to move. When she finally reached the healing potion and gulped it down, the poacher students were long gone. She smashed a fist against a tree, breaking her hand. She relished in the pain. In her opinion, it was well deserved.

"I must get stronger," she said through gritted teeth. "And smarter. I should have waited to see if they had more people. If this was a real battle, I'd be dead."

Retrospection didn't lighten her self-blame. She stayed on the forest floor for a while, lamenting her failure, apologizing to the creatures she'd failed to save. She'd inform the Enforcement Hall, of course, but without proof, all these students would get was monitoring from the school authorities. It would stop them from poaching, but they wouldn't get expelled.

"Dammit," she said, bruising her other hand against the ground. Tears left her eyes. "Damn!"

If one looked at this forest from above, they'd find it fist-shaped.

Thin clouds interspersed the blue sky. Currently, far higher than where Ebele could see, two people stood on a pair of little clouds. One was a woman in flowing red robes, her eyes shimmering with rage. The other was a shirtless man with his aura fully withdrawn—yet, even like this, he commanded the respect of the elements.

"I don't believe you," Vivi said. "Those guys just beat up your daughter. Are you really just going to stand there!"

"Ebele needs tempering," Jack's clone replied calmly. "A bit of bruising is nothing. If I take away this lesson from her, she might make the same mistakes in the future, when I'm not there to watch over her, and then she'll suffer for real."

"She's a child!"

"Which is the perfect time to fail and learn."

"She's lying on the ground! She's crying!"

"She'll be fine," Jack insisted. "Look at her eyes. See how they're clear? She's healthily frustrated, that's all. All that bothers her is her failure, not the pain. She experienced far worse when she insisted on diving into the Ice Pond when she was younger. This is nothing to her."

Vivi crossed her arms. "I don't believe you, Jack Rust."

"This is necessary. Trust me. The world is harsh, so we must be as well. That said..." His eyes turned to the ground again, looking slightly to the side of Ebele, where six disciples were hurrying through the forest with cages in tow. A few of them were injured.

Jack snapped his fingers, and the squealing pinkoars disappeared, teleported back to their nests. The disciples took a few moments to notice. When they did, their eyes went wide, and they fell to their knees, looking around and at the sky. Jack ignored them completely. A few moments later, the disciples bolted away at top speed, letting the injured fall behind.

Jack shook his head. "We can't play gods, Vivi. If we smother the world below us, it will grow weak, and weakness brings pain and sin. The same goes for our children. Since Ebele is determined on entering the cultivation world, we should encourage safe failures like this one, because only they can give her the lessons she needs to survive later in life. I could tell her to plan for hidden enemies a thousand times, but this single day will teach her the lesson far better than I ever could. If it seems harsh, blame her, not me—I'm just preparing her for the road she chose."

Vivi snorted. "Then why did you save the pinkoars, if we can't play gods?"

"That was just payment. I prevented some enforcers from reaching the area before, so I had to make up for it."

Vivi tried to remain angry, sighing instead. "Do you promise you love her?"

"More than anything in the world," Jack replied, his gaze growing distant. "I would destroy the galaxy before I let anything happen to my daughter. However, I won't always be by her side. That's not how life works. She needs to become strong. I just... want her to be happy..."

Vivi smiled, hugging him tightly. Her anger was gone. She was a cultivator, too—she understood the importance of personal strength, as well as the fact that a little bit of pain was nothing to the tempered mind. "For the ruler of a galaxy, you're pretty soft," she whispered.

"Really? I thought you said I was mean."

"That, too."

He laughed, then looked down. "Ebele is reaching the Academy gates. The danger is over. Wanna go prepare dinner?"

"No. I want to pay her a visit and see how she's doing."

"You know she doesn't like us appearing uninvited."

"I don't care. I'm her mother, I just saw her receive a painful lesson, and I want to make sure she's okay."

Jack chuckled. "Fine. Just send her a message we'll be visiting in an hour, if she's free."

"...I can do that."

"You know I love parenting with you, right?"

"I love it too. But you can be so stubborn sometimes."

"That makes two of us."

They kissed. "What about your other body, anyway?" Vivi asked. "It's been gone for fifteen years now. Any news?"

"No," Jack replied. "I get a vague sensation from my inner world. Something happened. Something major. I suspect we'll be returning to this world soon, and then I get to beat the crap out of Elder Hero. Can't let him be a bad role model for Ebele. They do share a Dao—for now."

Vivi laughed. "I'm sure she'd love to hear this."

The two teleported away, and the sky remained peaceful, as it always was.

CHAPTER SEVENTY-FOUR
RETURN WITH A BANG

Bobo leaned over his starship's door to peek at the portal to the Space Monster World. It had been a while since lightning stopped falling. The portal was slowly repairing itself—its defenses had held—but the surrounding space was much worse off. All ambient Dao had been sucked dry for endless light-years around it. The heavenly tribulation must have been cataclysmic.

Thankfully, that wasn't anything Bobo needed to worry about. He was just a little B-Grade scout of the Church, sent here to make sure the portal was alright.

It is, he confirmed. Time to return. Good job, Bobo.

"Halt!" a voice crossed space. "In the name of the Immortals, put your weapons down and walk over slowly!"

Bobo froze mid-step. He turned to find a bulky man hovering behind him. An early A-Grade.

I'm so dead.

Bobo had no backup. It was just him in one of the lightest starships available. If he could get inside and close the door, he'd be safe, but would the enemy A-Grade give him the chance?

Cutting costs my ass, he fumed inwardly. The Immortals can afford A-Grade scouts, so why did the Church send me!

He debated surrendering. Couldn't be worse than instant death. Before he could reply, however, a purple missile smashed into the side of the enemy A-Grade's head, taking it clean off his shoulders. Body and head exploded, leaving only a streaking purple line which raced for the end of the universe. Bobo gasped, then turned to look at its source.

The portal? he wondered. No. Is someone there? What's that?

The slowly-rotating portal to the Space Monster World flared to life. A majestic silver dragon rode out, opening its giant jaws to roar at the heavens. The sound whisked Bobo's soul out of his body, spun it around a couple times, then hastily crammed it back in.

Heavens! he thought, clutching his chest. *An Archon!*

Before he could comprehend what he saw, more people emerged. An entire army headed by A-Grades, with every soldier a B-Grade. The weakest of them were at Bobo's level, and there were even peak A-Grades in the mix. Before long, hundreds of space monsters had exited the portal, forming a small but elite army which could easily conquer galaxies.

The monsters are invading! Bobo thought with terror, but he didn't dare move. Even from a distance, that silver dragon could kill him instantly. He had no way to let the Church know either.

Just before he fell into despair, he spied two more forms. He hadn't noticed them at first, too small compared to the dragon they stood beside. A man and a brorilla, but not just any man, and not just any brorilla. Those were Jack Rust and Brock! The heroes of the Church!

Jack Rust glanced over, then reappeared in front of Bobo in a mockery of the distance between them. "Hi. I'm Jack. You're with the Church, yes?"

"I am," Bobo replied as if in a dream.

"Perfect. Can you let them know Jack and Brock returned? The space monsters will fight on our side from now on." He glanced behind Bobo. His face brightened. "Is that snacks I see in your ship? Nice! I hope you don't mind if I enjoy a couple while you tell me what happened in the last fifteen years."

News of Jack's return, as well as the monsters joining the war, spread like wildfire. All across the scattered Church forces, A-Grades rejoiced, B-Grades celebrated. Sovereign Heavenly Spoon laughed when he heard the news. "I knew it!" he shouted. "That guy's a cockroach—he can't be killed!"

"I'm happy they're back," Min Ling said with a warm smile. "We need every help we can get. I wonder how they convinced the space monsters."

"Knowing them, they probably bebro'd them."

"That's not a word."

"You'd be surprised."

In another part of the galaxy, Elder Hero clutched a transmission stone, crumbling it to dust in his grip. "You dare return... Fine. Come. No matter how they worship you, no matter what allies you find, you are nothing but a stepping stone on my path to glory. Your reputation will feed into mine."

He then glanced in front of him, where a massive sphere floated, filled with endless divine power. He grinned. "Now more than ever, your chances of victory... are zero!"

As for the New Cathedral, they accepted the news with all the joy one would expect. People took to the streets dancing. The celebrity campaign of Jack and Brock had died down in the last few years, but people still remembered him standing against an entire faction by himself, defying the heavens, rising above expectations. That was a true warrior, a true hero. The hope he'd carved in their hearts was reignited, memories of years past resurfacing.

The face of the Church was back, with new allies, and he was stronger than ever!

The Arch Priestess smiled as she read the piece of paper passed to her. "It's your disciple again, Boatman," she said from behind her veil. "He somehow convinced the monsters to fight for us."

Elder Boatman smiled under his hood. "Jack's progress has always been staggering. After fifteen years and such a grand show of his return, I suspect that his strength... will surprise us all!"

"Convene the Archon Council," the Arch Priestess commanded. "The arrival of the monsters changes our plans. We need to strategize."

Several A-Grades present rushed off to convey her orders.

"Should we invite Jack Rust as well?" a man asked. He sat leisurely on a chair, wearing a form-fitting yellow uniform with a red cape. His bald head reflected the lamplight.

The Arch Priestess thought about it, smiling with amusement. "As great as his contributions, he's not an Archon yet."

The bald man and Boatman exchanged glances.

As Jack descended toward the New Cathedral, the scene was vastly different than the last time he'd been here. He'd left in secrecy but arrived in full public view.

People crowded the streets. Most shouted. Some held banners spelling out "Welcome home, big bro!", "We believe in you!" and other similar slogans. A few people even raised Brock plushies into the air. Seeing that, Jack did a double take, finding many people wearing his and Brock's shirts amongst the crowd.

"Those things lasted fifteen years. Looks like they didn't skimp on the materials," he said.

"We're famous," Brock said, eyeing the crowds as their starship landed. "So many little bros."

"I think they're counted in the millions by now, Brock. Not just here, but everywhere in the universe."

"Not millions. Billions."

Jack turned around, shocked, but Brock had already walked ahead. He exited the starship with a hand held high, waving at the crowds, and Jack followed. The cheers were deafening. He consciously restrained his aura, lest these people actually considered him a god.

Which I am, actually. Sort of.

A person waited for them a few steps ahead. Their body was covered by a long cloak, while a scythe hung behind their back. Jack smiled and bowed. "Master," he said.

"No need for honorifics," Elder Boatman replied. "I suspect you've already surpassed me, or close. A-Grade, huh? Must have been quite a trip."

"You could call it that. The monsters are almost recreationally murderous."

"Sup, Grandpa Dead," Brock said.

A smile tugged at Boatman's lips. "Follow me. I know you want to sit here and enjoy the crowds, but we have things to talk about."

"What things?"

"Mostly about the space monsters. The Arch Priestess is hosting an Archon Council in a bit, where I represent you, so I'd like to know everything I can about them."

Jack raised a brow. "Why can't we represent ourselves?"

"You're not Archons."

"Neither are you."

"Yes, but I'm old and prestigious. It comes with perks."

Jack chuckled. "Brock and I will be there," he said. Boatman gave him a deep glance but didn't disagree.

"In that case," he said, "just tell me about your trip."

"It was fun. Somewhat risky, too, but nothing we couldn't handle."

They didn't rush through the city. Crowds still hollered around them. Jack told Boatman all about their trip, minus the most shocking details, while Brock talked about the propensity of space monsters towards brohood.

"Their aggressiveness is misguided," he claimed. "Brohood can fill the gap just as well."

"What about your side, Master?" Jack asked. "What happened while we were gone?"

"Not too many things, but all of great importance. The Old Gods returned, did you hear that?"

Jack nodded. "The scout who brought us over mentioned something, but he didn't know the details."

"Naturally. They arrived shortly after you left, but they—"

He paused as they passed under a particularly crowded bridge. The shouts of the crowd still deafening. Jack and Brock smiled and waved.

"They arrived in the midst of a decisive battle," Boatman continued. "I was there too, actually. Fighting Elder Hero. He would have killed me if the Gods were even a little late."

"Hero would have killed you?"

"Yes," Boatman replied, giving Jack a worried gaze. "I couldn't stop him, disciple. I'm sorry. He was already that strong over ten years ago. I shudder to think what he'll be like when you duel him."

"That's not what I meant," Jack replied calmly. "He dared touch you, my master and benefactor. I will make sure to crush him before I kill him."

Boatman paused, looking squarely at Jack. He kept his aura hidden, only revealing he'd reached the A-Grade, but his confidence was not something which could be mistaken.

"I hope you do," Elder Boatman replied, resuming walking. "After that battle—in which Hero escaped, by the way—the Gods ignored everything and charged at the Immortal section of this galaxy. Our armies didn't have time to follow. There was no preparation, no plan, just an attempt to stampede."

"Sounds about right," Jack said. "I did run into some clones of them in the Space Monster World, and they seemed decent, but they told me the real bodies are super arrogant."

"You met their clones? Where are they?"

"I couldn't free them yet, sadly."

"That's unfortunate."

"What about the Gods' attack on the Immortals?"

"They went in carelessly and paid for it. They returned injured, and with a casualty. The God of Mass has died."

That gave Jack pause. "A God died?"

"Nobody expected it. We didn't even know Gods could be killed."

"Who got him?" Jack asked. "The Heaven Immortal?"

"Probably. We don't know what happened exactly—the Gods won't say—but word amongst the Immortal armies is that Hero delivered the final blow. He's called the God Killer now. If he got any benefits from that, I dread to think about his current power level."

Jack shook his head. "It doesn't matter. How did the rest of the Gods take it?"

"Better than expected. They holed up somewhere to recover and told us to prepare for a final battle in a few years—currently, that day is almost upon us. With the Church's assistance, they're confident they can defeat the Immortals."

"Right. And we believe that?"

Boatman smiled. "No."

They'd reached the doors of the main temple. The wooden building towered over them, a smooth fusion of nature and architecture, vines crawling up its walls, the wood still alive. Boatman parted the doors just enough to pass, then shut them behind him. The crowd's cheers echoed muffled.

"Jack! Brock!" came a familiar voice. They turned over to find Sovereign Heavenly Spoon and Min Ling sitting on the pews.

"Hey, guys!" Jack replied, smile wide. Seeing them brought back memories. He was also pleasantly surprised to find they'd gotten stronger—Spoon was at the early A-Grade, while Min Ling had reached the peak B-Grade.

The woman jumped off the pew, rushing over to hug both of them. "You sure took your time," she complained sweetly. "We were worried about you."

"Some things can't be rushed." Jack laughed. "Have you been well?"

"Better than I want to admit. War is a terrible place, but it's the perfect training ground for us. I'm ashamed to admit I don't hate it."

"But you hate its consequences."

"Of course."

Jack nodded at her words. Brock stepped up, inspecting Min Ling and Heavenly Spoon with narrowed eyes. "Nice Daos. You bros are strong."

"Comes with the constant battling," Spoon replied. "We were actually on a mission, but they recalled us at the news of your arrival. I don't know why. Most importantly, now that you're here... How about a little sparring?"

Jack gazed at the sovereign. His aura had changed. From an aloof young man, he'd transitioned to a more somber presence. Something had happened to him... but, alas, that was the nature of war. Bad things happened to a lot of people.

"I'm afraid that ship has sailed," Jack said. "I'm sorry to say it, but you wouldn't stand a chance against either of us."

"Are you sure? I can fight a small realm above my own."

"We can fight several. Trust me. Not a chance."

Spoon didn't seem too disappointed. "I kind of expected that. There was probably a time when we'd be a good match, but, as you said, that ship has sailed. Happens."

Boatman coughed discreetly. Jack smiled at his friends. "Brock and I must go," he said, "but I'd love to catch up. How about we gather everyone and drink some wine tonight? I have some other friends to introduce to you guys."

"The monsters?" Min Ling replied, her gaze fiery. "Sure thing, Jack. It's a date."

He smiled at her, then he and Brock followed Boatman up the

spiral stairs. Their ascent was silent. Soon after, they reached the top of the Cathedral, where Boatman opened a set of wooden doors. A set of heavy presences blew over Jack and Brock. There were several people inside, all radiating the aura of Archons. It was the most oppressive room they'd ever entered.

"Hey, everybody," Jack said, calmly walking into their pressure. "It's been a while."

CHAPTER SEVENTY-FIVE

FINAL WAR COUNCIL

THOSE GATHERED EACH REACTED DIFFERENTLY TO HIS AND BROCK'S calmness. The Arch Priestess raised a brow. A bald man in a tight yellow uniform gave an intrigued half-smile—he seemed oddly familiar—while a completely naked, stunningly beautiful woman nodded in appreciation. Little clouds covered her private areas. In a corner, Great Silver gave them a deep nod—the monster Overlord had teleported in instead of parading to avoid spooking the crowds.

"Welcome," the Arch Priestess said. "I thought I instructed Elder Boatman to represent you in this council."

"You did, but given it was a stupid instruction, I chose to ignore it," Jack said lightly.

"Oho. You're confident. Think you have the right to participate in a council of Archons?"

She and Jack were only lightly jesting. Great Silver, however, growled with displeasure. "We follow Jack Rust, not the Church. If he doesn't participate, neither do I."

Every other Archon present raised a brow. The meaning of Great Silver's words was clear—he placed Jack above himself. For an Archon to do that was unheard of.

The bald man sitting in the corner laughed. "I don't mind this. However, if you want a seat at the table of Archons, you must prove yourself worthy."

Before Jack could respond, a heavy aura fell on him. The tiles cracked underfoot. It was clear this Archon was going all-out to suppress Jack with his aura—any weaker A-Grade would have already collapsed. Elder Boatman gasped before realizing Jack was unbothered.

Jack, under the pressure of this aura cascade, remained perfectly calm, his hands crossed in front of his chest and his face sporting a slight smile. "Are you done?" he asked.

The bald man was aghast, leaning forward to inspect Jack more closely. "I guess I am," he said, ready to retrieve his aura. Jack wouldn't let him.

"Good," Jack said. "My turn."

The world went still. Every Archon in the room froze, as if stared at by a giant, ancient beast. Jack's aura came as a subtle but steady breeze, blowing everyone into a new world of possibilities. For a moment, they saw through his body—planets for organs, a sun for a heart, rivers of stars for blood. Divine majesty filled the room, and everyone was beset with an instinctive urge to bow and worship. Yet, his aura was gentle, pushing everyone up instead of suppressing them.

Except for the man who'd tested Jack. He didn't experience it as a gentle breeze, but as a cascading waterfall. Jack's aura completely blew back his own, flipping it as easily as one would a cup, then descended on the man and smashed him into the floor. As he'd been leaning forward, he was pressed face-down, his nose shattering the tiles.

"One Fist!" the Arch Priestess shouted.

"Ah, I apologize for the disrespect, senior, but I believe you started it," Jack said.

As everyone was stunned, muffled sounds escaped the face

buried in the floor. Jack withdrew his aura—pressing him down like that was a matter of surprise, not force—and the Archon stood. Only now did everyone realize he was laughing. "Good, very good!" he said jovially. "Don't worry about it, Jack! It was my fault for testing you. I really shouldn't have, but I couldn't help wanting to experience the power of the Church's hero!"

Jack's smile turned genuine. He bowed slightly, withdrawing his aura completely. "It was no problem at all, senior. I went too far myself. Please accept my apology."

"Don't mention it. If you want to apologize, why don't you tell us about that thing you got going on?" the man replied, gesturing all over Jack's body. "I must admit I'm shocked!"

So was everyone else. Jack's aura matched theirs in quantity but far overwhelmed them in quality. Suddenly, the auras they subtly exuded before were nothing but jokes. They were saints flexing before a God. Jack's cultivation was one unified realm, and in comparison, theirs was just unremarkable.

Boatman was the most shocked of all. Jack had completely restrained his aura on the way, so this was the first time he'd sensed it. "How?" he croaked out. The energy which came from his disciple eclipsed his own so hard it wasn't even funny.

"I was lucky enough to achieve a complete breakthrough," Jack explained calmly. "I call this state the Universe of the Body. I believe it will let me break past the A-Grade in the future."

He didn't need to say it. Every Archon in the room knew instinctively that Jack had conquered the boundary they'd struggled their whole lives to reach. It was the same reaction Great Silver had shown—an instinctive sense of inferiority. The dragon himself hid a smug smile as he saw the other Archons' reactions. "You don't see this every day," he whispered.

"Can I ask," said the naked woman, her voice hesitant, "how did you achieve such a thing?"

It was the question burning everyone's mind. If Jack held the secret to advancing beyond the Archon realm, who cared about the war? This was the greatest revelation of the universe!

Unfortunately, he only shook his head. "I'm sorry to be the bearer of bad news. The Universe of the Body is meant for Physical cultivators. There could be other paths besides it, but for this one, the cultivator must start preparing from the C-Grade to achieve it. B-Grade at the very minimum. Anyone at the A-Grade has already lost their chance unless they reverse their cultivation, and even then, it's a long shot. For Archons already advanced in age, I'm afraid it is impossible..."

The Archons exchanged disappointed glances. Some of them may have had the talent to pursue a higher realm in their youth, but since they didn't know how, they'd lost their only chance. Jack saw the dream crushed in their eyes, but there was nothing he could do to help.

At least, they recovered admirably.

"It's a shame," the bald man said. "We were born just a little too early... At least, this lets us sacrifice our lives in this war without regrets. Congratulations, Jack Rust. You have opened a whole new avenue for the cultivation world."

Jack nodded in thanks.

"The two of us share a common origin, by the way," the man continued, a smile forming to cover his sadness. "My title is Archon One Fist. I also come from the Milky Way galaxy. I was one of the founders of the Exploding Sun—I've been told you studied in my faction?"

Jack's eyes flashed with understanding. That was why this man seemed familiar! How could he not realize it earlier?

He laughed out loud. "Not just that!" Jack said. "You were in my very first Dao Vision! I've followed your footsteps for a good part of my cultivation journey!"

"Really?" One Fist raised a brow. "It's my great honor—one you repaid in full by protecting my little faction. I wanted to rush over as soon as I heard what the Hand of God had done to them, but Church matters kept me occupied. It's a good thing you were there."

"It was nothing. I owed them a debt of gratitude. They're nice people, even long after you left the galaxy."

"I think we're all in agreement that Jack and Brock are fully qualified to join this council," the Arch Priestess said. "In fact, they're probably more qualified than all of us. Boatman, you may sit in as well."

"Thank you, Arch Priestess," Boatman said, still sneaking glances at Jack as he moved for an empty seat. Jack and Brock did the same. The seven of them sat in a circle.

"Shall we begin?" the Arch Priestess asked, her mood growing somber. "The Gods are almost fully recovered. We need to prepare for the final battle."

Everyone sobered up alongside her. "How close to recovery are we talking about?" the naked woman asked, then turned to Jack and Brock. "I'm Archon Truth, by the way. A pleasure to make your acquaintance."

"Likewise."

"A week at most," the Arch Priestess replied. "I've been contacted. They want us to be ready to march when they are."

One Fist snorted. "Do they think we're their pawns?"

"Well, they're my ancestors," Great Silver said.

"They certainly look down on us," the Arch Priestess said. "To them, we're just weak mortals. It's a pity they're right. They're ten extreme Archons, while we only possess four in total, and not all at that level. We also have the A and B-Grades with their formations, but overall, our war force is less than that of the Gods."

"That doesn't make us expendable," Jack said. "Or pawns."

"No, it doesn't. In fact, I suspect the Gods know about our plans to eventually revive Enas, and they plan on turning against us the moment we defeat the Immortals."

The revelation fell on the room like an anvil dropped from a mountaintop. "Why do you think that?" Great Silver asked.

"They're Gods. They're so arrogant they don't bother hiding their intentions. I can sense their disdain every time I speak to them—their plans leak out between their arrogant words."

"Are you certain?" Truth asked.

"Absolutely."

"Okay. Then, what can we do?"

"Only one thing," she replied, "which is also why I convened this council. We must blindside them and secretly revive Enas. He will protect us after the war is done."

"Revive Enas?" One Fist shouted. "You say that like it's easy!"

"It's possible now," the Arch Priestess said. "As you know, the Sage possesses the power to wake him up, and he just reached the A-Grade. He can use the entropy runic columns left by the Archons of previous generations. Provided no one messes with us, I estimate we have an over ninety percent chance of rescuing Enas from the black hole he's trapped in."

"But they'll certainly stop us," Jack said. "Both the Gods and the Immortals."

"Right. Unless they're busy fighting each other."

Boatman laughed. "There we go."

The Arch Priestess smiled back. "Here's my plan. We orchestrate what seems like the final battle. All the Gods and Immortals, as well as every eye in the universe, will swarm there. Then, secretly, we send a small elite force to revive Enas while they're busy."

"Say we can revive him," Truth said. "How do we make sure everyone gathers where we want them?"

"Jack can help us," the Arch Priestess said. All eyes turned to Jack.

"Me?" he asked.

"Yes, you. Your duel against Hero was scheduled to be in another fifteen years, but with the power you currently possess, I don't imagine fighting him now will be a problem. If you put out your challenge and we arrange the duel, the Immortals will certainly send over their armies to guard him—after all, Hero is their greatest rising star, a moral support of the army. If we and the Gods also arrive, they'll summon everyone. Then, it's just a matter of someone making the first move. The final battle will erupt by itself."

Jack considered it. "I could do that. What if the Gods suspect something is up? Or the Immortals? They're not stupid."

"They have no idea we can revive Enas. The Sage's existence and identity is one of our most tightly kept secrets. Without him, it would have been impossible. They won't suspect a thing."

The people present glanced at each other. "There is something I should say," Jack broke the silence. He told them about his encounter with Axelor's clone in the Hall of Trials, outlining what the God of Entropy had said about Enas.

"I hear that," the Arch Priestess said. "I don't think Axelor would speak the complete truth, but I never believed Enas was completely innocent either. He is the God of Life, not Love. However, I do believe that our teachings hold more truth than falsehoods. If we revive Enas, maybe he won't be utterly benevolent, but he'll still protect us."

Jack nodded. "You know better. I just said what I had to."

"Are you certain this plan will work?" One Fist asked.

"Reasonably so," the Arch Priestess replied. "We have a decent chance of succeeding. Enough to give it a go. Even if it doesn't work, it's not like we lose anything—the battle would happen anyway."

The people present looked at each other again. "I'm in," Great Silver said. "I have read the scriptures of my people. The Gods who created us saw us as nothing more than toys—I wouldn't find it strange if they decided to wipe us out."

"I agree as well," said One Fist.

"And so do I," said Truth.

"This will definitely not go as planned," Brock said, "but it's a good start. I'm in, my bros."

"I'm in as well," Jack said. "I look forward to beating up Hero."

"I don't think my opinion matters, but I agree as well," Boatman said.

"Then everyone is in agreement," the Arch Priestess said. "Good.

I have already recalled our important personnel and sent a secret elite team to Enas's prison. They'll be ready, and so should you. Once the Gods are almost done with their recovery, we set the plan in motion. It all ends in a few days. Until then... I wish you all a good rest."

CHAPTER SEVENTY-SIX

WINE NIGHT

Jack, Vivi, and Ebele were having a picnic on a lush hill. This wasn't Jack's main body, of course, but they shared a soul. He knew that the main body had just reentered the universe.

"How's school going, Ebele?" he asked.

"It's perfect!" she replied, stuffing herself with brioche bread. Crumbs rained on the blanket below. "My friends are all doing as great as I am, so we can be in the same classes. Norton got into core-dust, however—I can see how it gives him energy, but relying on that feels wrong."

Jack chuckled. "Back in my day, we used coffee."

"Not everyone has the expensive coffee you use, Dad. The regular kind just doesn't affect cultivators."

"It does if you drink enough."

"Don't encourage bad behaviors in your daughter!" Vivi said, her mood vibrant. "Focus on your studies, Ebele, but don't forget to have fun. It's equally important."

"If not more," Jack said.

"If not more," Vivi agreed. "Forging a great self is better than excelling in your studies. It's the foundation of everything."

"I know. You've only told me, like, a thousand times," Ebele complained.

Jack smiled. Since he shared memories with his main body, he could easily feel the difference between a warmongering, power-thirsting life and this simpler one. Both filled him equally. Of course, having memories and living them out wasn't exactly the same, but he was so glad he'd made this clone.

Being with his wife and daughter every day—or whenever she took a break from the Academy—was a blessing in and of itself.

I just hope, he thought, looking at the blue sky, the dream doesn't shatter tomorrow...

"Hey, Vivi, Ebele," he said. Both women turned to look at him. "I love you."

They blinked in surprise, then smiled sweetly. "I love you too, Jack," Vivi said. "Both of you."

"Me too," Ebele said. Thankfully, she was past being a teenager, so associating with her parents came easy. Jack smiled at their affirmations. He opened his arms wide, embracing them both.

"Did something happen?" Ebele asked as she hugged him back.

"Nothing happened and nothing will," he replied. "While I'm here, you'll always be safe."

"Um..." Ebele said. "Thanks?"

"You're welcome." They didn't know about the final battle happening tomorrow. They didn't need to. He would protect them... No matter what.

The night was breezy. Stars shone over the New Cathedral, shedding their light onto the top of the main temple, which the Arch Priestess had graciously offered to Jack and his friends. They could have drunk their wine between the clouds or in orbit, but there was a different joy to occupying the top of a tall building.

"To friendship," Jack said, raising his cup. "The only constant of the cultivation world."

"I thought the only constant was benefits," Min Ling said.

"Only if you suck."

Everyone laughed, cheering and then downing their cups.

"I like your universe," Strawpin said, looking up at the stars. "Our sky is just gray and red. Not... this."

Starhair wrapped his arm under her, Strawpin leaning in. "Every world is beautiful," he said. "For example, your world had you. All the stars in the sky couldn't compete with that."

She giggled, while Fiend Prince snorted in laughter. "Can you believe this guy? He was just a nobody before, and the moment he found a girl, bam! Prince Charming."

"At least I'm trying. You were an average dude, then you didn't find a girl, and bam! Still an average dude."

"Hey! I'm a genius, you know! The first disciple of Jack Rust!" Everyone laughed over his words. "Why are you laughing? Ohhh, is it sparring time yet?"

"No sparring this time," Jack said with a smile. "We'll have plenty of fighting tomorrow. Tonight is for relaxing and enjoying life."

"That's true," Brock said. "Let me change the subject, bros. How's everyone feeling?"

They looked at each other. "Right now?" Min Ling asked.

"Now and always."

"I'm apprehensive," Starhair said, his arm going slack around Strawpin's shoulders. "I feel we're on the cusp of a massive breakthrough. If we can just survive this war, everything will be great... but can we? A single battle will judge the universe's doom or endless prosperity. I know I won't play much of a part, but after spending time with all of you, I can't help feeling involved... and it scares me."

Jack gazed softly over his cup. "You've changed a lot," he said.

"I had to. Can't keep pissing myself every time an Overlord looks at me the wrong way."

They laughed again.

"It's not a single deciding battle," Heavenly Spoon said. He had broken the back of his chair and reattached it in a laid-back position, letting him lounge. A small silver spoon stuck out of his cup. "It's the accumulation of all our efforts over the years. Every choice we've made, every danger we've overcome, and every opportunity we've grasped with our two hands. We didn't know at the time, but everything led to this deciding moment. It's a relief, in a way. Compared to everything we've already done, our performance in tomorrow's battle matters little. The result is almost predetermined. We just have to play it out."

"I don't see it that way," Fiend Prince said. "I understand you're trying to compose yourself, but that is not the way of my Dao. Everything in the past only prepared me for this moment. I was sharpening my claws, and now is the time to use them. My performance matters."

"I side with Fiend Prince," Min Ling said.

"And I with Spoon," Starhair said. "What about you, Jack and Brock? You're the most accomplished individuals here. What do you think?"

Brock raised his cup and took a big sip. "I disagree with all of you. The performance of any individual is unimportant. It is our cumulative bro experience that matters."

Everyone gawked, then laughed. "That's so Brock," Min Ling said. As if drawn by an invisible power, all eyes slowly turned to Jack.

He'd been content to sit in his corner and listen to his friends converse. Sensing the attention on him, he smiled. "I'm just happy to be here. Sure, I relish the opportunity to fight at the highest level. I'll try my hardest and break myself to protect the world and my daughter. However... I can't help becoming emotional. Less than thirty years ago, I'd never even heard of the Dao, and I spent my days studying biology and teaching undergraduates in a lab."

"What's undergraduates?" Min Ling asked.

"What's a lab?" Fiend Prince asked.

Jack laughed. "The point is, back then, my world was so deceptively small. I could only see the tiniest corner of the tiniest corner of the universe. Even after the Integration, I remained a frog in a well for a long time. D-Grades were gods to me. I'd sworn enmity against C-Grades, whom I couldn't even fathom defeating at the time. But I kept adventuring, and my power kept rising, and eventually I stand here, at the top of the world, drinking wine with people who could have made all my past problems disappear with the wave of a hand. I stand side by side with Archons, and tomorrow I'll fight a war that the Animal Kingdom, my former nemesis, didn't even qualify to participate in."

He shook his head, wetting his lips with wine before he spoke again. Everyone waited.

"It feels surreal... Like it's all a dream. Me, just taking a stroll through the different power levels, living one fantastical adventure after another. I get emotional every time I think about how far I've come. I feel like it's taken such a long time, but it's only been, what... Thirty years?" He thought about it. "Okay, nevermind. That is a long time."

"Only to you," Starhair said, winking at Jack.

"How do you convince yourself it's real?" Spoon asked. "If everything feels like a dream, how do you know it's not?"

"Because of the pain. Pain and loss. They make it real."

"Welp, that took a dark turn," Strawpin said.

Next to her, Starhair shrugged. "I liked it. Jack for Arch Priest."

They laughed again. So did Jack, the weight over his shoulders slowly dissolving.

"So, tell us about that," Min Ling said, leaning forward and wagging a finger between Starhair and Strawpin. Her eyes held a tipsy light. "How did that happen?"

Starhair began, "Well, you know how bees fly from flower to flower? Sometimes, they—"

Strawpin slapped his shoulder. "We stayed in the Dark Canal for fifteen years," she said. "One day, I asked Dave here—"

"Your real name is Dave!" Jack interrupted.

"What about it?" Starhair asked back.

"I expected something better. Destructus or Gorgon or something. Dave the Long Hair Archon sounds silly."

"Everyone has a normal name beneath their titles," Spoon said, laughing. "Mine is Jonas—I think I've told you before. It's not like we know we'll become great when we're born, and we can't have everyone going around with epic-sounding names. You don't want your coffee served by Ostenslor, the Destroyer of Worlds. Better Jeff, or Tiffany, or Sop. Part of the reason why we all use titles is that Sovereign Jonas does sound silly."

"...Why am I still Jack?" Jack asked.

"Don't worry, bro. I also use my real name," Brock said.

"You can make your own titles whenever you want," Starhair said. "Of course, they're usually created *for* you by everyone else, but I guess you haven't lived long enough. Archon Fist sounds great."

"Too similar to Archon One Fist," Jack said.

"Then Archon Punch. Or force him to change titles—you're better."

"Can I be Elder Big Bro?" Brock asked.

"Sure. Who I am, the title police?" Starhair said.

"I also use my real name," Min Ling said. "And I still want to hear the story of Starhair and Strawpin, by the way."

"Oh yeah," Strawpin said. "Well, as we were just sitting there for fifteen years, I asked Starhair if he wanted to be my sex partner."

"So romantic," Spoon said with a laugh.

"It's not over!" she complained. "He said no at first because, in his opinion, being straightforward was 'weird' and 'creepy.' So then we had a silly courting dance where we went on dates and stuff. He kissed me behind the Hall of Trial's silver stele. That's also where we—"

Starhair coughed, growing slightly redder in the face.

Strawpin continued, "Anyway, that's how it went. Everyone else really looked forward to us becoming a thing, for some reason, but I think it's just because our names start with the same letter."

"That's not the reason!" Fiend Prince said. "We wanted you to become a thing because you're the hair duo."

"I have nothing to do with hair," she complained.

"Your straw looks like hair."

"I like your hair," Starhair said.

"And I like yours, sweety."

Brock tilted his head. "Weird mating rituals," he said.

"What can you do? Cultivators are weird like that," Strawpin said.

"It's a shame the Arch Priestess couldn't join us," Jack said with a sigh. "Too busy."

"Where did that come from?" Spoon asked. "You fancy her?"

Jack realized nobody knew about Brock and the Arch Priestess. "She's just young, like us. She would have fit in."

"She and I do the sex sometimes," Brock said, oblivious to everyone's shocked glances. He looked around. "What?"

"You and the Arch Priestess!" everyone said at roughly the same time.

"Yes. Why? Am I too handsome?"

"That's not the point!"

"Should you just be saying that?" Jack asked.

Brock shrugged. "It's not a secret. Besides, these are our bros."

"Oh. Okay."

Everyone still reeled from the revelation. Jack started pouring more wine into their cups.

"We should take care not to get too drunk," Spoon cautioned. "It's a big day tomorrow, remember? Jack has to beat up the rival genius, and then we go to war. I wonder if Hero's having wine with his friends right now."

"I don't think he has any," Jack said, still refilling the cups. "Didn't strike me as the type."

"Hmm. But every hero has a sidekick, right?"

"Not if you can't stomach sharing the spotlight sometimes."

"Jack's right," Min Ling said. "I was talking with some of our subterfuge experts the other day. They regularly tap into the Immortal army's off-the-records communications. Apparently, Elder Hero is a mega dick."

"How so?"

"Some guy from the other side put it nicely. He said, and I quote, 'Hard to live with a hero-complex princess.'"

"What does that mean? I'm a princess," Strawpin said.

"You are?" Min Ling asked.

"Yeah. My father runs a small kingdom in the outer provinces of our world."

"Oh. Then excuse my indiscretion, Your Highness."

"Now what's that supposed to mean! I'm as monster as the rest of you!"

Everyone laughed again.

The wine cups were emptied, then refilled. The pitcher kept going down. This was the highest grade of liquor, with such potency that one drop could intoxicate all fish in a lake. Even these high-level cultivators were affected, their conversation bouncing around all kinds of topics, ranging from funny, to ridiculous, to inappropriate. Brock regaled them with details on how he and the Arch Priestess courted each other. In return, Strawpin was all too eager to discuss her and Starhair's love life, which made the man go beet red.

"Some things never change," Jack said with a chuckle.

Only now did he realize how desperately he'd needed this. Even the most dedicated cultivator remained a person. Without unwinding, he'd eventually break like a string left taut for too long. This simple break, a night chatting and drinking with friends, completely unknotted and upgraded his psyche. He was ready to face the world tomorrow—quite literally.

They still had a battle to prepare for, however. A few hours later, after everyone had relaxed and enjoyed themselves, Brock was the first to stand. "We should go. Going into battle unprepared would be a shame."

"You're usually the one who starts the drinking," Jack said.

"Yes, but I'm responsible."

Jack laughed, then stood as well. "Brock's right. This was fun. Let's do it again tomorrow night?"

Everyone smiled as they followed. "You got a deal," Min Ling said, swiping the table, chairs, wine, and cups into her space ring. Everyone bade goodbye with smiles and promised to repeat this outing tomorrow. No one mentioned the alternative.

That night, for the first time in untold years, Jack slept. He'd never woken up more refreshed.

"Are you ready, bro?" Brock asked as they finished breakfast. The armies were assembling outside. The air smelled of war.

"I am," Jack said, walking out the door. "It's time to finish this."

CHAPTER SEVENTY-SEVEN
GOING TO WAR

The Sage hovered in pitch-black darkness. He'd been here for several months, preparing the ritual to free Enas—his sole equipment being twelve columns, each twelve-sided and inscribed with runic symbols. Despite their simplicity, their every rune had been carved by past Archons, containing enough total power to contest the laws around a real black hole.

They didn't need to destroy it, anyway.

Having placed the columns and connected them with green Dao tethers, the Sage stood in space, inspecting his work. "Just a little bit more..." he muttered, voice hoarse with desire. "A little bit more, and I'll be free..."

Jack floated upward. Brock was beside him as they left the New Cathedral, rising into the space beyond. They were welcomed by a sea of cultivators—thousands of them, the weakest being B-Grades. The antithesis to Jack's earlier days was striking.

All eyes were on him and Brock as they ascended—their entrance had been delayed on purpose. The other four Archons waited above the army, four dots emitting intense power. They were all releasing parts of their aura in preparation for war. Amongst them, the Arch Priestess shone like a brilliant sun, her aura easily eclipsing the others'. Jack still wasn't sure of his current level, but he knew she overpowered him as well.

As he rose, he also took in their army. Excluding himself and Brock, there were four Archons, thirty-something A-Grades, and around a thousand B-Grades. It was much too small a force to contest the end of the world, but every single participant was a powerhouse, someone able to dominate their corner of a galaxy.

Jack's friends were also there. Fiend Prince waved excitedly—he hadn't received any benefits as Jack's disciple yet, but Jack had explained to him and the others how he'd achieved the Universe of the Body. Further instruction would come after the battle, provided they survived.

"Welcome, Jack Rust and Brock," the Arch Priestess said. "Welcome, our champions!" She'd ditched her robes for white armor, hugging her body and accentuating her curves—the last thing anyone cared about right now. A veil still covered her tiger-featured face, while gloves and boots hid her hands and feet. She'd no doubt remove them before the battle.

The army cheered at her words, Great Silver's roar echoing through the void.

"Jack and Brock are more than just today's stars," the Arch Priestess continued. "In the Church's time of need, they rushed into the Space Monster World and secured an important alliance for us. Monsters, you made the right decision. Thank you for being here."

"How could we not?" Great Silver replied. "This concerns our future as well. If there is a chance, we fight!"

The monsters in the army—over a third of it—cheered. The Arch Priestess smiled under her veil.

"However, that is not the end of the good news," she said. "Jack Rust has managed to achieve a realm no one has seen before. While not above Archons, he's set the foundation to getting there. After we win this battle, he will spread his knowledge across the universe, heralding a new era for everyone. All of you, whether at the B or A-Grade, will have a chance to pursue the realms beyond!"

At this, every single cultivator present cheered with passion. They'd devoted their lives to pursuing the peak. There could be nothing more exciting than new frontiers. The void shook by their roars.

"To do that, we need to win the war today," the Arch Priestess continued, her voice dropping an octave. "The Immortals have ruled the universe for a billion years. They are tyrants, slave-drivers, sick, soulless automatons who pit us against each other to raise soldiers. Today is the day we end them. Our people will suffer no more. I know you all left your disciples and descendants behind to be here. We are the cream of the crop, the masters, the elites of the universe. We shall face an equal force and prevail, because they fight for conquest, but we fight for our lives."

The people were enlivened, masters growing emotional. Many were Elders. There was something primal about their spirited eyes, something which tugged at Jack's soul. Today, they would win, no matter what.

"We are a force for good!" the Arch Priestess shouted. "I believe I speak for everyone when I say that, even if we are slaughtered on the battlefield, none of us will think about retreat. This is where we make our final stand. The world will rise or fall according to our powers, so everyone, please... Give it your all!"

The cheers kept rising until they reached a crescendo. This entire part of the universe shook by their sheer power. Finally, the sounds abated, replaced by a pregnant silence.

Jack could sense it. A grim determination swept over the gathered cultivators. It was as the Arch Priestess had said—these were absolute masters of their generation, who came here fully intending on giving up their lives for the universe. Each could have run away, but none did. They showed up.

In truth, they didn't need any encouragement. Their hearts burned hotter than the brightest fire, their minds devoted to a single purpose. The Arch Priestess's rallying speech wasn't meant to inspire them, but to instill meaning in their deaths.

The priestess sensed the resolve of her warriors. She knew they were ready.

"Before we go," she said, "I want all of you who still possess System cores to remove them. We know the Immortals can use them against us."

Cries of assent rolled throughout the crowd. Jack gave a bitter-sweet smile as he looked inside himself, his perception landing on a tiny, isolated part of his body. A sphere of ephemeral cogs lay there—the System mini-core planted in each cultivator. It was what gave him access to the status screen, the Inspection, the Skills, the level power-ups, and various other benefits. He'd always known this day would come, as he knew the System was an enemy, but he couldn't help becoming emotional.

The System had been his oldest companion since the Integration, the raft on which he tightly held onto to stay afloat. The stats had been a constant relief throughout his adventures. However, everything ended.

He opened his status screen a final time, knowing he'd never see it again. He was long past needing it, anyway. Once he destroyed it, all enhancements it had already given him would remain, including stats and titles.

ERROR: PLEASE REPORT TO THE NEAREST AUTHORITIES IMMEDIATELY OR FACE EXTERMINATION.

Name: Jack Rust
Species: ???
Faction: Bare Fist Brotherhood (A)
Grade: A
Class: Paragon of Cultivation (Legendary)

Level: 550

Strength: 29,060
Dexterity: 29,060
Constitution: 29,060
Mental: 2,400
Will: 2,400

Dao Skills: Meteor Punch IV, Space Mastery IV, Death Mastery IV, Neutron Star Body IV, Black Hole IV, Iron Fist Style III, Brutalizing Aura III, Supernova III, Fist of Mortality III, Titan Taunt III, Immortal Commune I, Time Mastery IV, Life Mastery IV
Inner World size: ??? miles
Inner Cultivator Boundaries:
Highest: F-Grade
Average: F-Grade
Titles: Planetary Frontrunner (10), Planetary Torch-bearer (1), Ninth Ring Conqueror, Planetary Overlord (1), Grade Defier, Planet Destroyer, Challenger

Even the error message at the start, which he usually ignored, chimed pleasantly in his mind. Embracing the sentimentalism of the moment, Jack reached for the System mini-core inside him and crushed it, watching the broken cogs dissipate into energy. He felt nothing different.

Status screen, he thought. When nothing happened, he smiled sadly. Goodbye, System. I know I'm coming to kill you, but you were a damn good companion.

Maybe I'll create a better version of you in the future.

He refocused. Silence had fallen over the army as the last people were finishing up. Loss was in many eyes.

From above them, the Arch Priestess spoke, "It's time. Jack Rust, as the one with the highest Space laws here, would you do us the honor?"

Many of the Envoys and Elders, who didn't comprehend Jack's strength, were taken aback by this statement. He calmly floated upward, coming to rest on the same level as the Archons. An intricate device hovered between them. It looked similar to the teleportation cores of starships, except larger and vastly more powerful. As he connected his Dao to it, he could sense that a destination had already been set, and that its reserves were filled with an extreme amount of energy.

He willed it to activate. A blinding flash enveloped the entire army. The void sundered under them, and then they were gone, surrounded by swimming colors as they were dragged through a tunnel in the dimensional sea. They reemerged half a galaxy away, near the center, in a wide area devoid of stars and planets. Not devoid of people, though.

The Immortal army had arrived first. There were thousands of them, hovering through the void like almighty flies. Their B-Grades numbered in the thousands, their A-Grades and Archons almost doubling those of the Church. In addition, thirty-three A-Grade robots stood at the forefront, led by a single robot trailing void-ended wires. The Heaven Immortal, the current leader of the universe. They would have made for an unfair fight if not for the ten hulking behemoths dominating the void.

It was the first time Jack met the Gods in person. He'd fought a clone of Axelor and seen Enas in a vision or two, but their auras were a far cry from the real thing. Standing in the presence of Gods felt like a mortal gazing up a mountain, an ant looking at a dragon.

The ten gods were arrayed in a line, silently facing the army of the Immortals, their auras pressing down like veils of steel. Each was an extreme Archon, with Axelor rising even higher. The God of Entropy himself was a planet-sized ball of darkness covered in lashing tentacles—very different to the handsome young man Jack fought in the Hall of Trials.

The other nine gods were also titanic in size, though smaller than Axelor, and vaguely humanoid.

One was made of fire. Another, of stars. A third seemed normal, but everything around it was warped, as if it were drawing them in. The fourth was made of lightning, the fifth of blue and red sparks, the sixth and seventh of explosions, though the latter depicted fewer yet larger ones. Finally, there were two that only appeared as bodies of water, one resembling a rippling pond and the other a steady current.

As the Black Hole Church army appeared, Jack sensed the auras of the Gods clamp tight around him. His own aura reacted instinctively, fighting back, pushing against the Gods with a divinity similar to their own. All ten of them whipped around at the same time, their gazes landing on Jack, trying to see right through him.

He smiled. "Hi," he said, his voice crossing the endless miles. "Nice to meet you."

The Gods didn't respond. Unlike Axelor's clone, they felt impassive and inhuman, impossible to converse with. They probably could, if they wanted to, but their bubbling derision toward mortals clarified that wouldn't happen.

Jack sensed something more though. Their eyes had contained wariness against him, an emotion on the verge of turning into killing intent. Him, of all mortals, they acknowledged as a possible threat.

"***AFTER THIS, WE TALK,***" a powerful voice smashed into his mind. Axelor's.

Jack grinned. The God hadn't held back, but Jack endured the pressure as easily as a summer breeze. "*Sure,*" he replied, then turned back to the front.

Their three armies were arrayed in a triangle, with the Gods and the Church closer together. Technically, they hadn't come here to battle, but everyone knew how it would end.

A late A-Grade man stepped out of the Immortal army, captivating everyone's attention. The Gods shimmered with fury. Jack raised his brows—this aura was much greater than he anticipated. It also contained a hint of divinity, though it was pale, like a color which had already been washed off.

"Welcome, everyone, to the spectacle of my victory," Elder Hero said. His golden hair flowed behind his helmetless head, while shiny plate armor covered the rest of his body. He was almost unfairly handsome, with blue eyes, broad features, and a perfectly square chin as if chiseled from marble. He could give Superman a run for his money. Or Spongebob.

Hero took out his broadsword, aiming it at the Church army. "Jack Rust! Come out to die, if you dare!"

"Why wouldn't I dare?" The answer arrived easily, riding the currents of space. Jack appeared before his army, stepping into the massive empty space between the three forces. It was way too large, clearly meant for a much grander battle than this duel.

Hero laughed. "I heard you'd grown in power, and I must admit, your aura is quite impressive! However, don't think you stand a chance. Nevermind that it's only been sixteen years since our duel agreement. Even if you'd waited the full thirty, you still wouldn't be able to surpass me. For every talented genius of evil, the forces of good have a better one."

A smile tugged at the ends of Jack's lips. "You know, I'm impressed as well. I thought this would be a walk in the park, but you're actually pretty strong. I still haven't fought seriously since my last breakthrough. I look forward to exerting myself a little."

"Exerting yourself?" Hero laughed. "Those are big words for a cultist trying to revive an evil God. I should let your ploy foster, just so I can foil it more majestically later on, but since we're in the middle of something here, I guess killing you now will do."

"You speak a lot, but all you say is bullshit," Jack replied, cracking his knuckles. His aura spread out, upturning the void, shaking the world. Gasps rose from the two armies. "I heard you insulted my master," he said, assuming a boxing stance. "This fight is for his honor."

"Hah! Bring it, scum!"

The two greatest geniuses in the history of the universe clashed.

CHAPTER SEVENTY-EIGHT

JACK VS. HERO

RORY PICKLEMAN WAS A LATE B-GRADE ENVOY OF THE BLACK HOLE Church. His strength wasn't anything special, but he cultivated the Dao of Simple Honesty, making him perfect for carrying out top-secret missions. That was why he, alone, had been chosen to accompany the Sage into the old Ancient galaxy where Enas was imprisoned. A huge honor, as well as a huge responsibility.

I have to admit, it's going pretty well so far, Rory thought, sitting by the tea table they had prepared beforehand as he watched the Sage begin the ritual. A black hole was surrounded by twelve runic columns, each possessing twelve sides. The Sage stood before the black hole and chanted, an unintelligible sound which filled even Rory with energy. His body was rejuvenated.

The twelve columns connected to each other in a green polygon around the black hole. Its sides swayed as if the hole's rotation rubbed against them. While Rory couldn't see the black hole, he could perceive it, and noticed its rotation gradually slowing down. A green light appeared in its midst, growing ever brighter, as if approaching from an endless distance away. The same green light radiated from the Sage's body.

Rory couldn't contain his excitement. Of all the people in the universe, would he, a random Envoy, be the one to witness the return of Enas?

As Jack and Hero hyped themselves up, the Arch Priestess took something out of her space ring.

"Hmm?" Brock asked. "Recording stone?"

"That's right. I've already spread word, and this duel will be broadcast across the universe. The Immortals will also broadcast it in every corner of System space."

"Why?"

"Because each side thinks their champion will win."

She tossed the stone up. It automatically activated and zoomed in, capturing Jack and Hero, who were about to clash. At the same time, large screens flashed on the gathering fields of all high-grade factions across System space, including the Milky Way galaxy—after everything that happened with Jack, the existence of other galaxies and higher Grade organizations was no longer a secret.

The duel was broadcasted to every important eye in the world—except Earth, which was uncontactable to all.

Jack didn't know about the broadcast, nor did he care. He rushed Hero. Thanks to his new powers, charging through space at near light speed felt like strolling through the park. He arrived and casually shot a punch. Hero swung his sword against it.

Purple energy blasted Hero's defenses, carving a beam through space. The other man recoiled, blown away, retreating thousands of miles before stabilizing. He wiped his chin with a gauging expression.

"You have power," he said. "Good. It wouldn't be interesting otherwise."

Contrary to the strike he'd just received, he seemed in a good mood. Jack ignored his words and charged again. The budding universe inside him roiled with power. The astral rivers serving as his blood accelerated, the purple-sun heart pulsing with power. The laws of his universe circulated, feeding their essence into his, letting his fist command a field of power surpassing the physical domain.

As he punched out, it was like endless natural laws crashing down. A massive starry fist appeared to ram into Hero.

Hero fought back this time. A silver aura radiated from his body, encapsulating the space around him, changing its properties and making it uniquely his. As Jack's fist entered that space, he sensed it lose power as its Daos were no longer supported. It was like reality itself pushed against him.

"With the power vested in me by the people," Hero chanted, "I cast judgment!"

Jack had fought late A-Grades before. The power unleashed by Hero was far above them, a terrible torrent of reality-consuming silver. The greatsword rose above him and cracked down like thunder. It met Jack's fist, both attacks warping and consuming each other.

"You're good!" Jack laughed, even as Hero's gaze turned ghastly.

"You can resist my named attacks?" he asked. "Splendid! This makes my victory even worthier!"

"Don't bite your tongue!"

Jack shot out; a missile crossing space. He reached Hero instantly. A fist smashed into the other man's abdomen, ringing his armor like a bell. Another aimed for his head, blocked by a greatsword, which then turned and tried to cleave down Jack. He dodged, pelting his opponent with Meteor Punches which broke against his armor in a breathtaking light show. Light sparkled everywhere. The spectators' eyes reflected the glint.

When the two men exchanged strikes, they glimpsed into each other's psyche. All barriers fell during a physical confrontation. Jack could sense Hero's soul—a haughty thing, arrogance fueled by true competence. All his life, he'd been the best, a lonely peak looking down on the world. His moral superiority against "evil-doers" shared its foundation with his skill superiority over his struggling competitors—and it was exactly that superiority which Jack threatened.

At first, Hero's every strike landed as if disinterested, expecting to swat Jack away like a fly—a habit forged over a lifetime of excellence and a Dao built around it. Over time, Hero grew angry. Every strike was sharp now. His cold, handsome face turned fiercer, his mouth hardening into a straight line. It was imperceptible to most, but Jack, being so close and intimate, could see it clearly.

"What's the matter?" he taunted. "Is it hard to play hero when the other guy fights back?"

"What do you know about heroism?"

"Take a wild fucking guess."

The greatsword fell from the sky, orbited by a thousand angry stars. Jack punched up. A purple storm erupted, the stars extinguished one by one, metallic sounds roaring out as his middle knuckle met blade.

Hero's sword could cleave apart planets. If it touched a sun, the sun would be sliced in two. Jack's knuckle, by contrast, was something much harder. It was part of a universe, part of a whole, the apex of a fist clad in the highest natural laws. Unless Jack's fist broke, his knuckle never would.

A terrible shockwave spread down, covering a wide astral area below Jack. At the same time, the aftermath of his fist flew up, sliced in two by Hero's blade. The Archons of each army galvanized their powers to protect the onlookers as the Gods calmly watched on. Across the Spiral Stair galaxy, the clashes of Jack and Hero could be seen as pretty lights in the night sky.

And the battle ramped up still. Hero was an immovable mountain, armor and sword both standing at the peak. Jack was a force of nature, a fist calmly but firmly navigating the storm to strike the enemy.

With his cultivation fused into his body, teleporting was as natural as moving aside, the lines between the two blurred.

Attacking was the same. He'd fully digested his understandings, each strike flowing as a simple punch yet containing profound truths of the universe. He was a purple boxer in a river of silver, fighting against the current. Hero's aura cascaded over Jack, doing nothing, its level decidedly inferior to Jack's established divinity. As for the greatsword, it was even more ineffective—all strikes had been blocked or dodged. So far, Hero had received hits, but Jack hadn't. This infuriated the other man.

The greatsword flew over Jack's head, cutting a line in space. The void sundered for thousands of miles behind it. As Jack reared up to attack, one of Hero's hands left the sword handle, following his own momentum to pivot into a fist which struck Jack's chin. He flew back, somersaulting in midair.

"You punched me?" he asked with a grin, feeling his chin. "It would be funny to swap, but I don't have a greatsword."

"Silence, villain. No matter how strong you become, justice will always prevail. I must protect the people. If that means using less noble means than my sword, then so be it."

Jack arched a brow. "You talk a lot, and you sure love spouting bullshit. Does it help ramp up your powers?"

"Poking for weaknesses? How suitable for someone like you."

"I see," Jack said, cracking a smile. "Your Dao is based on belief. You spin the narrative in your favor, then grow stronger the more you frame yourself as the hero."

"I *am* the hero, little villain. You conspire with deranged cultists and dark gods. I work with the people of the universe, seventy-three galaxies standing behind my back. Tell me—who fights for the greater cause?"

"Your people of the universe are oppressed and enslaved," Jack reminded him. "The Immortals and their System force them to kill each other, disregarding life to create soldiers."

Hero snorted. "The world is always rife with struggle. People would kill each other regardless. Funneling that into creating soldiers is a necessary sacrifice to save the world from these false Gods you worship."

A hint of anger radiated from the Gods sitting to the side, rattling the space between Jack and Hero.

"You're merely preying on the weak," Jack said. "Your Immortals cannot even conceive the value of mortal life. We do. When your armies purged the Church from System space, how many innocent people did you kill? How many planets did you smite?"

Hero snorted again, a sound of clear derision. "You understand nothing. Let justice prevail."

Lord Longsword sat with his arms crossed and watched a broadcast playing on the big screen of his home faction. It had been a few decades since his foray into Trial Planet—his build had grown more mature and muscular, new scars decorating his face. His sword was even longer, hanging horizontal against his back and scaring the junior disciples to his sides.

After losing to Jack Rust, he'd worked harder than anyone and managed to reach the middle D-Grade after only a couple decades. He was even approaching the late D-Grade. The Elders hailed him as a genius and prepared him to be the new Faction Leader of the Wide Swirls faction.

Except all those achievements felt like nothing. There on the big screen, Jack Rust was fighting for the title of the world's greatest genius. They'd been on the same level twenty years ago, and now Longsword was nothing but an ant compared to Jack. The most humbling experience of his life.

Longsword, however, had matured over the past years. Instead of bursting with the anger of hurt pride, he smiled in self-deprecation. His fingers rubbed something in his pocket, from where a tiny giggle emerged.

"I'm just too inferior," he muttered. "I hope you win, Jack Rust."

Grand Elder Huali had arranged a viewing party. The entirety of the reborn Exploding Sun faction had gathered to watch Jack's duel, and they'd even invited all neighboring factions, the Sun disciples not losing any opportunity to brag about how Jack had studied with them for a bit in the past. There were even a few people who'd met Jack personally, or even sparred with him!

Huali's gaze was glued to the large screen, her eyes moist with tears. "Show me the power of Supernova..." she whispered.

Shol was beside her, deep in his proud drinking. He constantly laughed for no reason.

Back on Earth, there was no viewing screen to Jack's duel. There couldn't be, since they were outside System space. That didn't mean they did nothing.

Jack had arranged a banquet with all his old friends. Only Vivi knew the true reason: if the main body perished, so would the clone, and he wanted it to be amongst true friends. Ebele was there too, as were Gan Salin, Nauja, Edgar, Harambe, Captain Dordok, Brother Tao... Even his mother was present—Margaret Rust, the professor, deep in her waning years. She must have suspected that something was going on, because she'd dragged herself out of her house for the first time in months to attend.

Wine and food were aplenty. They talked freely, exchanging stories, sharing their lives. Edgar talked about the development of his Academy—he'd grown a mustache and a beard, and had overall shifted into a look much more fitting for a Headmaster than his previous one. His voice now contained command and dignity.

Jack sat back and enjoyed the pleasant atmosphere. There was a decent chance he'd collapse before the end of this banquet. He might as well enjoy it.

And, if the unfortunate truly happened, he'd make sure to teleport away in time. Wouldn't want to traumatize Ebele.

Hero charged, but Jack took a moment to grin before retaliating. His perception was sharp now, and he sensed the small but noticeable shudder in Hero's aura. That was a weakness of belief-based Daos—when founded on unsteady ground, all it took to shake them was a bit of Dao debate. It was the same trick he'd sometimes used against the leonines of the Animal Kingdom—and, if Hero had bothered to research Jack's background, he'd know that to engage in mid-battle trash-talk with him was suicide.

Though, maybe he had, and he was just overconfident.

Seeing Hero's approach, trailing the silver metallic aura of justice, Jack clenched his fist. Sparks rose from across his body. The Thunderbody technique was unusable now that he'd changed the fundamental nature of his body, but he'd been able to derive a new version based on the old one. Every spark that rose from his skin contained tiny stars, the essences of Jack's inner astral space. It would temporarily lower the energy density of his inner universe, delaying the progress of its cultivators, but that didn't matter. He'd make up for it later. This war was the convergence of everything, and he had to win.

He could have also used the Life Drop, but its energy reserves were still low, so he wanted to save it for when truly necessary.

Hero flashed above Jack, sword poised to strike. His red cape fluttered. He brought the blade down hard. "Divine Justice!"

Jack was done playing. His aura erupted as he drove up a fist, the world compressed inside it to the point of eruption. "Supernova!"

Hero's sword was washed away. A terrifying explosion filled the void, somewhat comparable to a real supernova, forcing the onlookers to turn away. For a moment, a new star appeared in the galaxy, brighter than any other.

By the time the spectators could look at the battle again, they found Hero flung away, his silver armor blackened at the front. Terrible wrath filled his face, while his flowing golden hair was singed at the ends. Before he could re-engage, Jack appeared in front of him, clad in purple lightning. His fist rolled forth. Hero's armor cracked as he flew back again, bright blood trailing his open mouth.

Jack used the overwhelming speed granted by his version of Thunderbody to flash around Hero, mercilessly pummeling him. He cracked a knee at the back of his armor, sending him flying upward, then smashed a fist into his chest from above. More punches landed, Hero's trajectory turning erratic. He was spinning in space, having lost all sense of direction, his mind shaking from the impacts. As he guarded his head and looked around, he saw a storm of meteors heading at him from all directions. He screamed as they landed.

The Heaven Immortal and the Gods looked on, transfixed. Hero was one of the greatest geniuses in the history of the cultivation world, assisted by every resource the Immortals could muster. Yet, here he was, losing to someone two small realms below him. This was historic.

"What a shame," the Heaven Immortal muttered, his voice electric. "If only we'd found him first, the Crusade would be over. Now he must die."

The Gods didn't make a sound, though they rapidly discussed amongst themselves. As for the Church army, they clenched their fists, inspired by the sight before them. Their champion was winning. They were no longer forced to hide in the shadows—thanks to Jack, they were able to step into the open, brazenly facing the Immortals with their heads held high.

Heavenly Spoon, Min Ling, Starhair, Strawpin, and Fiend Prince all had looks of admiration. Only Brock remained calm, used to his brother's feats of overwhelming strength.

As for Boatman, he slowly shook his head. "The new overcomes the old..." he muttered.

"Your disciple has surpassed you, Boatman, but that is cause for celebration," the Arch Priestess replied, unable to hide her pride. "In fact, he might have even surpassed me. He still hasn't activated his four-armed battle form, yet he can fight at the level of a weaker Archon."

"I wouldn't say that. As far as I can tell, the influence of his battle form should have decreased after Jack's recent breakthroughs. It wouldn't make much of a difference."

"Hmm. Perhaps you're right."

On the Immortals' side, an Archon leaned close to the Heaven Immortal's head. The robot possessed no ears, but whispering was a universal gesture. "Should we attack, sir?" he asked.

"No," the Heaven Immortal replied. "Hero is not done yet."

CHAPTER SEVENTY-NINE

WHAT IT MEANS TO BE A HERO

THE BLACK HOLE'S ROTATION HAD MASSIVELY DECELERATED, AND IT WAS slowly unraveling under its own weight. Rory watched as the green light grew brighter in its depths. Guided by the Sage's chanting and the twelve runic columns, the light began to form a portal of sorts in the middle of the black hole, out of which came a hand. It was perfectly human, yet grossly oversized—barely smaller than the black hole itself. Some of its nails were sharp, others trimmed.

Oh boy, Rory thought. If Enas is that big, he must have been super cramped in there.

The hand grabbed the edge of the black hole and pulled. More of the arm was revealed at an agonizingly slow pace. The Sage started laughing.

In the midst of the three armies, the flashes were settling down. Hero was revealed—though he still stood, he was clearly hurt. His hair was burned and disheveled, his handsome face bruised and bloody. Cracks ran down his armor, while his aura was unsteady, as if someone had poked holes into it. He breathed heavily as he glared at Jack.

"Do you know why I didn't end you?" Jack asked, hovering calmly some distance away. Even now, he was barely injured. "It's because I want the world to watch your downfall. A few years ago, you tried to kill my master. That was unacceptable. I promised to crush you before I killed you."

Off to the side, Boatman swelled with pride.

Hero snorted. "You will pay for your arrogance."

Jack gave a hard smile. His statement hadn't been the whole truth. He did want to humiliate Hero a bit, but he was far too experienced to let an enemy recover. The real reason he stopped attacking was that he sensed something inside Hero—an extremely pure and potent power buried into his body, on the verge of erupting. It filled even him with fear. If Hero decided to use whatever that was and Jack was too close, he might not be able to react in time.

Now, Hero couldn't mount a sneak attack. His pride wouldn't let him hold back after being manhandled so heavily. He'd be forced to activate that core of power, and, as long as he wasn't taken by surprise, Jack was confident in dealing with whatever Hero could throw at him.

The two crossed gazes, reading each other's calculations. Hero tsked. "Very well. I hoped I wouldn't need to use this here, but so be it. Let me show you the true power of a hero."

"Sure, and I'll show you the true power of an ass-kicking," Jack replied, but his mirth was cut short. The new power streaming out of Hero was no joke. Dark tendrils filled the void, spreading far and wide, carrying a weight too heavy for the mortal world. Jack could sense it like a bonfire in Hero's belly, something great in there burning itself to achieve new heights of power. Jack suddenly had an odd sensation, as if Hero grew denser, weighing millions of tons.

"INSOLENCE!"

Angry divine Daos assaulted them from another side. The Gods stepped in. The Heaven Immortal teleported at the same time, appearing before them like he'd always been there, and the Gods froze mid-step.

Jack's eyes widened, as did every other onlooker's. One robot blocked the path of ten Gods, wires trailing from behind it into rifts of space. It would have been impressive if this wasn't an enemy.

"HEAVEN IMMORTAL! WHAT DO YOU THINK YOU'RE DOING?" Axelor shouted, his divine voice shaking the fabric of reality. Yet, as imposing as he looked, there was no hiding the fact that he'd chosen to speak instead of attack.

The Archons watching narrowed their eyes. "Are they afraid of him?" the Arch Priestess wondered. "That can't be good."

"This duel was agreed upon," the Heaven Immortal replied calmly. "No one shall interfere."

"HE BURNS THE SOUL OF OUR SIBLING."

"The core was spoils of battle. Elder Hero can do with it whatever he likes."

The Gods' aura churned like an angry fire in which someone had thrown a vat of oil.

"DO NOT THINK WE FEAR YOU, IMMORTAL. WE ARE HERE TO DESTROY YOU. WE WERE WILLING TO WAIT FOR THIS MORTAL CHARADE TO FINISH, BUT SUCH DISRESPECT WILL NOT PASS."

It was quite clear they did fear him. Jack didn't know why—the Heaven Immortal's aura was no stronger than most Archons, noticeably below even the weakest of Gods.

In any case, even if they did fear him for some reason, Axelor was right. Since they'd fight anyway, they had little reason to endure such disrespect. A thousand calculations ran through Jack's mind. He had to act fast.

"*Let me fight him,*" he telepathically told Axelor.

"WHY?"

Jack explained his plan. The Gods, who were ready to attack, suddenly teleported back to their original positions. **"FINISH THIS BATTLE,"** Axelor commanded the world. **"AND THEN IT'S WAR."**

The Heaven Immortal hesitated, as if surprised by this development, then also teleported away. Jack and Hero remained alone in the middle of this vast starry field.

"You were saying?" Jack said, turning to his opponent.

Hero flashed with power. "In my name as a hero, I will end you."

The core of the deceased Mass God burned inside him, infusing his body with endless mass and his Dao with divine providence. Jack knew that for every moment they spent fighting in this state, part of the Mass God's essence burned away forever. He had to end this fast, though carrying out his plan wasn't simple.

The two flashed, meeting in the center of the void. Supernova met heavy sword. The clash between them was far more balanced than before, Hero's strength sharply increased by burning the core. "Divine Justice!" he kept shouting.

Fists met blade. Their strikes painted the world silver and purple, shedding new light in the galaxy's night sky. Stars were born and died. The belief of Hero's perceived people clamped around Jack like a vise, threatening to suffocate him.

"It's funny," Jack said between all-out strikes. "Your divinity is a pale imitation of the real thing, achieved through a shortcut, the same way your heroism is nothing compared to mine."

"What!"

Jack pressed the attack, not letting Hero act out his shock. Brilliant purple and silver rivers illuminated the void. "You are not a true hero," he said between punches. He paused to dodge the greatsword, then continued, "Your achievements were all given to you. Your masters are the world's tyrants. How could a true hero work for them?"

"You know nothing about me!" Hero cried out.

"That's where you're mistaken," Jack replied. Despite their frantic battle, he spared a hint of his power to make their voices echo undisturbed through the void, reaching everyone's ears. "Unlike you, I'm too experienced to underestimate any opponent. I had people research you before this. You were born as royalty to a B-Grade faction. Your early achievements came in the form of stomping the rebellions of starved farmers. You labeled yourself a hero as you committed endless atrocities against your enemies, who were nothing but oppressed people fighting for the future of their children. You pushed them into the ground and laughed upon their corpses."

"Lies!" Hero roared.

"Are they? Because that's what I heard about you. Your heroic achievements were always against the wrong people—as they still are. When you helped your family eradicate the space pirates of the Gentle Sun constellation, who were those space pirates attacking? Innocent people, or slave traders working for your father's interests? When you saved the plantations of planet Eresol from local bandits, were they really bandits, or were they people your family had starved, desperately trying to feed their families and escape your oppression?"

"Shut up!"

"The Immortals helped you frame yourself as the hero, but all you're doing is patting your own back!" Jack declared, laughing. "What hero? You're nothing but an enforcer!"

A tremendous wave of energy blasted Jack, headed by the heavy blade of a greatsword. He blocked the strike, flying back a bit to dissipate the blow.

"What do you know about me?" Hero asked, panting, his body still wreathed in the dead god's flames. "What do you know about being a hero!"

The flames dancing around him made a stark contrast against his white armor. They framed his bloodshot eyes in a scary light, making him resemble a hero less and less.

"I told you, I *am* a hero," Jack replied. "A true one, unlike you. I overcame terrible odds to save my planet from the B-Grade Animal Kingdom. I fought tyrants and stood up for the right thing. I almost doomed myself defending my values. Unlike you, who only ever fought balanced battles, I had to struggle for every advantage I ever received. In fact, you could say my current standing and power are the results of true heroism. I don't usually tout my own horn like this, but if we're talking heroes, I'm far more qualified than you to possess that title!"

Hero's gaze flared dangerously. Jack only laughed and pressed on, "You were unlucky to face me, Hero. Against anyone else, you might have stood a chance, but when daring to use your frail Dao before me, only matching my power because of desperately burning massive resources, you are completely inadequate. I am the living proof of your Dao's failures. A true hero stands before you, and that makes you feel so small."

"Shut the fuck up!" Hero roared, finally pushed past the limits of his patience. He barreled forward, sword poised to strike even as his aura wilted. All around Jack, space erupted with light. Silver beams emerged from hidden crevices in space, placed there during Hero's previous attacks, and lunged at Jack. A terrible mass of power besieged him, all of Hero's potential erupting in one calculated strike. A shocked expression emerged on Jack's face. Hero grinned manically.

"Die in the name of heroism!" he shouted. "Sword of the People!"

Silver swords fell on Jack from all directions. Hero's sword pierced in, carrying a dead god's power. Jack raised his gaze—and, suddenly, his shocked expression was wiped by a smirk. "I don't think so," he said.

Sparks and green light erupted together as Jack grew taller, with two extra arms. The silver swords fell on an invisible barrier around him, deteriorating like they'd weathered the endless passage of time. The silver sword pierced into that same barrier, but Hero desperately burned his own lifeforce to forcefully penetrate.

Jack's barrier of entropy shattered, having already dealt with all the silver swords and delayed Hero's main strike. In that moment of delay, a black sphere had formed in place of Jack's fist, sitting eerily still. He pushed it into the tip of the sword. Hero's silver greatsword pierced that darkness and kept going, its length gradually consumed by the black hole. Horror finally appeared in his eyes, but it was too late. Jack pushed the hole deeper, fully consuming Hero's sword and arm, then punching it into his abdomen, where it tore and swallowed his armor like paper.

The black hole pierced into Hero's body, but it wasn't as wild as it used to be. A thin barrier of entropy was draped around it, letting Jack control what it ate and what it didn't.

When the lunging Hero came to a standstill, his expression frozen into horror and disbelief, Jack's hand was in his stomach. He slowly pulled it back, revealing, that in place of the black hole, he possessed a regenerated fist. In it he held a dark, burning spherical core. He extinguished its flames with the strength of his own divinity.

Everyone rose to their feet. The Heaven Immortal teleported beside Jack, reaching out to grab him, but a dark tentacle slapped the hand away even as Jack dodged. The Heaven Immortal grabbed Hero's body and teleported back to the safety of its army.

"This is impossible," he said. "You extracted the god core. Give it back."

"It's my spoils of battle," Jack said, brazenly inspecting the core. "I can do with it whatever I like. Right?"

These were the exact same words the Heaven Immortal had used to defend Hero's actions before. Now, Jack threw them right back in its face, a crisp slap which echoed throughout the universe.

Axelor gazed at Jack with appreciation, while the Heaven Immortal considered its next words. "Taunting me is pointless. I possess no emotions," it said. "In return for sparing Hero's life, I will not kill you immediately. Return me the core, and I promise not to execute you after the battle either."

"Ah, but you see, Heaven Immortal, you're wrong about two things," Jack said, lazily flicking the god core up and down in his hand. "First, taunting you very much has a point. You may be emotionless, but I enjoy it. Second... While I did technically spare

Hero's life, you killed him when you took him over there. You see, I can't control entropy that well yet. Whoops."

"What are you—" Hero muttered through gritted teeth, still folded in on himself, when his eyes shone with new horror. "NO!" he shouted. The Heaven Immortal sensed it at the same time and pushed Hero into the empty space ahead of them, far from the army.

When Jack had pierced the black hole into Hero's body and retrieved the core, he didn't dissipate it. He just left it in Hero's stomach, perfectly covered in an entropy barrier which prevented it from eating him up. That same barrier absorbed all perception, effectively hiding the black hole so no one could notice it without careful scanning.

When the Heaven Immortal dragged Hero away, Jack truly lost the ability to control that entropy barrier. A hole formed, the barrier shattered, and Hero found himself with an active black hole in his stomach. What's worse, his body had regenerated, closing the wound. The black hole was sealed inside—and all it had to eat was Hero.

"NO!" he screamed again as his body warped. Bones snapped, flesh tore. His horrified face was distorted as it got sucked in alongside his armor, and all that was left of him was a black hole absorbing its surroundings like a whirlpool. It exploded a moment later, sending a dark shockwave through the void.

Everyone watched silently. The Heaven Immortal tilted its head. **"I rescind my words. You will be destroyed."**

"Try it, bitch," Jack replied, giving it the middle finger.

The Immortal army moved behind its leader. A-Grades flew in, led by Archons and followed by B-Grades. "Protect Jack!" the Arch Priestess shouted, and her army charged right back, all of them converging on Jack's location. The Gods had already appeared there, and Jack suddenly found himself surrounded by dozens of Archons, all ready to fight each other. War cries echoed. The first blasts of energy were launched. The Arch Priestess and Heaven Immortal were flying at each other.

"GIVE ME THE CORE," Axelor commanded.

Jack hesitated, and in that half second, the Time God rippled, and all the Gods shuddered with rage.

"YOU ARE AWAKENING ENAS!" Axelor shouted, his voice echoing so hard it paused the battlefield. Jack didn't even have time to panic. The Space God snapped its fingers, and a large portal appeared over the battlefield, falling over everyone and forcefully teleporting them. It wasn't a particularly powerful spell for a God. All Archons could have resisted, but they chose not to. The entire battlefield was sucked into the portal, leaving a large empty portion of space in the Spiral Stair galaxy.

At the same time, in a different galaxy far, far away, a portal appeared out of nowhere, spitting out two armies and ten Gods. A black hole in the middle of unraveling towered in the distance.

"Shit," Rory said.

Axelor waved a tentacle, and all the runic columns shattered, consumed by entropy. The black hole resumed its rotation, while a muted cry of frustration echoed through space. Jack was stunned. The Arch Priestess was stunned. The Heaven Immortal hesitated before resuming its attack, and the two armies clashed in a cataclysmic explosion which illuminated that entire corner of the universe.

CHAPTER EIGHTY

HIGH-LEVEL CHAOS

Rory looked askance at the two armies and ten Gods who'd just popped into existence. He glanced back at the black hole, where the twelve runic pillars had been destroyed. The Sage appeared beside him.

"Elder Sage," Rory said in a shaky voice, "what do we do?"

The Sage carried a calm smile. "This is unfortunate, but I have a feeling everything will work out. How about you go join our army while I wait here?"

Rory looked at the Sage's confident face, then at the army of the Black Hole Church which had spawned nearby. "Yes, sir!" he cried out as he flew over.

Jack looked at the new astral field around them. He didn't recognize the place—strange stars littered the void, not quite a galaxy, but clustered in large or smaller groups with vast swathes of void between them. There were also a few isolated ones, lazily drifting through the darkness. Through the gaps between clusters, other galaxies were visible. Jack couldn't make out the Milky Way—from afar, all spiral galaxies looked alike.

"I thought your universe only had galaxies. What is this place?" Fiend Prince said. Jack had retreated to the front of his army after the duel, where the eager monster was also waiting.

"The former Ancient galaxy," he replied. "The cradle of all life—except space monsters—which was destroyed during the First Crusade. Enas was trapped in a black hole near it."

"Wait," Fiend Prince said, gazing at the large black hole hovering nearby. "You don't mean..."

"That's right. The black hole you see holds Enas, the God of Life, and those funky rods were trying to rescue him."

Fiend Prince stared agape. The plan of rescuing Enas was top secret—besides Jack, Brock, Boatman, and the Archons, almost nobody knew. To them, they'd just randomly teleported to a different point in space. Nothing much seemed to have changed, but those in the know were devastated. With the Gods and Immortals here, saving Enas was impossible. They'd just have to fight and hope the Gods didn't turn on them afterward.

With the sudden teleportation putting a lull on the battle, Axelor turned to the Arch Priestess. **"WHAT IS THE MEANING OF THIS?"** he asked, his voice shaking the void. Hints of his aura rolled over the Church army, giving the cultivators a sinking feeling.

"Does it really matter?" the Arch Priestess said, rising over her soldiers. Her expression was bitter. "It's over now, anyway. Let's just fight the war."

"ENAS MUST NOT BE FREED."

"Yes, it will be as you say."

"That was an interesting plot you orchestrated, Arch Priestess," the Heaven Immortal's voice echoed, "but you failed. We will end this now."

The Immortal army washed over the cosmos again. They descended on their enemies like a swarm of unfathomably powerful locusts, blasting the void open with endless surges of power.

World-destroying attacks flew everywhere, annihilating the ambient Dao, ripping it apart as everyone wrestled for control. In moments, the ambient Dao was gone, replaced with the wild energy of thousands of inner worlds. Almost every master of the universe was present, whether they had to leave seclusion to make it or withdraw from their retirement. This battle would be remembered for billions of years.

The Church army, while fewer in number than their opponents, was equally imposing. B-Grades fell into formation led by A-Grades. Massive runic circles appeared, powered by clusters of inner worlds, to spray death upon the enemy. Jack watched lances the size of planets spear through the void, launched like they weighed nothing. Several A-Grade wizards combined their powers to form sun-like fireballs. A storm of Space Dao sliced apart an area the size of a solar system. Summons sprang into existence—colossal angels and monsters, twelve-headed hydras, ogres the size of planets.

The usually tame fabric of reality now pulsed rapidly, every tiny touch causing it to tear and open to the void beyond. Even that void was weaponized, certain high-level cultivators pulling it out in batches and firing it at their opponents.

In this chaotic melee, the worst were Time cultivators. Fighting in three dimensions was bad enough—they spread the battle into the fourth, creating glimpses of reality which had yet to be or already had been. Every B-Grade's Dao perception was short-circuited by the almighty chaos, forcing them to rely just on their sight to gauge the battlefield. In such a high-level conflict, they were little more than pawns. Only the strongest of them could fight freely. The rest remained close to their assigned A-Grades, adding their powers into formations.

Whenever a formation shattered, its members spread into the battlefield, fighting not to win, but to survive. Jack glimpsed many B-Grades getting sucked into dimensional gaps and disappear, or simply get torn apart in the aftermath of a more powerful cultivator's battle.

Many A-Grade cultivators were working by themselves, going head-to-head against the enemy masters. Dozens of these once elite confrontations now covered the entire battlefield. Jack spied Elder Boatman leading a squad of three A-Grades into battle, right under where Archon One Fist faced an enemy Archon clad in a mantle of chaos. Space around them was empty and desolate for endless miles, the tiny bodies of cultivators barely noticeable before the massive halos of their powers.

Sovereign Heavenly Spoon and Min Ling dashed into an enemy squad: a planet-sized green phantom tried to scoop up some cultivators and eat them, but an equally massive hammer smashed into it, eliciting a pained moan. Red lightning escaped a crack in the void to assault the hammer, melting it, while purple flames electrified its caster. The green phantom escaped the hammer's suppression, and scooped the enemy cultivator directly into its mouth. It burped before roaming deeper into the battlefield.

There was another part of the battlefield. A part which Jack wanted to rush, but which he'd been advised not to. In a distant region of the void, the ten Gods and the most powerful Archons of each side struggled together. They were far less people than in the main battlefield, but their battle easily overwhelmed anything else.

Jack was momentarily transfixed. The Gods battled in a rough group, throwing around their colossal powers like it meant nothing. A lesser cultivator wouldn't have noticed, but Jack saw in their Dao manipulations the signs of amateurs. They possessed great power but didn't know how to wield it properly—probably because they never had to. A significant measure of their power was wasted. They weren't *really* amateurs, just nowhere close to possessing the average Archon's wealth of battle experience. Despite that, they could match the mightiest of mortal Archons.

Jack briefly wondered whether the Gods had actually reached the S-Grade and just didn't know how to control their power. A wave of aura dispelled that notion. The Gods were clearly Archons, just deeper into that realm than any mortal had been able to reach.

Axelor himself was on a different level. His dark tentacles lashed around wildly, each carrying the power of a normal Archon. They were made of Entropy so dense it turned solid, and he had an entire planet's worth. If he desired to destroy a place like Earth, it would take nothing more than an afterthought, similar to a human flicking a switch.

Right now, that massive behemoth of a God had clashed repeatedly against the Heaven Immortal and the other thirty-two Immortals. They had arrayed themselves into a seamless formation to hold their own against the God of Entropy, forcing him to a standstill.

The other nine Gods and the Arch Priestess—the only representative of Church forces in that battlefield—faced the elite forces of the Immortal army. They didn't possess ten extreme Archons to match all of them—in fact, they barely possessed ten Archons total—but they were backed by dozens of A-Grades, all contributing their power to establish a wide array of formations. In a wild display of skill, they managed to stall the nine Gods and the Arch Priestess, who was an extreme Archon herself. Jack wondered what exactly their plan was, because both their extreme Archon front and the thirty-three Immortals seemed to struggle.

Because the Immortals needed to spend most of their forces on the Gods, only a few Archons and A-Grades were left in the main battlefield, but they were enough to match the Church army.

Jack and Brock had already been rushing to join the battle. They were equal to an Archon and a peak A-Grade respectively—their arrival could massively impact the main battlefield, which split in their wake. Jack shot a straight punch. It tunneled through the battlefield, dragging along many enemy A and B-Grades, swirling them along its path. It pierced through several formations before an Archon dove in its path, blocking it between crossed arms.

"Jack Rust!" she shouted, an Amazonian goddess somewhat similar to Vivi in appearance. "Your duel made my blood boil. Do you dare to face me, Archon Three Lives?"

Jack smiled. "Why wouldn't I dare?" he shouted back, registering that her title had little to do with her imposing physique. "Will you be alright, Brock?" he asked, turning to the side, only to find that Brock was already gone. A massive golden brorilla rampaged through another corner of the battlefield, cladding all allies it came near in a thin golden aura. The aura persisted as the brorilla moved, slowly conquering the battlefield.

Jack laughed, locked his stare onto Archon Three Lives, and charged.

Elder Boatman summoned a flood of death energy and sent it swooping forward, finally overwhelming his opponent's Chaos. He sighed as he looked around. *Back in my day, an A-Grade battle was the talk of the millennium,* he thought, taking in the dozens of A-Grade battles happening simultaneously. He sighed again. *Youngsters.*

Yet, he couldn't deny his excitement. It'd been a long time since he grew too powerful to fight often, and this war brought back all the passion his life had been missing for the last half a million years. He loathed all the deaths which came from it, but no cultivator could resist the allure of a good battle.

At least, most of us dying are old folk, he thought, gazing over the battlefield again. The majority of cultivators were past their prime. It made sense for a high-level battlefield, yet it still struck him as a pleasant sight. He was in good company.

His vision fell on the youngsters. The geniuses of the Church, packed into one tight squad and sent to pursue their luck. He and many others had agreed to keep an eye on them, step in if necessary, but that hadn't been the case so far. The geniuses performed admirably. He watched as a giant spoon slipped under an enemy formation and raised it all up. Red lightning and purple flames crackled around it, frying enemy cultivators, while an array of deep but weak Daos enhanced them both. Starhair, Strawpin, and Fiend

Prince had been sent to support Heavenly Spoon and Min Ling—the future pillars of the Church fighting together.

He turned his gaze to another part of the battlefield, where Brock led a hundred low-level cultivators into a rampage, and Jack faced off against an Archon.

I'll be able to retire peacefully in a few years, Boatman thought, *provided we win.* He spotted an enemy late A-Grade glancing over the genius squad and moving over. Boatman rushed to intercept her—far enough away that the geniuses wouldn't notice.

CHAPTER EIGHTY-ONE
PRAISE THE IMMORTALS

STRAWPIN CREASED HER BROWS AS SHE FED ENERGY INTO THE FORMATION core, a five-sided diamond crafted specifically for this purpose. Their squad's victories were nowhere near as easy as they seemed. They were constantly besieged by shockwaves not even aimed at them erupting all over. Her Dao perception was so overwhelmed she'd shut it off, relying completely on eyesight to navigate the battle, which meant she couldn't see in every direction at once for the first time in many years. It stressed her out.

A powerful tug slipped into her soul, requesting more power than she was putting out. She complied, also wiping her Dao off the energy she sent away, gritting her teeth as some of the straw floating around her dissipated. Overhead, Min Ling unleashed a powerful attack fueled by the energy she'd just received. An enemy A-Grade fell screaming.

"Are you okay?" Starhair asked, close beside her.

"Of course," she lied. "You aren't?"

"Of course I am," he lied back.

"I'm better than both of you," Fiend Prince declared through gritted teeth. A constant stream of crimson energy left his body to sink into the diamond. Strawpin would have laughed if she wasn't exhausted.

A powerful aura fell over them. Strawpin looked up in fear to find a peak A-Grade cultivator hovering above their formation, cold eyes taking them in. It was a species she'd never seen before—some sort of gray, taut-skinned humanoid. The cultivator aimed its palm downward to release a hail of needles. Heavenly Spoon and Min Ling turned to them, galvanizing their powers with a painful tug at the three peak B-Grades' inner worlds. A spoon-wielding green phantom, red lightning, and purple flames surged upward, wrapping around the needles in a colorful showdown. It would only delay the inevitable—they did not possess the power to fight a peak A-Grade.

"Leave my friends alone."

A powerful aura appeared nearby. Strawpin turned to find Jack, his body covered in shallow wounds and purple sparks, holding the lifeless body of an amazonian-looking Archon in one hand. He was panting, but not overly hurt. The moment he appeared, the enemy cultivator's eyes turned from cold and merciless to terrified—it tried to teleport away but found space around it sealed. Jack punched out, a river of purple power which crashed into the enemy and shattered their body, throwing away all needles just by passing by. The energy flow continued deeper into the battlefield, turning smoothly to avoid allies and only strike at enemies. One punch took down over a dozen enemies—most of them B-Grades.

"Are you okay?" Jack asked, looking over his friends.

"We are now," Min Ling replied, flashing him a warm smile. "Thanks."

"No problem."

He let the Archon's body drop and teleported away, escaping Strawpin's vision. As Heavenly Spoon and Min Ling looked for the next opponent, unperturbed by their near-demise, a golden aura flooded their surroundings. "Join the bro train," said a majestic, familiar voice. Brock smiled at them. "We're riding to victory."

Strawpin found herself assenting, sensing the golden aura wrap around her body and subtly tie her powers into everyone else's. Their previous formation collapsed, the diamond running it shattering into dust, as all five of them joined a massive golden formation centered by Brock and containing dozens of other cultivators. They formed the outline of a massive golden brorilla, with each cultivator's power not annexed, but contributing to the formation's uniqueness. Different energy signatures merged harmonically. Strawpin felt useful.

"Choo-choo," said the massive golden brorilla, diving deeper into the battlefield, trailing behind it a majestic golden aura. The enemies in its path were swatted away like bowling pins.

Jack was rushing through the battlefield, searching for a weak Archon to fight, when an imposing voice slammed into his mind.

"BRING ME THE CORE," Axelor commanded.

The God hovered in the distance, clashing repeatedly against a thirty-three-pointed polygon created by the Immortals. His dark tentacles found little purchase, and his attacks were growing wilder by the moment.

Jack paused mid-stride, hesitating. "If I bring you the core of the God of Mass, will you promise to let us all live afterward?"

"NO."

"I'm not sure you know how negotiations work."

"I AM A GOD. I DO NOT NEGOTIATE WITH MORTALS."

"Well, I'm kind of a god too, and I'm known to be quite stubborn sometimes, so you might want to reconsider."

"WE ARE ALLIES. BRING ME THE CORE OR WE RISK DEFEAT. MY ENDURANCE WON'T LAST FOREVER."

"If you don't promise to let us all live afterwards, I'm not giving you shit. Not yet, at least. I'd rather get both you and the Immortals exhausted so the Church can finish the job."

The God paused for far too long, then, "***I SWEAR IT. NOW BRING ME THE CORE.***"

"There you go! That wasn't difficult, was it?"

Jack had recently realized he was strong enough to defeat weaker Archons without a prolonged battle. That didn't mean he should approach the highly volatile clash of Axelor against thirty-three Immortals. He took out the core of the God of Mass—a dark, spherical thing the size of his fist, which he suddenly found himself wishing he had the System to identify. The void before him parted like a curtain into which Jack slid the core. Sensing the incoming teleportation, Axelor briefly let the space lock surrounding his body fall to receive it. He then quickly re-teleported it somewhere else.

The other Gods reacted immediately. They disengaged from the Archons and A-Grades they'd been fighting, a God made of stars reaching out to grab the core which materialized out of thin air in front of it.

"**MY FELLOW GODS,**" **it said,** "**LET US UNITE.**"

A bright light blinded the battlefield. Excluding Axelor, the other nine Gods melted into bright liquid, then gathered together in two large groups. One contained five Gods, while the other held four and the dead god's core. In front of everyone's stunned gazes, the two large masses of reality-making liquid solidified into new shapes—two new behemoths superior to even Axelor in size and aura.

One was perfectly solid, containing the essence of matter and physical energy. Even from afar, Jack felt such intense ripples of strength that he knew his nascent Universe of the Body couldn't hold a candle to this God's physicality. Without a doubt, this was the God of Matter. Everything in the physical realms fell under his purview.

As for the second form, it was an ethereal and formless, vaguely humanoid figure which seemed to contain every kind of energy. Its aura was equally imposing. This was the God of Energy.

Jack and everyone else were stunned as they watched the transformation occur. Thinking back to the different Gods, there were indeed five embodying physical properties or states and five pertaining to energy, if one decided to be loose with their interpretation, but he didn't think they'd actually combine like this.

Their reasoning became immediately obvious. The power of each of these new Gods was greater than the sum of their parts. They were even greater than Axelor, each emanating an aura twice as powerful as his. They remained Archons, however.

Floating between the two greater Gods, the Arch Priestess looked tiny. Her aura was a breeze to their storm. "You didn't do this in the First Crusade," she managed to say.

"WE DID NOT KNOW HOW, NOR HAD WE FELT THE NEED TO LEARN," one of the two new Gods replied, its voice pulsing with five different undertones.

"NOW WE DO," added the other God, four undertones to its voice, **"AND WE CAME TO WIN."**

They charged into the battlefield. The collection of Archons and A-Grades holding them back before gathered their powers, forming a massive, multicolored shield. Jack knew he could be punching that thing for hours and not even crack it. The God of Matter slammed into the shield, shattering it like glass. The God of Energy raised its hands and a reality-bending beam flowed out of them, smashing the gathered cultivators and sending them flying. Several died on the spot.

With the nine lesser Gods combining into two greater ones, their powers had increased massively. Watching the devastation they wrought, Jack wondered whether he'd messed up by giving away the core. If these two Gods and Axelor decided to turn against him or the Church afterward, there would be no resisting them. The Immortals and their army couldn't stop them either.

The two greater Gods, however, didn't share that thought. After blasting away the weaker enemies, they turned on the Immortals instead of barreling into the main battlefield. Two powerful gazes, along with Axelor's, landed on the Heaven Immortal.

"BRING OUT THE FORM WHICH KILLED OUR SIBLING,"

they said at the same time. "LET US CLEANSE ENAS'S SIN WITH THE APEX OF DIVINE POWER."

Facing such overwhelming might, the Heaven Immortal didn't appear flustered—if it even could be. It tilted its head. **"Very well. Your divine power is impressive, but this will go no different than last time."**

The Immortal formation shattered. Thirty-three robots went flying in different directions, and Jack, watching from afar, realized that thirty-two of them were lifeless. Only the Heaven Immortal remained, its form shrouded with ethereal cogs, a vision similar to the mini-System core which had existed inside Jack's body, only much grander.

The wires which extended from the back of the Heaven Immortal's head into spatial rifts were retracted, more of their length revealed as they pulled something out of the void. Complex machinery came into view. Jack felt a tug in his soul as he saw a sphere of polished cogs and gears completely suffused with magic. The energy contained in that sphere was the greatest amount he'd ever sensed, and that included the two greater Gods before him. He could tell that the sphere, only a few feet in diameter, was a marvel of magical mechanics—it contained compressed, endless miles of machinery interspersed with the Dao of multiple Archons—perhaps more of them than on the entire battlefield combined.

"By the System born, and by the System cometh," the Heaven Immortal chanted. Every cultivator fighting for the Immortals shuddered. Some clutched at their chests and others screamed as energy rose from their open mouths, corporeal gears tearing through their throats. Each cultivator spat out a smaller sphere of magic machinery, which all flew into a side-door of the Heaven Immortal's larger one. With every small sphere it absorbed, its power increased, as did the diversity and depth of its Daos. Even the Archons weren't spared, their cog spheres eliciting the greatest impact. Every cultivator who released a sphere was left drained, their innards riddled with wounds and their energy siphoned.

This sounded slow, but it took place in the blink of an eye. Jack didn't have much time to react. Everyone who tried to grab a sphere before it flew or teleported over were shocked, their bodies flung away by a burst of power.

"Arrogant flesh," the Heaven Immortal intoned. "You may not interact with my power."

Jack suppressed a shiver of fear. Those were the mini-System cores, he realized. I didn't know they could be ripped out in such a manner. They basically stole the cultivators' energy and copied their Dao understandings! If I hadn't removed my System core before coming here, would I be like them?

He suspected his Universe of the Body would interfere with the process, but he was glad he didn't need to find out. He wasn't glad for the massive amount of power now hovering behind the Heaven Immortal though.

The large sphere throbbed, shrinking into itself with every pulse. In a moment, it went from several feet wide to just a few inches, at which point the Heaven Immortal grabbed and swallowed it—a mouth was the only facial feature the robot possessed. The wires connecting the back of its head to the ball persisted, now crawling into his throat like futuristic worms.

The power radiating from his body spiked. It reached the level of Axelor before easily overtaking him. Even the two greater Gods paled before it. They frowned. **"THIS IS DIFFERENT THAN LAST TIME. YOU TRICKED US."**

The Heaven Immortal wiped its mouth, from which some green liquid had leaked, then smiled. Its mouth extended in a creepily wide grin which would have reached its ears if it had any. The wires and tubes still stretched into it, making for a grotesque sight.

Jack realized he'd been holding his breath. Shivers ran down his spine—not from shock, but from pure terror. The current Heaven Immortal was seriously pushing against the boundaries of the Archon realm. Jack was confident nothing could get stronger without a breakthrough.

“Nevermind,” he whispered. “Giving them the core was the right call. There’s no way they could have handled this monster before. They barely can now.”

“Behold the peak of mortal power,” the Heaven Immortal declared over a frozen battlefield, “and behold the start of a new age. The Old Gods fall as the New Gods rise. Praise the Immortal System. Praise the New World.”

CHAPTER EIGHTY-TWO

THE SPIRIT OF CULTIVATORS

THE WAR HAD SLAMMED ON ITS BRAKES. TWO GREATER GODS AND AXELOR stared down at the Heaven Immortal's enhanced form—a bunch of titans about to clash. Compared to their overwhelming auras, even A-Grades felt inconsequential, and Archons couldn't help a deep sense of inferiority.

Jack shook his head as he spectated from a distance. Even if he went all-out, he couldn't even come close to these beings. He couldn't even beat one of the extreme Archon lesser gods from before. Axelor was a step above them, the greater gods were a step above him, and the current Heaven Immortal was yet another step higher. Meanwhile, Jack was an early A-Grade. That was a gap no amount of talent could bridge.

Even the strongest Archons of either side were only at the level of lesser gods. When the big guns came out, all they could do was sit to the side and hope. As for the B-Grades and A-Grades fighting each other, that was just a joke.

The Arch Priestess shook her head in self-deprecation. She realized now that the only reason the Gods had summoned the Church was to hold back the Immortals' army from creating formations to assist the Heaven Immortal.

The two armies came to a stalemate, warily glancing at each other as they both surveyed the battle. The Immortal army had originally held the advantage, but the Heaven Immortal's transformation had sucked enough energy out of them that the two armies were now roughly evenly matched. There was no reason to fight. If one army tried to create formations and participate in the greater battle, the other army would just stop them, shedding blood on both sides for no reason. They might as well watch.

Even Jack was in the same position. The only one still moving was Brock, spreading his golden aura over more and more of the Church forces.

"**MORTAL CANNOT OVERCOME DIVINE,**" one of the two Greater Gods said, its voice echoing with five undertones. It was slightly stronger than the other.

"**My calculations indicate it can. I will prove it soon enough,**" the Heaven Immortal replied. Its aura erupted, a clinical white expanse carrying extreme efficiency but little spirit. It charged into the Gods and blew them up in an explosion which filled the galaxy.

Everyone in the two armies rushed away. Even the aftermath of such a battle wasn't something they could withstand. They made significant distance before turning around to watch again.

The Heaven Immortal was nestled between the three Gods. Its white powers contained blue streaks in the exact same color as System screens. At the same time, its moves contained every single Dao, changing properties automatically to counter the Gods.

Axelor moved first. He conjured tentacles of darkness, swinging them at the Heaven Immortal, who conjured white shields to block. Entropy was blocked by the concept of Infinity—it stood at a slightly lower level than Axelor's laws, but a little extra energy made them evenly matched. The tentacles clashed into the shields and were repelled.

The two greater gods attacked right after. One unleashed what looked like a solar beam, while the other charged and straightforwardly tried to punch the Heaven Immortal. The robot used a far too complex combination of physical Daos to block the beam, then twisted space to make the punch miss. In the same move, it unleashed a soul attack on both greater gods, sending them staggering.

"You are powerful yet incomplete," it informed them. "I possess all Daos in existence. You do not. The victor is obvious."

The Gods tried to fuse their powers, but there was something missing. In the end, the best the two Greater Gods and Axelor could achieve was to synchronize their attacks, but the Heaven Immortal conjured over a hundred different Daos in the blink of an eye and countered everything. Each of those Daos was demonstrated at the Archon level. Several clashes later, the Gods had been pushed into a definitive disadvantage.

"You cannot escape," the robot said. "I am faster and stronger. You should surrender your cores. Persisting is pointless."

The Gods roared. A massive energy beam as wide as a star crashed into the robot, which blocked it with a flat energy shield. The beam spread in all directions, impacting distant stars and shattering them, carving deep scars in the fabric of reality which took a long time to regenerate. The Archons of each army were working together to shield their people from the shockwaves—the Immortals' army was retreating even farther away, cheering for their leader.

"Arch Priestess!" Archon Truth shouted. "We should run as well! It's not safe here!"

The Arch Priestess did not reply. Her gaze was glued to the battle—specifically, Axelor.

Another exchange ended badly for the Gods. Jack, who spectated the battle, knew that nothing could change. These three Gods possessed great power but little to no variations. All they could do was use the same attacks over and over. The Heaven Immortal had copied the Daos of every B-Grade and above in its forces, as well as every powerful cultivator's who had ever existed within the System —it possessed nearly infinite Daos and great control over them. Countering everything the Gods could throw at it was simple. The only way for them to win was to overpower it, but that was clearly impossible, as its strength rose above theirs.

Jack's stomach dropped. This is a losing battle. We lost. Nobody can beat that thing. Even I... I'm not even close!

Consequent breakthroughs from his recent A-Grade transformation would take a very long time, as his inner cultivators needed to develop. By his estimations, he'd need to reach at least the peak A-Grade to be able to contend with the Heaven Immortal, and that would require centuries in the least.

Should I run away? he thought, hating the idea. If he escaped—which he wasn't certain he could do—he would be leaving everyone else to die. So many good people who believed in him. It would be a betrayal of his Dao, and would it ever recover?

He didn't need to consider it. Soon after he had the thought, he felt a tremendous pressure fall on him. His blood ran cold. The pressure wasn't suppressing him, just stalking him like a predator. He had the feeling that, if he moved, he'd die.

The Heaven Immortal is watching me, he realized bitterly. It's not stupid. It can let anyone else escape, but not me and Brock. We have the power to overcome it in the future—we must die today. If we try to leave, it will ignore the Gods and rush over here, killing our entire army in the process.

Is there nothing I can do?

He'd cultivated for such a long time, sacrificed so much. Yet, when it really mattered, all he could do was sit on the sidelines. He hated that feeling. Hated it so much. His mind spun with ideas, but all were fruitless.

The Arch Priestess ignored her subordinate's pleas as she focused on the single strand of survival she could see. "*You must do it,*" she said. "*Don't you see? If you don't, everyone dies!*"

"***MORTAL LIVES DO NOT CONCERN ME,***" Axelor replied. He was conversing with her mid-battle. His growing exhaustion and desperation echoed in his voice, making him sound like an old, sad whale. "***ENAS HAS SINNED. HE MUST NOT RETURN.***"

"*Let him fix the problem he created!*" *the Arch Priestess pleaded.* "*If the two of you combine as well, you'll be strong enough to take on the Heaven Immortal!*"

"***YOU DO NOT UNDERSTAND WHAT YOU SPEAK OF.***"

"*Are you stupid? You are about to die! Everyone is! How can you be so stuck-up that you don't see there is no other choice!*"

"***MIND YOUR WORDS, MORTAL.***"

"*Or what? You're going to kill me? You're already doing that!*"

"***I AM CONVERSING WITH MY SIBLINGS. WE WILL DECIDE.***"

"*Conversing? How stubborn can you possibly be?*"

A beam of clinical white light cut into Axelor. A third of his body was shaved off, turning him from a sphere into a thick half-moon. His pained moan echoed through the universe. The stars flickered in mourning.

"***WE HAVE DECIDED,***" ***he said in the Arch Priestess's mind.*** "***WE WILL FREE ENAS. USE YOUR MORTALS TO DELAY THE HEAVEN IMMORTAL. DO NOT HESITATE TO SACRIFICE THEM.***"

The three gods moved as one. The Energy God snapped its fingers, teleporting Axelor beside the black hole. It also locked down space around the Heaven Immortal. The Physical God stood between it and the black hole.

"Your last resort will fail," the Heaven Immortal said. "It has been calculated."

It turned into a ray of light which rammed into the Physical God. Tremendous powers clashed. The impact dislodged the void, momentarily robbing spacetime of meaning. The Heaven Immortal remained locked in place by the Energy God, but every distant cultivator felt their senses lurch.

Axelor waved his dark tentacles around the black hole. From a distance, Jack could perceive a forming barrier of entropy at a far larger scale than what he could accomplish. He instantly understood what was happening. Axelor was destroying the black hole, but he'd need some time.

"Cultivators of the Black Hole Church," the Arch Priestess shouted. "Heed my command. Protect Axelor with your lives!"

Jack shot her a glance. He understood her meaning, which was why he could see the pain hidden in her expression. She was commanding them to throw away their lives, and she hated herself for it. Maybe that was why she was the first to charge against the Heaven Immortal. A yellow-clothed arm blocked her way.

"We still need a leader," Archon One Fist said, his back to her, his cape fluttering heroically. "Don't worry, Arch Priestess. We came here prepared to lay down our lives for the future, for our disciples and descendants, for the cultivation world. This is what must be done, so each and every one of us will gladly lay down our lives. Isn't that right, cultivators?"

"Yes, sir!" the entire army shouted at once, Jack included. He looked around to find brave faces consigned to their deaths, wide smiles and fiery eyes. The sense of community which rose in him was hard to describe. These people were heroes, each and every one of them. He was proud to be here. His chest rose, and he released a battle cry, echoing everyone's sentiments.

"CHARGE!" he roared, and the entire army sprinted toward the cataclysmic battle. Everyone operated at their best—formations formed unerringly, cultivators scraped for every hint of power left in them. Archons Great Silver and Truth were at the forefront, radiating their Daos in all their majesty.

"We need you still, Arch Priestess," One Fist said. He turned around and gave her a dashing smile, alongside a thumbs-up. "Let us go first, okay?"

She did not respond. She'd loathed her mask, but today, she was glad for it. It hid her tears.

Thankfully, the Immortal army didn't seem too willing to intervene. They knew that to approach meant suicide, and they did not possess the Church army's resolve. Their side was winning, anyway—they remained watching from a distance.

The Gods stepped back to recover some power as the Church cultivators approached. The Heaven Immortal turned to them. **"Why are you doing this? It will certainly end in your demise. You are miscalcula—"**

He didn't have time to finish. Great Silver and Truth got in its face and detonated their inner worlds. The explosion was as powerful as the all-out attacks of the greater gods, if not more, flinging the Heaven Immortal backward.

"I've spent my life pursuing the peak..." a voice drifted through the void. "At the bitter end, am I finally enough?"

Archon One Fist appeared before the Heaven Immortal, red cape fluttering, bald head and yellow suit looking out of place. He looked tiny as he shot out a punch. Space shattered in a deep groove, the undulations stretching out for light-years. A fist physically met the Heaven Immortal's chest and was cut short by a combination of Daos uniquely crafted to counter him. His fist went flying, cut off at the wrist. He chuckled. "Still not enough..." he muttered as a white hand backslapped him, sending him careening across the void.

"Foolish cultivators," the Heaven Immortal said. "You're miscalculating. You should run away."

They ignored it. Dozens of cultivators flew at it, dozens of inner worlds detonating. The entire galaxy lit up in the fireworks of their last stand, the Church cultivators going out in a glorious blaze. Even the Heaven Immortal was pushed back, unable to deal with these explosions fully.

The people who'd detonated their inner worlds so far were a minority. Most cultivators arrayed themselves in solid formations between the Heaven Immortal and the black hole, a glowing golden aura pulsating over them and helping them fuse their powers. Jack and Brock were amongst them, as were the other young geniuses. For once, all of them stood side by side, ready to give their lives for the greater good.

"The young ones should stand at the back," an elderly A-Grade said, stepping in front of Jack and the others.

"Senior!" he replied, but the old man just gave him a warm smile.

"Don't rush to throw your lives away," he said. "Wait your turn. If you can survive, our sacrifice will have been worth it."

Jack wanted to reply, but the words wouldn't rise through his throat. He watched the old man fly into the second wave of attacks and detonate his inner world alongside another hundred cultivators, all in their waning years. Everyone else watched impatiently—not to escape, but to give their lives in turn. Jack grew emotional.

"Even if we fail here," he said aloud, "I want you all to know that fighting alongside you is my life's greatest blessing."

A woman laughed. "Those should be our words, Jack Rust!" Her words were followed by more cultivators speaking up.

"Right! Dying alongside you is a great honor!"

"Stand back, younglings. Some of us have waited our whole lives for this. Let us have our moment!"

Brock slapped a fist against his chest. "Bros..." he shouted, brorillian eyes getting teary. "I swear I will never forget you!"

"That's more than enough for us!" the cultivators in the third wave replied as they, too, flew at the Heaven Immortal.

"*Make me proud, disciple...*" a familiar voice echoed in Jack's mind. His eyes widened.

"Master Boatman!"

He glimpsed a dark-cloaked form hidden in the third wave of cultivators. A scythe teleported next to Jack even as the form under the cloak bloated, ready to explode alongside everyone else. "*If you survive this, take my scythe to my descendants. Consider it payment for my tutoring,*" were Boatman's final words. He looked at Jack through his hood and warped his wrinkled face into a genuine, youthful smile.

More fireworks filled space. Jack forced himself to look, enduring the searing of his eyelids which would quickly heal. "I swear, Master!" he shouted, taking the scythe into his space ring.

"Why are you doing this?" the Heaven Immortal's voice came distorted through the explosions. It didn't sound hurt, only frustrated. **"You are sacrificing yourselves! It is a bad move!"**

A white hand parted spacetime, bypassing the explosions to appear before the army. Archon One Fist was waiting right there, his bloodied body overshadowed by a wide smile. "It's because we are people, you idiot. Now fuck off."

He erupted in an explosion greater than even Great Silver's and Truth's. The Heaven Immortal was once again pushed back, releasing a roar of impotent fury.

"This makes no sense! I miscalculated nothing!" it roared out.

As the fourth wave of cultivators prepared itself, Jack looked back. The two greater gods were rapidly recovering their powers. Dying before them felt undeserved, but they'd need to be at their best to stand a chance against the Heaven Immortal, even after Enas returned. Even farther behind them, Axelor was done creating a barrier around the black hole. It was clearly straining him, the barrier so large, even he struggled to keep it up. But it was working.

In the exact same process Jack used, the black hole had nothing to absorb as entropy flooded it. Infinite time passed. It grew smaller and smaller until a giant human hand emerged from it and grabbed its side. The hole warped under the strength of its grip.

"I miscalculated!" the Heaven Immortal shouted with almost self-hatred. It sent a rainbow-colored beam of energy at the Church army, but the fourth wave of self-detonating cultivators blocked it successfully. By now, almost a third of the entire army had sacrificed themselves. Whoever remained swore to make their sacrifice worth it.

The black hole bent dangerously, then shattered like a pane of glass. Everyone held their breaths—the Gods opened their eyes from meditation, and even the Heaven Immortal paused to calculate the new arrival.

Enas was not a giant like the other Gods. Despite the hand which had appeared to crush the black hole, he was just a large, formless mass of green energy exuding deep exhaustion. It hovered there in the void.

"ASSUME A PHYSICAL FORM AND MERGE WITH ME, BROTHER," Axelor said, his voice also tinted with exhaustion. "THE TIME TO RIGHT YOUR WRONGS IS NIGH."

"INDEED IT IS," Enas responded.

Jack never had a strict father, but this is what he imagined it would sound like. It made Jack—and everyone else—want to stand on attention. It demanded obedience.

CHAPTER EIGHTY-THREE
A MONSTER FOR ANOTHER

THE GREEN LIGHT PULSED. IT TURNED INTO A BEAM AND DROVE ITSELF INTO the chest of a human standing nearby, too small for anyone to have noticed. He wore dirty clothes and had yellowed teeth, his hair disheveled. As the light entered him, his aura grew, expanding from the early A-Grade all the way to the Archon level, rising still until it was similar in power to Axelor's.

The Sage laughed. "After a billion years, I'm finally free!" he shouted in his normal voice. "Come, brother. Let's end this."

Axelor and Enas—who now occupied the Sage's body—melted into a black and green pool of light respectively, then mixed together, forming a yin yang shape in space. "You too, my siblings. Let us be reborn," the Sage's voice echoed.

The two greater gods glanced at each other. Then, they too melted into pools of ethereal light which dove into the yin yang diagram. An intense concentration of power shook the universe, once again dislodging space and time. The combined aura of twelve Gods rose through the Archon realm, advancing higher and higher until it slowed down. Then, with a pop, it burst through, its quantity lessening but its quality skyrocketing.

The Church army erupted into cheers. People shook in suppressed fury and joy, while others hugged the cultivators next to them and celebrated. “We did it!” they shouted. “There is hope!”

“All those sacrifices weren’t in vain!” a man shouted, raising his fists to the sky.

Jack held his breath, eyes shaking. “They broke through! They reached the S-Grade!”

“Bro,” Brock said from the side, not sharing Jack’s excitement. “Did you notice?”

“Notice what?”

“When Life Bro and Entropy Bro fused, they only spoke in Life Bro’s voice. Not both, like the other fusions.”

Jack took a moment to digest this. His eyes widened. “No way.”

The pool of light shone in all colors of the rainbow, then settled on green. The Sage reformed, his aura completely transformed, having risen to a quality similar to Jack’s except far grander. This was the true S-Grade.

“And so the God of All is reborn,” the Sage said in his regular voice, “except it is me. Goodbye, my foolish siblings.”

“They miscalculated,” the Heaven Immortal said. “You did not merge with them. You consumed them. How did that—”

“No spoilers,” the Sage said, appearing next to the Heaven Immortal and hitting it with a palm strike. A thousand different Daos formed a complex shield which was then completely overpowered and destroyed. The Sage’s palm smashed into the Heaven Immortal’s chest, and its entire robotic body exploded, its head and limbs flying in different directions. It was deader than dead.

Jack looked on, stunned. So did everyone else. Their cheers were cut abruptly. The Heaven Immortal, whom the Church cultivators had sacrificed themselves by the hundreds to delay, had been destroyed, just like that. The difference between Archons and S-Grades was tremendous. Unbridgeable.

The Church should have been celebrating, yet none of them

moved. Sudden fear left them frozen. An instinctive understanding that something was very, very wrong.

Enas turned slowly to regard them. A silent astral breeze lifted his robes. His green aura was tinged with hints of darkness, falling over him and obstructing his image, leaving only cold eyes and a hard, predatory smile. As his aura submerged the Church cultivators in frozen water, their relief turned empty, their joy was dashed. They all felt a sinking feeling at the pit of their stomachs, as despair, slow and steady, creeped over them.

The Church's teachings spoke of Enas as a loving father, but there was nothing loving about this figure. He was cold and calculating, while they were defenseless cattle. His gaze hounded their souls.

Silence stretched for a while. Far away, the remnants of the Immortals' army scrambled into a wild retreat, but Enas paid them no heed, only observing the Church cultivators. They instinctively grouped closer together like mortals in the winter.

Jack remembered the words of Axelor's clone. *Enas is no loving father,* he'd said. *All he cares about is himself.*

"We... We won, right?" someone asked, gulping.

"I think so," another replied.

"Why doesn't this feel like winning?"

The Arch Priestess was completely silent. Jack and Brock glanced at each other, then back at Enas.

"He's considering whether to kill us or not," Brock said.

"We made a mistake," Jack said through gritted teeth. He thought back to all those brave cultivators who gave their lives to let Enas be revived. Master Boatman, included. The scythe in his space ring suddenly felt accusatory, a token of Jack's failure. His gaze grew dark. He clenched his fists so hard his nails bit into tempered flesh. "We exchanged a monster for another," he spat out. "Robots, Gods... None of them care about us. Nobody's coming to save us. We messed up so fucking hard. All those sacrifices were for nothing."

His emotions warred between terror, regret, and grief. He and all other Church cultivators had fallen from the highest heavens to the pits of hell in a single moment. The God standing before them was something they could never, ever defeat, and they were completely at his mercy.

Enas—still looking like the Sage—moved his gaze slightly. It landed on Jack. Just the pressure of being stared at was so intense he could barely breathe.

"What are your intentions?" he managed to say.

Enas smiled coldly. "Isn't it obvious? Mortals have proven themselves too dangerous. To ensure my continued survival, I will purge all life from the universe except my own."

Jack expected something like this, but it still burned his heart. "Why would you do that?" he cried out, finding more of his strength. "You created us! We saved you!"

"Ah," Enas said, shaking his head. "If you created a bomb, would you let it sit in your living room until it destroyed you? Would you love it?"

"We are not objects."

"You are toys. A little experiment I designed to test my powers. It went pretty well, but it's time to bring it to an end. You will no longer be a threat after today, but others may follow in your footsteps. I cannot allow that."

Jack felt helpless. And stupid. So many of his fellow cultivators had given their lives, and he had been about to as well, just to create a monster even more unbeatable than the Heaven Immortal. He could see no way out. There was nothing in the universe which could stop an S-Grade.

He wanted to roar in fury. The Arch Priestess had gone silent from shame. Everyone looked at him to speak. He had to at least try.

"You can't do this to us," he pleaded. "We don't want to kill you. We don't want anything from you—we just want to live!"

"For now, maybe," Enas replied condescendingly. "But not forever. You do not understand the nature of your own consciousness. Mortality is an expanding inevitability, and sooner or later, someone will appear with both the will and power to threaten me."

"And you'll kill us all, just for that?"

"Tell me, Jack. How silly would you feel if your throne was usurped by a bunch of toys you made?"

"We are not toys, we're *people*!"

"To you, maybe. To me, you're just a bunch of stardust formed into shapes which make it move in patterns. You're not even alive, not in the same way I am. You're merely slightly more complex objects. Breaking you means nothing."

"You can't think that!" Jack shouted, anger rising inside him. "What are you even saying? You think we're not alive? My sacrifices and effort meant nothing? My son's life was nothing? All the brave people who sacrificed themselves for you today were *nothing*?"

"Yes," the God replied.

Jack was about to erupt. He would have, if he didn't know it would be useless. "You can't actually believe that! You are the God of Life, for God's sake! You need to respect life."

"No, Jack. I am the God of Survival. My survival," Enas said. "I do want to thank you for freeing me, though. My imprisonment turned out to be a fortunate event, but it would mean little if I was never released."

"Fortunate?"

"That's right. Existing away from the other Gods allowed me to develop a stronger individuality and be able to absorb them instead of merely fusing. My presence near System space let me distribute clones like the Sage you know, guiding the world's development to where the other Gods would need to fuse with me, so I could absorb and annex them. Delaying the Crusade until you were ready was challenging, but I succeeded. Now, your efforts are mine to reap."

"You make no sense."

Enas smiled coldly. "That's a really nice body, Jack. Better than mine. It would be a shame not to... acquire it."

"What?" Jack asked, but the God did not reply. He turned into a green meteor which charged straight for Jack, completely disregarding the gathered Church army.

They were flooded with the same dark feelings as Jack. Seeing the God approach, these brave cultivators snorted and raised their weapons.

"Jack is the future," a peak A-Grade said, leveling a blade at their God. "If you want to harm him, you'll need to get through us."

"Alright," the reply lazily drifted over.

A single green meteor flew into hundreds of the universe's strongest cultivators. Not one person retreated. A thousand different Daos rose to meet Enas, each glowing with the power to sunder planets. The green meteor crashed into them like a bowling ball against glass, shattering them all, opening the void wide, eradicating the meaning of spacetime.

Energy offsets flew everywhere as Enas appeared amidst the army. He waved his hands, conducting a symphony of death. Streaks of intense life energy followed them. Every time those streaks approached a cultivator, they pierced straight through his defenses, then infiltrated his body and overfilled it with life. It didn't matter if they were B-Grade or A-Grade. Everyone was the same in the face of absolute power. Bodies exploded like flesh balloons filled with blood. The explosions came close together, and blood rained through the void.

Entire squads flew toward Enas, passing through the gaps in his attacks. They unleashed their own attacks, only to have them split ineffectively against his body. It was like his mere physicality superseded all natural laws. Even their self-detonations were useless. The Arch Priestess flashed beside Enas. She was slapped away before she even made her move, instantly rendered unconscious and near-death. A bunch of healers rushed after her as Enas kept tearing at the army.

It was a massacre.

Some cultivators started getting cold feet. Heroism collapsed before desperation. They tried to run away, only to discover that a green sphere had surrounded their army at some point, its walls webbed. Anyone who touched it exploded in a shower of flesh and blood. In desperation, people tried shrinking to pass through its gaps, teleporting through it, or attacking it. Everyone exploded all the same. The green web was as holistic as Enas's body, countering all individual Daos. It remained based on the Dao of Life, but the sheer quality and quantity trumped everyone else's to the point where individual Daos did not matter. Even the Daos directly opposite that of Life were useless. God-killer swords were useless when wielded by ants.

A brave soul self-detonated against the web to save her people, but this attack proved as ineffective as the rest.

Enas snorted again. "Bunch of ants," he said. As people turned to look at him, they found he'd at some point teleported right next to Jack. Jack punched out a black hole, only for Enas's palm to grab his fist and snuff it out. Brock smashed his staff against Enas's head, but the God didn't even bother defending. The staff snapped on impact, and Brock's palm split as he was sent flying backward.

A green web appeared around Enas and Jack, forcing everyone to make some distance or die. The outer net remained as well, trapping the cultivators between two concentric spheres. After their comrades' gruesome fate, they didn't dare touch either.

Only Jack and Enas were left inside the inner web. Jack tried to pull out his fist but couldn't even budge it. Resolve filled his gaze. Before he could self-detonate, an unstoppable force shrouded his body, freezing him completely. Even the energy of his inner world ground to a stop. He was completely immobilized and defenseless.

Jack gazed at the face of Enas—a face which had once belonged to the Sage, who'd helped Jack many times in the past. He'd come to think of the mysterious ally as a friend. The betrayal hurt more than he expected. For a brief moment, Jack hoped the Sage would struggle against the God dominating his body.

But the truth was clear. There was no domination—the Sage and Enas had always been one and the same. He'd always been a traitor. Their interests just happened to align, and he'd only helped Jack so he could later steal his perfect body.

Anger filled Jack's eyes, but frozen as he was, the best he could do was glare.

At least, according to everything Jack knew, stealing his body could not be done. There was no way. As great as the difference between them was, it was nowhere near enough to achieve something that complex. Jack's soul was imprinted into every cell of his body, every strand of energy. He was one with his Dao. Stealing it away was impossible.

Yet Enas seemed confident, and that scared Jack.

The God grinned devilishly. "You're probably thinking I can't do it. But you've been dancing in my palm for longer than you think. Awaken."

Deep in Jack's body, Copy Jack opened his eyes. Green energy flooded out, far more than he should possess, and connected with the Life Drop to raise a storm of life energy which whipped against every single cell of Jack's body. His inner world was unaffected—it was his soul, vested into every inch of this world, that came under attack.

Venerable Saint Thousand Shell roared under the onslaught. It could barely shield itself against such power. It grabbed The Stone and Franky and retreated into the Life Drop, which was now completely empty. Its inside was the calm eye of the storm, granting them temporary safety, but the turtle realized to its horror that any control it had over the Supreme Blood was gone.

"Copy Jack!" it roared in angry disbelief. "What are you doing?"

Copy Jack, still outside the Life Drop, ignored them completely.

"Harboring nascent souls is a risky endeavor," Enas said slowly as the storm of energy in Jack's body grew stronger. "I remember how this one contained the will to travel and see the outside world. It was growing nicely, and it quite liked you, too. Too bad it was naive—once it touched my drop of blood, so many years ago, I destroyed its will and occupied its mind. How do you think the Sage could always find you and knew so much about you? I was watching, Jack. Always watching."

Even Copy Jack... I couldn't protect... Jack thought, but he didn't reply. He couldn't. He remained immobilized, and as the attack on his soul ramped up, so did the pain. Copy Jack had existed inside him for so long he was completely harmonized with Jack, allowing him to access every tiny bit of him.

It was like a grater passing over Jack's soul, again and again, striving to destroy his sense of self. A terrible force sought to delete him, wrestle away control of every fiber of being he possessed, to steal his body, power, and identity. Everything that he was would be gone.

Jack felt a pain greater than anything he'd ever endured before. Even the Trial of Will in the Hall of Trials paled in comparison. He would have screamed if his mouth wasn't immobilized.

"Surrender, and the pain will go away," Enas said. Jack shook in his grip, his body convulsing against the pain. The cultivators around them watched in mute despair, blocked by the inapproachable green web, while Brock had closed his eyes in fierce meditation. The golden aura around him undulated. Everyone else could only wait for the inevitable.

A few moments later, Enas frowned. Jack was still thrashing, but nothing else was happening.

"Why do you not yield?" he asked, a measure of strain in his voice. "You know it is impossible for you to resist. I saw your performance in the Hall of Trials—you'll never outlast me."

Jack was indeed in extreme pain. Anyone else would have yielded instantly—only his experience in withstanding pain let him last this long. He could sense that, the moment his will wavered, his soul would lose its support, and it would be wiped away forever. He would well and truly die.

No! he screamed through the pain, sensing his grip on reality lessen. *No!*

CHAPTER EIGHTY-FOUR

THE POWER OF BROHOOD

Back on Earth, Jack's clone had suddenly fallen to the banquet floor, convulsing and screaming in pain.

"Jack!" everyone shouted.

Vivi wore a dark expression. She knew about the war, but this was unexpected. What could be happening? She directed people to assist, but the healers weren't even close to the level where they could help him. She sensed his aura growing weaker, infused with a hint of wicked green. She had no idea what was going on.

Jack... she thought, eyes watering in powerlessness.

"Dad!" Ebele screamed, falling over her father. "What's wrong, Dad? Talk to me! Talk to me!"

Jack's pain came from the soul, so his clone suffered the same as his main body. He couldn't speak. He could, however, think through a blurred veil. If Enas took over his body, he would simultaneously take over his clone as well, and then wiping all life off Earth would be trivial. That included his wife, daughter, and friends, whom he'd foolishly gathered together.

"Dad!" Ebele screamed.

The clone looked up, seeing the teary eyes of his daughter. His grip on reality recovered because he simply couldn't afford to lose it. *I will not fail again,* he swore. *I will protect you, Ebele. No matter what.*

Enas was flustered. This attack was not easy on him, so he needed Jack to capitulate before he grew exhausted. He'd thought it was certain—how could a mortal mind withstand such pressure?

"Why are you persisting?" he asked. "How?"

"My... body..." Jack said telepathically, staring at Enas through frozen, bloodshot eyes. *"My... family..."* He paused. *"Are... not... for you... fucker."*

Enas's eyes widened. "You cannot possibly withstand this!" he shouted.

Jack's entire body vibrated in pain and unheard screams, but his eyes remained wide open and glaring straight into Enas's, branding his resolve into the heart of a God.

"I refuse to believe you can outlast me!" Enas shouted.

Another few minutes passed. The Church army stared at Jack and Enas helplessly, but with hope slowly growing in their hearts. Brock was still meditating. His golden aura grew stronger. To the side, the Arch Priestess had recovered consciousness, her expression hidden under her mask.

In the inner web, Jack persisted. He and Enas had locked gazes, fighting with their willpower. Jack's burden was much greater, but so was his responsibility to endure. The immobilizing effect on him had long since worn off as Enas poured all his power into torturing his soul. Jack flashed Enas a bloodied, closed-toothed smile.

"What kind of father..." he muttered, insanity entering his gaze, "would let his daughter get harmed?"

Enas's eyes widened. His own exhaustion was kicking in. He suddenly interrupted his attack to teleport away. Despite his exertion just now, he recovered to the peak of his power near-instantly.

The inner web disappeared alongside his teleportation. People rushed in to support Jack, who stumbled with a pained but triumphant expression. Contrary to expectations, Brock was still meditating. The golden aura around him and every other cultivator was growing steadily stronger, but it was nowhere near the level where it could threaten Enas.

Enas hovered in the distance, staring at the army. The outer web remained, trapping them in with him. His gaze was dark. “Don’t think you have escaped, Jack. We will resume after I crush these bugs. When I kill your family and everyone you know, then we’ll see how well you can resist.”

Jack’s exhausted eyes regained a hint of life. He struggled to his feet, pushing away the other cultivators to stand by himself in the void. “Fuck you,” he said. He tried to detonate his inner world, only to realize he couldn’t. It was extremely stable to begin with, and Enas had further enhanced that stability—in his current exhausted state, he simply couldn’t detonate it.

The God smiled. “Let me feed you some despair,” he said, then waved his hands condescendingly. The outer web disappeared. “Run, little mice. Try to escape me as I crush you one by one.”

The gathered cultivators glanced between themselves. They saw the despair in each other’s eyes. Some people prepared to run when a new voice appeared.

“No,” it said.

Jack laboriously looked over to find that the speaker was... some guy? He’d never seen this person before. He wasn’t even an A-Grade, just a peak B-Grade. Yet, this random cultivator, with his unassuming face and short red hair, dared to stand up to a God.

“I’m not going anywhere,” he said, crossing his arms. “I think I’m the only one who didn’t expect to die today, but fuck you, *God.* I won’t give you the satisfaction. If you want to kill me, come over here and I’ll do my damn best to give you the slap that you deserve.”

The cultivators about to run didn’t. There was no point anyway—they could never escape. One by one, they turned toward Enas, galvanizing their Daos.

"What's your name?" Jack asked the guy who'd spoken.

"Rory, sir. Rory Pickleman. My title is Envoy Shattersun."

"Shattersun... That's a good title. You are a fine cultivator, Rory Pickleman. May I have the honor of fighting by your side?"

"Honestly, you should just detonate your inner world to spite him."

"I would if I could, Rory, but I like your enthusiasm. My self-detonation ability is sealed. Best I can do is fight to exhaustion, then suffer a fate worse than death."

Rory considered it. "I can accept that. Alright, Sir Jack Rust. We might die, but at least we'll go down swinging."

"Damn right!" another cultivator shouted.

"Fuck you, Enas!" another said. "We may be weak compared to you, but at least we aren't assholes!"

"Let's die together, brothers and sisters! Show that God the honor he can never have!"

"That's right!"

"Let's go!"

"I'm all fired up!"

The cultivators all shouted, one after another, as both armies rose against an impossible opponent. Enas gazed at them ludicrously. "You're idiots," he said.

"We're the best kind of idiots," Jack said, moving to the fore of the army. "Let us show you the best thing about being mortal. Everyone, CHAR—"

"Wait," a voice cut him off. Everyone turned to find that Brock, still meditating, had opened his eyes. His expression was strained, but a huge smile dominated his face.

Jack had seen him meditating before but had forgotten about it in everything that happened.

"Brock?" he asked.

"You guys are the best bros I could ask for," the brorilla said, "and that matters."

Jack looked around, finally noticing the golden aura which had at some point spread over everyone—a form of ultimate camaraderie based on the resolve to live and die together.

It was brohood.

Fueled by everyone's selflessness and unity as the end approached, it had spread rapidly, its strength rising to new heights. Jack didn't think there was any point to it anymore, but he watched as the aura glowed brighter, tinging the void golden.

Others noticed, too. Everyone looked around in wonder, feeling their heartbeats combine into one. Enas also realized something was happening, and it made him frown.

"Everyone," a voice said, ringing clearly in the ears of every cultivator. "Not all is lost yet. True brohood never dies. If you are willing to trust me with everything you have, we still have a shot at victory."

Everyone stared at the golden brorilla hovering in the middle of the army, his body shining like a beacon of hope. The aura of golden light had turned into bright tethers connecting him to every other cultivator except Jack. The warm light spread into their hearts, and they suddenly believed.

"We all share a heart," Rory Pickleman declared, surprised by whatever was going on. "Go for it, Brock. We believe in you."

"Good."

The brorilla raised his arms slowly, panting as if the task was laborious. As he did so, everyone felt a power streaming into their souls, forcibly tearing open a portal. They suppressed pained grunts. The sensation was invasive, entering what was a cultivator's innermost sanctum, but nobody tried to resist. This might well be their only chance at survival. Moreover, bonded by their common emotions, everyone trusted Brock. He stood amongst them like a beam of sincerity, channeling all positive emotions into one potent brew.

The cultivators embraced the tether sticking into their souls, pouring all their remaining power into it. Many stumbled, driven to exhaustion. The tethers glowed brightly, and Brock lit up like a Christmas tree, all sorts of colored lights swimming around his body.

His arms finally extended fully upwards, and all the colors streamed above them, mixing and forming a sphere of pure gold.

While the process was ongoing, Enas snorted. "I'm still here, you know," he said with annoyance. He stepped through the void, appearing right in front of Brock, and slapped the air to release a burst of green energy. It rivaled the golden flood in intensity—most importantly, Brock was too busy controlling the energy to defend. Green tendrils spread out of Enas, immobilizing everyone nearby.

"Just die," said the God.

Jack flashed between Enas and Brock. The God's attack was massive. There was a chance Enas would cease the strike to avoid killing Jack—being the god of his own survival as he'd proven over and again—but Jack didn't count on that.

This was a great place to die, anyway.

"Keep your filthy hands off my bro," Jack said. The attack wasn't lessening at all as it hurtled toward him. He had no hope of surviving it. He looked back, giving a warm smile. "Give him hell, Brock."

Jack was confident his extremely tempered body would at least divert the green beam before being destroyed. He could secure Brock enough time to finish whatever he was doing. His life was a small price to pay for that. At the last moment, however, he was forcefully shoved aside. His energy fell into disarray. His eyes widened.

"Arch Priestess!"

The white-clad space monster stood in his place, facing the approaching green beam. White light streamed out of cracks all over her body. She reached up and tore her mask away, revealing the tiger-like face she'd always hidden.

She turned it to Jack and gave a pained smile. "Save them for me..." she whispered as her inner world detonated. The galaxy was washed white. A tremendous explosion threw Jack away. The void was seared clean as white met green, bravely standing in the face of a God's attack, carrying all of the Arch Priestess's shame, honor, and courage. A monkeyish scream echoed before the powers even finished clashing, and Jack spied Brock's face twisted in rage—she'd diverted some of her power specifically to protect him.

Dozens of cultivators had been tossed away, some gravely injured. Everything was in chaos in that moment. It was then that Venerable Saint Thousand Shell, who'd been quiet all this time inside Jack, chose to speak.

"She was young," he said in a heavy voice, "but she carried the responsibility of a leader. Don't blame yourself, Jack. Giving her life was the right choice."

Jack didn't reply, too shaken. The green light was finally swallowed up by white. Enas moved to attack again, his expression warped in annoyance, but it was too late. The golden sphere over Brock's head finished forming. It shone brighter than any star. Even Enas had to look away at its might.

"BROS!" Brock shouted, his voice ravaged by pain. "LEND ME YOUR POWER!"

The sphere brightened even more. It conquered the universe, filling it with brohood, momentarily refuting even Enas's Dao of Life. Jack couldn't look that way, but he suddenly felt a tremendous surge of power entering his body. He couldn't breathe. His inner world was filled with so much energy it almost cracked. His mind cleared. His soul lightened. His wounds and exhaustion disappeared. At that moment, he was absolutely certain that he possessed enough strength to turn over the world, a wave of his hand shattering galaxies. He felt reborn.

As his perception blitzed out, instantly capturing everything, he understood. Brock had borrowed everyone's power and given it to him. It wasn't just the cultivators present—Brock's call had crossed time and space to reach all the bros he'd ever made, as well as the infinite low-level cultivators of the Church who believed in him and Jack from the celebrity campaign so long ago.

All that near-infinite power had been funneled into Jack. He had no idea how strong he was right now. He didn't need to know.

Everyone around him faltered as if completely drained. They

couldn't even self-detonate. Brock was suspended midair, frozen by the infinite power coursing through him to reach Jack, frozen in place by the need to act like a medium for all this power. Only his mouth could move, and it cracked open in a grieving, desperate cry which echoed throughout the universe, through every small and large creature he'd borrowed energy from.

"SAVE US, BIG BRO!"

Enas teleported before Brock. Finally out of patience, his hand pulled back in a fist, ready to unleash the full power of an S-Grade God. The universe shuddered. Brock was defenseless. Jack appeared, moving even faster than Enas, grabbing Enas by the face and arresting his momentum.

"Keep your filthy hands off my bro," he growled, launching the God backward. Enas flew so fast he practically disappeared. The void shattered everywhere he passed, deep gouges carved in reality for endless light-years. Drops of green blood trailed Enas's path. He slowly came to a stop, staring at Jack in disbelief as he cradled his broken nose. Distance meant nothing to him, but his eyes contained wariness—everyone else's were suddenly awash with hope.

"How?" Enas said.

Jack raised his fist at him. "These bros let me borrow their power. They put their lives in my hands. You no longer get to touch them."

"I'm a God, you lowly creature. You don't dictate what I do."

Jack smiled. He punched out, and space lost all meaning as his fist met the God's stomach. S-Grade powers clashed. A massive explosion echoed, a supernova in the middle of empty space, shaking the entire galaxy and releasing a vast cone of purple energy. Enas bent over. He wiped a hint of blood from his lips, eyes shaking.

"This shouldn't be possible," he said. "How can you match my power? You're just a bunch of ants. You're far too weak!"

"But we are many," Jack said. "It was you who created us with this potential, Enas. You could have been a father, but you chose to be a tyrant. This is the day you pay for it."

CHAPTER EIGHTY-FIVE

JACK VS. GOD

Enas's face turned furious. Green aura emanated in waves, his S-Grade power finally fully activating. "I don't know how you got so strong, but you're delusional if you think you can defeat me."

Jack smiled. A torrent of purple and gold erupted from under his feet, making his magic trunks flap lightly, the two colors merging in the air like lightning strikes. Under the light, his eyes were sharp and confident. The pressure of merely releasing his aura was so strong that the distant cultivators turned wobbly, almost losing their ability to fly. The weaker ones vomited, but it did nothing to curb their enthusiasm.

Their eyes were full of hope. "Go, Jack Rust!" they screamed until their throats tore. "Save us!"

Spacetime between the two fighters wavered, shimmering like hot air. Their auras clashed, green against gold and purple, creating a river of power which spread to the left and right, stretching far enough to be visible from some nearby galaxies. Reality was already flaking. Withstanding this clash of auras strained it, so the actual battle might well break the universe.

Jack glanced at the gathering cultivators in the distance. They weren't nearly far enough away. "Let's take this elsewhere," he said.

"Hah!" Enas laughed. "You think I care about—"

Jack raised a hand and jabbed space. It shattered for several light-years around them. The universe crumbled around him and Enas, leaving them in a sea of swimming colors, where they had nothing to break.

Enas looked around warily.

"Don't think of going back," Jack said. "Opening a portal to the universe would take long enough for me to stop you."

Enas finally rested his gaze on Jack. "You also can't go back. You really want to kill me or die trying?"

Jack smiled. "When did you ever doubt it?"

As this tremendous power surged through Jack, forcibly pushing him to the S-Grade, he'd seen the path clearly.

The S-Grade was a completely new realm compared to everything before it. The breakthrough to reach it would be incredibly difficult, and the increase in power was vast to the point where even Archons were ants before a true S-Grade. That was why Enas had been able to so easily overpower the entire army. He simply existed at a higher level. He was transcendent. Mere cultivators could do nothing against him, be they F-Grades or Archons.

To reach the S-Grade was to raise the self to the level of a true universe. It was incomparable to an inner world, which was a tiny, mock universe. The S-Grade contained galaxies, heavenly Daos, and sprawling civilizations. Jack had only reached this level temporarily by combining his seed of transcendence—the Universe of the Body—with a tremendous influx of energy. He'd revert to his normal level when this was over, but he knew he'd return here in the future. He'd achieve it the right way. It was only a matter of time.

Since being S-Grade meant being a complete universe, the actual universe itself could technically be an S-Grade cultivator, though Jack doubted it was so. If it was sentient, it would have interfered by now. That did bring interesting questions to the fore—could the universe be the corpse of a dead S-Grade cultivator, with the twelve gods being remnants of their will? Could there be more worlds out there, or S-Grade beings traversing the infinite dimensional sea in search of new places to conquer? Was it a whole new frontier, or just an empty infinity?

Jack didn't know, but now was not the time to consider these things.

His own Universe of the Body was a real universe. It was newborn, far too weak to attain the S-Grade by itself, but it contained the seeds to that path. That was how he'd been able to absorb and utilize all the power Brock gave him. They used extreme amounts of energy to simulate a more active universe, letting Jack command power at the S-Grade. In fact, the energy he'd been given was so much he could only partly utilize it.

At the same time, Enas was a true S-Grade. He was the fused form of twelve Gods, each representing one corner of the universe. Together, they formed a complete being—a true God—who stood at the peak of Dao. His body wasn't a universe like Jack's, but he kind of served as the spirit of their universe, letting him borrow its power to confidently stand on the same level.

Jack gazed at Enas. "Can you answer some questions before we fight?" he asked, burning with curiosity.

Enas smiled. "No."

"It's okay. I'll figure out all the answers myself. I'll have time after I kill you."

"You're confident."

"I'm powerful."

"So you think. Let me show you true power."

Their auras reemerged, swooping out and combining to enforce reality onto a part of the dimensional sea. The natural laws were a tug of war dictated by the two of them. It formed a mini universe, not enough to truly separate from the dimensional sea, but enough to serve as a tangible battlefield.

Jack pulled back a fist, then shot it forward.

"Supernova!"

"Well of Life!"

Their energies clashed in the middle. Jack's punch unleashed more power than an actual supernova, obliterating the hastily-created spacetime in all directions. Part of their energy went to rebuilding it. Enas's attack was a green beam containing infinitely regenerating life force. It was easily destroyed by Jack's attack, but it regrew as it forcibly entered his body. Jack braced himself but felt nothing. He snorted.

"Have this back," he said. The Life Drop appeared in his hand—he'd already withdrawn the turtle and stones into his inner universe—and tossed it over. It turned into an Archon-level monster the moment it left his hand—a green, lumbering giant with sharp fangs and angry insanity. Jack punched and eradicated it. The Life Drop was gone forever.

"Is that how you treat my gift?" Enas asked. "After all the times it saved you?"

"I respect the Life Drop," Jack said, "just not you."

They clashed again. Enas was the God of Life—though technically in the realm of the soul, he favored physical attacks, just like Jack. The soul components of their attacks neutralized each other. Their punches met each other in world-shattering explosions. The mini universe they'd conjured broke and reformed all over. None of the two rushed things. They were both new to the S-Grade. As time passed, they grew increasingly familiar with their powers, their clashes becoming sharper and fiercer.

Jack no longer possessed the four-armed battle form, and even Thunder Body was far too low in level to enhance his current power. His speed and strength were transcendent, both sundering expanses the length of galaxies. He and Enas were two rays of light clashing repeatedly in space, as well as every other frontier. Their auras warred throughout the newly created cosmos—Daos clashed and were annihilated, Archon-level manifestations appeared and vanished, minor Gods blinked in and out of existence.

Those were all inconsequential. Jack gathered his powers into his body, focusing on the only real opponent—Enas.

"Black Hole!" he shouted. His fist crumbled, replaced by a swirling black orb. With his laws and power risen to new heights, this was no longer an imitation but the real thing. If shot into a universe, it would absorb matter and keep growing forever. He pushed it forward. Enas brought his hands together, wrestling control of the nearby universe and enforcing his own Dao of Entropy over the black hole, destabilizing it and forcing it to disappear.

"I have absorbed Axelor, boy!" Enas laughed. "You cannot use his tricks on me!"

"Fuck off," Jack said. A swarm of black holes appeared around him, orbiting his head before flying at Enas. The God brought his palms together again, combining them in esoteric seals which changed the Dao. Entropy formed precise counters which rushed at each black hole and neutralized it.

Enas possessed all the Daos of his siblings, it was just that he favored Life.

Jack mixed in a punch. It met Enas's forearm, blocked, while the shockwave destroyed half the universe behind them. Enas struck back, his hand formed into a claw. Jack parried. They each launched into a flurry of blows, two titans clashing physically.

The world around them was peeled away by the violence.

Jack's inner universe faced apocalypse. Planets were ruptured every time his organs took damage, and the sky above their heads was torn apart as his skin broke. Intense energy currents rushed everywhere, obliterating anything in their path. Jack felt the loss. These were living creatures he'd birthed—in a way, they were his children—and they suffered every time he took losses. Every fight meant their sacrifice.

This was the responsibility of a God.

His creatures died by the thousands each time he clashed, entire planets scoured of life, their development pushed back to the single-celled age. He split off a tiny part of his power to protect the cultivators of his inner world, but that was all he could afford. The grief fueled his resolve to win.

Their clashes were cataclysmic, and Jack was seemingly winning. His every punch drilled into the God's defenses, pushing him back, inflicting minor wounds. In return, subtle undercurrents of malevolent life energy entered Jack's body. They didn't cause any immediate changes, but Jack was no amateur—he kept his perception on the lookout, and before long, he noticed something. His face went white.

"Fool!" Enas cried out. "You dare engage in a melee with me? Watch as I destroy you from the inside!"

Jack's organs had turned into planets, but they also remained organs. They were made of his cells and were part of his body. Now, he could sense malevolent tumors growing rapidly inside him, expanding and conquering him.

"You gave me cancer?" he asked incredulously.

"That's right! The overwhelming, uncontrolled power of life! Now die!"

Enas pressed the attack, not giving Jack the time to deal with his inner problems. Jack snorted. Even as he fell on the back foot, his perception drilled deep into his body, reaching every good and bad cell. He saw their inner workings clearly. Then, he purged the tumors, letting healthy cells regrow in their place. He couldn't do it very accurately, given the chaotic battle, so he ended up using more energy than required.

It was a constant balancing act. As they clashed, more energy slipped into Jack's body, and more tumors appeared, which he had to purge before they expanded too much. That process demanded part of his attention, hindering his fighting and enabling Enas to take the upper hand.

The Sage had always fought from the back, at least in Jack's knowledge. Enas, on the other hand, was a fierce pugilist. His dirty robes fluttered as he landed strike after strike on Jack, boxing him in. Knees and elbows and fists rained alongside insidious blows. Jack dodged the fingers heading for his eyes and smashed aside a fist, then ducked under a wide blow only to be met with a knee to the face. He jerked back, but Enas was already there, smashing a palm into the small of his back and dislocating his spine. Jack willed it to reattach, then suffered a kick to the back of the head for doing so. He flew away, the world spinning around him.

In that moment of weakness, another insidious power took hold of his body. Jack sensed the power of life infiltrating him, fusing into his own to push it in a certain direction. Still recoiling, he didn't manage to stop it. His body started evolving in terrible ways. His organs were failing, his limbs twisting, his brain breaking. Ugly protrusions grew out of his skin, while his bones turned spongy. He was killing himself.

"Fear the power of life and evolution!" Enas shouted, green rivers emerging from him and diving into Jack's body. "You're already dead!"

CHAPTER EIGHTY-SIX

THIS IS OUR ERA

Jack gritted his teeth. The tumors he had to constantly purge were one thing, but this situation was even harder to resolve. A simple purging wouldn't work. Every evolution was spurred on by his own body, responding to the expertly designed fake stimuli provided by Enas—he was, after all, the original creator of human bodies. Moreover, the foreign life energy assimilated with his, polluting it. He had no way to purge it before it exhausted itself, but if this continued, he'd die long before that. His own regeneration now worked against him. His body was self-destructing through misguided evolution.

"You're trying to use evolution against me?" Jack asked, calm despite the deadly threat. "Did you forget who I am, Enas?"

"I know exactly who you are. An arrogant pugilist, a fake god soon to be dead!"

"I'm something much better," Jack declared. "A biologist!"

Jack's life energy turned into tiny streams, drilling into every part of his body, coming face-to-face with the evolutionary transformations.

"Two can play this game, Enas!" He created fake stimuli of his own. His body's evolutions were held back, slowly reversed as Jack rapidly analyzed the situation and provided the perfect stimuli to counter Enas's.

The God frowned. "You dare compete in understanding life against the God of Life?"

"So what if I do?"

"You'll suffer!"

The foreign energy went wild inside Jack. It produced all sorts of evolutions, various odd and intricate interactions to challenge Jack's understanding. Yet, even the most esoteric of those were countered by Jack. After years of meditations, he understood his body perfectly, and analyzed all changes to figure out how to reverse them. As the foreign energy inside him exhausted itself, Jack's body returned to normal, stronger than ever. Since Enas's energy had wanted to assimilate into his, he obliged, using it to recover some of his spent energy.

Enas's eyes looked about to pop out. "How did you do that? I created the human body! No matter what Daos you have, I understand it better than you. How can you match me?"

"You're forgetting something, Enas," Jack said with a bright smile. "I'm a biologist with almost a PhD, and I've studied a ton of books which I can now recall with photographic memory. I also possess the Dao of Life to round out any errors. I may not be able to compete with you in general understanding of the human body, but when it comes to *my* body, nobody can surpass me!"

Enas hesitated as his anger fanned hotter. "You're ridiculous. Go die," he said, falling back into the melee. Jack met him fearlessly. Over time, the differences in their fighting styles became clear.

Jack was a fist fighter. That was where his strongest attacks lay. Enas, on the other hand, used all of his body and every insidious attack he could manage. Fist met knee. Jack pushed away an elbow, then met Enas's headbutt with his own. They both staggered back and reengaged.

Jack was growing used to his powers by now. He felt much more efficient than earlier in the battle, but this improvement wouldn't last forever. It'd slowed down. Enas, on the other hand, just kept rising. He'd started off completely unused to the extreme powers he possessed, and even now, his combat efficiency was lower than Jack's, compensating with raw power. As time passed, he became better and better, continuing even after Jack approached a plateau.

"A fake god cannot stand against me!" Enas shouted, diving head-first into their erratic melee. "I created mortals billions of years ago! I gave you life and Dao! I have always existed above you! Your powers are only borrowed, and you will lose!"

Jack gritted his teeth. The more they fought, the worse his situation became. He wasn't really an S-Grade, just fighting with the powers of one, so he couldn't quite match Enas. The more time that passed, the stronger the God would become, while Jack had already reached his peak.

I need to do something, he thought frantically. But what? He is the twelve gods. He possesses the origin of every single Dao in the universe. I cannot overpower him in sheer force, and I cannot defeat him in the Dao.

How ignoble would that be. After everything that happened, all the sacrifices and hope thrust onto his person, Jack might fail to defeat Enas. Everyone would die. His friends, his bros, his family... He shouldered the hopes of an entire universe and was falling short. What's worse, he couldn't even see a way out. His entire cultivation was based around his body, which Enas could match and soon overpower. As for his energy attacks, those relied on his Dao, and Enas had reached the peak in all of them. As for soul attacks, they were never really his thing.

Defeat was inevitable.

Is there nothing I can do! Jack screamed inwardly.

Faces passed through his mind in flashes. Brock, Vivi, Ebele, his mother... His son, Eric... Even further back, he saw all the people who'd been important to him in his journey. Harambe, Edgar, Shol, Gan Salin, Dordok, Nauja, Huali, Heavenly Spoon, Min Ling, Boatman, Starhair, the Arch Priestess, Great Silver, Fiend Prince... These people and many others passed through Jack's mind. All of them were enjoying their lives or had sacrificed themselves somewhere down the road. He shouldered the responsibility of protecting them or carrying their legacy.

He even thought about the brave cultivators of the Black Hole Church who hadn't hesitated to detonate their inner worlds for a shot at victory. *His* shot at victory. All the people who'd stood by his side and declared they'd rather die fighting than running, and who later placed all their hopes on him.

And now, he'd fail? Just like that? He'd let everyone he'd ever met, everyone he'd shared life and death with, get squashed by an unfeeling, selfish god?

At the final deciding moment, would he let everybody down?

Am I so fucking useless?

Jack inwardly shouted in outrage, This is so unfair! I did everything right. I took on every opportunity, every risk, every bit of pain. My road was perfect. How can I be so close to victory yet fail at the final moment?

Jack roared in fury, punching out. Enas blocked easily, now content to defend more than he attacked.

"Tick tock, little mortal," he mocked. "Your time is coming."

The shockwave of Jack's strike spread into their mini universe, shattering part of its foundation, which their combined auras forced to reconstruct. Jack looked around him.

Constructing a universe... he thought, his eyes growing wide. Wait! I didn't utilize every opportunity! There is still one... The universe-creating woman!

There was one Dao Vision Jack still hadn't figured out. The highest-level one he'd seen. A woman sat in space, orchestrating a high-speed collision of particles which ended up creating a new universe. Too many interactions happened in a short time, and Jack hadn't possessed the mental energy to decipher them at the time.

Now, he did.

His mind looked back into the vision, rewatching it as he fought. The particles collided, shattering to unleash an entirely new world as if they'd always contained it. Time spread into a new axis, pulsing at its own frequency, and all other Daos spun around it to fall in line. They merged into one complete whole. One explosion, one world. Infinite interactions happening simultaneously, so many that even Jack's currently enhanced mind was strained almost to the point of breaking.

And then, his perception shifted, and everything made sense. It clicked. The infinite interactions outlined the underlying structure of the Dao itself. The image turned crystal-clear by his current S-Grade level, and suddenly all the mysteries of the universe were unlocked. He saw the Dao for the first time, the true Dao, how everything worked together brilliantly. It all fell together. The destruction and creation of worlds were his to command because he understood them.

Jack lost his breath, overtaken by sheer wonder.

"Birth of time..." he whispered, eyes growing distant. "All becomes one... I finally understand."

Mid-battle wasn't the best place to ponder on the Dao. As Jack's concentration lapsed, he'd received several good hits by Enas. A few bones had snapped and even his organs were wounded. Blood trailed out of him like stardust, painting his death in ethereal colors.

Enas smashed a backhand into Jack's mouth, sending him reeling, while even the tumors constantly growing inside his body threatened to escape control.

"What's wrong?" the God laughed. "Overcome by despair? Realized you're losing no matter what?"

Jack looked up, his eyes now focused. "The exact opposite. I'm about to punch you into a new world."

"Still with the bravado! Very well, mortal. Come and show me the—"

Enas's words were cut short. His eyes lingered on Jack's fist, then grew wide. There was a Dao there he didn't recognize. Something which spoke to him in a deep, primal level, a memory from before he could remember.

"What's that?" he asked in horror. "I understand all Daos. How can I not recognize it?"

"You don't understand all Daos," Jack said. "You understand all Daos in the universe, but the universe didn't create itself. This is something which has never appeared before. A concept just beyond your reach, which you could have easily grasped if you tried, but you never did."

Jack stepped forward. His fist glowed with a white light. In the space around it, all particles had disappeared, leaving only two, rushing around at speeds vastly eclipsing that of light. The woman in the vision had only been an extreme Archon—Jack was currently far stronger than that, so where she'd been forced to wait for the particles to collide naturally, he could control their trajectories. The imminent explosion was under his control. So were its consequences.

"This is impossible!" Enas raved. "You're *my* creation. You cannot rise higher than me!"

"You think we mortals are nothing but toys," Jack said, letting the particles build up even more speed. "That our progress is a joke, that we can never challenge you, that we will always be inferior. Well, I have news for you, *God*. We are neither toys nor objects. We are alive, as much as you are, if not more. You may have created us, but you do not control us. We can and will surpass you. We are the future—and the future is now. Your age has passed."

Enas stepped back in fright, eyes glued on Jack's fist. Jack teleported before him, fist pulled back. He shot it out. Enas conjured every Dao shield he could, hoping at least one of them would counter this unknown Dao. Jack's fist pierced through.

The particles collided, exploding to birth a new Dao of Time pulsing at its own frequency, a blooming new world held in Jack's grasp. He directed all its energy forward, guiding it alongside his fist. All of Enas's shields shattered like glass.

Jack punched the God in the face. "THIS IS OUR ERA! *BIG BANG*!"

An entire universe smashed into Enas's nose. His defenses were useless. He was blown away, shattering their mini universe. A bloody tooth flew out, falling into the dimensional sea, containing enough divine energy to spontaneously form its own world before collapsing.

Enas held his face, only a bleeding eye revealed. He shook in shock. "Impossible," he muttered. The power he felt from Jack's newest attack was enough to make him shiver. It rendered every Dao he knew useless. It stood at a higher level than anything he'd ever met, save for the universe itself. But how could he fight a universe? How could he rise beyond his origin?

Enas turned tail and ran. "I am the God of Survival! You cannot kill me! I will survive, and when I return, I—"

Jack appeared ahead of him. Their previous mini universe had shattered, but the one created by Jack's Big Bang was still there, letting him move faster through it than Enas could through the dimensional sea.

Seeing Jack's sudden appearance, Enas's eyes went wide with panic. "I will survive!" he screamed.

Jack didn't reply. His eyes were cold. Two objects orbited his fist: one was a pair of accelerating particles, the seed of a new world. The other was a black hole, which had just consumed the entire universe he'd previously created, reaching new heights of power. The apexes of creation and destruction fused. Jack's single fist held the secret of the universe, the underlying principles of the Dao.

He punched.

Enas screamed, releasing all of his remaining power in one universe-annihilating green burst. "I WILL SURVIVE!"

Jack ignored defense to keep attacking with everything he had.

The green energy seared his body in and out, demolishing his organs and all life on them, breaking his body, mangling his limbs. From one moment to the next, he was on the verge of death. But his fist kept going. It easily penetrated everything, enforcing order on the dimensional sea, to strike at Enas's face. Their eyes met, one holding confidence and the other unwillingness. Time slowed to a crawl.

"This is the end of my road to mastery..." Jack said. "Fist of the Universe."

There was a sound like a ringing gong. Creation and destruction intermingled. Two universe-level concepts fused, then unleashed in the mightiest attack ever witnessed since the creation of the universe.

Jack flew away. New Daos and concepts erupted everywhere, flooding the dimensional sea, warring to instill order amidst its chaos. A world took shape and collapsed. A black hole turned white. The colors of the dimensional sea parted, momentarily revealing a white expanse behind them before merging back together.

All of existence moaned in pain and fury as it was forced to endure Jack's mightiest strike, and Enas's body was right in the middle, shattering in infinite tiny particles which melted into the chaos. Not a single piece of him remained. The twelve Gods were destroyed.

Jack floated through the swirling colors, grievously injured, but alive. His ravaged inner universe had turned unstable, no longer able to support his S-Grade power. He opened a portal to the universe and let himself fly through it, arriving back where the gathered cultivators eagerly awaited news. It felt like home.

He finally let the borrowed power slip away, returning to his normal level, and chuckled through bloodied teeth. He'd done it. He'd saved everyone. He'd shouldered their hopes and succeeded. His gathered fear and pressure culminated into one, massive roar.

"FUCK YEAH!"

The God Enas was dead. Jack was victorious. The war was over.

EPILOGUE: THANK YOU FOR EVERYTHING

A MAN RESTED ON A LUSH HILL, ARMS CROSSED BEHIND HIS HEAD. HE enjoyed the wind, the sun, the grass blades caressing his back. His eyes were closed in happiness—or, more probably, he was asleep.

"Hey, Dad," a woman said, manifesting beside him. She seemed in her late twenties, but that was definitely not the case.

The man cracked open an eye and smiled. "Ebele."

"Mom says dinner is ready," the woman said, "but you don't have to come if you don't want to."

Jack laughed. "It's not often that my adventuring daughter comes to visit. I wouldn't miss it for the world."

"Shall we?"

"Not yet. Lie down, Ebele. It's important to appreciate the little joys of life every once in a while."

Ebele hesitated, but relented and joined Jack in lounging on the grass. He sensed her fidgeting but let the minutes pass in silence.

"It's nice," she finally said when she'd adjusted. She took a deep breath. "I should do this more often."

Jack looked up at the sun. The real sun. He'd long moved Earth back to its original place in the solar system, no longer wary of hidden enemies. His mind ran back to the end of the Crusade fifty years ago, when he earned true freedom for himself and the universe.

The cultivators of the Immortal army surrendered after news of his victory spread. Even their five remaining Archons did so. Of those, a couple later chose to escape to distant parts of the universe, but Jack put them out of his mind. They'd never dare to return.

All the surrendered cultivators were imprisoned and their backgrounds looked into. They were fairly judged. Those who committed atrocities under the Immortals were executed, but their families were spared—that was the term of their surrender. As for the innocent ones, they were simply let go. No need to foster more hatred.

This incited a shift in cultivator culture across the universe. With many bad apples gone and good ones remaining, the world became a better place, at least temporarily. Corruption had a way of sneaking into every house, but Jack wasn't going to chase it endlessly. Some things were meant to happen.

The war had also created a vast power vacuum, as many high-level cultivators had perished, including the majority of Archons in the universe. The new generation had risen to the task. They hadn't reached the level of their predecessors yet, but following Jack's instructions, they'd soon usher the cultivation world into an unprecedented era of prosperity. A handful of people had already achieved a fusion of their cultivation similar to Jack's Universe of the Body. They were Brock, Heavenly Spoon, and, surprisingly, Fiend Prince. Jack's teachings had made a difference.

All of them possessed the potential to reach the S-Grade in the future, but, of course, that breakthrough would be no easy task.

As for Jack, after cultivating for fifty years, he'd reached the late A-Grade and become the undeniable strongest person in the universe. That gave him the power to enact several changes.

He'd restructured the Bare Fist Brotherhood with the purpose of enforcing justice across the universe, making it as corruption-proof as possible. Thanks to his presence, it had attracted many young talents, becoming the foremost faction of the cultivation world.

Besides that, Jack had reconstituted the System, which had collapsed along with the Heaven Immortal, into a form similar to its previous one but no longer rewarding the killing of others or monsters. That slowed progression, but it was a price he was more than willing to pay.

He'd also visited the Space Monster World, releasing the clones of Axelor and the Space and Time Gods from the Hall of Trials. They were devastated at the destruction of their main bodies, but eventually adjusted. They stayed in the monster world and dedicated themselves to training up the young generations. Jack still visited Axelor's clone from time to time—he was a decent guy.

His comrades in the final war had spread to all corners of the universe, living their own adventures. As for the residents of the Black Hole World and Green Dragon Realm, Jack brought both these realms to the main universe, where they could live happily ever after. He personally made sure no one would go after them.

After dealing with all other issues, the main bodies of Jack and Brock flew deep into the uncharted universe, pioneering new galaxies for the cultivation world and heralding its expansion. Their entire world was still in its infancy, after all—occupying less than a hundred galaxies out of billions, the future was vast.

Jack also wanted to explore the dimensional sea and uncover its secrets, but that could wait until he and Brock formally stepped into the S-Grade. Until then, pioneering and helping the world prosper was the best he could do. He'd also crafted a few more clones which took over teaching the new generations of cultivators. People everywhere venerated him as an all-knowing sage, though he knew he wasn't perfect.

His clone on Earth was the happiest one. He spent most of his time with Vivi, enjoying their long lives. Ebele visited occasionally, in breaks between her various adventures, and they also had many friends on Earth to keep them company.

He often relaxed by himself and mused about everything he'd been through. His entire cultivation journey up to defeating Enas had lasted only thirty years, but it felt like several lifetimes compressed into one. The Integration, the tournament, Trial Planet, his guerilla warfare on Hell, the Cathedral, the Green Dragon Realm, losing his son and finding himself, the war against the Animal Kingdom, the Space Monster World, the Second Crusade... His life still felt like a dream.

I should write a book, he mused sometimes. *An autobiography.* He wasn't in a hurry, however. His life was far from over.

Of all the people who were part of his adventures, from beginning to end, he remembered them all. Maybe they would no longer walk together, but they would forever be part of each other. He'd never forget them, and he hoped they wouldn't either.

"Thank you for everything..." he whispered in the air occasionally, even when no one could hear him.

The professor had passed away ten years after the final war—while Jack had the power to reverse death, to a degree, he viewed it as deeply disrespectful to a life well lived. He let his mother rest, visiting her grave regularly.

"We die to live," he'd say when people asked him about that, refusing to elaborate.

He still looked at the sky sometimes, pondering the true secrets of the universe. Were there more universes out there, scattered in the dimensional sea? S-Grade existences roaming the true berth of the cosmos? Were there realms beyond the S-Grade?

He did not know the answers, nor did the God clones in the Space Monster World, but he'd find out. When the time came, his main body would break into the S-Grade and leave this universe behind. As for what would happen afterward... Jack really looked forward to finding out. Worst-case, if there weren't any more universes, he'd make them.

But not in haste. Jack had been through a lot, and in the end, he emerged victorious. He'd earned his rest. He would enjoy it.

And the future would always come.

THE END

Want to discuss our books with other readers and even the authors?

JOIN THE AETHON DISCORD!

THANK YOU FOR READING ROAD TO MASTERY 6

We hope you enjoyed it as much as we enjoyed bringing it to you. We just wanted to take a moment to encourage you to review the book. Follow this link: Road to Mastery 6 to be directed to the book's Amazon product page to leave your review.

Every review helps further the author's reach and, ultimately, helps them continue writing fantastic books for us all to enjoy.

Also in series:

Road to Mastery
Road to Mastery 2
Road to Mastery 3
Road to Mastery 4
Road to Mastery 5
Road to Mastery 6

Want to discuss our books with other readers and even the authors?

JOIN THE AETHON DISCORD!

You can also join our non-spam mailing list by visiting www.subscribepage.com/AethonReadersGroup and never miss out on future releases. You'll also receive three full books completely Free as our thanks to you.

Don't forget to follow us on socials to never miss a new release!
Facebook | Instagram | Twitter | Website

Looking for more great books?

An apocalypse LitRPG about an underdog who must do whatever it takes to survive against impossible odds. ***Stranded on an alien world. Surrounded by enemies. He must learn to fight... or die.*** *When the apocalypse strikes the world Kyle Mayhew calls home, he is thrust into a struggle for survival. Alongside his Central Health Autonomous Diagnostic Drone (C.H.A.D.D.), he will have to overcome mutated creatures, ruthless marauders, and his grandfather's legacy to carve out a new home. He might even find that he belongs...* ***Don't miss the start of this Apocalypse LitRPG about an underdog who must do whatever it takes to survive against impossible odds. This rational, Healer Class MC will rise from weak-to-strong together with his sort-of- insane AI companion.***

Get Oath of the Survivor Now!

A LitRPG Apocalypse Series about an IT worker who is given early access to a somewhat buggy System. ***Survive pocket dimensions full of monsters. Report bugs to the System. Survive.*** *Dex is just your average, everyday I.T. Professional. Eyes tired from working late, the strange glowing gem floating in the middle of his apartment didn't exactly grab his attention. Until it opens into a portal and starts counting down to his death. In a life-or-death situation, an autistic quality assurance engineer probably isn't your first choice for a hero. But he has a certain set of skills that catches the attention of the Daemon System as it implements a secret beta-test on Earth. The impact of the Essence Wavefront is imminent. With it, humanity will unlock access to fantastic power. To have any chance to survive against the countless invaders who will seek to take that Essence power from us, humans will need the structure of the System. And who better to ensure the induction of 9-billion humans goes smoothly than Dex, the self-proclaimed God of Q.A.? By reporting bugs while fighting for his life in pocket dimensions full of deathtraps and monsters, Dex will win rewards, earn Essence, and grow more powerful than he can imagine, all while slowly uncovering the truths of the upcoming horrific apocalypse. Because work-life balance is important, right?* ***Experience this unique take on a LitRPG Apocalypse, featuring a weak-to-strong MC who gains early access to a somewhat buggy but non-sentient System.***

Get Beta-Testing the Apocalypse Now!

A hilarious new Isekai LitRPG adventure perfect for fans of Dungeon Crawler Carl and Full Murderhobo. ***Conquer ancient dungeons. Get rewarded. Grow stronger.*** *After being killed by a high-velocity tree-hug, Arlo is transported to a new world where those brave and talented enough to conquer ancient Delves are rewarded with incredible power and abilities. Unfortunately for Arlo, there is no tutorial. He is immediately forced to tackle a Delve set to the highest difficulty with a party of adventurers who are not only strangers to him, but strangers to each other as well. Arlo has no armor, no weapons, no knowledge of the world at large, and his party is growing increasingly suspicious of his lack of preparation and paper-thin excuses for how he got there. There's also the fact that the System in charge seems to be treating Arlo's situation like a big, cosmic joke. Determined not to die again, Arlo forgoes putting any points into his highest stat, Intelligence, and instead dumps everything he's got into Fortitude. After all, who needs equipment or fighting skills when you can eat fireballs for breakfast and still ask for more hot sauce?* ***Mage Tank begins a new Isekai LitRPG adventure that features steady progression, intelligent characters who spend time making intentional build choices, and tons of laughs. It's not action all-the-time, but Arlo's life is replete with danger and, more importantly, consequences.***

Get Mage Tank Now!

For all our LitRPG books, visit our website.

AUTHOR'S AFTERWORD

Hey bros!

I just typed in the final words of the series. Bros... I can't believe it's over. Road to Mastery has been my project for the past two years, my continued obsession and companion. It not only pushed my skills to a new level, but also my life, financially and in a bunch of other fields.

Throughout these two years, despite the success and reader satisfaction that Road to Mastery received, I never allowed myself to experience it fully. It was incomplete. Anything could go wrong. That is no longer the case. The completion of Road to Mastery means I can finally stop obsessing over it, and it will always be there, never becoming worse no matter what. I cannot describe the relief that brings me. It also marks me as a true author, in my mind, in a more impactful way than anything so far. I feel so proud of what I have accomplished. So satisfied with myself. The positive feelings inside me are so many they fight to come out first.

That doesn't mean I won't miss Road to Mastery. I realize now, as I'm writing these words, that I will never write about Jack and Brock again. All the characters of this series are people I'll leave behind, despite everything I've shared with them. It is almost grief. However, life is change, and embracing it is the secret to happiness. Good and bad. This is the good kind of loss, and I hope that, after sharing this adventure with me and Jack—as well as our excellent narrator, Jeremy Frazier, who has my heartfelt thanks—you will embrace the ending of this series as a maturing opportunity. I know I do.

I might be getting emotional now. Anyway. I also have news for you.

Good news!! The series might be over, but it will return in new forms. Road to Mastery is being adapted into a **webcomic** as we speak! All of the art I've seen so far is great, and so is the script, so you should really look forward to it.

Also, I know you guys enjoy system screens and stuff...so I'm making a **video game!** The Road to Mastery videogame will feature Jack Rust as the pugilist alongside various other classes, and you'll get to fight your way through the Forest of the Strong, Jack's hometown, and the Integration Tournament. It will basically follow the plot of Book 1 with various changes to make it enjoyable as a videogame. Brock will be there too, and you'll get the chance to not only fight in a roguelike environment, but also build a unique combination of Daos (diverse power-ups) through every run.

Both the webcomic and the game should come around the end of 2025 or start of 2026, so...keep an eye out! If you want to not miss the news (because let's be honest, you'll have forgotten by next week) join my Discord server, where you can chat with me and other fans, and where I'll post regular updates on the videogame. Some concept arts are already there, including Jack's. The server name is Valeriosverse. Corny, I know, but I got other series too.

Speaking of other series. Road to Mastery might be over, but my journey as an author—my own Road to Mastery—is just beginning. Follow me anywhere to be notified about my next series, though Discord is by far the most reliable. Let's stay in touch—we're bros now!

I might write another series in the Road to Mastery universe in the future—a cultivator in Jack's Universe of the Body, or maybe a student in Edgar's academy. No promises though. For now, my next series is going to be Good Guy Necromancer—a story about a wholesome necromancer and his army of undead friends trying to save the world. It's less xianxia-style than Road to Mastery, and a little more slice-of-death (hehe) but still heavy on the progression.

That's about all for now. Thank you very, very much for being part of this journey for the past two years. Your presence and comments meant the world to me. You gave me a bunch of great ideas and feedback, as well as motivation to keep going when things got rough—that goes especially for the people who messaged me about how my story helped them improve their lives, or gave them something to rely on during hard times. Writing is a tough gig, but you guys are the reason it's worth it.

See you soon, bros!

To new words, to new worlds,

With love,

Valerios

www.ingramcontent.com/pod-product-compliance
Lightning Source LLC
Chambersburg PA
CBHW020719310726
48979CB00004B/987

* 9 7 8 1 9 6 4 5 0 5 2 2 0 *